# Stopwatch

More by Brooke Shaffer

The Timekeeper Chronicles

The Chivalrous Welshman
Time to Kill
Tick Tock
Windup
Stopwatch
Free Time (2020)

The Hands of Time
In the Hands of the Enemy (2020)

Singles
Of Saints and Sinners

# Stopwatch
## Book Four of The Chivalrous Welshman
## The Timekeeper Chronicles

Brooke Shaffer

Black Bear Publishing

ISBN:
Hardcover: 978-0-9991392-9-5
Softcover: 978-1-7336954-0-4
eBook: 978-1-7336954-1-1

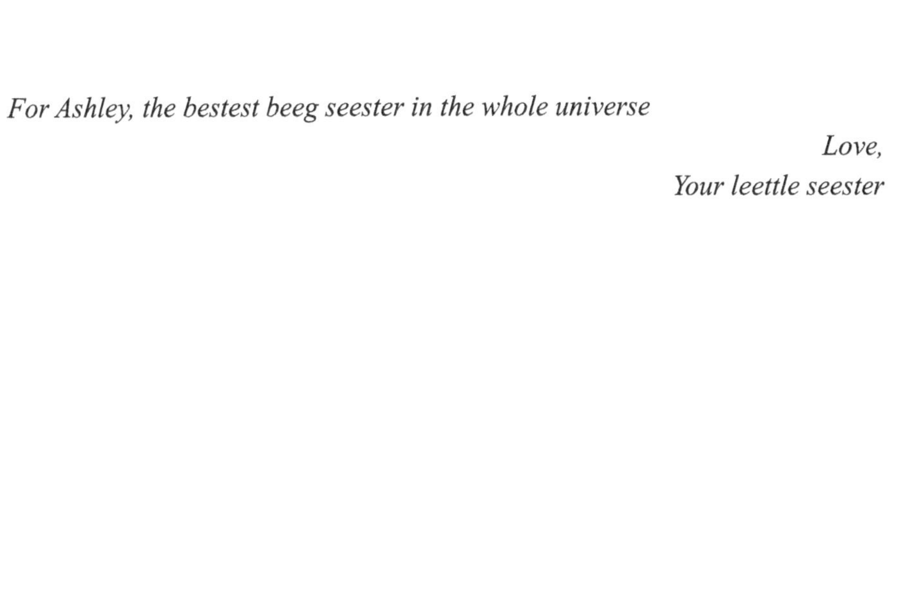

*For Ashley, the bestest beeg seester in the whole universe*

*Love,*
*Your leettle seester*

So this is Tommen," Micaiah said, leaning on the counter and looking down at the scrawny child who shrank back a few steps. "We've heard a lot about you." He looked at Walter. "You said the adoption officially went through?"

"Tuesday, yes," Walter answered proudly. He put his hand on Tommen's head, but something had caught the child's attention, and he wandered off to investigate. Walter kept his voice down as he added, "He's not leaving the family again."

Micaiah straightened. "I'm less worried about him than I am you." He turned on the faucet beside the coffeemaker on the counter. As he dumped the old coffee and rummaged in the cupboards for a fresh package, he went on, "Question is, are you going to tell him?"

Walter faltered. "I haven't decided. He's just starting to adjust; I don't want to surprise him or confuse him more."

"The longer you wait, the harder it's going to be. I mean, once he gets to be a teenager, well, things could end badly. That's the only way things really could end, once he gets it in his head that he's a man he doesn't have to listen to you. You don't need to suddenly dump an armload of fuel on that fire."

"I know what you're saying. I just don't know a good way to tell him. I've already Suppressed him, and I don't plan on taking him before the Hands any time soon. Telling him without showing him could end badly, too."

Micaiah flipped the switch on the coffeemaker, and it sputtered to life. He turned and watched the boy for a minute as he stood and just stared at the television, completely mesmerized by the moving images. He looked back at Walter. "You said he's just starting to adjust. Everything is new to him, and he's terrified. No, he might not understand the hows and whys, but he needs something solid and familiar to hang onto."

"But the explanations and everything else—"

"Walt, he's eight years old. He doesn't have to know all the details and all the Time involved; he just needs to know that you're there, and you're family. Do you even speak Welsh with him?"

"Not really, here and there. He does need to learn English, though, before I can put him in school, and he doesn't exactly have a bunch of friends who can help him. I'm all he's got."

"Exactly," Micaiah said severely. "You're all he's got. Don't be a stranger to him, Walt."

He stopped speaking as the boy walked along the large display case, marveling at all the baked goodies contained within. Gingerly, he walked up to Walter and tugged on his shirt. *"Fe merdr'i 'r rhôl 'na, os gwelwch yn dda?"* (Can I have that roll, please?)

Micaiah raised a brow. "What's he want?"

Walter showed him the roll in question, a kid-sized sticky bun which Tommen took gently, as if afraid it would disappear. As he bit into it, he mumbled, *"Diolch, Tad."*

Micaiah looked from the child to Walter. He didn't need to speak Welsh to know what Tommen had just called him. He sighed. "Have a nice day, guys." He leaned on the counter again and addressed Tommen. "Enjoy the sticky bun, okay? *Go dté tú slán.*" (Bye.)

# Chapter One
## Aftermath

Inauguration Day was supposed to be a day of excitement and anticipation, as eleven-slash-seventeen years of the same leadership came to a close and a new crowd of faces—or shrouds, anyway—assumed the mantel of leadership. Sure, there would always be grumbling about a particular candidate who didn't get elected, and trepidation that the new leaders would be terrible, but that was normal. That was to be expected.

But the atmosphere in the Wheel, surrounding the Coliseum, it was not one of excitement and anticipation with a few pockets of grumbling and trepidation. Rather, the entire Coliseum, inside and out, seemed to be an atmosphere of grumbling and trepidation with a few pockets of nervous excitement and anticipation.

Tommen had heard several stories from his dad about policing protests on the college campus. Most often, they were peaceful and eventually everyone got bored and went home. But sometimes, his dad described a scene that was like watching the crowd become a collective tiger, poised to strike. Just the right flutter of movement, indicating prey, and all hell would break loose. And that was when the peaceful crowd became an angry mob.

He was pretty sure that this was such a scene. Just the right word or movement, and all hell would break loose.

Tommen was torn between wanting to be as close as possible to hear and see what was going on—an impossibility anyway considering the crowds—and wanting to stay as close to the portal as possible in order to make a quick exit. It wasn't be a matter of if he would have to run, but when. He debated just leaving early and saving himself the trouble of potentially getting caught up in the running of the bulls. At the same time, from what he could hear and from what news got passed around through the crowd, everything was going as planned. The Hands handed over their shrouds without incident and all seemed well. Had they imagined the whole thing? Was it possible that this collective tiger would not strike?

The break came when the Coliseum guards started moving. Tommen saw it coming, though he couldn't quite say how. Maybe it came from understanding basic police tactics and how to move in such a way so as it round up as many as possible and gently herd them into an area. Maybe his paranoia superpowers were kicking in. Either way, once he saw the guards moving, he made sure to make himself as small and possible and just melt back into the crowd beyond the line of guards.

As the crowd quieted, Tommen heard a voice coming from inside the Seat, one he knew too well, one he'd hoped never to hear again.

"All during the elections, you heard about a False Zero Hour, one who was masquerading as the highest authority in the land with no one to rein him in." Cassius' voice carried over the crowd so even Tommen could hear him clearly. "You heard tales of Calis Cutthroat being this enemy, this False Zero Hour." Beat. "I. Am. He."

That was apparently some cue that the guards were waiting for because they turned from stealth mode to actively trying to push and shove as many people into the Seat as possible. That was also when the killing began. Any who tried to slip through the lines were struck down, whether by knife, fist, or some other means. Panic gripped the crowd, which only made it worse. Those who were not killed at the line were trampled by others, driven by instinct to escape.

Tommen took a few steps back, watching it all unfold, wanting to run but not wanting to look away. His dad was still in there!

*There is nothing you can do, and there are Timekeepers much more powerful than you trapped in there.*

Even as he thought it, the enormous gates started coming down. And still the guards pushed, killing anyone within striking distance. He looked behind him. Several had made it through the lines, or had been outside the lines to begin with. He jumped as someone grabbed his shoulder. Once the mini heart attack subsided, he looked to see Micah nose-to-nose with him.

"We have to go. Now!"

They got about three steps into a run, when Tommen pulled them to a stop. "What about my dad?"

"We couldn't leave together," Micah told him. "Too obvious. But your dad and Micaiah were right behind me. Come on!"

Tommen allowed himself a small measure of relief and kept pace with Micah, making a beeline for the portal. Some other alien beat them to it, but it was just as well. As soon as it stepped through, it was attacked and killed, nearly beheaded in fact.

"How are we going to get through?" Tommen wondered breathlessly.

"Very carefully," Micah said, not slowing. "Stay close to me."

The only thing left was trust and hope. Trust that Micah knew what he was doing and hope that it would work. Tommen stayed hard on Micah's heels, following him through the portal. It felt as though they ran into shrink wrap as Micah strained to put up a Band on the other side. They were not attacked or impaled, and once Tommen got his bearings, two dead Grandfathers lay on either side of the portal.

"What did you do?" Tommen asked.

"Tell you later," Micah said, pushing back the Grandfathers' cloaks, taking a knife for himself and handing one to Tommen. Well, to call them knives was a severe underestimation. Tommen had seen full swords shorter than these knives. Still, he gripped it hard and followed Micah through the Wheel.

The situation was not unique to the portal leading to the Coliseum. In fact, every portal had Grandfathers, waiting and ready to murder any who stepped through. But they were out of the Coliseum now and they could Band once again, moving into a Fast Band so it was as if everything else stood still. A couple times, one or two Grandfathers would recognize the Bands and break in. But Micah was no amateur. Rather than letting his Band be shredded and opening them up to an attack by several dozen Grandfathers, he would instead restructure the Band and absorb the attacking Grandfathers, to make it a more even fight.

Most often the fight did not involve the knives so much as Micah simply using a myriad of Time abilities to confuse the Grandfathers long enough to get away.

The Wheel proper was largely devoid of life, but not empty. It looked like everyone everywhere had been taken by surprise. Most of the strewn dead were average Time Agents from all disciplines, but here and there, Tommen spotted a couple secretaries. He managed a grim smile of satisfaction whenever he saw a Grandfather among them.

"You're sure my dad and Micaiah are close behind us?" Tommen wondered as they slipped through the last portal door before heading for the portal room.

"That's the last I knew of them, Tommen, I'm sorry," Micah said, not slowing. "Believe me, I wish I knew more and I wish I knew what the hell is going on. But we can't figure it out here where everyone in a black cloak wants to kill us. We need to get home."

When they got to the portal room, they found it completely empty. Not just of pedestrians or Grandfathers, but of portals, too. The whole room, where normally there were rows and rows of portals going to all corners of the universe, had been reduced to what amounted to a big, empty warehouse. Their footsteps echoed eerily.

"All the portals have been closed," Tommen stated dumbly.

"Yes, I see that," Micah said. "Makes this easy, then."

He went up to the nearest row, put a hand on the metal bar, and, with some effort, opened a portal to the bakery office. Sweat dripped down his forehead as he said, "Go!"

Tommen did not hesitate, but he jumped through the portal as if a T. rex was after him. It was kind of like doing a dive off the tall diving board and not exactly getting into perfect form at the entry. He hit the portal hard and it reverberated through his body, rattling his teeth, squeezing the air from his lungs, and slamming into his arm, making it feel as if it had been rebroken. Then he took the real physical hit as he stumbled into the office and over half a dozen objects in his way, like a table, a chair, and finally a door, instinctively putting his hands out and catching his injured arm once more, his injured fingers to be more precise. It was as though someone sent an electric shock up his arm, and it was all he could do to bite his tongue.

Micah was right behind him, though he was slightly more graceful, stepping through and more collapsing into a chair than tripping over it. He was breathing hard and sweating as if he'd run twenty miles through the desert. Tommen gathered himself and calmly stepped out of the office to retrieve a glass of water which Micah accepted gratefully and drank in two gulps.

"Thank you," he breathed, setting the empty glass on the table. He used his shirt to wipe his face. "Are you hurt?"

"I don't think so," Tommen replied, checking himself and trying to ignore the throbbing in his arm. "No, I think I'm okay. You?"

Micah nodded. "I'm fine."

"Why are you sweating so much?"

"I'm assuming it was the Grandfathers; they put a dampening field over the portal room. It closes all currently open portals and makes it nearly impossible to open a new one."

"But you did."

"I only said nearly impossible."

"Micaiah can do the same thing, too, right? He can open a portal through the dampening field?"

"He's better at it than I am."

Tommen found his own chair to slump into, feeling suddenly very weary. "Are we safe now?"

Micah sighed. "That remains to be seen."

"What happened in there?"

"Oh, I wish I knew exactly. The previous Hands were named and unshrouded, all according to plan, the usual bullshit from every inauguration that's more pomp than practical. Then they brought out the newly elected Hands, as well as the Zero Hour. Except the supposedly elected Zero Hour turned out to be Rifun."

"Rifun?" Tommen wondered.

"Yup. Think about it, though. Everyone had heard about Cassius and the False Zero Hour and the whole scandal. If someone was going to try something, stop Cassius from becoming Zero Hour, they'd only take out Rifun instead." He shrugged. "I don't know, it's only my theory. Anyway, the Hands transfer power like they're supposed to. The Zero Hour is always saved for last because...drama, I guess. But when the Bat goes to remove the Zero Hour shroud, the Zero Hour steps away and takes it off himself. And that was Cassius."

"That was when the guards started moving."

"Right. That was when your dad also said that it was time to go. We couldn't go all three together because it would be too easy to get caught, but we weren't going to be waiting around if you know what I mean. I went first because I was the smallest. Your dad would come next and Micaiah would generally stay with him to help if needed. Last I knew, they were almost right behind me. I slipped through the line of guards and went to find you and get you out of there."

"So there's no real way to know if they actually made it out. I mean, they'd be here already, wouldn't they?"

Micah sighed. "I don't know. Maybe. Maybe not. I wouldn't count them out just yet."

"Micah, we both saw the guards killing everyone, the Grandfathers, too."

"Tommen, it does Cassius no good to kill absolutely everyone. He might use those events to make a point and make the rest of those inside bend to his authority, but he didn't go through all the trouble of these elections just to murder everyone. He could have murdered everyone without needing to become the Zero Hour." He went on before Tommen could speak. "I don't know what his plans are. But I do believe that your dad and my brother are smart enough and resourceful enough to stay alive as long as they can and figure out a way to get home. Okay?"

Tommen nodded grimly, trying to hold it together. But as soon as Micah touched his shoulder, he lost it. Micah drew him gently to his chest, letting him cry on his already sweaty shirt. "I don't want to lose my dad again," he bawled.

"I know," Micah whispered. "It's frightening and unfair, and I don't want to lose them either. But the important thing is that you're safe, which was what your dad wanted most, whatever happened. He wanted you to be safe. Okay?"

After a second, Tommen nodded and pulled away, feeling like a stupid child. He took a tissue from a box on Micaiah's desk. "I'm sorry, I'm an idiot."

"No, you're not. You love your dad, just like I love my brother."

"Yeah, well, you're not the one sobbing like a child."

"Who says I don't want to? There's a time to weep and a time to be strong."

Tommen sighed and tossed the tissue in the trash. Micah went on, "Just like you said when your dad was in the hospital: I'm not giving up until they're six feet under. When they're six feet under, then I'll mourn. But it's not over until it's over. All right?"

It sounded silly, like a word salad of pithy little motivational quotes that might normally be found on the walls of yoga and karate studios. At the same time, half of it was directly quoting him. He sighed. A time to weep and a time to be strong. Just like last time, he supposed. Until his dad and Micaiah were six feet under, he wasn't going to give up. And this time, he had Micah beside him to help.

He grabbed another tissue from the box and tried to clean himself up and make himself at least a little presentable to the public, still sitting out there at various tables and booths, completely ignorant of the massacre that had just occurred inside another dimension. How quaint to be immensely concerned with the affairs of Hollywood and its idiot celebrities.

Tommen sniffed and wiped his eyes. "Okay, so what do we do?"

Micah leaned back in his chair. "I haven't actually figured that out yet, as far as a rescue plan goes. However, I do have an obligation to warn anyone and everyone who is still here on Earth to not go or even attempt to go to the Wheel. Who knows, maybe we'll get a bite as to a plan of action. In the meantime, you think you can run the store?"

"Um...Like, the whole thing?"

"Yeah." Micah glanced at the clock. "It's getting to be about closing time, once the dinner crowd leaves, so you don't have to do a lot of baking."

Tommen scoffed and shook his head. They'd just survived a massacre and been separated from those they loved most. And now they were talking about closing up the bakery like it was any ordinary Saturday. It made Tommen's stomach churn. It felt disrespectful, cowardly even. He'd done as his dad said and gotten out of the thick of things, but now he felt the need to use his vantage point on the sidelines to figure out a way to rescue them.

And they sat here talking about baking.

"I know what you're thinking, Tommen," Micah said. "I understand. But if I can't do anything right now, neither can you. And actually, you're going to be more help to me here. I'm officially promoting you to the temporary position of Sub-Lieutenant."

"Is that a position?" Tommen wondered.

"No, I just made it up, but I still need you. Go out and manage the store for a bit, and I'll call you when I have something, okay?"

After a second of hesitant consideration, he nodded and stood. He made it to the door when he stopped and turned. "Wait, so you said that you made up the Sub-Lieutenant position, but...that bit about managing the store...is that a promotion, too?"

Micah raised a brow. "Weren't you just feeling guilty about

working while Walter and Micaiah are still trapped in the Wheel?" Tommen felt his cheeks turn red. Micah managed a half-smile. "Prove you can do this, and we'll talk later. All three of us. And don't forget to take your translator off." Even as he spoke, he removed the one still in his ear.

Tommen had completely forgotten about the translator. He'd thought it was strange that he could hear Micah speaking English and Welsh at the same time. As he went to the back to punch in and grab an apron, he removed the translator and stuffed it in his pocket. The sounds around him became clearer as he first went to the counter to make sure no one was waiting, then retreated to the kitchen to see if anything was waiting for him in the ovens.

So Cassius had really done it. He'd not only won the elections and become the Zero Hour, but he'd launched a full military coup in the Wheel, murdering thousands, if not tens of thousands, and assumed total authoritarian control of Time. Had all four of them made it out of the Wheel, Tommen would probably be less concerned, but as long as his dad was a captive of that maniac, he felt rage burning in his gut and spreading throughout his entire body.

There were several pans still in ovens that he worked on, all the while coming up with dozens of different ways he wanted to torture and kill Cassius and Rifun. From a firing squad, to being drawn and quartered, to any number of obscene and obscure medieval tortures. Taking the two and taping them together with a bomb between them wasn't off limits either, as far as he was concerned, but he really felt his calling more toward the slow, painful deaths. Just as every second that passed by where Tommen wasn't sure whether his dad was alive or dead was agonizing, so he wanted those two to suffer. Just as Cassius had murdered those women so precisely, so he wanted those two to feel torturous pain.

Supposedly, people who were always cynical and angry and held every grudge since kindergarten were more likely to die young and with few friends. Tommen was certainly feeling that way now, as though his rage would make his blood pressure go so high that he would spontaneously combust. But, the way he figured it, there was no point in dancing around the kitchen whistling some cutesy little tune while baking a humble apple pie. He was angry, he was scared, and he wanted to pummel Cassius' face until it was puffy and bloated like the dough beneath his fists. He wanted to —

His thoughts were interrupted by a ding from the service bell on the counter. Clapping the flour dust from his hands, he went up front, nodding to the lady at the counter and quickly washing his hands.

"What can I get for you?" he asked, trying to sound courteous and not ready to rip someone's head off.

"Do you do custom cakes?" she wondered.

Tommen sized her up. Pretty thing, early twenties, blond, probably went to yoga every morning at sunrise and ran a marathon every other weekend. Probably had a salad for lunch with extra kale and drank a chocolate protein shake as her way of indulging. This cake would not be for her.

"Yes, we do, what's the occasion?" He reached under the counter and found the custom order slip and a pen. "Birthday, anniversary? Something off the wall?"

"I'll take C, final answer. It's kind of unusual, so I hope you don't mind." Tommen didn't mind the uncommonness of the cake so much as the way she hesitated and wouldn't get to the point. "It's for my sister. It's a congratulations cake; she just adopted two kids. We're having a party for her."

If there was a God, He certainly enjoyed sticking his little Tommen voodoo doll with needles. Most often they went straight through the heart, it seemed.

"Okay," Tommen told her. "Actually, it's not as unusual as you think. What are you thinking?"

She gave him the parameters and requirements and he calculated the total, ringing her up when she decided to pay in full upfront.

"So, if you don't mind me asking, what kind of kids?" he

wondered, knowing he was willfully jumping into a pool of sharks. "Boys, girls?"

"A boy and a girl," she replied. "Brother and sister. From China. Illegal twins, you know. We're all pretty excited."

If she would have said "from Wales" he probably would have run to the back of the store and beat his head against the back door, which was solid metal. He nodded pleasantly, saying, "Congratulations."

She thanked him, grabbed her receipt, and headed out. The dining room was beginning to clear as the dinner crowd finished up their more civilized meals and prepared to head out to the club or the bar or someplace where they didn't necessarily have to be civilized, where the whole point was to become uncivilized on a Saturday night. Tommen sighed as he thought about Micaiah who usually was one of those people, going out every other Friday or Saturday. He almost missed hearing him announce that he was leaving, and Micah lightly chastising him for leaving him alone.

He turned, ready to go back to his dough, when Micah opened the office door. "A second?"

Tommen tried to tell himself that it was because he was the unofficial, temporary Sub-Lieutenant, as well as a candidate for manager, and not because he was in some kind of trouble. Problem was, generally whenever he got called into the office, it was because he was in trouble, and the feeling of dread was hard to shake.

"Good news?" he wondered, looking around the office. Obviously their missing persons were not back.

"Good and bad news," Micah replied. "I called around the District, to Timekeepers, Harvesters, Merchants, every Time Agent in the District. The good news is that about seventy percent of them are still around. The rest I couldn't reach. I don't know if it was because they're sitting under Cassius' thumb right now or they just stepped out of the office for a minute, but I'm counting them as being missing.

"Bad news is that upper management is in chaos. The only District Captain I was able to raise was District Three. As for

Managers, I actually got a call from Region Nine Manager; he's the only one left of the Managers. Mi Chin the Gatekeeper is gone. There are a handful of Captains and Lieutenants left around the world, but they're mostly gone. A majority of the layfolk are still around, though."

Tommen folded his arms. "What does that mean for us? What do we do?"

"That means that for the time being, we report to the District Three Captain and he reports to the Region Nine Manager. I'm currently going through my list of others around the world who are at least Gatekeeper-trained." He indicated a file open on the computer. "If I can do that, we'll be in pretty good shape."

"What about Wardens or Dominions?"

"Acting as Gatekeepers, yes. But with the state of the Time industry and the Wheel, it does us no good to have such high-ranking officers. In fact, it's more likely to make us a target. Right now, we have to focus more on planetary needs and filling the gaps, figuring out who we have and who we don't have. When in chaos, establish order, set up a chain of command. Then you can work out your plan of attack."

"And what is our plan of attack?"

"I don't know yet," Micah admitted.

"What do you want me to do?"

"Right now, I just wanted to let you know what's going on, what's being done. You are a Sub-Lieutenant and even though it is unofficial and temporary, you still need to be kept in the loop as much as possible."

"Oh. Okay." Tommen looked at his feet.

Micah chuckled nervously, humorlessly. "Believe me, I know you want to go back and murder every one of those black-clad bastards, but it's not going to happen at this moment."

Even as he spoke, the office phone rang. He picked it up. "Bakery na hÉireann, Micah speaking." Pause. "Uh-huh. Yeah. Okay, thanks for keeping me updated."

"Who was that?" Tommen dared ask as Micah hung up.

"District One has an Acting Captain."

"That's good."

"It is. It's even an old friend of ours. Assim Foyez."

Foyez had helped Tommen escape the Grandfathers when he returned from Sifura's world with the cure to his dad's illness. Tommen thought for sure that he'd been killed or had his clock broken or any number of horrible punishments.

"That reminds me," Micah went on. "Sifura is alive and well, also. Or she was. She was present at the inauguration at least."

Sifura had been the one to take Tommen to get the cure in the first place, crossing desert and jungle and facing off against some of the ugliest creatures in the universe. She'd been injured in their quest and sent Tommen home early in order to not waste anymore time. But there had been a spy among the rescue party, and Tommen had feared that he'd done her in, despite her prowess as a Harvester.

It was too strange, too convenient. When the Grandfathers had chased Tommen with murder in their eyes, why had they spared his accomplices? It made no sense.

"What's the likelihood that the Grandfathers would actively chase us here?" Tommen wondered. "Would they actually, like, come to Earth and kill us all?"

"Well, they can try," Micah said, "but it's unlikely. Well, for you. Me, I'm not so sure. But Earth is Unengaged and unimportant; we contribute about as much to the Time industry as Guam contributes to the U.S. economy. Some participants are outliers—Lily, for example—but if they do come after us, it's because they've already desecrated the rest of the universe and are just mopping up the rest."

Tommen wasn't sure if he intended his words to be encouraging or not, and decided it was better to just take them at face value. They were safe for the time being. How long they were safe was unsure, but for the moment, they could take a break.

The phone rang several more times over the next minute or two. District Seven had an Acting Captain. Region Three had an

Acting Manager. A couple people within District Four had returned to their phones and were now informed as to the recent tragedy.

Tommen folded his arms. "How long do we wait before declaring our chain of command as good as it's going to get?"

"Probably not until tomorrow morning," Micah told him. "People need to know what's going on, and it's going to take time to tell them the truth as well as sort out who's here and who's not."

"But that's at least an eternity in the Wheel! What if they're already dead?!"

"Keep your voice down, Tommen, there are still guests in the dining room. If they're already dead, then it won't matter if we went now or waited a day. But if they're alive, we do them no good if we go in there with an ill-conceived plan and get caught ourselves. Do you understand what I am saying?"

Tommen sighed. "Yes."

"I know, Tommen. I know. I do. You want to go in there and murder the Grandfathers and free everyone. Part the Red Sea and deliver everyone to the Promised Land. I get it. But it's not happening right this second. Now, I either need you with me as a Sub-Lieutenant who can handle slow and uncomfortable information and make rational decisions, or you can just be an Apprentice and I'll do this myself."

Part of him wanted to just say, "Fuck it," throw his hands up, and let Uncle Micah do his thing, do all the work. He felt like a small child facing big problems, and he wanted the grown-ups to take care of it and make it go away. Like when he'd first come into the twenty-first century at eight years old, alone and afraid. His dad had done all the work to help him make sense of it all, explain it to him, and help him adjust to his new life. How Tommen wished he could have that again in this situation, surrender it all to Micah and just make it go away. Go to bed tonight and by morning his dad would be back, smiling and saying that it was all just a little misunderstanding and everything was going to be okay.

The other part of him knew better. The other part of him was his pa's son, his dad's son, the part that said that he was a man now and he had to face things like a man. No more hiding behind ma's skirts like a frightened child. It was time to bury his feelings, take the information—no matter how sad, how disturbing, how angering—and come up with a rational plan of action that saved more lives than it sacrificed, even if the only life he sacrificed was his own.

He took a breath and nodded, saying quietly, "I can do it. I can be your Sub-Lieutenant."

Micah nodded slowly. "Good. I was hoping you'd say that."

"What do you need me to do?"

"Your first priority right now is managing the bakery while we're open and making sure that no one notices anything amiss." He raised a brow and Tommen flushed. "And when you get time, I want you to make up a list of all the Regions and Districts with the current Acting or True Managers and Captains. I'll scribble them down on paper; I just need you to write it up so it's more organized. Can you do that for me?"

Tommen nodded. "Yes, sir."

"Good man." The phone rang. "I'll get back to you."

Tommen turned and left the office just as a customer walked up to the counter. He put on a good face and hoped it looked convincing. From his experience, there were only two acceptable options when it came to greeting customers and not letting on that something was wrong. The first was the nice face that everyone expected, the one that said, "Hi! How are you today? How's the wife and kids? Isn't little Johnny getting big!" The second option was the face that everyone expected from a teenager, the one that said, "I don't give a fuck about you or what you want because I hate my job, I'm just here for the paycheck, and I think that you should actually be catering to me." No one wanted to see the sad face and hear the sob story because that made everything awkward, and the mad face and the whiny story just left everyone feeling miserable.

The order was simple enough, and once the customer was gone, Tommen was faced with the task of doing full store shutdown alone. That meant going back and finishing his baking project, then working on condensing all the trays in the display case. It also meant cleaning the kitchen from top to bottom as well as the normal dining room duties—wiping down tables, sweeping and mopping, trashes, cleaning the display case once everything was empty, cleaning the coffeemaker...

Yeesh. And to think that Micah normally had to do it all by himself on the days Tommen didn't work, or mostly by himself; Micaiah didn't always leave early. Still, it almost seemed cruel of Micaiah to leave his brother alone to do all the cleanup.

As the last of the customers filtered through, Tommen tried to make up silly little scenarios about what Micaiah really did when he left early. He always said that he went out to bars and clubs and got laid—maybe not explicitly, but hey, when it's just three dudes in a bakery, talk happens—but even if he did do that occasionally, what if it was really just a cover-up for something else?

While his less serious scenarios involved Micaiah secretly being Batman and the like, he also considered the possibility that maybe he really did have another job. Probably not the normal kind, moonlighting as a bartender or a saxophone player on various street corners, but maybe as a true Timekeeper? He had a day job and couldn't just up and leave on a whim to go chase down some Runner in Vermont who'd stolen six minutes' worth of Time from some low-level Merchant. Maybe he worked a night shift, unofficial, unpaid, but it was his eight hours where he would respond to all things Runner, and other assorted Time shenanigans.

Tommen dumped a bit of bleach in a bucket and started filling the final cleaning bucket. It was kind of like when his dad had still worked Missing Persons, doing that for about six months after the adoption. It wasn't always about hunting down international terrorists who kidnapped the pretty daughter of some secretive ex-FBI agent. Most of the time it was a parent or relative doing the kidnapping. And sometimes, it was all about getting a vehicle description and direction of travel. His dad would be out at three in the morning, hiding on a side road or behind a bush, waiting for the kidnapper to try and make the crossing into Kentucky. He might sit there for ten minutes or six hours, only to learn that they'd gone north to Ohio instead.

Tommen told himself that it was just the stink of bleach that got him all teary now. *Fuck, but you're an idiot. What are you, a child? A girl? What would your dad say if he saw you like this, if you and him and escaped and it was Micah and Micaiah trapped in the Wheel?* He'd probably say the same thing Micah did. A time to weep and a time to be strong, but not until they're six feet under. Not over until it's over. To say nothing of the fact that if those had been the circumstances, he probably wouldn't be so torn up over it. Did that make him a bad person?

He rubbed his eyes on his shirt sleeve, feeling his sinuses burn as he turned off the water and hauled the bucket out to the dining room. Dipping a wash rag in, he quickly found several small cuts on his hand and wrist and he sucked in a breath through his teeth. Trying to work around a cast sucked. Couldn't get it wet, so washing his hands was difficult and that only made it harder to do his job seeing how he had to contend with frosting and icing and glaze and sprinkles that somehow, someway, managed to slip in under the wrappings and cause him to itch and scratch something fierce. Luckily he was able to dig them out with only moderate difficulty, like trying to lick a piece of silk out of your teeth after eating corn on the cob.

After he wiped down the tables and put away the bleach bucket, he started on trashes. He'd just opened up a new box of large bags when the bell on the counter dinged. He glanced at the clock. Well, technically they were still open. For another fifteen minutes.

It was a group of college students, as evidenced by age, school pride sweatshirts, and general drunken demeanor, suggesting that whatever they were up to tonight, it wasn't going to be studying—not the book kind anyway. As it was, of the ten people in the group, seven of them—yes, seven—appeared to be unable to keep their hands off their significant other, or others. Tommen didn't even want to think about why they decided they needed the last eight unsold donuts of the day. Not to say that his mind didn't go there, but something about present circumstances just didn't make it seem like much fun.

"How's it going out here?" Micah asked, standing in the office door and stretching, looking about as grouchy as Micaiah normally did after being cooped up in the office for too long.

"Just about ready to take these pans back to wash and lock the door," Tommen reported, trying to sound responsible, a polite balance of eagerness to be promoted in some fashion, without seeming to completely neglect why he was in that position in the first place.

"Is the kitchen clean?"

"Aside from a few last dishes, yeah."

"Damn. I was hoping for a distraction."

"Sorry...I think?"

Micah shook his head. "No, you're doing good." He rubbed his eyes. "Micaiah makes this job look easy. And I'm not even talking about the bakery stuff."

Somehow it just suddenly occurred to Tommen that Micaiah did as many Timekeeping duties as baking duties as he sat in that office for hours on end. He was the one who did all the leg work while Micah ran the bakery and Walter raised Tommen. He wasn't a baker who did a little Timekeeping on the side; he was a Timekeeper who did a little baking on the side, probably as a hobby just to keep him sane.

"You okay?" Micah asked, cutting into Tommen's thoughts.

"Yeah," Tommen answered, probably a little too quickly.

"Hang in there just a little while longer. We'll get them back."

There is a certain sinking feeling that one gets when one realizes that one's paranoia isn't really paranoia and all of one's fears are true. Walter had always known that the elections would end badly, but there had always been that last glimmer of foolish hope that desperately prayed for everything to go smoothly, that paranoia would simply remain paranoia. But when Cassius revealed himself, when the guards began closing in, when the gates came down and the guards and the Grandfathers began their slaughter, it wasn't fear or shock that twisted his gut. He did not become overwhelmed with a blind, bestial instinct to survive—though all of those certainly came into play at one time or another.

Rather, it was an almost sick kind of stoic determination and acceptance that drove him to hobble along, pushing and shoving in the pressing, suffocating throngs, trying to keep Micaiah close to hand. Maybe it was his police training, the knowledge that any call could be his last no matter how ordinary it seemed. Maybe it was lessons from his past life, the ability to size up a situation in a second, to weigh the odds—a knife against a beer bottle, fisticuffs against a gun, one-on-one or one-on-five—and conjure up either a plan of attack or plan of escape.

The problem now, though, was that neither was a viable option. And that's what made the feeling in his gut disgusting to him. His mind shut out everything that it didn't deem relevant in a bid to fight or flee, but when both of those basic instincts failed to work, his mind simply shut down and he saw and heard only what was immediately around him, as if he was just watching TV. Once the greater portion of the fighting and killing was over and he and Micaiah were safely snugged up in the middle of the thick crowd away from the guards and the Grandfathers, it almost became unreal. He had no fear left in him to flee, no strength with which to fight, and yet with no threat of death looming over him like a guillotine, it was about the same amount of suspense he would feel as a cliff-hanger at the end of a TV episode.

Did that make him a bad person? Wasn't he supposed to be fighting or crying or trying to run? Anything but simply sitting in the middle of the Coliseum like he was trying to be part of some Guinness World Record?

His mind came back to him as Micaiah spoke beside him.

"So, what are you thinking?"

Walter blinked and looked around. Everything appeared to have calmed down, at least for the moment. Here and there, someone tried to break the line, rush the guards, and were quickly cut down. But for the most part, the stampede had ended and now they sat or stood in nervous compliance, like sheep held in a pen, one by one being taken away for slaughter.

"Do you think Micah made it out and got Tommen to safety?" Walter found himself asking.

"I'd say he had enough time," Micaiah replied diplomatically. "Micah's a snake; I imagine he was able to slip out. And Tommen's no idiot. He would have seen something was up."

"There's a difference between seeing something was up and following my orders to run when he did."

"True. But there's nothing we can do about it from here. Right now, we have to worry about us and each other. So, what do you think?"

Walter took a breath. He was thinking that maybe after this was all over, he could retire and maybe talk Micaiah into becoming District Captain. It was a terrible thing to say, but there were advantages to having only yourself to look after. Micaiah wasn't distracted by a family or other ties; he certainly wasn't worrying about whether his son had made it out. Sure, he probably worried about Micah, but there was a difference there. Micah was an adult and they had equal training. Tommen was just a kid and only just made an Apprentice.

Walter closed his eyes and tried to get it together. Police mode wouldn't help here because he had no advantages at his disposal. He would have to either make an advantage or learn to simply melt into the crowd, come out on top by slipping out through the bottom.

"I'm thinking that Cassius is in control," he stated finally. Even as he said it, his thoughts came more into focus. "Rifun is his right hand. The Grandfathers are his police force because I don't see any Timekeepers rushing to his aid or defense. The majority of the killing has stopped, but it would be impractical to just keep us in here."

"Why do you say that?" Micaiah asked. "Small space, easily guarded."

"Guarded, but not defended. Just like you can contain a peaceful herd of cows, but if they get it in their heads to stampede, no fence will hold them. If we got in a single mind to stampede, we could overrun the guards and even the Grandfathers. Problem is, it would take a lot to get this whole group moving as one at once."

"True."

"The fact that nothing has happened despite the general calming down, I'd say something outside of here is holding them up."

"You think something happened outside the Coliseum?"

"I'd say it's possible, even highly likely. If Cassius wants control, he needs not only the Seat and the ruling power, but he needs at least the attention if not the fear of the layfolk. He'll probably have done something similar in the marketplaces."

Micaiah swore, but before either of them could say more, there was movement in the seats and Cassius took front and center stage once more.

"Now that I have your attention," he began mockingly, "let's begin with how this is going to work. With every transition of power, naturally there is fear of retaliation. Will my enemy, who now has power over me, seek to destroy me with said power? And the answer here is yes. Those who have actively opposed me in the past will be shown no mercy. But for those who do not know me and simply used my name as a foolish bedtime story, you may have the chance to receive mercy and bow to me."

Part of his speech sounded off to Walter. A man who got a kick out of killing and watching his victims die slowly and horribly didn't understand the concept of mercy except as weakness. Cassius was king, but Walter suspected that he didn't have as much power as he flaunted. Somewhere deep down, Walter suspected that Rifun was still the one calling the shots. Somehow, that did little to comfort him.

He knew enough that shows like *Criminal Minds* were more drama than criminal science, but he'd never doubted that heartless, soulless, highly-manipulative psychopaths existed in the world—after all, he'd been one himself at one point. And they were scary enough to deal with, hence the maniac standing above them now. But to know that there was someone above even *him*, manipulating that heartless, soulless, highly-manipulative psychopath...that was a whole new level of fear. Walter had heard of the peace that surpasses all understanding, but this was now a fear that surpassed all reconciling.

"Many of you here today are political opponents," Cassius went on. "And many of you will die. But some will not. However, because there are too many here to deal with right now, and because I can't risk you escaping and warning those waiting at home, you will be taken to the Judgment Wing for processing and wait for your executions."

Say one thing for Cassius, he wasn't the schemer of the pair. He didn't sit around a grand chessboard, making his moves and sacrificing pawns to achieve an endgame. He was all action and blunt words. Even more reason to consider Rifun to be the mastermind.

Somehow, no matter how many times he thought about it, realized it, and mulled it over, the thought still wasn't very comforting. It was the equivalent of "the butler did it" and yet, for as cliché as it was, it was much scarier in person. He shook his head to clear it. *Focus. Cassius basically just delivered your verdict and sentence. The ambiguous part is over with. You have the information, now what are you going to do with it? You have to fight and escape; there are no other options because you are being delivered unto death. They'll probably even make you carry your own cross.*

The guards did not take everyone out at once, but rather in smaller groups of a hundred or so. Considering the capacity of the Coliseum, Walter knew it was going to be a while before he and Micaiah went anywhere. The only thing he could look forward to was that with each group that left, there was a little more room to breathe.

They could have sat there for six hours or six days. Either way, it was long enough to get hungry, though no food was brought, just a bit of water to pass around. Walter was pretty sure he slept once, or at least dozed off. Every so often, a guard would approach Cassius, who still sat and watched over them, but what was being said, Walter could only guess.

As the Seat cleared out, the occupants slowly dispersed and found their own sections. Walter and Micaiah managed to find a few humans to group with. Two were Indian, one Vietnamese, one Ugandan, and one Peruvian. No one had any idea of the fate of their comrades or anyone outside the Coliseum. Eventually they lapsed into silence.

Walter slept a second time, lightly, and fitfully, as Micaiah had to shake him awake, saying that he was shouting and getting some unwanted attention from the guards and the Grandfathers.

Finally, their turn to be taken out came around. Walter privately wondered if the whole bit about being taken to the Judgment Wing was just a ploy to get them to cooperate, make it easier to kill them once they were out of sight of the others. Give them hope, a chance to potentially talk to the judge and straighten things out, then cut off his head once he was in the door.

But they left the Coliseum without incident. Walter glanced down the track corridors as they passed, all of them empty like the ancient Coliseum ruins. All the dead had been removed, and he could only imagine what the guards had done with them. Piled them up to decay, burned them, sent them to the Food Court to be spitefully and satanically fed back to the prisoners? It was all a guess.

Or so Walter thought until they finally left the Coliseum, filing through the portal into the rest of the Wheel.

Generally speaking, Walter enjoyed watching war movies, at least on occasion. And he had a certain appreciation for how realistic they were becoming, more like a true story and less like hero propaganda. But for all the detail and special effects that Hollywood was able to pull off, there was still no substitute for the real thing. To see real blood and real bodies and be in real fear of your life, there was no way that any production could ever truly capture that.

So it was how Walter felt as they walked through the Wheel. There was no way to sugarcoat it; a massacre had happened here. The guards and Grandfathers and an army of secretaries were busy trying to hide it, pulling bodies this way and that, but the sheer scale of the operation spoke mountains. Some of the victims had been lucky enough to be killed with one or two blows — a stab, a beheading, some form of projectile. Others showed signs of violent struggle and a slow, painful death. One beast the size of a grizzly bear had virtually no skin left on one side; it had all been skinned from him, the blood flow telling Walter that it had been alive at the time. At the same time, in massive hand-paws, it had the head of one Borelian Grandfather and the horns of another, with more flesh in its mouth, still twisted in a snarl of rage.

The majority of the dead were common Time Agents, and there appeared to be no real favoritism. Harvesters and Timekeepers lay dead beside one another, as did Merchants and a Scout here and there. Even the secretaries did not appear to have been immune to the slaughter, most of them dead in a position of fear as they ran for cover.

How much had they known? Who had been in on the coup? Why had anyone been dumb enough to throw in their lot with

Cassius? Walter was not disillusioned; he knew that he was one of the lucky ones who was able to profit from his work, but many suffered. Was the suffering really so great that having a pair of psychopaths in power was better than a corrupt council of Hands? Or was it that some were so tired of the road that Time had been on that they would take any alternative? Did anyone really know where this road led?

A long time ago, Walter had taken Tommen to Yellowstone; they'd driven out there so Tommen could see more of the country. They stopped at a few attractions along the way, just to make it interesting. Once, though, when they were driving through Colorado, Walter had gotten the bright idea to take a "shortcut." They were both tired of the interstates and highways and, being back in the mountains, Tommen wanted to explore some more, and Walter had tried to oblige. Long story short, he'd almost obliged them both over a cliff.

"I don't see them," Micaiah said quietly.

"What?" Walter turned to look at him.

"Micah and Tommen. I don't see them. Maybe they got out."

Walter nodded but said nothing. He desperately wanted to take Micaiah's word at face value. No bodies equals still alive. But there was always that niggle of fear in the back of his mind that said that their bodies had already been taken away. After all, it was a big cleanup job that looked like it was just beginning to turn the corner to see the end. How many bodies had already been taken away and disposed of? It was like Holocaust cleanup. Six million had been murdered, but only a fraction of the bodies had ever actually been found; most were lost to time, nameless and faceless, knowing only fear in their last moments.

Walter's heart leapt into his throat as someone suddenly broke from the group, barging past the guards and making a break for it. In one moment, Walter was terrified because of the sudden movement, then confused, then secretly hoping that maybe they would make it and escape.

First came the net, then the tripwire, then the blade that almost clove them in two. It took Walter a second to realize that it had all come from one of the guards, though the group never stopped moving. As they walked away, leaving the would-be escapee dead or dying on the floor, a Grandfather approached and knelt beside him. A pink Borelian hand reached out and touched the person.

"So," the Peruvian man said, "knowing that, what do you think our chances are?"

"I think I'd take that over whatever Cassius has planned for us," Micaiah said grimly.

"You don't think there's any way out?" the Ugandan woman wondered.

Walter sighed. "I think it's best to keep our thoughts to ourselves right now."

He tried to sound encouraging, as if he and Micaiah were secretly working on a plan and they didn't want to give away the details right in front of the guards. He hoped it was convincing, because he had nothing.

They continued through the Wheel and reached the Judgment Wing without further incident. It was the only place that seemed even remotely normal in the sense of a ton of people milling about outside the main entrance. It was only then that Walter realized that the dampening field that normally covered only select areas of the Wheel had been extended to everywhere. Time was lost to him. On the one hand, it frightened him. On the other hand, it was encouraging in the sense that his mind was coming back to him enough to even notice. How much good did that do him, though? Did it matter if the chicken fought back only just before the cleaver came down?

The enormous screen projected on the outside just above the portal into the Judgment Wing, once a frenzied list of candidates and their accumulating votes, was now a forbidding list of names as each person was processed. Name, rank, galactic coordinates of the home planet, and a small line of pictographs that Walter could only guess the meanings of. Some had only one or two symbols while others had up to twenty, like comparing the features of two similar items. This house had a fenced-in backyard but that one had an open floor plan. This person was Manager-trained but that one had actively opposed Cassius.

The line of people outside the Judgment Wing only traveled one direction. Hundreds of people marched forward, into the Judgment Wing, but the only ones who came out were guards and Grandfathers. Not even the secretaries, if there were any secretaries in there, returned.

It made Walter wonder where the secretaries fell in all of this. The rule of thumb had always been that anything said in the presence of a secretary would inevitably make its way back to the Hand of the Secretaries, thereby reaching all the Hands of Time. Now one was forced to wonder what the secretaries actually did with the information that got passed around. Had there been some sort of revolt within the secretaries? Had the Hand of the Secretaries been against Cassius and so doomed everyone under him?

"Do you think they will actually process us?" the Ugandan woman wondered. "Or you think they'll go straight to executing us?"

"Hard to say," Micaiah answered. "My bet's on the actual processing. Cassius is evil, but he isn't very smart. If he wanted to kill us, he would have done so. He wouldn't play these games."

"So you're thinking what I'm thinking?" Walter wondered.

"That Rifun is the real power behind this? Yes."

"Quiet!" one the guards snapped, swinging a blade toward them and missing Micaiah's face by an inch.

As they got closer to the portal door, fear began to creep into Walter's mind. He'd been here before, once, just one in a long line of prisoners being sent before a judge. Before, he'd certainly deserved it, a man who was a criminal, who had done many dangerous and stupid things finally receiving his due. Wages of sin and all that. Sure, he'd spent countless nights in jail, but there was only one instance where he'd been really afraid to stand before a judge.

"Hang him!" they'd cried. And by "they," he meant the rich family and associates of Mr. Balk, his former father-in-law. But in that instant, all he'd heard was, "Crucify him!"

Back then, the fear had been tempered with a calm sigh of acceptance. He'd done terrible evil and now he stood to face his punishment. This, though, was fear compounded by the cry of injustice. He'd done nothing wrong now save oppose a tyrannical regime and now he was persecuted for doing good.

"Hold it together, Walt," Micaiah said beside him.

Walter realized that his breaths had become fast and shallow, panicky. He forced himself to take a deeper breath and almost stumbled as a wave of vertigo swept over him. Panic was contagious and he didn't need to get everyone here killed. Not like it would be any worse now than later.

"Think of Tommen," Micaiah told him. "What would he say if he could see you now?"

He sighed. "He'd probably say that there has to be a way out, even if we have to fight." He shook his head. "Must be a family trait or something."

"We'll take every advantage we can get, I think."

They narrowly dodged another blow by the guards, Walter ending up on the ground as his leg gave out from under him. He gritted his teeth and found himself wishing for a pill or two. Strange thing to be wishing for, he thought, as Micaiah and one of the Indians came up under him and got him back on his feet.

At the same time, the way Micaiah spoke, it almost sounded like he had some sort of plan and was telling Walter to be ready to fight. On the one hand, it was encouraging that Micaiah seemed to have a plan—a bit shameful on Walter's part since he was the Captain and all. On the other hand, his fighting days were long since past. Yeah, he could defend himself and fight well enough—cheating with Time—in order to subdue a particularly violent criminal, but he knew he couldn't win in sustained hand-to-hand combat. Once he ran out of tricks in order to surprise an adversary and his short bursts of brute strength ran out, he was done. Time did wonders to slow the aging process, but he'd entered the industry when he was past forty years old, already past his prime. By the time the effects really took hold, and considering that aging never truly ceased, in the last ninety years, he probably had a bodily age of about fifty-five to sixty years old. He had experience and could still generally hold his own, but he was no spring chicken. He wasn't even a summer chicken at this point.

They inched closer to the Judgment Wing. When they were just about to the door, there was the shuffle of feet and other assorted appendages behind them as another group came up from the Coliseum. A few guards were relieved and they headed back through the portal, probably to retrieve another group.

"If the Coliseum has just as many rooms and the same dampening field, why bring us here?" the second Indian wondered aloud.

This time the blow connected and bright red blood spurted out from the man's radial artery. Walter stepped back as his companion and a couple others attended to him. A tourniquet was tied, but without proper medical care, he wouldn't last the night. The guard looked on, his — or hers or its — expression difficult to read, but putting Walter in mind of disappointment, like getting a huge tug on a fishing line only to pull up an old boot that had mistakenly gotten caught on a log.

Still they moved forward. Walter said nothing aloud, but he knew why they were brought to the Judgment Wing. It had nothing to do with the number of rooms or the dampening field. The real goal here was the black cells, the prison, the asylum where all violent Time criminals were kept. It didn't matter whether Cassius was going to kill them all or not, because the black cells would break them. They always did. If you weren't sentenced to die, just a few minutes in those cells and you would be begging for such a mercy. Sometimes the worst thing that could happen was being allowed to live after such an experience. There really were fates worse than death, and sometimes the worst one of all was life.

Walter jumped as something bumped into him from behind, but it was just the general push and shove of the crowd. He tried to take a breath, close his eyes, and calm his racing heart, but with every step it was like walking towards death. In between wild-eyed glances at the screen over the Judgment Wing portal, all those names of the people being processed, his mind also showed him memories of Beaumaris Gaol. The cold stone, the awful guards, the rotten food, the rats, the black cells. He remembered both times he tried to kill himself because of that fear, the hopelessness and despair.

He tried to keep Tommen at the forefront of his mind. Just like when he'd pressed on in his Time training and doing his best to wait for Tommen to come out of that cave, now he was going to have to press on and endure for the sake of getting back to him now. Where he was hopefully safe and sound at home with Micah, and not one of the bodies that the secretaries dragged away, never to be seen again.

"I'll go ahead of you," Micaiah said, breaking into his thoughts. "Stay close."

Immediately, fear turned to shame in Walter. Micaiah was speaking to him like he might speak to Tommen, a parent trying to comfort a child. Get behind me, I'll face the danger and protect you. Walter felt his ears turn red. He was the Captain. He should be the one to lead his men, go before them, ask nothing of them that he wouldn't do himself. He shouldn't be the one hiding, wrapped and drowning in fear as they stepped through the portal into the Judgment Wing.

Still, watching the screens as the people filtered through, wondering what the symbols meant and if it was better to have more or fewer of them, being able to identify which names belonged where as the line got shorter and shorter. Where the Hutch, a strange hamster alien secretary, had been in charge before, taking down information for voting, a Grandfather now stood doing the same job. Behind him, the Hutch stood, hunched and looking as if he'd been beaten and tamed and made into a veritable footstool, a servant for the Grandfather's every whim and order.

"Name," the Grandfather ordered as Micaiah stepped up, next in line.

Micaiah did not resist as he gave the Grandfather all the information he asked for, but Walter could see the frustration as he clenched and unclenched his fists. He was trying to work out a plan, but the rules had changed. Everything they had known about how the Wheel worked was shattered. Once all the information had been given, Micaiah proceeded down the corridor and out of sight.

Walter stepped up next.

"Name."

"Walter Forbes."

"Time Agent affiliation and rank."

"Timekeeper, Captain."

"Coordinates."

The Grandfather was shrouded, per custom, but somehow Walter got the impression of a bored, snobby teenager who worked at McDonald's. Just looked at the screen, never at the customer, pushing buttons and completely uninterested in anything but what they were going to do once they got off work. So not all jobs under Cassius were glorious and satisfying. Hey, someone still had to mop the floors, clean the toilets, and process the prisoners.

It was almost amusing as Walter answered the Grandfather's remaining questions. This wasn't the judge; this was the desk officer. This was the one who drew the short straw and had to deal with every single person who came through, no matter how dangerous or how petty. He was the switchboard, sending each person to the designated department.

"This information will be sent back. You will go to the holding cells to await the decision," the Grandfather told him mechanically, the same way he'd told Micaiah and probably every person before that. The same way that every McDonald's employee mechanically told incoming customers about their specials on smoothies or frappés or whatever else.

It actually helped to calm Walter down a bit as he was turned away and made to move, walking through the vault door, down the corridor to the three doors. There were fewer guards here, but he'd been marked with the one-way stamp. Even if he tried to go back and make a break for it, he'd be electrocuted by the force field in the doorway. He had no choice but to go through the second vault door where another force field would close behind him, forcing him to continue ever onward.

Apparently everyone received the same initial order because the door on the left was already open, one guard posted there, looking about as happy as the Grandfather-secretary. Had this guard hoped to be one of the ones on the outside, rounding up those in the Coliseum and bringing them for judgment?

The holding cells in the Judgment Wing were about as packed as the holding cells at the precinct on New Year's Eve or St. Patrick's Day. With exception of the obvious aliens, it was a familiar scene and even that helped Walter to feel more at ease. At least until the point where he was rudely reminded that he was on the other side of the bars this time.

He could not find Micaiah in the cell, instead spotting him a short ways down the hall in another cell. As far as Walter knew, Micaiah had never been in trouble with the law or done time, but the way he carried himself now was oddly familiar. He'd found his place in the cell and he'd defended it; no one else bothered him, even as Walter was being sized up. It wasn't that everyone locked up was a hardened criminal, but when you had no possessions and no power, you took what you could get, even if it's just one square foot of space in a tiny jail cell. Walter gave a bit and held a bit, just enough to send the message that he wasn't interested in fighting, though he would if he had to. But still, looking at Micaiah, he had to wonder.

Actually, he didn't know a whole heck of a lot about the twins. He'd heard their story of how they ended up in Time and some of their exploits afterwards up until they became his Lieutenants, but home life beforehand wasn't always discussed, and Micaiah in particular wasn't the most forthcoming. Did he have as much of a wild past as Walter? Wouldn't that be the irony.

Where the outside of the Judgment Wing had been a mass

funneling into a single-file line, the holding cells were more of a revolving door as guards came and went, delivering new inmates and taking out old ones. Some resisted and were killed, any excuse to be rid of another prisoner. A few inmates killed themselves before they let themselves be taken, and Walter wondered if they had really hoped to be freed at the end of the road only to realize that there was no hope of escape.

With the constant flow of people and aliens and guards and inmates, it was difficult to keep track of who was who, but he did notice eventually that he—and Micaiah who was still in his same spot just down the way—had been in the cell longer than normal. It quickly became that most all of the prisoners being taken out had come in after them. Since Walter highly doubted that they'd been forgotten, he suspected that they were being deliberately held. But for what purpose?

After a short time, he found out. One guard went for Micaiah and another came for him. He did not resist, but the way he was being handled made it difficult to keep up with his leg and he stumbled more than once. They were taken to the desk at the door where another shanghaied secretary looked harried as a Grandfather stood over his shoulder, watching, expression unknowable under the black cowl.

"Walter Forbes and Micaiah Durvin," the Grandfather stated.

"Yes," Micaiah said sarcastically.

"You have been specially marked by the Zero Hour as personal enemies to himself as well as enemies of Time."

"I always wanted to be wanted."

Walter went down as the guard swiped his cane from his hand and used it to hit Micaiah across the back of the shoulders. He grunted but did not go down except to help Walter back up. The Grandfather did not react, instead going on to say, "You are to be held for interrogation by the Zero Hour himself as well as the Council of Grandfathers."

Council of Grandfathers? Walter had never heard of such a

thing. Strange thing was, though, he had a hard time deciding if it was just one more aspect of their normally secretive nature that he'd never before needed to know about, or if it was a new thing that Cassius had devised in order to give more power to the Grandfathers and keep them happy and under his control. Either way, it wasn't a pleasant thing to consider. One Grandfather was bad enough, but getting more of them together was never a good thing.

"What about my brother?" Micaiah demanded. "What about Micah Durvin?"

Walter briefly considered asking about Tommen, but decided against it. Maybe it was cowardice, that he was too afraid to consider the possibility that he was dead or had been captured and sentenced to die. He told himself it was because he didn't want to bring Tommen's name to the forefront. *Don't point him out and maybe the hounds will pass him by.*

The secretary nervously ran through the records available, acutely aware of the Grandfather hovering over him like the Grim Reaper. Finally, the Grandfather answered, "No one has yet come through by that name. If he is not dead, we will be sure to deliver him with you, as he has been marked for interrogation as well."

It was the only hope they had going for them. Micah wasn't here and they hadn't seen his body. Maybe he really had escaped. And if he was gone, he had to have taken Tommen with him. He had to. It just had to be.

"Furthermore," the Grandfather went on, "until the Zero Hour is ready to interrogate you, you will be taken and held in the black cells of the prison."

Somewhere in the room, something gave out an unearthly shriek. It wasn't until Walter was beaten with his own cane until he hit the ground that he realized the shriek had come from him. No, no, no, no, no, no, no, no, he couldn't go the black cells. He couldn't go back there. The black cells. So dark and small. Crawling rats. Stinking of death and waste. The darkness and the hallucinations, the sounds and the false images. The guards, laughing. The other prisoners, screaming and begging and weeping and praying. Death and sickness. One scrape, one little cut, infection. Fever and chills, sickness made worse by rotting in your own waste. He couldn't go back there; there was no way he could. He would kill himself before he went back there.

Before he could do anything to compose himself, the guards hauled him to his feet and wrenched his arms and shoulders in such a way that he could not move, pulling back on his hair so he had to look at the Grandfather.

"The Zero Hour has also ordered this one to be bound and put in chains," the Grandfather continued. "He is to be watched and kept alive until the interrogation."

Before Walter could say anything or scream again, a gag was forced into his mouth. And it wasn't the high-tech gag that was commonly used in the Wheel, but an old, filthy rag tasting of oil and dirt and waste, one that Cassius himself had no doubt picked out specially for Walter. He tried to fight, but the guards held him easily. After a moment of watching the Grandfather smirk, they turned and hauled him out of the room of the holding cells, Micaiah and his guards close behind.

They went to the middle door. As it was painstakingly opened, Walter began fighting even harder, thrashing, his reflexive fear of pain being overridden by sheer terror and the need to survive. He wasn't going to go in there. He couldn't. Somehow, he would tear every joint out of place and break every bone, he would die before they placed him in there with the darkness and the screaming. He couldn't do it. He wouldn't.

Somehow, though, they managed to wrestle him past the force field and lock the door behind them.

There really were fates worse than death. Sometimes, the worst one of all was living.

# Chapter Three
## In Charge

Tommen reluctantly locked the front door and turned off the lights before heading into the office.

"Do you really think they'll still come back?" he wondered, trying to keep it together and stay positive, if for no other reason than to be considered for promotion. It still sounded selfish, but it kept him motivated when emotional reasons threatened to choke him.

"Even if they come back while we're gone, Cai has a key to the store to lock up after himself and your dad's car is still here," Micah told him, clearly trying to sound optimistic, like they were merely out for a walk and might get back a little later than expected.

"Do you think it's possible that Rifun will try to use them against us like he tried to use me against my dad?"

Micah frowned. "I think it's a possibility, yes. But if you think of it this way, it means they're still alive. And just like your dad came up with a plan to get you home safely, I think he's thinking of a plan to get home safely himself. And we should be planning on how to help them. All right?"

Tommen nodded. "Okay." He took a breath. "So, what do we do?"

"The calls have been fewer and farther between, but these are the names I have so far." Micah handed him a notebook with four sheets filled with names, including rank and location. "Most of those are the Masters and lower of our District, but more importantly are the people of upper management, Lieutenants and Captains and Managers. I haven't heard anything about an Acting Gatekeeper, but like I said earlier, that really isn't important right now."

"How do you want me to rewrite it?" Tommen wondered, flipping through the pages and scanning the names.

"Standard management style, but I'll show you later when we get home."

"Wait, what?"

"You can't go home by yourself. Not tonight. It's too dangerous."

Tommen's first thought was that he still had an English essay to write. Then he felt guilty and asked, "What if they don't come back? What am I going to do?"

Micah frowned. "I don't know. But we're not to that point yet. One thing at a time. And just remember, not until they're six feet under. Not over until it's over."

Tommen nodded. "Right. Not over until it's over. So what do we do next?"

"Next," Micah said, standing and stretching, "we are going to go home, get something to eat, and get some sleep. I know it sounds callous and unproductive, but you are no good to anyone if you aren't at full strength and energy. How's your head doing?"

Tommen shrugged. "Okay. I can work and stuff. I can use my phone and get on the computer for short periods."

"How about Banding?"

"I mean I can, but it's kind of like when I was just starting out, how I used to get really bad migraines really fast."

"Okay. Good to know."

"My dad was going to take me in on Monday if my headaches didn't improve."

"Did he make an appointment?"

"No, I don't think so."

Micah nodded and grabbed his coat. "Well, at any rate, talking about it won't do us any good here. Lights off, door locked?"

Tommen affirmed and they headed out of the office toward the back door. He cast a last glance at the old Cadillac, sitting alone in the parking lot.

"Maybe I should follow you in the car," Tommen said, stopping and gesturing toward the vehicle. "Keep it safe at your house and hopefully keep it from getting towed."

"Do you have your license yet?" Micah wondered.

"Well, no."

He could see Micah's hesitation. He didn't have his license and he wasn't exactly cleared to drive on account of his concussion. But leaving the car out was like having a big neon sign over it saying, "Rob me!" to car thieves, "Ticket me!" to cops, and "Tow me!" to tow drivers. If and when his dad came back, he really didn't need that hassle. And on the rare chance that he didn't come back, Tommen was going to need something to drive.

"Fine," Micah conceded slowly. "If you think you can, I'll let you."

"Awesome. Okay, I'll follow you."

"Ah ah. Hold up for a second. If you start feeling weird in the head, pull over."

"I will."

"And you know very well where we live, so you don't need to follow me that closely. If you don't feel comfortable going fast, then don't."

Tommen sighed. "I know."

"And if you need to call me, then pull over and —"

"Micah!"

Micah put his hands up in defense. "Okay, okay, I get it. I'm just making sure."

"I know."

"Although, now that I think about it, maybe I should follow you back to your house."

"Why?"

"I imagine you might want to take a shower and get a fresh change of clothes, at least. Plus it will leave your dad's car in the garage where it can't be seen. And you might also need the charger for your hearing aids."

Tommen groaned. "Okay, fine, we'll go to my house first."

"And no Banding either," Micah told him. "You need real experience behind the wheel and..."

But Tommen was already out the door and making a beeline for the car. It wasn't locked and the keys were in a secondary hidden compartment in the center console, right next to his dad's gun. It wasn't his police-issued one, just the one he kept in the car or on his person. Briefly Tommen wondered what the reaction would be if he took that to the Wheel and started killing Grandfathers and demanding that his dad and Micaiah be set free. He quickly decided that without unlimited ammo, it was a doomed idea. Even with unlimited ammo, it probably wasn't the brightest move anyway.

It was strange to drive without someone in the passenger seat, reminding him of this or saying something about that, or just making conversation. He was alone, not having to talk about school or work or anything else. In a strange sort of way, it almost felt like he was doing something wrong. Not illegal kind of wrong, which he was already doing by driving without a license or adult supervisor, but more on the level of forgetting to check mirrors or put on his seat belt, which, after he double-checked and triple-checked himself, he found was not true and everything appeared to be in order.

He couldn't decide if he wanted to brag about it later to his dad. He tried to weigh the risk factor between praise and getting his ass chewed. More likely Micah would be the one in trouble for letting him drive without a license or supervision. At the same time, his dad might choose to totally overlook it given the circumstances. In the end, Tommen decided it was best to not worry about it until the time actually came to worry about it.

He saw Micah's car pull around the side of the building into the main lot. The younger twin headed for the exit driveway but stopped and waited politely for Tommen. Taking a breath, Tommen shifted the car into gear and slowly pulled around.

It wasn't that Tommen didn't know how to drive or didn't normally feel confident, but this time he was driving alone and he was driving his dad's car. Getting it from the bakery to home was one thing, and his dad might be able to overlook it. But if he ended up in a ditch or in an accident or otherwise damaged the car, well, that was a whole different story. Regardless of circumstances, someone was going to get an ass-chewing for it.

Still, he did his best to follow all the rules as he remembered them. He made sure to follow the speed limit, always use his signals, and do everything that most people simply forgot about as soon as they got their license and were turned loose on the roads. He knew he would inevitably do something wrong, piss someone off, what have you, but his attention was focused solely on driving and the road.

Okay, that was a lie. Driving was kind of a relaxing event and, despite his best attempts at staying alert and vigilant of his surroundings, Tommen felt his mind wander several times. He thought about everything that had happened in the Wheel. He thought about school and how that would go if his dad wasn't back by Monday, or at least Tuesday. He thought about work, what would happen if Micaiah didn't come back. He thought about what they could be going through right now while he, Tommen, drove leisurely home.

His thoughts wandered to his dad's story about spending time in jail and prison. And not jail like the twenty-first century knew it, but old world prison, where rats abounded and prisoners were left to rot and die, in that order. Eighteen months in darkness, listening to the screams of the other prisoners as the guards beat them. Sometimes being beaten yourself for no other reason than the gaolers were bored.

He still couldn't imagine his dad being the man he said he was. Drunk and fighting all the time. It just wasn't possible. Of course, it was equally difficult to imagine him being a modestly wealthy British banker with a wife and daughter. Somehow it was just absolutely foreign for Tommen to comprehend that his dad...had been a dad.

Tommen was jerked back to reality when he felt the car start to slide on the road just as he got off the bridge toward home. He managed to save it, but pulled into the driveway at little more than a granny crawl. Micah pulled in behind him, but Tommen shut the garage door before he could say anything. Or so he thought as he turned around and Micah had Banded into the garage.

"Good God, what is that smell?" the younger twin wondered. "Something die in here?"

"It's just a few furs," Tommen informed him. Though in his mind he was secretly agreeing with his dad that they had to be moved. The smell was pretty overwhelming.

"All right, start packing."

"For how long?"

Micah faltered. Tommen didn't mean to ask a trick question, even if that was how it came out. He meant it honestly. How long did they expect that he would be staying? How long did they expect that Walter and Micaiah would be gone?

"Why don't you pack for three days?" Micah suggested finally. "Hopefully by then, we'll at least have a plan."

Tommen agreed hesitantly and headed to his room. It was like déjà vú, packing to go stay at the twins' house because his dad wasn't home. First he was in the hospital, now he was a prisoner. Tommen sighed. He just wanted things to go back to the way they were before he and Eric and Varad ever stumbled on that body under the bleachers. Ever since then, it felt like his life had done nothing but suck and try to take everything away from him. Sometimes his dad talked about retiring, both from the police department and from Time. Somehow, that idea seemed very appealing at the moment. Just settle down into a quiet, cozy life where bad things weren't sneaking around every corner.

Of course, that was highly unrealistic, and he knew it as he packed a few days' worth of clothes, transferred his English essay onto a flash drive, and grabbed chargers for his phone as well as his hearing aids.

"Ready?" Micah asked as he emerged into the living room.

Tommen shrugged. "I guess."

"Let's go then."

Tommen followed Micah out to his car and got in, trying not to look as sullen as he felt. He had to stay strong. He was the Sub-Lieutenant. It's not over until it's over.

*But when do you declare it over?*

Would Cassius really see fit to return the bodies of the people he kills? Would he keep everyone in suspense forever? If he didn't return the bodies, what would happen when Walter never returned to work, never showed up for anything at school? What would happen if he just vanished, an eternal cold case? Would it be the same as if he had died in the hospital? Would Micah become his guardian? What would happen to Micah if Micaiah disappeared? How would that affect the bakery?

Of course, on a larger note, if the bodies never returned, would anyone notice any odd correlation between all the people who went missing on the same day? Would it be considered terrorism? Would the whole world go into lockdown? Would there be some religious revival for all the people who missed their fabled rapture? What if no one noticed the connection? What if it's just another Tuesday for the guys at the office? How many people go missing on a daily basis? How many would have to disappear for it to be considered as a possible connection?

And if the bodies were returned, what kind of investigation would be launched then? Would anyone think to make the connection? Would there be a massive manhunt for some faceless killer? Would it be considered terrorism?

"You okay over there?" Micah asked, yanking Tommen from his dark thoughts.

"Huh?" Tommen turned to look at him. "Yeah, fine."

"Listen, I know I keep pushing you with the 'not over until it's over' and 'stay strong' business, but I know it's not easy. We both lost someone important to us and we don't know what's going to happen. If you need to talk, I'm here."

Tommen shook his head. "No, I'm fine. Just thinking about

what I'm going to do to those black-clad bastards if I ever catch one."

Micah grinned and managed a nervous chuckle. "Well, make sure you leave a few for the rest of us to pummel. I don't think there are going to be very many Grandfathers left after all of this. I think there's going to be more than one hostile person or race willing to fight for the honor of killing those black-clad bastards."

One of the few fights worth engaging in, as far as Tommen was concerned. He didn't even need to kill one of them completely, just beat within an inch of his life. Well, okay, yes, he would probably kill one just out of sheer passion and hatred.

Despite the slippery roads, they made it safely to the twins' house and even managed to plod up the driveway to the little metal overhang that served as a garage. From the outside, the house appeared to be like most other houses on the block—average, middle-class but with a nice view. But the vinyl siding hid a grand interior that spoke of the house's origins, when the neighborhood was slated to become a fine gated community for the rich and famous who wanted obnoxious vacation homes in the "charming little mountains." That never happened. Instead, the plans were scrapped and the few luxury homes that were built were listed at a fraction of their value, getting snapped up by opportunistic buyers like Micah and Micaiah.

So while the outside appeared to be no more than any other middle-class home, the inside reeked of wealth with real stone tile, gorgeous and rare hardwood floors, and all the best of everything that money could buy. It was the only time the twins really flaunted their wealth, and that only because everything had been here before them. Otherwise, they were fairly modest about their earnings. Part of it was simply their nature, and the other part was because they couldn't exactly claim their Time earnings on their income taxes.

Tommen slipped his shoes off and gingerly headed for the guest bedroom, the same one he'd used when his dad was in the hospital.

"I'm gone for a week and you clutter this place up again?" he said jokingly, stepping into the room.

The last time he'd been here, the room had been used as a sort of miscellaneous room to store all manner of boxes from stuff the brothers bought, most often for the shop. Boxes and manuals and a variety of packing materials had been scattered around. Tommen thought he'd managed to clean it up pretty well, getting the room almost completely cleaned. Now here it was again with boxes and plastic and papers strewn haphazardly from corner to corner and over the bed.

"Yeah," Micah said guiltily. "When it rains it pours, and when one thing breaks, they all do."

Tommen recalled how a number of small appliances and other things had gotten replaced around the bakery. The coffeemaker, the mini-fridge, a few lights in the display case. Well, it made sense, he supposed. Not that it mattered, and cleaning the room again would give him something mind-numbing to do so he could process everything that had happened in the last twelve hours.

"I'll grab you a bag and you can stuff all the packing stuff in it," Micah told him, disappearing back to the kitchen for a moment.

"Where are you going to be?" Tommen wondered, taking the trash bag. "I mean, like, what are we doing next? Food and bed, right?"

"Eventually. If you're hungry, by all means, *mi casa es su casa*. I think I'm going to go snoop around Cai's room for a few minutes, see if there isn't something lurking in there that might help us."

Tommen raised a brow. "You're going to snoop around in your brother's things?"

"Yes."

"I don't know if I'm more surprised that you don't already share everything or more amused that you're acting like a child. Going to snoop in your brother's things." He grinned.

"Twins we may be, but we're still individual people. He has his space and I have mine. But I think I'm going to have to invade his for a bit. This may come as a surprise to you, but Micaiah can be very secretive."

"Really?!" Tommen feigned shock. "I had no idea."

"Yeah, sure. Get to work if you want to sleep in that bed."

Tommen couldn't help but smile as Micah turned and headed down the hall. Yes, twins they might have been, but some days only their appearance was any evidence of that.

Piece by piece, Tommen reclaimed the bedroom, grabbing all the plastic wrappings, spongy packing sheets, packing peanuts, and bubble wrap—popping the bubble wrap until Micah yelled at him from down the hall to knock it off—and stuffing them into the giant trash bag. Eventually he found the walls of the room, the floor, the desk, and, at long last, he managed to uncover the bed. It felt like the project had taken forever, but the clock showed just barely an hour had gone by.

As Tommen closed the door after returning from taking the trash out to the bin, he noticed Micah coming down the hall from Micaiah's room, his expression difficult to read.

"Find anything?" he asked tentatively.

"Nothing useful," Micah replied grimly.

Tommen could tell he was lying, but he also knew that tone. It was an echo of Micaiah's tone when he was disturbed and deep in thought and did not want to be pressed for details until he managed to figure out whatever problem was plaguing his mind. Micah's tone was far less intimidating, but the implication was still there; he had found something, but he wasn't going to share it until he knew just what it was that he'd found.

"You hungry?" the younger twin asked instead.

Micah wasn't really asking Tommen if he was hungry; he was just looking for an excuse to do something to distract his mind. Still, Tommen agreed to food. He tried to help as much as he could, but Micah was not in much of a talking or helping mood. Like Tommen and lazily cleaning up the guest bedroom, Micah need some mind-numbing distraction.

"You'd tell me if it was something to do with me, right?" Tommen inquired cautiously as Micah chopped up some herbs.

Micah looked at him and Tommen wondered if he'd heard him. Then, "Yes, I would." He went back to chopping. "But it doesn't have to do with you. Actually it has to do with me."

That was a switch. Sure, Tommen wasn't privy to every aspect of the twins' personal lives, but he'd just always assumed they got along well and did things together like, you know, talk. About something other than work. Brother things. Tommen wasn't sure what he could use as an example, but, brother things, you know. Stuff that brothers talk about. Somehow it had just never occurred to him that they would have anything against each other, at least not privately. Apparently it had never occurred to Micah either, if his disposition was any indication.

"Is it anything I can help with? That whole talking thing goes both ways," he offered meekly.

Micah looked up again, and, for a second, Tommen was prepared for him to unload. Then he simply scraped the herbs off the cutting board into the pan on the stove. "No. Thank you for offering, but Cai and I need to talk first."

Tommen had his doubts, but he kept his thoughts to himself. He waited patiently for Micah to finish cooking then sat and ate in silence, trying to guess at the man's broody thoughts.

"So, here's what's going to happen," Micah said finally as they were finishing up. "Until we hear otherwise, District Four has no Captain. Walter is absent and no one who is Captain-trained is either here or admitting to it. Therefore, I'm the one in charge, and you are my Sub-Lieutenant. We have to be the ones to keep District Four running smoothly on all day-to-day operations while still thinking of a plan to rescue those who are still lost to the Wheel."

Tommen nodded once. "Okay. And how are we doing that?"

Micah went on as though he hadn't spoken. "Right now, we are reporting to District Five's Acting Captain. In our District we have five Masters, four Journeymen, and ten Apprentices, you included. Did you start on the chain of command list?"

"Uh, no, you said you were going to show me how you

wanted it done."

Micah stared at him like he was crazy, then he seemed to realize that he had actually said that and nodded. "Yup, I'll do that."

He kept talking, but Tommen quickly tuned him out as his words seemed to be more for his own sanity than any semblance of a real plan. He'd always relied on Micaiah, Tommen realized. He'd never been left alone like this. Likely he was a Lieutenant only because big brother Micaiah was, not because he really wanted to be one himself. Now he was having to take charge and having a blasted time of it. Still, he was doing his best, and Tommen bet that, given the circumstances, even Micaiah might have a little trouble if the situation were reversed.

"Okay, I'll show you how I want the command structure written out," Micah said at last, standing and taking his dishes to the sink.

At the same time, Tommen thought as Micah gave him a brief rundown of how he wanted things laid out, he could also see Micah turning into Micaiah because of this situation. They were twins; they could practically read each other's minds. Micah was alone and uncertain, but he also knew his brother inside and out. He knew what Micaiah would say and do, but instead of waiting for him to say and do it, he said and did it himself, or he tried to.

Actually it was kind of like how Tommen tried to imitate Teo, what he remembered of him, and suddenly he felt a rock of homesickness lodge itself in his gut. He managed to shake it off long enough to listen and comprehend Micah's words on how he wanted the chain of command, but once the younger twin was gone, the rock returned. He wasn't even sure why, exactly, even. He was gone. Teo was gone. Had been for ten years. One would think that eventually Tommen would get over it. Maybe it was just the brotherly love feeling he got from Micah for his brother.

He finished the list in good time and took it down to Micah who was again snooping through Micaiah's things. This time he sat in a comfortable office chair, feet on the desk, reading...a journal of all things? Tommen never pegged Micaiah as a journal keeping kind of person. Sure, he was kind-hearted underneath his grouchy demeanor, but even journals seemed too sappy for him.

"Interesting reading?" Tommen wondered.

Micah snapped the book shut and slammed it down on the desk as if it had been Micaiah who'd spoken. When he turned and saw it was only Tommen, he relaxed and rubbed his eyes.

"What time is it?" he asked rhetorically, looking at the clock on the wall. "Fuck, it's midnight already?"

"Afraid so," Tommen said, handing him the sheet. "I got that done."

Micah groaned and rubbed his face vigorously. He sighed. "Okay. I'm sorry, I don't mean to keep you up."

"It's okay. I mean, tomorrow's only Sunday."

"Yeah, and who's going to help me in the shop tomorrow?"

Oh. Hadn't thought of that.

"Luckily, Sundays aren't too hectic, but you'd still have to catch a ride with me in the morning since you can't drive. I'll let you sleep a couple hours in the office if you need to."

"Do we have a rescue plan yet?"

"Not yet." Something in his tone said that he was lying and he just wasn't going to tell Tommen his plan. "But let me worry about that. You get some sleep."

Tommen nodded, but before he left the room, he nodded toward the journal. "Interesting reading?"

"Very," Micah replied grudgingly. "I expect we will have a very lengthy discussion about its contents. Good night."

It was a dismissal and a warning worthy of Micaiah, and Tommen quickly ducked out of the room. At first he was confused. What in the world could Micaiah have hidden in those journals that would irritate Micah so? Not that it was any of his business, but it was a mystery that he saw that he felt obligated to solve. Some people might call it sticking his nose in other people's dirty laundry, but could they blame him?

Once the confusion wore off, his own irritation began to creep in. Sure, Micah had said that he didn't have a plan to rescue their missing friends, but his lips were the only thing that said that. Every other part of him had said that he had a plan, he just wasn't going to share that plan. Tommen might not have felt bad if he'd elected to stay an Apprentice and let him do all the work, but Micah had promoted him to Sub-Lieutenant for a reason. Even if the position was made up just for the circumstances, it was still a promotion, which meant that Tommen was supposed to help. How was he supposed to help when his commanding officer didn't let him in on the plan?

He closed the door to the guest bedroom, leaving it open just a crack, and carefully removed his hearing aids to put them on the charger. Strange how he'd gotten used to them and not having them in made his ears feel naked. At least until the cotton feeling kicked in when he heard low-frequency sounds. Even yawning sounded different to him now as he flopped down on the bed.

Today had been a fucked up day. He was tired of fucked up days. He was tired of spending his days looking over his shoulder, being assaulted at all hours by paranoia. He was tired of having to keep everything a secret from everyone except those who shared his secret, and those people kept getting kidnapped and taken away from him. And every time he came out the other side of another horrible event, some piece of him was taken away as well. His hearing, his arm, his brain. It was all too much, and pretty soon he wouldn't have anything left to give.

Fuck, he was tired of it all. Even sleep held little respite for him, given the nightmares he had. Sometimes he remembered them vividly; other times, when he woke, he knew nothing but the fear. He couldn't keep this up forever. Some days, he really just wanted it all to end. Some days, he really just wanted to end it all.

# Chapter Four
## The Visitor


Tommen could not recall the dream perfectly, but he remembered the musty smell of the warehouse and the sticky blood welling up from his dad's bullet wounds as he tried everything he could to keep pressure on them, stop them from bleeding even as he knew it was hopeless. He remembered the light as the enormous warehouse doors were finally powered up and opened for emergency crews.

Except that wasn't right. It had been nearly dark out when that all happened. Reluctantly, Tommen opened his eyes, even as his brain wasn't fully awake yet, and found himself staring at the ceiling light. Micah stood to one side of the bed, hands out defensively.

"What?" Tommen gasped.

"You were yelling," Micah told him slowly, his tone and posture giving the impression of a man approaching a snarling dog.

"I was?"

"Yeah. You were. It's okay. You're safe. You're in the guest bedroom just down the hall from me."

"Oh." Tommen wasn't sure where he expected to be, but the guest bedroom down the hall sounded familiar. And safe. Better than the warehouse, anyway. He sighed. "What time is it?"

"Just about time to get up anyway. Why don't you relax for a few minutes and I'll get something going for breakfast?"

Breakfast. Right. Food. That sounded good. Tommen closed his eyes, let out a breath, and nodded. Micah straightened. "You sure you'll be okay?"

"I will be."

"All right." He didn't sound entirely convinced, but there was nothing that could really be done. Nightmares were just nightmares, right? They couldn't be controlled, but they couldn't actually hurt you. Right?

Tommen sat up and rubbed his face. Fuck. Fuck, fuck, fuck. He just wanted all of this to be over. He wanted his dad back. He wanted to go back home and sleep in his own bed and have the biggest thing he had to worry about be his English essay which he somehow had to find time to write. Fuck.

Slowly, he eased out from under the blankets, feeling like he'd not only gotten no sleep, but he'd gone a few rounds with Tyler Freeman, too, and lost all of them. He was sore and every muscle ached. Even his bones hurt, his arm throbbing in the cast. As he stood upright, a tiny headache began pulsing right where he'd concussed himself. Every move he made felt like it was slow motion and he half-expected Micah to come banging on the door again, telling him to hurry up, they had to go.

Instead, when he finally emerged from the bedroom, he found Micah just doling out breakfast onto two plates, scrambled eggs, hashbrowns, and toast. He looked up briefly. "Feeling up to breakfast?"

Tommen ran a hand through his hair. God, it was getting long. He could almost put it in a ponytail. "Yeah, I guess. Probably should."

He finished out the morning routine in silence, struggling not to fall asleep in his eggs or swallow his toothpaste. Fuck, but he just felt slow, like someone had stuck him in a Slow Band or something. When the time came to head to the bakery, he slumped over on the shoe bench.

"I don't know if I can make it," he told Micah honestly. "I'm just exhausted."

"I know," Micah said sympathetically. "You think you can sleep in the car? Maybe laying across the backseat?"

Tommen shrugged. "At this point, I think I could sleep on anything. Like, I could probably sleep on a bed of nails right now."

"Well, the backseat is only heated leather, so that will have to do. Come on."

It didn't take Tommen long to figure out Micah's plan, and he felt like an idiot for not realizing or suggesting it earlier, but that was probably from the fatigue. The cold and snow outside managed to wake him up enough to drag himself out to the car and get in the backseat. He didn't think he was quite that exhausted, but he could honestly say he didn't remember feeling the car back down the driveway to the road.

Instead, he slept. He didn't think he dreamed, but he was fairly certain he didn't have nightmares either. By the time consciousness came around again, he still felt tired, but more in that Monday-morning-have-to-wake-up-for-school-after-a-busy-weekend kind of tired. When he sat up and looked around, rubbing his eyes and trying to bring everything together, he found that they were only about half a block from the bakery.

"How long did I sleep?" he asked blearily.

"It only takes about twenty minutes to get from home to the shop," Micah answered smartly.

"Ha ha. How long?"

"I figured I gave you about eight hours. Did it help?"

"Must have. At least a little."

"Good. Now then, I'm going to show you how we open the store."

"I thought you said I could have a few more hours in the office?"

Micah raised a brow. "I just gave you eight more hours. Now you can either go to sleep in the office for a bit, or you can earn your promotion and help me open the store."

Tommen sighed. Micah was the younger brother, but he wasn't an idiot. And Tommen really did want that promotion. Actually, he was less thrilled about the promotion than the pay raise that went with it. So he nodded and got out of the car, shivering in the cold while Micah found the key to the back door.

"The nice thing about Banding," Micah began, "is that where

most bakers have to get to the shop two or three hours before they open, we only have to allot for about half an hour. Gives us a little wiggle room in case something happens."

He flipped the light switches and the overhead lights slowly flickered to life, starting out as a dim yellow before brightening to a brilliant white. "Now then, this here..." He grunted as he lifted an enormous binder onto the table. "This is our Big Book of Have and Have Nots. It tells you everything you need to have at any given moment throughout the day, and the things you shouldn't have. It's generally used as more of a guideline than actual rules. So, today is Sunday so we're going to flip to the Sunday section and here we are. These are the things we should have at opening. As you can see, Cai loves his graphs and charts and, based on past sales, this is the projected product that we need for today at various times."

"Holy shit, so math actually means something in the real world?" Tommen said.

"Occasionally, yes. Once again, guidelines only. Believe me, people are weird and unpredictable. Most times, Cai is spot on and we end up following this to the letter. Other times, people will come in demanding things we don't initially have and none of this will get touched."

And that was how it was done. That was their big secret to keeping product rotating and flowing in such a way that there was always minimal waste. Tommen knew that Mr. Morrison at school taught a basic business class; maybe he could use the bakery as a case study.

"I'm going to get started on the dining room," Micah announced. "It doesn't take long. I want you to study this for a minute and get started on as many as you can keep track of. Don't push yourself too hard. You're still only learning as both Apprentice as Manager-trainee, and I don't want to waste a ton of product. Regardless of what's happening in the Wheel, Cai would shoot me if he came back and we lost a good ten thousand dollars worth of stuff."

Tommen could believe it and he agreed to keep the

experimenting to a minimum. He turned to the book while Micah headed up front. It wasn't difficult, really. In the mornings, people were looking for muffins, bagels, cinnamon rolls, that sort of thing. Cookies, brownies, and other sweets didn't go out until eleven. Pies were saved until about three or four o'clock. And those were just the obvious things. Other baked goods like garlic bread had their own numbers and times and special days, too. It was a wonder they—and by "they" he figured Micah—could keep track of just this, never mind throwing in all the actual baking and the Bands and everything else that just made it all more complicated.

"You get it?" Micah asked, returning just as Tommen was getting out the first bowls.

"Um..." Tommen began awkwardly.

"Don't worry, you will. It takes a while to get used to, and it's always changing anyway. I'll help you."

The helpful resolve lasted only as long as they weren't open. But once the clock ticked seven o'clock and the first customers of the day walked in, Tommen was back in his familiar spot on the counter.

The earliest customers on Sunday mornings were mostly pastors and church staff, looking for a quick breakfast before going to prepare to preach to the masses. This crowd was soon followed by the masses the pastors were preparing to preach to, all of them looking for a quick breakfast before going to sit in a pew for two hours listening to fire and brimstone while making a grocery list. Of course this crowd was also interspersed by the non-church group which included everything from working moms who finally had a day off to take the kids somewhere and do grocery shopping, to college students who were looking for a hangover cure right before going to work.

Tommen had only worked a handful of Sunday mornings; mostly he didn't start Sunday shifts until noon, maybe one o'clock. In one respect, it was a nice change of pace to see different faces and feel kind of important in his own mind. He was being trained to be manager. He helped open the store that day. He was special. On the other hand, it only served as a reminder of what a long ass day it was going to be.

The other awful realization came when a customer decided to be an asshole and dispute the charges on a cake he wanted to order. He was just irate that this ten-by-twenty cake cost more than the six-inch cake he'd ordered from them five years ago. Tommen listened to him complain for a minute and tried to explain the cost difference, but the man would have none of it and demanded to talk to the manager. Tommen honestly thought about telling him that he was the manager, but figured that lying wouldn't look too great. So he calmly went back to the kitchen to grab Micah who basically did the same thing he did. In the end, the man left without his cake.

Later, once the rest of the line had been dealt with and they could take ten seconds to breathe, Micah pulled Tommen aside. "So, how would you have dealt with that guy?"

Tommen explained his failed attempts at doing just that. Micah listened patiently, nodding occasionally. When he was done explaining, Micah said, "Good. Remember, you can do your best to remedy a situation, but you can't please everyone. Nor should you. He was fishing for goodies, possibly a free cake. Don't let yourself be intimidated."

The service bell rang then and Tommen returned to the counter, feeling pretty good about himself. He'd done well. He did exactly as he should have. He was the manager. Well, not really, and he wasn't going to try and pull that card until he actually had that card to play, but it just made him feel good. Wouldn't that be something for his dad to come back and see that his son had been made manager of the bakery?

Of course, that didn't seem too likely given that the decision would probably have to be joint between Micah and Micaiah, and he would need a lot more training, but it was a nice thought at least.

Pretty soon, noon rolled around and the church crowd came back. Old ladies in flowery blouses and sweaters, young families in jeans and nice shirts, children of all ages in common street clothes.

Some people were polite to the point of being obnoxious, others you would never suspect had just come from church the way they treated the other people in the store, Tommen especially. As if he were committing the greatest sin of all by working on Sunday. *News for you, lady, if I didn't work, you wouldn't be here demanding your lemon poppy muffin and cream cheese bagel with a cup of decaf.*

Still, the best he could do was grin and bear it and wait for them to leave. Once the after-church group left, business slowed to a crawl. Tommen felt fatigue creeping up on him again as the excitement wore off and the adrenaline died down. Once the dining room was empty of all people, he retreated to the kitchen where even Micah was so bored he didn't have any Bands going.

"Slow up there?" Micah guessed.

"Dead," Tommen told him.

"How you holding up?"

"Well, as long as I tell myself that my dad's at home and Micaiah's in the office, I'm okay."

Micah nodded. "Okay. Fair enough."

"Any word?"

"Not yet."

Once again, his mouth said one thing but his tone and body language said another. He was waiting for something but he wasn't going to say what. Frustrated but trying not to let on to his suspicions, Tommen returned to the front, taking the opportunity to wipe down and reset the tables, some of which had been moved so that larger groups could sit together. He got the tables back where they needed to be just as the door opened and a group of college students walked in.

It took them forever to figure out what they all wanted and another day to figure out who was paying. From one person wanting to treat another, to another person asking if anyone had another dollar or if Tommen had a penny cup. They must have been at the counter for a good twenty minutes before they were finally served and satisfied, making for the same tables that Tommen had just reorganized, moving them again so they could all sit together.

Thankfully they didn't stay long, but they left the tables a mess. Grudgingly, Tommen went back out with another rag to wipe them down and set them back. Again. He just tossed the rag back in the bucket when the door opened and another college student walked in. She was alone, but it was small comfort.

"Be right there," Tommen told her.

He took the bucket to the back and asked Micah to replace the water while he dealt with the customer. When he got back to the counter, he got a good look at her. Five-seven probably, Hispanic with bronze skin and thick black hair. He couldn't tell if her nails were fake or if she was just really talented with nail polish the way they had little stars and stripes and polka dots. Despite the cold she wore a low-cut top and denim jacket, as well as short denim shorts with black leggings that only reached about mid-calf. She wore heels that looked atrociously uncomfortable and carried a denim bag that looked like it had been bedazzled by either a toddler or a group of drunk college students. Most likely the latter. She also had a pair of sunglasses perched on top of her head even though it was overcast with light snow showers outside.

Basically, she was dressed for someone else's weather.

"What can I get for you?" Tommen asked politely.

"You don't do fancy coffee, do you? Mocha latte, cappuccino, that sort of thing?" she asked.

"No. I don't even know what those are, honestly."

"Too bad. But it doesn't matter, anyway. I don't have time to wait for all of that."

"Regular, then?" Tommen wondered, reaching for a cup.

Suddenly it was like someone took a vacuum and sucked the air from his lungs. He coughed several times and looked at the woman. She raised a brow.

"I said I don't have *time* for all of that."

Suddenly annoyed with himself for coming off so unprepared and weak, Tommen put everything he had into a mighty thrust, shattering her Band more by surprise than force. He stopped reaching for the cup and turned back to the counter. "Do you have something to say? Because I have work to do."

"You're an Apprentice." If he wasn't mistaken, she almost sounded impressed.

"And you are...?"

"Everything all right up here?" Micah asked, coming up front with a fresh bucket of bleach water. "Can I help you with something, ma'am?"

"Lieutenant Micaiah Durvin, I presume?" she wondered.

Micah visibly flinched. "Um, no. Wrong twin. Micah."

"Oh, I'm sorry."

"No harm done. And you are...?"

"Jenna Goldwin, Journeyman, District Three. Janice Riley is my Master."

Micah studied her for a moment. "Where have you been in the last twenty-four hours? Base Hours."

She looked thoughtful. "Well, I actually started out in Philadelphia yesterday morning, hopped a Greyhound to Ohio. Then I decided to rent a car and just do a little sightseeing on my way here. I'm actually heading home; I kind of did an east coast tour."

"My point, though, is that you haven't been to the Wheel lately," Micah said.

"Oh, no. I know the elections happened recently, but Janice said I shouldn't get too involved yet. My own studies are exhausting enough and I should use my time as a Journeyman to explore and grow without getting bogged down by politics."

"Smart lady. When was the last time you talked to her?"

"Um...a week ago? I give her weekly updates. I was actually going to call her tonight after I made contact with you. Why? I mean, you're tone and everything is kind of freaking me out."

"Then you haven't heard."

"Heard what?"

Micah threw up a Band around the three of them. "Maybe you

should step into the office for a minute."

Jenna did so, stepping around the counter and following them into the office. There were some things that made Tommen sick to see, and a girl looking uncertain, confused, and even a little afraid was one of them. He knew the news she was about to hear was not about to be pleasant, and he wished she didn't have to hear it.

"What's wrong?" she asked, taking a seat while Micah shut the door.

"Yesterday was the inauguration of the new Hands of Time and the Zero Hour," Micah told her. "Does the name Cassius or Calis Cutthroat mean anything to you?"

"No, but it doesn't sound good."

"Long story short, he's a Triage Harvester and a raving psychopath. Actually, he used to be the Zero Hour over a century ago. Yesterday, during the inauguration, he launched a coup and has crowned himself the King of Time. His right hand man is a man called Rifun Ndolo who is a Warden Timekeeper. Together, they trapped everyone at the inauguration in the Seat and slaughtered anyone outside its gates. In the Coliseum, the marketplaces, everywhere. They put a dampening field over the portal room to make it almost impossible to escape. It was a massacre. Hundreds, thousands, maybe millions of Time Agents from all over the universe are dead. We were lucky to escape, but ever since, there has been no word from the Wheel and the chain of command around here is pretty tentative."

Jenna stared at him, mouth wide open, red lipstick a sharp contrast against her white teeth and caramel skin. Finally she blinked, closed her mouth, and shook her head. "No. Wait. What did you say? I'm just...that's not right. No."

Micah nodded. "Yes." He gestured to Tommen. "His dad who also happens to be District Four Captain, he was captured. My brother, Micaiah, he's captured. They could be dead for all we know. We hope not, but it's unlikely Cassius is going to let them live after the hell we've been giving him the last six months."

"So what happens here? Earth-side? What about the

Grandfathers?"

"The Grandfathers helped him do it," Tommen told her. "That's how he was able to carry it out so effectively, because no one can stand against a Grandfather, especially not all of them at once."

"Oh my God," Jenna said. "Oh...my God." She dug in her purse and brought out her cell phone. "I have to call Janice. Oh God, she said she was going to be there. She wouldn't take me, but she said that she wanted to go because she said the politics this time around were really heating up and...oh my God."

"Go find a table," Micah said. "Banding and electronics don't go well together."

Jenna nodded and stood, eyes fixed on her phone as Micah opened the door for her and watched her leave. She bumbled her way around the counter and got to a table, Micah releasing the Band. Tommen watched sympathetically as her expression turned from hopeful fear into dread. Then the call apparently went to voicemail.

"Hi, Janice, it's Jenna with my weekly update." She sounded almost normal, just calling to give an update. "I made it to Charleston, West Virginia, where I wanted to meet with the District Captain and Lieutenants, but, um..." Her voice wavered. "One of the Lieutenants, um, Micah, he, uh, said that something happened at the inauguration and, uh, if you could just give me a call back, that would be really great. Thanks, bye."

Tommen grabbed a plastic cup, filled it with water, and took it to where Jenna sat, looking out the window, looking ready to cry.

"On the house," he offered.

"Thank you." She took the water and managed a small sip. "Your dad is the Captain?"

"Yeah."

"And he was taken, too?"

Tommen could only nod.

"I'm so sorry. It must be hard."

Again, just a nod. *Hold it together. Don't lose it here in front of her.*

"What can we do? Is there anything we can do?"

"Micah's working on a plan, but I'm just an Apprentice, so I don't know." Tommen shrugged.

"Well that's dumb. I mean, if half the people are missing or dead, everyone ought to be brought into the loop to share information and work out a plan to rescue the others. Fuck the hierarchy. Well, not completely, I mean, it is important and serves some purpose, but you shouldn't just be discounted for that. He's your dad. You at least deserve some information based on that."

"I do what they tell me. But if Micah, who's a Lieutenant, has problems, what can I do? If my dad couldn't get out, how can I get in?"

Jenna shook her head. "I don't know." She took another drink of water. "I don't know what I'd do if I lost Janice." She sighed. "How'd you break your arm?"

Tommen felt his face burn. "Um, skiing accident. It's fine."

"Obviously not if it's broken." She shrugged and took another drink of water. "Whatever."

"Can I get you some more water?" he asked.

At first he thought she was going to refuse, but eventually she nodded and handed him the cup. He refilled it for her then retreated to the kitchen where Micah was still working, though his expression was unreadable.

"I don't have anything for her," Micah said before Tommen could speak. "Normally, when a Journeyman comes in, they spend a little time here, me, Micaiah, your dad, we all give her a little training, a little wisdom, and send her on her way. The only thing I have for her right now is bad news."

"How about a plan?" Tommen wondered. "Like, a real plan that you're willing to share with the rest of us? Or at least your Sub-Lieutenant? Or was that something you made up just to make me feel better?"

"Tentative plans are wonderful things, but that's all they are. Tentative. Until we get something a little more solid, I didn't want to get your hopes up unnecessarily."

"You could at least tell me about the plans. Who knows, maybe I can contribute an idea or two? Fresh eyes, fresh mind."

"Your judgment is clouded."

"And yours isn't? I'm missing my dad, you're missing your brother. Everyone is missing someone. You think anyone's judgment isn't clouded?"

Micah set down his mixing spoon and looked at him. "Your judgment is clouded because of Rifun." That made Tommen stop. "Rifun still has a hold on you, he still has power over you. Like it or not, you're a pawn. An expendable pawn. As long as you are here, he has every incentive to keep your dad alive. If I send you into the Wheel on some ill-conceived, dangerous mission without a proper plan or proper protection, he gets you both. He gets you all. You, your dad, and my brother.

"Right now, I'm fighting other Lieutenants and Captains and Managers who want to send you in solely as bait. They're business-minded, and if the situation were reversed, I might even be one of them. Sacrifice the Apprentice, save the Captain, the Lieutenant, and who knows how many others? But they can't appreciate the nuances of the relationship between you and Rifun and how devastating it would be if he got his hands on you. The manipulation and the power that could be gained.

"And even if, somehow, you survived...you wouldn't survive. You're breaking, Tommen. I can see it, your dad can see it. It's too much for you. We don't want you to break, but in the event that you do, we want to be the ones to pick up the pieces. Not Rifun. I'm trying to save you, Tommen. Yes, I admit, I made you Sub-Lieutenant kind of to make you feel better, feel useful, keep your head up. I'm doing it to try and help you. Help me help you so we can help them. Do you understand?"

"I'm fine," Tommen insisted, even if his words and his voice sounded hollow. "I'm fine. I want to go. I want to help."

Micah shook his head. "No. You are going to stay here. We'll find another way."

"Yeah? How?"

"What about me?"

They turned as Jenna peeked into the kitchen. She blushed. "Sorry, I kind of eavesdropped a little. Listen, I don't know the backstory to all of this—but it sounds like it would be really interesting to listen to at some point—but maybe I could help."

Micah sighed and wiped his face on his sleeve. "I appreciate the offer, but—"

"I can," Jenna insisted. "Look. It sounds like you're trying for the whole ambush, frontal assault kind of thing. But that's probably what they'll be expecting. If the portal room is closed, they won't be everywhere in the Wheel. Most likely just the Coliseum and the Judgment Wing, maybe a few other places. One person could make it through easier than an army. It wouldn't necessarily have to be a rescue mission, just gathering a little intel. I could get in there and tell you guys what's happening, rather than you sitting out here and playing twenty questions with your rescue mission."

"One person can also get captured and we would never know about it."

"Then so be it. At least I could say I tried, and I would be with Janice."

Tommen raised a brow. "How old is Janice?"

"Well, she's actually ninety-two, but believe me, she doesn't look a day over twenty-nine." Jenna winked.

"Right," Micah said. "And how do you expect to just waltz in and gather information without being seen or captured? It's possible they've expanded the dampening field to include the whole Wheel. Even if they haven't, the Grandfathers are everywhere and they are on a seek and destroy mission." He briefly explained how the Grandfathers waited at each portal for someone to come through so they could kill them.

"Well, sitting here in fear isn't doing us any more good than trying and failing," Jenna informed him.

They were saved for the moment by a couple customers walking in. Tommen attended to them, trying to make it seem like just an old friend was visiting them and they were glad to see her, rather than a total stranger had walked in and was now telling them how it was going to be. Fresh eyes and fresh minds were one thing, but this was starting to get annoying. He reluctantly returned to the kitchen just as Micah and Jenna were walking out. Micah silently motioned for Tommen to follow them to the office where he picked up the phone and dialed a number.

"Brian Wilcox speaking," the voice on the other end said.

"Brian, it's Micah," Micah replied. To Tommen and Jenna, "Acting Manager for Region Four."

"What can I do for you, Micah? Are we sending Tommen?"

"We are not sending Tommen now or ever, but I do have a volunteer of another source."

"I'm listening." His tone said he would not be listening too intently.

"I have Jenna Goldwin here. She's a Journeyman from District Three, Janice Riley is her Master."

"Okay..."

"She's volunteering to go into the Wheel alone and gather information for us, find out what's going on. Maybe if we got some real intel, we can make a real plan instead of sitting around playing twenty questions."

"Absolutely not. No one goes into the Wheel alone."

"Even though you were willing to send Tommen in alone?" Micah's words dripped acid.

"That was a different plan. A good plan which you keep shooting down. If not for the present circumstances, I would come down there myself and —"

"Well these are the present circumstances. And I'd like to not make them any worse, thank you."

With that, Micah hung up. He sighed and pinched the bridge of his nose. "Okay, so, there goes any future ambition I had about advancing beyond Lieutenant." He glanced back and forth between the two of them. "All right. Suggestions?"

"Do it anyway," Jenna said, as if the answer was obvious. "You got out, you can get back in. Like he said, if the circumstances were different, he'd come down. Which means he can't come down. He can't do anything to you. And if this works, he won't be able to do anything to you because you'll be a hero."

"That's a big if, though. For all we know, there could be Grandfathers in the portal room just waiting for a portal to open so they can come through and kill those of us who escaped, or maybe just weren't even there."

"And it's just as likely to be empty."

"Schrodinger's cat," Tommen tossed in.

Micah looked at him. "You're agreeing with her now?"

"Every second we wait, my dad and your brother could die, if they're not already. I can't just sit around waiting for you guys to stop fighting and come up with something. Okay, so you won't let me go. I get it. I understand. But Jenna is willing to go and help. Why not let her?"

Micah sighed and rubbed his face. Tommen figured that by the time this was over, he would be raw from all the rubbing. Finally he rested his head on his fist on the desk. He looked toward Jenna. "Am I correct to assume that whatever plans you had just went out the window?"

"Yes," Jenna answered.

He sighed. "Okay. Fine. Go out and get something to eat first at least. God knows how long you're going to be sneaking around in there."

"What are you going to do?" Tommen wondered.

"I'm going to make a few phone calls. I'm not sending her in alone, that's for damn sure. Maybe I can find someone else nearby who's willing to go on this suicide mission with her. And maybe reduce the chances of it being a total suicide mission."

Jenna tried to argue, but Micah was adamant. She could go,

but she wouldn't go alone. Eventually she gave in. She and Tommen left the office.

"You work with him?" she hissed as she went around the front of the display case and looked over all the goodies. "Like, all the time?"

Tommen shrugged. "He's stressed. We all are. And actually, he's the easier twin to work with."

"Damn." Jenna shook her head. "I pity you. I really do."

Still, she picked out her baked goodies and returned to the same table as before. She brought out her phone and started tapping away. Looking at her, she seemed completely normal. If Tommen hadn't just witnessed the entire exchange since she walked in, she might have passed for any average college student, just out for a Sunday stroll doing a little self-help through retail therapy. She certainly didn't seem like the type who could control Time and bend it to her will.

Of course, what did that kind of person look like, anyway? Not a skinny, awkward six-foot-one teenage boy with a broken arm. Not a couple of twins who ran a bakery. Certainly not a homicide detective in his late forties, early fifties.

The blinds were down in the office windows, so Tommen couldn't peek in and check on Micah, and the phone conversations seemed to be civil enough that he couldn't eavesdrop too well. He tried to stay busy, but the day was slow and he got caught up on chores pretty quickly. Eventually, he was reduced to playing on his phone while waiting for either Micah or a customer.

Micah was the first to appear, though he dodged any and all questions by first heading to the bathroom.

"Did you hear or see anything?" Jenna asked, approaching the counter. "Does he have an answer?"

"I don't know," Tommen answered. "I didn't see or hear, but maybe that's a good thing?"

"Well, it means he wasn't yelling, but that's about it."

"If you're quite done gossiping," Micah said irritably,

returning and leaning against one wall of the office. "I have news."

"Did you find someone to help me?" Jenna asked, trying to disguise her spiteful annoyance as something resembling hope.

Micah nodded. "I did. He's on his way now. Shouldn't take him more than five minutes to get here. Then we can talk."

It didn't even take him that long because of a Band that delivered him straight into the parking lot. As soon as Tommen saw the dreadlocks, he knew who it was. Kyle was dressed a little more sensibly in thick pants and a sweatshirt, but he still looked more like he belonged on a surfboard.

"Who's that?" Jenna wondered, her expression spelling unadultered disgust.

Kyle quickly crossed the slippery parking lot, sauntered in the door and looked around, his gaze settling on Jenna like a teeny bopper boy who apparently just decided that girls don't have cooties anymore.

"Jenna, Kyle. Kyle, Jenna," Micah introduced, evidently getting some amusement out of it. "You're going to be working together for the duration of this mission. Kyle is an Apprentice from District Eight. Jenna is a Journeyman from District Three."

"Canada," Kyle stated dumbly. "From Quebec, then? *Parlez-vous francais?*"

"Oh my God," Jenna said, rolling her eyes. "Are you fucking serious? There was literally no one else who was willing to help? Please, there has to be someone. I admit there is every possibility that I could get captured, but I'm not going to just go in there and announce myself, thank you very much."

"He's done well by us in the past."

"Well, that's great for you, but I don't think—"

"He's here to help and he's what we've got," Micah cut in irritably. "In case you haven't noticed, but this is going to be dangerous and dirty work, so come down off your high horse and get in the mud where you need to be in order to carry out this mission. It's not always about the cavalry and riding in on a white horse to save your lover. This is who you're working with. Now I expect you to at least treat him with some respect and work together on this. Or else you're both captured and you're both dead. Got it?"

Jenna just blinked, as if she couldn't believe that someone had actually spoken to her in any way that wasn't fabulous adoration. It was actually Kyle who spoke first.

"So, what are we doing?"

Micah huffed once before giving him the abbreviated version of what happened in the Wheel. Kyle listened solemnly, not interrupting, even as Micah outlined the premise of the mission to the Wheel, gathering information and getting out.

"You think you can handle that?" Micah asked as he finished, looking like he just wanted to go home and crawl back into bed.

"I don't see why not," Kyle told him. "Sounds simple enough."

Jenna rolled her eyes. "Oh, please, we're not going surfing here."

"And we ain't goin' shoppin' neither," Kyle said, indicating her purse and high heels. "While you were spending your days playing pretty princess dress up, I was out causing havoc and trying not to get caught by the neighbors. I learned a thing or two about avoiding the fuzz. I'd still probably be on the run, but his dad caught me and kind of shanghaied me back into service." He nodded once at Tommen.

At this point, Tommen's money was on Kyle more than Jenna, but he judged it best to keep his mouth shut and just watch how this played out.

"I do have one question, though," Kyle said. "If the portal room is closed, they're going to know when a portal opens—because, you know, it's not supposed to—and they're going to know where it leads. What's to keep them from coming back through and killing or kidnapping you two, since it sounds like that's what they want?"

"Because the portal isn't going to stay open," Micah told them severely. "Once you are through, the portal will close. The dampening field makes it nearly impossible to open a portal in the first place, and it won't stay open on its own like on a normal day. I can't keep it open. It's going to close. But it is possible to essentially contact me through the threshold so I can let you back out."

"How do we do that?" Jenna asked.

Micah went into the office and returned with his translator. "Using this. And you're actually going to be contacting Tommen. Tommen, you still have your translator, right?"

Tommen dug around in his coat pocket until he found it. "Yeah."

"Go ahead and put it in, just the earpiece, and let me see the collar."

He did so, handing the collar to Micah and sliding the connector into his hearing aid with only a little difficulty, ignoring the blatant stare from Jenna.

Micah fiddled around with the collars. At one point, a loud low-frequency pulse blasted Tommen's ear and he wanted to rip out his hearing aid. But Micah nodded satisfactorily and handed Jenna the regular translator, saying, "When you're ready, hit the button there. It will relay a pulse to Tommen and he'll tell me to open the portal."

"How does that work?" Jenna wondered, putting on the translator.

"Better question, how do you know that it will work across dimensions?" Kyle asked.

"I've had to use it before. Only once. I don't know how it works, only that it does. But it only works at normal spots. It's not an automatic emergency exit. You will have to be in the portal room because that is where the portal will open. Do you understand?"

Jenna and Kyle both nodded.

"You think you can work together to get information that will help us bring everyone back?"

Kyle readily agreed but it took Jenna a second to concede that Kyle was her partner, whether she liked it or not.

"Do you think we'll need to take anything with us?" Kyle

asked. "I mean, I've got a pretty decent pocket knife, but I don't know how much good it will do."

"Doesn't matter what you have, you'll be on the defense. Remember, you're only there to gather information; the war comes later. All right?"

The duo agreed, though they still didn't seem too thrilled about having to work together. Tommen bit his tongue but his thoughts still ran wild. They were doomed. The mission was doomed. Tommen didn't know much about military tactics, but he knew enough that the team where the members hated each other would be the first one to get captured or killed. He held out very little hope that they would succeed.

Nevertheless, Micah took a breath and readied himself, like a kung fu master about to break thirty cinder blocks with just his pinkie. Even before the portal actually opened, sweat was streaming down his forehead and soaking his shirt. Normally a portal opened about as easily as a door. Now it sputtered to life like a live wire that just wasn't quite connecting and rained sparks everywhere.

Tommen braced himself for a hoard of Grandfathers to come swarming in, but none did. Instead, it looked about like any other trip to the Wheel. The bleak portal room, emptier than ever. No welcoming committee to be seen.

"Go!" Micah ordered, looking like he was on the verge of passing out.

Jenna cast another forlorn look at her rescue partner before stepping through, Kyle hard on her heels. As soon as they were through, Micah released the portal and it snapped closed. Tommen got Micah to a chair in the office and retrieved a cup of water.

"Thank you," Micah said, breathing heavily and downing the water in one gulp.

"Now what?" Tommen wondered.

"Now we wait. And hope they come back."

"You think they'll actually accomplish their mission?"

"Honestly? I don't know. But my faith in them is greater than in any plan thus far."

"How long before they contact us?"

"Depends on how much information they're able to get before having to flee. Just keep an ear out and let me know immediately when they do contact you."

Tommen assured him he would and headed back out to the bakery to pass the time.

# Chapter Five
## Prison

Walter lost track of Micaiah after they entered the asylum. But then, he'd lost track of a lot of things once the Grandfather had announced his sentence. The last thing he remembered was being beaten with his own cane before being uncomfortably manhandled out of the holding area. After that, he knew nothing but the blackness.

Darkness did terrible things to a man, regardless if he'd been there before or not. For the one who'd never been exposed to the darkness, it started out simply enough. After ten minutes, the spasms of the eye began as the eye tried so hard to see a wall or just the hand in front of your face that it started to play tricks. After half an hour, the real hallucinations began. Seeing things even though you knew it was impossible to see anything. Hearing things without being sure whether those things were actually there or if it was your brain starting to panic. Smelling things, too, from musty cave smells to roses you knew were impossible. Twenty-four hours in the darkness and the retina began degenerating, causing not only hallucinations but headaches as well as the eye tried to stave off weakness. Four days and mania started to set in, but that was assuming that the person knew it had been four days. There was no Time in the darkness. No Time, no emotion, nothing but the darkness and the hallucinations and the fear.

For a man who'd already spent time in that darkness before, he skipped those first four days and went straight to the mania and the fear. He was smart enough to know he wasn't really seeing anything, but still his mind insisted that he could see something in front of him. The sounds he could not speak for. He knew he was in an asylum where Time criminals were left to rot and there were any number of sounds and smells that could be floating around.

Walter knew that this darkness would not be like the darkness before, in Beaumaris Gaol. There, it had been possible to catch the smallest glimmers of light from the gaolers' lanterns as they passed by, and he always saw the light at least once a day when food was delivered. Sometimes, if he was really, really good, he'd been let outside. This would not be like that. There was no light from lanterns passing by. There was no food or water. And if and when he was set free, it would be only so he could be taken to his execution.

Most of what he experienced there in the black cell was unreliable. He saw things, heard things, smelled things, but with no light and no point of reference, he couldn't be sure of any of it. It could be real, it could be his mind. It didn't matter anyway. The only things he could count on were the rattling of his chains and the screaming. Most often, he wasn't sure where it came from, but he always figured out that it came from him. He was the one screaming. He couldn't figure out why he screamed or how it started, considering that it generally took a concerted effort to do so. But every time it left him feeling exhausted. No one ever answered, either to scream back at him or tell him to shut up. The darkness was always quiet after the screaming.

Sometimes he wondered if the darkness wasn't all in his mind, if the asylum was like some twisted version of the Apprentice review. Maybe he'd been drugged somehow and was spending some quality time inside his own mind, his fears, his conscience, his soul, all the things he wished he could hide or undo. At least something like that he might be able to handle. Drugs, a bad trip, that he could handle. But things like that always ended. Bad trips always ended.

The darkness, however, never ended. It just simply was. There was no way to keep track of time here. He could talk to himself, sing if he wanted, work out some made-up puzzles in his head, but always, time would slip away from him. The darkness was like the non-Borelian way of clock breaking. Fear overcame him again as he considered the possibility that maybe that was what had been done to him. There were fates worse than death, and having your clock broken was certainly one of them. To have that basic instinct of time, to count the seconds and be aware of the passage of time, stripped away.

But that was half the point of the darkness. It stripped away time and thought and reason and emotion and sanity, until all that remained was a hollow, screaming shell of a man.

Several times, Walter managed to collect himself enough that he almost felt human again, rather than a disembodied soul left to wander in the abyss. He tried to force himself to be calm and collected. Just think of his son. Think of Tommen. He had to get back to him. Had to get back to him or die trying. Cassius was going to kill him anyway, might as well go down fighting, right? He wasn't going to be led like a sheep to slaughter. He would fight and take as many Grandfathers with him as he could.

But his resolve lasted only until the screaming began again, until the next hallucination. He couldn't tell real from fake, despite the tiny voice inside telling him that none of this was real. He was imagining things. He tried to close his eyes and bring to mind anything and everything. He knew what the Judgment Wing looked like and how to get out of the Wheel. Leaving the Wheel meant going to the bakery, the office where he and the twins had had so many officers' meetings. He pictured the precinct and his coworkers, Jim and his inability to ever find a utensil that could write. He pictured Charleston, draped in a snowy blanket. He pictured his house, anxiously scolding himself that he'd left before finishing the painting job in his bedroom.

He pictured Tommen, tall and lanky, as socially awkward as his pa had been. What would life have been like if Walter had been a better man and Time hadn't gotten involved? Would Tommen have ever met young Victoria? Would he have known his cousin?

What would life be like if Walter had been a better man? He probably never would have left Wales. He'd probably still be married. Might even have more children. If he'd been a better man, he'd probably still be living in London, a wealthy banker. He'd be able to afford the finest luxuries for his wife and maybe help his parents to retire so they didn't die in their farm work with nothing to show.

He probably would have had a better relationship with his younger brother, the kind he was supposed to have where he set the example and kept his brother out of trouble.

What would life have been like if Walter had been the man he was supposed to have been, his pa's son, pride and joy? There were too many possibilities to really consider, and none that he really wanted to ponder right now. But that was the problem with sitting in the darkness. The only thing you can look at is your own soul with no convenient distractions. The darkness offers nothing new to look at, no hope of a future. So the only place to look is back. Some people had wonderful lives that they loved recounting and sharing with their children and grandchildren. Walter had only shame. His book contained life lessons from the school of hard knocks, not something ordinarily shared around the Christmas dinner table.

Maybe he'd already died. Maybe they'd already killed him, and this was his punishment. It wasn't quite fire and brimstone, true, but the darkness and the terror was much in evidence. He didn't remember standing before Almighty God to give his account, but maybe he didn't need to. Maybe his actions spoke so loudly that he'd been charged, tried, and convicted long ago with no hope of being saved, whatever the priest said. Walter thought hard but could not remember the man's name.

Maybe he'd taken the shortcut to Hell. While he knew it was certainly justified, he couldn't help but let out a small wail at the thought of all his efforts to change himself and raise a good son had been in vain. Nothing mattered and he was dead.

"I'm dead," he whispered hoarsely, his throat raw from lack of water.

"You're not dead."

Walter jumped in his chains and looked around uselessly. Then, there just in front of him, was a face. It was lit in a way that suggested this person—human, and a stranger from the looks of him—was sitting in front of him with only the smallest of lights between them, a dying match perhaps. Walter couldn't make out his features well except that he had a firm jaw and a long nose. He could see the light in the man's eyes, but that was all; otherwise he was draped in shadow.

"Who are you?" Walter asked. "No, you're not real. None of this is real."

"What is real in the darkness?" the man said. "I'm as real as any of your hallucinations. What does it matter?"

"So even my own mind has turned against me and my hallucinations have produced a personification of my conscience. Why? I know I'm a guilty man. I know I've done terrible things. I don't need a phantom to tell me that. What are you doing here?"

"Perhaps I am your conscience. But perhaps I'm not here to guilt you. Maybe I'm here to comfort you."

"Giving a cup of water to man in the desert dying of thirst."

"So you would rather have the guilt trip? Why, because it makes you feel noble? As your conscience, let me give you a little piece of advice. Guilt is useful for many things. When it's useful, we call it conviction, your mind telling you that something is wrong and it's your fault and you need to make a change. Do you know what we call guilt when it's not useful, or when that conviction gets ignored?"

"No."

"Diarrhea."

Walter blinked. The man went on. "A child screams when he poops his diaper, but he doesn't want it changed. He doesn't like the poop, but it's warm and familiar and it's all his. He wants to wallow in it despite screaming that he wants his diaper changed.

"You felt that conviction decades ago after losing your wife and child. You acted on it and you made a change in your life. Something like that takes time to overcome, yes, but here you are over a century and a half later, still wallowing in it."

"I told Tommen the truth," Walter pleaded pathetically. "Isn't that enough?"

"It was a nice gesture, but you are still a dog returning to its vomit."

Walter shook his head. "No, you're not real. It's the darkness. It's doing things to me; it's playing tricks."

"And you're letting it!" the man snarled. "Don't give the darkness power! Don't let it win!"

"But it's here! I'm surrounded!"

"And so you can attack on all fronts! One shred of light holds the darkness at bay! When you turn on the light in a room, do you see the light and the dark struggling for power? No! Light always wins!"

"I have no light!" Walter barked back. "There is nothing but darkness here! We're in an asylum! It's the epitome of darkness. It is the kingdom of darkness!"

"Then be the light!" the man roared. "Turn off your night light and face the darkness yourself!"

"I can't do it myself!"

Walter's words echoed in the empty room. He watched the stranger through blurry eyes as tears streaked down his cheeks into his mustache and beard, body racked with silent sobs.

"I can't do it," he repeated, almost inaudibly. "I can't do it alone."

The stranger said nothing, just watched him with kind eyes. Finally he nodded, picked up his match that had been lying on the floor and said, "I know. You know. And don't be afraid. I am with you."

And he blew out the tiny flame.

Walter screamed again, deliberately this time, though he couldn't say just why. He was frustrated, angry, hurt, and the man—whether real or hallucination—had plunged him back into darkness. He'd left him alone right after saying that he would be with him. He'd turned his back and left Walter to die. Even if he wasn't already dead, he was going to be. He wanted to be. Anything but the darkness. He couldn't stand it anymore, couldn't take it. He just wanted out of it. He wanted it to end. He wanted anything at all to happen because this was just madness; he was going mad. This place was causing him to lose his mind in a way that made Beaumaris Gaol look like after school detention. It wasn't right. It wasn't fair. He had to get out, couldn't get out, must get out. Any way he could, he had to get out. Even if it meant his death. He was going to die in here. He was—

He jerked awake in such a way that it put him in mind of a Hollywood exorcism, the way his body contorted. Every muscle ripped apart in agony as he tried to shift position. His hands were numb from tight shackles cutting off circulation while he could still feel blood slipping down his arms. His shoulders and back were tied up in ten kinds of knots, doing terrible wonders for his still-injured shoulder blades. His abs were tight but he couldn't tell if that was from his positioning or because he was starving. His left leg was cramped something terrible but gradually loosened the more he worked it. His right leg, however, was like a charliehorse from Hell above the knee and it jumped and spasmed uncontrollably. Slowly but surely, as he managed to wiggle feeling back into his toes and foot and get his lower leg moving, the pain subsided to a dull throb.

He sighed weakly. He didn't know how long he'd been here, or how much of his madness came from his sleeping or wakefulness. That was the thing about the darkness. It stole everything, bit by bit. Never a sound, never a trace, never able to be retrieved or regained. What pieces of his mind he lost here would stay here. Even if, by some miracle, he did make it home, he would never be the same. He wouldn't be the same police officer, wouldn't be the same Captain, wouldn't be the same man. And he wouldn't be the same father.

With a quiet resolve, Walter searched for every memory he had of Tommen, from Teo commissioning him to find his boy, to Tommen stowing away in the back of the car so he could go to the inauguration. He gathered up all the memories and stitched them together haphazardly like an old blanket. It was pitiable defense against the darkness and whatever lay out there, but if it could work for a child, maybe it could work for him. Just this once.

One more hour. It was a tactic that was taught in the military. If a soldier was captured and he was going to be waiting awhile, after all the hope had gone and memories dissolved into bitter tears, there was only one thing left: Can you survive one more hour? Even if your captors beat you and whip you and strip you and dehumanize you and demoralize you, can you last one more hour? It only takes twenty-four hours to make a day, and by the time you've survived a hundred more hours, you've survived four days. Just one more hour.

Problem was, Walter had no way to tell time. He could count, but he always slipped up eventually. And even if he could keep a decent string going, the ghosts and hallucinations always whispered to him to confuse him. Nineteen, thirty-four, seventy-two, eleven, six, fifty-one. And he had to start over.

One more hour.

At the same time, they were doing nothing to him. He wasn't being dragged out of his bed to be beaten. He wasn't sleeping on a cold stone floor. There were the shackles to keep him in place, and they cut into his wrists, but that was the extent of the physical damage. That and the cramping. Otherwise, there was nothing. He was alone and in the dark, but they were doing nothing to him. He was just sitting alone here in the dark.

One more hour.

Maybe he could turn the tables on them. Maybe he should try to make friends with the hallucinations. There was little to be scared of from a man who heard and saw things. He was more to be pitied as he battled the demons that existed only in his head. It only got scary when he made friends with and started listening to those demons, keeping them as close companions and counsel. That was when things became real. That was when the threats had to be taken seriously. Maybe he could use that same tactic, confuse the guards long enough to make his escape.

One more hour.

That was one thing he'd learned in his life. He'd been on both sides of the law, so he knew how everything worked. He was an officer who'd once been a criminal, so he knew how the criminals thought, how they were going to move and react. It gave him an edge. Maybe it was time to use that in reverse. He was a cop, knew how to think like a cop, so maybe he ought to revert back to being a criminal. If they were going to treat him as such, maybe he ought to oblige. The key was all about playing his cards right.

One more hour.

That was when things got interesting. It was probably safe to assume that some of Cassius' guards used to be criminals, so then it became a huge game of cops and robbers, where all the robbers had once been cops and all the cops had once been robbers. It turned into one huge psychological game at that point, an enormous game of chess as each side tried to read the other. What was the other man thinking? What was he now and what had he been? What did he do? What does he want? How does he think? How did I think when I was where he was?

One more hour.

It was probably the only part of Walter's imprisonment that he could say he remembered clearly, with a stoic determination and peace that surpassed all understanding. The fear and the darkness still enveloped him; no magical, heavenly light had suddenly come down to light his path. But he could feel it now, almost as an entity unto itself, a living, breathing organism. And while he could feel it all around him, sniffing at his heels and his hands like a pack of hungry hounds, it did not seem to consume him anymore and he could breathe without feeling like he was drowning. His mind was his own again; he could think full, clear, coherent thoughts. He had drive and resolve.

*Yea, though I sit in the valley of the shadow of death...*

One more hour.

And so the hours went by. Whether or not they were true hours didn't matter. He concentrated on his memories, on his heartbeat, on his breaths. With the same determination that got him out of Beaumaris Gaol, he sat in the darkness and waited.

When he woke again after falling asleep unexpectedly, he almost couldn't process what it was that had woken him. Then he wasn't even sure he was awake as he saw light. At first glance, his tired, weak eyes were surprised and he immediately squeezed his eyes shut as hard as possible and looked away, blinded and overwhelmed. When he managed to open them again, just a tiny sliver, someone or something was coming toward him, but he couldn't make it out against the light. It got closer, blocking more of the light until Walter could almost stand to open up his eyes fully.

He heard something smack the floor at his side. And then another smack on his other side. It took a second for him to realize that the shackles had been undone and his hands had fallen limply to the floor. Within just a few seconds, the pain in his wrists came to life and he moaned. Gradually he tested his fingers one by one until he was fairly sure he still had all ten of them. The muscles in his arms felt like lead even as his shoulders and back muscles continued twisting in knots, trying to untangle themselves after being held for so long in a single position. His head drooped forward and he wasn't sure if this was real or if he was still hallucinating. At this point, it probably didn't matter.

The pain he got from being hauled to his feet was very real, though, he determined. He was little better than a rag doll as a guard came on either side of him to hoist him upright. His left leg was bad enough and could barely take his weight, to say nothing of his right leg. Eventually, he was simply dragged under his armpits.

The light, while he knew it was normally very dim in the asylum, now seemed far too bright. He squeezed and squinted and tried to ease into it, but it was like returning to the gym after ten lazy years and trying to do anything more than a short walk and tiny five-pound weights, and even that, figuratively speaking, seemed too much for him now. He found himself wishing for sunglasses even as a headache began shooting arrows through his skull.

Obviously, no one would oblige him. The good news, though,

was that by the time they reached the first of many doors leading from the bowels of the asylum to the room with three doors, his eyes had adjusted enough that he could look down at the shadows around his feet without much problem. The motion did little to help his headache, however, and several times he thought he was going to be sick.

As he was dragged through the asylum, his mind was active, but his body didn't want to respond to his commands. Even his mind seemed divided. One part was telling him to perk up, be alert, take stock, take notes, get ready to make an escape. The other part was divided between relief that he was finally out of his cell and fear of whatever came next. And while he battled conflicting thoughts and emotions and other things he didn't even have names for, his body remained limp. His wrists were cut and bleeding, and being dragged through the corridors, his ankles and feet scraping the ground, they weren't going to look too much better by the end of this.

By the time they reached the fifth door, Walter could lift his head and look around briefly, enough to take in his general surroundings. His eyes still hurt and his head was beating like a drum, but he was determined to power through as much as he could. His mind still chased itself around in circles, and he could experience resolute determination, unbridled relief and joy, and the old familiar terror, all in about the space of fifteen seconds.

Walter did not know his way around the asylum as well as the guards, but he was fairly certain they'd passed the corridor leading to the exit. Not that it mattered with his condition, but he tried to remind himself that it was significant in some way and he should probably start making a mental map for later. When he tried to recall their path thus far, however, his brain failed him and he was still just at the mercy of the guards and wherever they dragged him.

It wasn't actually a very long trip from start to finish, from cell to wherever they were going. He counted about two hundred steps before they finally stopped in front of a door, and he knew he'd missed quite a few at the start. As they waited, some part of Walter's brain and body connected, enough that he tried to get his feet under him. His right leg felt like he'd taken a few more bullets and possibly an arrow to the knee, but his legs were able to support him along with the help of the guards—if their disdainful postures could be considered helpful.

The door opened then to reveal a room dimly lit by just a couple candles on one table and a few more around the walls. Just as Beaumaris Gaol might have been. One part of Walter jumped to red alert suspicion, that this was deliberately planned just for him. Another part of him was grateful to be able to relax his eyes a little until they could better adjust to the bright light outside.

He barely got to process this before he was shoved in the room. He stumbled and the guards grabbed him and roughly dragged him to a chair on one side of the table. He was made to sit and again he was shackled, his wrists on the table, his feet on the floor. His heart leapt into his throat, but he was exhausted from all the fear and emotion and trying to stay strong in spite of it all. So he largely betrayed nothing, or hoped he did, not putting up a fight but simply waiting for the guards to do their job and leave, which they did without saying a word.

He didn't have to wait very long before another door opened across the room. A tall humanoid figure stepped in the room, but it wasn't until he got closer to the table and the light of the candles that Walter was able to make out the unmistakable face of Cassius.

Unlike what Walter might have expected, Cassius hadn't decked himself out in regal robes and jewels and a crown to proclaim to all, near and far, that he was king. He was still dressed in simple jeans and a T-shirt with an open jacket, and work boots that, contrary to the first time he'd seen them, were much more worn. He sat across from Walter, but not as a king or a judge with a domineering presence and authority. Rather, he sat the same way most gangbangers and petty criminals sat when being interrogated. It was a laid back posture, one that said, "I don't give a fuck what kind of authority you think you have because I'm not afraid of you and I'm not squealing."

Except now the positions were reversed. Cassius was not the one under the gun, and his posture was one of mockery; he had Walter. He knew it and he loved it. He reveled in it, like any criminal who, upon release from jail, goes out for revenge against a cop and finds it.

"Good morning, Walter," Cassius greeted, amiability soaked in sarcasm, like a child who wants to squeal with excitement but can't.

"Is it?" Walter wondered. "It's hard to tell."

"You know, I've been waiting for this moment for a long time."

"How long have I been down?"

"By Base Time? Only about twelve hours. But I had a little fun adjusting the cell Time; it's as easy as changing the thermostat. You've been down about four months." Cassius shifted position to something like business casual. "I have to say, I expected you to break a lot sooner than that, given your history. And from what I'm gathering, you haven't actually been broken yet."

"Are you going to send me back until I do?" Walter tried to keep fear from wavering his words.

"No. It was more of an experiment. I listened to you rant and scream and wail. Prisoners do that when they still have hope, you know. Even if they're sad or angry, they will scream because of the agony. They go silent when all hope has left them, when they have no resolve left but to die. You haven't quite reached that point yet, but it's no matter."

Pause.

Cassius shifted again and his expression changed to something menacing. "Do you know who I am?"

"Cassius," Walter answered. "Calis Cutthroat. Sorry to say I don't know your real name, but I know you were one of the gaolers at Beaumaris."

"Yes. Mi Chin figured that one out." He did not sound overly concerned by it. "You know, I remember you, Walter. I remember the day you first walked into your cell. I remember the day you were sent out to be sunk. And how you escaped. You disgust me. You were a drunkard, a fighter, given the world and you squandered it. You left your wife and child to die and then murdered those who had once been so good to you. And yet you still seem to think that by seeking out your little brother's son and raising him as your own that you are somehow vindicated of all responsibility."

"You can talk," Walter cut in. "You who murdered countless innocents for your own disguises."

Cassius grinned. "I wasn't done." Beat. "You've lived on both sides of the law, Walter. Earth-side, you are the law. But that law cannot help you here. But I can."

"Oh, so we're going for good cop, bad cop. You need two for that, don't you?"

Cassius laughed. "Rifun was right. Sarcastic to the last." He sighed. "But it doesn't have to be the last. The Hands were corrupt and everyone knew it. Everyone saw that something like this would happen; all that needed to happen was for someone to push the big red button. Now we have the opportunity to build something flawless."

"All men are flawed," Walter told him nobly. "And as such, anything they build will be flawed."

"Ah, still clinging to that old religion? I can respect that, but know this: mankind, the entirety of the universe, with Time and the Akari, is on its way to perfection. We need only provide the cornerstone for it. Provide the cornerstone and the building falls into place. You have a spot in this kingdom, Walter.

"Think about it: No more corruption. No more changing laws based on the whims of the Hands and the bribes of the elite. Absolute law. Laws that can be enforced. If there is a law, you enforce it without worrying about whether this Hand or that Hand will seek retaliation."

"Instead I have to worry about all the black laws that I don't know about and whether you will come after me for perceived offenses, coupled with evidence you will manufacture. I'm not an idiot; I know how the Communists work."

"A clear conscience is a good way to get to sleep, but it offers no hope for the dead." Cassius was quickly losing patience, Walter could tell. "I am offering you a way out, a way to stay alive and do the job you've always wanted to do as a Timekeeper. Why can't you see that? You die, you lose your life, no one will notice or even remember that you existed. Stay alive and you will be known. Not as a drunkard, a fighter, a shame to the family. But as a good Timekeeper, a keeper of the peace in the Time industry."

Walter studied him, reading his gaze, his expression, his posture. He grinned. "Tommen's alive. And you don't have him."

"I don't—"

"You promised to kill everyone who actively opposed you. I have no doubt that you've been making good on that promise while I've been down, but that's the only reason you would be sitting here talking to me and offering me a way out. As long as I'm alive, you know that Tommen and the others will come for me. You want to use me as bait." Walter shifted as much as he could, his back still tied up and sore. "But you don't need Tommen. All you want is power. Which Rifun promised you. He's the real mastermind here. You put on the show to attract all the attention and let Rifun work his magic in the background, is that how this works? Rifun wants Tommen for his psycho Akari cult, God only knows why, and you want power. So he comes up with a plan to get what you both want. Am I correct to assume that Rifun is somehow sifting through all your prisoners to look for more apprentices for his cult? Or—?"

The next thing Walter knew, he was on the floor looking up at the ceiling. Same room, from what he could tell. His head throbbed and when he tried to move, he felt sticky blood under him. He was free of the shackles, however, and he managed to get his senses sorted out enough to try and move and get up.

Just as he got up on one arm, steel-toed boots connected with his back and he pitched forward on the floor. The room was spinning and he stayed down for just a second to let the nausea pass. Damn. Something had happened and he wasn't entirely sure what, other than a beating. He coughed a few times and slowly got to a sitting position. When he did, something came up under his arms and deposited him limply back into the chair. Cassius walked around the table and sat across from him, breathing heavily, but looking a bit calmer.

"So, we're going to try that again. Hi, my name is Cassius."

"Walter. Pleased to make your acquaintance."

"Do you know who I am?"

Walter could feel blood in his mouth and more in his mustache as it dripped from his nose. Had he at least gotten one good blow in? It didn't look like it. "You were a gaoler at Beaumaris Gaol."

"And who am I now?"

"The Zero Hour."

"Very good. Who are you?"

"A prisoner." *Once more under your grubby thumb.* But he was smart enough and lucid enough not to say it out loud.

"You are a prisoner right now. But you can become more. I have the power to elevate you, Walter. You can be a Timekeeper again, and not just a lowly Captain on some insignificant planet. You can work here, in the Wheel, or anywhere you choose. You can make a difference, be the officer you always wanted to be."

Walter chuckled. "Power...is only your ambition. It's true, I enjoy being a cop and a Timekeeper, but being an officer was never my ultimate ambition. My only ambition for the last almost hundred years has simply been to find my nephew and be a good father to him." He spit some blood on the table to make a point. "You may kill me, but at least I will not die in shame before my son. And when I'm dead, you and Rifun will have lost him forever, too."

Walter was ninety-nine percent sure Cassius was going to launch himself across the table and murder him right there, but the other one percent won out and he stayed right where he was. Fatigue permeated his bones, but Walter refused to give in. *Not now, not in front of Cassius.*

"You know, being king isn't easy," Cassius started. "There's a lot of work that goes into ruling a kingdom. I know where your boy is hiding; he's not that good at it, and your other little Lieutenant isn't very good at protecting him. But being king—and with Rifun also busy—I can't just go and get him myself. And it takes a special talent to be able to get through the dampening field in the portal room, so almost all of my Timekeepers and Grandfathers are out right now, too. But there is another weapon I have at my disposal, one that was banned over a thousand years ago along with the last Cult of the Akari. Do you know what they are?"

"Can't say as I do."

"As with all bad translations, their name is not as fearsome as anything I might have come up with, but they are called Trackers. In years past, when relations were better, the Akarin used to send them out to track down wily Time Agents. They're like bloodhounds, able to track down even week-old Time wakes from an uncoordinated Apprentice. Nice, strong Lieutenants? Well, might as well hang a steak around your neck and release the hounds. It is also said that they can track down those who bear the Akari, which your boy just reeks of, according to Rifun."

"If you train them to track down Bigfoot, you might win more converts to your cause," Walter said sarcastically.

But Cassius was beyond amusement now. "They'll find your son, and they will bring him to me. Unless you agree to my terms and work for me."

Walter shook his head. "No. I taught my boy better than that, and I know he would expect nothing less from me. You are going to have to kill me first."

Cassius sighed and ran his tongue over his teeth. He leaned back in his chair. "Very well then. We'll see just how much like you your son is." He made a motion and six guards entered the room. Two of them seized Walter and hauled him to his feet while Cassius addressed the other four. "Send out the Trackers. Bring me the boy." To Walter's guards, "Take him back to his cell. He'll be in the next round of executions."

With that, Walter was dragged out of the room, the light from the outside momentarily blinding him. He squeezed his eyes shut and did not resist the whole way back down the corridor, through multiple doors, and finally to a stop before a rather small door, comparatively speaking.

There was a terrifying moment between being standing in front of the darkness and landing in the darkness. Even though he was fairly certain that this was his cell, the same cell as before, there was always the fear that there would be nothing there. No walls, no floor, just a pit, where he would fall and fall and suddenly there would be nothing. Absolutely nothing. Not even anything to comprehend the nothing. A total non-existence. Perhaps worse was the thought of heaven or hell, that there would be an eternity and he wasn't good enough to make it to the good eternity.

A thousand prayers went through his mind as he was pushed into the darkness, being cut off abruptly when he hit the floor. Before he could fully comprehend even that, he was picked up and dragged back to the wall where his arms were wrenched uncomfortably backwards, bleeding wrists locked in again. Then the guards turned and left, the last of the light fading until the darkness closed in again.

Four months before. Would it be four months again? Would Cassius be standing outside the cell like a mischievous child, playing with the Time thermostat, still trying to break him before sending him out to be executed?

And had he made the right decision? The dead can't make decisions. The dead can't make a break for it. Maybe he should have chosen to work for Cassius and bought himself more time to figure out how to escape. Except Cassius wasn't dumb; he knew that was exactly what he'd do, and he would make some arrangements to ensure that never happened. Truthfully, they would most likely involve Tommen, use each as a hostage against the other. The only way to end the stalemate was to remove one of the factors, and the only way to remove one of the factors was to die.

"Well, that went well."

Walter turned to see the same shadow man as before, squatting just a short distance away, match flickering to give some light to see, but not enough to show his face.

"Who are you?" Walter asked again. "You're not my conscience."

"Oh?" the man said, shifting so he sat cross-legged. "And how did you come to that conclusion?"

"The conscience doesn't comfort. That's not what it was designed for."

"Did I comfort you?"

Did he? "I don't know. But you said you would be with me, and then you left, and then I felt...I don't know...better. At peace."

"There are many ways of being at peace. There's the...accepting your death kind of peace, the beautiful sunrise kind of peace..."

"It was a peace and a quiet resolve, that I could keep going."

"That works, too."

"You're not my conscience."

"Then what am I?"

Walter sighed. "Some might say that you're...a ghost. An angel. M-maybe the Holy Spirit..."

"Yes...?"

He shook his head and managed an insane grin. "My son would say there's no such thing, or that there has to be a more reasonable explanation for such things, other than just 'supernatural.'"

"And you're your son?"

"Well, no."

"What would the reason be for the peace you had, then?"

"I don't know. Look, is this going to be a regular thing? If you are a ghost or an angel or a spirit, are you going to be haunting me? Have I seriously gone insane here and now you're going to be following me around for the rest of my life?"

The man shrugged. "Well, if I'm your conscience, I'm never going to leave you alone. You can ignore me, but I won't leave. If I'm a ghost or a demon, then you have to find a specific way to make me leave. If I'm an angel, then it's probably not a good idea to ignore me, but you can and suffer the consequences. And if I am, as you say, the Holy Spirit, then, boy, are you screwed."

"Why? What do you want from me?" He went on before the man could answer. "And why do you say *the* Holy Spirit and not *a* holy spirit? In order to make that distinction, you would have to know the significance between the two."

"So either I'm of God, or you're insane."

Walter wished he could rub his face or at least beat it against a wall. He was insane. He had to be.

"There comes a time, Walter, when you have to put your money where your mouth is, when you have to decide what you believe and how far you're willing to believe it. You certainly believed a great deal as you knelt at the altar of the church right after making a seventy year leap into the future."

"And if I say that I believe, you're going to unlock my chains and cause an earthquake to magically open the door, is that it?"

"Are you asking or telling?"

Walter groaned and shuffled a bit in frustration. He was insane. He had to be. Things like this didn't happen, not really. He was insane. He was hallucinating and his scary, apparitional conscience was chiding him for...what? Not going to church enough? Not singing old hymns while locked in this dungeon?

And what if the man—ghost, angel, demon, whatever he was—what if he did unlock Walter's chains and unlock the door? What would he do then?

"Okay, so what if I—?"

He turned to ask the man another question, but he was gone, match and all. The only thing left was the darkness.

Walter closed his eyes—not that it made much of a difference—and tried to take a calming breath. He was insane. He was hallucinating. Better yet, he was hallucinating angels come to save him. How quaint. The mind was a terrible thing when left in the dark.

He tried to sleep, tried to think of what circumstances he might recreate that the man might come back, but each time he was alone as ever.

Cassius hadn't divulged when the next round of executions were supposed to take place. As Walter did his best to count the minutes and the hours and stay sane, he could almost say with certainty that Cassius was again playing with the Time thermostat in the cell. How long would he be kept in here this time? Another four months? Four years? Would Cassius simply turn the dial and leave so he would die before ever going out to be executed?

Walter shifted and shuffled, tried to get comfortable, tried to relieve the strain on his shoulders. He was momentarily amused by the thought of having to take even more extended medical leave because of all the therapy he was going to need after getting out of here. That was assuming that he was going to get out of here and go home. That was his brain clinging desperately to any kind of hope it could find.

That was how men broke, down here in the darkness. They looked for strong bursts of hope, a smörgåsbord of hope to sustain them, when really they just needed little bits here and there. *Let the hope fly under the radar. Keep it tucked deep inside you where it can't get stolen. Hope takes time to replenish, but replenish it will. Just stay calm.*

Eventually, Walter did manage to sleep. He knew he slept because he saw light in his dreams. It was just a small light, a little lantern that he carried with him down the hall to a large wooden door. The room behind the door was decorated sparsely for their station. An enormous window let in the light of the full moon, making the lantern almost unnecessary. Fear had brought him here, but all seemed well. The crib that sat along one wall was undisturbed. He approached it quietly, hoping not to disturb the tiny bundle that lay tucked among the blankets.

She was already awake and she stared up at him with huge blue eyes and little wisps of blond hair just starting to darken.

"It's okay," he told her. "I'll look after you. No one will ever hurt you. Not while I'm here."

# Chapter Six
## Infiltration

Even as Jenna stepped through the portal into the Wheel, she had a sudden regret for her choice of shoes that day. Unsteady going through, she stumbled and just about broke her ankle as she went down. Instead, the snap she heard came only from her shoe. She didn't have time to take it off, however, before Kyle came bumbling through the portal after her, almost landing on top of her. She scooted out of the way and he landed where she'd been just a second before.

"Clumsy!" she hissed.

"You didn't do much better," he growled, indicating her shoe.

She snorted indignantly and removed her high heels, grumbling the whole time. She'd just bought these, and they weren't cheap either.

"Why did you even wear those?" Kyle asked.

"I didn't exactly have an emergency trip to the Wheel and a rescue mission on my agenda today, thank you. At least I try to dress decently when I go out in public."

"Hey! When Micah called me, I was home getting something to eat. Not exactly out in public. And I didn't have this on my agenda either but at least when I get dressed, I get ready for anything."

"Yeah, and your pocketknife is going to save us?"

"More than your makeup bag will."

Kyle broke first, rolling his eyes and sending a shiver of satisfaction up Jenna's spine. He shook his head. "Listen, we're both here on the same mission. We need to gather as much information as we can and get back so the others can form a plan."

"Why? We're here. We're the ones getting the information.

Why should we turn it over to others who aren't here, haven't been here, and don't know shit about what we're seeing? I mean, we can pass on information, but it always gets skewed and misinterpreted. Yeah, let's gather intel, but then why don't we do a little rescue work of our own?"

"Because it's too dangerous."

"They're not launching a full assault because it's too dangerous. They're sending us two in because two can do more than twenty. Why not take advantage of that? We don't have to save the whole universe at once, but imagine if we came back with a few prisoners, hm? Inside intel is the best intel."

Kyle sighed and rubbed his face. "Either way, we still need to get some information about what we're up against. Why don't we do that, and then we can discuss how to proceed?"

"Who's discussing? Fine, we'll gather intel, but if I see a chance to free some prisoners, I'm going to do so."

"Fine. At least give me the translator. If you get captured, I'm not sticking around to get strung up next to you."

"Some help you are. Fuck, I hope you're not going to say you were in the Marines or something because I wouldn't believe you."

"This isn't the Marines. This isn't an Army operation. This is two dudes going into hostile territory with no weapons and no backup and only one way out. Now give it to me."

"No! What if you get captured?"

"Then it will only be because you did."

"What, you think I'm—"

"Sh!"

Jenna was unprepared for Kyle suddenly throwing himself at her, and it knocked the wind out of her lungs. He put one hand over her mouth as he dragged her back against a wall, trying to press himself into a slim cubbyhole as far as he could, holding her tight against him.

With no portals in the portal room, they were near the entrance, just off to the side of the translator dispenser. The door to the Wheel proper was wide open, but now someone stood there, looking around. From a distance, Jenna couldn't tell if it was a guard or a Grandfather, but she figured it didn't matter. Either one was just as likely to capture and kill them. She held her breath; she could feel Kyle's heart thudding against his chest even as his dreadlocks obscured most of her vision and tickled her nose.

For ten long seconds, she waited for the alarm to sound and for guards to come rushing in to seize them both. Then the guard or Grandfather turned and walked away, grumbling something.

Still Jenna and Kyle waited another minute or two before moving from their hiding spot. Jenna's first instinct was to gasp for breath after being so tightly packed, but she forced herself to breathe calmly and make no sounds.

"Okay," she whispered, "so we really have to work together."

"You think?" Kyle hissed.

"Hush! Do you want them to come back?"

He sighed. "Fine." He pinched the bridge of his nose. "We should start in the Coliseum. That sounds like where all the action is."

"And if all the action is there, how do you expect to get in without being seen?"

"I don't know, but where do you expect we're going to get any information worth writing home about? The bathrooms?"

This was going to be harder than she first thought, Jenna realized. In most movies, there was always a convenient corner to hide in, a conveniently placed room with conveniently important information conveniently left out in the open. But this was real life. Worse, this was the Wheel. Portals got them from one place to another. There were no doors or curtains to hide behind. And they weren't going to find the secret master plans left out in the open for all to see. If they wanted good intel to take home, they were going to have to go straight to the heart of the matter, to the Coliseum. And that was just an assumption; there was no way to know for sure where everything and everyone was without going and looking for them.

"I haven't been to the Wheel in a while," Kyle went on. "You're going to have to lead."

"Why haven't you been to the Wheel?" Jenna asked, stalling. She hadn't been the to Wheel much either, truthfully, but she wasn't going to tell him that.

Kyle flushed bright red. "I, uh, I'm not exactly an Apprentice. I mean I am, but..."

"You're a Runner."

"Yeah."

Jenna rolled her eyes. "Great. They pair me with a criminal. Guilt by association and being an accomplice ups my sentence."

"I don't know how much worse of a sentence you can get after execution."

She sighed. "Okay, listen. I know the Wheel pretty well and you know how to avoid the police. I'll tell you where we need to go and you get us there. You think you can manage that much?"

"I don't think I need to repeat the fact of how different the circumstances are this time around, but I'll nod and go along with it."

"We don't have much choice."

"No, darlin', we don't. So, lead the way."

Jenna nodded decisively and approached the door. She barely got two steps toward it when Kyle grabbed her arm.

"Lesson one. Don't just go waltzing up to a door where anyone can shoot your ass. Go along the wall and hide as often as possible. When you see your opening, take it and don't look back."

This was so far out of her league. She did some 5k runs and a friend once talked her into doing Tough Mudder, but this was so much more than that. It was like going from a 5k straight to a marathon while under heavy artillery fire and having to crawl through mud pits filled with razor wire. She hoped that her new approach to the door was taken as caution and not as the fear that was actually paralyzing her.

She shouldn't have done this. She shouldn't have volunteered. She should have just waited for a plan, a real plan. But she was here now and she wasn't about to chicken out. She especially wasn't going to show weakness in front of Mr. SoCal here.

"Do we have an opening?"

Jenna jumped as Kyle whispered in her ear. Then she realized she'd been staring out at the first portal for probably two minutes. She didn't see any guards or Grandfathers, but then, if there was a dampening field over the portal room, then this place wasn't likely to be of the highest priority to keep watch on. Supposedly, no one could escape through here and they certainly weren't expecting anyone to enter through here.

"Yeah," she said finally, giving the area an intentional sweep. "Yeah, we're clear."

Kyle surprised her again by darting out in front of her and running, grabbing her hand and dragging her along behind him. They broke through the portal and stopped. Before Jenna could comprehend her surroundings, they were on the move again, Kyle finding a wall staircase to press himself against and somewhat hide behind.

"That's how you do that," he told her, working to control his breathing. "We're not shoe shopping here. You have to make decisions fast and be able to process information even faster."

"I know that!" Jenna hissed, even as she was silently thankful for his quick thinking.

"So. Where do we go from here?"

Jenna was still trying to collect her swirling thoughts, but she carefully twisted and poked her head out over the staircase to look around. This area was generally considered to be the hub of the Wheel, though all the portals didn't take you absolutely everywhere in the Wheel.

"Two guards," she reported. "Down at the far end of the room on the right wall."

"What's the fastest way to get to the Coliseum?" Kyle asked. "What's the next portal we have to go through?"

She looked around, trying to remember. Then, "About a hundred and fifty feet down on the ceiling. Go through that one, then it should take us to—"

"I just wanted to know the next one. And you're sure it's that one?"

"As sure as I can be."

Kyle sighed. "It'll have to do."

"Hey. If you haven't been here enough to know, that's your fault. So unless you want to be the navigator, I suggest you pipe down."

"You first. Get down."

They got down, both of them acutely aware that the staircase was the only thing hiding them from the view of the guards as they approached. Thankfully, the guards chose a different staircase to get to the floor where they started walking away again.

"God, I forgot how fucked up this place was," Kyle breathed.

"You're telling me," Jenna agreed.

He cautiously looked up over the stairs. After a minute or two, he said, "Okay. When I say go, we have to go and keep going. Don't look back until we're sitting down again like this. Got it?"

"Got it."

She understood his words. After the first time, she understood what that would entail. That didn't necessarily mean that she was okay with what they had to do. She had little desire to make another sprint for the door like a dinosaur was after her. Still, she had to do it. If she ever wanted to see Janice again, she had to do it. She at least had to try.

"Go!"

Kyle took off, but he did not grab Jenna's hand this time and pull her along. In her surprise, she lost about five seconds just trying to process it, and then another five scrambling after him and trying to get her body to move the way it was supposed to. As she stepped from the wall to the staircase that took her to the ceiling, she found that she was holding her breath as she futilely tried to keep from making any noise. Still, she didn't want to burst out gasping or coughing, so she held until her lungs threatened to burst, pushing out the last bit of energy she had to get right up on Kyle's heel as he disappeared through the portal.

As soon as she was through, Kyle grabbed her hand and dragged her to a safe spot. Once she got her breath and was able to see straight, she found that the safe spot was actually a vendor booth in a marketplace. Looking around, it took her a second to realize they were in one of the lower marketplaces and it was emptier than a ghost town.

Normally, the lower marketplaces were so packed, it made a tin of sardines look good. People and aliens pressed together, all jostling to look at wares that Merchants enticed them towards. Sales and bargains and arguments mingled with the din of conversation and the shuffling and movement of people and goods. Now, the booths sat empty. Not even a free sample Time capsule was left, loaded or discarded. Many things appeared broken, as if there had been a huge fight here. Seeing as the marketplace no longer appeared needed, things had been repaired just enough to get them out of the way but otherwise just left to rot.

Perhaps the strangest thing about it was how open the marketplace was now, how far apart the booths seemed. If she hadn't seen this place when it was packed full, Jenna might have complained and pointed out how many more booths could go in the empty spaces to fill the place in a little.

"It's...empty," she said.

"Kinda spooky," Kyle agreed. "I don't see any guards, but I still want to be careful. Where's the next portal?"

Jenna took a breath, tried to think, tried to focus. Suddenly it was dawning on her that there had been a massacre here. People had died. It had been like shooting fish in a barrel with nowhere to run.

"Jenna?" Kyle pushed into her thoughts. "Stay with me. Where's the next portal?"

Next portal. Right. The one that would take them to the Coliseum. She took another calming breath. "Okay. At the other end of the marketplace, there should be two portals. One leads to another marketplace like this one and the other goes to the marketplace hub. From there, we should be able to find a portal to the Coliseum. Or closer to it."

"All I needed to know. Come on."

He did not stand up and walk through the marketplace normally. Instead, he chose to slide behind the booths, crawling on the floor and keeping one side pressed against the wall. While he paid attention to what was in front of them, Jenna kept an eye out behind to make sure they weren't being followed. She still didn't see or hear any guards, but she was liking this mission less and less.

"Doing okay back there?" Kyle asked.

"Yeah, fine," she answered and shuffled faster to keep up with him.

"I'd tell you to go back if you're afraid, but I have to be able to leave, too."

"Who says I won't go and leave you here?"

"Because if you're that inexperienced and that much of a bitch, you must have some ulterior motive for volunteering for this in the first place."

"Well why are you here?"

"Micah asked me to be. And I promised Walter that I'd look after Tommen. Tommen's safe, so now I figure I should pay my debt to him for not turning me in when he should have." He paused and looked back at her. "Your turn. Boyfriend got captured?"

Jenna sighed dramatically. "No, my girlfriend."

He shook his head. "Fuck."

"You got a problem with it?"

"Okay, I ain't religious or nothin', but that just fucking weirds me out. Dude on dude, chick on chick. It ain't natural. I mean, I'm sure you're okay—a bitch, maybe, but maybe pretty chill with your friends—but that just creeps me out."

"Then I guess it's a good thing you're not the one I'm fucking."

Kyle shuddered noticeably. "Yeesh, now I'm going to have nightmares."

"You can always go back if you're scared."

"Of what? You? Psh, I'm not afraid of you. Not when we have to get around guards and Grandfathers and who knows what else."

Under the circumstances, that did seem like the greater threat. Jenna had any number of smart replies that she'd developed over the years for dealing with such people, but she quickly decided that maybe now wasn't the time. Maybe once they'd rescued Janice—okay, and Walter and Micaiah—and gotten the hell out of here, then they could have that little chat.

"Okay, we're here," Kyle said, stopping abruptly. "Anyone behind us?"

Jenna gave the area a good look-see. "No, nothing."

"Well, I can tell you which portal leads to the hub."

"Yeah? Which one?"

"The one with guards on the other side."

Jenna looked around Kyle. The portal to the hub was there. As he said, there were guards on the other side. She only counted three, but there could have been any number of guards elsewhere in the room that they couldn't see.

"Shit," she hissed. "How are we going to get past them?"

"Is there another way around?"

She racked her memory. "I don't think so. The marketplaces all eventually circle around each other, lower and middle markets. If there are guards there at the hub, though, there will probably be some in the auctionhouse hub, too."

"Yeah, but the marketplace hub is generally more populated than the auctionhouse hub. If there are any there, I'm betting it won't be as many. Come on."

"Wait a minute. Who made you leader?"

Kyle paused. "Um, you did. You're the map, I'm the mover. You tell me where we're going and I get us there. So far, I think it's been working out. Unless you have a better plan?"

No, she just didn't want to feel like she was just plodding along like an obedient puppy. Finally she shook her head. "Not really."

"So let's go."

They slipped around the portal leading to the marketplace hub and instead went through the one leading to yet another marketplace. This one, too, was empty and unguarded.

"Why do you think they leave them unguarded?" Jenna wondered aloud.

"Nothing here," Kyle said thoughtfully. "Nothing to steal, nothing of significance. If anyone's going to try anything, they'll have to get through any of the hubs which are guarded."

"So they're guarding from the inside out, not the outside in."

"Uh, sure, whatever you said."

"They're expecting the threat to come from the inside rather than the outside."

"I don't think they're expecting any threat at this point, honestly."

Well, that made sense, too, Jenna supposed. Still, someone had to have noticed that a portal opened up in the portal room when it shouldn't have.

"Okay, we've got a portal here on the floor and a couple more on either wall," Kyle reported. "Where are we heading?"

"The one on the floor is another lower marketplace. The ones on the walls take us to middle marketplaces."

"Middle it is, then."

The intermediate marketplaces each had a guard, but they were easily bypassed. Only when they were finally confronted with the portal to the auctionhouse did they stop to catch their breath for a second.

"Do you think we could infiltrate the guards?" Jenna asked. "You know, knock them out, steal their clothes, that sort of thing?"

Kyle shook his head. "No. Guards are like Grandfathers and Hands; their rank is confirmed by their DNA. Every time they enter the Wheel, they're endowed with their weapons, defenses, and special privileges. When they leave the Wheel, everything is saved for them the next time. We might be able to move around the outer part of the Wheel, like here, but the auctionhouse, and especially the Coliseum and the Judgment Wing, we'd be found out."

"Well, fuck."

"Not a bad idea, but believe me, I already thought about it."

Jenna rolled her eyes but he didn't see. Of course he'd already considered it. She shook her head. "Okay, so what about the auctionhouse hub?"

"I'm only counting two guards. Where exactly is the next portal, once we get in there?"

"Um...let me think." Jenna wasn't rich; she didn't go to the Auctions. She'd only been in the auctionhouse hub once just so Janice could show her what they were. At the same time, the Auctions were extremely exclusive and they didn't want just anyone wandering through there.

"Okay, I got it," she said. "So when we go in, in front of us there will be a row of portals leading to the Auctions themselves. The portal leading out of the marketplaces is on the other side of this portal that we'll go through."

"Then what?"

Then what? She didn't know then what. Well, actually, maybe she did. "After that, I think we'll be in a large atrium looking room. It's kind of a hub, except it leads to places like the Food Court and the Archives. And the Archives is part of History Hall which connects the Archives to the Judgment Wing and the Coliseum."

"So we're talking ramped up security."

"Most likely."

"Damn. All right, so we're going to have to move quickly and find a good place to hide as soon as possible."

"Sounds like it."

"When I say go, we go."

"Got it."

That was probably one of the longest three seconds Jenna could recall. Still, she was ready this time when Kyle gave the signal and dashed toward the portal.

There were only two guards in the auctionhouse hub and their backs were turned when she and Kyle entered, did a perfect pivot that any dancer would be jealous of and slid into the portal on the other side of the portal, this time entering a large atrium, as promised. Jenna did not immediately see any guards, but soon Kyle had her pulled back in a small crevice, much like he had in the portal room.

They had been saved only by the fact that the portal itself blocked them from most angles. Otherwise, there were about ten guards and two Grandfathers that Jenna could see milling about the room. Jenna knew that to their right somewhere was the Food Court, as well as another portal that led to History Hall which would be the Archives, the Judgment Wing, and the Coliseum.

"Where do we need to go next?" Kyle asked.

Jenna told him about the layout. "How are we going to get past them? Forget the guards, what about the Grandfathers?"

"I'm working on it."

And then there was the fact that no matter how far they got in, they had to be able to get out, too. Jenna felt her hopes of returning with a handful of freed prisoners go out the window.

"The window."

"What?" Kyle looked at her.

Rather than explain, she started digging in her purse, trying not to make much noise.

"Hardly a time for your makeup," Kyle said as she brought out a small jar of cream.

"You know how this really isn't at all like the movies, where the heroes get really lucky all the time?"

"Um, duh?"

"Well, I'm making my own luck."

She chucked the jar of cream as hard as she could, hearing it shatter and, oddly enough, thinking only that she'd just wasted sixty dollars.

But it had the desired effect. Well, sort of. A couple guards heard or saw it and soon the whole pack was barking at each other. While they were distracted and the Grandfathers moving closer to where the thing had crashed, Jenna and Kyle took off along the wall toward the Food Court and the portal to the Archives.

Instead of jumping through the portal, though, Kyle grabbed Jenna's hand and ducked into the Food Court hub. Unlike other hubs, there was no portal between the atrium room and the Food Court hub, just a small archway—okay, a large archway to accommodate larger aliens—that afforded them a brief hiding spot.

"What did you do that for? I don't have anymore jars of cream to distract them and get us out of here!" Jenna whispered harshly.

"But we're close enough to the Archives portal to see what we're getting into," Kyle said. "I don't feel like running straight into a Grandfather, do you?"

Jenna conceded the point and together they peeked around the corner toward the portal.

"We have to assume that there are going to be guards and Grandfathers everywhere," Kyle said. "Whether the Coliseum or the Judgment Wing, they're going to be there if nowhere else."

"So what do we do, O Enlightened One?"

Kyle sighed, but then they apparently got their answer. A couple guards took positions on either side of the portal just seconds before a large group of aliens of all sorts walked past. If Jenna had to guess, they were probably prisoners, as haggard and hopeless as they looked. Then the group passed by and the guards followed.

"Leave your purse here. Let's follow them," Kyle said, looking around the atrium for just a second before moving, leaving Jenna behind.

She caught up to him just as he passed through the portal. No huge alarm was raised and neither of them was murdered on the spot. Jenna would have been happy to hurry to catch up with the group, but Kyle seemed to have the right idea, trying to match the demeanor of the group and plod along slowly and unhappily.

Then the call went up from another guard. Jenna didn't have a translator, but she didn't need one to know that she was being insulted and told to hurry up. One of the guards from the back of the group dropped back and shoved the two of them forward, pushing them into the group. They complied and squeezed their way in more toward the center.

"Okay, so we're in," Jenna hissed. "Now what do we do? Wherever we're going, I don't think it's out to lunch."

"Now we gather information and hope that we can get out before we're executed."

"You're asking me to put my trust in you based on that kind of hope? No thank you, I think I'll be looking for my own way out."

"You wanted to save some prisoners? Well, here they are. Save them."

Problem was, she wasn't sure how.

So they just went with the group, plodding along sullenly, but keeping one eye out to keep track of who was in the group. They were the only humans as far as Jenna could tell. Without translators, they couldn't ask after anyone by name, not that she expected anyone to know who Janice was.

They walked away from the Judgment Wing, looming eerily behind them, to the portal to the Coliseum. The group, about a hundred in number if Jenna had to hazard a guess, got bottlenecked at the portal and they were made to wait. They went through one by one, but even then it seemed unusually slow. When it was her turn, she understood why.

She'd only been to the Judgment Wing once, when Janice was showing her around and showing her how everything worked. She knew that the Judgment Wing used special stamps for the Timekeepers and the Runners they brought in. Timekeepers got two-way stamps, so they could pass in and out unhindered. Runners got a one-way stamp, so they could get in, but if they tried to get out, they would be electrocuted by an invisible field that guarded all the doors.

As they each passed through the portal to the Coliseum, a Grandfather stamped their hand with one of those stamps. If Jenna had to guess again, it was probably the one-way stamp, meaning if they tried to escape, they would be electrocuted or die in some other grisly fashion.

"So what's your next big idea?" she hissed to Kyle as they continued on toward the Coliseum.

"Still working on it," he told her, but his resolve sounded like it was wavering. He was as lost as she was.

From the outside, the Coliseum seemed to be the only thing unaffected by the whole coup thing. It still appeared lively and busy. Maybe not as busy as a normal day, but there were people milling about.

As she got closer, she found that anyone who was milling about was either a guard or a Grandfather. And here, the guards seemed to change, too. Outside the Coliseum, they'd seemed to be little better than street thugs patrolling their turf on the streets. Here, in the Coliseum, they were less like thugs and more like true military personnel. Their posture, their disposition, even the weapons they carried—from strange alien biological appendages to knives to firearms to things Jenna didn't even have a name for—all spoke of real security. They weren't dealing with some tired, retired, sleeping door guard now. This time, they were being guarded by the Navy SEALs, but not in any way that made Jenna feel safe.

They passed through the first entrance into the first track around the Coliseum. Here, running among the soldiers and Grandfathers, Jenna spotted a few secretaries. They seemed less like accomplices in the whole thing and more like the unfortunate souls who got sold into slavery, some sort of bonus prize for the winning team. They ran around like headless chickens while orders were barked at them from all directions.

Perhaps the most obvious change, though, was that the enormous iron gates that passed by all the tracks and led straight into the Seat of the Hands were open. This was where they were made to walk. The whole walk was lined with guards, the innermost gateway being lined with Grandfathers who parted for their arrival.

It was slow going to the Seat, and Jenna found her mind wandering even as she told herself she had to look around, take mental notes, gather intel. But the thing about gathering intel was that they had to report it back to those who sent them. Well, so far, gathering intelligence was going great. Couldn't be better. Now how to get it all back to Micah and the others...she had no idea right now.

It was easily an hour before they even set foot in the Seat, and the line was still long. Inside, Jenna could see the stadium was busy and filling up quickly. Moving in closer, she could see the seats had been divided into sections of sorts, the lines being made obvious by the guards and Grandfathers. But what were they being sectioned off for?

Getting even closer, Jenna could see a stage had been erected in the middle of the Seat, where the Hands were supposed to have made a smooth transition of power. On this stage, Jenna could see a table, someone seated behind it. It looked like a Borelian, but she could not make out the color. About twenty feet back and to the right, she saw several more figures. One was a shrouded Grandfather. Another was a pink Borelian.

The third figure was a human. Tall, maybe a peep over six foot. Compared to Jenna, he was white, but his skin was still darker than Kyle's. He had long brown hair tied back in a ponytail that might have reached his waist if not for the bulk of a gray hoodie. Otherwise, he wore jeans and tennis shoes, as if it were just an ordinary Tuesday.

*So that's Rifun,* Jenna realized. He was one of the ones who caused this whole thing? He certainly didn't seem the type, so either he was more evil that anyone gave him credit for, or else the Time industry and the Hands really had been that unstable that the faintest breeze could have toppled it, never mind this storm.

"Any ideas?" Kyle murmured in her ear.

"Um...maybe. I think that's Rifun there." She nodded toward the man.

"It is. I've seen him before. What are you thinking?"

She got halfway through her idea when she saw Rifun say something to the pink Borelian and the Grandfather, then turn and walk away, disappearing into the tunnel off to one side. She almost wanted to jump out and shout at him to stay and wait and maybe listen, but she refrained. At the same time, her plan kind of depended on him being there.

"Okay, what's your other plan?" Kyle asked.

Jenna just shook her head.

They moved closer to the stage. As each person took their turn at the table, Jenna tried to find some semblance of order, of predictability in how things were going. Some prisoners were sent to one section, other prisoners a different section. Looking around at all the sections in the stands, Jenna could only conclude that they were being intentionally divided, but for what purpose? One section seemed to be populated by very large species, though there were some smaller species among them. Same with sections containing primarily very small species that might contain a few larger aliens. Other sections were a mix. Some sections were vastly populated, while one particular section had maybe two dozen, total, out of perhaps a hundred thousand. And still there were some aliens that were escorted back down the line and out of the Coliseum, perhaps back to the Judgment Wing.

They moved closer, now one of the next in line. Jenna saw that there were actually five tables with five Borelians working, though that still seemed woefully understaffed given the situation. Even the DMV wasn't this bad, she thought. Bring in about fifty desk workers, get the line moving, maybe get on with whatever little scheme Rifun and Cassius were concocting? At the same time, if they were now the end-all power in the universe, why rush things? Take the time to do them right, save more trouble down the road.

"What do you think?" Kyle asked nervously as they moved up to be the next in line.

"Stick to the plan," she told him, trying to keep her own voice from shaking.

"What plan?"

Before she could answer, she was made to go up on the stage and meet with one of the Borelian DMV staff.

She instantly felt the gaseous side effects. It came from a color imperceptible to humans, but the side effect was confusion and a general feeling of loneliness. In general, it made the unsuspecting victim easier to manipulate, easier to bring down their mental barriers, get them to talk.

"Coordinates," the worker asked.

While Jenna had no sympathy for Borelians, this one's demeanor was far from threatening, and she suspected that he—or she—was just another desk worker. Kingdoms and empires and glorious futures were great, but in the moment, it was a hell of a lot of paperwork. She gave the worker her coordinates.

"Species?"

"Human." Was there another option to choose from?

"Rank?"

"Journeyman Harvester."

"And...your name?"

"Walter Forbes."

While the underpaid DMV staffer did not react to that, simply input the information on his tablet-like device, Jenna did notice that she had gotten the attention of the pink Borelian who was still standing politely back from the tables. Jenna did a risky thing and met the Borelian's gaze.

Her thoughts were interrupted by the common worker. "And are you willing to swear allegiance to the new order of things, under the command, direction, and authority of Cassius Hand and Rifun Ndolo?"

*Never in a million years.* "Yes."

Still unimpressed. "Secretary."

A secretary hurried over to the stage. Jenna gladly stepped away from the small gathering of Borelians and followed the secretary up the stairs into the stands. She looked back to see Kyle was also being led away, but to a different part of the stands. They were separated. They couldn't be separated. Oh, this was not good. What had they gotten themselves into? Was there any way this ended well?

"Your place is here," the secretary said finally, admitting Jenna into one particular section of the stadium seating, one of the largest groups.

"Where is here?" she asked.

"Secretaries," someone answered.

"I don't understand."

"That is to be our job," a large, weasel-looking alien told her. "We are assigned work in the new way of things. Now, we are simply secretaries. Our duties will be decided later."

Assigned work? Duties? Wasn't this all supposed to be mass execution, doom and gloom, someone had to come charging in on a white horse to save the day? What were all these logistics? What was all this logic that said that Cassius and Rifun couldn't just slaughter everyone and it was better to put their subjects to better use? They'd committed a tragic coup and ordered a massacre only the night before, and now they were running the unemployment line?

But then, was there even such a thing as a velvet coup? Who was she to judge these things? Maybe things would be better.

She shook her head and looked around. Several of their guards were Borelians. Maybe they were intentionally chosen to make their charges compliant, maybe not, but she had to remain on alert. They were on a mission here. If only she knew where Kyle had gotten off to.

Down below, she saw that the pink Borelian had walked off the stage and was missing from the center completely. That had to be Isthim, Jenna reasoned. She would be the only Borelian who knew Walter and Micaiah by name and would want to relay it to Rifun.

She looked around the Seat but could not spot Kyle or his dreadlocks anywhere. She didn't see Walter or Micaiah either. She especially didn't see Janice and her heart feared the worst. She looked down at the line of aliens streaming out of the Coliseum, and endless line of prisoners here to be assigned to their new place in the new way of things.

After a short time, movement in the center caught her attention. Isthim had returned, but Rifun was easily three strides ahead of her. They went to the center stage and approached the table. There was a conversation. Guards were summoned then released. One went toward the second set of stairs where Kyle had been taken. The other came up the first set of stairs and made for the secretary section.

"Walter Forbes," the guard commanded. "Come with me."

He walked a few more steps and repeated the same thing. Jenna waited until the fourth call before finally gathering her nerve and standing. She wordlessly followed the guard back around the stadium to the stairs. On the other side, Kyle was already on the ground and heading for the stage.

Jenna's heart hammered in her chest as her feet hit the ground. Rifun and Isthim had disappeared, and the guards took her and Kyle through the tunnel into the dungeon that was the domain of the Bat. There Rifun and Isthim waited.

For a long moment, no one spoke.

"You are not Walter," Rifun said finally, looking at Jenna. To Kyle, "and you are obviously not Micaiah." He paused, then grinned. "Well, I don't know who you are, but we've been waiting for you nonetheless."

Jenna didn't like the grin he had on his face, and she gasped and jumped a little as Rifun put a hand on her arm. It was his right hand, and it only had three fingers. The nubs where his index and middle fingers were supposed to be feel weird on her arm and she shuddered. He took Kyle's arm in his left hand.

He looked at Isthim. "Keep things running smoothly, darling. I have an errand to run."

Isthim dipped her head and ducked back into the tunnel. Meanwhile, Rifun led them through the inner track and through several passages until they reached the straight track which was under heavy guard. The Grandfathers and a few guards grumbled and murmured among themselves, but they parted to let them pass. They walked under the first iron gate, through the corridor, under the second iron gate, past another line of guards and Grandfathers, and out of the Coliseum. Jenna tried to tell herself that it was a good thing; they were putting more distance between them and the Coliseum. On the other hand, she wasn't sure she wanted to know what new fate awaited them now, especially since Rifun said that they had been expected.

"W-wait," she said, putting on the brakes as they neared the portal. "They gave us stamps. We can't go back through."

Rifun said nothing, simply pulled harder, forcing her along. They paused just before passing through. Another group set for assignment waited on the other side. The guards looked ready to make a fuss until they saw who it was holding them up. Rifun spoke with the Grandfather giving out the stamps, and the Grandfather removed the stamps, allowing Jenna and Kyle to pass through harmlessly.

"Where are we going?" Kyle asked. "How did you know to expect us?"

"We're going to have a little chat, and then your questions will be answered," Rifun replied amiably. "Then we will see about your futures. You may not have one."

Well, at least he was honest, Jenna figured. They retraced their steps through History Hall, passing the portal where they'd slipped in and making for the Judgment Wing.

The last time Jenna had been in the Judgment Wing, it had been overseen by a hamster secretary called the Hutch. Now, as with everything else it seemed, it was run by a Grandfather. The Grandfather gave them another one-way stamp and sent them on their way, through the first enormous vault door and down the hall to a second vault door and a room with three smaller vault doors. The one on the left was open a crack, but Rifun went to the one in the middle.

"Tell Cassius I'm here," he ordered the guard. "And I have

friends."

Jenna wasn't sure how she felt about being called a friend of this wacko. Still, the guard agreed and disappeared into the room behind the vault door. They waited in silence for about ten minutes before the guard returned and opened the door wide for them.

The middle vault door led to what Jenna could only describe as a prison. And not just a prison, like how most Americans understood prison, but this was like high-tech. Each cell seemed tailored to the prisoner it held. They passed cells of varying metals with doors ranging from simple bars to mesh to completely solid. The cells also varied in size. Small cells were grouped together, stacked up next to large cells, like housing a bunch of lab mice next to a Great Dane kennel.

The whole place was a maze with hallways going off in every direction, doors open and closed, leading to even more places Jenna didn't want to think about.

They finally stopped in front of an unsuspecting door, like the kind you might find in any given school, except that it was enormous in order to accommodate all sizes of aliens and creatures. Rifun opened the door and pushed Kyle and Jenna in ahead of him.

The room was sparse, to put it mildly. A table with two chairs on either side, candles on the table and around on the walls, just enough to give some ambient light without seemed overwhelming.

"Have a seat," Rifun said, intentionally bumping into them from behind as he made for one side of the table.

Before any of them could sit, another door opened and the man Jenna could only assume to be Cassius walked in. He didn't look like anything particularly menacing. He didn't have pale gray skin or black eyes, nor did he seem like a scary, imposing super bodybuilder type, or even the quiet and brooding type. At the same time, something about his very presence exuded menace and evil. Maybe it was his posture, his demeanor, his expression. Whatever it was, it gave Jenna the chills, and an image of tomorrow's headline flashed through her mind: Tourist Found Dead in Possible Hate Crime.

Except the hate would have nothing to do with her sexuality, but the sheer, obscene pleasure of murder.

"So, the rescue party arrives," Cassius said. "Please, have a seat."

It was not a request, and Jenna and Kyle dutifully sat.

"I have to say, I expected more, but maybe I expect too much."

"Ah, but we are being rude," Rifun interrupted. "We haven't been properly introduced. You may know me, I am Rifun Ndolo. My counterpart here is Cassius."

"Kyle," Kyle said levelly.

"Jenna."

"Tell me, Kyle, Jenna, how did you get here? I put a dampening field over the portal room. You are the first ones to break in."

"The same way Micah and Tommen broke out," Kyle told him with a hint of sarcasm. "Your dampening field isn't impermeable."

Cassius grinned and now Jenna saw where the evil was starting to become obvious. "No. Indeed it is not." He shifted in his seat, completely changing his demeanor. "So, Micah and Tommen are alive and well, are they?"

"All they want is for Walter and Micaiah to come home," Jenna said, searching for a heart string. "They don't care about Time, and Earth isn't significant. Just send them home and they'll be fine with not interfering with anything else."

"I like you, Jenna. Searching for a soft spot, hoping to strike a bargain perhaps. There's just one problem: we have no emotions to play. We're giving people new life assignments and killing those who refuse to go along in there, in case you haven't noticed. We're burning down the world so we can be kings of the ashes and build our own kingdom. You're right, two insignificant people from an insignificant planet shouldn't mean much. But if we start with the mercy now, where will it end? We'll be weak. We'll be overthrown."

"And we might have even let them go, if they didn't represent such a significant investment to us," Rifun went on. "Tommen is of particular interest to me. I've lost him, though. And he won't come back if I don't have something to lure him here."

"His dad," Kyle stated. "You're sick."

"Be that as it may, it's business."

"I am curious, though," Cassius said. "Portals cannot stay open while the dampening field is in place. How were you intending on getting back?"

"We were going to free Walter and Micaiah, and Micaiah would open a portal back home," Jenna lied, hoping it was convincing and she wouldn't have to tell them about the translator. Her purse was still hidden in the little Food Court nook, or so she hoped.

"Ah, such a noble plan," Rifun sighed. "And you were hoping to find them before you were set to be executed, correct?" Kyle and Jenna glanced at each other. "Do you even know where they are?"

"No," Kyle admitted.

"Are they even still alive?" Jenna asked quietly.

"They are," Cassius confirmed. "For the moment. Though they are due to be taken out momentarily, I believe. I don't think they'll take mundane assignments and subservience to us very well."

"You know, this is all very special," Rifun said, slapping the table like he was laughing at a joke. "I think Walt and Micaiah ought to know how close they were to freedom. I say we send these two with them and they can all go together."

"That is an idea," Cassius mused. "Send them out, then. And send word ahead that I am going to oversee this one personally."

He made a motion and a couple guards entered the room. One hauled Kyle to his feet while another took Jenna and stood her up like she was little more than a Barbie doll.

"Can I ask one question?" Jenna asked as Cassius and Rifun stood and prepared to leave. The duo turned, brows raised. "I came here for someone else, too. Her name is Janice Riley. She's a—"

"Dear, do you know how many people have been through today?" Rifun said, as if asking a child how many snowflakes had fallen during a storm. "I can't keep track of them all. Besides, you'll be joining her soon enough. Or if she's still alive, just wait a little while and she'll come to you."

With that, Rifun and Cassius walked away, and Kyle and Jenna were taken out by the guards.

# Chapter Seven
## Escape

Micaiah had never done time in any sort of major prison, but he had no illusions about it, especially when he knew his prison was going to be populated with aliens from all corners of the galaxy and run by a deranged psychopath. To him, he figured, it was just another prize-fighting arena. Not that Walter's reaction was any comfort. He'd seen Walter vulnerable a time or two, and he respected him for it. Never had he seen such a meltdown, a fear that surpassed anything Micaiah could comprehend. Not only did the fear bleed over a little into his own mind, but it instilled a paradox of respect and pity for his Captain; the only way his greatest fear could be so well-exploited would be if it was the same man who exploited it both times. And that was just cruel beyond all words.

They were separated after that. Walter was beaten into near-unconsciousness and carried off to his own cell. Micaiah put up decidedly less of a fight, figuring that no good would come from it now; if he was going to escape, it would be outside the Judgment Wing. He still hadn't worked out the details of the escape, and it was only made more complicated by being separated from Walter; ideally, he wanted to deliver them both to safety. The last thing he wanted was to face Tommen and have to tell him that he'd been forced to abandon his dad.

He was taken to a cell that, had it been lit, would have been as unremarkable as any other room in the Judgment Wing. But it wasn't lit. The cell was completely dark. No candles, no tiny windows, not even a glow beneath the door. Once he was pushed in and the door closed and locked, it was like the darkness came alive and folded him into itself.

Eons ago, Micaiah had done some caving at various locations around the world. One of the things that was always reiterated—barring cave or tunnel collapse, equipment malfunction and injury, all the really bad stuff—was the effects of total cave darkness. The retina was a muscle and it had to be used; it wanted to be used. In such absolute darkness, it couldn't be used. The first thing that came around was hallucinations, as the eye tricked itself into thinking it saw a wall or a floor, the hand in front of your face, or a way out. Other hallucinations came into effect, too, after a time, mostly auditory.

"So, they got you, too."

Micaiah whirled. There, about twenty feet away, a man sat on the floor cross-legged. He had only a match that dimly lit his features so he looked like a ghoul.

"I haven't been here long enough to start hallucinating," Micaiah said.

"Haven't you?" the man asked. "How do you know?"

"I just got here."

"The darkness plays tricks right from the start. Your clock may not be broken, but you still have no sense of time in here."

"That's the point of clock breaking, to strip away that inherent sense of time. I still have that; I'm not an idiot drooling on the floor."

"Then why are you still arguing about it?"

Micaiah sighed and rubbed his eyes. When he opened them, the man was still there. He hadn't moved an inch and the match still flickered.

"Who are you?" Micaiah asked evenly. "Did Cassius capture you as well?"

The man shook his head. "Cassius did not capture me. He can't touch me."

"Then why are you here?"

"I am here because I am needed here."

"Prison chaplain then. Fantastic."

"Do you want to talk?"

"Oh, a sarcastic prison chaplain. Even better. Maybe I have been here long enough to hallucinate. Apparently my conscience manifests itself as a sarcastic prison chaplain."

"Could be worse."

"You're right; you could be my brother."

"Would that be so bad?"

Micaiah sighed, feeling suddenly guilty. "No. Actually, it'd be pretty good to see him right now."

"Why don't you go to him, then? You have the power."

"I might, except Walter and I got separated."

"And...?"

"I can't go back without him, not if I still have a chance to save him. I couldn't face Tommen otherwise."

"And at what point are you going to throw up your hands and just save yourself? How do you really know that Walter isn't dead already? How do you know that they didn't beat him so bad that he's going to die in his cell, whatever Cassius said about taking you out for public execution?"

"I don't. But until I'm up there on the chopping block, I'm still going to hold out hope that we can all go home."

"All? Every single being here? Can you do that? You think you can save them all?"

"Okay, fine, get technical." Micaiah rolled his eyes. "'All' meaning me and Walter and, probably, any other humans that it's possible to save."

"Only humans? That's racist."

"Well what am I supposed to do? I can't very well just show up to work dragging along six different aliens with me. I don't need to take a one way trip to New Mexico to some secret government bunker."

"You can't save them all."

"No. I can't. Right now, I'll be happy to take Walter, myself, and, yes, any and only humans. Sorry, but I can't do it all."

The man nodded. "Very good. I think we've made some excellent progress today." And he blew out the match.

Micaiah stood very still after that, listening for any indication that the man was moving and where he was going, but he heard nothing. Gingerly, he felt his way in what he believed to be the direction that the man had been, but he found nothing.

Now what had that been all about? Had the man ever really been there in the first place? Or was it a hallucination? If so, had his conscience really manifested itself as a sarcastic prison chaplain type person? Why in the hell would it do that?

Groaning, Micaiah found a place to sit and drew his knees up to his chest so he could beat his head on his knees. No, he could not allow himself to succumb to the darkness. Guiltily, Micaiah told himself that he could not allow himself to end up like Walter. He had to stay strong. He had to stay sane. He had to hang onto anything that would bring some semblance of order and decency and sanity to this godforsaken place.

He repeated recipes from the bakery, both proud of and yet disgusted with himself that he knew all of them by heart. In his next life, he was not having anything to do with baking, thank you very much. He sang — or tried to sing — a few Irish hymns, having to stop every so often to think about the words. It had been decades since he'd been to a proper Irish church; his ma would be repulsed by it. He repeated a few Irish prayers and blessings. Not because he believed he would actually receive an endless supply of fruition and potatoes, but because they were the only prayers and blessings he knew. Did God care if he'd forgotten the old prayers? Was it too late to start any of that? Did he get points for trying?

Micaiah took in a breath. Hope and religion was fine, but he couldn't be thinking about it like he was going to die at any moment, even if that was entirely within the realm of possibility. He had to stay focused, stay on task. His mission right now was to be able to walk out of this black cell with his sanity in tact. God knew that whatever length of time Walter spent in a black cell, he was not going to be in any shape to do anything for a while. If there was an escape attempt in their future, it was probably going to be Micaiah doing all the heavy lifting and having to drag Walter through it all.

Maybe he should convince the man to retire. All of this bullshit wasn't good for him. Between Rifun taking his son, nearly dying, having to relive his past, now being forced face-to-face with that past by psychological exploitation, Walter was going to end up a terror-stricken vegetable before the year was out. And the year had only just begun. Maybe he, Micaiah, should train to become a Captain and take his place. That wouldn't be bad. Go dark during the training, come back to a new life of his construction with a new promotion.

Micaiah knew with about ninety-nine percent certainty that his clock hadn't been broken. He also knew that between the time he'd been pushed in and locked up, to the time the door opened again and light blinded him, that it hadn't been very long. For one thing, his beard had barely grown at all; it was just getting to the point where it was possible to tell that he didn't have a nice, full, solid color, but a mismatched patchwork of brown, red and blond.

He stood as the door opened, squinting in the light. It was dim outside, he knew, but after—what, ten hours?—sitting in the dark, he might as well be looking at the sun.

The guards took him out much the same way they took him in, with a little more force than necessary. Micaiah wasn't sure of the reasoning seeing how he was still stamped so that he couldn't get out through conventional means. Thankfully, his eyes adjusted quickly enough to the light and he was able to look around at his surroundings with minimal difficulty. Not that there was much to see beyond rows and rows of cells.

He was hastened to a room that was reminisce of the corridors, small and dimly lit, except this room had a table and chairs. He was taken to one of the chairs and shackled in, wrists on the table and feet on the floor. He could see dried blood still on the wrist shackles and he forced himself not to think about what had happened to the last guy who had been here. Then the guards left him there alone.

He did not have to wait long before another door opened. Honestly, he'd been expecting Cassius. After all, he was the king and he, Micaiah, among others, had conspired against this new king. Only fitting that the king himself should come down to taunt and gloat and bring down his hammer of justice. Instead, it was Rifun who walked in. Jeans, sneakers, sweatshirt, he certainly didn't look like the evil businessman who sat behind a mahogany desk stroking an evil cat. He didn't even sit like it, instead leaning back leisurely like they were a couple dudes out to get a couple drinks and a couple girls.

"I have to say, Cai, I'm impressed," Rifun began. "You are every bit the older brother that Walter wishes he could have been."

"Don't tell Micah," Micaiah told him. "Sometimes he goes on a tirade and desperately tries to prove he's the older twin."

"Ha! You and Walter are very much alike; I think you've worked together too long. Sarcastic to the last. But your sarcasm covers up your fear, in much the same way that, the way you flaunt your physique and always take the initiative over Micah, always being the go-getter while leaving Micah behind, it covers up your little brother and hides him from prying eyes."

"I'm sure I don't know what you're talking about."

"Oh, I think you do. You know, not twenty minutes ago, Cassius and I got out of another meeting similar to this one. Two people, a man and a woman. Kyle was his name, classic surfer from Southern California. Her name was Jenna. Nice girl, pretty, shame she's a lesbian. They weren't here during the hostile takeover. And yet, they got in, despite the dampening field in the portal room."

"There are more corners in this Wheel than you realize," Micaiah said.

"There are, but I don't think they crawled out of one of those corners. You see, they got in via your brother. And your brother escaped through that same dampening field."

"You're right. He doesn't take the credit or the glory, but he is every bit as talented and powerful as I am."

Rifun grinned. "You are not talking about Time, though, are you?" Micaiah felt a bead of sweat snake down his spine as Rifun stood and slowly walked around the room. "You know that we know that you are an Akari-bearer. You and I go way back, more than Walter can appreciate with his little serial killer case. Back then, you managed to throw us off the trail. You rejected us and we fell back, and you had us completely convinced that, even though you and Micah are identical twins, that he was the unfortunate object of fate and did not inherit the ability to wield the Akari." He nodded. "As I said, you are a big brother to be envied."

Micaiah glared at him. "I did my best."

"Yes, the prize fighting wasn't your most intelligent choice of professions, but you did what you had to, am I right? Tell me, does Micah know? Or does he simply think that he is incredibly talented and he just knows what every other Timekeeper Lieutenant supposedly knows?"

"He knows his abilities are above and beyond, but he doesn't know why. I trained him in a few things, but he doesn't know everything I know."

Rifun shrugged. "Too bad."

"What are you going to do to him?"

"I haven't decided, actually," Rifun answered, sitting back down in his chair, leaning back like he was considering a tough decision. "On the one hand, I have every reason to expect that he's just like you and will reject us the same way you did. I might as well just save myself the hassle and execute him, too. On the other hand, he's already half-trained. You got him through the tough stuff. Now, when I tell him the truth, we already have a starting point to work with. Plus, if I get Tommen in on the deal, having a partner might be motivational for both of them, especially since both you and dear Walter are on the chopping block."

Micaiah shook his head. "They'll never agree to it."

"Fear is a powerful motivator. Love is an equally powerful motivator. More often than not, the two go hand in hand. After all, you should have seen poor Walter when we dragged him up out of his hell earlier. Had he been an Akari-bearer, I am certain he would have done anything I asked of him."

"Tommen isn't his dad."

"Isn't he? True, he may not have spent years in the black cells of Beaumaris Gaol and become psychologically fragile and afraid of the dark, but think of everything he's been through. Stumbled on a dead body, got in a fight with a couple of psychomaniacs, nearly drowned, was kidnapped and held for ransom, almost died himself at a police shootout, held his dying father in his arms, traveled halfway across the universe to look for a cure that had no guarantees of working, lost his hearing, endured the most unethical exam in the history of exams, witnessed and almost did not escape a political coup, and now he sits at home, wondering what's become of his father and his friend. Do you think his fragile sixteen year old brain can take much more of this? He thinks he's Superman, but he's far from it."

The worst part was, he was right.

"Maybe," Micaiah conceded cautiously. "But all it will take is one little tip-off and they're gone. They may not be able to go dark properly like normal, but they'll disappear."

"That's precisely what I'm expecting." Rifun straightened. "Which is why we've already sent out Trackers. Do you know what those are?"

Micaiah sighed. Yes, he did know, but he did not want to show it. "No, but if the name is any indication, I expect they track things."

"They can sniff out a Time wake that's a week-old. They'll find Tommen and Micah and they'll bring them to me. Just in time to watch you die. Then we'll see what love and fear really mean to them."

Micaiah studied him. "So then, what happens next?"

"Next?" Rifun raised a brow. "Next, you and Walter and your little failed team of rescuers will be taken to the Pit where you will be executed. That's all there is left. No grandeur, no flourish, no last words and moving speeches. You will say your name, your rank, your crime for actively opposing Cassius, and your sentence of death. That's all."

Rifun stood. A couple guards walked up behind Micaiah and undid the shackles. He barely had time to process the tingling in his fingers before he was hauled to his feet. Rifun approached him and leaned it to whisper in his ear, "Perhaps your brother will make a better choice than you did, hm?"

Then he backed away and nodded once to the guards. Micaiah was roughly spun around and marched out of the room, back down the corridor and back to his black cell.

Micaiah was left in the darkness once more. At first he was paralyzed, afraid to move as he let his mind relax and considered the implications of the conversation. Rifun was going after his little brother. True, only by a couple minutes, but no matter what the pipsqueak said, Micah was still his little brother. Then his mind was paralyzed with another agonizing decision, whether it was worse that his brother be executed with him, or if he should stay alive but under the thumb of Rifun and Cassius. He quickly decided that life under psychopaths was no life at all.

Of course, he didn't want his brother to die, either. Grouchily, he forced his body to respond to his commands and, with one hand on the wall, he made laps of the cell. The corners felt like regular ninety-degree corners. Assuming that, the cell wasn't very big, maybe ten by ten. Bigger than expected, actually. Then he considered that the mystery man who'd been in the room had looked about twenty feet away. He paused in his pacing. Definitely a hallucination, he decided.

He only made three laps of the cell when the door opened again. Micaiah tried the eager compliance thing in hopes of not being roughly manhandled, but to no avail. At least they didn't clap him in chains or anything like that. Instead, they removed the one-way stamp from his hand and marched him through the prison, out of the black cells, out of the open cells, and out toward the large vault door. As they went, they met up with other guards who marched other prisoners.

Micaiah looked around, trying to spot Walter or Kyle or the girl, Jenna—or any human at all—but he did not see any in the corridor between the vault doors. Eventually, the guards got tired of his rubbernecking and jabbed him in the back so he stumbled. He managed to catch himself before he went sprawling on the floor and got his feet under him just as he went through the main vault door into the lobby-like area of the Judgment Wing.

"Micaiah!"

At the sound of his name, Micaiah stopped and looked around. Again he was hit from behind and he pitched forward. He ended up falling into two pairs of arms, one belonging to Kyle, the other to a woman he assumed was Jenna. They helped him to his feet and he looked around. Guards stayed to the outside of the group, but the group itself was allowed to mingle freely. Not that there was a lot of mingling going on as it looked like a scene out of a bad zombie movie.

"Oh my god, we're so glad we found you," Jenna said. "You are Micaiah, right? I mean, you look like Micah."

"Yeah, I am," Micaiah said dumbly. "Have you seen Walter anywhere?"

"No, not yet." Jenna frowned. "Listen, we have a way out. Well, sort of."

"Yeah. Me. Any idea what happens from here?"

"Do we ever," Kyle growled. "They're going to march us out of here to the Pit."

"What's the Pit?"

"We don't know.  Sounds like they've been doing a little redecorating in some areas of the Wheel."

"No, that's not possible.  Not him.  Not unless..."

"Unless...?"

Before Micaiah could say anything, Kyle and Jenna looked behind him eagerly. Turning, he saw Walter being led meekly into the group. If there was ever an image of defeat, it stood within their midst.

Micaiah knew that the black cells could be adjusted like Bands, and it looked like Walter had spent quite a bit of time in a Fast Band in his cell. His beard had grown out, he'd lost some weight, and overall he just looked like he'd spent another eighteen months in Beaumaris Gaol. Except Beaumaris was middle school detention compared to the hell he must have gone through in his solitude.

Micaiah went to him. When he reached for him and touched his shoulder, Walter flinched away and looked ready to come unglued. Then his face registered recognition and he fell forward into Micaiah, sobbing. Micaiah awkwardly put his arms around him and let him cry. How long had it been since Walter had seen another human being? Weeks? Months? Years?

Eventually the shaking sobs abated and he just lay there on Micaiah's chest. He murmured something.

"What?" Micaiah asked dumbly, shifting so Walter could speak into his ear.

"They took my cane, but they will not take my boy. I can still run and fight if I have to; just give the signal."

When Micaiah took a step back and helped Walter to stay steady on his feet, he did not see the defeat that his posture projected. Rather, he saw only fierce determination. Micaiah nodded gravely and motioned for Kyle and Jenna.

"You said you have a way out. What is it?"

"Micah," Jenna said. "He modified a translator so we could somehow communicate across the dimensions without the portal." She explained a bit how it worked, at least to her knowledge, but Micaiah knew what she was referring to. He was the one who'd originally developed that little translator hack.

"As far as I know, it's still in my purse in the little Food Court nook," she concluded. "But I don't see how we can get back there."

"Better question, how did you get here? What route did you take?"

The two explained it as well and as fast as they could, but about the time they got to the middle marketplaces, there was a shrill, ear-piercing whistle and everyone fell silent. After a second of looking around, all attention turned to the Grandfather who had taken over the Judgment Wing.

"Every one of you here is being taken to the Pit where you will be either executed or have your clock broken," the Grandfather announced bluntly. "You will go into the Pit and stay to the right. You will move around the Pit counterclockwise and you will be escorted to staircase to the right when it is your turn. You will state your name, your rank, your crime, and your punishment. That is all."

The Grandfathers were known for being physically menacing in their black shrouds. They were not known for being menacing in their speeches or delivering spooky threats. In that area, they were generally pretty blunt.

Then they were moving, the guards closing in and pushing and prodding like a line of cowboys trying to get a herd of slow-moving cattle to giddyup. Once they were outside the Judgment Wing, their guard compliment dropped from about a hundred to about ten or fifteen.

"Hurry up, tell the rest," Micaiah hissed to Jenna and Kyle, making an excuse of helping Walter so they could all get close together.

"There isn't much to tell after that," Kyle said. "The marketplaces are nearly empty and the portal room only had one guard that we think probably came from another area. Either way, up until we got to the auctionhouse hub, we didn't have much of a problem."

"Can either of you fight? At all?"

"Any fighting I did was just enough to run away."

"Good enough. Jenna?"

"Um, well I did...no. Not really. Nothing that matters."

"Appreciate your honesty. Listen, I'm going to try and create an opening. Walter can't fight—"

"I can if I have to," Walter protested weakly.

"Jenna, your job is going to be to get Walter to the portal room safely," Micaiah instructed. "Kyle, you are their primary defense. I'm going to create an opening and I'll be with you, but I might lag a little behind. Are there any other humans in the group that you can see?"

"Not that we've seen, no," Kyle answered.

"All right, so it's just us four. Jenna, grab your purse if you have a second to do so. If not, don't worry about it too much, but it would be really helpful if you got it. Or at least the translator. But no matter what, get to the portal room. Does everyone understand what they're doing?"

"I can fight," Walter repeated. "I'm not completely helpless."

"I understand," Jenna confirmed, taking Walter's hand and coming up under him like he was limping, which he was.

"I got it," Kyle said, nodding and getting just a step ahead of them. "Just give us the word and we'll run. You're the boss."

*That's what I'm afraid of,* Micaiah thought woefully.

The group did not move very fast, giving Micaiah time to think, but also time to hesitate. He had to consider his actions, but also the reactions. Newton's law, after all. The easy way would be to simply kill the two guards at the atrium portal and slip out that way, their biggest challenge then being the guards and Grandfathers in the atrium itself. Problem was, word would spread quickly and there was no shortage of guards that could be sent after them from the Coliseum or this "Pit" or anywhere else. No matter how fast they moved, there were enough portals and enough ways through the maze that was the Wheel, that they would be intercepted long before they reached the portal room.

At the same time, there were plenty of guards and Grandfathers on hand in the Judgment Wing, too. More Grandfathers than guards, lamentably.

"Um, so, you do have a plan, right?" Jenna wondered as they passed the portal to the atrium.

Micaiah glanced at the portal guards and considered them for just a moment. Once they were past, he nodded. "I do. Fall back, as far back in the group as you can. This might hurt. And do exactly as I told you. Remember, we're already on our way to be executed, so they can't do anything worse to you."

Well, there was that whole clock breaking business, but it was all relative anyway. Still, the trio nodded and slipped backwards in the group while Micaiah moved more to the front. He had no belief that he could save everyone in the group—he wasn't even sure he could save the four of them he was trying to save—but more bodies meant more confusion, and surprise would be the only thing that really gave them a head start.

The group paused and became bottlenecked at a new portal erected on a rather plain raised platform as each person had to be stamped with a one-way stamp once they got in. Micaiah was the sixth one in line, but he stopped when he got to the portal. A guard jabbed him in the ribs and he almost tumbled through, but he Banded. He stopped himself.

Around him, everything had stopped, and yet, he could see the beginnings of surprised expressions making their way across a number of faces. And for the Grandfathers whose faces were shrouded, he could see offensive postures forming. It became harder to hold his Band against the dampening field that seemed ubiquitous in the Wheel now. He didn't drop it completely, but rather let it sift slowly through him, like sand through his fingers.

As he did, he looked at the portal to the Pit. He reached out and touched it. He did not go through it, but he felt the portal. Felt its place in Time, in Space, felt its absolute coordinates within the physical continuum, touched it like a pane of glass. Except this pane of glass was more like the mirror from *The Matrix* as he felt it and it felt him, coming out to touch him as well. He felt inside the portal, felt its inner workings and everything that made the portal tick, like reaching into a pool of water and feeling the individual atoms that made up the hydrogen-oxygen bond.

Then he blew them apart.

The shockwave lifted Micaiah off his feet and threw him fifty feet easily. He landed flat on his back, stunned and momentarily wondering if he'd just paralyzed himself. The world around him was spinning and his ears were ringing. Still, somewhere in his mind, he knew he had to get up and keep moving.

Drunkenly, he got to his feet. Chaos was everywhere as guards and Grandfathers and prisoners had been thrown in all directions. Some were still lying on the ground, wiggling pitifully, as dazed as Micaiah felt stumbling around on his feet. Others lay on the ground completely still, their life status impossible to determine at a glance. Elsewhere, people and aliens bumbled about in a state of confusion.

Micaiah turned and ran away from it, not entirely sure why but knowing that this was the way to go. Had to get this way. He recognized the portal coming up; it went to the Judgment Wing. Reflexively, he Banded as Grandfathers came swarming out of that portal, drawn to the confusion and the spectacle. But trying to Band now was reminisce of that scene from *Star Wars* when Luke, Leia, and Han are in the garbage compactor, trying to find anything to keep the walls from closing in, but to no avail.

Still, his Band held up long enough for him to get to the portal and reach inside that one. A majority of his brain told him not to do it, that he'd probably kill himself if he tried. The other part of him wondered what alternative there was; he was already marching toward his death.

He figured he must have destroyed the Judgment Wing portal, because when he blinked awake, he was again on his back, but this time he'd landed on top of someone. He coughed, knowing this only from the physical exertion as his ears were ringing and everything was cloudy. He slid more than rolled off of whatever or whoever he'd landed on, his body weak and exhausted, smacking his face on the floor. When he looked up, he saw another portal. He couldn't remember where it went, but he knew it was significant somehow. He couldn't destroy a third one. That really would kill him.

Slowly, he got his hands under him and pushed. He fell again. Got one knee in position, got one arm under him. Gradually, low-frequency sounds started coming back to him, but there was little to hear beyond screaming, moaning, groaning, and all the sounds of confusion and chaos.

He flinched as something grabbed his arm. Looking up, he saw a girl. Hispanic, pretty, bleeding from a cut above her eye.

"Come on!" she was shouting at him. "We have to go!"

Go. Go, go, go...go, go, go, go, go. Go. Go...to the portal room. To go home. Because they were otherwise trapped here and they were relying on him to get them out. And they were Walter and Kyle and this girl was...Jaime? Jennifer? Something like that anyway.

Micaiah got all the way up once before drunkenly losing it and landing heavily on his knees. Still, the girl pulled in his arm and got him through the portal. He clambered into a large atrium room where a couple guards were in offensive position, but seemed uncertain as to what to do. There should have been more guards, Micaiah found himself thinking. And maybe some Grandfathers. Unless they'd already gone back through the portal to see what all the fuss was about.

"Hurry up!" the girl—Jenna, that was her name—said, pulling on him. "We already got the translator. Kyle took Walter ahead to find a place to hide until we caught up."

Kyle took Walter. Ahead. They were going to hide until Micaiah and Jenna caught up. What idiots. Hadn't Micaiah explicitly told them to keep going to the portal room no matter what? Oh well, it wasn't like there was a whole lot they could do about it now anyway. Still struggling to get his feet under him, Micaiah followed Jenna to a portal and slipped through.

"This doesn't look like the auctionhouse hub," Micaiah stated, feeling like he'd just gone to the dentist and been numbed.

"Oh, shit," Jenna hissed. "Maybe it was the one on the other side of this portal."

"No time." Looking over his shoulder, Micaiah could see that the guards had made up their minds and were heading straight for them. "We have to move. Follow me."

They'd ended up in a wares market, one of the few marketplaces that didn't sell Time, but little intergalactic odds and ends, an intergalactic flea market of sorts. It was as empty as any of the marketplaces Jenna had described; there weren't even any guards meandering around.

"Should we stop a minute so you can rest?" Jenna wondered. "Holy fuck, you, like, exploded a portal from the inside out."

"I did," Micaiah confirmed lamely, putting a hand to his forehead as he felt a late migraine well up, probably a concussion. "There's a way to do it subtly, but I wasn't going for subtle."

"Should we stop and rest?"

"No. If we stop and rest, that will just give the guards and Grandfathers time to get around to anywhere and everywhere. We have to keep moving."

He started off with a left foot going right and almost tripped himself. Yes, he wanted to stop and rest, but they just didn't have the time. Still, he took ten seconds to catch his breath and try to make it so the world wasn't spinning so bad.

"Where do we go from here?" Jenna wondered.

"The wares markets are all connected." Micaiah squeezed his eyes shut. "Eventually they hook back up with the intermediate markets and we can go from there. Hopefully Kyle is smart and they don't wait too long for us because we may not run into them before the portal room."

"They won't stop for very long. I told them not to. Just long enough to see if we'd catch up, but to keep going like you said."

"Well, hopefully they listened. Let's go."

And somehow he still had to break through the dampening field to open a portal home. He was going to kill himself trying to escape his own execution. Well, if his plan worked out, he wouldn't be doing all the work. Still, depending on what time it was at home, that could be a big if.

They crossed the wares marketplace easily, giving their pursuing guards the slip simply through the confusion of all the portals on the floor, walls, ceiling, everything that made the Wheel nearly incomprehensible to anyone who didn't spend a lot of time there.

There were eleven wares markets in all, but they only had to go through five before finding one that connected back to the intermediate markets.

"Does this look familiar at all?" Micaiah asked as they ducked behind a booth. Far down the market, a couple of guards walked about on patrol. "I know it would be easier if this place was full and bustling, but I have to ask anyway."

Jenna looked around as much as she dared. "No, not really. One marketplace looks about the same as any other right now."

"I was afraid you'd say that."

"Which way do we go?"

"That way." He indicated a portal on the ceiling. He wasn't supremely confident that that one was going to be their one-shot wonder and take them straight out, but one was as good as any other in the messy web of marketplaces. He searched for the staircases and found them fairly close at hand. "Okay, when I say go, we go."

"Following you, chief," Jenna told him.

Micaiah watched the guards, trying to determine their movements. They'd been lucky so far, and if they managed to make a clean getaway, then they might be able to sit and rest a minute in the portal room before going home. But until they were actually in the portal room, they had to remain on their toes. So far, Micaiah was struggling with that last bit.

"Go!" He made a leap of faith and moved from their hiding spot. Jenna followed.

The only saving grace was that despite going up on walls and ceilings, the gravity was such that it was always against the surface, so no headrush on the ceiling or weird vertigo on the walls. It really saved Micaiah's brain, as fried as it felt.

Just as they were leaping through the portal, however, he heard the alarm sound. They landed in another intermediate marketplace and just kept running. Micaiah blinked rapidly to clear his vision and gritted his teeth against the pain, but there was no time to slow down now. They had to make it to the portal room. Now that the alarm had been raised and the guards knew where they were and where they were heading, they had no choice but to make a last mad dash for safety. For home.

At one point, as his vision blurred and his steps became uncertain, he felt Jenna take his arm and lead him on. They ran. Guards be damned, they ran. Through one marketplace, and another. By the third marketplace, Micaiah had a good idea of where they were and diverted course. Around a wall, on a ceiling, back down the other wall, through a portal and now they were in the lower marketplaces. There weren't supposed to be guards here, but Micaiah could see them filtering in. They were coming from somewhere and they would all be converging at the portal room.

"Hurry!" Jenna yelled unnecessarily. "Which way?!"

Micaiah's head was pounding and he could barely think. He figured it must have just been habit that he chose the portal he did because suddenly he recognized the marketplace they stepped into, knew exactly which portal would take them to the portal room. As they ran, the guards and Grandfathers closed in. A few threw things at them. Micaiah felt something graze his cheek, but he didn't slow down. They were just approaching the last portal to the portal room when something pierced the back of his leg.

He went down hard, feeling the projectile push back through his right calf as he landed on its head. He cried out in pain but managed to crawl the last twenty feet through the portal. Jenna was already in the portal room and he saw Kyle and Walter there, too. Kyle was frantically messing with the translator while Jenna screamed at him to hurry. The sounds were muffled and his vision was blurry through the pain. He could hear the blood thundering through his ears, could feel it, warm and sticky, flowing down his leg to his foot.

Taking a breath, Micaiah stood, right leg more useless than a sausage, left leg taking all the weight. He turned. As he did, every adversary that had been bearing down on them and were just inches away from crashing through the portal stopped. And waited. They knew what he had done back there, to the Coliseum portal. To the Judgment Wing portal. Not all of them had been there, but for those that did, oh, they knew. There was the rage, the passion, the heat of the moment. But there was also the fear. He should not be able to do those things. Probably good that he'd been sent to be executed, but then he'd changed that plan. He'd done something. What would he do next?

Acutely aware that shock from his injury was going to overwhelm him any second now, he hopped up to the portal, white-hot pain searing up his leg as he dragged it along, through his knee, spreading through his body with each step. The guards on the other side did not step back, but he saw a few of them waver, lower their weapons, glance uneasily at the guy next to him.

So Micaiah reached out and he felt the portal. He touched it, played with it, felt the little bits of mechanisms and space dust and everything that held the portal together. He felt the coordinates of the room on either side of the portal and how they were manipulated, squished and squeezed and stretched until all that remained was this door right here, standing in the middle of nothing. And the portal reached out and touched him as well, felt his coordinates and his place in Time and Space. Felt that he was part of it, he understood it.

And it was through this understanding that Micaiah only had to convey his thoughts of what he wanted the portal to do. He felt the internal mechanisms and dust shiver and shudder as it processed and protested. But just as they had a friendly understanding, there was also the greater understanding that Micaiah had the power to force the portal to do what he wanted; he was just being polite. Finally, he felt the portal give in and agree.

Behind him, Micaiah could sense Jenna and Kyle and Walter bracing themselves for another enormous shockwave as the portal shivered, shuddered, and finally sealed up. But there was no shockwave this time, at least, not on their side. On the other side, however, with all the Grandfathers and guards present, it would be the biggest shockwave that that little portal could muster up.

"You did it," Jenna said, awed.

"Yeah," Micaiah said, feeling weariness spread through his limbs. "I did it."

As he turned, he went down on one knee. Kyle and Jenna rushed to his side while the best Walter could manage was a tired, determined limp.

"We need to get you to a hospital," Walter stated.

Feeling dizzy, Micaiah looked back at his leg. Well, it wasn't an arrow, but rebar wasn't exactly a better alternative for having your leg impaled on something and blown to shit. It was only about a foot long, smooth all around but the ends were jagged and he was bleeding something good from that gaping hole that really wasn't supposed to be there.

"Jenna, do you have anything like a sash or a scarf in your purse? We need to get that stabilized," Walter said, taking command.

"Wouldn't it be better to pull it out?" Kyle wondered.

"It's loose enough that it might fall out anyway, and the blood loss would kill him. The only other option is a tourniquet."

"Um, I have a scarf," Jenna offered meekly, holding out a fashion scarf that looked like it wouldn't even be effective to hang someone. Still, Walter took it and tried to wrap it around the rod to stabilize it.

"It's too smooth," he said, frustrated. "And the hole is too big, it's coming out anyway." He got down to look Micaiah in the eye. Or as best as he could. Micaiah could barely see straight anymore. "Cai, I'm going to have to wrap your leg in a tourniquet, and then we might have to pull it out."

"I have some Tylenol," Jenna said, rummaging in her purse.

"Tylenol is a blood thinner," Kyle told her. "We're trying to stop him from losing too much blood."

"Here we go," Walter said, sliding the scarf under Micaiah's knee and tying, pulling as tight as he possibly could. "It's not going to be perfect, but it'll cut off the blood pretty good."

Micaiah groaned as he pulled tighter and tighter, feeling the pressure of the circulation being cut off. Oh, it hurt like a mother. It hurt like a damn mother. Even when Walter announced that it was tight and tied and the best they could do, the pain kept building. Oh, mother, it hurt. He was going to pass out.

Instead he just got sick. He didn't have much to get sick on considering he hadn't eaten, but he still got sick.

"Okay, now let's get you home," Walter said. "Jenna, Kyle, on either side. Give me the translator."

They did as they were told. As Micaiah was helped to his feet, the bar fell out on its own, but he couldn't even feel it. The only thing he felt was the godawful pain building up in his leg, around his knee like he'd blown it out, his hip like it had come out of joint. Fucking hell, mother, God, fuck, it hurt. Oh, it hurt something awful. Fuck, maybe execution would have been better.

Then there was a light in the dimness of the portal room. Walter twisted to shield his eyes as a portal struggled to open up. Micaiah had had every intention of meeting Micah halfway and opening the portal fifty-fifty like they always did, but he was too weak to do much more than reach out and touch it, connect with Micah's strength just enough to let them know who it was and that they were there. He felt another surge of strength come through the portal as Micah redoubled his efforts to get it open and stable..

"Walter first," Micaiah found himself saying. "Then we'll come through and I'll close it behind us."

There was no time to argue; it was like Atlas holding up the world, trying to open a portal through a dampening field. Walter went through first. Then Kyle, Jenna, and Micaiah between them. Normal portals were difficult enough, having the air squeezed from your lungs and the strength sapped from your body. This was more like trying to shove a watermelon through a hole the size of a lemon. A rebirth as it were.

Assuming they survived the trip.

# Chapter Eight
## Outlaws

After a long day of no messages, signals, leads, or brain-exploding pulses through his hearing aid, Tommen reluctantly headed to bed around ten o'clock. He plugged his hearing aids into the charger and Banded the unit so they charged quickly, then replaced them in his ears so he could hear the signal if it came through during the night. Oddly enough, the foremost thought in his mind was how he was going to tell Micah of the group signaling him when he would be at school and Micah at work. Would a text be fast enough?

He wasn't sure what woke him at first, but when his brain was rattled a second time by a fog horn going off right next to his hearing aid, he just about jumped out of bed and ran down the hall. Just as he was about to pound on Micah's door, it went off again.

"I hear you, I hear you," he growled and banged on Micah's door. "Micah! Micah! Open up! It's them!"

He could heard some crashing around inside and a moment later, Micah was at the door. "Are you sure?"

"Yes, I'm sure. I don't make up these things I'm hearing." Even as he spoke, it went off again. "Hurry up! Open the portal!"

Sleepily, Micah made his way out to the living room where a portal was struggling to form and open. It took a concentrated effort and Tommen wished he knew how to open the portals so he might be able to lend a hand, like how the twins opened portals fifty-fifty. He hoped that good vibes would be enough, even if his good vibes were more likely anxious vibrations that made him shake and pray to whatever god was out there that his dad would be coming home, too.

He literally whooped for joy when he saw his dad step

through the portal, even if he did almost fall flat on his face. Just a step behind him, Kyle and Jenna came through, holding Micaiah up between them. Kyle and Jenna made it through all right, but where Tommen saw that Micaiah was initially conscious, he passed out as soon as they were through the portal. His two helpers were unprepared for this, and they went down with him, just about on top of Walter.

"Dad!" Tommen cried, sliding in beside him when the portal finally snapped closed.

The first thing he saw was the bloody wrists as his dad fought to get on elbows and knees. The marks were indicative of shackles or manacles, with small holes, like needle sticks, into the veins as if he'd been given an IV. The second thing he saw was that his dad had a full beard. Not just a few days' growth, but a real, full beard. The third thing he noticed was that he'd lost some weight. Not like those weight loss commercials or anything where the models went from five hundred to one fifty, but it was pretty noticeable.

"Dad, are you okay?" Tommen asked fearfully.

"Get...Get Micaiah...to...hospital. Now," his dad whispered, still on his elbows and knees.

Tommen looked over where Kyle and Jenna had untangled themselves from Micaiah. Upon inspection, Tommen saw the tourniquet and the blood staining pretty much everything below the knee.

"He was impaled," Jenna said. "It was an arrow or maybe a spear of some form, but it fell out when he got up."

"Should we call an ambulance?" Kyle wondered, digging around in his pockets for a phone that was apparently no longer there.

"It'll be faster just to take him ourselves," Micah decided. "Tourniquet looks good. Help me get him to the car."

"I'll get the door," Tommen offered, standing and racing to the door while Micah, Kyle, and Jenna situated themselves and prepared for carrying.

As they shuffled through the door, Micah spoke. "Tommen,

stay with your dad. Catch up later. You know where the keys are."

Tommen nodded and closed the door behind them. He watched them for a second before returning to the living room where his dad had managed to get up on one knee and support himself with the aid of the coffee table. Without being asked, Tommen got under his other arm and helped him to the couch.

"Are you okay?" Tommen asked. "What did they do to you?"

His dad simply sat quietly for a minute, his gaze somewhere else entirely. Tommen saw tears streaming down his cheeks even as he tried to hold it in. Finally, "The dark. They put me in the dark. In the black cells."

Tommen slowly backed up until he was sitting in one of the chairs. His dad continued.

"The black cells can be adjusted, Banded just as we can Band, so that the time you think you spend in the cells is far longer than the actual time you spent there."

"H-how long did you stay in the black cells?"

"The first time was four months, even if it was only a few hours. The second time was eight months." Now his dad looked at him. "I spent a year in prison. In only one day." His composure wavered. "I haven't seen another human being in eight months. I haven't seen my son in a year."

He held out his arms and Tommen went to him. As soon as they touched, his dad lost it, bawling and shaking so hard, Tommen thought he was having a seizure. After a minute, he started crying as well.

"It's okay, Dad," Tommen said, sniffing hard. "I'm here. We're together."

Another minute or two passed and finally his dad pulled back, wiping his eyes on grimy shirt sleeves. "I'm sorry, I shouldn't...I mean...A son shouldn't see his father cry."

"Why not? It makes you human. It means that you actually came out of those black cells. You're not still there."

That set his dad off again, but it didn't last long. Finally he relaxed, leaning back on the couch, and Tommen thought he was going to fall asleep.

"Maybe I should get you home," Tommen suggested. "Get you cleaned up."

His dad sighed. "That would probably be the decent thing to do before going out in public."

"What happened to your cane?" Tommen wondered as his dad got to his feet.

"Um...they beat me with it. Before taking me in. I haven't seen it since."

"Oh. Sorry."

His dad shook his head. "You didn't know."

Tommen rummaged around in Micaiah's coat until he found the car keys. He turned and looked at his dad's decidedly less-than-winter clothing and said, "Maybe I'll warm the car up first."

His dad simply nodded, and he made a mad dash through the snow. He turned the car on and cranked the heat. Just after midnight. Nope, he was not getting any sleep before school today, that much was for sure. He Banded the car so it would heat up faster, then went back for his dad who was just coming out of the house. In just a few minutes, they were on their way.

"So...if you don't mind my asking...how did you not go insane?" Tommen inquired cautiously. "I mean, I thought the darkness did things to you."

"It does," his dad said quietly. "And it did. And I don't know how it will affect me in the long run. I just know that this time...this time I had hope. I had no hope in Beaumaris Gaol because no one cared for me. I didn't even care for me. But this time, I had hope that I would see you again. I didn't know if it was real hope or foolish hope, but it was hope, and I clung to it desperately."

"Do you think you'll be able to go back to being a cop?"

"I don't know, honestly. I hope I can. It would look strange if I suddenly didn't after I told them I could, but how would I explain the sudden onset of mental health issues?"

"Delayed PTSD? I...I don't know."

"We'll see. I still have a while left on my medical leave."

Tommen cast a sideways glance at his dad, and it didn't do much to reassure him. He told himself that once he got cleaned up, got a shower, a shave, and some good food in him that they would both be able to think a little more clearly and have a rational discussion. Kind of like when Tommen first got home after his hostage ordeal.

They pulled up to the garage and walked in to the smell of vinegar and brains. His dad openly blanched, and even Tommen wrinkled his nose at the smell.

"You're moving them first thing after you get home tomorrow," his dad told him.

Tommen might have protested except he couldn't help but smile that for one moment, his dad came back to life before limping up to the door and shuffling inside. Once inside, Tommen noticed that his dad didn't turn on any lights. When he himself did so, his dad turned his face.

"Does it hurt?" Tommen wondered.

"There is no light in the black cells," his dad told him. "And the eye can degenerate just from lack of use. Yes, it hurts."

"Oh. Sorry." He flicked the light off. "But at the twins' house...and the car."

"I had my eyes closed, usually. And...there were times when I was able to see light. Like when they brought bits of food and water."

"Did they have to feed it to you?" He noted his dad's expression—or his general body language indicating surprise. "Your wrists. They had you chained up, didn't they?"

His dad did not reply except to say, "I'm going to take a shower. When I'm done, we'll go visit Micaiah in the hospital."

Tommen nodded even though it could not be seen. While his dad went into his room to gather up a few things, Tommen went to his room. He probably should have stayed in the kitchen and prepared some food, but he just wanted to be back in his own room again. It felt like he hadn't spent a lot of time in his room over the last month or so.

"Tommen."

He turned and froze as he saw his dad standing in the doorway with his gun. Shit. His dad had gone off the deep end in those cells. Fuck, he was going to die. Fuck, fuck, fuck, duck?

"Duck!" his dad barked.

Tommen did so, covering his ears as his dad raised the gun and fired. His blood froze as something screamed. Then it was over, and he stood, turning. There on the floor on the other side of his bed, some ugly alien creature with seven legs and something like the head of a parasaur lay dead. His dad lowered his gun and, through eyes barely open, went around to the creature. He kept the gun on it at all times as he nudged it with his foot.

"What...the *fuck*...is that thing?" Tommen asked.

"My guess, a Tracker," his dad answered. Apparently satisfied that it was dead, he set his gun down and indicated to Tommen to turn off the lights, which he did.

"A Tracker?"

"I hadn't heard of them before, but apparently they can search out Time wakes a week old."

"How did you know it was here?"

"Rifun said he'd sent some in order to get you and Micah and take you to him. Walking through the house, some things were disturbed. When I walked in your room, I saw it in the corner."

"F-f-fuck."

For once, his dad didn't chastise him. Instead, he held the gun out to him. "I'm going to take a shower. You see any more, shoot, then ask questions."

"No arguments here."

Thankfully, though, no more came out to say hi. Tommen kept the gun close to hand, though, as he went to inspect the thing more closely. It was like a seven-legged parasaur Labrador mutant with oily, kind of blubbery skin. When Tommen pulled his hand away, it was like touching sticky slime or something. He went out to the kitchen and wiped his hand on a washcloth, considered it, then tossed the cloth in the garbage.

His dad wasn't in the shower long, but when he emerged from the bathroom by the light of only the few nightlights in the house, it was almost like he'd never left. In fact, it was almost as if he was just getting ready for work.

"So what are we going to do with it?" Tommen wondered, following his dad as far as his bedroom door.

"Take pictures of it for one. We need to show the twins and probably others. Then we'll have to dispose of it, but I don't need to give the garbage man a heart attack."

"You think I should dump it somewhere in the woods?"

"Maybe try the same area you set your illegal traps."

Tommen felt his cheeks turn red, and he did not reply.

"Are you going to be okay going to the hospital?" Tommen asked as his dad finished getting dressed and headed back out to the kitchen. "I mean, their lights aren't exactly dim."

"I don't know how well they'll work, but I still have the goofy glasses from the last time I got my eyes dilated."

The lights were just an excuse. Really Tommen was worried how much longer his dad could keep up the tough guy charade before everything came crashing down. You didn't just walk out of a year of solitary confinement in total darkness and go waltzing around town on some errand or another. Most people went into therapy. The rest...well, the rest committed suicide.

Still, there was no dissuading him from it, and Tommen was himself curious to know how Micaiah fared.

"I just remembered," his dad said as they got in the car. "Are you okay to drive? I seem to recall you have a concussion."

"Um," Tommen began guiltily. "I can do it. I mean, I still get headaches, but I can do it for now; I can do what we need to do. And we need to go and see how Micaiah's doing."

He started the car and backed out.

"All right," his dad said as he began backing out. "Tonight's an exception. But starting tomorrow, until you—"

"Dad. It's okay. I got this."

Neither of them said anything as he almost hit the mailbox, but he could practically hear his dad laughing internally. At least, he hoped he was laughing internally. Even a nervous chuckle would do. Or a polite tee hee. Something to let Tommen know that not all hope was lost. He wanted his dad to come home, all of him.

The drive back into the city was quiet and uneventful. It had snowed basically all day Sunday, but the actual accumulation had been only an inch or two. The roads were still good, and Tommen felt almost confident in his driving abilities.

"What's today?" his dad wondered.

"Um...January 17$^{th}$ technically. Why?"

"Couldn't really remember."

"Oh."

"And you're in...eleventh grade?"

"Tenth," Tommen admitted grudgingly.

"But your girlfriend is in eleventh."

"She's not my girlfriend. I don't even know if I would call her a friend. She's my table partner in AP Physics."

"Right. I knew that."

But Tommen could hear the frustration in his dad's voice. In a year, clinging to hope and memories, how many of those memories had branched out into his own wishful thinking? Had he envisioned seeing Tommen graduate? Marry and have kids? How many lifetimes and what ifs had he gone through in his mind in that darkness? Where was his mind at now? Would he ever really be able to come back to the present and live in the now?

Tommen forced himself to focus on the roads as they approached the hospital and he turned into the parking lot. In the middle of the night, parking was relatively easy to find.

Once in the hospital, a nurse directed them to a small waiting room where Micah, Kyle, and Jenna sat, solemn, silent, and a little bloody. They barely looked up as Tommen and Walter walked in and took a seat.

"How's Micaiah?" Walter wondered softly. He wore the shades from the eye doctor but still put a hand up to block the light from above.

Micah sighed heavily. "Well, he's alive, to answer the question before it's asked. He's alive, but that's not the part in question."

"Then what is in question?" Tommen asked.

It was a moment more before Micah answered. "The rod—whatever it was—blew through both tibia and fibia, your lower leg bones. They're going to make an attempt to save them, but they were seriously talking amputation."

It felt as though a rod just slammed through Tommen's chest.

Micah went on. "The only good news is that he'll be able to keep the knee. But...the rest is toast."

For a second, Tommen couldn't breathe. He couldn't even comprehend it. Yeah, he saw amputees sometimes on the street or in the shop, but they were war veterans who went out on the battlefield, faced down terrorists and IEDs and all manner of awful things. They were purple heart recipients and the poster people for the VA and other veteran organizations. They weren't...average guys like Micaiah who worked in a bakery. They weren't people who just happened to be in the wrong place at the wrong time and got captured by a psychomaniac. They weren't people who risked everything just to get home.

Or...were they? Was there any real difference?

"How was he when you brought him in?" Walter asked.

Micah shrugged tiredly. "He was semi-conscious. Couldn't really get a coherent thought out of him, though he knew his name and address, so that was good. I guess."

"Did the doctors say how long it would be?"

He shook his head. "They didn't give a time, but once they made the decision to amputate, I mean, it doesn't take as long to cut off a leg as it does to save it. That's just my opinion. It's still going to be a couple hours at least."

"You still have to go to school in the morning," Walter said, looking at Tommen.

"I want to see him when he wakes up, though," Tommen protested.

"He won't be leaving here any time soon, certainly not before you get out of school," Kyle said. "Besides, you won't want to see him when he wakes up."

"He's right," Micah agreed. "I'm going to have to be the one to tell him, if he doesn't figure it out in his drug-induced stupor. And you know him. He'll be stark raving mad. You don't want to see that. Wait until he's a little more calmed down."

Well, there was a point to that, Tommen figured. Micaiah wouldn't take the loss of his leg lightly, and he was going to lash out at anyone and everyone around him. Best not to be in the immediate line of fire.

"And how are you holding up, Captain?" Kyle inquired.

"I don't know yet," Walter answered evasively. "The sunglasses help. I'm just glad I could see the Tracker so I could shoot it."

"Tracker?" Jenna wondered.

So Walter briefly explained the incident in Tommen's room, from how he knew to shooting it dead. He described the beast as best he could with Tommen throwing in details here and there and showing them the picture.

"So you're telling me that there are things out there that can literally smell Time," Micah said. "And somehow they have the ability to jump back and forth through the dampening field. And Rifun sent them specifically to track down me and Tommen and take us to him."

"Yes."

"Shit. Because today just couldn't get any worse."

"Yes. Which is what brings me to my next point. I think...actually I strongly suggest that everyone—at least from Lieutenant down if not Captain down—should be Suppressed."

Micah opened his mouth but no words came out. Finally he blinked and shook his head as if to clear it. "Suppressed? Everyone? Like, everyone in the world kind of everyone?"

Walter nodded gravely. "Everyone. Probationary to Lieutenant, if not Captain. If Rifun sent the Trackers after you and Tommen, there's no reason to think he doesn't have others out there also. With the internal portals to the Wheel all but destroyed, it should slow down Rifun for a day or two. And if his Trackers can't find us, then it leaves him blind, and it buys us time. And while the Wheel and the Time industry is in chaos, Time does us no good anyway."

"Um, excuse me. Walter. Time is how Cai and I run the bakery. We didn't get to be such an anomaly by the sweat of our backs alone. And if Cai's going to be out for a while, I'm going to pretty much be running the show by myself."

"Then may I suggest taking on a few new hands to help?"

Micah glanced at Kyle and Jenna. Walter continued, "Kyle's a runaway anyway. I can't speak for Jenna, but if she's supposed to be a traveling Journeyman, well, her studies have been cut short. Plus it will help to keep an eye on them."

"That's great and all, but it's not like Rifun doesn't know where we live. If that thing was in Tommen's room, who's to say there won't be one waiting for me when I get home? Or get to work in the morning?"

"I didn't have to use Time to kill the one in Tommen's room." Walter sighed. "And anyway, I wasn't asking for your opinion. Once I get some sleep and food in me, then I plan on going to the Regional Manager—or whoever is in charge—and delivering my suggestion."

Tommen was pretty sure he looked as shocked as he felt. His dad was the District Captain, and his word trumped Micah's ninety-nine days out of a hundred. Rarely, though, did he pull rank like that, the "I'm not asking for your input, I'm telling you how it is because that's what I'm going to do." It proved to be enough to shut Micah up.

They sat in silence after that. Tommen figured he must have

gotten some sleep because the next time he looked at his watch, it was about five o'clock. He couldn't remember much of his dream except that it had to do with a bear he thought. Huh, must have been some dream about the D'Bok. He yawned and stretched and looked around the room. Everyone else was sleeping. The only one who didn't seem peaceful was his dad as he twitched and flinched, almost like he was seizing.

After another yawn and another stretch, Tommen got up and wandered off to find a bathroom. When he found one, he paused. Were Trackers intelligent? Would they follow him and wait until he was alone? Or were they instinct- and mission-driven, not caring if they were seen by others? Didn't matter, he supposed. He still had to pee, and he wasn't about to go back and ask daddy to hold his hand.

When he returned, he settled in as if to go back to sleep, but he'd only just gotten comfortable—or as comfortable as he could be in the hard chair—when the door opened again and a doctor walked in. Tommen nudged his dad with one foot and Micah with the other. His dad snapped awake, and for a second, Tommen was almost afraid he'd go off on them. But he saved himself just in time and woke Kyle and Jenna even as Micah came around, yawning hugely and setting off a chain reaction around the room, doctor included.

"How's Cai?" Micah asked softly, looking like he hadn't slept well.

"He's just out of surgery; he'll be in recovery for a couple hours for observation. Then you can see him," the doctor answered calmly. He wasn't a particularly tall man—Tommen was taller by at least half a head—and he had a little extra weight on him, but his demeanor was oddly reassuring, a man who knew what he was doing and did it well.

Micah sighed. "So you took the leg."

"Yes. There was too much bone missing, and the soft tissue damage was irreparable. We were able to save the knee."

*Small comfort,* Tommen thought bitterly.

"When can I see him?"

"Once he's out of recovery. He'll probably take kinder to seeing you than me, at least initially. After that, I imagine an officer may want to speak with him."

"An officer?" Walter echoed. "What for?"

"He said he didn't remember what happened," Micah protested.

"And in such a state of shock, that is to be expected. Once he comes around, though, he might remember something. I'm not saying I think there was foul play involved, but something like this doesn't normally happen out of the blue."

"Isn't that the definition of an accident?"

"If he took yesterday off and disappeared, we just want to rule out the possibility of an assault."

Micah sighed. "Okay. Makes sense, I guess."

"A nurse will come and get you when he wakes up. You said you live together?"

"That's correct."

"When everyone is calmed down and rational, then we can discuss home care and physical therapy."

"Okay. Thank you."

The doctor left them alone then, each to his own thoughts. They'd taken the leg. Micaiah was missing the lower half of his right leg. The next time Tommen saw him, he would be missing part of his leg. Somehow, it just didn't even seem real, even though he'd had ample time to consider and accept it.

"So, what story do we want to come up with for the officer?" Micah said after a few minutes of silence.

"Whatever story we do come up with, we have to make sure to tell Micaiah," Walter pointed out. "Unless we want to be investigated for felonious assault."

"How about a hit-and-run?" Jenna suggested. "He was out running, gets hit by a car, driver takes off. No witnesses. Explains the impalement to some degree. And if he hit his head, he doesn't remember a thing."

"I don't think amnesia works like that," Kyle told her.

"Why not?"

"It's the best we've got," Micah said tiredly. "Besides, we give Micaiah the outline so we're all on the same page, and he fills in the details because, after all, he's the only one who knows what happened. He just doesn't know it yet."

It was a solemn agreement that they came to, having to fabricate such a ridiculous and overly simplified version of events. In Tommen's mind, it almost seemed more cruel than the lies they told about any of their injuries. Walter had been shot and poisoned, and there were a ton of witnesses, even if those witnesses hadn't really understood the extent of the incident. Tommen, too, had sustained hearing loss from a gunshot which multiple people had seen. He'd also broken his arm and gotten a concussion in the terrain park, again, that multiple people had seen even if they hadn't understood the true underlying cause. Micaiah, though...his accident happened purely within the Wheel, within Time. There were no witnesses, no tabloid stories to try and explain away. He'd just...been out for a jog or something and been hit by a car. Why he'd been out jogging at eleven o'clock at night was a different story, one that he'd have to come up with himself, but it just seemed...cruel the way this was going to play out. No one would ever know what a hero he'd been or why he'd paid that price. Just an accident, they'd say.

"Well, at least we know," his dad said, interrupting his thoughts. He looked at Tommen. "But you still have to go to school today."

Tommen rubbed his eyes, feeling the fatigue creep into his bones. "I'm exhausted."

"I know. And I'll Band you one last time so you can get a few more hours. But as for you..."

He reached forward and put his hand on Tommen's head. Almost instantly it was like walking into the Coliseum or the Judgment Wing as a huge, heavy curtain came down over his Time abilities. It was like putting on nearly-black sunglasses the way his ability to see and feel Time was obscured and taken from him. He gasped involuntarily and was left reeling for a minute, trying to reconcile what had just happened.

"You really think it will help more than hurt?" Micah asked. "Remember why you taught Tommen to Band early in the first place."

"I know," Walter replied. "But now I'm considering a much larger threat than Tyler Freeman."

Strange to think how, in the space of just six months, Tyler Freeman had gone from being the most menacing menace on the face of the planet, whom Tommen dreaded seeing everyday and loathed just hearing his name, to an almost non-entity. Not to say he wasn't threatening or couldn't do some real harm, but his motives seemed petty and childish compared to what was going on now.

His dad went to Kyle next. The surfer was more than a little skeptical, but he took it like a man. Or he tried. The shock on his face was pretty self-evident. Jenna was up next. She tried to keep her chin up and tough it out as Kyle and Tommen had failed to do, but even she was not immune to the surprise and the shock of having one of her senses removed. Then Walter went to Micah.

"For the sake of your brother, I'll wait on Suppressing you two until he's awake and lucid enough to know what's going on."

Micah dipped his head. "Thank you. I'm still skeptical, but I trust your judgment."

Tommen found himself questioning whether his trust was misplaced. Did Micah know what had happened to his dad in the Wheel? Did he know about the black cells? Could he comprehend what horrors haunted his dad at night, the reason he slept with a night light? Or did he simply dismiss it as a fear of the dark that he never outgrew as a child, in spite of his time in prison? Still, there was nothing to be done. They were all going to be Suppressed and that was the end of that.

"We're living as outlaws now," Walter told them. "We are Timekeeper-trained, but no more than that. As far as anyone off our planet is concerned, we are wanted for crimes against the crown." He managed a bit of sarcasm in his voice. "So far I have no reason to expect that anyone left here will turn us in, as turning us in means turning themselves in. However, it would be in everyone's best interest to minimize all talk of Time, even among ourselves. For the time being, we must simply be...normal."

"Are you going to be Suppressed, too?" Micah wondered. It was a simple question with no accusation that Tommen could detect.

"I am not opposed to it." Though his tone suggested he would welcome it, actually. "However, if the Manager approves of the overarching measure, he may want one person in each District who is not. I will leave that as his call."

Micah simply nodded and said nothing more.

"Up," Walter commanded as he made his way back to Tommen. "You still have to go to school."

"What about the car?" Tommen asked, stalling.

"Kyle can take you home," Micah decided. "Then he can drive it back to the house later."

Kyle agreed and plodded along behind them, out the doors and into the cold. It wasn't snowing, but a chill wind had picked up, suggesting more snow later in the day. They lost the car for a minute or two. When they found it again, Tommen's first instinct was to Band it so that it would heat up faster and be toasty warm when they got going. But it was like trying to view the Mona Lisa from behind a heavy curtain. He knew it was there; he could envision it and just feel it, but he could do nothing about it.

Kyle elected to drive. Walter took the front seat and Tommen slipped into the back, laying down across the seats and falling asleep even before they pulled out of the parking lot.

He figured his dad must have Banded him to get more sleep, as promised, because when he woke, he knew that he'd been asleep a lot longer than half an hour, looking at the clock. He sat up and stretched and looked around.

"Where are we?" he murmured.

"Almost home," his dad answered tiredly.

When he looked closer, Tommen recognized the neighborhood, streetlamp to streetlamp as he could see it. A couple neighbors were just getting up, little kitchen lights turned on, morning news on the TV. They passed the newspaper bike as it started down Maple Street, street tires replaced by fat tires, the cyclist bundled tightly against the cold, flinging newspapers to the dozen or so houses still dedicated to reading print news.

"Right here." His dad pointed to the ranch-style home that sat dark between a couple neighbors who didn't believe in taking down Christmas lights until July.

Kyle pulled into the driveway.

"Nice place," he observed mildly as Tommen fought with his seatbelt.

"Need a cup of coffee?" Walter offered.

"No, thank you. And thanks for suggesting the job. I don't think Micah will go for it, but it was a nice gesture."

"He might surprise you in the end. As long as you don't mind haircuts or hair nets."

With that, they headed to the front door where Tommen fished for the hidden key and let them inside.

"I'm going to bed," Walter announced, finally letting his shoulders slump and his head bob a little. "Are you okay to get yourself around and get on the bus and everything?"

"I'll be okay," Tommen promised. "You go get some rest."

His dad said nothing, simply headed down the hall. A second later, Tommen heard his door click shut. Then he went to the kitchen table and collapsed in the chair, rubbing his face like he might be able to wake up from a bad dream.

Fuck but this sucked. Make no mistake, he was thrilled that his dad was home again, but he still wondered whether all of his dad had come home. How many more blows could either of them take before one of them broke beyond the point of being able to come back at all? Tommen was tired of the fighting and the running and the politics. Maybe in another life, he would have been thrilled to be a Timekeeper and learning all this cool stuff, become an officer like his dad. But this...this was no game. This was life and death and some pretty bad shit that he really didn't want any part of.

Maybe it was for the best that they were all Suppressed. True, they would never be able to unlearn what they knew or unsee what they had seen or undo everything that had happened, but they would be normal. They would be able to mingle and interact normally with other people. No more secrets, no more lies, no more double life. This could be exactly what they all needed. A way out.

Of course, that also meant that he couldn't putter around the house and then just Band to make up for lost time. He actually had to get his ass in gear and get ready for school.

He did a quick check of his room to make sure nothing was waiting for him. The Tracker thing was still dead on the floor, but he wasn't sure quite what to do with it at the moment. He couldn't Band and take it up to his trapping locations, but he didn't need to give the garbage guy a heart attack. Well, maybe if he just bagged it, double-bagged it, then tied it off. The garbage guys didn't necessarily go rooting around intently in people's garbage.

It took longer than he wanted it to, but he had to get it done before confidently turning his back and getting ready for the day, pulling out a clean change of clothes and heading for the shower. After staying up pretty much most of the night, he felt dirty and gross, to say nothing of his dad hugging him after spending a year—a year!—in prison.

So, Tommen, how's your dad doing?

Well, he's still going to physical therapy, trying to lose a little weight while he's off (or at least not gain any more), oh and he just did a year in an inhumane black prison cell with no light whatsoever for a year. Yeah, he's fine. He'll be back to work on Monday, sure thing.

By the time he got out of the shower, got dressed and double-checked his backpack, he barely had time to pack his lunch and run out the door to the bus.

"Running a little late, are we, Tommen?" the bus driver asked.

"Just a little," Tommen said wistfully, making his way to the back of the bus.

Life without Time was going to be harder than he thought, and his abilities were little more than party tricks. He was actually going to have to pay attention to the clock and allot time for stuff. No more, Oh, well, I can probably fit that in a Band between these other two things that I have to do one right after another. It was going to be, Oh, well, let me see if I can pencil you in. How does next Tuesday sound?

It meant that he was actually going to have to take time to do his homework and get it done before bed so he didn't cut in on sleeping time, plus he still had to make room for cooking and eating. Not to mention he had to work after school, too, though he suspected that was going to be slightly less traumatic as far as time and planning was concerned. And then there was the ever-important socializing that he had to do. But when was he going to get that done? When was he going to have time for any of this? How did normal people do it?

*Priorities*, a small voice whispered. *Normal people have priorities. Once they eliminate what's necessary, they delegate their remaining time into what they consider to be important. So, Tommen Forbes, what do you consider to be important?*

Well, everything was important to him. Maybe not school, but that was a necessity. Work was equal parts important and necessity, but the necessity part ruled that out. Eating was essential to life, and sleeping was usually high on his list when confronted with an either-or situation, rare though they had been up to this point. Homework was part of school but semi-optional, depending on the class and what the assignment was. Socializing, well, he didn't have too many friends anymore so he might be able to get away with cutting time out of that.

Then there were his new responsibilities of having to look after his dad. Whether or not he admitted it, his dad was going to need help. On top of the injuries he'd already sustained, which were still healing but had apparently regressed some in his time in prison, he had new injuries that had to be cared for. His wrist injuries hadn't looked quite so awful once they'd been cleaned and treated, and anything else had probably healed during his time; most injuries heal in a year. But then there were the psychological injuries to consider. He'd managed to play tough guy for a short time after escaping the Wheel, but he was sleeping now and the adrenaline was wearing off. What kind of man would wake up in his dad's bed this morning? Tommen doubted it would be the same tough guy.

Plus there was every chance that he was going to have to assist Micah in caring for Micaiah in some way. Probably not an in-home nurse or anything like that, but it could be driving Micaiah places. If he did return to work, Tommen might end up being like his personal assistant or a gopher, going places and doing things when he couldn't.

Well, maybe that last bit was an exaggeration. Micaiah would need help, but he still had his pride. He wasn't going to accept help lightly. Big things like driving, he wouldn't have a choice, at least at first. Little things like getting around the house or around the office, those he would do himself whether he ought to or not.

Tommen tried to keep everything straight in his mind about what was going on and what would need to be done. He tried to envision it a hundred different ways, but even as he was thinking that, the bus pulled up to the school. He couldn't even Band in order to finish his thoughts and get them all organized before heading into his own prison. Then he quickly decided that wasn't a fair or accurate statement, not after seeing his dad.

If nothing else, school was simply a government-run daycare. They had babysitters who ran little classes to learn things; they went to the little library, played on the little computers, even had little foodies and snackies in the middle of the day.

But school was not a prison. Prison was prison. His dad had been in prison and would suffer for it, probably for the rest of his life. Micaiah had lost his leg trying to escape that prison, and he would certainly carry that scar with him forever. With all of them Suppressed and Micah having to keep watch over the bakery, the responsibility ultimately fell to Tommen to ensure that everything went smoothly and everyone was getting the help they needed. They were officers, but he was an outsider and could see things from a different perspective. Given how much time he had to spare at daycare, he figured he should be able to come up with a few decent plans of action and be able to prioritize. Now was the time for him to man up, step up, and take the lead.

# Chapter Nine
## Footloose

The last thing Micaiah remembered was lying on his back under a bright light, Micah holding his hand and telling him everything was going to be all right. Actually, that was the only thing he remembered between stepping through the portal in the Wheel and waking up in bed, his head feeling like a lead balloon, his chest feeling as if a full grown elephant was sitting on him. His whole body just felt numb, as if he was encased in concrete, or maybe a block of ice. The room was blastedly cold, which he thought was odd. Maybe it was just him.

Gradually, vague images and sounds began sorting themselves out and he realized, not too quickly, that he wasn't at home in bed. These were not his sheets or his blankets or his pillow. This was not his room. Once he figured out what was not, he started trying to sift through his brain to put names to what was. His brain felt fuzzy and sluggish, but he managed to find a heavy door, ugly wallpaper, and even uglier linoleum. Shit, was he at Walter's house? No, except for the kitchen, Walter still had shag carpet, though it was no more beautiful than the linoleum.

Then his gaze wandered to some of the things on the wall. There were two paintings, one across from his bed and one by the door. The former was an eagle soaring over mountains, and the latter was some still life painting with a quote that he couldn't seem to read because his brain wasn't working quite right yet. To the left of the door was a small cabinet arrangement, all of it industrial, including the tiny sink.

His vision went from the cabinetry and focused on the stuff in front of it, beside him in fact, beside his bed. It was another bed, but it was empty. It, too, had the same white sheets and white blankets and a white pillow, all of it looking as though it had been washed far past its usefulness. Around it, computers of one form or another stood blank and silent.

*Where am I?*

It hit him then that he was in the hospital. Head still heavy on the outside but swimming on the inside, he did his best to survey himself. He had an oxygen tube under his nose and an IV in each arm. When he turned his head to look at the fluid bags, his vision swam, and he had to close his eyes to regain composure. Yes, he was in the hospital, but he had no intention of getting sick, especially when his only option was to be sick all over himself.

When he opened his eyes again, he was able to glance at the IV bags long enough to see that one of them was a blood bag. On one side of his bed, various monitors and computers hummed and blipped, reading every vital his body put out. As he studied that, he became aware of the sticky nodes on his chest and the meter thing on his finger.

Were he feeling mischievous, he might have seen how fast he could get someone in the room by removing one or two meters, see what would happen if his heart rate suddenly dropped to zero. But he barely had the energy to consider such a nasty little prank, never mind get around to actually pulling it off. Maybe later, once he'd slept off whatever drugs they'd given him.

He relaxed and tried to pull his thoughts together to figure out what had happened. He remembered collapsing several portals in the Wheel and racing to make it to the portal room to escape. He remembered being injured and he remembered escaping. The details of it all, though, were pretty sketchy. Again, probably because the drugs were screwing with him. He just needed a short nap and then everything would be fine.

Micaiah figured he must have slept at least a little more because when he came back around, his body felt better even as his stomach and head felt as if he were being tossed around in a barrel lost at sea during a storm. Keeping one eye closed and the other open just enough to look around, he searched for a bag or a pan or something so he didn't have to get sick all over himself. His closest option was a small pan that he figured might normally be for pens and small tools, but right now, it was his only saving grace.

As he was getting sick, the door opened and a doctor of some form walked in.

"I see you're awake," he observed mildly. "I'm Doctor Kohler."

Micaiah vomited a second time before collapsing back onto the bed, onto the starchy pillow. "Can I have some water?"

"I'm afraid it won't help; you'll only puke it up again."

"I'm going to be puking anyway. At least let me rinse my mouth out."

The doctor allowed him that much. As much as he just wanted to chug a couple gallons of water, it wasn't the first time he'd been under the influence of anesthesia; he knew that this was only the beginning.

"How long have I been here?" Micaiah asked, breathing hard and hoping he could get five minutes without being sick.

"Well," the doctor said, looking at his watch, "it's about quarter after seven in the morning. You came in just after midnight and were admitted into surgery within half an hour."

He thought on that for a second before nodding gingerly, feeling his stomach roil again, letting him know that another bout was coming. "Is my brother here?"

"He is. Actually, he's been very anxious to see you."

"Well, don't let him in just yet. I don't need him to see me like this."

Kohler nodded graciously. "I will tell him that."

"And unless you need to prep me for surgery again or change fluids, I would rather you weren't here either."

"You would rather suffer alone. I will respect your wishes to the best of my ability, but know that nurses will be in and out regularly to check on you."

"They can skip the welfare checks; I know where the magic button is."

"Not your first rodeo, huh?"

"No. Essentials only, please."

"Do my best. Just let someone know when you're ready to talk."

Micaiah promised him he would, knowing that it would be a while before that happened. The doctor moved the bed remote, the help remote, and the TV remote within reach and got him a proper sick bag with pitcher of water. Well, one of the better doctors he'd gotten, Micaiah figured.

He managed to hold off until the door closed before getting sick again. He wasn't even sure what he was throwing up; he still hadn't eaten in probably twenty-four hours or more. So really it was just stomach fluids and probably other bodily fluids he couldn't afford to lose, hence the IV bag. When he was done, he thought about turning on the TV, but he knew that the screen would only aggravate his headache and make him even sicker. In the end, he decided that maybe he just needed to sleep it off a while.

The third time waking up, he felt almost normal. His headache had gone and his stomach still felt a little queasy, but he felt more like himself rather than a stranger in his own body, trapped in concrete.

*"Madainn mhaith, a Mhaicín."* (Good morning, Sunshine.)

Blearily, he looked over to see Micah sitting in a chair against the wall, flipping through a magazine.

"I told the doctor I didn't want to see you yet," Micaiah complained.

"I know," Micah said, not looking up. "He told me. But I got your room number and slipped down here anyway."

"Why?"

"Because I'm your annoying younger brother and don't care what my older brother tells me to do or not do."

Now he looked up and grinned. Micaiah felt himself returning the smile as Micah stood and approached to give him a gentle hug.

"How you feeling, bro?" he asked, straightening and taking a step back.

"The anesthesia's killing me. Or it was."

"Yeah?" An odd expression crossed Micah's face. "How's...how's the rest of you feeling?"

"My head hurts a little, stomach's still kinda queasy, arms are sore from these needles, but I'm okay."

Micah blinked. "So...you don't notice that anything's wrong? Like, seriously, you...haven't...noticed?"

"Noticed what?" As he said it, he took a quick, personal inventory.

"Cai...they had to amputate your leg."

Micaiah stared at him, looking for some evidence of a joke, but the only emotion he found was dead seriousness mixed with pity. Without breaking his gaze, Micaiah moved his hands down to feel his hips and thighs.

"No," he said, his heart beginning to race, every beat caught on the monitor. "No, I can still feel them. They're there."

"Below the knee, where the rod went through the bone. Doctors said too much was lost and the soft tissue was irreparable."

"No," Micaiah repeated. "I don't believe you."

Micah reached over his lap to the bed remote and sat him almost completely upright. He looked down. Yes, there was his left leg, hip, thigh, knee, lower leg, foot. He wiggled his toes just to be sure. But then there was his right leg. Hip, yes. Thigh, yes. It even looked like his knee might still be in tact. But then it just...ended. It was strange, he knew that there was supposed to be another half of a leg there. The lower leg and then his foot.

He shook his head. "No. You're lying. No. It didn't happen."

"I'm afraid it did," Micah said softly.

"No, I can still feel it. It's there."

"It's only in your mind, Cai. It's gone."

Micah reached for the sheets to flip them up, but Micaiah

clamped down on his wrist. "Don't. No. I don't believe you. It didn't happen. It's not real. This has to be a dream."

His younger brother did not speak immediately, simply leaned him back so he wasn't completely upright, returning the remote to its original position. Then, "I'm sorry."

Micaiah had a tart reply ready, but his stomach chose that moment to gurgle and boil, and he only just made it to the sick bag. Once, twice he vomited. By the time he was done and had washed his mouth out, he couldn't do much more than lay back and relax.

Gone. It was gone. His lower leg was gone. Cut off. Like a choice chunk of meat. Except there had been a rod or something through it. Destroyed the bone, mangled the muscle. Irreparable. And in that split-moment decision, the doctors turned from meticulously trying to save the leg to sawing it off completely. Gone forever. Couldn't get it back now. No oopses here.

"No foot?" he asked, looking at Micah who was studying the floor.

Micah shook his head. "No foot."

"No ankle?"

"No ankle."

"No lower leg?"

"Nope, no lower leg."

"No knee?"

Now Micah looked up. "Actually, you did get to keep your knee."

"Well what fucking good is a knee if I don't have a fucking leg?!" Micaiah roared, just about coming off the bed at his brother, being stopped only by a sour stomach that drove him back to the sick bag. As he puked again, a shift in his stomach told him he was nearing the end of his misery.

"I'm sorry, Cai," Micah said softly. "I saw the wound myself. Even I couldn't have seen a way to save it."

"Well, you're not a doctor."

"And I'm not an idiot. It was gone, Cai, even before they took it off."

Micaiah opened his mouth to speak when the door squeaked open and Kohler walked in holding a file folder.

"Why didn't you tell me?!" Micaiah snarled.

Kohler paused only briefly in his walk. Then he resumed, saying, "You were in no state of mind to be able to process the news at the time, assuming you hadn't noticed already. And your brother said he wanted to be the one to tell you."

"There was nothing you could have done?" Now Micaiah's attitude was reduced to a pathetic whimpering.

Kohler turned on a lightbox on the wall and slapped up some X-rays. A few were standard, but some had red marker marks on them where the doctors had estimated the rod to be, its direction, and other notes Micaiah couldn't read or understand. All he knew, looking from the X-rays, was that the rod had not just broken his bones, but it had completely blown them out and removed them. They were probably still scattered over the floor of the portal room.

"Do you think you can handle some pictures?" Kohler asked.

"I'm not squeamish," Micaiah told him.

Kohler handed Micaiah some full-sheet pictures.

Micah hadn't been lying. Half his leg had already been gone even before they took a saw to it. How he'd managed to get back up and stand on it long enough to collapse the portal was beyond him. But there it was. Or wasn't. There was a big fucking hole right through the middle of his leg. There were bone shards, the top and bottom pieces of what little bone shaft was left, and marbled hamburger that had once been his muscles, tendons, and ligaments and other fancy words for soft tissue. And blood. There was quite a bit of blood, too. And through it all—literally—was a big fucking hole.

"No," Kohler said. "There is nothing we could have done. As you can see, there wasn't anything to save."

"Except the knee," Micaiah said numbly.

"Except the knee."

He handed the pictures back to the doctor.

He couldn't even make it all fit together in his mind. That had happened. He remembered it happening, feeling the rod pierce him and drive him to the floor. He remembered the pain all through his heroic last stand with the portal. And then Walter and the others were around him, trying to stabilize the rod. When they couldn't do that, they had to tie a tourniquet. His memory got fuzzier the more the pain spread through his body as the circulation got cut off and backed up into his body, his body panicking and trying to figure out what to do.

And now that was all over. He'd lost it. It was gone. Cut off. Amputated. He was an amputee. He was a charity case. His life was over. All done. His leg was gone, and he was finished. Things would never be the same again. How could he expect to carry on?

Carefully, he reached down and moved the sheets back. Yes, his leg was gone. There was the stump wrapped in layers of bandages, a drainage tube dripping down to a bag hanging off the side of the bed. Looking at it, he could feel a small, stinging pain right in the center of the site, but otherwise, it didn't really hurt which was probably the thing he found most strange. He couldn't make out his knee amid the bandages, but internally feeling around in there, he knew it was still attached. Well, at least he had that going for him. It wasn't much, but he figured it was the best he could have hoped for, given the circumstances. He moved the sheets back to cover it up.

There was a phrase: Life sucks and then you die. Micaiah figured he was pretty well-versed in that first part by now. Life was sucking pretty hard right now, no doubt about it. So when did that second part come into play? Was that an automatic thing, or did he have to help it along a little?

After a moment of silence, Micaiah took a breath and asked as calmly as he could, "What do I do now?"

"Now," Kohler began, equally as calm, "we put together a plan for how to proceed, which will include myself as the primary overseeing doctor. It will also include a physical therapist—"

"Why? I've got no fucking leg!" Micaiah tried a nervous laugh, but the tears started coming.

"The physical therapist will start you on an exercise regimen that will keep the muscles from contracting as you heal. This is especially important since you still have your knee. You want your knee to function correctly or else we'll have to go back in."

Micaiah just sighed.

"Then you will also need a prosthetist who will help get you fitted for a prosthetic in about four weeks."

"Seems kind of soon after surgery," Micah commented.

"It's only a preliminary fitting. The 'permanent' prosthetic as it were wouldn't be ready for a couple months after that. It's simply to get you started using one, becoming comfortable and familiar with the idea, use, and care of a prosthetic."

Micaiah didn't want a prosthetic leg; he wanted his real leg. He liked it better. It had been with him for so long, why give up now?

"And through it all, we highly recommend a therapist for support," Kohler concluded. "Your brother sounds like a good guy, and he tells me you have a lot of friends rallying around you, but sometimes it helps to talk to someone who doesn't already know you."

"How long do I have to be in the hospital?"

"Normally, a planned amputation would see you out of here in about four days. Because of the nature of your injury, I want to keep you for at least five to seven. But regardless, in the time that you are here, a police officer is going to want to speak with you."

"Officer?"

Micah nodded. "There weren't any witnesses to your hit-and-run. Or that's what the speculation is. Cops just want to see if there's a crime to be investigated."

Hit-and-run. So that was the story they'd concocted to explain how a rod got blown through his leg. Well, not like he had anything better, but there was going to be quite a bit of memory loss involved.

"Fine, whatever," Micaiah sighed. "If I have to talk to him, send him in."

"I can probably stall for another hour or two if you want,"

Kohler offered. "If you want to take a little time to collect yourself."

"I said send him in."

The doctor nodded and left the room. A moment later, a female police officer entered the room. Any other day, Micaiah might have been interested enough to ask her out for drinks and maybe a little more. Now, though...he couldn't even begin to think of a reason why any woman should look at him other than to scorn and walk away. He felt ugly and repulsive, even to himself. He didn't want to be himself; he wanted to be someone else. Someone with two real, functioning legs.

"Micaiah Durvin?" she began.

"That's what the wristband says," he answered, raising his left arm and shocking himself with his own wit.

"My name is Officer Golden. Can you tell me what happened to you last night?"

"Fuck if I know. Everyone seems to think I got hit by a car."

"Were you?"

"I don't know."

"Where were you last night from, let's say, ten pm to midnight?"

Micaiah let out a breath. He had to come up with a story, one that couldn't be reliably cross-referenced.

"Let's see...I took the day off work yesterday so I could just fucking relax and get some work done that didn't have to do with work." He paused as if going through a mental list of the things he did. "I hadn't eaten all day so I made myself some dinner around six...and I didn't get to it for some reason. Oh, I hadn't gotten the mail, and I wanted my newspaper. Sunday paper, sale ads, you know. I did that...went back up and ate my dinner. It started to snow..." He cast a quick glance at Micah who gave an almost imperceptible nod. "Micah had already gone to bed, and I didn't feel like dealing with an icy driveway in the morning, so I went out to shovel. Actually, I went out to snowblow, but the damn starter gave out. So I shoveled. Then I wake up here."

"Do you remember anything about the vehicle? Make, model, color...type?"

"Um...truck, maybe? Like a small pickup work truck? I just..." He sighed and closed his eyes. "I just get a glimpse for a fraction of a second, and I'm not even sure that I remember it right. I'm sorry."

"It's all right," Golden assured him. "I'll ask around your neighbors, see if maybe one of them saw something."

"That late at night and with our neighborhood?" Micah scoffed. "Not likely."

"Well, we can hope, right?" She fished out a business card and handed it to Micaiah. "If you do remember anything, give me a call."

Micaiah nodded. They exchanged meaningless pleasantries as she left. When she was gone, Micaiah took the bed remote and leaned back until he was almost flat. "I wish it was that easy. Then maybe some real justice would get done."

"It will," Micah said simply. "Just not today. And, not that you really need anything else sprung on you today—"

"They take my arms, too?" Micaiah held up his hands. "Nope, still got those.  Or did someone else get hurt?" Fear flashed through his mind.

Micah waited patiently. "Everyone else is fine, but Walter thinks everyone should be Suppressed."

For a second, Micaiah couldn't even remember what that meant. Then, "Wait, like, Suppressed so we can't use our Time abilities?"

"Yup."

"Why?"

Micah told him a tale that Walter hold told him, about being attacked in the home by a Tracker and what their purpose was and how they operated.

"Walter thinks that simply keeping our heads down isn't enough. He wants us to lay low, real low."

"But we need Time. Or hasn't he gotten his pastry recently?"

Micah hesitated. "Problem is, I can see both sides. The Wheel is cut off, the Time industry is imploding, Cassius rules, and Rifun is doing the cleanup work around the universe. This is Walter's way of throwing the hounds off our scent. It's not a permanent measure, just long enough."

Micaiah sighed. "Micah...you don't know what happened to Walter in there. He was kept in the black cells. Same as I was, but I was only held for the true Base Time. Twelve hours or something. Cassius fucked with Walter, okay? He kept him locked up for something like six or eight months. In the space of a single day. Okay, Walt is fucked in the head. He might hold it together long enough to get by for a time, but he's not going to crash lightly."

"So you think we shouldn't be Suppressed?"

"No, I don't. If nothing else, I think we need to train harder. Okay, fuck the Wheel, and fuck the Arena. Figure out who's here, who's left. Masters, Apprentices. Train. Work out our own system. Do things our own way. Gatekeeper is the Grand Master and on down the line."

Micah nodded. "Okay. Well, you can hash it out with Walt when he comes to see you."

"Why? I'm crippled anyway. Wait. The fuck are you doing here? What about the shop?"

"Don't worry about it. Oh, but that does remind me that I have to pick Tommen up from school." Micah glanced at the clock. "Still got a little time, I guess. He wants to see you, too, though. Everyone does."

*Well, I don't want to see them,* was Micaiah's first thought. Then a guilty strain hit him and he silently amended, *I don't want them to see me weak and vulnerable.*

He sighed and looked away. He didn't want visitors. He didn't want pity or sympathy. He didn't want a prosthetic or physical therapy or any of that. He wanted his damn leg. His real leg. He wanted to go back in time and redo what had happened. Maybe if he'd zigged instead of zagged, or if he hadn't hesitated that last half-second. If he could somehow tell himself or tell Jenna which portal they had to go through instead of getting lost, maybe they would have made better time and beat the guards to the portal room. Any number of tiny factors that could have saved him this pain and humiliation.

*That's what you get for not being careful and not taking the lead. That's what you get when you trust someone who has no fucking clue what they're doing or where they're going. You could have just Banded for ten fucking seconds to collect your head and get out the right way instead of letting yourself getting dragged every which way, getting lost in the process. But no. You left your fate in the hands of a Journeyman. An idiot if the results are any indication.*

"Talk to me, Micah," Micaiah sighed.

"About what?" Micah asked politely.

"Anything but this. Anything but this and Time and any of the shit that happened this weekend."

He couldn't even remember what they talked about or if it really made him feel any better. The only thing he could think about was his missing leg. He kept looking down at it, or where it should have been. He could feel it, but it was gone. Phantom limb, something he'd always ascribed to war veterans and people who had a real reason for losing their leg, like war or cancer or some other life-threatening disease, not because some idiot got them lost during a high-stakes escape and cost them time, allowing their pursuers to catch up and mortally wound them. His leg was fucking gone.

He barely even noticed that Micah left to pick up Tommen from school. The most he remembered during that time was that his stomach had settled enough that he could handle water without puking it up in ten minutes.

"Cai," Micah said, poking his head in the door sometime later. "Tommen wants to say hi."

Micaiah sighed. No. Go away. He just wanted to be left alone to sulk by himself. Furthermore, if he ever dared show his face again in public and go back to work at some point, he wanted the kid to still have some fear of him. Seeing him now....he would only ever evoke pity. That's the only reaction he would ever get from anyone ever again. Pity and sympathy and little baskets of food because...that was what people did?

"Fine," he sighed. "Might as well send him in."

Tommen had apparently been standing near the door because he entered the room before he even finished the statement.

"Hey," Tommen said awkwardly.

Micaiah knew his expression in an instant. Tommen was trying to maintain eye contact, but he wanted to look. He wanted to see the stump. He wanted to see where his leg ended. *Yes. It's gone. It's true. There's your proof.*

"Morning," Micaiah replied cordially, trying not to take it out on the boy. "Or afternoon or whatever fucking time it is."

"Afternoon. You feeling better?"

"Anesthesia's wearing off, so that's a good start."

"But...I mean...how...?"

"How's my stump of a leg?"

Tommen halted as if he'd just been slapped. He glanced at Micah for some sort of direction. This was no man's land for everyone. Tommen didn't know how to approach him. Micaiah didn't know how he wanted to be approached. He just wanted to be normal and carry on like normal. But he didn't get that option. He didn't get to go back to that normal. This was going to be his new normal.

"Want to see it?" he offered just as awkwardly. He didn't really want to show it to Tommen, and the kid didn't look like he really wanted to see it. Was it pretentious? In bad taste? Would it be enough to just settle the curiosity once and for all?

"Um...sure..." Tommen said, taking a hesitant step toward the bed and slipping around to the other side.

Micaiah raised the bed some so he could reach the sheets and pull them back.

It was still a surprise to see, and it didn't repulse him as much as he expected it to. It was more of a curiosity, like a freak sideshow at a circus. Hey, come look at the funny man with only one and a half legs. Here, throw some rotten fruit at him, see how he futilely tries to scurry away.

"You got to keep your knee, though, right?" Tommen said.

He covered it again, even though he really felt like staring at it for a while, a puzzle to be figured out. "Yeah."

"So it shouldn't be too bad, with a prosthetic."

Micaiah sighed. "And we're done here."

Tommen got a look on his face like his puppy had just been kicked. "I'm sorry."

"I know. Out."

The teenager hurried out of the room, looking puzzled and frustrated. Micah stopped him at the door and whispered something before letting him outside. Then he shut the door and looked at Micaiah.

"He's just trying to help and be supportive," Micah told him, as if they were an old, bickering married couple.

"Well, he can do it when I'm feeling better," Micaiah retorted lamely.

"And you won't feel better unless you let people help and support you. Imagine what he would be like if we just held off about his hearing until he felt better."

"That's different."

"Is it? He lost a part of himself, just as you did. He didn't want to get hearing aids or admit to anything being wrong no matter how obvious. He still doesn't like them and I bet he'd take his normal hearing back in a heartbeat if he could, but he's adjusting. He's learning to cope. He's getting better. And what are you going to do?"

"Not engage in this conversation, for one."

"Maybe, but you still have to live with me and work with me. The best you can do to me is ignore me, but you will not be alone. And your phone has been ringing, too. I think you know who it is."

"I don't care. I'm not talking to anyone right now. I just found out today that I lost my leg, and you act like I should just go back to work tomorrow. I can't."

"I'm not saying you are. Or you should. Your wound needs to

physically heal, just like any other wound. But once the doctor says you can be up and around—or even just sitting behind your desk being cranky while you work—then you are going to come back to work."

"Yes, Dad."

"Yeah? Want me to pull out a bag of Mom, too? Because I can sit you down and fuss over you and poke and prod and try to make everything better immediately. Cai, I'm your brother. I'm not Mom or Dad, but I will be if I have to."

Micaiah sighed and rubbed his eyes. This was turning into more of a nightmare by the minute. Problem was, since the anesthesia wore off and his mind was coming back to him, he was feeling too good to buy time by getting sick, and too awake to buy time by claiming fatigue.

"I...appreciate...that you want me to get better and get back on my feet quickly." He winced at his own pun. "But for God's sake, Micah, it's not going to be today. I can't process it all at once. It's like telling me that you brought in a top-notch construction crew for this big project of mine, and they're all working before I've even given them the blueprints. Just...let me be for a little while."

Micah went and sat in one of the chairs along the wall by his bedside. He nodded slowly. "Okay. I get it. On a few terms."

"I'm the sick one here; where do you get off setting terms?"

"A few terms. First, Walter will want to see you. Today or tomorrow, he wants to see you. Just let him know you're okay."

Micaiah sighed. "Fine. Next?"

"I'll tell them to lay off on seeing you for a little while, provided that you don't shut me out. Talk to me. I'm your brother. It doesn't even have to be about this. It can be about work or TV or whatever. Just talk."

"Sounds fair."

"I'm probably going to be bothering you a lot because you're going to be off work a little while, and I'm jealous."

Micaiah shook his head. "Believe me. This is no vacation you want to take."

"I know. But you'll make it. You always do. That's why, even though we're twins, I've always looked up to you."

*But who do I look up to? Does anyone want to know that, or do they just want to feed off of me?*

Micaiah agreed to his brother's terms, unsure how he felt about them. He endured the visit from Walter the following day. Apparently he'd spent an entire year in the black cells. His eyesight was still adjusting to light, and he was going to visit an eye doctor about it, but otherwise he seemed no worse for wear. Micaiah had his doubts. There was no way that someone with Walter's darkness issues could spend another year in the darkness without going insane. Still, the visit was pleasant enough, despite being Suppressed in the end, and soon Micaiah was left alone in his hospital room.

The week he spent there, despite denying any visitors besides Micah, felt like a non-stop carousel of doctors and specialists. He was introduced to Sean Higaki, the physical therapist assigned to him. That whole day—or what felt like a whole day—was spent learning various exercises to keep his knee limber and useful so that it would be easier for Francine Jacobs, the prosthetist, to work with him. How he was supposed to do the exercises a minimum of two times a day was almost beyond him for how much pain they caused him.

But, Doctor Kohler said that a little pain during the exercises wasn't a bad thing. It was only if he experienced pain otherwise during downtime that he should be worried. And they had a chat about changing bandages, keeping the wound site clean, looking for infection, and home care. They also spoke at length about falls and other bad things that could and were statistically likely to happen, and what to do about them. Mostly, it just boiled down to call the doctor and get in as soon as possible.

It wasn't until Friday that he was allowed out of bed not in a wheelchair. With a pair of crutches and an eager med student tailing closely behind, he took himself to the bathroom.

Being upright, his leg felt like a huge lead weight was attached to it, and yet it wanted to float away it seemed. He had muscular control over the appendage, but there was no grounding, no counterbalance to gravity as he moved.

Saturday morning, he woke up feeling kind of alone, and guilty that he'd told Micah to keep everyone off his back. His brother had done so, but Micaiah had little doubt that he was reporting his every cough and sneeze to anyone who was interested. So, reluctantly, and with not a little trepidation, he reached for his phone. It had lain on a tiny table nightstand, untouched since Monday but not silent. He had literally hundreds of unread messages and emails, and dozens of missed calls. Oddly enough, they were split pretty evenly between personal messages, people wanting to know what had happened and how he was doing, and business messages, replies to things he'd been working on at the end of last week. Like that fucking advertising. He'd meant to get back with the guy.

Micaiah set his phone back on the stand and leaned his bed back some. Maybe he could ask Micah to do it. No, that wouldn't be fair. Without Time, Micah was working full steam at the bakery. He'd even been forced to hire temporary help, that being Kyle and Jenna, with a temporary-but-possibly-permanent promotion of Tommen to a manager's position. There was no way that any of them would be able to just pick up on all the extra work that had to be done. Tommen could do stock orders and scheduling, and Micah could do payroll and accounting. They wouldn't have the time to worry about the advertising or any of the little projects that Micaiah had had going.

At the same time, he couldn't just return to work like nothing had happened. Nothing hadn't happened. He'd lost his fucking leg. He couldn't do all the moving and maneuvering around in the kitchen, and he didn't feel like having to stand and balance on the counter, going back and forth in the display case.

And it almost seemed cruel to just go back to the office. The hiding he wouldn't mind, at least for a while, but it just...didn't seem right. To return to the office and keep making phone calls and sending emails and carrying on. Last week he'd been unjustly kept in prison, sentenced to execution. He'd lost his leg in a last bid to escape. And he was just supposed to sit in his chair in the office, trying to negotiate the price of a billboard? It was awful and laughable and any number of things Micaiah didn't have a name for. He just couldn't do it.

He looked up as the door opened and Micah walked in with a backpack, followed by Kohler with a file folder.

"You mean there's a world beyond this room?" Micaiah asked snidely.

"There is," Kohler replied, meeting his snark. "And you get to join it." Micaiah sighed. "I know we already went over them, but here are your home care papers. On this last page I wrote down the names of all your doctors and specialists with their phone numbers if you need to reach them. And just remember, if you have any questions or concerns, don't hesitate to give one of us a call."

"Where do I sign to get out of here?"

Kohler raised a brow but brought out another sheet. "This page acknowledges your continuing treatment with your doctors and authorizes us to treat you in matters of physical therapy, prosthetics, and so on."

Micaiah skimmed through the page and signed, figuring he wasn't going to get out of it no matter what.

"Your brother brought you a bag of clothes. Whenever you are ready, you can check out and head down to the pharmacy; I've forwarded your scripts to them, so they should be ready when you get there. One is a painkiller. If you find yourself taking more than four in a day, give me a call. There is also an antibiotic to help keep the wound clean and not infected. And there is a muscle relaxer, to keep things from getting too tight and uncomfortable. Just remember that a little pain and discomfort during the exercises in not a bad thing, but if it doesn't stop, doesn't go away, go ahead and take one. If it still doesn't help, give me a call."

There were more minor instructions and banal departing pleasantries, Kohler not failing to emphasize calling him for anything and everything. Micaiah knew it was for a good reason, but he really just wanted to go home and sleep in his own bed. Enough of the scratchy sheets, the IVs, and the doctors and nurses coming and going at all hours of the day. He just wanted some peace and quiet.

Eventually the room cleared out except for Micah who held out the backpack to him.

"I don't need help, Mom," Micaiah said as he scooted to the edge of the bed and brought out the clothes, untying the hospital gown and slipping the shirt over his head. He wished he was as confident as he thought he was when he got to the boxers and pants. He wiggled into the boxers but stopped when he got to the pants.

The first thing he noticed was that one of the legs had been pinned up with safety pins. The reason was obvious, but still, it just...no. *No.* It couldn't be for him. Because he lost his leg. He was going to have to do that for all his pants. All of them. Every single pair. Tailor them to fit his missing leg. Well, maybe not all of them, if he got a prosthetic, but... Was he really thinking that? Was he honestly considering his future with a fake leg? Fucking hell.

"Are you sure you don't need help?" Micah asked cautiously, barging in on his thoughts.

Micaiah realized he'd been staring at the pants for probably a minute or two. Finally, "No, I'm not sure."

He got the normal leg on easily enough, even managed to get the pinned leg on over his stump without issue. He just had to be able to stand and bring it up around his waist. Micah stayed on his deficient side, promising not to touch him unless he was actually going down. Very carefully, Micaiah stood up, feeling every muscle in both legs clench, fighting to maintain balance when the normal expected counterweight—either the crutches or his lower leg—was suddenly absent. He got his pants up, but the motion cost him his balance. Thankfully, he was able to fall back and sit on the bed.

"I'd say you did good, for your first time," Micah offered helpfully.

Micaiah did not reply as he brought out the socks and shoes.

Plural.

"Are you patronizing me?" he asked.

"Patro—oh. Oh, shit, I didn't even...I just grabbed a pair of socks out of your drawer, but...oh, shit, I didn't even think... I'm sorry."

It was still about the only normal part of the process, besides the shirt. Force of habit dictated he put his right shoe on first, except he didn't have a right fucking foot anymore. He let the shoe drop to the ground as he brought his left foot up and dressed it.

"Let's go," Micaiah sighed, turning and grabbing his crutches.

Micah grabbed the empty, or almost empty, backpack while he hauled himself to his feet—foot. He'd been all eager to go home, but now he almost didn't want to leave the hospital. Somehow it felt like defeat. As if he was accepting that his leg was never coming back and he was going to move on to a normal life. In the hospital, it reeked of death and sickness and despair, true, but also of hope and possibility, like the stereotypical commercials showing doctors standing around a file or around a lab table, doing what appeared to be some sort of serious discussion or research. As long as he was in the hospital, there was the chance that some doctor would burst into his room screaming, "Eureka! I have found it! There's a way to save your leg!"

Signing the discharge papers felt like giving up, signing his life away, telling the doctors that it was okay that they hadn't been able to save his leg, he'd plod along anyway, like everyone else and yet not like everyone else. He'd give up, keep his head down, and try to fit in with the rest of them.

"I'll bring the car around," Micah told him as they headed for the door.

"You think I can't make it?" Micaiah asked hotly.

"I don't know if *I* can make it. It's a little slick. And I don't think you want to sign your discharge papers, go out, slip and fall, and have to come right back in again."

Fine, so he had a point. At least he made Micaiah feel a little better by slipping and falling thirty feet from the door, thus prompting a hospital volunteer to run outside with a hugebucket of salt.

They were heading home soon enough.

"How's the shop?" Micaiah asked levelly.

"Working our asses off. Production is a smidge lower, but no one's really seemed to notice."

"What do you have Tommen working now?"

"Well, in trying to keep with child labor laws, I can't put him on as full-time weekend manager. So I made him the Saturday manager plus two days during the week."

Their conversation lasted only until they got home. Micah helped Micaiah inside, still trying to talk, but he was done. He just wanted to be alone. Ignoring his younger brother, Micaiah headed down the hall to his bedroom where he locked the door and flopped down on the bed.

Life without Time was unusually hectic. If something had to get done, Tommen had to hurry and rush, instead of just making more Time as he needed. Not just one part of this was getting up for school in the morning during the week, and for work on Saturday mornings. Early Saturday morning.

Some days his dad felt good enough to take him to school, and other days he rode the bus. His dad's eyesight had normalized about two weeks after getting home, or normalized within his ability to drive and do most tasks. Even so, however, he sometimes ended up in bed with severe light-induced migraines. Like this Friday morning, as Tommen woke up alone.

He was starting to get the hang of getting around quickly, but more than once he had to run out the door without breakfast or with breakfast in hand. He still wasn't quite willing to get up earlier. And he ended up hurrying down the driveway, backpack in one hand, peanut butter toast in the other.

"Morning, Tommen," the bus driver said, his tone irritated at his tardiness. Again.

At the very least, he didn't have to worry about Tyler Freeman anymore. His cronies and his younger brother gave Tommen death stares and taunted him in the halls, but so far none of them had actually gotten physical. Tommen dreaded what would happen if any of them did challenge him and he still didn't have his Banding abilities.

Since his skiing accident, Tommen's head had cleared up enough that he was able to resume his normal hybrid English class, spending a couple days in the computer lab and a couple days in the classroom itself. For that he was grateful; he wasn't sure how much more he could have taken if he'd been forced to stay solely in the classroom. He hated Mrs. Righting and he was fairly certain she hated him, too. Whatever her role in getting Tyler expelled, he was pretty sure she didn't hold him in much higher regard.

It wasn't absolutely impossible to Band electronics, but that ability was far above his skill level anyway, so when it came to taking tests online, he'd become more accustomed to having a time limit that he couldn't manipulate like he could in math or history or any of that. That still didn't mean that he enjoyed being confined to the same rules as everyone else.

But he finished his English test with good time to spare, leaving him plenty of time to goof off. He knew he should probably be rationing his time, prioritizing since he couldn't manipulate, and working on homework for other classes like everyone else, but even so, he didn't find school all that interesting. Or important, really, in the long run. He understood its purpose, understood what his dad said about making sure he had some brains to back up whatever he said about himself in future lives, but all the same, it was just government-run daycare.

He headed to Economics with about as much enthusiasm. Thankfully, Morrison decided to forgo the planned test in favor of showing them some documentary that he'd been waiting on from the library for at least forever and it was the only day he would be able to show it to them.

The only thing about turning the lights off in the room in order to see the movie was that it made it more difficult for Tommen to putter around on his phone, especially since he couldn't just slip it away if and when Morrison caught him.

"Are you working today or do you have play practice?" his dad had texted at some point in the last twenty minutes.

"Today is work," Tommen replied. "Monday is play practice."

"Aren't you in class?"

"Maybe."

"Why aren't you paying attention?"

"You texted me."

"Pay attention, Tommen."

He could almost hear his dad's exasperated sigh. Since returning, his dad had been texting him more and more while he was at work or school. Tommen figured it was because of being in prison for a year; he was terrified of losing everything so he texted Tommen to make sure he hadn't vanished into thin air. Given some of the shit they'd gone through over the last six months, he really couldn't blame him. Supposedly, his dad had even had to kill another Tracker that had made its way to their house.

Time. Couldn't live with it, couldn't live without it. He palmed his phone as Morrison looked up from his desk, then slipped it back in his pocket for the remainder of the movie. Could be worse, he guessed. Could have been the test they were all preparing for.

Although, speaking of tests, he wasn't too thrilled about the one coming up in AP Physics either. Normally he was okay with it, but this would not be a normal test. First and foremost, he had no Time abilities. He couldn't just make himself more time if he needed to figure out an equation. But, secondary to that, this was going to be a partner test. He and Becky would be working on the same test together, getting the same grade. Supposedly the test was super short and each one was different to avoid cheating, but he couldn't understand White's logic. Collaboration was great, but on a test? Seriously?

There was nothing he could do about it either way, and when White said to go ahead and begin the test, Becky flipped over the paper and they began the test. Three questions only, story problems, ones that required thoughtful, detailed setup. It actually went better than Tommen expected. Becky was good at identifying the underlying problems and matching them to equations, while Tommen could quickly work out the pure math portion of it. He went to lunch feeling pretty good about it.

Probably the only good thing that had changed about Tommen's school day was that he no longer dreaded lunch. Becky was right about bringing in more people to sit with them at their table, but it wasn't as awful as he'd first assumed. Few people actually cared that he was hearing impaired and he'd gotten to know a few people at the table. Lisa's family wasn't rich; her designer clothes came from her modeling gig. Ollie didn't refer to himself as "gay" but as more of a "creative explorer" whatever that meant. Robert had scholarship offers from places like Yale and Harvard, but he didn't parade it around because he, too, was the object of school bullies. Dolores was an exchange student because of a lottery that let impoverished families have a chance at sending a child anywhere in the world for student exchange.

Okay, so life wasn't all bad. Some things had actually gone pretty well since the beginning of the year. While this relieved Tommen and he felt like he might be able to breathe again for a spell, it also grated on his paranoia powers and made him super suspicious that something really bad was going to happen.

"I stopped by the bakery the other day," Becky said as the bell rang and they headed down the hall, his locker coming up first. "You got some new hands? Are you still working there?"

"Oh, yeah, I actually got promoted to weekend manager," he answered, feeling his ears turn red.

"Really? That's cool. What brought that on?"

"Well, Micaiah—one of the owners—was in an accident and he had to spend some time in the hospital; he hasn't returned to work yet."

"Aw, that's too bad. Not too badly injured, I hope?"

Tommen squirmed a little. Micaiah had his pride and trusted that his friends wouldn't just go blabbing to everyone about how they knew a one-legged man; Tommen wanted to maintain that kind of trust and respect. He replied, "The worst injury was the one to his pride."

"Of course it was." Becky rolled her eyes in exaggeration. Of course, men and their ego. "But as long as he's all in one piece and on the mend, that's what counts, right?"

All in one piece. Sure. That one piece is slightly smaller, but yeah, he's still in one piece. "Yeah, he's good. He will be."

"Cool. I'll see you Monday, then."

She scurried off, vanishing into the throng of people, a child-sized adult, expertly weaving her way amongst the mass jungle of legs and textbooks that met her at eye level. Tommen watched her go, knowing that they both had to get to class, yet wanting her to stay, just so they could sit and talk or walk and talk without a table full of people to overhear their conversation.

He made it through Web Programming without too much issue. That class was still a bit of a delicate balance, simply because by that time, normally, he would have already been through his online English class, plus done quite a bit of Banding throughout the day, putting him at a precarious position as far as headaches went. But, without the Banding, he got through it and finished out his day in art class.

By the time he got on the bus, he was feeling pretty good, actually. School didn't suck balls, and there was just something awesome about going into work when you know you have power. Granted, it wasn't much, since they all still had to do the same crappy jobs — twice as hard and twice as fast without Banding — and they were still under Micah's rule, but yet, he was over Kyle and Jenna. He was their boss. He was in charge. When Micah wasn't around or wasn't available, he called the shots. He made the decisions. The idea of it just made him giddy. That and the dollar raise wasn't bad either.

"Afternoon, everyone," he said, walking in the door.

"Hey, Micah could really use you in the kitchen," Kyle told him at the counter.

Tommen simply nodded and headed back to drop off his things, punch in, and grab an apron. Also since becoming manager, he spent less time on counter and more time in the kitchen doing the actual baking and decorating. When he finally got his hands washed and dried, Micah was busy mixing some kind of dough. He nodded to a pan of steaming cupcakes just to one side. "Those need decoration."

"Got it," Tommen said, feeling his power nostalgia die as he set to work. Kyle was a grunt and Micah was the owner, but everyone worked. He got out the utensils, moved the pan to a clean spot so Micah could continue his work, and started decorating. "How's Micaiah?"

"Bitchy, as usual," Micah replied. "The physical therapist was in today for therapy and evaluation."

"Yeah? How's he doing?"

"Well, he says that everything is looking good and healing like it's supposed to. Supposedly, he's been cleared to drive, too."

"Cool. He's probably itching to get back here and see what mayhem we've caused." Tommen grinned but Micah did not return it.

"Do you see him here?" Micah sighed. "He still won't leave the house, even to get the mail. With the hit-and-run story we've perpetuated, it might make sense. But still." He shook his head. "I don't know what to do for him."

"He hasn't turned into some hermit, has he? Like, doesn't shower or shave, only comes out of his room for food?" Tommen arranged the cupcakes on a tray to go out, then moved on to taking out pans of cookies from the ovens.

"He hasn't gotten quite that bad, thankfully," Micah chuckled. "He cooks for himself and gets around the house pretty okay, does his exercises. He does bathe; he just has to do it a special way, but that might have changed today." He shrugged incredulously. "He just refuses to leave the house. So instead, he texts me all day to complain and gripe. But that's okay. I told him that if he wanted me to keep people away from him, then he had to talk to me. No silent treatment."

"Maybe me or my dad could visit," Tommen suggested hopefully.

Micah shook his head. "I thought that, too, but he's just...he just wants to be left alone for a while."

"And maybe someone should visit anyway and say, 'Hey, asshole, there are people who care about you who want to see you and help you to get better.'"

Micah laughed. "As amusing as that would be, don't do that. He's got his pride. And..." He let out a breath. "And there is more going on in his mind than either of us can really appreciate. Believe me, I am thinking about what I'm going to do when it does come to that point, but in his mind, it's still too soon. And for now, I'm respecting that."

Tommen sullenly agreed. "Probably not easy for you to be his caregiver, is it?"

"Pft. What caregiver? He won't let me be his caregiver. Anytime I try to help, he practically beats me to death with his crutches." Tommen snickered. "I'm serious. He's taken a few swings at me. Finally I just backed off and figured that he'll need me if he falls and has to get back to the hospital." He shook his head. "Idiot." He huffed. "But anyway, how are you doing without your Time abilities?"

Tommen shrugged. "Okay, I guess. I mean, I don't have as much time to get stuff done, but it hasn't really been a problem so far."

"Oh, what's a little challenge?" Micah poured his batter into a pan and took it to an oven. "You learn what you know when you're under a little pressure. School's good for you, Tommen, even though you don't think so now."

*No, learning is good for you. School just sucks.* But he kept his mouth shut and went about his duties as needed. Prepping this, mixing that, baking, decorating, and occasionally switching spots with Kyle or relieving him so he could take a break.

Part of Tommen was pretty sure that even though his dad said he'd Suppressed Micah and Micaiah, that he really hadn't. Micah hadn't hired enough people to cover the amount of time and labor it would take to crank out their normal production, and yet somehow they were running at about ninety percent what they had been. He didn't see any Bands, but he still suspected that something was going on.

"So how are you holding up?" Tommen asked as Kyle returned to the counter. He couldn't say he was particularly interested, but he figured that, as manager, he should keep good relations with those under him.

"I have a steady job, a steady paycheck, so I'm good," Kyle said, not looking at him. "And Jenna's not working today, so I'm doing even better."

Tommen sighed. Other than coming together for a common cause in getting Micaiah to the hospital—two weeks ago—Kyle and Jenna had been at each other's throats. Kyle said she was a bitch who made everything about her sexuality. Jenna said he was an asshole who was intentionally being a dick because he hated lesbians and the whole ilk. Tommen had tried to solve the problem, failed miserably, and turned it over to Micah, who also failed miserably. The best solution they could come up with, short of firing them both, was to keep them on different tasks at different times, and make sure that their days off were back-to-back, that way they had two whole days of not having to see each other.

In the end, Tommen ignored the jab and returned to the kitchen to start on cleanup. As Micah pulled out the last of the baked goods, Tommen set to work on cleaning the ovens. At least with Kyle working, Tommen didn't have to worry about cleaning up front, so cleanup time felt like it got cut in half. But maybe that was just him.

"Tommen, your dad's here!" Kyle called from the front as Tommen was wiping down the large prep table.

"Okay!" he called back. *Not like I'm just going to drop my rag and run out the door with this stuff unfinished.*

"When do you get your license?" Micah asked as he emptied the sinks and started washing them.

Tommen paused and thought a second. "Um, I start the next driving course in March. After that, I have to take the road test which should be in September or October."

"Have you started looking for a car?"

"I kind of glanced through the ads, but I don't really want to start looking until I get closer to the actual road test."

"Don't put it off too long. It takes time to get to know a vehicle, and everything has to be pristine, on the nose when you take your test. They'll knock you for the dumbest things."

"I know. It's just been kind of on the backburner lately."

"Hey, I totally understand. But while life is a little calmer now and a little less hectic, you should take advantage of it. Since Time isn't taking up so much time, now is a good time to get your personal life in order."

*What personal life?* Tommen wanted to ask. He had no personal life. He had school. When he didn't have school, he had work. And when he didn't have work, he had the school play. And when he didn't have school or work or the play, he was doing important things like eating and sleeping. He had no personal life.

To outsiders, it might look like he had plenty of time at home to putter around and do his own thing. To some extent, that was true. His dad was plowing forward with the remodeling, and Tommen helped him when he could. But there was the other end of that spectrum, when he had to take care of his dad.

Tommen knew he could never begin to understand the horrors that prison—both back in Wales and in the Wheel—held for his dad. He couldn't imagine the fear that the darkness and shadows held for him. But he knew what it was like to look at that fear from the outside. On nights when his dad was shouting so loudly in his sleep, the only kind thing to do was wake him up, and even that was taking a serious risk as he came out of his nightmare like a bull ready to charge. Or, last week, they'd been walking through the grocery store when one of the lights in the freezer aisle flickered and burned out; Tommen had been fully prepared for his dad to drop to the ground wailing and screaming. Instead, they'd had to leave the aisle and find a quiet spot for him to collect himself and keep moving.

As he headed out to the car now, he tried to gauge what kind of a day it had been, whether they would be going home to finish up some project, or simply go straight to bed. His dad didn't drive well at night anymore either; he did it only out of necessity to pick up Tommen, but made him drive home. If Walter Forbes expected that he would be able to return to police work, Tommen was pretty certain he was in for a big surprise.

"Hey," Tommen greeted, throwing his backpack in the backseat and getting in the driver's seat, trying to sound friendly and cover up the dread that twisted his gut.

"How was work?" his dad asked, though his voice was strained. So it had been a bad day. Go home and go straight to bed, then.

Tommen shrugged. "Work."

"Micaiah come back yet?"

"No. Micah said the therapist was at their house today, and apparently he's clear to drive now."

"That's good." He sounded tired, as if he'd tried to sleep but found only terror. "How was school?"

"Same as always. Did you get any more remodeling done? You said you wanted to start on the cupboards."

"I did," his dad confirmed, shifting in his seat and seeming to come back to life a little. "I got most of the layers of paint stripped off. Figure I should be a little more careful now and try to find the original wood on purpose."

"Makes sense. You pick out a stain yet?"

"Not yet."

Tommen had read about soldiers returning home with PTSD. They weren't always violent; sometimes they just sat there. And stared. To everyone else, they stared into space. To them, they were back wherever their hell was, watching it go around and around and around and around, never ending. Tommen had never actually seen his dad do such a thing, but truthfully, they didn't see each other a whole lot during the day. Somehow, it wasn't difficult to imagine his dad sitting in his recliner, all the light in the house, but unable to see for the darkness that surrounded him.

Sometimes he wondered if it might be a good idea to contact Steggmann or someone at the police department and see if they couldn't possibly confiscate his guns for a short time. Only the Tracker attacks prevented him from doing such a thing. That, and the fact that he had no good story to give them as to why his dad took such a dramatic downturn, and why his expected fears didn't seem to line up with the events in question, the kidnapping and the warehouse and whatnot.

They made it home in good time, Walter leading the way in the event of another Tracker, but again the house was clear. Tommen followed behind meekly, slipping off to his room to drop off his backpack.

At the very least, his dad was able to keep himself busy with the remodeling. It was probably just as well that he had something to occupy his mind other than the nightmares. He'd managed to finish the paint job in his bedroom and had gotten new carpet installed. Other than some minor adjustments, his room was done, a brand new creation. The bathroom had also gotten repainted, but he was still putting off a new shower-tub and tile work. The living room hadn't been touched, but supposedly a new color was already picked out, as well as the possibility of hardwood floors. As for the kitchen, he was just getting around to that, starting off by scraping away all the decades of paint that coated the cabinets, sanding them smooth, and finishing them off with a nice coat of stain.

Tommen still considered repainting his room, just to go along with all the changes; his dad was already planning on replacing the carpet anyway. But he knew that it would probably be pointless to do so. He'd only picked out the current color—a green he couldn't comprehend—because it had a cool name on the sample card. As far as he was concerned, one gray was the same as any other. If his dad wanted to repaint it so it would match the new carpet, so be it, but he had no real opinion on the matter.

"Are you hungry?" his dad asked from the doorway.

"Yeah, I guess," Tommen replied.

Some days, Tommen wasn't sure if it was stress, lack thereof, or Time that caused him to not be hungry when he might normally be hungry. The usage of Time royally fucked with the body, resulting in slowed aging—or, as in rare cases, accelerated aging—and slowed metabolism and other normal bodily functions.

"If a Timekeeper stops using Time, how long until he starts aging again?" Tommen wondered, following his dad out to the kitchen.

"Depends," his dad answered.

"On what?"

"How long he's been exposed to Time, his skill level, how much he uses in a day, the nature of his disuse."

"What do you mean?"

"Suppression will cause a reversal faster than simple disuse. Like a lot of things, the body can become dependent on it. Even if he isn't actively Banding and using his abilities, his body may still use it within itself in order to keep the metabolism normal, or its version of normal."

"So, say, what about you? Or the twins?"

"Me? Well, the Acting Manager agreed to Lieutenants and under, but he still wants Captains to be active. I choose not to use my abilities, but I imagine my body is still leeching Time here and there. As for the twins, hard to say. They have Lieutenant skills but their use of Time is nearly constant. It might be sixty, seventy years before aging would have any effect on them again, maybe only fifty because of the Suppression."

"Sixty or seventy years?" Tommen's brows shot straight up. "Are you serious?"

"Once again, depends on exposure, skill, and use."

"So what am I? Like, six months?"

His dad shook his head, something like a tired smirk trying to twist its way onto his lips. "Time has barely begun to affect you in such a way. You're looking at early twenties before you start to see a noticeable change, that is, no change at all."

"Oh. Apprentices and Journeymen don't really get much out of the deal, then."

"Only the ability to control Time. Not like that's a huge deal."

Tommen grinned. So his dad wasn't completely lost, not if he could still make snarky, sarcastic comments when the occasion demanded.

Dinner ended up being some leftover pot roast with mashed potatoes, gravy, and scratch biscuits. For as lax as they two old-fashioned mountain men had become, the one thing that always had to be homemade was the biscuits. There was just no good substitute for fresh buttermilk biscuits coated in flour and drizzled with honey.

"You said your play practices start Monday?" Walter asked as they took their plates to the living room to eat.

"Um, they started a couple weeks ago," Tommen told him. "Mondays, Tuesdays, and some Thursdays."

"Right, you told me that."

"I mean, I don't have much to do right now because, you know, nothing is done. The set's not done and they're still reading from the script for their lines."

"What are you doing again?"

"Backstage help. Moving props and making sure people know when to go out."

"So if there's no set and no props, you have no work."

"No, but it's helpful to know the lines so I know them."

"And because there's a certain girl involved that you want to see?"

It was getting harder and harder to deny it in front of his dad, or in front of anyone else for that matter, so he just kept his mouth shut most of the time now.

"When are you going to ask her out? I've never seen you hold out this long."

Tommen felt his ears burn. "Well, I don't know..."

"Oh please, there has to be a reason. You won't even tell me what she looks like or show me a picture. Is she hideous?"

"No."

"Only got one eye, hunchback, pegleg like Micaiah?"

Tommen squirmed in his seat. "Well, not exactly. She's...she's a dwarf."

"So you won't ask her out because she's short?"

"Not just short, like, she is a literal textbook dwarf. Like, three-foot-eight or something like that."

"And why does that matter? Non-dwarf short people ask for your help all the time to do stuff, so that's nothing new."

"It doesn't matter. It's just...weird."

"The fact that it bothers you this much means it does matter. Does she like you?"

"I don't know. I haven't asked and I haven't heard anything."

"If she said she found it weird that you're so tall, how would that make you feel?"

Tommen sighed. "I know. I know it shouldn't matter. I mean, she's a really cool person. I don't know. If you met her, you'd understand."

"How can I meet her unless you ask her out? Have her over for dinner or something. You can't say you're still embarrassed about the house because it is getting remodeled."

Yeah, and Tommen could feel that excuse slipping away a little more every day. Once the living room got redone, it was over. No more excuse there. Even the kitchen by itself wasn't half bad, it was all about the living room.

"You're not going to work after practice, are you?" his dad asked after a minute of embarrassed silence.

"Huh? No. It'll be too late and the bakery closes early."

"So I'll have to come get you."

"If that's okay...I can probably ask Micah; he'd probably enjoy a quick break in the middle of the day." Tommen watched his dad, trying to judge his expression. The days were getting longer, but slowly, and it was still pretty dark out at five o'clock.

His dad shook his head. "No, no, that's fine. Just thinking about how I'm going to plan my day, what I need to get done and what time I should get cleaned up to come and get you." *Nice excuse.* "And who knows, maybe I'll get there just a little early to catch the end of practice. I'll get a little early access to the play and I might even embarrass you in front of your girlfriend."

And so it was that come Monday after school, Tommen was torn between wanting to make every excuse to visit Becky, and using every excuse to stay away from her. He wasn't even sure if he was horrified or relieved when Layman intercepted him on his way to the auditorium.

"Afternoon, Tommen," Layman greeted.

"Hi," Tommen said suspiciously. He hadn't gotten in any fights lately, at least not that he could remember. He was trying to keep his nose clean, really he was.

"How's your dad doing lately?"

"Um, he's okay. Not back to work yet, though. But soon."

"Glad to hear it. And how about yourself? Everything good at home?"

"Yeah..." Where was this going?

"Your arm is healing okay? And your head? After your...I heard it was a skiing accident?" Layman raised a brow.

"Yeah, I'm fine. What are you...? No. You're insane. Me and my dad are cool."

"I didn't say anything," Layman said, but his tone said a whole lot more.

"You don't have to," Tommen informed him. "It was a skiing accident. Even got video of it. My dad is fine, and he'll be going back to work hopefully in the next few weeks."

"Good to hear. Enjoy rehearsal."

Tommen pushed past Layman into the auditorium, fuming. Did the man actually think that his dad was unstable and abusing him? What an asshole! What a fucking asshole. For fuck's sake, what the hell?

He tried to keep calm as he took a seat and waited for the director with the rest of them. A broken arm and concussion wouldn't normally be enough to rouse that kind of suspicion, would it? Maybe Layman had run into his dad at some home improvement or hardware store and they got to talking. Maybe his dad had said or done something that tipped Layman off.

Well, either way, they were cool. Suggesting anything otherwise made his blood boil. If Layman only knew some of the things they'd gone through, he might—

"Hey."

Tommen looked up—or, more accurately, to one side—as Becky sat down beside him, her huge beach bag full of sewing materials taking up the seat next to her and heavy enough to effectively weigh it down.

"Hi." Tommen grinned stupidly.

"I saw you talking to Layman. Everything okay? I mean, you don't have to tell me, I'm just curious."

She'd gotten better about that, the nosiness. She could still be an endless fountain of questions, but her discretion was better.

"Um, yeah," Tommen answered, looking at the seat in front of him. "No, it's good."

"Doesn't sound good." Her tone was a question all its own.

Tommen shrugged. "Layman was always good about keeping me and Tyler apart and respecting that I was always acting in self-defense and never threw the first punch. But some days I'd like to deck him just as much."

"I don't think you'd get very far if you did that."

"No, not likely."

They didn't get to speak more before Mr. Martin the director appeared and whistled for everyone's attention.

"All right, quiet down," he said, the lead role model for how to project a voice. "The sooner we start, the sooner you can all get out of here to your homes or jobs or other appointments. Today we'll be going over the opening scene and the transition into the second scene..."

Tommen tuned him out for the most part, paying only enough attention to know when certain key words and terms might involve him. They were still about two months out from the show. There had been some debate as to whether it wouldn't have been better to hold the play before spring break, send everyone off on a light note and something to talk about. Had the rehearsals been more frequent and longer than an hour or two at a time, and were the cast and crew not only more experienced but more mature, that might have been possible. As it was, three weeks in and Tommen knew the lines better than some of the actors just by sheer exposure and repetition. The only reason the actors themselves didn't know the lines was because they were usually too busy cracking jokes about them—clean on stage, and very, very dirty offstage. Not that Tommen didn't participate in the merrymaking a little, but it was killing their production; the final blow would be dealt on opening night.

That was to say nothing of the set. The framework was built, a project done by the architecture and woodshop classes, and only because it was a class project did it get done. Robinson had enlisted the help of his Art Therapy and AP Art classes, but that was a disaster idea from the beginning. Other than the two students who happened to overlap both classes, the former was for the outcasts and the latter for the snooty overachievers, just like any advanced placement class. The AP kids automatically assumed they were in charge and did nothing but disparage and discourage the therapy kids and use them as gophers. The therapy kids pulled pranks and otherwise got revenge. In the end, out of a good twenty-five pairs of helping hands, only six were left and most of them had lives that needed tending to more than the set.

So in Tommen's opinion, the play was doomed. The only part of the production that was mum on the complaints was the sewing department, e.g., Becky. She wasn't the only seamstress, of course, but she was the only student seamstress. Robinson and Martin had come to an agreement that appropriate, properly-fitting garments probably shouldn't be left to the hands of horny, sex-driven teenagers who barely knew what a sewing machine was. Once Becky presented her professional portfolio, she'd been ushered in as the leader, but her team consisted of Robinson, his wife, and several volunteer moms and grandmas.

"Tommen, where are you, Tommen?"

Tommen came back to life as he heard his name. Slowly he pulled himself upright in his seat. "Um, here."

Martin pointed to him. "Tommen, help Becky move some of her things, then I want you here with me."

Of course, those in assembly all made the "ooh" noise as if he'd done something wrong and being next to Martin was a punishment. Actually, in theater, it was anything but. He was going to be next to the director. Most likely he was going to be running around for this thing or that thing, taking notes and memos to various members of cast and crew, but he was going to be the director's assistant. He would be writing down all of Martin's notes and observations, privy to his secret musings about the play.

Basically, he was going to be important. Like being manager at the bakery. He enjoyed it. Yeah, it was a lot of responsibility and he wasn't sure about opening by himself on Saturdays, but he could do it. He liked it. He finally got his reward for his hard work; he was recognized. He had power.

"Okay, let's go," Becky said, jerking him from his thoughts.

He didn't say anything, following her and hoping he hadn't missed too much of an important conversation. Becky didn't call him out, so he figured he must be doing okay so far.

He ended up following her out to the parking lot where a large minivan sat with its back hatch open wide, an older woman reaching in and dragging out several clear plastic tubs with all manner of sewing items, from fabric to needles to thread and mashed up paper. It was almost dizzying to think that such a box of junk was going to turn into breathtaking costumes for the play.

"*Megfogtam a kádakat a zöld fedéllel, mint te megkérdezte,*" the woman said. *"Mindez volt?"* (I grabbed the tubs with the green lids like you asked. Was this all?)

*"Úgy néz ki,"* Becky said, inspecting the tubs. (Looks like it.)

The woman looked past her to Tommen. "Who's your friend?"

Tommen felt his ears turn red as he made the connection even before she spoke. "Mom, this is Tommen."

"Oh, the boy you keep telling us about?" Her eyes glittered with mischief. "Very nice to meet you, Tommen."

"Thank you." Thank you? "I mean, um, nice to meet you, too. Mrs. Polski."

The lady Polski grinned and shook her head as she grabbed a tub. Tommen moved forward quickly to grab another one. Becky grabbed a third, probably the lightest one though she still looked a little strained. Mrs. Polski was still talking. "You know, Becky, you should tell him the story of that name." She lowered her voice. "It's a good one." She winked at Tommen.

"Mom, you know that's a story I keep in reserve," Becky told her, though her tone suggested she was itching to tell it anyway.

Tommen took the bait. "Reserve for what?"

"For any boys I date."

Her words stung more than Tommen thought they should. She saved that story for the boys she dated. She wasn't going to tell him the story which meant they weren't dating. He hadn't really thought they were—he'd been going to great lengths to deny it—and they didn't really see each other outside of school, though she did sometimes drop by the bakery. But still...he liked her. It was pretty dang obvious he liked her. And she had picked him to help her. Didn't that mean she liked him? Or was he just a convenient choice, given the circumstances?

Of course, maybe she'd had that little exchange with her mom for the sole purpose of telling him in a roundabout way to officially ask her out. They could have easily spoken in Hungarian or whatever language in order to keep him out of the loop, but they'd deliberately used English. Had they? Was he reading too far into this? Maybe they were using that exchange to secretly...femininely insult him. After all, they both used the word "boy" when he was clearly a man or near enough. Maybe they were calling him small and weak?

He batted back and forth in his mind the likelihood of Becky—whom he would honestly like to see get into an argument with Micaiah one time—going from blunt and nosy to secretive and girly. She didn't pull punches when it came to her opinion or the way things ought to be done, so why would she suddenly change?

On the other hand, if her dad was Jewish and her mom was Catholic, maybe this was one area where she was obligated to be a little more traditional. Girls didn't ask boys out on a date; it's just the way things were. He had to be man enough to go up to her and talk to her and ask her out. The first two he had little problem with. It was that third thing that scared the shit out of him. He couldn't even say why. He had a fair relationship with her dad, and her mom wasn't clawing his eyes out. She was obviously dropping hints...wasn't she? Was this what dropping hints looked like? He was more accustomed to girls who all but screamed "fuck me on the first date" so this was largely uncharted territory for him.

Maybe he was just seeing signals that weren't there, looking for magical signs in random leaf patterns or other mystical bullshit. Maybe his mind was in overdrive. On the other hand, if he really wanted to hear that story—and by default, date her—why not just ask? What's the worst that could happen, right?

He didn't really want to consider those possibilities; there were too many of them.

They marched single-filed into the classroom. It was the classroom used for architecture, mechanical drafting, and other assorted hands-on classes. It was less than ideal given the omnipresent layer of dust—of both the dust bunny and sawdust kind—but it had all the measuring tools the seamstresses could want, as well as a number of sharpening tools for their scissors. There were probably other things around the room that Becky could find to use if she put her mind to it. That much Tommen had learned in Physics:

don't leave her alone with any objects you don't want dismantled and potentially put back together into something entirely different. Didn't matter if her contraption worked or not, she would be proud of it and felt the need to show it off.

"Just...set them on the table," Becky instructed, huffing.

Tommen set his down and reached for her tub, relieving the burden and keeping an eye on her as she found a stool at one of the tables.

"You okay?" he wondered.

She put a hand to her forehead and checked her insulin pump. "I think I need a candy bar or something."

Her mom dug in one of her coat pockets, bringing out a handful of wrapped chocolate candies. "Something for just such an emergency. I'll go grab you something to eat."

Becky simply nodded her thanks and unwrapped and ate the candies two at a time, coming back to life after only a minute or two.

"Seriously, like, are you okay?" Tommen asked.

"Yeah, I'm fine," Becky told him, moving to brush off a table. "I just lost track of myself, that's all."

"If you're sure. I mean, I don't want to see anything happen to you."

She raised a brow and for the second time that day, he felt his ears turn red. "The Chivalrous Welshman strikes again."

Well, he'd meant it. In the I-don't-want-to-have-to-call-an-ambulance-and-explain-to-your-dad-what-happened-and-why-we-were-alone-in-a-room kind of way. Anyone else would have felt the same, or at least he hoped they would.

After a second, she looked up from the bins at him. "Don't you have to be down with Mr. Martin?"

"Yes. Right. Um. Yeah. Thanks. I mean, you're welcome. For the help. Bringing the things in. Glad you're okay. Yeah, I'll just...I'll go."

He spent the entire walk from the classroom to the auditorium cursing himself and his stupidity. He should have known, should have remembered, should have helped her, made sure she was okay, then removed himself with all the grace and flourish as befitting the Chivalrous Welshman and gone about his business.

Problem was, he did help her, did make sure she was okay, and he really had left with all the grace and flourish as befitting him. That is, he had none. No grace and no flourish. The Chivalrous Welshman had no real victories to speak of, so he wasn't exactly well-practiced in the art of shaking hands, kissing babies, and sweeping fair maidens off their feet. More than likely, he would get his hand broken, make the baby cry, and drop the fair maiden. Then fall on top of her.

So he entered the auditorium feeling sullen and deflated. Yeah, he was the manager at the bakery, but so what? He still did all the same grunt work as the others, still had to deal with the angry customers. Actually, he had to deal with the angry customers more since Kyle and Jenna deflected them to him. And yeah, he was the director's assistant, the one who got his coffee and wrote down every word he said, but with no real voice or opinion of his own that would be heard and acted upon.

"Oh, you're here," Mr. Martin said, turning around as he walked down the aisle. "I didn't think you'd be back so fast."

"Figured my place was here," Tommen told him, trying to keep as much edge out of his voice as possible.

"Good. Here's a notebook and a pen."

Tommen couldn't even say why or how he'd gone from on top of the world to surly and sullen. The day just seemed to be a rollercoaster of elation and fury. Maybe it was just one of those Monday things. Four more fucking days of the same fucking thing. First school, then three days of play practice and three days of work. Damn monotony.

Not that he had any desire for any of the excitement he'd been exposed to lately, but he could really do with some excitement, probably of the nicer Time variety. He was supposed to be training as an Apprentice, learning all sorts of cool new things. Forget simple

Banding; that was just a party trick to keep the probationary interested, a taste to whet the appetite of the meal to come. He wanted to learn how to do some of the things Micah and Micaiah could do. Collapsing portals, holy shit. That was a party trick, except it wasn't a trick. Of course, there was a long ways to go between Apprentice and Lieutenant, but still, baby steps, right? Building blocks. Just keep putting one block on top of another and soon you've got yourself a tower.

Point was, he wasn't supposed to be stuck here in this auditorium with this shitty production. He didn't really want to be here anyway. How had he gotten mixed up in this in the first place? Wasn't because Mr. Layman and Mrs. Wendell had suggested it as a way to cope with his stress, that was for sure.

Nope, he'd joined because he was following a girl. Wars had been started over similar circumstances, so he figured that being stuck here was comparatively better.

What if he left the play, just got up, walked out, and never came back?

Well, for one thing, that wouldn't send a very good image to the Powers That Be. Layman already thought Walter was abusing Tommen, and dropping out like some emo, depressed kid wasn't going to help that ill-conceived notion any. To say nothing of how Mr. Martin, Mr. Robinson, and the rest of the staff would treat him if and when they found out. God forbid the Chivalrous Welshman quit anything he started. Problem was, he didn't really have a good reason to give as to why he would quit. His dad was on the mend and he didn't have to work three jobs to support a drug addict mom and six destitute siblings in elementary school.

But, of far greater importance than the Powers That Be was Becky and her opinion of him if he quit. Would she shun him? Would she hound him with questions to which he had no good answers? Would she think less of him because he quit? Would she think more of him if he admitted he couldn't handle it?

Problem was, he really could handle it if he put his mind to it.

After all, if he left the play, the only thing he would be trading it for was more shifts at work. An hour and a half of boring ass rehearsal...or four hours of boring ass work? The only reason he even considered work was because then he got a paycheck for his trouble.

Rehearsal plodded along slowly and couldn't have ended too soon. He gave Martin back his notebook and the detailed notes therein, noting the director's expression when he saw just how attentive Tommen had been. *Yeah, imagine how much more I could have done if I wasn't sulking this whole time.*

He headed for the door to the parking lot, then paused and went back to the sewing room. To his shock and horror, his dad was standing near the doorway, chatting with Becky and her mom while they packed up their things.

"There you are," his dad said when he noticed him. He seemed completely normal. "Ready to go?"

"H-how long have you been here?" Tommen asked, his gaze darting back and forth between his dad and Becky and her mom, both of whom smiled, giggled, and said things in Hungarian.

"Long enough. Got your backpack and things?"

"Yeah."

"All right, I'll be out in the car so you can say goodbye."

Tommen's breath caught in his throat as his dad said that and left the room. He felt frozen to the floor, unable to move or do anything as Becky and her mom put the lids on the tubs. Finally, he got his legs to move, then his arms as he carried a tub back out to the van, all in silence.

"Thank you, Tommen," Becky said as the tubs were loaded up.

"*Croeso,*" he mumbled in reply. "Er, you're welcome."

"See you tomorrow in Physics."

And that was that. No "I had a good time" or "We should do this again" or any of that. No goodbye hug or kiss. He simply got out of their way as the van backed up and pulled out of the lot. A second later, he turned his back and crossed the parking lot to where his dad was waiting.

# Chapter Eleven
## The Precinct

"So, Walter, how are you feeling?" the physical therapist asked as the session ended and they headed to the reception counter.

"If not for the remodeling, I'd be going insane," Walter answered him, trying to sound the appropriate mixture of annoyed by the therapy and eager to get back to work, without letting on about the real insanity he was afraid he was slipping into.

"Good news for you then, because these papers here—" He grabbed a few from the printer and searched for a pen amid the mess of papers. "—are going to get you back to work."

"I'm good to go?" Walter took the papers in disbelief.

"Well, that's up to your commanding officer, I would think, but everything on my part says you are clear to make a comeback."

"But I still need PT."

"Four more weeks, yes. Just to be sure. But honestly, it's not all that uncommon. Police officers put up with a lot of shit, and not all of it from the outside. How many guys you know go to a chiropractor or PT or something else on a regular basis? How many of them wear knee braces or elbow braces? Uh huh, that's what I thought. Truthfully, you're in a lot better shape than some who are on active duty right now. My opinion, of course, I have nothing but respect for you and what you do."

"I understand. Is there anything else I need from you?" Walter looked through the papers.

"If there is, just give us a holler, and we can fax the papers wherever you need them."

Walter thanked him and left the doctor's office, completely

cane free for the last three days. His leg still ached and he still limped a little, but he was walking on his own two feet again. That was more than he could say for Micaiah, sadly. He occasionally texted or called and left a message, trying to be polite and respect his space but wanting to let him know that he cared. Micaiah rarely responded beyond one word, dead end answers, and Micah would only shrug and say that he was doing okay, still coping, not quite coming around just yet.

Didn't matter a whole lot, he supposed, inasmuch as Time was concerned. Supposedly Micah had been attacked by a Tracker one morning at work, but quickly took it out with his concealed carry. Other than that, Time lay dormant among them. Well, not completely dormant. Walter hadn't been Suppressed, but he chose not to use his abilities.

He told himself it was because of the Trackers, but the deeper reason lay hidden, known only to his own mind. In a way, Time frightened him. After what happened in the Wheel, in the Judgment Wing...in the black cells...even for as skilled as he was in Time, he knew it was useless against Rifun. And that terrified him.

It terrified him even more than some of the other people on the road as he drove from the doctor's office to the precinct. He only had to hold it together for a little while, enough to pass the psychological evaluation. After that, he could get back to work, get back to his routine, and get back to his regular life. Remodeling was nice and all, but even that stress was starting to wear on his nerves. He'd gotten the kitchen cabinets done and he had the new flooring for the living room and hallway coming next Tuesday. The only real thing he had left was the shower and tile in the bathroom which he'd have to get a contractor to do, and the wallpaper in the living room and kitchen. He just wasn't sure if he was ready to deal with the mess of removing wallpaper.

He arrived at the precinct and parked. It was a moment before he went inside.

"You think any harder, smoke'll be coming out your ears."

Walter was roused from his thoughts at Cynthia's voice. She grinned. "How ya doin', Walt?"

He handed her the doctor's papers. "You tell me."

She took the papers and looked them over, bringing her glasses down off her head. "Well, according to this paperwork, I'd say you are doing a lot better than you were a little over a month ago."

"Amen to that." He leaned on the high counter. "So, what's the news around the water cooler? What am I coming back to?"

Cynthia raised a brow and gave him a mischievous look. "Think you're coming back that fast, huh?"

"I figure there are a few more hoops I'll have to hobble through. Just give me the highlights."

She grinned and shook her head. "Walter, Walter. Let's see, we've hired five new guys since the first of the year and they're eyeing a few candidates coming out of the academy this spring. Eric Wilson is on leave for a week; his wife just had their second. And Jim and Terry are working together now since you've been gone. They work well, but it's just not the same as you and Jim."

"Terry can be a bit of a stiff, but he's a good guy."

"I'll get these to Steggmann and have him call you," Cynthia told him, filing the papers. "He's swamped with meetings this morning."

Right, first Friday of the month. The best time to do meetings because everyone involved would be out of the office and conveniently unavailable over the weekend for any inquiries. By the time Monday rolled around, everything was forgotten or seemed unimportant, so there was rarely any opposition.

"Of course," Walter said. "Apparently I've been away a while."

"It'll be good to have you back, but don't waste your time pining for your cubicle. We've all heard the stories about how you're bringing your house out of the seventies."

"Sixties. And believe me, it's long overdue. Thanks, Cynthia."

He left the precinct and went to sit in his car for a minute, unsure what to do next. He'd fully intended on speaking with Steggmann, but completely forgotten about the meetings. And what had he expected anyway? A how-do-you-do, pat on the back for his recovery, and sent to work an eight hour shift? He still had to undergo the psych eval, and assuming he passed everything with flying colors, he was still looking at another week or two before he was back on the clock.

Well, might as well get some lunch before heading home to keep working. He headed in the direction of the bakery, then diverted to a nearby deli. Micah had enough to do without him barging in and wanting to talk. Tommen would be in soon, but he didn't want to bother him either. From what everyone said, he was doing a good job, training to be manager; Walter didn't need to mess that up by going in and distracting him. The boy was becoming a man, facing more evil than any human being should ever have to, and that included more responsibility at work, having to balance work and school, which included the school play.

And if things went the way they were looking, it would also mean throwing a girlfriend into that balancing act. There was a joke to be made about Becky's short stature being easy to balance, but if his five-minute conversation with her and her mother had been any indication, she was no petite flower. Her mother actually described her as more of a bulldog, not the biggest of the dogs but definitely a force to be reckoned with, with equal parts bark and bite.

Personally, Walter couldn't see the relationship lasting more than a few months, but it would be entertaining to watch while it lasted. Tommen would be sent spiraling in all directions as his confrontational attitude and personal code of chivalry were suddenly pitted against each other with just this one girl. Oh, to be young and in love again.

He was in the middle of his sandwich when his phone rang. It was the precinct.

"Walter Forbes," he answered.

"Walt, it's Greg," Steggmann said. "Cynthia said you came by today. Dropped off your PT paperwork. I got a chance to look at it and from what I can see, it says you're good to go."

"Well, I hope that's what it said, else I need new glasses."

"Listen, I'm on a tight schedule today with a ton of meetings. Why don't you come in Monday morning and we'll have a chat? I'll see if I can't get the shrink down here for your eval, too, so we can knock out two birds with one stone. But that's only if you're interested in coming back soon. You still have some time."

"Can't think of anything I'd rather do."

"Great. How does seven sound? Or maybe eight, since I imagine you're pretty accustomed to sleeping in now."

Sounded atrociously early either way he put it. Still, eight o'clock wouldn't be bad; he could drop Tommen off at school and head over, and he told Steggmann as much.

"Excellent," Steggmann finished. "I'll see you on Monday then."

He hung up before Walter could say more. If he had to guess, the man had probably escaped his captors and hidden out either in the storage room, the bathroom, or one of the unused offices, in order to make a few phone calls and do some work besides just the meetings.

Oddly enough, for as much as he'd been looking forward to getting back to work, now that he was going to meet with Steggmann, he found that he didn't particularly want to. He just wanted to get cleared by the doctor and start back to work. He was even okay if he had to go part-time for a little while until his therapy was fully and completely over. He just hated all the meetings and the evaluations and the hoops.

But for all his misgivings, he still found himself in Steggmann's office early Monday morning after taking Tommen to school. In the event that the shrink was able to come in, he'd been careful not to take any of his pills. He still used them for the pain, but the last thing he needed was to be pegged as some kind of addict in his recovery. He thought that he was managing his pill use very well, but he wasn't going to take any chances here today.

Still, the way his leg was cramping, maybe he should have taken one when he first got up; it would have worn off a little by now, right? Enough to stave off suspicion?

The door opened and Steggmann walked in, heading for the small coffeemaker in the corner of his office and filling his mug. "Get you some coffee? You look like you could use it."

Walter felt like he needed a cup or five. Maybe it was just his normal restlessness or his anxiety over this meeting and the eval and coming back to work, but he felt as if he hadn't slept eight hours total over the whole weekend. Tommen had had to wake him up a few times in the past, but he couldn't recall that that had been the case recently. Still, he politely accepted a cup of coffee, hoping it came across as good humor. *Ha ha, you've been off for five weeks, you've been sleeping in until noon, now you have to get up early. Still want to come back, Walt old boy?*

"So, Walt, how the hell are you?" Steggmann asked, leaning back in his chair but still not looking relaxed.

"Been better, but I've sure been a hell of a lot worse," Walter answered.

"Amen to that. Believe me, I never felt more relieved than when your boy made a fool of me. Your name was included at the memorial speech because everyone expected you to die that day or within the next couple days. Then Tommen tells me you made a miraculous recovery and were awake and talking." He shook his head and took a drink. "Other than therapy, what have you been doing with yourself?"

Walter described the remodeling endeavor. Steggmann's brows went sky high.

"You mean you're actually bringing your house into the twenty-first century?"

"Can only try."

"And how's your kid? I heard he had some permanent hearing loss or something?"

"Yes, he has to have hearing aids now."

"How's he taking it?"

"He's...adapting. I think what kills him the most is the actual putting in and taking out of the hearing aids because it's a constant reminder of what happened, but other than that, during the day, I think he's just gotten used to it. For the most part."

"Not easy for a teenager who thinks he's invincible."

"No, but he'll get used to it."

"And things between you two are okay?"

Walter nodded and took a drink, buying time to formulate an answer. "Some days I think he still thinks I'm dying—well, maybe not dying, but crippled and incapable. Only injured, not helpless, and I'm getting better. I don't even need a cane anymore."

"I saw that. Good for you." Steggmann shifted in his seat, his demeanor telling Walter that friendly talk was over and now they were going to get down to business. "As for any physical concerns, I can't say that I have any, at least nothing severe enough to keep you out a little while longer, as long as you believe you are physically capable of returning to work. If you're doing your own remodeling, you must be in pretty good physical shape, and the PT seems to agree. Watching you this morning, I don't get the feeling that you're straining and just trying to put on a good face while your leg is secretly killing you."

"Everything feels pretty good," Walter confirmed. Even his shoulders were feeling better since his shoulder blades had healed.

"That's good to hear. But you know that the only ones around here in perfect shape are the kids from the academy, and even a few of them have problems. Physical things are easy to fix and manage. The main concern, as you may well have guessed, is what's going on upstairs. Psychological problems. This is especially a concern for you since it was your son being held hostage."

Because Walter could have forgotten that in two months. Still, he nodded politely and took another drink of coffee. "I understand. And if I didn't think I could come back and do the job, I wouldn't be here."

"Well, there's thinking you can do the job, and getting out there and realizing your demons aren't sitting at home watching TV."

Walter understood that notion all too well. It wasn't just about the night light either. Certain smells were liable to set off his mental red alert, his instinct to flee, the most common smell being heavy rot and decay, with sewage being a close second. Certain actions, even observed in broad daylight would confuse him for a second, make him question where he was. Once he picked up Tommen from school and saw one boy dragging another under the arms in some game or joke, and for a full second, Walter only saw a guard carrying off another prisoner.

The worst part was the knowledge that he couldn't stop it. He could control his reaction, wrangle the fear and beat down his flight instinct, but he couldn't control the fear. He couldn't not smell the stench of his own waste and decay as he lay in his cell. He couldn't not see the prisoner being taken away, to die cold and alone, forgotten by the rest of humanity.

Spending another year in a similar hell hadn't help any either. In fact, it only made things worse. Seventy years removed and he'd been able to muster his courage and manipulate a little Time in order to get his police job in the first place. This time, though, he wasn't so sure. He still had the ability to Band Time and buy himself some breathing room, but that would only fool the shrink. Steggmann was right; his demons wouldn't just sit at home and watch TV. They'd be right up there with him on the frontlines. The last thing he needed was to have some panic attack in the middle of a firefight and put his guys at risk.

"So, I have the shrink coming in at eleven," Steggmann was saying. "What will happen is he will talk to you, interview you, ask you about what happened, what's happened since—"

"And how that makes me feel?" Walter wondered, trying to interject some humor into the conversation. It fell flat.

"—and all the stuff that a shrink does. He'll make a determination, he'll tell me, we'll talk, then I'll call you and we'll talk.

How does that sound?"

Walter's first thought was that it sounded like he'd just completely wasted his time here and he could have slept in a little later. But he didn't say that out loud, instead opting for the more polite, "Sounds like a plan. Is there anything else you needed me for? As far as sticking around here?"

Steggmann shook his head and chuckled. "No, you're free to return to your bed for a few more hours."

How he wanted to, but between the coffee and being up for this long, Walter knew he wasn't going to be able to get back to sleep, no matter how exhausted he felt. The best he could do was finish moving the living room furniture out of the way so the flooring guys could get in and start working tomorrow. Tommen had helped him move the big stuff yesterday, so all that was left were end tables, lamps, and the picture frames so they didn't get accidentally knocked down and broken.

He actually ended up returning to the precinct a little early as it didn't take as long as he thought it would. He could have Banded and closed the gap, but he didn't want to risk another Tracker attack. Cynthia greeted him again as he walked in.

"The doctor is waiting for you," she said in a mock-pretty-young-receptionist voice.

"Which one is it?" Walter asked suspiciously.

"Tequila."

The doctor's last name was literally Tequila, supposedly because his grandfather had been a nobody who became a somebody by his excellent bartending and legendary homemade tequila in Costa Rica. Whether by some humor from his parents or a mistype at the hospital, his legal first name was ironically Martini. Dr. Martini Tequila. Oh, the man had heard it all.

But if anyone cared to get to know the guy, he was actually a decent fellow. He wasn't the type of shrink who made his patients feel uncomfortable or awkward; he was one of the few who could actually have a decent conversation with his patients while still getting whatever information he needed, at least for his professional evaluations. Walter had been to see him several times after catastrophic incidents, so he had a pretty good idea of how this was going to go. The problem with Tequila being so good at his ease of conversation was that there was no good way to guard against it, no way to game the system, at least no way that Walter knew of.

"Good morning, Walter," the man greeted as Walter walked in the door.

Even now, Walter knew that this was part of the evaluation, whether he admitted it or not. It was equal parts infuriating and encouraging. Encouraging, because it was the ease of conversation and the confidence builder. Infuriating, because that meant that the man was always analyzing and evaluating and couldn't take two seconds to just simply be friendly.

"Morning, Martin," Walter replied.

"Greg told me you've been through quite a bit in the last couple months."

*Is that all it's been?* "Maybe a little more than the average person, but I figure I'm no worse for wear."

"Well, we'll see about that. Can I get you something to drink? Coffee, tea, water?"

Walter accepted a glass of water and Tequila got himself a fresh cup of coffee.

"Believe me when I say I have a pretty good idea of what happened —" *After talking to all the other survivors plus some of the other guys who were close friends with the people who died.* " —but I guess you have a unique perspective. Why don't we start there?"

It was the first and last real "break" that Tequila had for the entire session, the only time he actually sounded like a shrink and was asking what happened and how that made him feel. Walter was positive that their conversation was very specific and very directed, but it felt so natural. Anyone can lie to a shrink when they're acting like a shrink, and probably a lot of people did. But when having a normal conversation, even if it was carefully constructed, it felt rude for Walter to fudge details and play down events and even outright lie, even if eighty percent of it was absolutely necessary because of Time.

But that was how it went down. For the next two hours, they simply talked. Walter did most of the talking, but Tequila asked polite, if direct, questions and waited patiently for him to figure out his thoughts and put things in order as he remembered them.

He didn't particularly enjoy remembering the events of the warehouse, although in his own private thoughts he found it fascinating how far away it all seemed. Out here in the real world, it was still a pretty fresh wound. Walter was over a year removed from it, not that the circumstances of his absence was anything to celebrate. Still, it was as though he'd stepped ahead of the rest of the group and was looking back on everything, seeing everything with a bird's eye view now.

Maybe it helped him, maybe it didn't. The best that he could do was choose his words carefully and hope that he portrayed himself as stoic and determined to get back out there on the job again, and give away nothing of his time in the black cells. If he gave away some fear, he hoped it was reasonable fear, or what might be considered reasonable; no one could be expected to be fully and completely recovered by now, right? Just recovered enough to stay focused on the job and not freeze up when it mattered most and put more lives at risk.

On the other hand, what if he was going about this the wrong way? What if Tequila thought he was being too careful? Would he think he was hiding something? Would he think he was trying to be too tough, too strong? They didn't work together, so what Jim might describe as being thoughtful and careful, Tequila might interpret as being suspicious in some psychoanalytical way. Was that fair, then? Had any police officers ever been dismissed because of misinterpreted words and body language? How did you fight something like that?

What would happen if Walter failed this evaluation? Would he be given a second chance after some more time? Would they offer him a different position, something other than homicide? Or would they simply dismiss him, send him off with some kind of severance package? He racked his brain, trying to bring to mind any others who had failed the evaluation and what had happened to them. He could think of a few people. A couple had no business going back into any kind of police force in any position. But the others...he couldn't remember what had happened to the others.

Well, there was Pat. He'd taken retirement rather than go back to work, but what had gone on during his evaluation? Had he been in some sort of crisis, trying to reconcile what he knew to be true and the sudden reality of rock monsters?

An even worse thought crossed Walter's mind: what if Tequila was going to somehow cross-reference his conversation here with the testimonies of the others involved? It wasn't just about the bare facts, though they were important and Walter had done his best to keep everything "true," but it was about the attitude, the emotion, all the little things that shrinks looked for.

This could be harder than he thought.

Still, he did his best. The worst he could do was not answer or lie, but in conversation format, either of those options was nearly impossible. He wasn't sure how comfortable he was supposed to be in order to pass, but he tried to bring to mind all the other times they'd sat and spoken, how he'd behaved, maybe some things he'd said or how he'd said them.

Or could Tequila tell that was what he was doing? Was he watching for some subtle cues, little movements or slips of the tongue that Walter wasn't even consciously aware of? Was he overthinking the whole thing? Was it showing? Was he sweating? Maybe he should just take a breath, calm down, and reapproach this whole thing like a rational human being.

"Well, it's been good talking to you, Walt," Tequila said suddenly as Walter finished up some narrative or another. What had they been talking about just now anyway? Something about Tommen and the school play, maybe. Sounded right. "But I think I have everything I need."

"So what's the verdict? Am I clear to return to work?" Walter asked, standing and following him to the door.

"I'll talk to Greg and we'll decide how to proceed from there."

"Is that a good or bad thing? I'm not a shrink, I can't read subtle cues."

Tequila laughed. "Don't worry yourself, Walter. You don't have to be a shrink to read me. Trick is, most people think you do, so they trick themselves into thinking they can't."

Walter shook his head. "We're going to talk to Steggmann, then?"

"No, I'm going to talk to Steggmann. After we've talked, then we call you in."

"Feels like parent-teacher conferences, except I'm not the parent or the teacher. How long do you expect it to take?"

"There's how long I think it will take, and how long it will actually take. My money's on how long it will actually take, which I'd say is maybe an hour. Plenty of time for you to grab lunch and come back." He chuckled. "Parent and teacher will call you in when they're ready."

It was another test. It had to be. To see how he would react to being called a child even though he himself had started the metaphor. He didn't like it, but he was too slow to come up with a convincing reaction otherwise. Instead he simply frowned, grunted his reluctant assent, and elected to head out for lunch.

He hated this waiting game; it was like hitting every red light through traffic. Start and stop, start and stop. When was he going to hit the green light and just cruise right through?

Actually, maybe it wasn't so much like hitting every red light, as hitting road construction, the one lane kind with the flag turner who could stand there and make you wait for an hour if he wanted to because he had nothing better to do that day, at least until quitting time. Right now, Tequila was that flag turner. Walter sat looking at him, waiting for the go ahead, but it just seemed to take forever.

He spent his lunch trying to decide if the man was being coy about people trying to read him. Then he tried to dissect his words, figure out whether the meeting he and Steggmann were in now was a good one or a bad one. If there was no problem, it shouldn't take long, right? Tequila was only there as the shrink, reporting on his mental status; Steggmann was the one who would actually decide whether Walter would be returning to homicide or some other department, the number of hours per week, and so on. And that ought to be decided while the subject of their conversation was present. Right?

Even when he returned to the precinct, taking it just a little slower, a little longer, looking for a good parking spot instead of the just the first one he saw, Cynthia shook her head and informed him that they weren't ready for him.

"Any idea how it's going?" he asked, trying not to sound desperate or whiny.

"If they're not shouting, I can't hear," she told him. "Sorry."

"Does it usually take this long?"

"Well, normally it takes longer, but that's usually because Greg's busy doing three things at once."

So there was hope. Not really wanting to stay and wait, but not wanting to keep leaving and coming back, Walter elected to sit and read a magazine, try to take his mind off the whole thing. It didn't help that the current issue of the premier police magazine was on officer mental health, especially since the uptick of violence in cities had resulted in a number of police officer deaths.

He set that magazine aside and opted for the newspaper.

He'd barely gotten halfway into the article when the door opened and Steggmann poked his head out, looking at Cynthia.

"Cynthia, call Walter and—"

Walter stood.

"Oh, you're here." Why did he seem surprised? "Come on in."

Walter tried not to read too far into Steggmann's friendly, if unusual, choice of words, just accept them and follow him into his office where Tequila sat, looking completely at ease.

"Have a seat," Steggmann offered unnecessarily. "Coffee?"

"Better not," Walter answered, now growing suspicious. "So when can I come back?"

"Well...not right now."

His expression must have said it all because it was Tequila who answered the unspoken question. "You're not all right, Walter, as much as you may think you are, and as much as you want others to think you are."

"How do you figure?"

"The most obvious factor was a combination of how much of a ghost you were through the entire conversation and how you were trying to play me."

"What do you mean?"

"We talked, yes, but it was like you weren't even there. You were somewhere in your mind trying to figure out my questions and how you thought I wanted them answered in order to pass a test. You were picking and choosing how you talked about things. It was like you knew things happened one way, but you were going to retell it a different way.

"On top of that, descriptions of your home life afterwards are less than encouraging, and it doesn't take a shrink to see that you don't sleep well."

"Sorry, I was anxious about having to cram for a test," Walter replied coldly.

"And the mood swings, those were evident in our discussion, too."

"I don't appreciate being dissected."

"Now, Walter...if we didn't know each other, you might have one leg to stand on in that argument. But we've talked before. I know you. And I know that you were thinking about those previous times and how you could try and emulate them. I say emulate, because you couldn't do it genuinely, and you knew it."

Damn him. He knew Walter too well. He knew Walter and he knew his lies. The only problem was that some of them were lies that could never be spoken of, no matter how much time passed. It just wasn't possible, not unless he wanted Tequila to brand him a madman and lock him up in the loony bin.

"So what happens now?" Walter asked, trying to remain calm. Mood swings, his foot. He was mad because he wasn't going back to work. What other reaction was he supposed to have? Most people would probably be overjoyed, but he enjoyed his work; he wanted to return to it.

"You have a couple options," Steggmann told him. "First, you can leave. I can ask Cynthia to look into what you have available as far as retirement, partial retirement, severance, and so on. You will have an honorable discharge for your service and sacrifice. No one will think less of you for it."

"Next."

"Second, you can wait a while longer. Dr. Tequila recommends twelve weeks but—"

"Twelve weeks?! We've gone from six weeks to twelve weeks?"

"But..." Steggmann continued, "I am willing to pull it back to nine weeks, and that's the most I'll do. It'll give you more time to recoup, finish up whatever vacation projects you've started, and you'll be coming back in the summer which means less winter driving." Actually, that didn't sound half bad. "At the end of the nine weeks, you'll come back for another evaluation."

"What happens then?" Walter wondered, shifting in his seat.

"If you pass, you can come back to work. No muss, no fuss. The caveat, however, is that if you don't pass, you don't come back. And we go through the process of you leaving as we discussed."

That really didn't sound too bad, really. Nine to twelve weeks to get his mind back together and figure out how to play Tequila and actually win this time. But the stakes were pretty high, not that he expected any less. He couldn't stay on leave forever and they couldn't keep waiting for him to recover, assuming he ever did. There was that possibility, too, that he would never be able to return to police work.

What, then, did that say about his future as a Timekeeper?

"There is a third option, too," Steggmann went on. "The doctor advised against it, but I am willing to offer it. And that is, you can come back to work. However, you will be limited to one eight hour shift or two five hour shifts per week, desk work only. Recording, filing, shredding, all the fun stuff."

"I'd be the office grunt," Walter stated. "A glorified intern."

"That's one way to put it. But it would get you back in the office."

He sighed. "What's the stipulation here?"

"Tequila evaluates you every two weeks for twelve weeks, then he renders his decision. Same possible outcomes as before."

Walter rubbed his eyes. So on the one hand, he could have twelve more weeks off. He wouldn't be working, but he would still get paid and it would give him time to figure out how to outsmart Tequila.

There was just no way he could take this seriously when the guy had a name like that.

On the other hand, he could get back in the office — albeit as a grunt. No matter his honor and prestige, the errand boy always got tormented. But he would have regular meetings with Tequila. That could help him in that he might be able to figure out the questions and answers and be able to direct his own progress, at least according to the shrink. As long as he didn't let on that he was trying to get the best of him. Tequila would be waiting for that since he'd already tried to do it once.

God, maybe he wasn't ready to come back to work. Any other time, he would have nodded and agreed. Now he was trying to figure out how to game the system. *Don't do it, Walt. Don't go back there. You're an honest man.*

"Can I have time to think about it?" Walter asked, suddenly feeling very tired.

Steggmann nodded graciously. "Of course. Call me tomorrow before lunch and let me know what you've decided, otherwise I'm going to assume that you are retiring."

Well, that was certainly some pretty good motivation. Tell us you want to come back or don't come back.

Walter thanked them both as earnestly as he could muster, which, in all honesty, wasn't all that much. He didn't feel grateful at all. He had twelve weeks to get his act together or his career as a police officer was over. He didn't even feel relieved that they were generous enough to give him twelve more weeks. On that point, he felt rather insulted. He needed more time, like he was somehow deficient and he was getting special treatment in order to catch up with everyone else. To continue the metaphor, he needed summer school if he wanted to stay with his friends.

Actually, if he had to pinpoint an emotion, it would probably be anger. It wasn't fair to be mad at Tequila, even though he was the one who'd made the call to deny Walter his return to work. Steggmann wasn't a fair option either, since he was just going by Tequila's recommendation and he had to look out for the good of the department, and his own ass.

It was really easy to be mad at Rifun and Cassius. They'd started this whole thing, from the first woman being murdered all the way up to the coup and keeping him prisoner. If they hadn't started this, then everything would be normal. Christmas wouldn't have been hell on earth for a number of families, Tommen wouldn't have lost his hearing, Micaiah wouldn't have lost his leg, and Walter would be back to work. Actually, he never would have stopped working.

But in the end, he supposed the anger was directed mostly at himself, even if he didn't want to admit it. Ultimately, he'd started all of this. Him and his stupid, wanton ways. The drinking, the fighting, all of it leading to Beaumaris, when hell really began. If not for that, Cassius would have had nothing on him, and the worst he might have gotten was Base Time imprisonment, like Micaiah.

And what was he going to tell Tommen? He'd been just as excited for Walter to go back to work. To face him now and say that he had failed the psychological evaluation, that he was still unfit for duty...how could he tell his son that? Tommen's star was rising as he got promoted at work and was doing better in school, and he had the school play, even if that was fueled almost entirely by a girl he was too afraid to ask out on a date. No, he didn't need to be burdened with the knowledge that his dad was coming apart at the seams. All he would need to know was that Walter was going back to work in a limited capacity, just two days a week, to make sure he would be able to return to full-time work. That was it. Nothing about the evaluation or anything that followed.

"Greg," Walter said, halting at Cynthia's desk as Steggmann walked him out, "Actually, I do know what I want to do. I'll come back for a couple days a week. I'm sure if I get back to work, get back into the swing of things, that everything will turn out all right."

Steggmann studied him for a long moment, then nodded. "All right. I made the offer, so I'll stand by it. Is Thursday too soon?"

Walter almost felt guilty that he hesitated, running through the remodel projects going on. Floor guys were working in the living room tomorrow...shower and tile guys wouldn't be out until Saturday... "Thursday works. And Tuesday?"

"Excellent. Tuesdays and Thursdays. How does nine to two sound?"

Walter opened his mouth to reply when the door opened and Jim stood there, looking a bit harried.

"Si—hey, Walter, how ya doin'? Anyway, sir, we've got a live one. Or a not so live one." His gaze darted to Walter as if wondering whether he ought to be privy to such information. *And the insults just keep coming.*

"Where?" Steggmann and Walter demanded simultaneously. Steggmann gave Walter a look and he shrugged.

Jim rattled off the address.

"Wait, I know that place," Walter said, but he couldn't for the life of him remember why exactly, only that it was a place he dreaded going. Oh, wait...

"You're not going, Walter," Steggmann told him. "You're

coming back on desk duty only. You stay away from this case, got it?"

Walter sighed. "Understood."

"Good. We'll see you Thursday." Even as he spoke, Steggmann was following Jim back through the office, the door swinging shut behind them.

Cynthia gave Walter a sympathetic look. "Sorry, Walter. Tough luck, I guess."

"Even tougher luck for the poor person involved," Walter commented dryly.

"Well, that is one way to look at it, I guess."

"Is there anything else you need from me?"

She shook her head. "No, you're all set. Enjoy your afternoon, Walter. Good to have you back."

Walter thanked her and headed out to the car. He was back to work as errand boy, yes, and Steggmann had ordered him to stay away from the case, true. But he knew that address and he wasn't about to let this case just pass idly by. It was the culmination of the case that had led to the warehouse, the reason—whether true or not—why Walter was having the troubles he was having. Because Cassius and Rifun wanted Lily Guile dead. And it sounded like they just might have succeeded.

Walter did a quick check of his gun and extra clips just to be sure as he started the car, drove to a spot between cameras and out of good sight line and Banded. Even after just a couple weeks without using it, it was like eating a giant pixie stick after giving up sugar for Lent. It was natural, but slightly unfamiliar. Still, he kept it together as he navigated his way through traffic, passing the band of police cars on their way to Lily's condo. There were the obvious patrol cars, a couple unmarked cars, Steggmann's vehicle, plus the investigation van.

Technically, Walter figured as he found a parking spot and turned off the car, this could be considered tampering with a crime scene, contaminating it, potentially messing up fingerprints or destroying fibers and other evidence. On the one hand, Walter knew his way around a scene well enough to know how to avoid most of those things. On the other hand, if he was right, there wouldn't be much evidence anyway, none that they hadn't already found.

So, keeping his Band as tight as possible and keeping an eye out for Trackers, Walter got out of the car and headed inside, electing to take the stairs rather than try to Band the elevator or drop the Band completely just for the one trip, which, if anyone was paying attention, might seem a little odd that the elevator was working on its own with no one apparently inside. Best use the stairs.

When he reached the penthouse, he saw that the door was wide open, a frenzied couple standing in the doorway. They'd been the unlucky ones to find her, then. And what drew them up here, exactly? Walter wanted to ask, but he wasn't going to have the chance, not if he wanted to have a job come Thursday.

Carefully, he stepped through the door into the actual apartment. It looked like the last time he'd been up here, filled with gross displays of wealth, and not the kind that said, "This carpet cost more than your condo." This was the type of wealth that would make even a billionaire weep if he knew the cost and the true exoticness of the items contained within. This went far beyond the princess and the pauper.

But to the average person, it looked like a very wealthy person lived here. Walter was still surprised that Lily didn't hire a maid to do all her cleaning. Or maybe she did and it just wasn't a human maid who came in and out to do all the literal dirty work.

Walter, however, was more taken by the fact that nothing looked disturbed. At all. Not even in the cleaned-up-after-the-crime kind of way. It was more like walking into a house where the owner had died a month ago, and everything was exactly as it was before. A coat hung over a chair, a grocery list half-made, items out on the bathroom counter, a house just waiting patiently for its inhabitants to return. There was no evidence of forensic countermeasures, but no evidence of a struggle either. Nothing slammed on the ground in a fit of rage, or knives where they wouldn't be expected.

Looking at the carpet, Walter saw that he was leaving impressions on the carpet. As for the couple outside, the man probably could have made impressions, but the woman would be too light. If she could be used comparatively, Lily didn't make much impression on the carpet either. But other than Walter's steps, there weren't any others that he saw. Either she had been dead that long and the carpet fluffed out again, or some piece of this puzzle was missing.

He checked the bedroom. The bed had been made, but still looked like it had been slept in. The only thing that jumped out was that the huge lock on her chest had been broken, the lid opened, and the contents stolen. Walter never knew what was in that chest; he'd always figured it had been Lily's trillions, locked up right under everyone's noses, there for the taking. And taken they had been.

Walter backed out of the room slowly and turned toward the bathroom. No Psycho killer here; Lily wasn't hanging out of the tub with Hershey's chocolate circling the drain. Really, the bathroom looked like the only room that might have been left alone completely. Call it a hunch.

Heading to the kitchen, the first thing he noticed was the smell. A pan had been left on the stove. Maybe it had been clean, maybe not, but now there was some serious fuzz coating the bottom of it, and some spots on the stovetop that had been missed. Taking a breath, he strategically opened the fridge and involuntarily gagged, almost vomited. Everything had gone to hell. He closed the door quickly.

He took a step back and tried to keep from throwing up. He tried to think and get a timeline going in his mind. Inauguration coup had been...three weeks ago? Already? Didn't feel like that long. That meant that Lily had either been at the inauguration, or she'd gone or been taken to the Wheel shortly thereafter. She'd been gone three weeks. They'd known that she was missing, of course, and they'd known why, but what excuse had been given to the hospital? How had they not noticed her missing?

Well, Time giveth and Time taketh away. If it was possible to completely build a new life from the ground up, it was equally possible to tear a life apart, too. All Cassius would have to do was type up a letter of resignation and whatever other paperwork to send to her boss at work and away she went. On leave, on vacation, whatever excuse had worked for the last three weeks.

But for all the investigating around the condo he'd done, he still hadn't found the most important thing: the body. And the only place left was the patio.

Walter had never really liked Lily, but he had no desire to see her dead. Given the circumstances, he had even less desire. But to the patio he went.

She'd been dead for some time. He could see that immediately. And if he had to guess, she'd probably been dead about three weeks. She was curled up in a fetal position, mouth open in a scream, open wounds now dry. Around her, there was no blood, no signs of struggle whatsoever. She'd died in the Wheel, probably cold, helpless, and alone. But she couldn't just stay missing from Earth forever, so Rifun or Cassius or one of their goons had simply dumped her here, a cruel irony that the same wealth which had brought her the world had also brought her death.

Out of the corner of his eye, Walter saw something move. He whirled and brought up his gun, but it was only the pet snake. Or—what was it called? Some kind of water beast? Was it immune to Time as well? Still, he put away his gun and sighed.

"Lily said that you're supposed to be smart, kind of like a dog. Well, we don't need dog smarts right now. We need people smarts. So if you're smarter than a dog and at least smart enough to give a witness description of the person who dumped her here—not that it's hard to guess—it would be appreciated."

The water beast said nothing, just flicked a tongue at him. Sighing again, Walter cast one last glance at Lily's body lying there in the snow, and walked away.

# Chapter Twelve
## The Ask and the Answer

How was your first day back to work?" Tommen asked as he got in the car after play practice.

"Took a lot more getting used to than I thought it would," his dad replied honestly. "Also took a few minutes for the new guys to realize I wasn't a new guy."

"They try to pull rank on you or something?"

"Or something. How was play practice?"

Tommen tried to judge his dad's mood. He'd been a bit of a scattered mess when he announced he was going back to work, trying to figure out what remodeling projects still needed to be done, when the contractors would be out, and how to get it all set up around his new, temporary work schedule. So far it had seemed to do him good; he seemed more focused—or occupied, anyway—and Tommen hadn't had to wake him up in the middle of the night lately. Still, there was that little voice in the back of his mind that said to keep an eye on him because his demons wouldn't give up that easily.

"It was okay," Tommen answered finally. "Still not doing a whole lot."

That was an understatement; they'd been doing the same thing for the last three rehearsals and it still didn't feel like they were making much progress. The only thing that was going well was the sewing and costuming; they were set to be done by the end of the month, six weeks before opening night.

"So if you're still not doing much, what do you do for an hour and a half?" his dad wondered.

"Take notes for the director, mostly. Run errands."

"Director's assistant isn't all that bad."

"No, it's not. It's just boring."

"Well, once people get their act together and things start taking off, I'm sure it will be a lot less boring."

"Hopefully they'll get their act together soon, then. The set hasn't been touched for the last couple days because everyone's working on the decorations for Snowcoming."

"That's next week, isn't it?"

"Yeah, it is."

"Are you going with anyone?"

Tommen blushed hard and he hated himself for it. "Well, no. I kinda want to ask Becky."

His dad raised a brow and gave him a sideways glance. "How much is kinda? I seem to recall past dances where you would ask half the girls in your class in the space of just a couple days. It's been at least a couple weeks and you haven't asked anyone, let alone the girl you actually like."

"I don't—!" Well, okay, maybe he did like her. A lot. "—have anything to wear."

"Yeah, I was thinking your tux from Homecoming might be a little small on you now. Lucky for you, though, you know an excellent seamstress. I'm sure she could help you out if you asked."

Dammit. "Yeah, but...it would be weird. Like, 'Hey, will you go with me to the dance? By the way, will you also fix my tux? It's a little small for me.'"

"You might have a point there," his dad conceded. "Well then, maybe you'll have to take some of your newly-acquired riches from your promotion at work and put it towards a new tux, even if you have to rent one."

Tommen didn't want to do that either, but saying so would sound incredibly selfish. He'd already signed up and paid for his next driving class, so that excuse was out. Any of his other major savings projects were so long-term that taking a hundred out to rent a tux wouldn't even be noticed. Mostly he just didn't want to spend the money.

He shifted in his seat. "What if she says no?"

"I highly doubt she'll say no."

"Why, did she tell you that when you talked to her and her mom?"

"In not so many words."

"And you're sure?"

"When have you ever feared rejection?" His dad mustered a weak laugh. "I'm still trying to figure out why you are having such problems with this one girl."

"Because she's not an ordinary girl. She's not like the others."

"Oh? How is that?"

"Well..." *The other girls I just wanted to date and hopefully sleep with at some point. Becky I actually want to get to know and stuff.* "She's...forceful. She's not a pushover."

"That much I could tell."

"But if she's so forceful normally, I mean, why wouldn't she have asked me already? I mean, I'm not complaining, but it just seems like...I don't know."

"She's definitely a strong personality, but she still comes from a traditional family. As the man, you have to approach her." He went on before Tommen could speak. "That means you have to overcome whatever fears you have of other people's opinions and whatever reservations you have about her appearance and personality, and actually talk to her and ask to be seen in public with her as an item."

Tommen hated it when his dad overanalyzed things and pointed out exactly what it meant for him to be the man and overcome his problems.

Fuck.

He'd never had problems before. Maybe because previous girls already had a lot of guys asking, so he felt the need to dominate the competition. Becky had no throngs of guys asking for her hand at the dance. She was the freak in the corner, and to ask her was to be associated with her. Yeah, they sat together at lunch, but that was different.

*Of course it was different, because she approached you. She's not the freak in the corner, you are. She befriended you first, and she brought more friends to the table. Maybe you could at least return the favor?*

"I don't know how I would ask her, though," Tommen protested lamely.

"Well," his dad began thoughtfully, "you could always wait until you see her at lunch—because you should be focusing on your work during class—catch her at her locker and ask her to go to the dance with you."

"I can't do that!"

"Why not?"

"What if she's already going with someone else?"

"Fine, lead in with that."

"Dad, it's not an interrogation. I'm not putting her under the gun here."

"Oh, I have every confidence that she'll have you under the gun easily enough if you drag it out too much."

Tommen rubbed his eyes. Why was this so difficult? Both trying to ask Becky to the dance and get advice from his dad. His first mistake was confiding in his dad, obviously. His only two methods were interrogation and blunt questioning. Tommen had to do something different. He had to be cool, smooth, easy-going. Nothing was worse than talking to a girl and being a sweaty, nervous wreck. If he took too long and didn't ask quickly, that's exactly what would happen. But he couldn't just go up to her and demand an answer like she'd killed somebody.

Tact, that was the word. He needed to have tact. Tact and diplomacy, telling people to go to hell in such a way that they look forward to the trip. Except this was asking a girl to the dance in such a way that she was actually okay with going with him. Huh. Somehow that sounded better in his head.

"Come up with a plan yet, Casanova?" his dad asked as he pulled in the garage.

"Not really," Tommen admitted.

"As long as it doesn't involve any crazy plans and climbing up a tree outside her bedroom window." Walter got out of the car and headed inside.

"I don't even know where she lives," Tommen told him, following him inside.

"Even better."

"What's that supposed to mean?"

"Nothing at all, especially if you don't get up the nerve to actually ask her to the dance."

Yeah, there was that. The more he thought about it, the more Tommen realized that he had only a week to ask her, even though it felt like the dance was tomorrow. It would probably be better to ask tomorrow, though, or else he would be a nervous wreck the entire weekend. But then, asking her tomorrow would give her the weekend to change her mind, because you just couldn't change your mind the week of; it was an unwritten rule.

So he approached Becky with cracked confidence the following day after school, having spent every class planning how to say it but lacking the nerve to take advantage of downtime during Physics and lunch. He found her at her locker, just about to head out.

"Hey," he greeted lamely.

She turned and grinned. "Hi. What's up?"

"Um, are you going to the dance with anyone?"

"You mean as a date?" She took his redness as answer enough. "No, no one's asked."

"Why not? I mean..."

"Most people don't want to be seen with a dwarf, at least not in that way. And anyway, I can't dance." She slammed her locker shut and shouldered her backpack. "Why?"

Tommen felt all nerve leave him, ripping a stripe of yellow along his spine. "Oh, um, I just...I was just, um, wondering. I have to get going. I don't want to miss my bus."

Her expression killed him as she nodded sullenly. "Yeah, that would be bad."

Every step he took out to the bus, he told himself he should run back and just ask her. But he never did. Just kept walking, got on the bus, went to work.

"You look like a ghost," Micah observed as he walked into the store. "Something happen?"

"Nothing happened," Tommen grumbled as he headed back to punch in.

No one inquired further, and, as expected, he spent the weekend mentally pummeling himself. Such a fucking coward! He should have asked her. Just gone right up to her and asked her. Will you go to the dance with me? Will you go to the dance? With me? Will you go? To the dance? With me? With me to the dance will you go? How hard could that be? It's like, seriously, why was asking her that question so much harder than asking her what she got on some answer on the Physics homework?

Still, he started a hundred texts that were never sent. Will you go? Will you go to the dance with me?

He might have sent one of those questions if it didn't feel like its own form of cowardice. He was still old-fashioned that way. If he was going to talk to a girl like that, he should do it in person.

Monday came around finally, but Tommen was no closer to having stored up enough courage than he had walking away Friday afternoon. He did his best to find some courage reservoir deep inside him, but found that that reservoir was limited in its use to cleaning the bathrooms at work, and either running away from hideous beasts and Rifun or else turning to stupidly fight them. When he tried to tap that reservoir for asking a girl to the dance, however, he found it dry.

So he showed up to Physics the sweaty, nervous wreck he'd feared to be when talking to a girl. Becky greeted him, but he could hear the reservation in her voice. She was sizing him up, psychologically picking him apart, weighing the odds of him actually asking her to the dance, wondering whether she should go anyway in hopes that he would be there and they could just hang out.

Maybe he could do that. Maybe he could ask her to go just as a friend. He didn't have a date, neither did she, so maybe they would go together as a couple hopeless bachelors. Or bachelor and bachelorette? He'd done it with Eric and Varad plenty of times; was it possible to do that with a girl?

Even as he batted the idea around, he knew he wouldn't do it. He liked her and she was expecting him to ask her; if he asked her to go just as a friend, he would feel like he was shortchanging her. No, they had to go together, like together-together, or not at all.

But did that mean that their entire friendship hinged on just this one question? If he didn't ask her, and he ended up not going, would they still be friends come next Monday? Maybe, but could he really face her after that?

Why the fuck did this have to be so difficult?!

The lecture ended with about five minutes left of class, "plenty of time to get started on your homework" according to Mrs. White. But as was to be expected, pretty much everyone packed up anyway and started talking quietly.

He could ask her. Right here, right now. *Just do it. Ask her. Will you go to the dance with me? That's all you have to say. Just say it. Ask her. Before the bell rings, you must ask her.*

Taking a breath, he turned to look at her, hoping he at least appeared calm and collected even as he felt sweat snaking down his neck and his heart thudded hard against his chest.

"So, has anyone asked you to the dance yet? I mean, over the weekend?" he mumbled foolishly. *Good going, Casanova, that'll win her over.*

"No, not yet," Becky replied.

Her tone was decidedly less hopeful than it had been on Friday. Had she given up on him asking so quickly? Well, maybe she had been waiting for at least a text over the weekend. Three days of uncertainty. Maybe she didn't understand his little code of having to ask her in person. That was his fault, not hers. Still, she'd spent two whole days not hearing a peep from him, all the while expecting that he would ask her.

Mustering every last bit of courage he had and praying his voice didn't break, he opened his mouth to speak when Mrs. White beat him to it. "Becky, can you come here, please?"

He covered up his embarrassment with a cough at the same time the bell rang and all hell broke loose, throngs of students streaming through the halls toward the cafeteria.

*Okay, so you were definitely going to do it. That wasn't any fault on your part, just bad luck that Mrs. White needed her. But it's okay. You still have that little bit of courage; just keep it at the forefront. Lunch is here, plenty of time to talk without interruption. And hey, lunch is usually pretty loose conversation, so it should help you relax some before actually asking her. Right?*

Well, that's what he told himself, anyway, as he grabbed his lunch and made for the cafeteria with everyone else.

Tommen was the first one to arrive at the lunch table. Strange things happened during Snowcoming season, when everyone was finding dates for the dance. People actually wanted to sit with their dates. So that meant some major changes were happening as people shuffled from table to table. Girls and boys from different tables argued over whose friends to sit with that day. Several regular people at Tommen's table were missing while a few new ones joined them with their dates. Luckily, most of it would be back to normal come the Monday after.

Becky did not show up until probably halfway through lunch.

"Everything okay?" Tommen wondered, trying to keep calm and hoping that average conversation would help him.

"Yeah," she answered. "The grading program mysteriously deleted most of my recent grades, so Mrs. White had me turn in everything again. Thankfully I still had most of it. Normally I clean out my binder on Fridays."

"That's good."

"So what were you going to say?"

"Huh?"

"There at the end of class, when Mrs. White asked to see me, it looked like you were going to say something."

There it was, the suspicion, the hope, the unasked question that he would ask because she could not. *Will you go with me to the dance? Will you go to the dance with me?*

"Um..." He swallowed hard and took a nervous bite of his sandwich. He grunted as someone bumped into him. He looked around but couldn't see who it was. All he saw was people. People from his class and other classes, staff as well, teachers and other faculty. All the people who knew him. The gossip would get around.

He felt his courage desert him as he shook his head. "Nothing. It was nothing. I mean... I just..."

Tommen finished his sandwich in two bites, tossed the rest, and left the cafeteria, heading for his locker. His mind screamed at him. *Coward, coward, coward. You're no man. Still a boy, afraid to talk to a girl because she has cooties. So what is it? Not like it would be your first date ever. Is it because she's different? Do you really have a problem with her dwarfism? Are you ashamed to be seen with her? You're okay with her as a friend, but is that because it requires comparatively little commitment and is easier to terminate? Going to the dance with her, dating her, that not only requires a level of commitment, but association. You're just starting to recover your identity after losing Eric and Varad and having your hearing damaged, are you afraid a dwarf for a girlfriend will somehow damage your image?*

Another thought crossed his mind, then. Maybe it was because he knew that it wouldn't last. Few high school relationships did, and fewer relationships still did not end with the two parties remaining friends. There was too much emotion to just set aside. Once a balloon was popped, the pieces couldn't be salvaged and reinflated. It was done. Over with. Maybe he was afraid of losing his only friend to a dumb, fleeting relationship.

At the same time, his past girlfriends had been fleeting because he'd just hoped to sleep with them. He'd only been interested in using them. Becky he wanted to get to know. He wasn't planning on marrying her—fucking hell, wouldn't that be a nightmare—but maybe a different mindset would help to sustain this relationship more than a couple weeks. At least until the end of the school year. Then he could decide what he wanted to get out of it, whether he just wanted to fuck her and be done with it or keep going a little longer.

There were times when he missed having an older brother. But wishing would do him no good. And existential crises of the future wouldn't help him in the present. At this point, he either had to ask her by the end of the day or else he was going to go insane. And that was an even worse way to end a friendship.

"Hey."

He whirled to see Becky standing behind him. Her expression was unreadable. "Are you okay?"

"No," he blurted before he could stop it. "I...do want to ask you something...I've been wanting to ask you something...since Friday, all weekend, all day...I just...I don't know how to ask. I'm not...really good with words."

"Well..." She glanced at the clock. "Lunch has eleven minutes left. I can wait."

"That's not going to help. It'll only make it worse."

"Then I suggest you get asking."

Fuck. Fuck, fuck, fuck. God, why did this have to be so hard? Why was talking to a girl he liked the most difficult thing in the world? He'd fought ugly cats and demented bears and a psychopath, and even those things had seemed easier to deal with than this right now. Fucking hell.

"Um...so you know the Snowcoming dance is Friday..." Tommen began.

"Yes..." Becky goaded.

"And I keep asking you if you're going with anyone..."

"Yes...I mean, no...I mean, yes, you ask, and no, I'm not going with anyone." She laughed nervously. Good, so she was nervous, too. Oddly enough, that made him feel a little better.

"So...I was wondering if, maybe...you might like to...to go to the dance. With me. As a date. And maybe...afterwards we could...have, I don't know, dinner sometime. Or lunch, I mean. Maybe not dinner. Dinner's too formal. But maybe lunch. And a movie? Or something like that? If you want. I mean, I'm not trying to push. I'm just, kind of, you know, asking what you'd like to do..."

Tommen quickly realized that his voice had gone from a nervous talk to an almost incomprehensible mumble, and he was staring at his feet or the walls or anything but the girl right in front of him.

But when he finally looked at her, he found that she was caught between a grin and a nervous laugh as she nodded. "Yeah. I'll go. To the dance. With you, I mean. I'll go to the dance with you. Yeah. That would be great."

Tommen wanted to melt from his relief. "Oh. Okay. Thanks." Thanks? "I mean, that's great. Yeah, so, um, I'll pick you up? Maybe? If that's okay? I know your dad is a little more traditional, so he might not...what I mean to say is that I...don't actually...have my license yet. So my dad will still have to ride." He found himself staring at the floor again, ears burning. "If you wanted to get picked up, I mean."

"That would be nice."

"Cool. So, uh, I'll pick you up at, like, six-thirty?"

"Sure."

"Great!"

"Don't you need to know where I live?" Now her familiar snark and sarcasm was coming back. *Good going, Tommen.*

"Oh, um, yeah."

She gave him the address, but he paused when she told him the street name.

"Wait, that's, like, just down the road from where I live. Are you the ones who bought the little brown house with the — "

"Mosaic walkway? Yeah, it is. I mean, we are. Or my parents. They bought the house, yeah. So which house do you live in?"

"You ever go up the road a little ways and see the one with all the renovation junk waiting for pickup?"

"The one that's like nothing but stuff from the sixties?"

"That's the one."

"Oh, wow." She grinned and spat a laugh which she tried to turn into a cough. "Guess I won't tell you my initial thoughts about the people who must live there."

"What's that supposed to mean?"

"Oh, nothing. Just know that my opinion of them has significantly improved all of a sudden."

He got nothing more out of her on the subject and pretty soon, the bell rang, signaling the end of lunch and the impending doom of fourth period. Actually, it wasn't all bad. Actually, it wasn't bad at all.

She'd said yes. Once he finally got his guts together and told himself it was do or die and asked the question, she'd said yes. Yes, yes, she'd said yes. For a fleeting moment, he felt like running through the halls whooping for joy. Then he thought himself foolish. He'd only asked her to the dance; it wasn't like they'd gone against her father's Jewish matchmaking and gotten unexpected approval to marry. It was just the Snowcoming dance.

And yet, while he tried to play it down and contain his excitement, tell himself it was no big deal, he felt guilty for doing so. After all, if it wasn't anything important, then it shouldn't have been so hard to ask her. Asking her for help with homework was no big deal. Asking her to the dance was a much bigger deal. So he had to allow himself some excitement.

He wished he could tell someone. Before, he would have told Eric and Varad and then basked in their jealousy. He wasn't going to tell his dad, at least he wasn't going to text him right away; he'd tell him after school. Maybe. He couldn't say that he had a ton of other even semi-friends who he really wanted to tell. Still, he wanted to brag to someone.

Eventually, he ended up texting Micaiah, hoping a little good news might bring him some cheer, even if that came in the form of a sarcastic reply.

"Guess who got a date to the Snowcoming dance?" Tommen

typed.

He wasn't sure what Micaiah did all day, but Micah was fairly adamant that he did not leave the house in any way, shape, or form, and he was basically ignoring everyone. So when fourth period passed by with no answer, Tommen could only assume he, too, was being ignored. He figured it shouldn't have hurt as much as it did, only except that he was worried about Micaiah.

That worry lasted only through fifth period dot-painting, but was quickly replaced by the same exhilaration he'd felt before once the last bell rang and he headed for play practice.

But as he got closer to the auditorium, the worry started to return in a different form. What if she changed her mind? What if, at some point in the last two class periods, she decided that she didn't want to be seen with him? Knowing her, she'd probably tell him bluntly, or maybe she would at least have the decency to suggest that they go just as friends. Sure, it was an unwritten rule not to change your mind the week of the dance, but Becky had a penchant for bending, breaking, or ignoring rules when it suited her.

She seemed deep in thought as she entered the auditorium and sat next to him, a certain broody look that Tommen had come to understand meant that she was not aware of the existence of other people beyond obstacles in her way of wherever she needed to go.

"Hi," he said.

That seemed to snap her out of it, whatever "it" was, and she looked at him. "Hi."

"So...we're still going to the dance, right?"

"Huh? Oh, yeah, of course. I'm not that wishy-washy. If I didn't want to go, I would have told you so. But it was pretty funny to see you squirm a little. Honestly, it's not the first time someone's asked me to a dance, but it is the first time that someone has seemed interested in going beyond that, and not just to their bedroom." She rolled her eyes. "Pigs."

"Um...right." How was he supposed to respond?

"No, no, we're good. No, I was just thinking of some

costuming problems we have to fix today."

"Like what?"

It was like asking a NASA scientist why the rocket wasn't working and expecting them to reply, "It's not going *vroom, whoosh!*" The technical jargon she espoused on him then was well beyond his expertise in sewing. He was happy he knew how to thread a needle and fix a hole in his pants. She was going on about this stitch and that stitch and grains and a dozen other things he wasn't even sure were real words or concepts except that she used them so fluently. From what he could gather...something about the costumes wasn't right and they had to fix it before they could move on.

Tommen wasn't sure what the fuss was about, really. Listening to the chatter, these were going to be the nicest costumes the school had ever had bestowed upon them from anyone, and that was coming from the director, the other adult help, even Layman. If the costumes were even half as nice as everyone was reporting them to be, Tommen doubted that anyone would nitpick a few missed stitches.

"Are you at least getting to do stuff?" Becky asked as Mr. Martin had some private chat with one of the other adult helpers.

"Not really," Tommen answered. "I mean, I'm helping Mr. Martin, but all of the set and stage stuff has been put on hold until after the dance." Because the crew was reportedly down to five total workers, including Mr. Robinson, so hands and time were both in short supply and priority was given to the props for the dance.

"Oh. Well, if you're feeling strong, I have some more tubs you can help bring in."

It was a prod, a goad, a stick in his pride to suggest he couldn't somehow help because he wasn't strong enough. Tommen knew it, and Becky knew it, too, judging by her expression. Spiteful bitch. Damn, she was hot.

Did he just think that?

"Okay, everyone, eyes up here!" Mr. Martin said, even as someone else whistled shrilly. "So, we're working on a few different scenes today, and if we can all keep our heads together, we should be out on time..."

Like that was going to happen. Tommen rolled his eyes but snapped to attention as his name was called.

"Yes?" he wondered uncertainly.

"Tommen, I'm putting you in charge of backstage, including the set," Mr. Martin told him. "I know we have few hands to spare, but do what you can; we need to get going on it so it's not a last-minute rush. Think you can handle it?"

Tommen could feel all eyes on him. "Uh, yeah, sure. Where is it?"

"Well, some of it is in the art room, some of it is scattered around backstage or the prop room. Find it, bring it together, build it, make it work."

So it was that Tommen had less time than he wanted to help Becky bring in her stuff, though he felt largely excluded anyway seeing how she and her mom spent the entire time chatting away in Hungarian. It didn't take a rocket scientist to figure out what they were talking about, especially when he heard his name several times, but it was almost insulting to be standing right there, being talked about, and he still didn't know what they were saying. Maybe he ought to look up some Hungarian phrases, spook them a little and make them think he understood, see if their attitude changed any. On second thought, no, they'd probably find some clever way to turn his little plan against him. But still...

And at any rate, being backstage manager kept him busy enough once he realized the scope of the project. Mr. Martin had been downplaying just how bad things were. When he'd said that pieces were scattered about, he wasn't talking about whole pieces of a larger set, but little tiny pieces of larger pieces of whole pieces of a bigger set. Random pieces of wood, nailed or screwed together with some sloppy handwriting marking it as "1" or "2" or "Back" stashed in the weirdest places turned the whole thing into one giant Easter egg hunt, except there was no knowing what size or shape or condition the eggs were going to be.

By the time the end of rehearsal rolled around, Tommen had a mess of pieces and parts, more to find, and nothing to show for his efforts, or so it felt. Mr. Martin praised him on finding what he did, even going so far as to compliment him on the amount of stuff.

"I had no idea that this much was just laying around," he said. "You did a good job. If you think you can turn this into a real, working set, go for it. But I'm not going to push; I know you probably have a lot on your plate already."

"No, it's fine," Tommen told him, willing it to be true. "I mean, it's just finding the stuff that's hard. Once I get it all out in the open, I'm sure I can come up with something."

"Very well then, I will leave it in your capable hands. If you want to stay after rehearsals and work some, let me know and I'll leave the doors unlocked."

"Not today, my dad's probably waiting for me."

And he was, again talking to Becky and her mom.

"I hope you're not embarrassing me," Tommen said, walking up.

"Of course I am," his dad said, not missing a beat. "It's what I'm here for. But don't worry, Becky's mom is doing a fine job embarrassing her as well."

Looking in, there was no mistaking the expression on Becky's face, the one where you just wanted to melt under the table, find a convenient drain, slip down into it and die. She cast him a helpless glance and he found himself amused by it. Getting a little taste of her own medicine. Still, he took the cue.

"Well, I have homework I need to get done."

His dad gave him a look, regarded him for a moment, but nodded. He glanced back at Mrs. Polski. "Good talking to you." He looked back at Tommen. "Are we going now or do you need a minute to say goodbye to your girlfriend?"

Now Tommen's expression mirrored Becky's. Goodbyes were halting and awkward, much to the amusement of the parents in the room, and not soon enough they were walking out to the car. Tommen grudgingly got in the driver's seat.

"Why did you do that?" Tommen whined.

"Do what?" his dad chuckled.

"You embarrassed me in front of Becky."

"So? I have to make sure she understood that she's not going out with a graceful, hunky—"

"Daaaad..."

His dad just laughed. Well, at least someone was feeling good. "Okay, okay. So, how did it go? Stick a note in her locker? Red rose at lunchtime?"

"You think I'm going to tell you after what you just did?"

"Of course you are, because you're a teenage boy trying to conquer the world and you want to brag about how you got a date to a dance you normally wouldn't care about."

Fuck he hated it when his dad was right. Well, Tommen certainly wasn't going to tell him about his miserable failures, the stutters and fillers and all the times he tried but couldn't get the words out. Instead he gave the condensed version, the one where he didn't make a complete ass of himself.

"Have you thought about what you're going to wear?"

Tommen shrugged. "Not really. I mean, nice pants, nice shirt should be okay, right?"

"Sure, if I'm the one you're trying to impress. Now, what are you going to wear if you're trying to impress Becky?"

"I don't know..."

After all the trouble he went through just to get her to go with him to the dance, why was the rest of this not easy? Why couldn't he just automatically have something decent waiting for him at home? Why did he still have to go out and either rent or buy something to wear?

"How's the play coming?" his dad asked, blessedly changing the subject.

Tommen gave him the rundown of the day's events, including being made backstage manager and all the little pieces and parts of the set he'd found lying around everywhere.

"That's a lot of responsibility. You think you can handle being backstage manager and bakery manager?"

"Sure. I mean, nothing's changed except now I can actually tell people what to do around the set."

"Good. Because think of it this way: if things don't work out between you and Becky at the dance, you still have to work together on the play."

Yeah, because he really needed to worry about that right now, too.

# Chapter Thirteen
## A Meeting After Midnight

It was probably a bad idea to go out, really, without telling anyone. Oh, he'd left a note, but Micah wouldn't be home for a while, or so he hoped. With any luck, Jack would be calling Micah before long to come get him.

Lucky Jack's Pub was a favorite haunt, and Micaiah had mixed feelings about going somewhere familiar. On the one hand, familiarity might be good for him. On the other hand, everyone knew him. They'd known him before. They knew who he was. They'd look at him differently now. Well, it was seven o'clock on a Tuesday, so it was past the dinner rush on a dead night; he might get a little peace and quiet here.

The pub was a little larger than the bakery, as far as seating went, and about half the seats were at one of two bars. Jack's bar did the beer, wine, liquor, soda, and soda mixes. The other bar did all the fancy mixed drinks, the ones with layers and flowers and other foufou decorations. The kind that some bartenders did years of schooling to learn how to make. And there were some tables and booths scattered around the dining room with a decent dinner menu. But in all honesty, probably eighty percent of all the sales were from alcohol alone. And that was what Micaiah intended to contribute to tonight.

"Hey, Micaiah!" Jack greeted as Micaiah seated himself. The man emerged from the kitchen and met him at the bar. "Been forever, man. At least a month or so. Was wondering where you got off to."

"Nowhere good," Micaiah replied lowly.

"Sounds like you need a shot."

"Make it two with an order of your hot wings."

"Holy shit, he's in a mood tonight."

"Actually I'm not," Micaiah told him, pinching the bridge of his nose. "Just do it. Please?"

Jack nodded but kept one eye on him as he relayed the order to the kitchen. Micaiah knew the look; it was one all bartenders got when they were sizing up a customer, trying to determine if their heavy drinker was likely to be a happy drunk or a violent drunk. Micaiah knew he was more likely to be the latter tonight, but when he considered the whys and the hows and the how nots, he lost all angry motivation and put himself in the third class: the melancholy drunk.

He wasn't actually planning on getting drunk, but he needed to feel the fire in his belly and do something to change his outlook. The painkillers he'd been given he decided were too risky, especially when he figured he had better options available to him.

"So, where have you been the last month?" Jack asked conversationally as he poured Micaiah's first shot.

How Micaiah suddenly wished the place was hopping so they didn't have to have this conversation.

"Spent the first week in the hospital," he said, downing the shot. "Since then, I haven't left the house until tonight."

"Not even to go to work?"

"Nope. I haven't touched work. I've thought about it, but that's about it."

"Damn. You okay? I mean, I've heard of taking a little time after a hospital stay, but a month at home...that would drive most people insane. You look all right, but...mind if I ask what you were in for?"

He hesitated for a second, but grabbed his crutches and got off the stool. Moving around forward he'd mastered easily. Backing up was a little more difficult, but eventually he got to where Jack could see him and his pinned-up pant leg. For a second, the bartender just stared.

"Oh, fuck."

"That's what I said," Micaiah said, returning to the bar. "Among other not so nice things."

"Fuck. What the hell happened?"

"Hit-and-run. Some asshole in some kind of work truck hit me while I was shoveling the driveway. Put some rebar through my leg, blew the bone to shit. Couldn't save it."

"Fuck," Jack said a third time. He filled another shot. "On the house, dude. You need it. You lose your knee, too?"

"No, I got to keep that. Not that it's doing me a whole hell of a lot of good."

"What about a prosthetic?"

Micaiah shrugged. "I'm supposed to go in Thursday for a preliminary fitting."

"Hey, it's something, ain't it? Technology can do wonderful things nowadays. You'll be up and at 'em before you know it."

"Please, Jack, I'm just getting used to the idea that my leg is fucking gone. Okay? It's gone. Not coming back. I don't even want to think about all of this right now."

Jack put his hands up in surrender. "Hey, I totally get it. Believe me, I do." He looked up as the door opened and a group of college-age kids walked in and sat at a table just in front of the bar. "I'll be right there, guys!" Back at Micaiah. "Listen, I'm sorry to see your latest lot in life. But I'm glad to see you're out and around again. Don't go getting drunk on me, okay? You need to talk, I'm here. I ain't much of a therapist, but I know how to listen."

Micaiah gave him an imaginary tip of the hat and watched as he made his way around the bar to the group of kids. They seemed to be too absorbed in themselves to notice anyone else in the universe. Jack took their drink order. As he was filling it, the evening waitress returned, smelling like cigarettes and other smoking materials. While the order was being handed off, another group of people came in, this group looking like some young business group. Suddenly, a normally dead Tuesday night turned uncharacteristically busy.

"Hoppin' place," Micaiah observed dryly as Jack served up his hot wings.

"Normally this is your scene," Jack told him before getting flagged down elsewhere at the bar.

*And normally I'd have two legs. I might still have my rugged good looks upstairs, but there's something unappealing and even frightening about a man with one and a half legs.*

He figured he could always change things up a little. He didn't know any of the women here; they wouldn't know the difference if he'd been hit by a car or if it was a war wound of some form. He might be able to drum up a little pity. And yet, the dishonesty of it struck him. Strictly speaking, his was closer to a war wound, but without explaining which war, it sounded self-serving and grossly disrespectful. But saying he'd been hit by a car was a flat-out lie, not to mention it wasn't anything particularly heroic on his part. It wasn't as if he'd been rescuing kittens from a burning building or anything.

He started in on the hot wings. Damn, he'd forgotten how much he liked these things. Or maybe it wasn't so much that he liked the hot wings as he liked not having to cook. Everything tasted better when someone else made it. Except hospital food. No salt, no butter, no fat, no flavor. And after one week of that and three weeks of his own cooking, he was ready for someone else to do the work.

He was about halfway through the dish when the seat next to him finally got taken. Business had been getting steadier throughout the evening, to the point where Jack had to call in extra waiters and extra bartenders.

"Aren't you even going to say hi?"

Micaiah coughed as he finished his wing and wiped his fingers on the napkin. He looked beside him at the woman who spoke. His age, about five-foot-four, black hair that landed about mid-back. With her darker skin, most assumed her to be Latina, maybe Native American if they wanted to be a creative guesser. Only those who knew her knew it was, more specifically, Alaska Native. Eskimo and whatnot, although she always corrected people. Inuit, she said.

Her clothes were modest, comparatively speaking at the bar

scene. T-shirt and dark jeans, tennis shoes, light winter jacket, hat with a fuzz ball on top, mittens that could be peeled back and turned into fingerless gloves.

"How did you know I was here?" Micaiah asked, moving on to the next wing.

"Micah told me." At his expression, she continued, "He went home early because he was worried about you. Said you haven't been yourself lately."

"That's because part of me is missing."

"Cai..."

"So what are you doing here?"

"Checking up on you. You haven't answered your phone for anyone. No calls, no texts, no emails. You haven't checked in at all. Micah got word to us that you wanted to be left alone. For a while, we respected that and tried to give you space. But to ignore even me? You can't stay holed up forever."

Ah, Micah. Such an annoying little brother sometimes, even if it was only by a couple minutes. It wasn't long after Micaiah had shut himself up in his room that first day that Micah confronted him about some of the writings in his journals. Their discussion had been brief, in part by Micaiah's volatile mood, but Micah now knew: the Akari was real, and they were both Akari-bearers. He'd given him a few people to contact, a circle of confidants as it were, and told him to go ask them everything.

"I'm not holed up," Micaiah retorted. "I'm here."

She sighed. "Why don't we get out of here, then? Head to a nice little hotel?"

He raised a brow. "You're joking, right?"

"No, actually I'm not."

"Kayla, I don't know if you've noticed, but I'm not exactly here to find someone tonight."

"Good. Means I get to have you all to myself. Come on."

"Where?" Micaiah whined. "I don't exactly get around like I used to, and I don't feel like falling and putting myself back in the hospital again."

"How much have you had to drink?"

"Two shots before, and I intend on having another once I'm done."

Kayla shook her head. "Skip the shot after; we'll grab something on the way if you want."

No, he didn't want. He wanted to finish his wings, get his shot, and go home. Actually, at this point, he wouldn't mind skipping right to going home. On top of that, it was the one night he didn't actively try to seek someone out, and yet someone found him. Was it some sort of karma or cosmic irony? Not that he was complaining who it was, but still... Did it have to be tonight? Maybe in another three weeks when he came back out of his hole and maybe felt a little better.

"I'll think about it," was all he said as he picked up the last wing. He managed to get Jack's attention long enough to get his last shot, even as Kayla gave him a disapproving look.

"Are you even supposed to be drinking with the meds you're taking?" she asked.

"Oh, probably not," he answered, using the little wet cloth to wipe his fingers before fishing out his wallet.

"I thought you said you didn't want to end up in the hospital again?"

"I said I didn't want to fall on my leg."

"That's easier to explain than meds and alcohol. Something like that might be taken as a suicide attempt. Then you really won't be able to hide away in your hole."

Well, she did have a point, but Micaiah oddly didn't feel as defensive about it as he might normally. Was it because the alcohol made him a little more compliant, a little less irritable and quick-thinking? Or was that some Freudian or Jungian analysis, that while he tried to tell himself that it was good to get out, he was secretly hoping to land in the hospital for something or, worse, actually secretly trying to kill himself?

"Come on," Kayla said again, putting a hand on his arm. "Let's get out of here. Me and you, little hotel, our own little hole to hide in for a while."

Any other night, he would have gladly taken her up on the offer. Now the idea tasted bitter in his mouth. He'd had his alcohol, and it was only making him moody, so he wasn't in much of a mood for more. And his overall sour mood that had hung over him for the last month had effectively killed his libido, so he wasn't really expecting to get any even if he wanted to. He wasn't even sure that he wanted to. It was kind of like, his normal nights out were all really good trips, but then every so often, along came a bad trip. One that he just wished would end so he could go home and sleep it off.

At the same time, he was getting to that point where he knew he shouldn't try to drive home. He wasn't terribly inebriated, but between the alcohol, his mood, and the roads, he didn't need to wake up in the morning to find that he'd lost his other leg, too.

"Fine," he finally conceded, fishing out a couple twenties and placing them under the plate, right where Jack knew they'd be.

As he reached for his crutches leaning against the bar under the bartop, Kayla stopped him and handed them to him. Fuck, now he was going to have to use crutches after drinking. What had he been thinking? Well, he'd been thinking like he used to, when he hadn't had crutches. He forgot to factor that in because he'd never had to before. And now he was probably going to fall flat on his face, jam up his leg, and have to go back to the hospital.

Kayla didn't say a word as she led him to her car, opening the door for him and putting his crutches in the backseat once he made it into the front seat.

"I don't think I've seen you like this since that little escapade to Yurik six years ago," Kayla observed as she got in the driver's seat.

"Well, that was equally stupid, but at least everyone made it out alive and in one piece," Micaiah told her sourly.

"From what I heard, your escape from the Wheel was anything but stupid."

He shook his head. "It was stupid to wait so long. If Walter hadn't been with me, I could have left at any point." He sighed. "Maybe I should have."

"And left him to die? Cai, that would tear you up even more than this."

Problem was, she was right. Again. He could deal with the loss of a limb easier than a death that he had the power to prevent. He could never have left Walter to die in the black cells or on the executioner's block in the Wheel. The other problem was that he felt like he was barely dealing with the loss of his limb.

He sighed. "Were we going somewhere?"

She nodded as she got her seatbelt on and started the car. He leaned his seat back a little and tried to relax, tried to take in the ride as a favor because he'd been drinking and not because she pitied him. He'd managed to left-foot drive into town. With the roads and the slow movement of traffic, he might have even said he'd done it well. So at least he knew that if he ever wanted to go anywhere, he had the ability to do so, and he didn't have to rely on Micah or Tommen or Walter or anyone else for a ride. What was it Walter had said over and over? Only injured, not helpless?

Not that it made him feel any better. If nothing else, he felt worse once he'd come to realize how contradictory his two mindsets were. On the one hand, he just wanted to be normal and do everything himself. On the other hand, he knew he could never be the man he was and that made him feel helpless and terrified.

"We're here," Kayla said. She touched his arm and he jolted awake. Had he fallen asleep? No, more of a doze. As he sat his seat back upright, he couldn't quite say where they were or how they'd gotten there.

It was a hotel a little ways outside the city, a large chain hotel for guests who wanted a view of the mountains without having to go too deep into Charleston traffic. Of course, they also paid the price for that kind of exclusive view, and Micaiah briefly wondered who was going to foot the bill for all this. He flinched at his own pun. Damn it.

Kayla grabbed a backpack from behind her seat while Micaiah

fumbled with his crutches, which she ended up helping him retrieve anyway. Unsure of the salt job on the sidewalk, he ended up following her into the lobby where a tired night clerk met them at the counter.

"Good evening," she greeted. "Checking in?"

"Well, we don't have a reservation," Kayla told her. "What do you have available?"

"We're kind of in a slow time right now; what are you looking for?"

"King bed, if possible. A view, obviously. And is breakfast paid or complimentary?"

"We have a complimentary cold breakfast. If you want the hot breakfast, you'll pay for that at the counter in the morning."

"Okay."

"Were you interested in a jacuzzi card in addition to your complimentary pool and fitness card?"

Kayla glanced at Micaiah who shook his head. "Can't."

"I guess not," Kayla told her.

Payment was exchanged for room key and soon they were on the elevator to the fifth floor. Supposedly their room faced west so they could have a view of the city and the mountains and not be disturbed in the morning by the sunrise.

It was a nice room, actually. Not exactly the honeymoon suite, but no Motel 6 either. Kayla dropped the backpack in the plush chair at the window along with her winter clothing. Micaiah sat on the bed, took off his shoe and coat, tossed them in the general direction of the chair, and lay back in bed, feeling something like a hangover start to creep up on him.

"So," Kayla said, laying next to him and kissing him even if he did not readily return it, "tell me what happened."

Reluctantly, he did so, giving her as complete an account as he could recall, from the inauguration coup to being thrown in prison, to escaping that prison and waking up in the hospital with his leg missing.

"So Rifun knows that Micah is an Akari-bearer as well?"

Micaiah nodded. "Yeah. And Micah knows, too, now."

"Obviously, if he contacted us. How did that come about?"

"After we were taken, he went through my journals to see if maybe I had some insights I wasn't sharing." He rolled his eyes. "And that's where he found one thing and that led to another. He didn't say anything while I was in the hospital, but he confronted me about it when we got home. I gave him Doug's number and told him to call him and set up a time when they could both go fly a kite."

Kayla laughed and Micaiah's heart soared. God, he hadn't heard her laugh in a long time. At least a month or so, which, all things considering, was just short of forever and a day.

"Yeah, according to Doug, Micah didn't sound too happy or all that convinced when he first called," Kayla said. "But they've been talking regularly, so I think it's starting to get through to him."

"He hasn't said anything to me about it, but we also haven't spoken a whole hell of a lot since I've been home. I guess that's my fault, though." Micaiah shrugged.

"You've been struggling. With the elections and the loss of your leg and everything else. I just hate to see you try and go it alone."

"Maybe it's time I came in, then."

She shook her head. "Not yet. Right now, Doug says everyone should just stay put, keep your head down. No one's going in or out right now."

"And what about you? Why are you here?"

"Because once I heard that you were out and about, I decided that no one is going to stop me from seeing my husband, not as long as we're both this side of the grave."

He scoffed. "Just barely."

"But you are."

"I know. And I should be grateful." He shook his head. "Fucking Rifun. And Cassius. Fuckers cost me my leg."

"Forget them. They are in another dimension, trapped there because of you. Because of your bravery, your willingness to stay and fight for your friends and your Captain." She kissed him; this time he returned it. "And that makes you my hero, too."

He felt her hand go under his shirt, then down to his waist where she unzipped him. He sighed and closed his eyes. "I don't have the leverage."

She grinned. "Not having the leverage isn't the same as not having the willingness. Now then, let's try that again, shall we?"

He felt his heart skip a beat as she stripped off her shirt and pants and lay down beside him. "I don't think—"

She put a finger to his lips. "Then don't think." She got his shirt off, then went down and unbuttoned his pants, sliding them down and gently moving her fingers back up to do the same to his boxers. "And if you're that worried, we can always start with something that doesn't involve your legs at all."

There was something tantalizing about the word "start" but he was momentarily distracted as she took him in her mouth. Something between a groan and a sigh escaped his lips and he felt his whole body catch, as if it wasn't sure whether to tense up or relax completely. A minute later, he got distracted again as she removed her bra and panties, swung one leg over and sat on him.

"Fuck," he said, chuckling and shyly lifting his hips just a little.

She grinned again and took his hands so he could caress her. "Why, yes, that's the idea."

There were times when Micaiah was content with sitting back and enjoying the ride. But seeing his wife naked and sitting on him now, when he hadn't seen her—never mind fucked her—at all in over a month, he couldn't just lay here like a bump on a log, could he? Her eyes glittered with amusement as she seemed to sense the will and the desire coursing through him, warring with the fear and uncertainty.

"Cai, it was just me and you when we were both dumb virgins," she told him. "You have nothing to be afraid of. We'll just have to learn the *ins*—and *outs*—of it all over again. Together."

He still wasn't sure, but she knew him well enough to keep his mind distracted and his body busy. God, this was exactly what he'd needed. Get out of his hole, go out, see his wife, and get laid. Hard. Yeah, he could still do it. His leg might be gone, but that had no bearing on the mechanics of its upstairs neighbor. It's noisy, slippery, hard upstairs neighbor who had been dormant for the last month but now came back with a roaring vengeance.

*That's right, Rifun. You tried to take me; you even got a little piece of me. But you didn't kill me. And I'm still on top. I'm still top dog around here. I still got it. I can still do it. And one day, I'll fuck you, too. Right up the ass with a nice piece of rebar. And then...and then...*

Reality came back to him as light-headedness overcame him. It didn't last long, and as his world returned, he took quick stock of himself. Somehow he'd ended up on top, his left leg doing the supporting, his right stump dug hard into the bed with a surprising amount of leverage, but with pain added into that. Slowly, he withdrew from Kayla and shifted to lay down beside her, breathing hard and trying to keep his head together. He was spent. Actually, he was fairly certain that he'd been able to do it twice. God, that was a lot of work, especially after a month reprieve.

"Shit," he breathed, closing his eyes and trying to get his breathing under control.

"You okay?" Kayla wondered, moving stiffly to curl up under his arm.

"Fine, just...a little more pressure than I wanted to put on my knee."

She sighed contentedly and giggled. "I don't think we've done anything that rough in years."

"Even longer since you enjoyed it that rough."

"So was that really so bad?"

"No," he admitted, "but I do think I need to go to the bathroom and check my knee."

"Check it here." He looked at her. "I want to see it."

She got up off the bed. She first went to the bathroom and grabbed a couple hand towels, then went and flicked on the lamp closest to Micaiah. She handed him the towels which he set aside for the moment. He hesitated when she sat down on his right side, but he carefully removed the dressing. It wasn't even really a dressing like a gauze dressing, just a sock and a bandage to keep it clean and dry and supported.

"How long do you need the dressings?" she asked.

"Thursday I'm supposed to go in for a preliminary fitting for a prosthetic," he answered. "If everything goes well, then I should be able to take off most of them."

The last layer came off, revealing bare knee and tucked skin lined with scars. The actual stitches and sutures had been removed, but according to the doctor, it wouldn't be truly healed all the way through for another year and a half. Still, other than a little redness from the workout, it didn't seem any worse for wear, nothing that was going to send him in before Thursday anyway.

Kayla surprised him by touching it, starting at his hip and running her hand down to the knee. "Does it hurt?"

"A little sore, given what we just did, but no, it doesn't hurt normally." Although the phantom limb sensation was deadly in its own right sometimes.

She nodded and watched him wrap it again before sliding to the edge of the bed and reaching for his clothes. As he pulled on his shirt, he caught her staring. "What?"

She shrugged. "I don't know. I guess it's just...strange. Kind of weird." She scoffed and shook her head. "I'm your wife and I wasn't present for any of it."

He sighed. "Does it offend you?"

"What? No! Of course not. It's...just going to take some getting used to, that's all." Kayla frowned. "I just wish I could do more."

Micaiah did not reply as he wiggled into his boxers and grabbed his pants. Over the last month, he'd figured out how to get dressed by himself at least. Part of this was due to a necessity-induced heightened sense of balance. He'd still had to install balance bars in the shower, but simple getting dressed he could do.

"Are you hungry at all?" Kayla asked from the desk where she flipped through what looked like a binder full of menus for local takeout and delivery places.

"Not really," Micaiah answered. "Still full from dinner."

"Well, I haven't had dinner yet. So I'm going to order me a pizza. Sure you don't want anything?"

"I'm sure."

He ended up eating a couple slices of her pizza anyway as they sat in bed and watched a movie on TV. He chalked it up to nervous eating, as Kayla sat on his right side and simply rubbed his leg. Up and down, slowly, gently, hip to knee and back again.

"You know that once you get a prosthetic, you will be able to cover it up," she said, "at least when you go out in public."

"I know. But I'd still have the limp."

"It'll take time, but you can learn to walk without a limp, even with a prosthetic. People have done it."

"True. But that won't be today or tomorrow. Until then, I guess I'd just have to limp like Walter."

Kayla grinned and shook her head, but stopped short when she saw his expression. "What?"

"Limp like Walter," he repeated, half to himself.

"Yes, you said that."

"No, no, no, I mean...I have an idea."

"For how to...not limp? I'm confused."

"No. For how to get rid of Cassius and Rifun."

"What are you talking about? People from all over the universe, hundreds of different groups, they've already tried. So far, we're the only ones who are able to get through the dampening field, and even we don't have an effective plan. The intel you guys brought back was invaluable, but you didn't exactly bring the schematics of the Death Star with you."

"That's because we've had them this whole time."

Kayla took an even breath. "Okay. I'll bite. What's your plan?"

"Surrender. And demand a Time Trial."

She jerked away from him and turned to face him. "Are you fucked in the head?! A Time Trial?!"

"Cassius and Rifun have done away with almost everything we once knew about Time and the Wheel and the Hands. They upended the justice system when they gave all power to the Grandfathers. But they still enjoy the sport and the spectacle."

"Yeah, Roman style. Throwing people to the lions."

"Exactly. So what's the one thing they're most likely to give in to?" He went on at her look. "The Time Trials are violent and bloody, something they love. And if one of us goes in asking for one, after all the trouble we've caused, they might do it just to use it to make an example of us."

"Okay, I follow. But who is this 'us' you're talking about?"

"Walter, Tommen, Micah, and me once I get my prosthetic."

Kayla blinked. "What? No! Absolutely not. Fuck no. You are out of your *fucking* mind. I disapprove. Actually, as your wife, I *forbid* you to go." She cut him off. "You were already seized once and threatened with execution. You were literally on your way to be executed. You were lucky to escape; you don't even know how lucky you were. And even then, you still almost didn't make it, and you lost your leg in the process. Or had you forgotten that bit during our little mini-vacation here tonight?"

"I haven't forgotten," Micaiah said quietly. "But that's why this is going to work."

She sighed and made a gesture. "Proceed."

"The Akari works independently of the Time dampening field in the Wheel, clearly, which means that we can still use Disguises. Rifun wants me for my power, as well as Micah's. He also wants Walter in order to get to Tommen. Send Walter in, disguised as me. Have him call me—disguised as him—Micah, and Tommen as the Testimonies. When the Time Trials begin, I drop the Disguises, Band using the Akari, and shoot Rifun and Cassius dead."

Kayla searched his face. "You know, that sounds like a great idea on paper, but it won't work. Even if Walter does agree to it, do you really think he'll last that long in the black cells? Again? He just escaped a year in that hell. If he has to be you, he has to be strong in a way that we don't know he can be."

"Walter sat in the black cells for a year because it amused Cassius. Because they had a shared history. I was kept for the Base Time because there was no point in doing otherwise."

"But going back, they might do it just to get to you, especially before a Time Trial. Why not ask someone else?"

"Because we need the limp. Walt and I both limp on the right side. Yes, a limp can be faked, but in the heat of the moment, it can also be forgotten. And then where are we? Besides, I'm sure he would take great joy in being there when Cassius dies."

"Okay, so Walter goes along with it and you make it to the Time Trials. Somehow you even manage to get your gun in there. You still have to face the Day, the Bat, the guards, and an army of Grandfathers. Regardless if Cassius and Rifun are dead, they will come after you."

"I know. Even with the Akari, it still might not be enough. It's a risk I'm willing to take."

Kayla didn't say anything for a long minute as she returned to her spot under his arm. The movie went through another segment before cutting back to commercial. Even then she did not speak. Micaiah grew a little nervous, wondering just how mad she was at him. Then, "When we became Akari-bearers, we knew the risks. When we got married, we knew there was every chance that we would not only be separated, but that we could die without ever seeing each other one last time, even if we promised not to let that happen if we could help it." She looked up at him. "Refine your plan. Make it so you have every chance of coming home alive and well. And for God's sake, tell me when you plan to do it and before you leave, that way I can see you, at least one last time."

Micaiah nodded and kissed her on the lips, then the top of her head. "I can't promise that the plan will be absolutely foolproof or that it will work, but that much I will promise. I'll work on it and make it better, and I'll let you know when we plan on carrying it out. Because I want to see you, too. I'm tired of this once a week business."

She chuckled. "Oh, it's good for us and you know it, to be apart for a short time. After fifty years, we ought to be more like a bickering old couple on the front porch instead of lovers escaping to hotels on the weekends."

"What are you talking about? We are a bickering old couple, Aklaq. We're sitting here talking about my latest medical procedure, and you won't let me go out and save the universe with my friends, even knowing that any day could be our last before we keel over."

"Ha ha, very funny. Smart ass."

Kayla fell asleep before the end of the movie, leaving Micaiah to turn off the system and take the pizza box from the bed to the trash. Normally he would have his own backpack with a change of clothes and small toiletries, but this was one getaway he hadn't planned on. The clothes he couldn't do anything about, but he did end up going down to the front desk to ask about toothpaste and a toothbrush, which they readily supplied.

"Is there anything else we can do to make your stay more enjoyable?" the night clerk asked pleasantly. "Is your room suitable for your needs?"

"It's fine," Micaiah told her, shoving the items in his pockets and feeling his ears turn red. "Thank you. Good night."

He could feel her eyes on him as he hopped away to the elevator and headed back to the room.

"Cai?" Kayla wondered sleepily as light from the hallway spilled into the room as he tried to get in as quickly as possible.

"Just me," he said, the door closing noisily behind him. "Had to get a few things."

"Oh. Okay."

"Go back to sleep; I'll be there in a minute."

Actually it was more like ten minutes, but he doubted she really noticed. And anyway, lying there in bed holding her in his arms, nothing else mattered. Not Time, not the Akari, not Rifun, not even his leg or lack thereof. It was just him and his wife, curled up under the blankets.

In the morning, he woke alone, but the light was on in the bathroom and he heard the shower going. After a minute or two, it turned off and the door opened.

"Good grief, what's up with that?" Micaiah said from the bed.

Kayla paused as she walked past, combing her hair. "What?"

"The towel. What the hell?"

She grinned, set the comb on the table, and unfastened the towel, letting it fall to the floor around her ankles. "Is this what you want to see?"

"Well, I want to do a little more than see, but..."

Quick as a snake, she slithered into bed beside him, tucking up close under the blankets. "I guess it's safe to say you're feeling better."

"Oh, I'll show you how good I'm feeling."

His intentions were a little grander than reality as he was a little more conscious of his leg. He was still trying to adjust to part of it being gone, and it was still sore from the night before. He got the job done, but it felt half-assed.

"It was still good," Kayla told him, laying beside him for a few minutes before getting up and heading for her backpack. "Maybe you can think about it a little over the next week. Or don't think about it. Spontaneity seemed to work for you last night."

Micaiah wasn't sure he wanted to come back next week at this point, and watching Kayla get dressed only made him feel worse. Eventually he roused himself enough to get his boxers and T-shirt on, and head to the bathroom.

"Shit," he hissed, taking the little hotel hand mirror and checking out his stump. Some places were just red, others had the beginnings of what looked like a blister or rug burn. But through it all, purple bruises blossomed like cover moss, sending tendrils around the redness and blisters.

Should he call? Was it really anything that bad? Even if he did call, and he wasn't bleeding out, would they really get him in before his appointment tomorrow? Worse, would this affect his fitting? Would it be pushed back because of this? Fuck, he hoped not. Not when he just got his brilliant idea. Recovery was going to take long enough by itself; he didn't need to jeopardize it more and drag it out even longer. Every second wasted was another second that Rifun and Cassius stayed in power, slaughtering and enslaving thousands and expanding their influence through the universe.

"Everything all right, my love?" Kayla asked, knocking on the door.

"Just great," Micaiah answered grudgingly, setting the mirror down and adjusting his crutches. "Is there enough soap left for me?"

"Should be."

By the time he got out of the bathroom, feeling even more clumsy and conspicuous, Kayla was already dressed and ready to go, though she did only have a backpack. Silently, Micaiah resolved to take her on a real vacation sometime, where they would need suitcases for their clothes and needs, plus another suitcase just for souvenirs.

"You okay?" Kayla wondered softly, and Micaiah realized she was heading out, but he stood in the middle of the room still.

He shrugged. "I guess."

"Want to talk about it?"

"What for? Talking won't regrow a leg."

He pushed past her before she could say more and headed for the elevator. A family already stood there, waiting. Looked like mom, dad, and four kids all under the age of ten including one infant.

"Morning," the dad greeted, upbeat and clearly ready for whatever fun the family had planned that day.

"Morning," Micaiah replied, trying to at least sound courteous, even if he didn't feel like it.

He was completely prepared and expecting one of the anxious little kids to blurt out some obnoxious question about his missing leg, but none of them did. One boy was busy pulling on the girl's braids while the other boy pushed the elevator button over and over again until it finally got to their floor. Once on the elevator, it was actually the mom who spoke.

"Are you a veteran?" she asked.

Micaiah sighed and did not look at her as he answered, "Only of a car accident."

The children remained unusually oblivious to the whole thing but the air around the parents turned into an awkward silence. Micaiah and Kayla got off the elevator and headed to the front desk while the family went out on their big adventure, a little more hurried by the parents.

"Here is your receipt," the front desk clerk said, taking a sheet of paper off the printer and handing it to Kayla. "Hope you guys enjoy your day. Don't forget about breakfast either."

Kayla thanked him and they headed out to her car.

"Why don't we go out to breakfast?" she suggested. "Micah said you've been cooking for yourself, but you still look like you've lost some weight." She cut him off. "And I don't mean that."

Micaiah shrugged. "What good is it if I can't even make fun of myself?"

"It's not making fun of yourself, it's torturing yourself. And making everyone else miserable, too. Now. Breakfast. You choose or I choose, but we're going."

Micaiah named some restaurant, but on the way there, he couldn't even remember which one he'd named. He still felt very conspicuous and self-conscious, but where that had once defeated all other motivation, the idea of going out to breakfast sounded...good. Like a candle had been lit in his darkened state of mind. He didn't want to be seen, but he wanted to go out. He wanted to do stuff again and be part of the world.

"You seem better this morning," Kayla observed, pulling into the parking lot of an Ihop.

"Yeah, a little."

"That's good. I'm glad. Come on, let's get a table before all the old people get here."

As expected, after they got their table, the clock ticked eight and a steady stream of elderly folks walked in the door, all here for coffee, pancakes, and gossip thirty years dry.

"I did a little thinking on your plan this morning," Kayla said after their drinks came and orders were taken. "Only because we both know him and know how he can be, do you want me to take it to Doug and see what he thinks?"

"Not even close," Micaiah answered. "Let me work on it for a while. If I need help, then you can bring him in. But we both know that as soon as he hears about it and agrees to it, he'll take all the credit."

"I know. That's why I ask. On the other hand, does that mean that you're likely to go ahead without him at all?"

"If I have to."

"Regardless of his ego, Doug is a good person and a good strategist; he does have ideas to help. And it's generally not advisable to cross him."

"All the more reason to do it without him. I don't like having to tiptoe around or be afraid of my leaders. What?"

Kayla was smiling. "There's the Micaiah I know. See, you're not so different. You just needed a little vacation, a little pick-me-up."

"I'll need a lot more than that by the time we're done. First we need to make sure Rifun and Cassius are taken out of power. Permanently."

"I wasn't talking about your plan."

"I know what you were talking about. And believe me, I'm grateful. But in all honesty, revenge is about the only thing motivating me right now. That, and you."

"Nice save."

"But I'd like to save the normal life talk until after this plan goes through or falls through."

He could see that his words hurt her a little, like she thought he was suddenly making tons of progress, but it wasn't for the reasons she assumed. He was grateful for her forcing him out on one of their usual weekly excursions, but his motivation to keep going was just a little different right now.

"Okay," she agreed reluctantly. "Just remember what you promised me."

"I haven't forgotten."

"Good. Then promise me one more thing."

"And what's that?"

"If you're not going to bring Doug in, at least keep me in the loop. Include me if you can."

"I don't want you to get hurt."

"Nor I you. But whether it goes through or falls through, we do it together. Got it?"

Micaiah knew where she was coming from, but it was the last thing he wanted to do. She shouldn't have to put herself at risk because of his revenge. Still, for better or worse, right? He nodded. "Okay. I promise."

# Chapter Fourteen
## Snowcoming

Tommen ran off the bus into the house, making a beeline for his room, barely remembering to stop and take off his shoes before walking on the new hardwood floors. Still couldn't get used to them as he went slipping, sliding down the hall to his room where the smell of fresh, new carpet still permeated the air.

"Everything all right?" his dad asked from his bedroom, poking his head out and looking around.

"I have to get ready for the dance," Tommen told him, maybe a little more sharply than necessary.

"Is that going to take you all afternoon?"

"Dad, it's three-thirty. I have to pick Becky up at six-thirty."

"She lives right down the road."

Tommen huffed and rolled his eyes. "I have to get ready."

Of the roughly two and a half hours he figured he had to get ready, one full hour was spent just in the shower making sure he was scrubbed pink, clean of any speck of dirt or dry sweat, and ensuring that he had cheeks so smooth he could be accused of not being able to even grow a beard. That was one thing he'd discovered recently: he could grow a pretty awesome lumberjack beard if he had to. But the night of Snowcoming dance was not one of those times. In fact, it would probably work against him, so off it went, not that there had been much there in the first place. But just in case.

Then, once he was well and cleaned by water, he spent another fifteen minutes making sure he was toweled clean as well, using the bath towel, hand towel, and washcloth to get into every little nook and cranny.

"Tommen, are you still in there?" his dad asked, impatiently knocking on the door.

"No, it's your other son, Mike," Tommen replied, grinning to himself.

"Very funny. For goodness' sake, Tommen, I think you're clean enough. And you will recall that the remodel did not include an addition; I need to use the bathroom, too, you know."

"Be right out."

It was still probably ten minutes before he actually left the bathroom—he had to make sure there wasn't anything stuck in his teeth, after all—narrowly avoiding his dad who shouldered his way in and slammed the door. Tommen shrugged it off and went to his room.

He'd decided to just go ahead and buy a suit. It wasn't a tux, but it was the high school equivalent. His dad had helped him pick out a few good shirts, white, yellow, blue, and of course, red and green, something for any occasion. Different pins on the sleeves told him which was which, and he picked out a tie to match, fussing with the knot for a while before surrendering to the magic of the Internet.

He got all the way to the vest and coat before he paused. Should he go all out? Would that be too pretentious? Would it be too formal? What if he walked into the dance looking like he was expecting a wedding? He could probably use the excuse that it was cold outside. Oh, maybe he could do the whole put-the-coat-around-the-girls-shoulders trick. That would be good, wouldn't it? Or was it too corny?

In his indecision during the week, he'd tried to ask Becky what she would be wearing, see if he could judge the best course of action by her actions. But she'd stubbornly refused to tell except that her dress would have green in it, so he should make every effort to coordinate, even if he had to ask for help.

Well, shirt and tie was pretty nice, but he wasn't trying to impress his dad. Still, he didn't want to seem overly formal or enthusiastic, so maybe he could go with just the vest. A little more noticeable, a little more formal than most without seeming cocky. He didn't have a flower or little decorative napkin, so he would just have to go without it. He was just getting his sleeves buttoned when his dad looked in.

"Are you going to eat before you go?"

As if on cue, Tommen's stomach grumbled. He paused in his finagling to look at himself. He was hungry, but he couldn't eat and risk getting his clothes dirty, not after he'd spent the last two hours making sure everything was clean. His dad apparently read his mind, as he sighed and said, "You can either take it off, put something over it, or eat carefully."

Tommen decided the best he could do was put a blanket around himself and eat as carefully as he could, acutely aware of everything on his plate and making sure it got from plate to his mouth without falling off the fork.

When he was done, he had to have his dad spend several minutes using a lint roller to get the blanket fuzz off him. He should have seen that coming. Blankets meant lint which meant little specks of lint and dust all over his clothes. But it was better than spaghetti sauce all over his front, he figured, a lot easier to clean and less shameful to his wallet.

"How much time do I have left?" he asked once the lint roller was put away. The clock read five-thirty. He had half an hour to get everything done that he needed to do.

First, he had to brush his teeth again. Then, hair. Since the shower, it had dried, which meant he had to re-wet his hair while trying to not get his clothes wet. Not like they wouldn't dry, but he still didn't want to get them wet. He'd finally gotten his hair cut after letting it grow out over Christmas break, but he was probably due for another haircut in the next couple weeks. At any rate, he had to make sure that there were no tangles or snarls before he could even think about how he wanted to part it.

That gave him pause. He didn't know much about hair styling, even though he knew it was pretty simple for guys. But how did he make a part that didn't look stupid? Maybe he should just comb it all back and forget the part. No, that just looked terrible. Well, what if he started at the top of his head and just combed down? No, that looked like a cross between a bike helmet and a bad British haircut from the sixties. Top part? Side part?

"You could just let it dry and comb it out like you normally do," his dad said from the doorway.

"I didn't spend this much on clothing to not worry about my hair, too," Tommen informed him, staring at himself in the mirror and debating. "After all, I am trying to impress Becky."

"Well, right now you're impressing the hell out of that mirror."

"How much time do I have?"

"It's...ten to six. You've got time."

"I have ten minutes."

"It's not going to take half an hour to get to her house. Even if you wanted to show up a little early, you've got at least twenty-five minutes, if not a whole half hour."

Tommen sighed and combed his hair another way. No, too...twenties. Like he was going to go to school to see the Sisters. Maybe he should just let it dry and comb it normally. It was already almost dry, so it wasn't like he couldn't wet it down again if he decided he didn't like it.

"So, what are we thinking?" his dad wondered.

"I think...I think I need to pick out a cologne," Tommen decided.

"What do you mean 'pick out'? You've only got one."

"Yeah, but..."

"You want to look through mine?"

"Yeah, I mean, if you're not using them tonight."

His dad raised a brow but nodded. "All right. You're right. I don't really use them anyway."

That was an understatement. The only time his dad wore cologne was at funerals for fallen officers and occasionally to fancy black-tie PR dinners that Steggmann told him he had to attend or else. So, yes, he had four different bottles, but each one had only ever been used two, maybe three times.

Tommen picked out a fragrance he liked, then returned to the bathroom to contemplate his hair some more. It had dried and he combed it out. He liked it, but was that just because he was familiar with it, because it was the hair he had every day? Maybe he should try something different, make himself completely different from head to toe. That would surprise some people, wouldn't it?

But he wasn't going to impress other people. He was going in order to impress Becky. What would she like? Was she okay with the dry, ruffled hair he had every day? Would she like it wet and parted?

His mind went a thousand different ways in the space of only a second.

"I know I said you had time, but now you're cutting it close," his dad told him.

"Okay, okay," Tommen said, turning to leave. He gave one last glance in the mirror, at his dry, everyday hair. Well, it would have to do, a little bit of ordinary to keep him sane, he supposed.

He hadn't bought new dress shoes, but his old ones worked just fine. Wasn't like he wore them enough to wear them out or anything, and they still fit, which was a bonus. Then he grabbed his coat and headed for the garage, being momentarily confused when his dad got in the driver's seat.

"But, I was going to drive."

"And when you get your license, you can. But if she can't sit up front because of her stature, then you're going to go back and sit with her."

Tommen still got in the front passenger seat, at least for the drive all the way down the street to the little brown house with the mosaic walkway.

"Go get her," his dad said, putting the car in park and leaning his seat back. "Just pretend like I'm not here."

"Yeah, up until her dad tries to murder me."

"Just go knock on the door."

Well, no backing out now. Taking a breath, Tommen got out

of the car and headed up the long narrow walk to the tiny front porch and the unassuming front door. If both her parents were in the medical field, he might have assumed they were pretty loaded for cash, but the look from the street was as ordinary as anything else in the neighborhood. Maybe they were like the twins who kept a wealthy interior hidden behind an ordinary exterior in order to keep attention away from themselves.

He knocked on the door.

A minute later, it opened and Dr. Polski stood there. The man was easily of retirement age, but he was still a forceful presence. Tommen didn't like to consider how imposing he must have been in his younger days.

The conflict was as evident on Dr. Polski's face as it was in Tommen's gut. As doctor-patient, they got along well enough, Tommen learning to trust him with a devastating problem while he tried to help Tommen get past his self-consciousness and back to a normal life that just needed a little aid. As father-of-the-girl, the man was inclined to protect his own and drive away all intruders no matter the cost. Now that Tommen was both patient and boy-hoping-to-date-girl, he had to find a balance in how to treat him. Tommen's role wasn't too difficult; he just had to show triple the amount of respect and proper deference to both doctor and father.

There was every chance this might not end well.

"H-hi, Dr. Polski," Tommen began, chiding himself for sounding weak and feeble. "I'm here to pick up Becky for the dance." He tried to make it sound like a statement and not a question.

"I don't think she's ready yet," Dr. Polski informed him, his voice remarkably calm for the occasion. Was he plotting Tommen's demise even as he spoke? This really might not end well.

"I'm ready," Becky said indignantly from somewhere inside. "It takes me less time to get ready for a dance than it does you to go to work."

If Tommen didn't know better, he might have wondered if Becky was his wife rather than his daughter, judging by her words and tone. It amused him, but he was careful not to do much more than a small smile, lest Dr. Polski think he was somehow secretly insulting him.

Not three seconds later, Becky appeared, effortlessly moving under her dad's arm to stand out on the tiny porch. For a second, Tommen was stunned. He was used to seeing her in jeans and a T-shirt, hair in a ponytail because she couldn't be bothered to do much else with it.

Now she stood before him in a stunning silver dress that went all the way to the ground to cover up her orthopedic shoes. A white stripe—she'd probably chastise him for calling it that and give him, not only the proper name for it, but how to cut and sew it—ran from her chest to the ground, decorated with straps and small beads. The chest and shoulders, however, were immediately recognizable; she'd used the furs he'd sold her, a couple tan rabbit furs. She carried a little silver handbag trimmed with the same fur. With hair done up and makeup on her face, she was nearly unrecognizable.

The one thing she didn't do, however, was flaunt it. Tommen had barely processed her beauty when she said, "I'm ready. Is there a reason we're standing out in the cold?"

"Oh, um, no," Tommen answered, feeling foolish. "Whenever you're ready."

"Well, I just said I'm ready."

Her dad bent down so she could kiss him on the cheek, then pushed past Tommen to head toward the car. Before Tommen could follow, Dr. Polski spoke.

"Back by eleven if you want to talk about dating her more. Back by ten-thirty if you want me to like it."

"Yes sir."

Tommen took the chance to slip away, making it to the car just in time to open the door for Becky who gave him a knowing look before getting in. Then he went around the other side and got in beside her.

"I thought you were driving?" she wondered.

"Well, I didn't think it would be fair for me to drive and you sit back here. I try to be considerate, at least on a first date," Tommen told her, not missing his dad's smirk in the front seat as he pulled away from the curb and headed toward the school.

"That's sweet."

It was hard to tell whether she actually believed him, or if she somehow knew that it had been his dad's idea. Either way, she was quickly learning discretion and knew enough to not say anything.

He swallowed hard. "Um, you look very pretty." *Pretty? That's the best you can come up with?* "Did you make your dress yourself?"

"Well, you're not going to find it in the kid's section of the department store." She laughed. "Yes, I did. I was actually already working on it; the dress was getting old, so I decided to spruce it up a little. It's actually green, in case you were wondering. Do the furs look familiar?"

"I was wondering."

"They're wonderfully done and easy to work with. Do you have any more? I don't know how trapping season works or anything like that, so I don't know what you have or what you're allowed to have or anything like that."

Tommen didn't miss the look his dad gave him from the front seat. "Well, I always have a few somewhere, but my buckets are empty right now." *Because it's a lot harder to outrun the game warden when your only advantage has been taken away.* "I'll see what I can find and maybe I'll head out soon."

"That would be great. The first ones I just wanted for my own experiments to see how I liked them; obviously I do. If I got a few more and actually started to make a few things and showcase them, I might be able to win over a few clients..."

Becky disappeared into her own little world, but she wasn't gone long before they pulled into the school parking lot.

"Okay, you crazy kids, call me when you're ready," Walter told them.

"Thanks, Mr. Forbes," Becky told him as Tommen got out and

went around to open the door for her.

She slipped more than stepped out, and Tommen quickly found himself facing another dilemma. How did he hold hands with her? Should he hold hands with her? Was it too soon on a first date? He'd done it before with other girls, but Becky was not like other girls. And then there was the point that he couldn't just casually bump into her and take her hand; her hand he would have to reach down for. There was nothing subtle about that. And was it even appropriate, given how it would seem more like holding a child's hand? Or that's how it would look anyway.

By the time he'd even considered his dilemma, they had already reached the front door. Classmates and a few adult chaperons milled around outside. Once inside, the first person to greet them was none other than Mr. Layman.

"Good evening," he greeted amiably.

"Hi, Mr. Layman," Tommen said, trying to sound anything but grudging and spiteful.

"Let's keep the surprises to a minimum tonight, hm?"

"Every intention."

They made their way to the gym where this dance looked about like every other, just the decor was slightly different. Since it hadn't really kicked off yet, no one was on the dance floor, instead preferring to hang around the walls and bleachers, the largest group huddled around the food and drink tables.

Homecoming dance had been themed Alice in Wonderland, per the school play. However, the planning committee evidently thought that because the play itself was actually closer to Snowcoming dance, then both major dances needed to be themed the same. But they obviously couldn't be the exact same because that would be totally lame. So Snowcoming was officially themed Alice Through the Looking Glass. Which was supposed to be different...somehow?

Regardless of what the planning committee said or thought, it was basically the same. Tommen saw the same light-up roses, the same failed paper mâché dragon creature. The only thing really noticeably different was that a bunch of mirrors had been brought in. Tall, full-length mirrors; tiny hand held mirrors; wide landscape mirrors; mirrors with almost no frame; mirrors with enormous, elaborate, decorative frames, even a few carnival fun mirrors. Some mirrors had colored lights placed in front of them, turning the whole place into a sort of inverted disco ball.

"Whoa," Becky said. "Psychedelic, man. It's like the sixties and seventies in here. I'm almost expecting someone to come up and offer me some ecstasy."

"Weirdly enough, they just might," Tommen told her seriously.

"So what did Layman mean, about keeping surprises to a minimum?"

In the dim light, she couldn't see him blush. "Well, at Homecoming in October, I—well, me and a couple friends—we kind of found a body."

"A body as in...dead body?"

"Yeah."

"Oh, cool! Where was that?"

"Out in the soccer fields, under one of the bleachers."

"Sweet. Wait, why were you under the bleachers?"

And there went Tommen's hopes of having a girlfriend for more than one dance. "Well, we kind of sneaked off to do some stuff."

"What kind of stuff?"

"A drink and a smoke."

He could feel her eyes burning into him. "You do that often?"

"Not since that. And not since I lost my two best friends."

"Huh." She was still studying him, probably with a million questions running through her mind but unable to decide whether she wanted to unleash them all at once, save them for a later date, or skip the whole thing and just dump him right there. "So was it like CSI out there or what?"

"Not like you see on TV. But I was kind of busy answering

questions and hoping my dad didn't kill me for being out doing what I was."

"Well, that would make sense. They catch the guy?"

"Um...well, they know who did it but they haven't gotten him yet."

"Is that the case where you said your dad got hurt and stuff?"

"Yeah, it is."

"Oh, I'm sorry. I didn't know."

"No, it's all right. Obviously, he's better now."

Well, this date was turning out to be a real drag so far. *Thank you, Mr. Layman. Because you couldn't just say something like, "Good evening, Tommen. You look handsome tonight. You clean up well, don't you? Good evening, Becky. You look very nice tonight. And don't you two look so cute together? Have fun. Enjoy yourselves at the dance and don't cause any mischief, ha ha ha." No, you just had to bring up last time, didn't you? Asshole.*

"I've never actually been to a dance before," Becky said, jumping to another subject. "What exactly are you supposed to do? I mean, I don't dance."

"That's kind of the whole point of a dance," Tommen told her. "But a lot of people mill around, hang out, chat, do some of the party games they have set up, take endless pictures, eat lots of food, that sort of thing. I've been to dances before, but I don't usually stay long."

"Oh. Well, let's see what kind of games they have."

Lame ones, in Tommen's opinion. He was never a corn hole toss kind of person. If he had to pick a lame party game, it would probably be the darts because then he could throw them at other people. Problem was, they seemed to have upgraded from standard darts to magnetic ones. They still hurt, but at least it wouldn't take someone's eye out when the game devolved into teenager antics and shenanigans.

Still, Becky gave him a run for his money in a couple rounds of the corn hole toss, proving to have superior hand-eye coordination and throwing judgment. She said it was because she was better friends with the ground than he was. Problem was, that was actually a likely explanation. Not necessarily about being friends with the ground, but being shorter, closer to the ground.

"At my old school, there would be a lot more people, but it was also a lot more strict and a lot less fun," Becky commented as they raided the snack table.

"What do you mean?"

"My school had metal detectors and all sorts of high-tech security stuff. And you wouldn't believe some of the things that got confiscated on a daily basis: knives, shivs, even guns. Gang violence was huge. Like, your fighting with whatshisface probably wouldn't have even been a blip on the radar as far as school officials were concerned."

"Sounds like prison."

"In a way, it kind of was. Bars on the windows, automatic locks on the doors, cyber security on par with the government, it was halfway to ridiculous. Some of the freshmen there were tougher than the seniors here. It wasn't a happy place to be."

"Which school was this?"

She told him the name. "All you need to know is that it was in southern California."

"So, if all your family is here and your dad had a successful practice, why move out there in the first place?"

"Well, they did it for me. From the minute I walked into kindergarten, I was bullied. I mean, kindergarten bullying is different from high school bullying, but I still felt it. I was isolated and made fun of."

"But in kindergarten, everyone's short," Tommen said.

"Disproportionate dwarfism. My limbs are disproportionately small. Doesn't matter if it's in kindergarten, it's pretty obvious. And I heard a lot of mean names tossed my way."

"And California?"

"My parents were hoping that the...liberal state of mind would be beneficial for me. They hoped that the tolerance touted in

California would help me be accepted and I would be able to find friends and have as good a life as anyone else." Becky rolled her eyes. "First day of first grade, 'Hey, is there a lot of hot air in your head or is that your brain? Nerd!'" She sighed. "I moved schools multiple times, even spent a few years being homeschooled."

"Why not move back sooner?"

"My parents liked the weather, and they got better jobs. My mom got a decent nursing job and my dad had a full practice again with no shortage of new clients if he ever needed them. So we had a nice house, nice cars, nice stuff, and took good vacations when we were able. It wasn't all bad; except for the people, I actually liked California.

"Then my parents got old, started approaching retirement age, and they wanted to get back to familiar pastures, be with the family, so on and so forth. And here we are."

"And here we are." Tommen nodded.

After a minute, Becky spoke again. "Let's get out of here."

Tommen felt his heart sink. "Oh, you want to go home?"

"I didn't say that. I just said let's get out of here. I don't dance; you're obviously not having any fun. Why don't we skip out of here and go get some pizza or something? You get the pizza, I'll get the breadsticks and drinks, we'll call it good."

"Oh, um...sure. Yeah, I mean, if you're sure..."

"Believe me when I say that I've decided the dance scene isn't for me. But it was nice to visit just to say I did it once. I even had a date." She winked at him and his stomach did a backflip. "But there's not much to do, at least nothing that's going to take up a few hours. Might as well go make our own fun."

Tommen's mind went a thousand different directions in the space of half a second. "Right. So, I guess I'll call my dad."

His dad was surprised and a little suspicious, but was waiting for them all the same by the time they made it to the parking lot. Tommen opened the door for Becky again and again sat beside her in the backseat.

"You guys weren't in there very long," Walter observed. "Everything...okay?"

"Dances are boring," Becky declared. "Are there any pizza places open this late?"

"In the middle of February? Not likely. But there are a few places we can check."

"Any place will do, but pizza sounds good."

"If you don't mind my asking, I noticed you have a pump. Can you have pizza?"

"Yes. I just have to keep a close eye on things. No worries, though."

"If you're sure because here we go."

For being a large city, Charleston was fairly quiet at night, at least during the winter as everyone hunkered down to wait out the latest impending storm. This night was unusually clear, so there were a few more people out and about, but as expected, most businesses were long since closed.

"Looks like the pizza places are closed," Walter observed. "Do we have a second choice?"

Becky looked at Tommen. "Is there anything still good at the bakery this late at night? Are they open?"

Tommen looked at the time. "Yeah, they'll be open. No guarantees on what they'll have."

"Your expression says you don't want to go anywhere near that place if you don't have to."

"If you want to go, then sure. I don't know what else we'll find open."

"Or," Walter interrupted, "we can go back to our house and make something. We've got stuff for pizza. Or your house, Becky, whatever you kids want."

Becky shook her head. "No, that's okay."

"So...bakery it is?"

It was the last place Tommen wanted to go, especially when he had to open in the morning, but, oh, the things he would do to impress a girl. Problem was, it was tough to gauge how impressed she was. He could be doing all this for nothing.

Kyle was just wiping down the tables when Tommen and Becky walked in. He took one look at Tommen and whistled. "Hey, good lookin'. You clean up nice, don't you?"

"Not like you'd know," Tommen retorted. "What do you have left over that's good?"

"Left over?" Kyle headed back around the counter. "Lots of stuff. Left over that's good? A little harder to say. We've got some danishes, but they might be a little iffy. Got a mean loaf of garlic bread. Got a few slices of pie, half a dozen cupcakes, what's your pleasure?"

"I like pie," Becky said. "What do you have?"

"We've got apple, cherry, and blueberry."

She ended up with cherry and Tommen took blueberry. He tried to pay for both, but Becky insisted not on a first date. She said it wasn't worth him wasting money trying to impress a girl when there was every possibility it wouldn't work out. Tommen blushed and Kyle gave him an incredulous look, but there was nothing to be done. When they sat down to eat, he asked her about it.

"I just don't want to see you wasting money on me," she said, shrugging. "I can buy my own dessert."

"Yes, but I want to do something nice for you," he told her.

"Is that because you like me and want to do something nice, or because you think that now that we're dating, or have that potential, that you have to make stupid sacrifices in order to try and impress me because you're afraid that I'll dump you if you don't?"

"Fine. How do I show you that I like you and I want to do something for you without seeming desperate or...cliche...y?"

She smiled. "You're already doing it."

He sighed. "I don't speak female. What am I doing?"

"You're hanging out with me. Anyone can buy stuff, but you are willing to be associated with me."

"Oh. Okay."

"And..." She hesitated. "You push back."

"What...do you mean?" He wasn't sure he wanted to know what she meant.

"Most guys find me too forthcoming, at least in a dating sense. Once they see that I can be just as bold and witty as they are, I don't know, I guess they're intimidated. They back off and, well, they friendzone me."

"Interesting. I thought that only happened to guys."

"No, no, it happens to girls, too. Just less frequently, I think. Either way, you're not like that."

"Well, you're not a pushover who's just looking for sex on a first date. At least I hope not."

Tommen found himself stunned by his own words. Wasn't he normally the one looking for sex? Hadn't he totally wanted to fuck Emily after taking her to the homecoming dance? Hadn't that always been his goal, to date a girl long enough to get laid, and not be a virgin when he got to college? Shit, maybe his own perceived code of chivalry was actually starting to wear off on him.

Still, she smiled and looked ready to say something when an Irish voice cut her off.

*"Bhuail, bhuail, bhuail, cé hé an lánúin álainn seo?"* Micah said as he walked up. *"An féidir liom coinneal a thabhairt duibh?"* (Well, well, well, who is this good-looking couple? Can I bring you a candle?)

"I'd say something, but I'd like to keep my job tomorrow," Tommen told him.

"Wise man." Micah looked at Becky. "I'd say he's a keeper."

"Are you here to kick us out?" Tommen wondered.

Micah looked back at him. "No, not yet. Still got some stuff to do in back." He set a small paper bag on the table and took their dirty plates. "I'll take those. That's for your dad when you go."

"Thanks. How's Micaiah? Any better? Last I saw him, he was still in the hospital trying to cope." *I also screwed up the conversation and he threw me out of his room without even lifting a finger.*

"That's your brother, isn't it?" Becky wondered. "What

happened?"

Micah briefly explained the story (lie) about being hit by a truck and so forth. He finished by saying, "Actually, he's been doing a lot better. He went out the other night, finally, so he's starting to come around."

"That's good." Tommen nodded.

"Is he getting a prosthetic?" Becky asked.

Micah shrugged. "Mm...he's getting one. Whether or not his pride will let him use it...remains to be seen. I think he might learn to like it, though. He's always complaining about the chafing from the crutches."

He looked ready to say more when there was the sound of shattering glass from the kitchen. Then, "I'm okay!" from Kyle. Sighing, Micah excused himself and went back to figure out what happened.

"I think that's our cue to leave," Becky said, carefully sliding out of her seat so she didn't trip over her dress.

Tommen reluctantly agreed. On the one hand, he didn't have to clean up and lock up. On the other hand, it meant that the night and their date was over, which meant they would be heading back to her house to drop her off, which meant he was going to have to face her father again. The prospect was daunting, but it seemed there was no getting around it, not if he wanted a second date.

"Oh, good, I was just about to come in to warm up," Walter said as they crossed the parking lot and got in the car.

"Micah said this is for you," Tommen told him, handing him the paper bag.

"Excellent. I will have to save that for tomorrow." He started the car. "So, kids, the night's still young, unless one of you has to be up early tomorrow. Anywhere you want to check out and see if it's open?"

It was a taunt. *What will you choose, Tommen? Will you take the out, plead fatigue, and go home to get some sleep? Or will you name someplace to go, sacrifice yourself and your sanity in order to impress a girl?*

Well, given the conversation they'd just had, it actually turned out to be a pretty easy answer. He glanced at Becky as if uncertain. "I know I mentioned seeing a movie, but I don't know of any that wouldn't end before ten-thirty or eleven."

"Got a curfew or something?"

"Or something," Becky answered, her tone difficult to judge. Was it dismissive, the, "Don't ask about it." Or was it grudging, the, "I'm practically an adult but I still have the curfew of a teeny-bopper."

Either way, Walter shrugged and obliged. "All right, then. Curfew it is. Next stop, Becky's house."

Now was the true test of Tommen's deodorant as they pulled out of the parking lot and headed toward home. It might not have been so bad except Dr. Polski knew where he lived. Worse, they were neighbors. If he was in any way disappointed or angry, there was nowhere to run and hide. He hoped his anxiety wasn't obvious to Becky.

"So, you kids have a good time?" his dad asked conversationally.

"Dad, you can stop calling us kids," Tommen told him.

"Oh, you'll let me? You're still my kid, I'll call you what I want."

"You're embarrassing me."

"And you two are so cute."

"Dad!"

Well, at least someone was having a good time. Even Becky seemed a little uneasy, but whether it was from Walter's patronizing or something else on her mind, Tommen couldn't tell. They were both saved, however, by the appearance of Becky's house in the distance, and a moment later, they were pulling up to the curb. Tommen got out and made it around just in time to open the door for Becky. Even if she didn't want it, maybe her dad would see it as a show of good faith. Plus they were back an hour early. That had to count for something, right?

Or maybe he would suspect that the date hadn't gone well.

Was Tommen going to have to face the wrath of a father of a scorned daughter? Maybe he would see the early return as a sign of weakness, that Tommen was so afraid of him that he would cut out potential fun date time just to make sure that he was pleased, rather than seeing to it that Becky had as much fun as she possibly could. There were too many variables. He hoped his deodorant held up.

Becky kept both hands firmly on her little handbag as they walked up the path toward the front door.

"So, no dancing and weird table service notwithstanding..." Tommen ventured. "Did you have a good time?"

"I did," she replied matter-of-fact.

"Well, we're back a little early, but hopefully, after your dad I talk, then—"

She laughed. "Oh no. No, no, no. He will be doing the talking, and you will be doing the listening. And if you don't piss your pants, then that's a good start. Good luck."

Perhaps what startled him more was the fact that he'd never heard her swear. Ever. Not even an "oh my god" or anything like that. Sure, some people might debate the actual profanity level of "piss" even as it related to urination, but it still caught him off guard.

When they reached the front door, Dr. Polski opened it to meet them. Becky gave Tommen a brief, polite goodbye before ducking inside. Just that was enough to jolt Tommen back to reality and he felt his heart leap into his throat. Dr. Polski did not invite Tommen in; rather, he stepped outside and closed the door.

This could end very badly.

"Normally I'm watching the clock and counting the seconds, wondering where she is," he began. "Tonight I'm caught by surprise. What happened? Not interested in a second date?"

"Um, yes?"

"Is that a question?"

"No. I mean yes. I mean, I would like to go out on a second date. We just...left the dance early. She said she wasn't really interested. So we went and got something to eat instead. That's all, I swear."

"Don't swear unless you're prepared to give an account for it."

"Yes sir. I mean, no sir. I think?"

Dr. Polski was old. There was no doubting that he should probably be retired. But he was no nursing home poster child. He still had some fight left in him, that burning need to defend his family from all intruders. Good grief, how had his other kids managed to get married? Or was Becky just special? No, it was probably the same story for all his kids. Maybe his grandkids, too.

After a moment of knee-knocking scrutiny, Dr. Polski relaxed his stance just a little. "You work, don't you?"

"Yes sir."

"Do you work Sunday night?"

"No, I have it off."

"Good. Come over for dinner. Five-thirty. Then we can all sit down and have a chat. How does that sound?"

"Sounds...tasty?" Tasty? What the fuck?

"Excellent. We will see you then. Have a safe ride home."

Tommen debated the intentions of Polski's last statement. He highly doubted the man was truly that concerned for his safety for the whole quarter mile stretch of road between their houses. Was it simply an automatic farewell, something he said to everyone regardless of his opinion of them? Was it a slight to let Tommen know that he knew that he didn't have his license yet and still had to be carted around by his dad? Was Tommen simply overthinking things?

When Tommen reached the car, he almost got in the backseat again, catching himself at just the last second and heading for shotgun.

"He got a restraining order out for you already?" his dad asked, pulling away from the curb.

"No, not until after dinner on Sunday," Tommen replied sullenly.

"At least he invited you back."

"Yeah, a lion invited me to dinner."

His dad shook his head. "You know, if you were still back living at home, this would be standard protocol, not the exception. You'd have to walk five miles to her house and have to get all dressed up in your only other change of clothes, bring a few flowers, and still have to face your gal's pa. And her brothers, too. Just like you'd have to inspect every man who came calling for your sisters' hands."

"Please, Dad, not now. And besides, back then, I wouldn't have known any better. It's a different world now."

They pulled in the garage and his dad killed the engine. "The world doesn't change nearly as much as you think it does. There's good and there's evil, and every generation is simply a new variation of it."

"When did you get so philosophical?"

"Since you needed a philosophy lesson, seeing how you have nothing else to hang onto."

Tommen rolled his eyes as he got out of the car. Should have just kept his mouth shut, but no. Like Becky, he was inclined to have the last word.

"But anyway," his dad went on as they went inside, "did you at least have a good time?"

"I guess."

"You guess? Would you have rather been working?"

"No, but...I don't know. I mean, she wasn't too interested in the dance, and I would rather not have gone to the bakery afterwards."

"Why didn't you say something, then? I'm sure there were other places open."

"I don't know. I mean, it wasn't that big of a deal..."

"You were trying to impress a girl."

"Whatever. I'm just...I'm going to bed. I have work tomorrow."

His dad looked like he had a hundred witty comments on his tongue, but thankfully he decided not to voice them. Instead, he simply nodded and said, "Yeah, and I guess I have to take you in, too, don't I? I hope you're not showering again."

Tommen shook his head. "No, you're safe. I'm just going to take these off."

Even as he spoke and headed down to his bedroom, he was undoing the buttons on his shirt. Normally he slept in his clothes, but he knew better than to do so in his good clothes. He wasn't even sure what to make of the date. In the middle of it, it had been great. He got to go to the dance with a date, hang out with Becky, make a fool of himself at some point he was sure. But looking back, the dance had been pretty mediocre overall, but neither of them had been too interested anyway. They'd been disappointed by the early closure of the pizza places and ended up going to the bakery. The fucking bakery.

He set his alarm and flipped off the light, laying in bed but unable to sleep. Maybe it hadn't been such a great first date. Maybe they should have skipped the dance from the getgo, gone to see a movie and have a real dinner at someplace that wasn't serving leftovers. Maybe they should have pushed the time limit just a little, forced Dr. Polski to sit and count the seconds.

It was a while before Tommen was able to get to sleep, but he still had a rock of dread sitting in his stomach when his alarm went off the next morning.

# Chapter Fifteen
## A Promotion and a Plan

Micaiah woke and stared at the ceiling. In the last five weeks, he'd gotten pretty accustomed to sleeping in, not having to wake up at the ass crack of dawn every fucking day. Not that seven was much better than five, but it was a natural wake up. He'd also adjusted to not having the use of his Time abilities. Not that the Akari couldn't make up for everything and more, but he figured it best to keep a low profile. Wasn't as though he'd been doing much lately anyway. Stayed home for almost a month after getting out of the hospital. Strangely, he couldn't recall much during that time. It was all a blur, broken up only by visits from the physical therapist.

His thoughts started coming back to him more clearly when he finally decided to leave the house. Yeah, he'd gone to a bar, but he'd gotten to see his wife again. After so long. Fuck, he owed her more than this.

That had been Tuesday. Wednesday after breakfast, he'd surrendered and gone to the DMV to finally register for a handicap tag and plate. He didn't want to, but halfway across a parking lot was a long way to hobble.

Thursday he'd gone in for his preliminary prosthetic fitting. He and the prosthetist had had a long chat about the whole concept of a prosthetic leg. What he needed, what he wanted, what he expected to do, and a ton of minute details he never would have considered important, like whether he wanted any "tattoos" on it. He just wanted to walk again; what was so difficult about that? But replicating the human body was not a perfected science just yet.

He'd even been given a temporary prosthetic, something to

use and adjust to while a more permanent one was made. Thursday he'd spent an hour with the prosthetist and the physical therapist learning how to put it on, take it off, and just generally stand up and make basic movements with it. Friday he'd spent another hour and a half with them just trying to get from one chair to another. Now he had twice weekly appointments with the therapist to look forward to, because one just wasn't enough.

They'd told him that they didn't expect him to wear it all day at first. Start with an hour and try to do a little more every day, they said. Use crutches, use a walker, use a treadmill, however he felt comfortable getting around and getting used to it.

He didn't want a prosthetic. He did want to walk. Not hobble, walk. But he wanted his real leg, where he knew all the little nuances and movements in the muscles. Not a prosthetic. Problem was, he didn't have any other option. It was the prosthetic or nothing.

The only comfort he got, he figured as he pulled on the sock and the prosthetic afterwards, was that because he'd been able to keep the knee, his was a much simpler machine than if he hadn't, only the ankle and foot motions needing to be recreated. It was small comfort as he forced himself to stand before grabbing the crutches to help his balance as he headed out to the kitchen.

"Well, look who's up and walking around," Micah said, pouring himself a cup of coffee.

"What are you doing here?" Micaiah asked. "You're supposed to be at the shop."

"That's the magic of hiring a manager. I kind of like the idea; we should keep him permanently."

"He's sixteen. We can't overwork him too much. And he doesn't have Time, so he can't just make extra time for whatever he needs to do, like school work."

"Lucky for you, I am actually heading in. I'm just taking my sweet ass time and the opportunity to sleep in for once."

"It is pretty nice, isn't it?"

"You're going to be nursing that, aren't you? Just so you don't have to get up early again."

"Absolutely."

"How's your knee doing?"

"It's...doing okay actually." Micaiah limped along slowly into the kitchen. "It's weird...I actually got used to not having a leg, having that support under my knee. Now I have support and the ability to walk again, but it's just..."

"You don't have the calf muscles."

"Right."

"Hey, I'm proud of you, dude. Seriously. Like, I'm pretty sure that in just two days, you're already moving faster than some old people at the grocery store."

Micaiah laughed. "You think so?"

"Absolutely."

"Well, I'm going to have breakfast and try to not fall down the stairs to go work out."

Micah finished off his coffee. "Guess I better get going to work then, make sure they haven't burned down the store."

He left not long after that, leaving Micaiah alone to finish his breakfast and make his way downstairs. It took him far longer than he thought it should, and was almost a workout in itself. It was a stupid thing to do, really, considering he hadn't gotten to stairs in therapy, but he figured it was just his stubborn determination coming back to life.

With no work to occupy his time, he probably should have spent more time keeping in shape and not letting himself get lazy, especially with his stump. But he'd only been down not even half a dozen times in as many weeks, and each time he felt like a miserable failure halfway through. Either that or his knee and phantom lower leg would seize in a cramp so awful he'd once dropped the bar on his chest and he'd counted himself lucky that he hadn't broken his sternum, or worse.

He resolved to do just a small workout, half of his normal routine. When that went off without much of a problem, he turned to the treadmill. Could he do it? Could he really keep any kind of decent pace? Would the machine go that slow? His early morning workout was typically a mile or two run, but he'd been known to do half marathons on this thing.

He started out like a coward, one foot on each side of the track, fussing with the controls until he got it as slow as it could go before actually stepping on.

In his mind, he actually likened it to water skiing, being prepared for the tug of the boat as you started off, but being unprepared for just how much of a tug you would get. It took him half a dozen tries to be able to just get walking without slipping and sliding and falling, and by that time he was too worn out and embarrassed and frustrated to do much more than about the equivalent of the length of the driveway. And he still had to get back up the stairs.

Still, necessity is a powerful motivator, and get back up the stairs he did, limping forlornly back to his room to remove his prosthetic and get ready for the day, starting with a shower.

By the time he emerged from the bathroom, he'd recovered some of his self-esteem, but he paused as he considered the prosthetic. He'd spent much more than an hour in it and he wasn't sure how he felt about it yet, never mind all the pain and embarrassment it had caused him so far. Even if it was largely his own fault for not knowing how to use the thing.

In the end, he decided that he'd had enough of it for a while. Maybe later once he'd shaken off the events of the morning.

Heading out to the car, though, he started having second thoughts, wondering if maybe he shouldn't have worn it, just so he could have another shoe with some traction. But he made it without incident, starting his car and using the Akari to Band and warm up faster. It probably wasn't the best idea since Walter had reported two Tracker attacks, Micah one, and there had been scattered reports around the Region of similar incidents, but so far, no Akari-bearers using the Akari had been attacked. Maybe it was just luck, given how few there were, but maybe it was that the Akari was invisible to them. Or maybe it was because they were originally trained to be friendly toward it. Who could know? Rifun and Cassius obviously didn't, but the fact that they were aware of Trackers and their uses was a little disconcerting.

Micaiah didn't dwell on it as he backed out of the driveway, still moderately uncomfortable with left foot driving. Not because it was left foot driving, but because he had no right foot backup in case something went wrong. But traffic was more forgiving on a Saturday morning as a majority of the working class slept in, and he got through town easily enough, heading toward the bakery and his parking spot, everything coming so naturally it was like he'd never been gone.

He fumbled his way through the back door, emerging into the kitchen area just as Tommen came around the corner to see who was intruding on their turf. Immediately, his face lit up.

"Micaiah!" he exclaimed loudly. "Hey, guys, Cai's here!"

Should have seen that coming, Micaiah figured as Kyle came from the front and Jenna came from elsewhere in the kitchen, both of them overjoyed. Jenna hugged him tight while Kyle and Tommen gave him simple bro hugs.

"Micah said you were starting to come back around," Tommen said. "How you feeling?"

Micaiah shrugged. "Been better. Been worse. Where's Micah?"

"Where do you think?" Kyle said, smirking.

Sure enough, Micah was in the office working on something or other on the computer. Nothing had changed, really. The desk was still covered in papers, the bins were usually full, and of course, there were a dozen messages on the answering machine. The only thing that really changed was who was sitting in the big, comfy chair.

"You're in my seat," Micaiah said.

Micah swiveled around and grinned. "Hey, you're here! You should have told me; I would have given you a ride."

"You think I'm going to be here all day? Not a chance. I have things to do."

"Well, aren't we Mr. Important? So how long are you here?"

"Oh, long enough to make some phone calls and get back in the swing of things. Get a few things organized."

"Before I mess up your system too badly?" Micah folded his arms and raised a brow, but it only lasted a second, before he dropped it and breathed a sigh of relief. "Hey, go for it, dude. Office work is not my thing. You can make all the phone calls and arrange all the deals you want."

As Micaiah moved toward the chair, Micah stood and hugged him. "Good to have you back, Cai."

"You are such a sap," Micaiah told him. "But thanks."

"Holler if you need anything."

"Yes, Mom."

Micah closed the door behind him, leaving Micaiah alone with the paperwork. The first thing he noticed was that all the piles had been rearranged. Incoming was where Paid should have been, and Stock Orders were in the Outgoing pile. He sighed. Ultimately, nothing had really changed. He spent a good hour not just moving the piles back where he wanted them, but sorting the papers in the piles, getting them where they needed to go, printing things that were missing. Just as well that Micah didn't want to do office work; who knew how many invoices had gone unpaid or uncollected?

He might be here longer than he thought.

"Micaiah?"

He turned to see Tommen poking his head in the door. "Angry customer. Doesn't believe I'm the manager. Wants to talk to the owner. Micah said to get you because he's busy."

Nope. Nothing changes.

Micaiah sighed and grabbed his crutches, debating the whole way out to the front counter whether he should have brought the prosthetic anyway just in case. Then he wondered why, seeing how he would still be using his crutches anyway, and no one would be able to see it with the display case and counter in the way.

"Are you the owner?" the angry customer, a woman looking within a few years of retirement, demanded. "Or at least the manager? I mean, my God, I've never heard of any place putting a sixteen year old in charge, especially these days!"

"And the way he stood out as respectful and responsible among the other disrespectful, irresponsible sixteen year olds is why he got made manager," Micaiah informed her. "But I'm here, and we're not talking about him. How can I help you?"

"Yes, I ordered a raspberry tart and the man gave me cherry! What if I had been allergic to cherries?"

"Then I imagine I would be speaking to a paramedic right now instead of you." He noted her expression. "Do you still have the tart?"

"No. I forced myself to finish it, as repulsive as it was. But I think I ought to get a free raspberry tart, if not now, then next time I come in. If I decide to come in again."

"Unfortunately, ma'am, without proof that the tart you received was cherry and not raspberry as you ordered, I'm not inclined to give you anything, especially since you willingly finished it and waited until now to tell anyone. I hope you'll come again and things can be put to rights, but I have a hard time believing your story, especially since you literally ate all the evidence. In good faith, however, I am willing to offer a small coffee or other drink."

"Well, don't you have cameras? They could show that he reached for the wrong one."

"No, they wouldn't. Is there anything else I can help you with?"

"Your sidewalk is icy, and the corners of your rugs were flipped up. I could have fallen! I put your rugs back to rights, but you really should salt your sidewalks."

Maybe it was the coup and his time in prison. Maybe it was the loss of his leg. Maybe it was because he was growing weary of this life. Maybe it was just his old self coming back. Whatever the reason, Micaiah was done with the bullshit. He spoke as he hopped around the counter. "You know, I've been walking around this store for quite a while today." Lie, but how would she know? He stopped at the end of the counter where she could see him. "And I have yet to have a problem. I'll consider your words and advice, as it is very cold outside and starting to snow, but I won't be intimidated or threatened. Now then, if there is nothing else I can do for you, have a nice day. And do be careful. After all, snow and ice is very uncommon around here in the middle of February."

The woman's gaze went back and forth between the gap between his knee and the floor, and his expression, one that he hoped conveyed how tired he was of this exchange. At his dismissal, she took a breath, turned her nose up, and left the store in a huff. A few customers behind her in line and around the store snickered or shook their heads and rolled their eyes. Micaiah turned and headed back behind the counter toward the office. He cut Tommen off before he could speak, saying, "I'm allowed to do that. You're not. You still have to play nice."

Tommen closed his mouth. His shoulders slumped as he assented.

"One more thing," Micaiah said before disappearing into the office. "Make sure the sidewalk gets salted. I don't need a nightmare becoming a reality."

He spent about another hour or two tidying up the office and getting it back to roughly the way he'd left it. Even if he did get everything organized and pristine, it would only drift back into the mess it was destined to be. It was a work desk, after all, inherently cursed to disorganization.

It was around one when he emerged from his den again, roused from the dull monotony of office work by hunger.

"How goes things?" he asked Kyle on the front counter.

Kyle shrugged. "They're going okay."

"You had lunch yet?"

"Yeah, like an hour ago."

Upon questioning the rest of the staff, it appeared that only

Micah hadn't eaten yet.

"I'm going to make a quick run to the deli," Micaiah told him. "Want to come, or you just want me to bring you something?"

"Um..." Micah looked uncertain for a second before nodding. "Yeah, I'll come. Just give me a minute to get this in the oven."

Within ten minutes, they were heading down the street to the deli in Micaiah's car. Normally it was a decent lunch hour walk, but Micaiah was in no mood to hobble that distance.

"What made you decide to come in?" Micah asked.

"Kayla," Micaiah admitted.

"How is she?"

"Better since I'm out and about, I guess."

"That's good. Did you some good, too, I see."

"Yeah, she did me real good." He smirked when he saw his brother's expression. "No, I just needed to get out of the house, get back to some semblance of normalcy."

"But...? I sense there's something else going on in your head. Come on, Cai, I'm your twin. I can practically read your mind."

"In the office," was all Micaiah said as he parked the car, grabbed his crutches, and got out, hurrying for the relative warmth of the deli, Micah close behind. They ordered lunch and sat to eat.

"How's Tommen been doing as manager?" Micaiah wondered.

"He seems to handle it well," Micah answered. "He's still not sure about his powers and limits when it comes to angry customers, but he's good with the responsibility otherwise. Kyle and Jenna don't have a problem with him. I feel comfortable letting him open on Saturdays and close on his working nights."

"Maybe we ought to make it permanent then," Micaiah suggested.

Micah shrugged. "I have no problem with that."

"The only thing I might suggest is that we might need nametags."

"Nametags?"

Micaiah explained the brief exchange with the angry lady. Even as he spoke, Micah nodded. "Yup, yup. A couple people have said that. Your woman sounds like the only one who's actually been angry; most are just shocked. One compared us to McDonald's, but you know how that goes."

"Since it's more than just the three of us, nametags might be in order," Micaiah repeated. "One for me and you, with some label that says Owner. One for Tommen that says Manager. And Kyle and Jenna get their own tags, too. Assuming that's our decision to keep Tommen on as the manager."

Micah nodded. "As I said, no argument from me. He's responsible, knows what he's doing, and does it well. And he knows when to ask for help."

So that settled it. The twins finished their lunch and started back toward the bakery.

"Are you going out tonight, then?" Micah inquired. "Did you and Kayla make plans?"

"She hasn't said anything about it," Micaiah answered. "I really haven't given it a lot of thought."

"Why not? What's on your mind, Cai?"

Micaiah grinned as he parked the car and got out. "Thought you could read my mind? After all, you are my twin."

"I said practically read your mind," Micah said, following him into the store. "Come on, Cai, what gives?"

But Micaiah ignored him. Instead, he found Tommen and called for him in the office, bidding him close the door.

"Am I in trouble for what happened earlier?" Tommen asked meekly. "I tried to handle it, I did, but she just didn't believe me when I said—"

"Stop staring at my knee and look at me," Micaiah told him. Tommen looked up guiltily. "I know what she said. I believe you. Micah's told me that it's not the first time it's happened. And you can't please everyone. She probably wouldn't have been happy if I offered to give her the keys to the store. All right? She was fishing for freebies and trying to intimidate you and me into giving her stuff. That's all that was."

"Okay," Tommen said, looking relieved.

"That being said, Micah and I did discuss your performance as manager recently, both today and by his accounts of the last six weeks or however long I've been gone."

"And?"

The poor boy's expression was comical, like he wanted to appear hopeful without seeming arrogant or cocky, and all that resulted was something like a cross between a first kiss and a sour lemon.

"We've decided to keep you on as manager," Micaiah told him. "So everything you've been doing over the last however many weeks, keep doing it. Opening, closing, stock order, cash counting and bank drops, personnel management, lord of the castle when we're gone, all of that. The only difference is, you'll be using my paper filing system instead of Micah's; pay attention to where everything goes."

"Yes sir," Tommen said, grinning from ear to ear.

"One more thing. Since it's more than just the three of us now, and because of the little snafu today, we've also decided to order nametags. Ours will say Owner, yours will be Manager, that way no one gets confused or doubts your position, though they still might."

"That would be great! To not be doubted, I mean."

"Did Micah have you sign any paperwork when he made you manager?"

"Yeah, it was a bunch of stuff about accepting the position and the pay raise and a whole bunch of other things. He said there would be a copy in my file."

"I'll look for it, but I thought I'd ask just in case. You would have been a little more confused about it if you hadn't done it."

"Probably."

"Congratulations. Now if you would be so kind, send Micah in."

Tommen nodded and turned to leave. As he was about to

walk out the door, he looked back. "It's good to have you back."

Micaiah only dipped his head and made a motion, telling him to get a move on.

It was about ten minutes before Micah showed up in the office, still wiping wet hands on a paper towel, apron covered in flour and who knew what else.

"I take it you told him our decision," he said, pulling up a chair and collapsing into it.

"I did," Micaiah confirmed. "I'd say he took it well."

"Uh huh. Right. So why am I here? Am I being demoted?"

Micaiah nodded. "Yup. Just one of the grunts." He shifted in his seat. "Actually I wanted to tell you about the...plan I came up with the other day."

"Am I correct to assume this doesn't have anything to do with your new prosthetic?"

"Ninety-eight percent accurate. It does depend a tiny bit on it."

"Okay, this ought to be interesting."

"I'm going after Rifun and Cassius."

Micah nodded and ran his tongue over his teeth. "Huh. Nothing subtle about that, is there? And how do you hope to accomplish this is a way that doesn't involve losing your other leg or any other part of your body?"

"I'm going to go back to them and demand a Time Trial."

"I said a way that *doesn't* involve losing parts of your body. That is the opposite of that. I really hope there's more to this plan than that. You would be slaughtered. And that's with both of your legs."

"It's not going to come to that, because with any luck, Rifun and Cassius will be dead before it even begins."

Micah put his hand over his face and sighed. "You are very good at being blunt to the point of rudeness, and also being vague to the point of insanity. What's your plan?"

So Micaiah told him, about sending in a decoy disguised as him, declaring the three Testimonies, where one of them would be him in Disguise. With Rifun and Cassius both present and within range, he could use the Akari to Band in spite of the dampening field, getting in enough time to murder them both. Then, hopefully, he could Band and get everyone out before the Day or the Bat came after them.

"It's still a work in progress," he concluded. "I told Kayla and she made me promise to include her somehow, as in, take her with me. I don't know quite how I'm going to do that, or if I even will."

"Well, a promise is a promise," Micah said. "And if you promised your wife something, you better try your damnedest to make good on it."

"Believe me, I know. Going over it again, though, I'm not sure how I can effectively include her and still keep her safe."

"You think that might have something to do with the fact that you are calling for a Time Trial?"

"One that won't begin because—"

"Cai, your plan, you have one shot to get it right. There is no escaping otherwise. There are no do-overs. Even if you somehow manage to escape the Wheel a second time, in tact, they won't fall for it again. No more do-overs for anyone ever again."

"All regimes fall sooner or later," Micaiah said. "I'm just trying to make this one fall sooner."

"Believe me, everyone would like that very much. It's just...I can't see how it's going to work."

"Why not? I understand your objections, but give me specifics."

"Okay, one: you want Walter to be your bait, knowing that he's not right in the head and the place he is most likely going to be sent is back to the black cells. We both know that Walt's a dedicated guy, but we don't need him coming back to us as a vegetable. The way Tommen talks, he's back to work, but just barely it seems. And you want to send him to the frontlines for a third time.

"Two: the only reason you're asking for Walter is because you both have a right-side limp. Decent reason, and I get your logic, but think of this way. Walter is healing. He's getting better. His limp is improving. You say you want to wait until you get your permanent prosthetic and get comfortable in it. How long is that going to take? Probably a little while. Long after Walter heals of his limp, you will still be gimping. I think you underestimate the time it takes to be that comfortable in a prosthetic, and overestimate your own abilities.

"Three: Rifun and Cassius are Akari-bearers, or they think they are. They certainly have comparable abilities. They can overpower the dampening field just as well as you can. And I'd be willing to bet that they're a little quicker on the draw. You might get off one shot, might even get lucky and hit one of them, but there is no way you'd be able to kill them both before they'd rip your Band to shreds and kill you. And the rest of everyone in attendance.

"Four: Even assuming that everything up to that point goes according to plan, we both know that the Day and the Bat are not...natural. They're not normal secretaries, Time Agents, whatever they are supposed to be. Call it a hunch, but I don't think they'd be much affected by your Banding either.

"Five—"

"Okay, I get it," Micaiah interrupted testily. "I get it. It's risky. It's dangerous. There's a good chance I won't come back alive, even if I do succeed. There's a good chance I'll fail anyway, and obviously not come back alive."

"Well, I'm glad you've come to terms with it."

"And what do you suggest?"

"I suggest you stay out of it. You did your part. You brought back information, inside knowledge. You basically crippled them, at least for a time. And you paid a price for it. Stay here for a while. Relax. Let your body heal. You can only push it so far before it breaks and you can't repair it."

"If that's what it takes to bring down Cassius, then so be it."

"Oh really? Is that what you told yourself as you lay in the hospital for a week? Is that what you were thinking about when you shut yourself up in your room for a month? Did you lay there and think, 'Gee, this was totally worth it. What a hero I am, giving of myself in order to defeat Rifun and Cassius. Maybe I'll go back and see if I can't—'"

Micaiah's fist connected with Micah's nose even before his brain fully processed what was happening. Micah tipped over backwards in his chair and lay on the ground, stunned. After a moment, he groaned as he picked himself up. Micaiah could only stare. Blinking rapidly as he realized what he just did, he spun around and grabbed the box of tissues.

"Oh my God, Micah, shit, fuck, I'm sorry. I didn't mean..."

"Yes, you did," Micah said calmly, taking a few tissues and putting them to his bloody nose. "Of course you meant it. I antagonized you and you reacted."

"I'm sorry," Micaiah repeated. "I didn't even think...I didn't..."

"Why do you think Kayla wants to be part of this so much?" Micah repositioned his chair, out of Micaiah's reach this time, and sat down. He took the tissue box from Micaiah's outstretched hand. "Because she loves and cares for you, yes, but because in your wedding vows, you promised that if you could help it, you would go together. 'Let not one be the coward' I believe were the words, or something close enough. If you were going to face life-ending danger, then if she could be by your side, she would. And if she were to face the executioner's block, then you would, too. Side-by-side. Always. And you made sure that I would remember that bit because you knew you would forget."

Micaiah rubbed his face. He remembered. He often forgot, but now that Micah brought it up, he remembered. Even Kayla had tried to remind him of it, and it had completely gone over his head. Shit. He shook his head. "She's accompanying me on a suicide mission."

"Exactly."

He sighed. "How can I make it not a suicide mission?"

"I don't know," Micah admitted, throwing away bloody tissues and reaching for more clean ones. His nose and left cheek under his eye were beginning to turn colors and swell up. "I'm not a strategist or a tactician. I just bake bread and do what my older brother tells me."

Micaiah scoffed. "No, you don't."

"Ah, you're right. I never listen. Except when it makes sense. Right now, you're not making sense."

He sighed. "I'm sorry. I shouldn't have hit you."

"Hit me? Cai, you fucking punched me."

"All right. I'm sorry I punched you."

"S'all right. It'll go away."

As if to prove his point, Micaiah Banded his brother with the Akari, healing his face in only about thirty seconds. When he was done, Micah blinked rapidly and shook his head, touching his face where it should have been tender and swollen. "You know, we're not supposed to be Banding."

"We're not supposed to be using Time," Micaiah corrected. "Walter said nothing about using the Akari."

Micah shrugged. "All right, you got me there. And it probably wouldn't look too good to the others if I walked out of here with a black eye and swollen face."

"I don't think it would." Micaiah sighed. "So what do you think I should do?"

"I told you, I don't know. Ask Kayla; maybe she'll have some insight." Micah stood. "I'm just going to head back out, if it's all the same to you."

Micaiah nodded guiltily. When Micah got to the door, he called him back. "Micah. I'm sorry. I am."

"I know."

And he slipped out of the office.

Micaiah held his breath for a count of ten and repeated four times before he was able to quell the anxiety and need to vent his frustration on whatever breakable thing happened to be within range. Had he honestly just punched his own brother? Where in the fuck had that come from? Was that what his vengeance looked like when it was uncontrolled? Poetic, maybe, but it still offered no solutions.

And there were worse things to think about anyway. Kayla

had seen right through his plan, knew it was a suicide mission and so tried to insert herself into it. Had Micah not said anything, would he really have gone through with the plan, intent on his revenge and sacrificing his own wife in the process?

After a minute or two of silent contemplation, he spun around in the chair and pulled out his phone.

"Hello?" Kayla answered.

"Hey, it's me."

"Hi! Hey, how are you?"

"Well, I'm working so—"

"That's great! So you're feeling better?"

"Yeah, somewhat. Almost like I never left. Think we could talk about it later?"

"And by later you mean...?"

They met at another hotel later that evening. They arrived separately, about an hour apart. Micaiah found Kayla just coming out of the pool, glittery bikini standing out against dark skin. She saw him and waved, hurrying to grab her towel and sandals.

"You and your towels," he said, tsking.

She kissed him and whispered, "Follow me upstairs and you can take it off if you want."

Well, it wasn't the reason he wanted to—okay, it wasn't the main reason, but it was always a good reason to meet her. By the time they were finished, he almost couldn't remember why he'd called her in the first place. Of course, wasn't missing one's wife enough of a reason?

"Why do we keep meeting here?" Kayla sighed, pulling the blanket up around them. "One of these times, we'll have to go to your house or mine."

"I don't think Micah would appreciate that," Micaiah laughed.

"Why not? He seemed to get a kick out of it after his breakup with Lily. Fine, we'll go to my place."

He sighed. "We sneak around in order to minimize—"

"I know, minimize the risk of becoming emotionally

compromised by hiding the fact that we're married, instead making it seem like we split up after your last Time Trial. I know, I know. It's like a bad movie, the hero surrenders in order to save the girl. And either he already has a backup plan in case of such contingencies or the girl dies anyway."

"Aren't you the optimist?"

"Speaking of plans." She stretched out against him and rolled over on her stomach. "How's your plan coming?"

"It's not."

He told her about the discussion in the office, including his disagreement with Micah.

"You punched your brother?" Kayla interrupted.

"I don't even know what came over me. I mean, I'll beat up on him kind of as a joke, you know, older brother kind of thing, but I've never actually...hurt him. Not intentionally."

"You punched your twin brother."

"He left, but he did remind me of our vows, and showed me that my plan was a suicide mission."

"Your twin brother. Your younger twin brother. You punched him."

"I've gone over it in my mind, but I can't think of anything else."

"You punched—"

"Yes, I punched my brother," Micaiah cut in. "I said it. I know it. I feel bad. I apologized. Can we please move on to something more pressing, like overthrowing an oppressive, tyrannical regime?"

Kayla sighed. "Okay."

"Why did you ask to be included in my plan? Was it because you knew it was a suicide mission?"

She didn't answer for a long moment. Then, "Yes. I could see that from the very beginning. I didn't say anything, though."

"Why?"

"Cai, when you get a plan in your head, when it's logical and clear-headed, it's brilliant. When you make plans based on need and helping people, they're awesome." She paused. "When you make plans based on personal revenge, it's do or die, sometimes more literally than you realize."

"So you were just going to let me — ?"

"No, of course I wasn't going to let you do anything. I was hoping you would come to the realization on your own, especially since it involved a few more people and a lot more time. And if you didn't, then I would tell you eventually, yes."

Micaiah was silent for a minute after that. He was an idiot. A stupid, one-legged idiot. He took a measured breath. "My greatest fear is losing you," he confessed. "And if I lost you because of my own stupidity, I would never forgive myself."

"I know." Kayla kissed him tenderly. "But I'm not as helpless as you think."

"What do you think I should do?"

"Well, there's what I think you should do, and what I know you're going to try to do anyway, so I might as well try to guide you as best I can." She giggled when he gave her a look. "Obviously, you're not just going to sit at home or in the office and go through the motions with your therapist."

"Got that right. I have to put up with the guy twice a week now."

"It's for your own good, dear."

"Yeah, yeah, whatever you say. What were you going to say?"

She hesitated. "Honestly, I would turn it over to Doug. Let him take the credit if he just has to have it; you'll still have your revenge, I'm sure. I don't think it really matters whose name is on the parade float as long as Rifun and Cassius are gone."

"But...but..." Micaiah said with mock-offense.

"Cai, you know we'd have to go dark afterwards anyway. You would never get to bask in the glory."

He finally nodded. "Okay."

"Doug can look at it from a more level-headed point of view. He'll come up with something."

Even as she spoke, she was reaching for her phone, punching in a number and putting it to speakerphone.

"Doug Templeton," came the answer.

"Doug, it's Cai and Kayla," Kayla told him.

"You're not naked in a hotel room, are you?"

"Just ignore any weird sounds you hear; you're on speakerphone."

Micaiah had to cough to keep from cracking up laughing.

"Duly noted. Micaiah, how are you doing? Haven't heard from you since your...escape. I expect a full report."

"It'll have to wait a bit," Micaiah said. "But I'm doing all right."

"Good, good. Hey, your brother has the potential to be as great as you, once he gets over his shock and fear and all the things that normally accompany an eye-opening."

"I don't doubt it, but that's not why we're calling."

"Well, I'm sure Kayla's filled you in on a lot, but I'll just reiterate that no one is coming in or going out."

"She told me, but that's not it either."

"Don't keep me in suspense, guys, out with it."

So Micaiah gave him the basics of his plan, not mentioning the fight with Micah and pretending like including Kayla had always been part of it. When he was done, everyone was silent for a long time. Finally, "You came up with this all on your own?"

"Yes sir," Micaiah confirmed.

"Has anyone told you how idiotic this sounds? It's a suicide mission, you know that."

"That's why we're asking for your input, Doug," Kayla said, though Micaiah could see from her expression how much she hated asking him for any kind of help. "Help us make it not a suicide mission. Everyone comes home."

"In one piece," Micaiah added.

"Oh, I understand that," Doug chuckled. "Okay, well, it sounds like you weren't idle in your downtime. Good to hear. Listen, why don't you let me chew on this for a while, see if I can't come up with something a little more likely to succeed and a little more likely to get everyone home alive and in one piece as you said."

"How are things going?" Kayla asked. "Has there been any news at all out of the Wheel?"

"Tighter than a Ziploc bag, sorry to say. We've had reports of Tracker attacks across all Divisions, but only when Time was used. Akari-bearers seem to be largely unaffected."

"What are the Trackers doing?"

"Those that aren't killed by their targets? Some targets are killed outright, usually explained away as a dog or bear attack or what have you. Others disappear. One Merchant was attacked when he was having dinner with his wife. Tracker was unconcerned with the wife, got its jaws around the Merchant and they just vanished."

"Vanished?"

"That's how the wife described it. Vanished. I can't tell you much more than that because I don't know more than that. The only thing we can assume is that they go back to the Wheel."

"Any pattern to who dies and who vanishes?" Micaiah wondered.

"Nothing we've been able to determine so far, but without access to the Archives and other Wheel databases, we're working on pre-coup information, and public information at that. What nasty little lists Cassius and Rifun kept, they likely kept to themselves."

"Imagine so."

"Listen, I'll let you get back to your date night, and I'll contact you if we come up with anything."

"Thanks, Doug," Kayla said politely and hung up. She shook her head. "Sometimes I hate that man."

"More than sometimes," Micaiah agreed. "But like you said, he's our best resource for rethinking a plan and getting some fresh input."

"But still...come on, let's find a movie or something."

The hotel room came with a bag of popcorn and a bowl, and

soon they were watching a movie on TV.

"Do you think...?" Kayla asked, yawning. "Do you think that we could spend our next life actually together, as husband and wife?"

"I'm sure we could," Micaiah answered. "We've done it before. But it would have to be after all of this shit with Cassius and Rifun gets sorted out."

"Considering our only options so far are kill or be killed."

"You are very good at being an optimist, you know that?"

"I consider myself to be a realist. I have to be, at least for the sake of children."

"Children?" Micaiah shifted so he could look at her.

She sighed. "I want kids, Cai."

"I thought we agreed that kids are a bad idea? There's our line of work and especially the state things are in now. Aklaq, that's why we can't even live together right now."

"But when all of this is over." She closed her eyes. "I want...I want kids and to have both of us raise them and live in our own house...I want a normal life, Cai. Just once. Walter's done it."

"I call that special circumstances. Besides, kids grow up. Unless we brought them with us into Time at least, we can't just dump them off somewhere the next time we go dark. That's a lot to force on a child. Look at Tommen."

When she didn't reply, Micaiah kissed the top of her head. "I don't mean to kill your dream, but with so much going on already...can we maybe put it on hold for a little while?"

She shrugged. "I guess." She went on before he could say more. "I know you're right. It's just...I was going to bring this up earlier, but figured I would wait until after the elections. Let the transition of power go over, then talk to you about going in and building a new life. Maybe even take a little time off from the rest of the gang."

"I know. I had plans, too. All of them supposed to be after the elections. We'll just have to put them off a little while longer. What's a few more months after fifty years of marriage, hm?"

Kayla shrugged again and stayed silent. After a time, he could feel her fall into deep sleep. The popcorn was gone and the movie nearly over. Micaiah gently moved her off him and she rolled away, grabbing the blanket and pulling it tight to her body. He got up and used the bathroom, looking over his stump before turning off the light. It seemed to have fared better this night than the other night and looked no worse for wear from the prosthetic. Maybe he could give it another shot and try to get more comfortable. He'd only had it a couple days, after all.

Wearily, he hobbled back to the bed, pushing the blankets back and stretching out alongside Kayla. How nice it would be to do this every night.

# Chapter Sixteen
## Scrutiny

Sunday came around way too soon for Tommen's liking. On the one hand, he was excited to see Becky again. He'd texted her a little on Saturday, seeing if he could weasel out some of the details of the dinner, but the most he'd gotten was that he should at least look presentable. He didn't have to show up in the suit he'd worn to the dance, but no jeans and T-shirt.

"You're not going to spend another two hours in the bathroom, are you?" his dad wondered.

"Not planning on it," Tommen answered.

But there was no guarantee. The time needed to appropriately prepare for a situation was directly proportionate to the person he was trying to impress. For the dance, he'd been trying to impress a girl, Becky. That had required approximately three hours. Now he was going to dinner to impress Becky's father. The time needed to prepare for that was...half a lifetime? It felt like it.

"Fine, what time do you want to leave?"

"Oh, I'm going to walk."

His dad raised a brow. "You're going to walk? It's ten degrees with snow on the way later."

"I know. I'm going to walk. It's only a quarter mile, max."

"I'll drive you. Actually, since it's only a short distance, I'll even let you take the car on your own. If you can promise you won't do anything and crash it or hit someone else or anything."

Tommen was ready to decline, then paused. He could do that. Quarter mile, pft, that was nothing. And it might serve to impress Becky and her dad. Yeah, his next driving course didn't start for a couple more weeks, but still, it was a display of maturity and early responsibility, on top of his being manager at the bakery.

"Okay," he said finally. "I'll drive."

"Have to get ready first."

Picking out a pair of pants was easy enough, he never chose a color he couldn't see. Shirts, however, were a different matter. To his eyes, his only options were blue and yellow. Thankfully, pretty much everything went with black, so he picked a shirt at random. Since Becky hadn't said anything about footwear, he hoped that simple tennis shoes would suffice. If her house was as upper crust as he suspected, he would be taking them off anyway as soon as he got in the door, if not before.

"Just remember," his dad said when he finally emerged from his room, "if you're driving, I won't be able to save you if something goes wrong." He smirked as he said it.

"If I'm driving, I'll be able to get to the car a lot faster than waiting for you to come," Tommen told him.

"I can still Band. I was referring to the fact that I won't be walking down the icy sidewalk."

"Oh. Yeah, okay. You might have a point there."

Truthfully, Tommen had adjusted to not having his Time abilities. Not to say that he didn't miss them or want to use them from time to time—okay, most of the time—but he no longer felt lost when he instinctively tried to throw up a Band and nothing happened. Instead, he simply took the impact of running into a mental brick wall and carried on. He could feel where he ought to be able to feel Time and manipulate it, but there was an unbreakable pane of glass between him and it, and the most he could do was stare forlornly through that window.

Walter held the keys out to him, but snatched them away when he reached for them. "You know the rules. You follow the rules. You get one chance. Got it?"

"Yes sir," Tommen said.

After a moment of consideration, Walter handed him the keys

for real and Tommen headed out to the garage. He got in the driver's seat, fully expecting his dad to climb in beside him and still surprised when he didn't.

The rules. Right, follow the rules. Seat adjusted, seatbelt, mirrors, steering wheel, and don't forget the garage door. The last thing he needed was to take out the garage door, especially with his dad watching right there at the door to the house. That would not go over well. One chance and he didn't need to blow it before he ever left the garage.

Okay, garage door open, check mirrors, back out slowly. He'd barely crossed the threshold when he heard a yell. Tommen slammed the brakes and looked around. He saw his dad on the step, laughing.

"Just making sure you're paying attention," he said.

"Dad!" Tommen whined.

"Have a good time. Remember what I said. One chance."

Rolling his neck to try and calm his frayed nerves, Tommen started backing up again. *Okay, pause at the street and look around. See anyone? Still a little dark this time of day, enough that people should have their headlights on. No cars. Don't see any pedestrians in the immediate vicinity, but the Miltons' dog is loose again. If it runs into the street, is that one of those things where the insurance company says it's better to hit it than try to swerve and potentially lose control? Can I use that excuse?*

Not that it would matter, since both he and probably his dad would get in trouble for him driving unaccompanied. The officer would show up on scene, take one look at him, shake his head, roll his eyes, and ask where Walter was. Then, when his dad got there and told the officer that he'd let him take the car without having a full license, the officer would shake his head, roll his eyes, and probably give them both a lecture. Even if no tickets were formally issued, Tommen would be under the eye of every cop in the city and around the county, and Walter would probably be in a little hot water at work.

So he took extra caution as he made it out into the street and headed down the road. *Follow the speed limit, going a little under if you have to. Keep a constant search pattern, always looking for kids chasing balls, riding bikes, playing games — yeah, when it's ten degrees out — and for stupid loose dogs that roamed the neighborhood.*

Thankfully, the Miltons' dog stayed out of the road, even if it stood on the sidewalk and barked its head off as he went by. No, don't look at that. See it, assess the threat level, and move on to the next potential accident.

All this in just a quarter mile, Tommen mused as he finally approached Becky's house. Normally there weren't any cars nearby, but now there was one in the driveway outside the garage and two right on the curb where he wanted to park. Well, he wasn't much for parallel parking and he didn't want to overshoot too much. But he also didn't have time to sit around in the road looking for a parking spot, not that he had a ton of options anyway. Plus there was a car coming up behind him, going a little faster than the speed limit. Actually, a lot faster.

He ended up pulling in behind the second car on the curb, waiting a second until the speeding car flew by. Tommen was just about to get out when he looked and realized that he'd blocked someone's driveway. Sighing and hoping no one had seen his blunder — or understood that he'd just pulled over for the car (that was his story and he was sticking to it) — he started the car again and elected to just back up until he was out of the way.

He stayed there a minute longer, nervous and hesitant. It came more from the car and driving than anything, really. He took a quick inventory of the stuff in the car. He knew his dad kept a gun in the center console, but that was locked at all times, and he didn't think there was anything else of value lurking around. Well, even if there was, like his dad said, if someone really wants it, they'll get it. Just make sure the car is locked so they have to work for it a little.

Shit, he was really doing this. Likely they'd already seen him. There was no backing out now. He took a look at himself in the mirror, making sure he was as properly attired as he could be. Hair combed, nothing in his teeth, shirt unwrinkled. Fuck, he was just going to dinner so he could date a girl, not ask to marry her. Still, he checked himself over and then got out of the car, making sure he locked it.

From the looks of things, he wasn't the only one who had been invited to dinner. There was movement everywhere, in every window it looked like. Becky had said she was the youngest child, but there were definitely some young children running around, so those had to be grandchildren.

The walkway had been shoveled recently, but a fine layer of frosty fuzz was forming on the stones again, showing Tommen's nervously short steps. He hadn't brought a coat and only now did he consider that Dr. Polski might want to have another chat with him on the porch before admitting him into the house. He stopped as the door opened before he even got to the porch. To his relief, it was Becky and not her father.

"Hey, I thought that was you," she said, grinning. "Good grief, didn't you bring a coat?"

"Uh, no. No, I didn't," Tommen admitted shyly.

"Well, come on, let's get you warmed up. Stomp off your shoes and you can put them somewhere on the mat."

It was similar to walking into the Durvins' house, the change from outside to inside. Outside: nice, polite, unassuming, just one house of many on the street. Inside: beautiful, lavish, as much care into the selection of items as the number of them. The entry was an area all its own with a closet full of jackets, a long line of mats and rugs for shoes of all sizes, plus two small benches to sit on to don and doff (because sophisticated people used words like that).

Stepping out of the entry, Tommen was presented with three options. The first, a staircase immediately in front of him, solid oak with an intricately carved railing and a runner that, if Becky had said it was imported yak hair from Nepal, dyed and woven by poor peasant women, he would not have doubted her. It led upstairs to an open landing as well as rooms which he could not tell what they were.

To the right of the entry was the kitchen and dining room, just as big as, or maybe bigger than the ones in the twins' house, and they were just as rich. Blown glass pendulum lights cast colored light around the kitchen, while softer white lights lent their brilliance to all the major working areas. Real stone tile created an invisible wall between the working area and everywhere else which was laid with real hardwood floors. Solid granite countertops were momentarily hidden by heavy cutting boards, sharp knives that Tommen could tell didn't come from just any old kitchen store, and food that looked fresher than any food had a right to look. Maybe he was just hungry. The dining table was a long, huge thing with probably twenty chairs around it, plus some booster seats and high chairs. Somehow, the children's seats just cheapened it, like putting them at the royal table where the queen was to dine. It was something you just didn't do.

On the other side of the staircase was the living room. It, too, was laid out with the same hardwood floors. No carpet here to get dirty and torn, though there was an area rug which, again, if he'd been told that it was yak hair, he wouldn't doubt it. Furniture consisted of a large couch, a smaller loveseat, two recliners, and a beanbag chair, along with a small mix of end tables and a coffee table. A fireplace was inset into one wall, but Tommen could tell it was gas and not real wood. It was the only cheap-looking part of the room, and even it looked expensive. A flatscreen TV was mounted on one wall, turned to the news.

Past the living room proper was something like a hallway, though it wasn't quite a proper corridor. There was one door on the left, closed, which, if Tommen could guess from the size, was probably a bedroom or an office. Another open door led to a bathroom; Tommen figured it was safe to bet that it was much nicer than his bathroom at home, regardless of the recent renovation.

"Wow," he said, feeling very much like his eight year old self when he first walked into Walter's home. All that space just for one person? A whole room just for him? A bathroom inside the house? Hot water, as much as he wanted? It was all too much. "You live here?"

"No, we just rent it on weekends and every other Tuesday," Becky said smartly. "Of course we live here. Three bedroom, two bathroom."

Even as she spoke, they were almost trampled by a storm of children, four of them all looking to be under the age of twelve.

"And more nieces and nephews than I care to count," Becky sighed.

"Who all is here?" Tommen wondered uncertainly.

"A couple of my brothers decided to 'drop by' tonight for dinner. And they brought their families."

"You sound suspicious."

"Oh, please, my dad called them to come check you out." She shook her head. "Seriously, you only want to date me. Not like you're asking to marry me. But whatever." She paused. "Anyway, come on, I'll show you around and introduce you."

Her oldest brother Danny was in the living room, watching TV. He also happened to be the oldest child overall, which meant he was almost fifty, which meant that he was here with his own grandkids, the eldest being eleven. If Tommen had to guess, he was more amused by the situation than seriously scrutinizing Tommen and considering him a threat, and they spoke pleasantly enough for a minute.

Becky's other brother, Andrew, was the fourth of the ten total children, forty-four years old, also with his brand new shiny granddaughter who was less than a year old. He, too, was more amused than threatened by Tommen.

Uri, the fifth child, forty-three years old, was married but was at dinner only with his wife. They had children, grown, but no grandchildren yet.

"David couldn't make it," Becky explained. "He's Aaron's dad, my nephew who goes to school with us."

"Ah," Tommen said, unsure what to make of it all.

"And, finally, you know my mom."

They went into the kitchen where Mrs. Polski was busy at the stove while a couple other women were doing this and that, all chatting excitedly.

"Mom?" Becky prompted.

"Oh, Tommen, welcome," Mrs. Polski greeted when she turned and saw him, always smiling, always charming. "Good to see you. Dinner is almost ready."

"Thank you," Tommen replied meekly. This was all way out of his league. He almost felt guilty for not being Jewish or Catholic, that was how out-of-place he felt.

"We'll be upstairs," Becky told her.

"Yes, of course. Go have fun."

Tommen's mind went a hundred directions at once.

He followed Becky upstairs. The landing was carpeted, a thick, plush white carpet that was, somehow, still white. There were two rooms upstairs, a bathroom and, as he might have guessed, a bedroom.

"My brothers tell them to stay downstairs," Becky said as she removed the child safety lock, "but they never do. Problem is, the older ones are getting old enough that they can take these off on their own."

"Guess you'll have to get creative," Tommen offered.

"Preaching to the choir, sir."

She opened the door and they went inside, Tommen stunned first by the size of the bedroom. It was like his room, his dad's room, and the bathroom combined. The walls were yellow—well, an unknown color—but that was barely decipherable under huge swaths of posters and art work and pictures and, for reasons *completely* unknown to him, fabric. One quilt took up almost half a wall, hanging over an enormous table where several sewing machines and enough fabric and assorted accessories to open a sewing store sat and waited patiently for its master to return. He recognized several of the costumes for the play, laid out with various alterations and notes pinned on them.

On the other side of the room were bookcases stuffed with,

not only books, but movies and CDs, again, enough to open a small entertainment store. They ran from the closet where glass doors made the room appear even larger, to the nightstand next to a tiny bed with a quilt for a blanket. The only real section of wall that wasn't plastered with stuff was above the bed. There was only a simple cross-stitched piece depicting a chicken and some word in Hungarian that Tommen didn't know.

"What's with the chicken?" he asked.

"That was from my grandparents on my mom's side," Becky explained. "When they heard that I was diagnosed with dwarfism, they sent that for me from Hungary. It's an Americauna chicken. They're small and they lay weird little blue and green eggs. Anytime that they spoke of me, they always called me their little Americauna."

"Oh. Sorry."

"No need. They died when I was three. My mom says I met them once, when they visited the last time, but I don't remember."

Tommen nodded, trying to find something else to talk about. A large window between the bed and the sewing madness overlooked the rest of the neighborhood, the majority of which was ranch-style homes. A window seat was covered in small sewing projects so he could only bend over to look out.

"Nice view," he observed.

"Yeah, it's not bad. A little depressing compared to the sunshine of California, but it's kind of nice to look at the glittering snow on a sunny day."

"So do I get to hear the story now?"

"What story?"

"About your last name. We did have our first date at the dance after all."

"Yes, and tonight is when we find out if we'll continue to date."

"Have you dated other guys before?"

Becky frowned and looked away. "Well, like I said, most guys are a little intimidated by my boldness. Most never made it past the first date. Some my dad didn't approve of. When they found that out, they dumped me anyway and went on to other conquests, so it wasn't all bad. I've only ever dated one guy, really. But his family moved. We tried to keep in touch, but then my dad said we were moving, and we just decided it was better to end it."

"Oh."

"Why, did you think you were the first?"

"Given the situation, I was kind of hoping I wasn't."

She shrugged. "My dad's super traditional, as you might have guessed. He says I can go on as many first dates as I want, but anything after that, it goes through him."

"Um, right."

"It's not as tough as you think."

"Where is he, anyway?"

"He should be home soon. Fridays and Saturdays are his weekends."

"Right, Sabbath and all that." He paused. "So which are you? If your mom is Catholic and your dad's a Jew, which are you?"

"I just tell people I'm a Catholic Jew and leave it at that."

"But what does that mean? And how did they get together anyway?"

"They met in med school. My mom was having trouble with her immigration papers and whatever, and my dad and grandpa were able to help her get them sorted out so she could stay and continue her education."

"Did you know those grandparents?"

She shook her head. "No. They died long before I was born."

"And what was their last name?"

Becky raised a brow. "Officially? Polski."

"But they were Polish. Come on, what's the story?"

"Okay, okay." She went and sat on her bed. "So, their actual name was Worczeski. When they came over to America, they didn't speak a word of English. Not a word. They tried asking around to see if anyone spoke Polish and could act as a translator. Well, a customs officer approaches them and asks for a name. They think he's offering to translate, so they ask him, 'Polski?' He takes it as their name, thanks them, and walks away. When they finally got their papers, their name was listed as Polski."

"Why not legally change it back at a later date?" Tommen wondered, finding a small spot on the window seat.

"They never learned enough English to do it. I mean, they could ask, but it was also a matter of finding a lawyer and a judge who could and would honestly help them. My dad could translate, but their trust in the American legal system was slim and they didn't want anything to get messed up." Becky shrugged. "I don't know. I just know that they had the means, they just didn't have the will or the trust." She chuckled. "The interesting thing, though, is that, obviously, all us kids heard the story. So if you ask any of my brothers what their name is, they'll tell you Worczeski. Because they changed it back when they got married."

"Well, that's got to fuck up the genealogy." *Yeah, because you can talk.*

"Not really. My mom keeps records like you wouldn't believe. So does the Church. And since my dad's Jewish, the temple keeps records, too. Believe me, no one's getting confused."

"What about your sisters?"

"Took their husband's names, like women do."

"Well, hate to tell you, but it's a changing world out there."

"Maybe. But not here. Not that much, anyway."

*Clearly, given the reason I'm here.*

Downstairs, they could hear a thunder of small children running through the house.

"My dad's home," Becky said. "Wait for it..."

Suddenly it was like the whole upstairs was shaking as the thunder got closer and closer, running up the stairs, and soon the room was swarming with children. Where they all came from, Tommen could only guess.

"*Becky, Sabah khan!*" one told her excitedly. (Becky, Grandpa's here!)

"*Makirah,*" Becky said. "*Terdu lenekomah takhtonah vtifreshu mekhadi!*" (I know. Go downstairs and get out of my room!)

The children ran away, giggling as they did. Becky shook her head as she put a few things to rights which the kids had knocked over or messed up in some fashion.

"Hebrew, right?" Tommen asked, unsure how mad she was at this point.

"Yes. We all learned it, but Uri and Andrew are the only ones of the boys to have actually followed Judaism after our dad, so their kids learned it, too."

"Oh. Cool."

He followed her out of her room, waiting anxiously as she reattached the safety lock and headed downstairs where her dad was just coming out of the entry way.

"So, he showed up," Dr. Polski said, looking directly at Tommen who stopped in his tracks.

"Yes sir," Tommen said, as he couldn't think of anything else.

"Good for you."

And that was it. The doctor went into the kitchen to kiss his wife and she informed him that dinner was just about done, even if it took a good five minutes to round up the kids and get them to listen long enough to help set out placemats and dinnerware.

"It's not always like this," Becky assured him. "This is just a special occasion because you're here for the first time. If and when you come over again, it'll just be the four of us, maybe one or two of the kiddos depending on if it's a weekend."

"Well, if and when you come over to our house, it'll just be us three. Maybe even us two depending on if my dad's working late."

Not that he expected that anytime soon. His dad was back to work, but there was more going on. The way his dad still fought his demons and the way he kept silent about being back to work said more than words ever could. He was back to work, but just barely.

"First thing's first. You have to survive tonight."

Survive. Not the most comforting choice of words, and he was forced to wonder what her intentions were by using it.

"Where's the bathroom?" he asked, pretending like he didn't already know or couldn't guess.

"Down there." She pointed past the stairs to the open door. "And make sure you lock the door unless you want an audience."

It was a welcome thing, actually, to be able to lock himself in a room. He was nervous as hell, and he really couldn't figure out why. He was just having dinner at his girlfriend's house with his girlfriend's family, of which only one member seemed to not like him. And that one was the one who would decide whether she was still his girlfriend by the end of the night.

He didn't like being told what he could and couldn't do. It was one thing when it was a logical rule—for instance, don't set yourself on fire and don't cheat on your college entrance exams—but to be told that he wasn't allowed to do something nice for someone he liked, that grated on his nerves. He liked Becky. He wanted to do nice things for her, buy her dinner, take her places, be her friend and confidant. Why the fuck should he have to ask for that kind of invitation?

He jumped as the doorknob jiggled and a couple of tiny fists pounded on the door. Elsewhere in the house, he heard yelling. The child answered in something not English, and ran off. Tommen took a breath and zipped up his pants. Fuck, this was way too stressful.

But then, maybe that was the point. Get him off his game, shake his Mr. Cool facade and see who he really was.

Fuck, he hated this. But he had to get through it. He wasn't going to let himself be shaken by a couple annoying little kids and an interrogation. He'd been interrogated by police, surely he could handle one doctor. He wasn't going to be told what he could and could not do.

He jumped as there was banging on the door again.

"I gotta go potty!" a young voice whined.

"All right, all right," Tommen said grouchily, drying his hands and opening the door. He'd barely made it out of the bathroom before the door was slammed in his back and he stumbled forward.

"Sorry about that," an embarrassed mom said meekly, hurrying forward to tap on the door and inquire as to the child's status.

Tommen figured it was probably safer to just head toward the dining room. The table was set up as if they were expecting the president as the guest of honor. It wasn't just one plate and a few utensils, this was everything straight from an etiquette book. Big plate, little plate, saucer, bowl, cup, glass. Thankfully they used only simple utensils so he didn't have to try and guess between half a dozen different knives and spoons.

"Do you always eat like the president's coming over?" Tommen asked Becky as she set out a quilt's worth of potholders and her mom and sisters-in-law brought out the food.

"No, only when we have a lot of company," she answered. She lowered her voice. "And when my dad wants to show off and boast without boasting."

"Ah. Got it."

So this was Dr. Polski's way of saying, "I'm rich. You're not. My daughter is accustomed to the utmost finery. What do *you* have to offer?"

*Not much,* Tommen thought as Becky showed him his seat. He expected to be placed next to Dr. Polski so the man could keep an eye on him at all times, but such was not the case. Dr. Polski was at the head with his wife beside him, then Becky, then Tommen, and the rest were arranged in such a way as to keep parents with their children. They seemed to have it down to a science, and he decided it was just best to go with it for now.

"Don't sit down yet," Becky hissed just as he was about to pull out his chair. "They have to pray first."

"They?"

His question was answered soon enough, as the doctor and his Jewish sons stood behind their seats and began reciting some hymn or prayer. The hair on the back of Tommen's neck prickled, but he also noticed that Mrs. Polski stood with her head bowed, lips moving in her own silent Catholic prayer. This was just too weird. Next dinner was going to be at his house, where he cooked the food, he took the food to his chair, and he ate the food. With none of the finery, pomp, or circumstance.

He followed suit as the prayers finished and they sat to eat. His expectations of being grilled immediately were put on hold as dishes were passed around.

It was almost like Thanksgiving. Turkey, roast beef, potatoes and gravy, salad, casserole, bread, and several dishes he could not identify right off hand. He would have settled for spaghetti, tacos, maybe breakfast for dinner, but this...this was all too much. No one else commented on it, though, so Tommen could only assume that this was not uncommon. These people ate like kings on a regular basis and never batted an eye. It actually made him feel humiliated.

An odd thought crossed his mind then: was this how his dad had felt when he met and married his wife? A lowly country Welshman, suddenly elevated to a status almost equivalent of a lord, never being allowed to forget his origins, always made to feel dirty and unwelcome no matter what he did.

"So, Tommen," Dr. Polski said. *And so it begins.* "Becky tells me you were promoted to manager of the bakery where you work."

"I was. Or, I am. The manager," Tommen answered dumbly.

"How did that come about? Are you going to school for business?"

"Well, no. The twins own it, and I've worked there for forever it seems like—"

"I've been an audiologist for over forty years; you have a long way to go before you hit forever at a job. Please, continue."

"Um, right. Anyway, one of the twins was in an accident and it put him out for a while, so there was a gap that needed to be filled. I knew the job the best, so I got made manager."

"What kind of accident?" one of the wives wondered.

"He was hit by a car and lost his leg." No point in lying about it or trying to fudge it.

"Oh, that's terrible. He's okay, though?"

"He literally just returned to work yesterday."

"How much of the leg?" Judging by Dr. Polski's tone, he wasn't trying to grill Tommen; he was genuinely curious as a doctor. How it was significant to an audiologist, Tommen didn't know.

"He was able to keep the knee. He's got a prosthetic now that he's learning to use."

Mrs. Polski said something in Hungarian that made her kids snicker. One of the sons, Danny, looked at Tommen. "What grade are you in, Tommen?"

"I'm a...sophomore."

"Isn't it taboo to date someone not in your grade?"

"Maybe, but I'd have to be an idiot to date anyone in my grade."

"How do you come to that conclusion?"

"Because they're selfish and shallow, just looking for a few free dinners and a little sex afterwards."

Tommen wished he had his Time abilities so he could slow down and see everyone's reactions. As it was, he caught only a fleeting glimpse of Dr. Polski as he raised a brow but said nothing, instead taking a bite of his food.

"So, what do your parents do for a living?" Uri asked conversationally.

"My dad's a cop," Tommen answered shyly.

"And your mom?"

He felt his cheeks burn. "Um, I don't...have a mom."

"I'm sorry. Do you mind if I ask what happened?"

Well, that was the question, wasn't it? Becky knew, or she knew what he wanted her to know. How far did he trust her family? It wasn't like they were a bunch of big-mouthed freshmen looking for a new story to spread through the rumor mill; they were mature adults who were curious as to why he didn't have a mom.

At the same time, this was his second date with Becky—if it

could be called that—and his first with her family. How much did they need to know right off the bat? Finally, he took a level breath and answered, "Actually I do mind, thank you."

Uri did not get offended or become upset, simply nodded graciously and returned to his eating.

"Becky tells me that you met your wife in med school," he began tentatively. Maybe if he did a little ego stroking and conjured up happy images, then the guy might soften up a little, warm up to him.

It was Mrs. Polski who answered, the unintended recipient of the warm, fuzzy feelings. "Yes. I came over to America as an exchange student in high school. I always wanted to be a nurse, and I was sure that an American education would help me. So I came back to go to university. I was not done with school before my visa came due, and there were problems trying to renew it. Thankfully, Ioshua knew what to do and with his help, I was able to stay, and he helped me again with my citizenship papers. And less than a year later, we got married."

Danny said something then in Hungarian. Judging by the reactions around the table, it made everyone uneasy, and Mrs. Polski rebuked him for it.

"What did she say?" Tommen asked Becky quietly.

"Nothing," she replied, too quickly.

*So, even rich families have dark secrets. Interesting.*

He wasn't sure if he was relieved or suspicious that a majority of the conversation for the rest of the meal was not about him. Sports, weather, politics, religion, it was all there, in all languages, but he was conspicuously absent. He was not talked about, nor did he offer his opinions or insights. Instead, he waited for the meal to be over, which seemed to be a more communal affair than simply getting up and walking away at will.

He followed Becky's lead, taking his dishes, scraping them, rinsing them, and then playing Tetris in the dishwasher. Afterwards, they retreated to her room.

"What did your brother say at dinner that made everyone so uncomfortable?" Tommen asked, hoping that the solitude might reveal an answer.

Becky shook her head and rolled her eyes as she sat on the bed. "He was telling them not to forget the part where they were pregnant with him before they were married which was the real reason they got married."

"Oh." So it was that kind of secret. "Well."

She shrugged. "It is what it is, I mean, it was fifty years ago. I don't know why they still walk around like their parents are going to whip them for it. Whatever. It's their little dark secret that they like to keep to themselves. So don't tell anyone."

"No problems from me, boss."

"Got that right."

"So, what good little Catholic Jew listens to heavy metal?" Tommen wondered, looking at some of the posters on her walls.

She just shrugged. "Metal worship. Is there a reason heavy metal can't be Christian?"

"Because it's the Devil's music?"

"Does an electric guitar automatically become evil based on the notes it plays? Would you feel better if the Devil played the fiddle?" She gave him a look. "Different strokes for different folks."

"Uh-huh. Right. And the horror novels here? Looks like you have quite a Ted Dekker collection going here."

"Yeah, but you don't see Karen Kingsbury, do you?"

He shook his head and took a step back. "You have more surprises in you than Pandora's Box."

She shifted her seat. "I think that's a compliment. At least, I'm going to take it as one. So...thanks, I think."

"Your dad is cool with us being up here, right? I mean, we are alone and stuff. He's not going to come barging up here thinking we're...you know..."

"Having sex? Not likely. More likely they'll send the kiddos up here randomly to check on us. The whole reason I got this room—actually this entire floor—is because they have a hard time getting up and down the stairs. And they know I like privacy when I'm working."

"Oh. Makes sense, I guess. I mean, it looks like you have a lot of projects going."

"Mostly it's the play. But some of the other women who are sewing started spreading the word and I have a few client projects in there, too. Obviously those take precedence because they're paid projects, but they are small and few in number, so I have lots of time."

Tommen nodded absently. "So, when will your dad tell me if I can keep seeing you?"

"Well, you haven't run out the door screaming, though a couple times it looked like you wanted to. And he hasn't thrown you out, which is a good thing. He'll probably talk to you when you leave tonight."

"Is there, like, a curfew, or a get-out-by?"

"Not really, but it would probably be safer if you left sort of within the realm of everyone else. Or whenever you need to get home to sleep before school tomorrow. So, you might want to text your dad and tell him."

"Oh, actually I drove."

"You have your license?"

"No, but...my dad thought it might be a little more impressive if I came on my own. And it's only a quarter mile or something, so it wasn't like I was going to be going anywhere that I might get caught. Unless I did something stupid, but, you know." He shrugged.

She sighed. "I wish I could do that. I wish I could drive. When I was a kid, I had an electric Jeep that I could drive around in, but I think that's about as close as I'll ever get."

Tommen wanted to sit down and comfort her in some way, except he wasn't sure how, or even if he should. She didn't say it like a grief-filled longing, more like a resignation to circumstances. It was like someone comforting him for not being able to use his Time abilities, awkward and unwanted.

There was rustling and commotion downstairs.

"Sounds like someone's getting ready to leave," Becky commented. "I'd wait a few minutes."

"Kicking me out so soon?"

"Trying to help you out."

"Well, good to know you're in my corner. Doesn't seem like anyone else is."

"Oh, please. My brothers liked you. Believe me, you'd know it if they didn't. You should have seen what they did to one of my sister's boyfriends."

"What'd they do?"

"Let's just say...there's a particularly green patch of grass in the backyard."

He raised a brow. "More to the story?"

"Eden was always the rebel, or so I was told. You'd never know it now, but I guess she used to be quite the black sheep. Didn't care one bit for our dad's rules on dating. Came home one day with some weirdo punk freak and announced that they were engaged and there was nothing anyone could do about it. Well, the boys banded together and they did something about it. And that's all I know. So count yourself lucky that you're still standing here."

Tommen took a level breath. "Right then. On that happy note, I think I should be heading out."

As he turned, she started laughing. He paused. "You were BSing me the whole time, weren't you?"

"Well, only most of it. There's no patch of strange green grass out back. But Eden was a rebel, and she did bring home a supposed fiancé. There was a fallout between him and the family and the two of them walked out, vowing to never return. That night, he raped her, she got pregnant, he beat her and left her, and she changed her ways."

He was simultaneously amazed and curious why he should care. Yeah, probably time to leave.

He got downstairs just as Andrew as his family were walking out the door, Mrs. Polski seeing off the last of her great-grandkids, at least from that clan. She turned just as Tommen was sitting down to put his shoes on.

"Oh, leaving already?" she wondered.

"School tomorrow," he told her, unsure if it was a lie.

She nodded. "Yes, school is very important." She looked at the clock on the wall. "I should actually already be getting ready for work."

"Graveyard shift?"

"A morbid saying in the hospital, but yes. The graveyard shift."

She left, presumably to get ready for work, and Dr. Polski came in. Tommen stood as he approached. "Dr. Polski, I—"

"Outside," the doctor commanded.

With a helpless look at Becky who only mouthed, "Bye," Tommen headed outside, desperately wishing he'd brought a coat even as he felt like he was being led to a firing squad.

"Did you enjoy dinner?" Dr. Polski inquired politely.

"Mrs. Polski is an excellent cook," Tommen replied, hoping it was the right thing to say.

"She is." Pause. "You remember why you had to come over tonight?"

"In order to impress you so I could continue dating Becky?"

"Is that a question?"

"No?"

Dr. Polski raised a brow. "You might have noticed that very little of the actual conversation tonight was about you. Words are only ten percent of a man. Actions are the other ninety percent. Do you know what I saw in your actions tonight, Tommen?"

*The look of a man before he pisses his pants in fear?* "No, I don't."

"Fear, as might be expected, but deference. You are willing to take a little heat and a little criticism to get what you want, and, I hope, the humility to accept when you don't get what you want."

Tommen felt his stomach sink with his hopes trapped inside. He looked away. "Yes sir."

"I wasn't done," Dr. Polski said, mildly irritated. "You may continue to date my daughter." Tommen looked up. "But know that I and her mother and her siblings will always be watching. Know, too, that she is no pushover, and I expect that any relationship be driven by mutual interest, not by force of will." Tommen elected to keep his mouth shut. "Do you understand?"

"Yes sir."

The old man straightened and turned. "You may find your hands full with her."

Tommen wasn't sure if he should go back in or stay on the porch or just leave. His musings were answered a second later as Becky came outside, pulling on a coat.

"He said he likes you," she told him.

"In a very roundabout way, I guess that's what he said," Tommen said, feeling his limbs suddenly turn to jelly.

"It's a good thing anyway."

"Yeah, I guess I should be grateful I'm not ending up a green patch of grass in your backyard."

"You should."

Beat.

"I guess I'll see you at school tomorrow," Tommen said finally. "You know, since I have to hurry home so I can get sleep for it."

She raised a brow. "Uh-huh. Right. Well, that's the nice thing about having a car, you don't have to wait for the whim of others."

That was true. He had the car. He could leave anytime he wanted. But he'd already said he was leaving, so he might as well make good on his word. They exchanged farewells and he headed down the walkway, shivering.

He said yes. Dr. Polski said yes. He might not have said that he liked Tommen, but he'd said that he could date Becky. That was a yes. Tommen waited until he was in the car before giving a small fist pump of victory, and even then he was nervous about being seen and his gesture interpreted the wrong way. But it was a victory, in a way.

They were free to date, to go out to dinner and a movie or do whatever they felt like.

Shit, now he had to turn around. Well, there was always the driveway he'd blocked when he first arrived. Eight o'clock on a Sunday, there were almost no cars on the road, running or parked. Still, he was careful to cut a wide berth around the person's mailbox, then slowly inch out into traffic. Yet another test of his deodorant, but it seemed to hold up pretty well under the circumstances.

Tommen could see the TV on in the living room as he pulled into the driveway and opened the garage door. Careful not to hit anything in the garage and trip at the finish line, he pulled in and parked the car.

When he got out of the car, all the tension and excitement suddenly left him and he almost ended up on his face as his limbs again turned to jelly. It was over. He'd won. He stumbled drunkenly to the door where it was opened in front of him and he almost ran into his dad.

"Are you okay?" his dad asked, taking a step back so Tommen could fall into the chair at the tiny kitchen table. "Look at me."

Tommen turned to face his dad but he shook his head. "I'm fine. I'm great."

"You don't look black and blue."

"No, no, no. He said yes." Tommen laughed stupidly. "He said yes. We can date."

"You didn't have any alcohol, did you?"

"What? No. I'm just...relieved." He grinned. "He said yes."

"You said that. So here's the next question: what are you going to do now?"

Tommen took a breath, but it caught and he could only manage a small sigh. Finally he said, "I have no idea."

# Chapter Seventeen
## Alice in Wonderland

Of course, the first thing that had to happen was Becky had to come over to their house for dinner. She was courteous enough, and amazed at the transformation between the sixties junk that was still in the process of being removed and the more modern decor that now graced the house, but Tommen could see the uncertainty as she realized that maybe, just maybe, they weren't as rich as her family. Tommen worked at a bakery for a little above minimum wage and his dad was a police officer and the only major source of income. Even that was starting to pinch as the medical leave ran out and still he was only working three days a week. Supposedly he was going to grab another day around the beginning or middle of March, but his tone was dubious.

Truthfully, Tommen wondered about his dad, worried about him even, but he said nothing about it. For one, his dad was a grown man who both had his pride and ability to take care of himself. And for two, Tommen had too many other things to worry about, not the least of which was Becky, whatever she claimed about being able to take care of herself.

They studied together often, which wasn't a new thing, but at least now they didn't have to deny that they were dating. It made for some interesting gossip at lunchtime, as well as at the school play. The Powers That Be had decided to make opening night the Thursday before the official start of spring break, which made the final performance that Saturday night. It brought all kinds of backlash from families who were supposed to be leaving Saturday morning, Friday night, even Thursday night, and not a few people had to drop out of the play.

"So, this is the correct date now, right?" Micah asked, taking down the old poster from the bulletin board in the bakery and putting up the new one. "Because if anyone asks, I'll be referring them to the manager."

"And I'll send them to the director," Tommen told him. "That's accurate as of today. I mean, I know why they changed it, but it's only going to hurt us. We weren't going to be ready the first time, now they moved it up two weeks. Means we only have a month left."

"You never know; theater has a way of pulling itself together," Micaiah said, limping out of his office, trying to transition from crutches to cane on his prosthetic and having a blasted time of it. "Speaking of which, where do I get tickets?"

"You want to go?" Micah was as surprised as Tommen.

Micaiah shrugged. "Why not? If you're nice to me, I might even buy a second ticket for a friend."

A look passed between the two, one Tommen didn't care to interpret even as it piqued his curiosity. It was obvious that the "friend" Micaiah spoke of was not Micah. Tommen might have to do a little crowd searching at some point.

"I'm always nice to you," Micah told him, even as his expression still didn't line up with his words and strained tone. Still, he went back to the kitchen to continue his work.

"Suppose I should change your days off, then," Micaiah mused, looking at Tommen.

Tommen simply nodded and let him go without another word. Both twins were acting a little suspicious lately, though it was tough to say if Micah wasn't reacting to Micaiah's odd behavior. Maybe it stemmed from his escape from the Wheel and loss of his leg, but he just seemed a lot more sentimental lately. He still didn't take shit from asshole customers or others he dealt with, but on the whole, when he wasn't dealing with asshole customers and the like, he just seemed a lot more...terminal, if Tommen had to pick a word. Like he was facing certain death and decided that some arguments weren't worth pursuing. Maybe it was just him.

"Tommen." Micaiah poked his head out of the office. "It's just the actual show dates that are different; all the rehearsals and such are still the same?"

"Yeah, they are," Tommen confirmed. "Monday, Tuesday, Thursday."

And, being Friday, that meant that the next Monday rehearsal was the start of the four week countdown. They had exactly eleven rehearsals left to pull together a conglomeration of clunky movements, forgotten lines, and general bad acting. Tommen didn't necessarily expect Broadway or anything, but for goodness' sake, people, do you even look at the script when you're not in the auditorium?

Well, not like there was much he could do about it. He could build all the wonderful sets he wanted, but it wouldn't save the show. And he figured that he had done a pretty good job of set-building. The stairs didn't break and the platforms didn't cave in when the actors stood on them. The walls didn't fall over when someone bumped into them. But, like his architect predecessors, Tommen still couldn't find too many people able and willing to paint the darn thing. He did his best, though, so it wasn't his problem that it was still mostly blank.

"So what are you going to do if opening night comes and it's still not finished?" Becky wondered when he went to visit her that Monday after school. As usual, she was bent over her sewing machine, zipping clothes through it one way, turning, folding, pinning, and zipping them back through again like it was nobody's business.

Tommen shrugged. "Then I guess we'll have to tell the audience to use their imagination."

"Yes, but you're the one listed in the credits. You'll be the one they blame."

"I'm only the builder. I'm not a painter."

"Well, if things keep going the way they are, you might have to learn how to paint here real quick."

The worst part was, she was right. There was no differentiating between set Builders and set Painters in the flyer. He'd seen the preview of it on Martin's computer one day, and his name was listed right there: Set Building Manager: Tommen Forbes, 10th grade. And again: Backstage Manager: Tommen Forbes, 10th grade. He sure seemed to be in charge of a lot of things lately, and yet it still seemed like nothing was getting done. Wasn't that the point of being in charge, to tell people what to do in order to get stuff done? Well, lead a horse to water and all that.

After a little searching, he managed to rustle up some painting supplies and get them sorted, but then he spent the remainder of the rehearsal going through the script to figure out what kind of scenery was actually called for. Then he had to figure out where to put that scenery in a way that it would be able to carry throughout the performance without looking too out-of-place when it wasn't needed.

Painting was harder than it looked, and he hadn't even opened a paint can yet. He ended up leaving that night without ever cracking one open.

"You seem frustrated," his dad observed when he picked him up.

"I hate this play," Tommen told him. "No one does what they're told or even what they're supposed to do, we're super far behind, and somehow we have to pull it together in a month."

"Hm. Welcome to the real world. Adults aren't much easier to work with, trust me."

"Did you get your extra day or no?"

"Yes, I did. Starting next week I'll be working Monday through Thursday."

"That's...a good thing, isn't it?"

"For now it is, but if they move me back to full time and everything the way it was, I'll be on Wednesday through Sunday, which really means Wednesday through Monday, or Tuesday through Sunday."

Tommen nodded grimly. No rest for the weary. If his dad got cleared to work, work him they would. "When do you find that out?"

"Sometime between spring break and the first week of May."

"So...after the play?"

"Yes, I'll be able to make it. Which night would you recommend?"

None of them, Tommen thought cynically. "Friday. Thursday is opening night, so it's going to suck. Saturday is the last night, so no one's going to care, so it's going to suck."

His dad raised a brow. "Would it be correct to assume you're only still in this because Becky is?"

"Is that a bad reason?"

"Can't say either way except you've done nothing but complain about the play for the last few weeks."

Becky told him the same thing, especially as the week of the show got closer.

"I understand you're frustrated, but what I don't understand is why you seem to think that you have to be the one to fix everything," she told him as she took a break and rummaged around in her bag for some food.

"Because I can't stand half-ass work and it feels like I'm the only one in this entire production who's actually doing work."

Even as he said it, he could see the fire in her eyes and he knew he'd said the wrong thing.

"I've been doing work," she informed him. "I've been doing this work on top of my other work. You know, the stuff I get paid for?"

He sighed. "I know. I'm sorry. You do good work. You probably work more than I do."

"I work. You work. We did our part. Sometimes we did other people's parts. But their responsibility is their own. You can't control everything."

If admitting she was right made him look like a dick, did he still have to admit that she was right?

Probably.

But he didn't.

Because he was a dick. And still frustrated about the play.

But that was the problem with having a production done almost entirely by teenagers. Too many chiefs and not enough Indians. And it wasn't even like there were just a ton of people trying to be in charge. Everyone who was supposed to be in charge was in charge; they just couldn't find any Indians to work. There was very little clashing of ideas as John the Worker thought his ideas were better than Joe the Manager; more, it was that Joe the Manager couldn't get John the Worker to work because...fuck you? He had other things to do, better things. It was infuriating.

By the time the last rehearsal came around, Tommen had even less confidence in the play than he had going into it. Going into it, he'd been naive and a little idealistic. Now he was a third of management, Becky was a third of management, and Mr. Martin was a third of management.

"I'm going to be glad when this is over," Tommen lamented as he and Becky waited for his dad to come and pick them up.

"You and me both," Becky agreed. She looked like she didn't get much sleep. The costumes were long since done, but she still had to oversee costuming, hair, makeup, and hospitality for the shows, and her working client base had grown to almost its maximum capacity. "This is one of those times when I miss my old school; this is just ridiculous."

*It's one of those times when I miss my Time abilities,* Tommen thought ruefully. If he didn't have to pack everything in and cram like normal students, if he could Band and just take ten seconds to calm down, look around, and remember which way was up, he was sure his attitude would get better, even a little.

The old Cadillac pulled up to the curb and they got in. At least one good thing was happening: spring had sprung (well, sort of) and it was warm enough now in the middle of April to be able to wait outside in the growing sunshine.

"How was rehearsal? Ready for the play?" his dad asked.

"No," they answered simultaneously.

"You're not exactly giving me the confidence to want to buy a ticket, especially since neither of you is actually on stage."

"We'll see how Thursday goes, but I'd say save your money," Tommen told him.

They dropped Becky off at her house before going home. Once they were inside, Tommen tossed his backpack on his bed and approached his dad.

"What's up?" he wondered as he found something to eat, bringing out bread and a few sandwich goodies.

"Dad, I want my Time abilities back," Tommen said.

"Well, I'm about ninety-five percent certain I'm going to say no, but I'll bite: why?"

"I can't do it without them."

"Do what?"

"The play. I need to be able to stop and slow down and just...calm down. It's too chaotic."

His dad did not look at him, simply portioned out some ham onto a slice of dry bread. "You've been doing all right so far. For goodness' sake, you've only got the shows left. Three shows, one, two, three. Then you're done."

"The rehearsals we can stop and pause and correct; the shows we can't."

"That's right. As the saying goes, the show must go on."

"Dad, I can't do it. I have too much to do but I can't as long as I'm trapped in Base Time."

His dad raised a brow, then went back to his sandwich, digging for some mayonnaise in an almost-empty jar to spread on the second slice of bread. "If want my opinion, you've been doing better about it than I thought you would, especially given the play. If you would have asked me a month ago, I might have even considered it."

"What's changed?! There haven't been any reported Tracker attacks in a month. I'm supposed to be an Apprentice! I'm supposed to be learning and doing stuff, not...Suppressed and plodding along with everyone else!"

"Need I remind you what was supposed to happen at the inauguration? That didn't happen. A lot of stuff is supposed to be happening or not happening right now, but we don't have the luxury of 'supposed to.' We have what is and that is how we're going to take it."

"And when is that going to change?"

His dad dropped the knife in the sink and turned. "I don't know. Believe me, Tommen, when I say that we're not idly sitting by. You are, because you're an Apprentice. But the higher ups, anyone who is able to get and stay in contact, they're trying. They're trying to stop Rifun and Cassius and bring an end to this madness. Just because you're not in the middle of it doesn't mean it isn't happening."

"But—"

"Tommen, stop. Can't you see what I'm trying to do? I'm trying to give you a normal life. Just like you've always wanted. Work, school, friends, a girlfriend, without all the chaos of Time. You think that by adding Time back in that it will help? In the short term, it might. But eventually it's just one more thing to add to your life." He sighed. "When Rifun and Cassius are removed from power, then if you want them back, I'll undo the Suppression."

"And when will that be? What if they're in power for a decade? A century? I could die waiting for them to be removed from power."

"I find that hard to believe."

"You said it yourself that you don't know when it'll happen." He took a step forward. "Please, Dad. Okay, you said that in the short term it might help. So do it just for the play. Thursday, Friday, Saturday. Please. I can't do it."

For a long moment, Tommen was sure his dad was going to refuse. Finally he nodded. "All right. I'm willing to compromise to that. Remind me Thursday morning and I'll lift the Suppression. As long as you understand that Saturday night when you get home, it'll be coming down again."

"That's fine. I just need to get through the play."

"Okay. As long as you understand that. But until then, clock is ticking and you have homework to do."

Tommen nodded and headed to his room, bringing out his books and notebooks. Six weeks until finals and then he would be a junior. His classes weren't terribly difficult, just boring, except for Physics of course. And he had Spanish again so he could have fun and banter with Mrs. Perez.

He actually had no intention of giving up his Time abilities if he could help it. Probably a foolish notion since he, you know, lived with his dad, but he could hope, right? Maybe if his attitude improved enough and nothing went wrong, then he'd consider letting him keep his Time abilities, provided he didn't go crazy with them.

Nothing going wrong with his Time abilities, however, was much different than things going wrong with the show opening night.

The first problem came when several of the cast were out sick. According to semi-credible sources, said cast members really were sick with varying accounts of either strep or flu. So lines had to be reassigned and a few things fudged. Tommen was just thankful he didn't get pulled to be on stage as a backup. His problem was that with some of the cast out sick, some of his backstage people got pulled to fill the gaps that had to be filled, and he didn't have many hands to start with.

The second issue arose when Rachel, the girl playing Alice, decided that her costume made her look fat and she just couldn't go out on stage looking like "a puffed up marshmallow." It led to a pretty intense fight between Rachel and Becky which apparently put some genuine fear in the spectators—from Becky. Eventually Becky—backed up by Mr. Martin—told Rachel that she either wore the costume and looked like a puffed up marshmallow, or she didn't get to make her stage debut at all. Rachel relented. Personally, Tommen thought the costume was very, ahem, form-fitting, but then, anorexia has a way of tricking the mind he supposed.

Well, at least he had his Time abilities, so when he was able to move faster, he could. It was strange how he'd gotten so used to not being able to Band, but once the Suppression was removed, it was like stepping back into an old pair of shoes.

He glanced at the clock. Five-thirty. One hour until doors opened, an hour and a half until it began. With the set finally completed, his work was largely done in that area, with exception of various props that had to get moved and taken out. He didn't have to get nervous until the lights went down, so why was his anxiety through the roof right now? And it was like Becky said, their part was done. They did their work, let the rest of them crash and burn.

Tommen sighed and rubbed his face. He'd done his part and he would keep doing his part for the show. He shouldn't be worrying about what everyone else was doing, both in terms of not being able to control every aspect of the play, and because if everyone else knew what the fuck they were doing, he wouldn't have to worry about it. Fuck, he hated theater. He didn't want to do this. He wanted it to be over already. Three days, three shows, suddenly it seemed impossible. *Why don't we just jump to spring break already? No one gives a fuck about this shit anyway.*

But, peeking around the curtain when the doors opened, someone must care about this shit. Because here they came. Mostly it looked like parents and grandparents and siblings. Oh, and teachers, because they were morally obligated to support the students even if they thought the play was shit, too. The rest of them probably didn't know any better. As far as ninety percent of the people in the play were concerned, it was going great.

*Yeah, tell yourself that when you're staring into the lights with no clue what your next words should be.*

"How you are doing, Tommen?" Mr. Martin asked, coming up behind him.

"Doesn't matter," he answered. "Nothing I can do about it now. Show must go on, right?"

"Very true. Very true." But the way the director said it was like he was wondering if the show was going to get enough momentum to go anywhere at all, let alone "on." It was never a good sign when even the director was less than confident in his own production.

When he was gone, Tommen Banded. Ten minutes until start, he needed to extend that a little so his head didn't go spinning off his shoulders. He went out on stage.

It was a full house, or near enough. Parents, grandparents, siblings, teachers, all intermixed with total strangers, people who had seen posters like the one on the bakery bulletin board and thought, *Huh, I'm not doing anything that night, maybe I'll go to that.*

Just as he was about to head backstage again and let Time resume, something caught his attention, or rather, someone. There, in the front middle section, about halfway back on the aisle, was Micaiah. But it was his companion that really got Tommen's attention, because it was a woman. She had dark skin and dark hair, but she didn't really resemble Jenna as a Latina. Native American, maybe? Micaiah had his arm around her shoulders, so there was definite familiarity. Girlfriend? Since when had Micaiah ever seen a woman outside of a bar or hotel? Maybe he was getting sentimental.

Well, Tommen figured as he headed off stage, he'd been looking for something to calm him down and occupy his mind other than this shit play. That was certainly something to think about. Micaiah seeing a woman. Like, actually seeing her, not just taking her out for an easy fuck. Damn. He dropped his Band.

"Hey, are we ready?" Hayley asked. She was one of his backstage hands, probably the most useless of them. She was an expert at acting busy while getting absolutely nothing done.

"Yeah. Hey, you want to just man this spot right here? I'm going to go to the bathroom."

She nodded enthusiastically as he started off. He had little doubt she would be there when he returned. He'd essentially ordered her to do nothing, and that was one thing at which she excelled.

Ten minutes until the show began and their reputation as anything resembling a decent and well-organized theatrical performance ended, Tommen mused as he locked the door and undid his belt. Ten minutes until the newspaper writer hoping to plink out a cute little story of aspiring actors and amazing talent instead showcased the horrible monstrosity that was—

Tommen's thoughts were interrupted by his paranoia alarm. Immediately he threw up a Band even as he hurried to finish and stuff everything back inside.

His first instinct was to turn around, but his better judgment told him to step to the side first. He did both simultaneously, stepping to the side and turning just in time to see slavering black jowls crunch down around where he'd been just a second ago.

"Oh, shit!"

The words were knocked out of him as the beast took a swipe at him, thunking him in the shoulder. It hurt like hell, but didn't seem to do much actual damage. Fuck, and he'd just gotten his cast off, too.

The thing lunged for him. Tommen Banded and slipped around it, but became acutely aware that it didn't seem affected by his Banding. If nothing else, it seemed to feed on it.

Fuck, fuck, fuck, fuck, fuck. The only reported effective measure against Trackers was something quick, decisive, and deadly. There was no running and hiding. But in a bathroom, what did he have? Soap and water? Could he really hope this thing was like the Wicked Witch of the West? He had a paper towel dispenser. Other than that, he had shit.

But he had Time. The Tracker might not be affected by it, but everyone else would be, and it would let him get out of this bathroom at the very least.

Slowly, Tommen backed up to the door. The Tracker approached him like a dog, snarling, ready to strike. Carefully, so as not to alarm it, Tommen reached up behind him and unlocked the door. Then, just as the thing leapt at him, he Banded, and flung the door wide open. It knocked the Tracker back a step. Tommen grabbed the door and when it lunged again, he bashed it as hard as he could, sending it skidding across the floor, and pulled the door closed behind him as he ran.

He had no illusions about being able to outrun the Tracker, but outmaneuver maybe, at least long enough to get out on stage. He could hear the thing behind him, heavy paws thundering across the wooden floor, knocking aside everything in its path. Tommen dodged left and right, using every bit of the chaos that was backstage to his advantage until he got out on the stage in front of the curtain. There, he flung his Band out toward the only person in the room who he knew might be able to help.

"Micaiah!"

Micaiah looked around, initially confused until he saw Tommen jump off the stage.

"Tommen, what—?"

He cut himself off as the Tracker crashed after him.

"Oh, shit."

"Help!" Tommen screamed uselessly, running straight for him.

"Bring it here!" Micaiah ordered, standing and shuffling awkwardly out of his seat into the aisle. He reached down and grabbed his cane. "Brace me!"

Tommen got behind him and braced him as best he could. The Tracker was right on his heels. As it made a killing leap, Micaiah took his cane and drove it as hard as he could through the beast's mouth, into its skull and out the back of its head. The impact was hard and Micaiah dropped the cane before it got all the way to the handle. The Tracker fell dead. Micaiah stumbled backwards into Tommen and they both went down.

"Are you okay?" Micaiah asked, breathing heavily and rubbing his knee. He picked himself up and offered a hand to Tommen.

Tommen could find no words at the moment and just nodded, his whole body beginning to shake as the adrenaline wore off.

"What are you doing, Banding?"

Tommen felt the tears come, even as he scolded himself for it.

"I'm sorry, I didn't mean to. I just couldn't do it."

"Couldn't do what? Tommen, it's okay. I'm more confused than angry." He stood again, shakily, like he wanted to offer some comfort but didn't know how. "Why don't you start at the beginning?"

"I hate this play. It's stupid and it's not going to turn out. It's just too crazy and I couldn't handle it, so I asked my dad to lift the Suppression. He said no, but he compromised to do it just for the play so that way I could Band and just relax if I needed to for a second."

"That's how you knew I was here."

Tommen nodded and hurriedly wiped his eyes and face. "Yeah." He took a level breath. "Who's your friend?" He nodded to the woman.

"A friend." Micaiah's tone was dismissive. "You going to be all right?"

After a second of hesitation, Tommen nodded again. "Yeah, I think so. Fuck, that was scary though. I was in the bathroom."

"I see. Before or after you took a piss?" He smiled. "Why don't you go back to wherever you were, the bathroom or wherever, drop your Band, and not do it again?"

"What about—?" But when he looked, the Tracker had vanished, leaving only Micaiah's cane, which he painstakingly bent to pick up.

"That happens sometimes," Micaiah said. "Now then, don't Band for the rest of the evening. When your dad comes to pick you up, I'll have a word with him."

"You'll make sure he knows I didn't do it on purpose, right?"

"No one calls the Trackers on purpose. Following Time is just something they do. It's not your fault. Go on. Show's about to begin."

Right, the show. That thing that was happening while he was running from Trackers and shit. That thing that he hated but, comparatively speaking, wasn't looking too bad right now, seeing as he had the option. He took a breath and looked around. Everything appeared normal.

"Yeah. Okay."

Micaiah returned to his seat and removed himself from the Band. Did his girlfriend—ahem, friend—have any clue about what just happened?

Tommen hurried back to the bathroom and dropped the Band. The theater came to life around him as the back doors opened and the cast came streaming in. Reluctantly, he joined the chaos, relieving Hayley of her post and preparing for the rest of the evening's horrors. Fuck, he just wanted to be anywhere else. Anywhere but here. At least he could keep himself busy for a few minutes, picking up everything the Tracker had unceremoniously knocked aside. Very little was damaged; it looked worse than it was.

And then it happened. The lights started going down and the chatter in the audience died. Tommen felt his heart dance around in his chest. Maybe he could just Slow Band his way through. The too-recent memory of the Tracker's slavering jaws put an end to that thought pretty quickly.

"Good evening, ladies and gentlemen," Mr. Martin said on stage. "Welcome to the 2014 South Charleston High School Drama Performance. Our chosen play this year is *Alice in Wonderland*. My name is Gary Martin; I am the director and I have never been more pleased..."

*Lie, lie, lie.* Tommen tuned him out. A couple years ago, he and his dad had come to see the Les Miserables performance, and that Tommen could have believed him when he said he was thrilled to be part of it and see all the hard work that went into it. This, though...this was like congratulating a kindergarten class on some cutesy performance of Noah's Ark or something. No one really believed that it was the culmination of anyone's existence because it was simple and easy.

"Now I give you, *Alice in Wonderland.*"

Applause, applause, total blackout. Lights up and...enter stage left.

Tommen more or less just closed his eyes and pretended it was already over. He tried to bring to mind anything that would help distract him, but any time he finally got good and distracted, he was needed for something. Someone was not where they were supposed to be, someone was missing a prop, always something that he figured he should not have to deal with. People should have what they need, be where they had to be, and generally do what they were supposed to do. What was so difficult about taking basic responsibility?

As expected, lines were missed or mixed up. A few girls tripped on their skirts or other assorted accessories. A few guys tripped on the girls' skirts or accessories. There was laughter where there should not have been laughter. There was no laughter where there should have been laughter because the one delivering the punchline fucked it up completely. Props were dropped, cues were missed, and everything that Tommen feared could go wrong, did go wrong. Murphy was alive and well, as they say.

Intermission was supposed to be a relief, but it only seemed to prolong the inevitable and increase the dread. Mr. Martin came backstage to have a little pep talk.

"Hey, guys, you're doing great," he told them. "A few bumps and bruises, but you know what, it's still awesome. You guys are the only ones who know what's supposed to happen. Something goes wrong, run with it. And relax. Your audience still loves you."

Again, Tommen tuned him out. He wanted to believe him, wanted to believe that everything was going to be okay, but experience taught him otherwise. They were fucked and they all knew it.

Mr. Martin finished his little pep talk and headed out. There were still a few minutes left in intermission. Tommen wished he could make some excuse to slip away, and he was still too afraid of a second Tracker attack to stretch out his time in a Band.

"Ladies and gentlemen, if you would kindly filter back in, make your way back to your seats, the second act is about to begin," Mr. Martin announced, trying to keep up his enthusiasm.

Problem was, it was only halfway into the first of three shows, and already most of the cast looked like they wanted to crawl under a rock and die. Now they were realizing the consequences of being unprepared and not giving a shit. Actors on Broadway didn't just pull this stuff out of a hat, and now they seemed to understand. Well, all aboard the sinking ship.

Everyone in, conversations hushed, and...blackout. Lights up a little and...begin Act Two, stage right. This was where things started really heating up, preparing for the final battle. But, in Tommen's opinion, if they couldn't even get the simple, silly stuff right, what hope did they have for the intense sequences where choreography and line delivery really mattered?

It was, in truth, a terrifying prospect. If it went down in flames, would any of the cast even come back tomorrow? Or would everyone suddenly mysteriously come down with the flu? What if Tommen did that? Wasn't like he did a whole lot backstage anyway, so his absence probably wouldn't be noticed. The only thing that kept him from entertaining the idea was that his absence would be noticed in that he was the manager of several different things. If shit went wrong — when shit went wrong, he'd be the next guy up.

*Why did I ever agree to do this?*

*Because you were infatuated with a girl, dumbass.*

*Why did I follow her to the play? To impress her? Couldn't I have just impressed her in Physics class?*

*Apparently not because here you are.*

Oh, such a wonderful fucking day. And they'd all have to answer for it tomorrow in school.

Teachers would quiz them: *why did the play suck?*

And they'd have to answer: *Because we didn't give a fuck during rehearsals and it came back to bite us.*

*But we thought you were just so in love with the play and were working hard to make it great.*

*No, we were in love with the* **idea** *of being in a play and having our names next to a character's name like we were some kind of Broadway star. The actual play, the part where we live up to that title, we didn't give two shits about.*

And there were inevitably slip-ups. Lines missed and, toward the very end, Tommen heard a hard fall when there wasn't supposed to be a fall at all. Well, maybe if Alice broke her leg, they wouldn't have to come back for two more nights of shame. And Rachel wouldn't have to put up with a marshmallow costume and Becky wouldn't have to put up with her.

So the best thing for everyone, really, would be something really awful and tragic and devastating to the cast and crew so they couldn't come back. Maybe Tommen should have led the Tracker on a little more of a chase around the set to tear it up, bump into a few of the actors, cause a little mayhem, destruction, and possibly a few injuries. That would have gotten it canceled for sure.

But they had only a few more lines to endure, then the first part of the torture would be over.

And...there it was. The last line delivered, actors walk off stage. Applause, applause, all very formal and expected but hardly appropriate, Tommen thought. Well, they couldn't boo and throw rotten fruit; it might damage the poor little actors' self-esteem.

The applause died down for a moment until the cast was summoned out for a final bow. Normally this was where the peacocks really spread their feathers, but looking at them going out, it seemed more like a line of chain gang prisoners heading out to the quarry. They took no pride in their work; at this point, they were just going through the motions. And to think they still had two more nights of this.

Still, they did their part and the audience picked up the applause again. Mr. Martin got up on stage.

"There was a lot of ambiguity around this performance, as many of you know. We didn't even have a set opening night until a couple weeks before."

*Yeah, use that to save it. Don't tell them that the ambiguity revolved around whether or not we were going to have a performance at all,* Tommen thought as he found a box to sit on and brought out his phone. *Don't tell them about how ninety-nine percent of the cast didn't care, and how we had a small exodus because of the "opening night" ambiguity that eventually got settled only once everyone already made vacation plans. No one is going to come see another SCHS performance ever again, even if future ones do get the hard-working treatment they need.*

But that was neither here nor there. They were done for and everyone knew it. The cast was dismissed off stage ahead of the audience so they could all mingle in the lobby. Tommen suspected that a few of them were going to disappear early so they didn't have to face the shame, or so they could go cry in the bathroom. A disappearing act sounded like a pretty good performance to do, if not for having to find Micaiah and stick with him until his dad arrived. Tonight was just a terrible night for everything it seemed.

Once the general sounds of the audience filing out was reduced to the quiet murmur of a few left behind to chat amongst themselves, Tommen left his hiding hole and headed out. Micaiah still sat in his seat, but his lady friend was gone.

"Where's your friend?" Tommen wondered casually.

"Gone out ahead of me," Micaiah replied, again, his tone dismissive of the subject. Not that Tommen wanted to know what they were going to be doing later; he could guess well enough. "Your dad here?"

"I don't know. I was just waiting until the majority of the crowd was gone."

"Ah." Micaiah grabbed his cane and stood. "Well then, we might as well go and mingle with the others."

"Why?"

"Because that's what you do. Make nice and move on."

"But it was terrible."

Micaiah gave him a gentle look. "It was exactly what I expected to see from a high school play staffed by amateurs. There were slips and falls and a few missed lines. So what? You live and learn. Some here are going to take everything personally and never return to the stage ever again. Most aren't going to take everything personally; they'll try again during high school, maybe college, but then real life takes over. It happens. And this just becomes a fun, silly memory. One or two are going to take the failures here and try to overcome them and they might just make a career out of it."

"But—"

"It's high school, Tommen. It's life. Don't take it too seriously because no one gets out alive."

Tommen had read that on some cutesy little home décor sign once. He'd always thought it amusing but never really applicable. Well, now there seemed to be a little wisdom behind it.

The lobby was still pretty full of people, but Tommen noticed something else: the sullen air that surrounded the actors seemed to have lifted. Maybe they'd all been given the same pep talk Micaiah just gave him. So maybe they would limp through the next two nights after all.

It was probably fifteen minutes before Walter actually showed up, and by then a majority of the people had cleared out.

"Well, I didn't hear anything on the scanner about the school burning down or a mass run of suicides, so it couldn't have been that bad," he said.

Tommen shrugged. "I guess."

"So how was it?" Walter looked at Micaiah.

"Not as bad as they think it was," Micaiah informed him. "It's safe to come. Well, relatively speaking."

Walter's expression turned severe and he Banded the three of them. "Why do I get the feeling you're not referencing the play anymore?"

"Before the play, Tommen was attacked by a Tracker. He knew I was here, so he came to me and I had to...dispatch it." He looked forlornly at his cane where the only evidence that anything had happened was a small dent at the end where it had gone through the beast's mouth and skull.

"Are you all right?" Walter demanded of Tommen.

"Yeah, I'm fine," Tommen said. "Worst it did was swat me." He was going to have to check for a bruise later.

"What I'm getting at, Walt, is that we probably shouldn't be standing here in a Band right now," Micaiah pointed out.

"Nothing else has happened tonight?" Walter asked.

Tommen shook his head. "No, nothing. At least, not in that sense."

"All right. Well, Micaiah's right. We shouldn't be standing around in a Band." He dropped it and his tone turned casual. "Have you said good-bye to Becky yet?"

"No, not yet. She's probably busy snapping at people for ruining their costumes or something."

"Well, go say good-bye and then we'll head out. I'll be here."

Tommen nodded reluctantly and made his way down to the costume room. Only a few people remained. As expected, Becky was griping over things that were damaged, destroyed, misplaced, or a whole host of other things that interfered with her way of doing things.

"Need a hand?" Tommen offered cautiously.

"Yeah. One to sort the work, one to do the work, and one to *smack all the people who couldn't take care of a costume for a few freaking hours!* Okay, these are sturdy costumes, not the nylon stuff you find at Halloween stores, but real fabric. Cotton, broadcloth, that sort of thing. I've seen some of these girls take more care that they don't damage their fluffy nylon scarves during the school day than they do of these costumes. I mean, my goodness. You don't have to like it; you don't even have to wear it outside the play. At least have a little respect for someone else's work!"

Short but tough, that was Becky. She rustled around some more in one of the costume racks before actually stepping out to meet Tommen. "Are you leaving?"

"Yeah, my dad's here."

She nodded and took a breath. "Okay. Okay, okay, okay. I'll see you tomorrow in class, then."

He knelt so as to be closer to her height as they hugged. The first time they'd actually hugged, Tommen had tried bending down, but Becky had grabbed his collar and told him to get down on his knees, darn it. It looked like hugging a child, and at first it had seemed like it. Now there was just something nice about it. Like getting in the backseat with her. It was their thing that they did together. No one else had to like it.

As promised, his dad was still in the lobby waiting for him, but Micaiah was nowhere to be seen.

"Micaiah leave?" Tommen wondered.

"Said something about going on a date," his dad replied, seeming uncertain whether to consider it just another one of his one night adventures or if he was actually going on a real date. Given that Tommen had seen the woman and the fact that they had been together doing something other than sitting at a bar or at a hotel, there was every chance that it was a real date.

"Oh. Okay," was all he could manage.

"Well, we better get going. You still have school tomorrow."

Despite the school being a gun-free zone, Walter—even as a cop who should have known better being off-duty—still kept his conceal carry on him. Tommen saw how he kept his arm ready in case he had to draw in the event of another Tracker attack. But they made it to the car unmolested.

"So, how was the play?" Walter asked.

Tommen gave him a rundown of the play, all the missed lines, slips, falls, and other stupid things he attributed to no one giving a fuck during the rehearsals. In return, his dad gave him a speech similar to Micaiah's. It was only a high school play; no one expected Broadway greatness. Maybe if he relaxed a little and stopped seeing every mistake as a neon sign saying "Mistake" then he would see a lot fewer of them.

"Only two more nights, Tommen," his dad sighed. "Count it down. Two more openings, two more intermissions, two more epic final battles. I'll be coming tomorrow, and Micah said he might show up on Saturday, so you have that to look forward to."

"But—"

"Tommen. Relax." They pulled into the garage. "Get something to eat and sleep it off. Even if it was as terrible as you think it was, if you stay up, you'll only brood on it."

Worst part was, he was right. Tommen silently agreed and got out of the car.

Come on, Tommen, it couldn't have been that bad."

"What wasn't that bad?" Micaiah asked, walking in the door. It was Jenna who'd spoken.

"The play," Tommen grumbled.

Ah, back to that again. The last show had been Saturday night, and from Walter's story on Friday and Micah's on Saturday, the play hadn't been as bad as the cast and crew had feared. It was a high school play. Like high school, it was finite and ultimately insignificant. But even on Monday morning, he was still going on about it and how bad it was.

"Is he still going on about the play?" Micah asked as he approached the counter.

Micaiah nodded. "Yeah. But he's doing his job, so that's all that matters, I guess. At least for now."

"He has to give it up eventually, right?"

"We can hope."

Thankfully, Micaiah had the office he could hide in so he didn't have to listen to Tommen's complaining. It didn't last long, really, only all of spring break that week. But once school got going again and everyone got to hear the glowing reviews, the bitching died down.

"Sounds like a bad dream," Sean, his physical therapist, commented as they went through the standard preliminary exercises during his regular Tuesday appointment at the clinic.

Micaiah shrugged. "Not really. Just another day at the office."

"Hey, guys."

They looked over as Francine, the prosthetist, approached. Micaiah hadn't seen much of her lately, not since he'd gotten more used to his prosthetic. He was still using his cane sometimes, but he'd figured out the treadmill so he figured he was on his way to free walking again. She had a package with her.

"Good news," she said, handing Micaiah the package. "Your permanent leg came in."

"Seems a little sooner than expected," Micaiah said, finding a chair to sit down and open the thing.

"First week of May. Actually, it's a little later than expected."

"So there should be no reason to have any problems, then."

It looked about like he expected, as close to a realistic-looking leg as technology could manage. Without being told, Micaiah unstrapped the one he was wearing and tried on the new one.

"How does it feel?" Francine asked, having produced a clipboard out of God knew where.

"Better than the other one, actually," Micaiah said, surprised at how true it was. The first felt good, felt like it was supposed to, but this one almost seemed to disappear. No pinching or rubbing or anything. And the balance when he stood was better, too. "I like it."

He never could have imagined saying such a thing when he had been lying in the hospital, but now it felt like he was getting his life back. Hopefully he wouldn't be throwing it away anytime soon.

"That's a good thing. Keep the preliminary anyway, just in case something happens to this one." Ha ha. Something. What could possibly go wrong? "Your running leg should arrive in another week or two."

Micaiah nodded. He didn't like the thought that he had to change legs between walking—or light, painful, hop-jogging as he'd haphazardly discovered on the treadmill—and running, seeing how he was probably going to be doing a hell of a lot of running in the near future. But, with the plan he had in mind, he might be able to get away with, instead of running on his walking leg, but walking on his running leg.

"And," Francine went on as he continued his exercises, "as requested, the foot and ankle are modified to be able to operate a motorcycle."

"Good. I might have to try it out in the next few days." *And hope I don't screw myself and land back in the hospital.*

But, he figured that if he could re-learn to walk in the middle of winter, getting back on a motorcycle in the middle of summer should be a piece of cake. The next, problem, though, was getting Micah to give him a time of day to go with him to get it out of storage. It took almost a week.

"Are you sure you want to ride it home?" Micah asked as they pulled in the storage lot. "We can always call someone with a truck and just take it home so you can—"

"No, Micah, I'm going to ride it home," Micaiah told him for at least the fifth time. "I'll know by the time I reach the driveway whether I'll be able to do it."

"And what if you can't?"

"I can. And I will. Here's the row."

They turned into the row and went about halfway down before reaching Micaiah's storage unit. He didn't keep much in storage, mainly his bike. As he lifted the door, it sat there waiting for him, like an eager puppy. Except this was a custom-painted 2013 Honda with matching helmet.

"How long should I wait before calling an ambulance?" Micah asked from the car.

"Thanks for the vote of confidence," Micaiah said, shaking his head. Self-consciousness about being on the bike again and potentially making an ass of himself was quickly replaced by cold determination. He was not leaving this place without his bike.

Sitting on the bike and moving it went well enough he figured. He at least had the strength and balance to push his way out. The real test came when he got it straight in the row, Micah sitting back and, when he looked, munching invisible popcorn. *Gamal.*

His first experience on the motorcycle with his prosthetic was a lot like his first experience on the treadmill. He managed to lay down the bike twice before figuring out positioning and movement. By then, both he and the bike were quite dusty and dirty, with a little gas and oil spilled. He was a little scraped up and frustrated, but he finally rode around the lot and back to the car no worse for wear. One thing he'd learned well, both when he first got a motorcycle and his prosthetic: how to fall safely.

"Still want to take that thing through the city?" Micah wondered.

"Have to get it home to wash it somehow," Micaiah informed him, trying to sound confident even as his wounded pride throbbed painfully.

"Whatever, dude. Want me to lead or follow?"

It was an embarrassing ride home, Micaiah thought, as he struggled to shift gears and adjust to a new way of balancing around corners; his left side was heavier than his right side, what could he do? But at least he didn't lay it down in the middle of traffic, and that was the most important part, he thought. Still, pulling in the driveway and up the hill was less of a victor crossing the finish line and more like a loser limping across, having wounded his knee five miles back.

"You all right?" Micah asked, pulling up beside him as he got his helmet off.

"Fantastic. Go back to the shop; I'll be there in a bit."

"Sure?"

"Yes, I'm fine. Go."

Micah still seemed uncertain, but there was still work to do. As he backed out of the driveway, Micaiah headed inside to change his clothes and lick his wounds. His prosthetic did not appear damaged and the stump was clean, but each time he'd felt the bike going, he'd made sure to lay it down on the other side. So it was the left leg of his pants that was ripped and his left leg that was bruised and scraped.

As he was reaching for his sock, his phone jingled. Checking it, it was Kayla.

"Hey, handsome, you busy tonight?" the text read.

"Well, I didn't have any plans as of yet, but I just got my bike out of storage, so I guess we'll see," he replied.

"Ooh, nice. Got room on that thing to take a girl for a ride?"

"Not right now. I need to get a better feel for it on my right side."

"Makes sense."

"But there's always room for a ride of a different kind."

"Sounds good to me. Where do you want to meet?"

They made plans and left all other conversation for later. Micaiah grabbed his sock and his leg, momentarily stunned at how casual this had become. He set the prosthetic aside and just stared for a second. His leg was gone. The bone had been blown to shit and he remembered the pictures of the gaping hole. And yet, here he was, almost six months later, walking around and riding his motorcycle. It was surreal. He went about his daily life, and the only thing that had changed was that part of his morning routine was putting his leg on.

He shook his head and fitted said prosthetic to his stumpy knee. It was all too philosophical for his taste at this point. Maybe later he would figure out why this had to happen, but for now, he was just glad that he was back to normal living.

He made it back to the bakery without incident, though he was pretty sure that if he had hit the little silver car, it would have been the car's fault for pulling out in front of him, not because he'd missed his gear shift when he had to hit the brakes. But that was neither here nor there as he locked his bike to the light pole and took his things inside.

"You made it," Micah said as he pulled a batch of cookies out of the oven.

"Astounding, isn't it?" Micaiah retorted sarcastically. "I'm even taking it to dinner tonight."

"Got a date?"

"Yes, I do. Dinner and a show."

Micah rolled his eyes and shook his head, but he couldn't help but grin. Before he could say anything, however, Tommen appeared around the corner.

"Hey, Micah. Or Micaiah. There's a guy here who wants to see you."

"Flattered, but I only date women," Micaiah said. "What's he want?"

"Says he's from OSHA, here to conduct a random investigation."

"Shit. Fine, I'll see him in the office."

This was not how he wanted to start his day. This was almost as bad as laying his bike down twice in the gravel drive, but this time the government was involved. So, really, this was worse than laying the bike down twice in the gravel drive. This was like laying his bike down and skidding into lava while a gas-hauling semi barreled down on him.

Still, he entered the office and dropped off his things, taking a second to Band and calm himself down. Wasn't like there hadn't been random inspections before, but usually they were from the Health Department, making sure their bleach water was clean and no one was wearing sandals or anything. Micaiah briefly wondered if he shouldn't have worn pants, but he figured that shorts were pretty safe while in the office.

"Micaiah Durvin?"

*Here goes nothing.* Micaiah turned. "Yes?"

The man held out his hand and crossed the room in two strides, no small feat considering he probably couldn't have been more than five-eight. "Hi, my name is Dan Pickard, I'm with OSHA, here to do a random inspection."

"So what brings you our way? Did we win the lottery?"

"You might say that."

"Have there been complaints?"

"A few concerns that have popped up on our radar. I'm sure they're nothing, but we are required to investigate them."

Something about the whole thing was fishy. Micaiah folded

his arms and tried to relax, take control of the situation. "If you don't mind me asking, do you have some kind of credentials to prove who you are?"

"Of course." The man rummaged around in the breast pocket of his suit. "I'm not here to shut you down or anything, just take some notes and observations so we can take you off the radar. You guys have been pristine for the ten years you've been in business, so I'm sure it's nothing, as I said. Here you are."

To Micaiah's eyes, the ID he presented looked genuine. Something about it still struck him as being off, but paranoia with no evidence never ended well. And having a funny feeling? Well, he got funny feelings in his leg sometimes, but those never amounted to anything either. Finally he handed back the card. "All right. Where do we begin?"

Once they were outside the office, Micaiah Banded and pulled Micah in with him.

"What's up?" Micah wondered.

"Something's not right," Micaiah told him. "I don't know what it is, though. Something about this guy. I'll humor him, but you watch him."

"You got it, boss."

Micaiah dropped the Band and he and "Dan" headed into the kitchen to start.

So they spent the next hour or so going over every inch of the store, making sure everything was as safe as could be. Then they spent another hour or so in the office, ensuring that everyone had the correct workplace safety training and had signed certificates in their files, and a dozen other things Micaiah wasn't even sure was technically covered by OSHA.

This was not how he wanted to spend his day. He had too many other things to do. Calls to make, emails to reply to, payroll, ordering, advertising, all of them much more important than sitting here with someone he wasn't even sure was a real government agent. At least not the United States government.

"Is there anything else you need to see?" Micaiah asked once he sensed things were starting to wrap up. At least he hoped they were starting to wrap up.

"Not that I need to see, per se, but there is one more concern that I need to address, and is actually the main reason I came out here today. I wanted to save it for last so I could see it in action." *And to waste two and a half hours of my time, apparently.* "Your manager is Tommen, correct?"

"Yes..."

"The problem that I have, or rather, that OSHA has, is that he is sixteen years old. You have the proper documentation for his school work release as well as his acceptance of the management position. Unfortunately, the two don't play well with each other."

"What are you saying?"

"I'm saying you can't have a sixteen year old as your manager. If he was a family member, there might be a little leniency, but he's not and there is none. It's the combination of the hours he's working and the work load. We can't have it. You can keep him as a regular employee, but not as the manager."

"Even though he wants to be manager? He signed the paperwork."

"Even so. Personally, I'm glad to see a teenager with such good work ethic. If he keeps it up for another year, two years, then I'm sure he'll make a great manager for you. Until then..." He shrugged.

Micaiah leaned back in his chair. "How exactly did you get tipped off about him, anyway?"

"Well, you might call her a mutual friend, though I don't think you would think of each other in that way. Let's just say that she will be glad to know that you're feeling better and can properly address the needs of your customers in the winter time."

*Fucking bitch with the raspberry tart! So that's what this was all about. Revenge. Fucking hell.* Micaiah shook his head. *Unbelievable. Well, that was the power of the elite when they didn't* get everything they wanted. Which probably meant that the man here was either a relative, or else owed her something. Either way. Fucking bitch.

The man seemed to sense that Micaiah understood exactly what had transpired, for he got a particular look of smug satisfaction, one that Micaiah wanted to beat off his stupid face. After a moment, the man dug around in his slim briefcase and brought out a couple papers. "This is a paper saying that you understand everything we discussed today. And this one is you saying that you will comply with any and all required changes within thirty days."

Problem was, there was no getting around it. If Tommen was the only "required change" he might have told the man he'd see him in court. But there were other things around the store that he'd missed or neglected that did need changing or updating. This was an all your eggs in one basket sort of thing. He couldn't not comply. Making sure the man saw his glare, he signed the paperwork.

"Excellent. Thank you very much." All the papers got swept up back in the briefcase and Dan stood. Micaiah stiffly followed and made sure to give him an extra tight handshake. "Like I said, you have a good business here and there really isn't anything of real concern that can't be fixed. Remember, you have thirty days to comply with the changes, and someone will be back to check on them."

*And the only one that they'll really be concerned with is Tommen as manager,* Micaiah thought, seeing the man to the door. Normally he might offer one of the goodies out of the case, but he was hardly in any kind of hospitable mood.

Once the OSHA inspector was gone, he motioned for Micah to join him in the office.

"I thought he'd never leave," Micah said, taking a seat. "I didn't really see anything suspicious."

"Because we were both expecting some kind of Time attack," Micaiah sighed. "Not that kind of attack this time."

"We're not being shut down, are we?"

"Not quite." He explained what the man had said about

keeping Tommen as manager. As Micah listened, his eyes got wide and his lips parted. Then his features screwed up as he tried to make sense of it.

"So the paperwork means literally nothing?" Micah wondered. "We're not working him any more hours or anything."

"He said it doesn't matter. He's not allowed to stay on as manager."

"I don't buy it. There's something not right about this. I mean, you go to the mall and all of the stores are managed by teenagers."

"That's what I was thinking, but I wasn't going to try and debate the point with him here. Besides, it's not just about OSHA and how crabby they are." He explained about the cranky woman and the raspberry tart.

Micah shook his head. "Bitch."

"That's what I thought."

"So what do we do? Call Tommen in and tell him he's being demoted?"

"No. I don't intend on telling Tommen anything yet, not until I can dig a little deeper into the legalities of the whole thing. If we get to the end of the thirty days and there's nothing we can do, yeah, we'll tell him."

Micah sighed. "Fuck. What do you think that lady has against teenagers that she would go to these lengths just to get him demoted?"

"Fuck if I know. But it doesn't matter now, I guess."

Micah only grunted. "Just perfect. You think he'd leave because of it?"

"Tommen? I doubt it. Even if he can't wear the manager badge, he can still keep the pay and do the work. I've seen no reason not to trust him as manager."

"True. So it's not all bad, I guess. Just...un-fucking-believeable."

"You're telling me."

"Is that all he was really here for?"

"I think so. There was other stuff, but that was all understandable and fixable."

"Nothing like the government to fix something that isn't broken." Micah stood and stretched. "But if it's all the same to you, I'm going to head back to work."

"Be my guest."

When he was gone, Micaiah turned back to the desk and the monster of paperwork spread out over it. There was so much he'd wanted to do while stuck playing tour guide, but now he couldn't think of anything. Well, might as well get some emails sent out and a little research done. There had to be some loophole that he could exploit, if not something he could find to refute that asshole entirely. Sometimes the government relied on people being too afraid of the government and too intimidated by its intentional complexities and confusion, but Micaiah wasn't fooled. He'd sift through all the bullshit and find something.

Maybe in his next life he should be a lawyer. Hey, they made good money, and if he and Kayla did finally decide to have kids, God knew they'd need a better income than what a baker and an interior designer could come up with.

He leaned back in his chair and stared at the computer screen. He needed to get out of here. Ten years as a baker. It wasn't that he hated the job, he just needed to move on. He needed to get his life back, take a vacation, a real vacation that didn't involve him going to the hospital. Problem was, the Wheel was closed to him, and Doug had decreed that no one was coming in. So until something changed, until Cassius and Rifun were taken out of power, he was stuck right where he was: in front of a computer screen in the office of a little mom 'n pop bakery.

It seemed to take at least forever for the clock to get around to six, and when it did, Micaiah couldn't have gotten out of there soon enough. Maybe his time off had done him some good, showed him that there really was a world outside of the bakery. He'd had time to himself, when he wasn't worrying about this order or that order, and he also wasn't expected to be on call for any goings-on in Time. A whole month when he'd been free, and now he was somehow expected to just return to the way things had been. This wasn't even about his leg anymore; this was about his sanity.

He was still anxious about riding his bike, especially in rush hour traffic, but he had no other options. Carefully, he pulled out to the road and waited for a clearing. He gave up several normally viable openings, but the last thing he wanted was to miss a shift and end up getting creamed from behind. He didn't need to call Kayla from the hospital. Again.

His fears were largely unwarranted as, when he did finally pull out into traffic, he neither missed a shift nor laid down the bike. Actually, as near as he could tell, everything went just how it was supposed to. His biggest problem was that he could no longer rely on muscle memory for the movements of his right leg; he had to make a conscious effort. But, he figured that if that was his biggest problem, it was easy enough to deal with.

He headed to the first place he'd gone once he'd tired of his pity party: Lucky Jack's Pub. It was a pretty hopping place for a Thursday evening and he counted himself lucky to find a spot at the bar.

"Well, Micaiah, good to see you back," Jack greeted. "You're not going to bite my head off tonight, are you?"

"So far, I'd say you're pretty safe," Micaiah told him.

"Good to know. Getting the usual?"

"Hopefully."

"You got it."

He wasn't actually supposed to meet Kayla until seven, but he figured it was smarter to arrive a little early and get something to eat first, that way he'd have a little time to digest before rushing into any physical activity. Jack returned with his shot.

"So, how's the knee?" the bartender asked cautiously.

"Knee's good. Rest of the leg isn't bad either, considering." Micaiah upended the shot.

"Got a prosthetic, did you? Good for you."

"Aye, I reckon so."

Before either could say more, Jack got called away. Micaiah looked around the room. The hard liquor bar was full, as was the foufou bar. Most of the tables in the dining room were full, mostly college kids and young adults with a light sprinkling of overworked, underpaid, middle-aged Americans.

If he and Kayla got back together, lived as man and wife, he'd probably have to give this up, especially if they had kids. Or at the very least, he'd have to cut back. But if he cut this out, he could take Kayla to see a movie, go out to a nice restaurant, even go on a real, extended vacation. True, every so often they did go see a movie or go to a restaurant, but they couldn't do it often, and they couldn't be too familiar. Such was the price they paid for security, and with Rifun and Cassius having total power, they had to tread even more carefully. In a word, it sucked.

"So," Jack said, returning, "since I've got ten seconds, tell me what's been going on. Three months ago, you walk in here with half a leg and almost bite my head off. Now you walk in totally fine and in a great mood. What's up?"

"Call it an attitude adjustment," Micaiah told him. "Don't get me wrong, I still miss my leg, but the prosthetic has helped me get my life back. I'm back riding again, so I can't complain too much. You might have seen my bike out there."

"I thought that was yours."

"Oh, please, you can't miss it."

"That bike out there is yours?" a new voice wondered.

Micaiah turned to see a blond standing just off to the side. He was forced to wonder if she was even old enough to be in such an establishment.

"Depends on which one you're talking about," he replied.

"The one with the white bear on it."

"That'd be mine."

"It's nice. Most guys choose eagles or tigers or something."

"Well, I like to be different." He indicated his leg.

"I see that. So what's the story? War wound? Scorned lover? Prison break out of the Wheel?"

And there was the code word. Micaiah and Kayla didn't always meet directly, lest someone figure out their relationship. Sometimes they sent a third party in their place, or used a disguise. The only side effect was that it made Micaiah look like a player and Kayla seem...open, but labels couldn't hurt them the same way death could, so they put up with it. Besides, after fifty years of marriage, they had to keep things a little interesting, and this girl seemed ten kinds of kinky.

"The story is whatever you want it to be," Micaiah told her.

"Oh, it's one of those." She grinned mischievously. Where had Kayla found her? Or, even better, was it Kayla in a Disguise?

"Why don't we get out of here? Go somewhere?"

She pouted a little. "We could. What are you up for?"

"I'm good with just about anything."

"Oh really? Do you have a brother? I especially like twins."

This was new. Still, Micaiah played along and nodded. "I do, actually. Where should I tell him to meet us?"

Micah was less than thrilled about being called away from work, but it was closing time anyway so he relented. He was even less thrilled at the prospect of meeting up for a kinky date. He knew that Micaiah went to meet his wife, which was why he didn't say too much about his going out, but he also knew that the dates weren't always—how did he put it?—Good Book approved.

Perhaps the only thing that got him to come out was the fact that he was never asked. Micaiah knew his brother wanted nothing to do with it, so the fact that he asked him now was an oddity worth investigating.

"So other than a strange little meeting—" Micah's polite way of saying kinky sex out loud in public. "—any idea what this is about?" He met Micaiah in the lobby.

"They haven't told me anything," Micaiah answered as they

got in the elevator. "But then, they haven't been in much of a 'talking' kind of mood."

"I'm afraid to ask, but I will. What do you mean?"

"Oh, you'll see."

"Cai, I'm not exactly in a mood for games. Okay, you do your kinky sex with your wife, fine, whatever, but either tell me what's going on, or—oh."

His words were cut short as they entered the hotel room and he saw what lay within. To put it mildly, trying to describe it would portray enough adult content so as to make a nun blush and scar small children for life.

Micaiah removed his shirt as Kayla approached. "Now then, what were you saying about telling you something or other?"

Micah blinked and shook his head. "No, I can't...Cai, this is..."

The blond, Julie, sauntered up to him and touched his face. "Can't what? It's okay, we can work around it."

"What? No, it's not that. I can do that. It's just—"

"Prove it. Your embarrassment says otherwise."

Micaiah, now completely naked, shrugged and held his hands out. "Take it or leave it, dude. And tell yourself you won't regret it."

He could already see his brother straining. He hadn't gotten laid in years. But once Julie touched him, it all went downhill from there.

At one point, Micaiah wondered whether one of the neighbors was going to call the front desk and file a noise complaint. On the other hand, if the neighbor had even an inkling of what was going on, he may not have wanted to subject a hotel staff member to the sight, asking someone to come and make them quiet down.

By the time they were done, Micaiah wondered if he wasn't going to have a heart attack from all the excitement.

"Shit," Micah breathed from the next bed, chest heaving, eyes closed.

"Tell me you hated it," Micaiah told him.

"I shouldn't have—"

"Tell me you hated it."

"But I—"

"Tell me you hated it and it was probably the worst thing to happen to you today. Tell me, little brother."

Now Micah looked at him. "Fuck you."

"Sorry. I'll do a lot of kinky things, but I'm not gay and I don't like you that much either."

"Fuck you." Groaning, he sat up, much to Julie's dismay. "I have to take a shower."

He disappeared into the bathroom, and a minute later the shower turned on.

"Is he always like this?" Julie asked.

"A dick? Yeah, he's pretty much always like that. A stiff? No, that's kind of new for him."

"He might come around a little now that he's been loosened up," Kayla said, nuzzling him as she lay on top of him. "But at least you were fun."

Micaiah kissed her. "Anything for you."

She grinned. "Well, in that case, I have a list of demands."

"Ah, can I amend that statement?"

She kissed him. "Nope. Too late. You already said it."

Even as she spoke, she rocked back and forth on his hips. He groaned and shook his head. "I don't think it's ready to go again just yet."

Kayla sighed and kissed him a third time. "Too bad." She stopped rocking and slid off to one side.

The shower stopped and a minute later, Micah called out, "Are you guys done being kinky?"

"No," Micaiah answered. He rolled his eyes. "Get out here, Micah."

After a moment, the bathroom door opened and Micah walked out, fully clothed.

"So was there a point—?"

"Good grief, Micah, take your clothes off and get back in bed."

Micah folded his arms. "Was there a point to this excursion or what?"

"Yes, there is," Kayla said, sounding exasperated. "We just thought that maybe we could get you loosened up a little before getting down to business. I see that effort was wasted."

Micah seemed unsure how to respond. Nevertheless, he at least took his shirt off before reluctantly climbing back in bed beside Julie.

"Now then, are we ready to get down to business?" he asked irritably.

Micaiah was not at an advantageous angle, but he could tell Kayla was giving Micah some kind of look. To make a point of it, she stretched out beside Micaiah, a long, sinewy pose, complete with a sensual sigh. She looked at Micah again. "Now we're ready."

Still she needled Micah's impatience by taking her own sweet time setting up a few pillows in such a way that she could be heard without obstruction.

"Obviously you know that Cai came up with a plan to take out Rifun and Cassius," she said.

"You mean that suicide mission?" Micah corrected.

"That's the one. You also know Doug, our superior."

"I've talked to him, but I don't really know him."

"Well, we'll save you some painful discoveries. He's kind of a dick who will take credit for anything he can, anything to make himself look good. But he does have some background in strategy and tactical analysis and a whole bunch of other things. And so, swallowing our pride, we turned the plan over to him."

"I'm assuming that he had some insight."

"He did, actually."

"Is it still a suicide mission?"

"Possibly, as all missions to the Wheel will be until Cassius is removed from power." Micah looked ready to speak, then considered her point. Finally he shrugged and she continued. "It's volunteer only, but the crux of the plan involves having both of you in it together."

Micah nodded slowly. "So that's why you brought me here. You were trying to get me to feel good so I would say yes to whatever crazy scheme you guys came up with."

"That would be the idea, yes," Micaiah told him. "It's possible to potentially Disguise someone as you, but it would be easier if you were there in person."

"Uh...huh. I see. Does this ingenius plan still involve the Time Trials?"

"It does," Julie said beside him. "But Doug has come up with a few safety features in the plan in the event something goes wrong."

"I don't see how it could go right."

"You don't even know what the plan is," Kayla said.

Micah sighed. "Okay, fine, I'll at least give you that much. Tell me what the plan is. And don't go giving me this whole, 'You have to agree before we'll tell you' kind of deal."

"We wouldn't do that, not with the stakes so high."

"All right. Hit me."

"The general idea remains the same. Micaiah goes to the Wheel, surrenders on the condition that he is granted a Time Trial. So far, everyone agrees that that will be an offer Cassius and Rifun won't be able to refuse. In a Time Trial, he is allowed to call three witnesses—or 'Testimonies' I believe is the word they prefer. He is also able to call a Stake, someone who will stand with him as a double-or-nothing gamble. At maximum, we can get five people in there, less one Micaiah."

"So, Johnny, who are the other four contestants?"

"Ideally, we'd like to use you as the Stake."

"How did I know that was coming?"

"The other three would be Walter, Tommen, and Doug. All three of them are prizes to Cassius and Rifun, something to be captured, conquered, however you want to put it. Naming them all but guarantees that they will not only agree to the Trial, but given how overconfident they'll be and how intent they will be on claiming their prizes, it might buy us just a few seconds to carry out the rest of the plan."

Micah sighed and looked contemplative. Well, Micaiah figured, at least he wasn't rejecting it outright like he'd feared. "Okay, I'm following so far. How are we all going to get out alive? Once the Trial gets going—"

"The Trial won't even have a chance to start. When Micaiah is brought out to be presented and his Stake and Testimonies are named, that's when you, Micah, will have probably less than a second to draw your weapon and kill both Rifun and Cassius. Then we escape by any means. If necessary, Doug can create a portal."

Micah shifted his position, nodding emphatically. Micaiah suspected an impending sarcastic remark, which there was. "That's a nice idea, except for the part where I somehow smuggle a gun into the Pit or the Coliseum or wherever the hell they're hosting these things. There are guards there, or did Cai neglect to mention that in his report? Hundreds and thousands of guards."

It was Julie who answered. "Objects can be disguised just as well as people. We've done it before."

"And what if the shit hits the fan?" Micah asked. "What if everything goes horribly wrong and we all end up getting captured? We'll be executed."

"That's almost a guarantee," Kayla acknowledged. "The question then becomes, what are you willing to risk? Do you really enjoy being a baker that much?"

"I enjoy living and being alive in general."

"Always having to watch your back? Wondering when Rifun's going to come knocking at your door?"

"Cassius and Rifun think they have the upper hand," Micaiah said. "And, in all reality, they do have the upper hand. They're expecting everyone else to play defense. If we take the fight to them, we might have a chance."

Micah squirmed a little. "You know, I might have a little less problem with this if you would have come to me, oh, sixty years ago." He gave Micaiah a look. "As it is, I'm just starting to figure this out, whatever 'this' is. Why would I want to risk my life for it?"

Micaiah sat up and fixed him in a stare. "Because I am. Do it for me, if not for them. I'm going, Micah. I might not come back. I'd rather have you there with me, too, rather than have you die alone and afraid when Rifun comes for you."

That's when Micaiah knew that he had him. It was time to face facts. Cassius and Rifun were in power and there was no foreseeable end to their tyranny. They were capturing and enslaving and executing people left and right from all the Engaged Civilizations, but it was only a matter of time before they worked their way down the tree and got to places like Earth. Then it wouldn't be a simple thing like a Tracker attack, but possibly armed guards who were not so easily taken down.

Micah was silent for a moment. Then, "All right." He let out a breath. "All right, fine. I'll do it. I will help you on this insane suicide mission, but only because I know that you're going to need me to save your sorry ass so you don't lose your other leg in the process."

Micaiah grinned. "Good to have you on board, little brother."

Micah gave him a look. "For fuck's sake, Cai, we're fucking twins. Stop calling me your little brother."

Micaiah kept grinning as he stretched out and sat up long enough to remove his prosthetic before laying back down under the blankets. "Well, get a good night's sleep anyway, little brother, because it's going to be a long day tomorrow."

"Wait, we're doing this tomorrow?"

"Unless you'd rather schedule it for next Tuesday after your dentist appointment?"

"I guess I didn't realize it would be so soon."

"It won't be," Julie told him. "At least for you. He's going tomorrow, but it might be a day or two before you're called as the Stake and Testimony."

Micah let out a breath. "Okay. I guess."

He made to get out of bed, but Micaiah called him back. "You better not be leaving this room. We paid for four people to sleep in this room tonight, and four people are going to sleep in this room. Or else you owe me—and by me, I mean Kayla—" he added quickly at a look. "—a hundred and thirty bucks."

"Can I at least go to the bathroom? Please, Mom and Dad?" Micah asked sarcastically.

"Do you need help, dear?" Kayla asked, matching his snark.

He blushed and they laughed as he walked away.

"I think he's starting to come around," Julie observed. "How receptive do you think he'd be to a morning wakeup call?"

"I'd leave the poor boy alone for now," Micaiah told her. "He's had a lot thrown at him this evening. He needs time to digest."

She shrugged and settled in under the covers. Micaiah rolled over and held Kayla close.

"I worry about you sometimes," she sighed.

"And other times?"

"I want to be the one to kill you myself."

"Got it. Where do I stand now?"

"On one leg."

He rolled his eyes and shook his head, but he was amused more than he was frustrated. After a moment, she went on, "I don't want you to go, but I know it has to be done. We've pissed off Rifun and Cassius too many times to just fly under the radar and hope that Suppression will spare us. They're coming. Sooner or later."

"Which is why we want to catch them off-guard," Micaiah said matter-of-fact.

"We only get one shot at this. You know that, right? They know that the Akari can get us through the dampening field, so they're going to suspect something's up."

"We're fighting fire with fire. We just have to do our best not to get burned. And hope that they don't know the full extent of what the Akari can do."

"That's an awful lot of hope."

"It's all we have."

She nuzzled closer. "No, we have more than that. We have

each other."

"You know, for being one hell of a badass Inuit warrior princess chick, you can be such a sap."

"And that's why you married me."

Well, he couldn't deny it. There was movement from the other bed as Julie rolled over. "You guys are so annoying when you get cute, you know that?"

"You're just jealous," Kayla told her.

Still, it was getting late and, as he himself had said, they had a big day tomorrow. Micah emerged from the bathroom and hesitantly got in bed next to Julie.

"You okay with this, bro?" Micaiah asked seriously. "I mean, I know you're young, but if co-ed is too soon..."

"Fuck you, Cai," Micah told him.

"Good night to you, too, *a Mhaicin*."

After a minute or two of settling, rolling over, and settling again, things quieted down and they drifted off to sleep, each acutely aware that it might be their last night.

# Chapter Nineteen
## Wanted: Dead or Alive

Micaiah didn't remember his dream except that when he woke up, he was already on edge. Cautiously, he opened his eyes, half-expecting to see Rifun sitting in the chair in the corner. The room was still fairly dark, but from what he could tell, no one was in the room who wasn't supposed to be. He rolled over and looked at the clock. Four-thirty. Shit. And with the way he could feel his body waking up, reminding him of all the aches and pains he already bore — to say nothing of the new ones he accrued last night — he knew he wasn't getting back to sleep.

He sat up slowly, as much for his headache as to not disturb Kayla who'd rolled away from him in the night. Sighing, he reached for his leg. Normally he might just get up and hobble along on his crutches, but he'd forgotten to bring them. Something about them not fitting in his motorcycle saddlebags.

His mood only darkened as he quietly got ready. What if this was all for nothing? What if, on some off chance, they denied him a Time Trial? What if the plan fell through during the Trial? To that end, what if this was the last time he saw Kayla? Guilt pricked at him. They should have kept it to themselves, made love only with each other by themselves, one final thing that they alone shared to take to their graves.

He looked at her, her sleeping form getting closer to the edge of the bed. He went to her, getting in beside her and pulling her close to his body, away from the edge. He Banded her, just enough that she would wake up without losing any sleep. She yawned and stretched and twisted to look at him.

"Good morning," she murmured, kissing him sleepily.

He did make love to her then, Banding them both so no one could disturb them.

"You're feeling better," she observed when they were finished.

"Just wanted to make sure you knew I love you," Micaiah told her, kissing her again and holding her like he might lose her.

"I know. And I love you, too. And I would be lying if I said I wasn't scared."

No more was said after that. No more needed to be said. Micaiah dropped the Band but waited a few minutes before getting up and continuing to get ready. By the time he was done in the bathroom, Kayla was almost ready and Julie was just getting out of bed.

"Should I wake him?" Julie asked, nodding toward Micah who was still sleeping soundly.

Micaiah nodded. "Yeah. We gain nothing by delaying, and he'll have to get to the shop eventually."

Micah was less than pleased to be woken up, but swore and panicked when he saw the time.

"I'm supposed to be there already," he said, scrambling to find his shirt. "Kyle's probably waiting, wondering what's happened to me."

"So you're not even going to say good-bye before I go?" Micaiah wondered.

"Huh?" Micah looked at him. "Wait, you're going now?"

"Not immediately. We're going to check out of the hotel and head home. Then they'll send me to the Wheel and it's all up in the air from there."

Micah sighed. "Don't do it, Cai. You've done enough. Let someone else go."

"I can't. I'm already committed. Are you?"

He seemed hesitant. Then, "I still don't know about this whole Akari business, but I said I'd do it for you, and I'm going to do it for you. I just...I wish there was another way."

"So do I," Micaiah said, putting his hands on his brother's shoulders.

Micah sighed uncertainly and they embraced, neither sure if he would see the other again.

"You take care of yourself, brother," Micah said, tears in his voice. "I don't want to bail your ass out of there, but I will. And then when we're back home, I'll kick it, too."

"I'm sure you will," Micaiah laughed.

There was a slump to Micah's shoulders as he left the hotel room, but he did not look back. Micaiah stared after him for a minute or two before turning and gathering up the last of his things.

Suddenly he found himself staring right in the face of his mission. He was going to go home, park his bike like any ordinary day, then go to the Wheel and try to topple a tyrannical regime or die trying. Self-consciously, he looked at his leg, where the knee ended and the prosthetic began. Last time he'd been in the Wheel, he'd always had the option to escape; he'd held out for Walter's sake. This time, though, his goal was not about escape, but release. Release from darkness the prisoners. Sounded poetic. Must have read it somewhere. But it seemed to sum up the situation quite nicely.

There was probably another way to do this. Might be that there were a thousand ways to do this and he just happened to pick the worst one. He wasn't going with the expectation of coming back. Living...living would be a bonus.

He turned as Kayla put a hand on his shoulder.

"It'll be all right," she told him. "I know it."

"I wish I could share your confidence."

"Come on. Least you can do is have a good breakfast before you go."

Yes, because he was simply going on vacation or a business trip, where he would need the energy to deal with long lines, crowded atriums, and grouchy persons.

"If this is my last meal, I do have a few ideas in mind," he told her, following her down to the lobby. "And they don't include a hotel breakfast, no matter how gourmet."

"It won't be your last. And when you get back, we can go wherever you want."

Micaiah was in no real mood for food, but he partook of the complimentary breakfast anyway as it was just being served. Warm pancakes, eggs, sausage, and buttery biscuits were normally enough to brighten any sour mood, but not today. There was just something about the prospect of it being his last meal that robbed him of his ability to taste and enjoy.

"There's still been no intel from the inside?" he wondered.

"Place is locked down pretty tight," Julie answered. "It'll be easier getting in than getting out."

"What about the Trackers? What if they come back through the portal and go after you?" He looked at Kayla.

"Then we'll just have to kill them," she informed him.

They checked out of the room and walked out to the parking lot. Even in late May, the mornings were still pretty crisp, and Micaiah found himself wishing he'd brought a jacket for his bike. But, it was neither here nor there, and in less than an hour, it wouldn't matter anyway.

Less than an hour. It was like watching his own death clock, seeing the seconds tick down and second-guessing each one as it was whisked away into the past. What the fuck was he getting himself into?

It was a strange thing, he mused as he pulled in the driveway and parked his bike, that he was more upset that he didn't get to ride his bike as much as he'd wanted. He should have pulled it out of storage earlier.

Kayla and Julie pulled in behind him and they silently entered the house. Micaiah's stomach was doing flips and twists and contorting every which way. He went down to his bedroom to drop off a few things, pausing in the doorway as he exited, wondering if he was ever going to see this place again and sleep in his own bed.

"Thinking about it won't make it easier," Kayla said behind

him.

"But it's harder to think about not thinking about it," he answered.

"Come on. No time like the present."

"Present. Future. Past. It's all the same, isn't it?"

"Not for us."

They went out to the living room where Julie was mentally preparing to break through a dampening field. The two women would open the portal and Micaiah would do his best to close it as quickly as possible without getting sucked into the Land In Between.

"Ready?" Julie asked, rising from the recliner.

Micaiah was unprepared for Kayla's sudden assault, flinging her arms around him, pulling him close, and kissing him desperately. "I love you."

He kissed her back. "I love you, too. And I'm coming home."

She nodded and took a breath even as tears started streaking down her cheeks. "May the Author write you a happy ending."

"For both of us."

Kayla nodded again and stepped back, wiping her eyes and trying to regain stoic, impassive composure, ready to carry out this mission and praying she wasn't sending her husband to his death.

"When you are," he said.

A small portal flickered to life, like a campfire trying to catch wet wood in a windstorm. It took some doing, and Micaiah eventually had to lend his strength, but the portal opened. It wasn't stable by any means and he stepped through quickly, cinching it shut like a noose.

He was not immediately assaulted or apprehended in any way, so he counted that a good start. Fighting to maintain balance and stay alert amid the seasickness, he straightened himself and looked around.

He was in the portal room; that much he could tell. But it was not the portal room as he remembered it. He remembered the portal room as being technology and engineering on flagrant display, maintained around the clock by an army of secretaries in order to keep traffic moving smoothly with as few fatalities as possible. The portal room now looked like something from a post-apocalyptic movie. Aside from being quite a bit darker, it seemed to have fallen into disrepair. There weren't exactly sparks and open wires and rust and rats scuttling in the darkness, but it was just...unmaintained. Certainly explained why they'd had such trouble opening a portal to get in the place. Without all the engineering and hardware to focus the dimensional energy, it was up to the instigator to make sure that the home and the destination connected, and that the destination was where they wanted to go.

Micaiah took a few tentative steps toward where the portal into the Wheel proper used to be. Cassius and Rifun were evil bastards, but he couldn't imagine that they would really let the portal room go to trash. Yes, evil dictators and tyranny always saw the collapse of infrastructure, but the portal room was the only way in and out. Okay, maybe not the only way, but it was certainly the easiest route, and Micaiah saw no reason that they would avoid the portal room.

He reached out and touched the wall. Or maybe they really had said to hell with it. Maybe, after he'd collapsed the portal, they'd sealed off this room to die. Maybe they'd created a new portal room elsewhere. Maybe they'd created their own private portal room, all the easier for them to slip in and out without worrying about sudden intruders.

If that was the case, though, then he'd come all this way for nothing. If the portal room was in such a state, then it was likely the rest of the Wheel was, too. Or most of it anyway. It was hard enough trying to evade the dimensional focusing of the portal room on a good day. Now, even though it was weakened, he would not only be evading that focus, but trying to break into some other part of the Wheel where he did not fully grasp the coordinates of the destination and was still fighting a dampening field. It was like trying to shoot a target that was hidden behind a brick wall while blindfolded and dodging return fire.

He took a step back. So that was it then. Cassius and Rifun sealed up inside their own little castle, playing masters of the universe. Suddenly it all seemed utterly laughable. And yet pitiable. And yet liberating.

Out of sheer curiosity, he walked over to the translator dispenser, almost completely draped in shadow. When he tried to access it, he got only a small spark of life before it fizzled out. How...expected.

Shaking his head, he turned back toward the empty rows, where, on a normal day, hundreds of thousands of portals to hundreds of thousands of worlds would be open and brimming with life; where walking down a row was like walking a tightrope across a canyon. Get shoved just right and you went tumbling into another world. And hoped you didn't get eaten immediately upon arrival.

But if Cassius and Rifun were sealed inside their little castle, he wasn't going to be the one to free them. If they did have another portal room set up somewhere, even a private one, it was going to take time and a lengthy investigation to find it without being detected. Either way, his work here appeared to be done. His entire mission had amounted to nothing. Maybe he should head to work and scare the shit out of Micah.

Just as he was about to try and open a portal back home, he heard something. In the empty darkness, it could have come from any direction, and he wasn't even sure what the noise was. It might have been the growl of an animal, something scuffing across the floor.

Cautiously, he looked around, trying to keep his body still and move only his head. He heard the noise again, closer this time, he was sure. He should have brought something with him. Even a knife would be helpful. So much for a clean getaway. He just had to make sure he didn't lose his other leg this time.

He was not ready for this. He was only just walking on his leg—or running, in the case of his running leg. His skills were limited to those two tasks. Those, and riding a motorcycle. Fighting he hadn't gotten around to yet.

He heard the noise again and managed to move just in time as a Tracker met thin air where his body had been just a second prior. It landed and used the momentum to swing back around and swipe a huge, ugly paw at him, followed quickly by a snap from large, drooling fangs. Micaiah danced back, fought for balance, tried not to go down.

The Tracker stalked toward him, and Micaiah got the impression of a tiger, stalking its prey. It was not a comforting thought. He also got the feeling that he was being watched, elsewhere in the darkness. Were there more Trackers around? Without the portal into the Wheel, was this room used as a sort of stable for the Trackers?

The Tracker launched itself at Micaiah who couldn't move fast enough. He might have, except his leg slowed him down, and the imbalance more than the Tracker plowing into him caused him to fall.

Oddly enough, he was more pissed that he was going to die because of a Tracker and not because he was facing off against Cassius and Rifun. He was ready to die, but he wanted it to be on his terms. Being mauled by a slobbering extraterrestrial bloodhound was not what he had in mind.

But said slobbering extraterrestrial bloodhound did not kill him. It didn't even scratch him or bite him. It simply stayed on top of him, its weight impossible to overcome, and bad breath almost impossible to stand for longer than a few seconds.

Then there was a burst of light behind Micaiah. He struggled to wiggle and look where it was coming from. The light disappeared and the Tracker got off him. Taking a deep breath, he stood, trying to seem ready for anything.

"Well, it's about time you stopped by," Rifun said. "We were beginning to worry about you." He grinned as his gaze dropped to Micaiah's leg. "It looks like we have more in common than I expected. We really must sit down and catch up on old times."

Micaiah didn't like his tone or his words. They were too ominous. They'd been expecting him. Maybe not him, but someone. And they had a plan to deal with whoever stepped in their front door.

Well, he just had to make sure that his plan was better than their plan.

"I'm here to —"

Rifun held up a hand. His right hand, gloved to conceal the missing fingers. "Now, now, you don't just walk into someone's house and start chit-chatting away. You say hello, take your shoes off, ask them how they are, and suggest that you go and sit in the living room or at the kitchen table. So, we've already said our hellos. I would tell you to take your shoes off, but that might be in poor taste." Micaiah fought to keep his temper in check. "We can see visually how each other has fared recently. All that's left is to retire to another room and speak privately."

"Yeah? What did you have in mind?"

Rifun regarded him a second longer before making a gesture, then turning and walking away, opening another portal. Micaiah followed a short distance behind with the Tracker trailing closely, ready to kill on its master's order.

"Looks like you executed the housekeeping staff, too," Micaiah observed.

It wasn't just the portal room that seemed to have fallen into disrepair. The whole Wheel looked like something out of some weird science fiction post-apocalyptic movie. Everything was dark, empty, abandoned, the ghost town of the modern world.

"Yes, it is rather bleak, isn't it?" Rifun agreed mildly. "Suffice to say, your little party tricks set us back a while. Once things got back on schedule, we decided that, since half the Wheel was blown to hell anyway, why not scrap the whole thing and start over? So we're undergoing a bit of a...renovation. Pardon the mess."

So that was the reason for the ghost town look. It had, truly, been abandoned so Cassius and Rifun could modify the whole Wheel to their own tastes. The question was, though, did they actually possess the power to create, or were they limited only to modification? Micaiah took an even breath. It didn't matter, he told himself, because they would be dead soon, anyway.

"Actually, I came just to make sure you were all right,"

Micaiah told him cheekily. "We hadn't heard from you in, what's it been? Six months? We thought something bad must have happened."

"Ah." Rifun gave him a knowing look. "I see. As you can see, however, I am just fine. As is Cassius. Though we do appreciate the concern. And fear not, for our plans will be back underway by the end of the year. Just a shame that you won't get to tell all your little friends the good news."

Secretly, that was what Micaiah was afraid of. He was ready to die as long as Cassius and Rifun went down with him, but he still had his innate self-preservation instincts. He was ready to go, but he was going to find every way to live, too.

"Does Micah still not understand his potential?" Rifun asked conversationally.

"I haven't told him anything," Micaiah lied.

"Protective to the last, aren't you?"

"You'll notice which twin is walking behind you right now."

"Yes. And I must say, it is much easier to tell the two of you apart now. Tell me, Micaiah, did you know you were going to lose the leg, or did you just wake up with it gone?" He paused as if considering. "I can't imagine it was a welcome change, either way."

"No more than your fingers."

"Very true. And some might say that my loss was the greater, seeing how you are getting along wonderfully, while I sit at my desk, going through the same penmanship exercises I did as a child, trying to force my left hand to do what my right once did so naturally. I must say, computers have made the universe much, much simpler.

"Did you know, there are places in the universe where a severed limb cannot only be reattached, but, in the absence of the detached limb, also regrown?"

"I've heard stories."

"The stories are true. But for us common folk, it is sorely inaccessible. The races who control such technology often won't stoop to even conversing with outsiders. And on the off chance you do get them to talk to you and admit to such technology, it has its limits. For example, it can only be used within what we would approximate as fifty-nine hours of the injury. By the time I heard about such technology—or rather, that it actually existed—I was already far past that threshold. That is, assuming such a threshold exists and wasn't merely a means to get rid of me." He turned his head to look at Micaiah. "From the looks of things, you're long past fifty-nine hours into your injury."

"Yeah, about six months into it," Micaiah told him flatly. "What's your interest in it?" *Other than sizing up my weakness.*

"Why shouldn't I be interested? We know each other well, and, despite your adamant refusal to be my Apprentice—or, perhaps now, my compatriot—I hold you in high regard and I am concerned for your well-being."

"Does this mean you're not going to execute me?"

"No. But I would like you to know that it was a split vote. I did not want to see you executed, but Cassius had the final say."

"Here I thought this was a partnership. Though, I always imagined it would be Lily who was crowned Time Queen, but I digress." Micaiah shrugged, trying to shake off his nervousness.

Rifun barked a laugh. "Ha! Always ready with the sword of wit. Though it is true that Cassius would be nothing without me. Have you heard the story of how we met and got in this business?"

"Do I want to hear the story?"

"Hm, perhaps not. It will do you no good now except perhaps to pass the time in your cell. It is a fascinating read, actually."

"Maybe later."

The next portal they stepped through finally took them out of the Old Wheel, where the darkness and emptiness put Micaiah on edge.

The new Wheel was far less dungeon-y, secret lair-esque than he might have imagined, given who the designers were. If he had to hazard a guess, he might have said that Rifun was the one in charge of the design. He'd always struck Micaiah as an actor of sorts, partial to Shakespeare especially, and the new Wheel reflected that. Where the

Old Wheel had been *Relativity* meets *Star Wars*, the new Wheel was more like *Relativity* meets Shakespeare.

The Old Wheel had been consistently fucked up; no matter which room one entered, all the wall faces were pretty much the same: translucent, tastefully colored to break up the monotony, modestly sci-fi-ish. The only exceptions to this had been major areas like the Coliseum, the Archives, the Judgment Wing, and so on.

The new Wheel, however, was pleasantly different, and Micaiah was fairly certain Rifun was taking him on a roundabout tour of the new construction. The lower marketplaces were stunning reconstructions of 1600's England, the streets and architecture, all convoluted to suit the fucked up physics of the Wheel, but still remarkable, even beautiful. The middle marketplaces were as pleasant gardens, like what one might imagine in *A Midsummer Night's Dream*. Not surprisingly, the auctionhouses were dressed far more regally. Not quite "castle" but more like a mix between a nobleman's courtyard and his receiving room.  Here and there, secretaries moved things about, decorating, setting up, under the watchful eye of loyal guards.

"You should have become an architect," Micaiah said, unable to conjure up any emotion except pity. To have such talent wasted on such evil was a crime in and of itself.

"I was, once, actually," Rifun told him. "It pleased me greatly, too. Imagine how much happier I was once I discovered I could also build using Time and the Akari."

"You are no Akari-bearer."

"Perhaps, but seeing how you are the one set to be executed, we will be using my definition of things."

Wisely, Micaiah said no more, for his thoughts were elsewhere. Things had changed. Like, really changed. The paths through the Wheel had changed. More worrisome, however, was that the scenery had changed. He'd been fully prepared for an escape from the Coliseum. What if it was no longer a Coliseum? What if they'd turned it into a medieval castle? What if they'd made it all but impenetrable? They were gearing up for a thousand-year dictatorship, and they had the power to secure it. Worse, Micaiah had given them the isolation needed to carry it out without interruption.

Shit.

On top of that, while some executions had taken place—they had to have—it appeared as though a good majority of those from the inauguration had found new purpose in Rifun's new Shakespearean paradise. Most of them appeared to be secretaries, but other than being under the watchful eye of the guards, he couldn't say as any of them looked mistreated in any way. Other than the initial coup, this was hardly the bloodbath overthrow he'd envisioned, and it could make sympathy harder to conjure up. The Hands had been corrupt, but Rifun wasn't beating them within an inch of their lives, and things looked almost okay, ready for business to resume.

Fuck.

At some point, they left the marketplaces and other general congregation areas, and they ended up in what looked like a ye olde towne square. Fucked up to the fourth dimension, true, but a town square nonetheless. The first thing Micaiah noticed was the gallows right in the middle, but rather than a noose, the frame held a portal. Elsewhere, portals were integrated into common doorframes, a medieval sign with the universal Time symbols depicting its destination. This place appeared to be the hub for the Judgment Wing, the Archives, the Arena, the Coliseum, and the Pit portal, still lodged safely, if eerily, within the gallows frame.

"As you can see, things have changed a little bit," Rifun said, making for the portal marked for the Judgment Wing. "But some things...never change."

He was probably speaking metaphorically, as the Judgment Wing they walked into was not the same one Micaiah remembered from the elections. Before, the Wing had seemed to be more of a bank vault set-up. This new Judgment Wing was made to be more like a 1600's courthouse.

The first room they entered, however, while decorated

differently, still had the same old procedure for processing criminals. The Grandfather in charge, along with the hand-stamping and other modern technology, kind of threw off the whole feel of the place, in Micaiah's opinion.

They were directed to go through another door at the back of the room. The same familiar force field parted for them as they walked through and sealed up behind them, trapping Micaiah. The whole route was basically the same, just with different decor, as they approached the room with three doors. As expected, they went through the left door.

The holding cells were eerily empty and they went straight through the side door that would take them before a judge. Normally, judgments were carried out by Gatekeepers, Wardens, or Dominion Timekeepers, the responsibilities rotating through the entire intergalactic roster, kind of like jury duty. And about as fun. This time, though, the one who sat in the place of the judge was a Grandfather.

"Everyone knows what you've done," Micaiah said. "Why do you still bother with the shrouds?"

"Small changes," Rifun told him, depositing him in the testimony box and stepping off to the side. "One thing at a time. We're in no rush. Have to make sure we do everything right the first time, right?"

*More than you know.*

"Micaiah Durvin, Lieutenant Timekeeper, Quadrant One, Parsec Eleven, Sector Five, System Four, Planet Thirty-Eight, Region Four, District Four," the Grandfather recited, reading the information off a panel which had been transmitted from the stamp on Micaiah's hand.

"That is correct," Micaiah confirmed.

"You have been brought before this court, charged with treason. This carries a mandatory death sentence. Warden, do you have any thoughts?"

"Just one," Rifun said, stepping forward. He looked at

Micaiah. "Why come back? Earth is such an insignificant place; you could have lived for a good decade or more before I came. You have a life, and a twin brother to look after. Why do you come here to your death?"

"I didn't come here to go to my death," Micaiah informed him. "I came to make a bargain."

Rifun grinned. "Ah. So the noble Micaiah Durvin does it again, able and willing to sacrifice what's left of him in order to protect those he loves. Some might say you have a Messiah complex."

"I demand a Time Trial."

That made Rifun shut up. Micaiah went on. "If I win, you leave Earth alone in whatever grand scheme of yours you have planned. Like you said, Earth is insignificant anyway. It would make no real difference whether we're Engaged or not."

Rifun folded his arms, and Micaiah could see the wheels turning in his mind. "And if and when you lose?"

"You've already pronounced me dead. So you get me, my Stake, and my Testimonies."

"Who do you expect to call?"

"Micah will stand as my Stake. Walter, Tommen, and Doug will come as my Testimonies."

At the mention of Tommen and Doug, Rifun's eyes lit up and his posture changed like that of a dog who's just heard the word "bacon." After a moment of ominous consideration, he said, "I'll meet your bargain, and I'll even raise you."

"What more could you want?" Though Micaiah wasn't sure he wanted to know the answer.

Rifun chuckled. "I want to know that this was a group effort and that you are all truly willing to sacrifice yourselves. If and when you lose, Doug will have his clock broken, Tommen and Micah will become my Apprentices, and you and Walter will be my personal servants. You will have your clocks broken in that you will never be able to use Time again, and you will swear a holy vow that you will serve me faithfully with no thought of treachery for the rest of your days." When Micaiah hesitated, he went on. "It's easy to die for a cause. It's much harder to live with the failure."

"Speaking from experience?"

"If you would have asked me six months ago, I might have said yes."

Now what was that supposed to mean? He could easily be referring to the time before he and Cassius were in power, but the way he said it was much more sinister.

"At any rate," Rifun said, returning to his normal, cheery, Shakespearean self, "we will need time to consider your proposal. As I am sure that you are tired and wish to get off your feet, I will allow you to do so. I'll even let you have your own cell. With recent housecleaning, quite a few have opened up."

Micaiah's stomach twisted, not because he was going to be thrown in jail, but because of the way Rifun worded it. How many had been slaughtered, and it was no more significant to him than simply clearing out an overcrowded hotel. Had the man no feelings whatsoever? True, Cassius was a violent, bloodthirsty bastard, but at least he felt. He felt rage and hatred and a sickening lust and pleasure for death, but he felt. Rifun, however, showed virtually no emotion, at least not with such passion. Everything he did was with an air of sarcasm and self-satisfaction.

Even as he was escorted out of the courtroom by a guard, Micaiah pondered the conundrum. Throughout this whole adventure, from the murders last fall to just now, no one had been able to definitively say who was the dominant one of the pair. Cassius had the power and the ability to rule with fear, but Rifun had the tactical mind and ruthless cunning to carry out any plan he conjured up. Really, it was impossible to tell where one stopped and the other started. Or, could it be that even that was all an illusion, too?

Thankfully, he was not taken to the black cells, instead being escorted to one of the holding cells. There were hundreds of different cell blocks, each one designed for a specific species or weak point, just enough to keep a prison in without having to go overboard on security. For example, humans couldn't fly, so there was no reason to have an electrified net in the ceiling. But, Endari were ferociously strong, so they would need something a little stronger than standard iron bars.

Strictly speaking, Micaiah could probably bust out if he really wanted to. It would take all his strength and focus, but he gave himself a generous sixty percent chance that he could make it out alive.

"Then why don't you go?"

Micaiah startled and whirled around. In the corner of the cell, a man sat, carefully pouring wax into a mold and setting the wick. Although the light was decidedly better in this cell, the man still appeared to be draped in shadow, and the most Micaiah could make out was black hair that was just able to be tied back, and the leathery skin of a man who did hard outdoor labor.

"Who...?" Micaiah began. He shifted his weight. "You're the man from the black cell, aren't you?"

"I could be," the man said, still pouring wax.

"Are you my conscience?"

"I can be, if you like. Although, I believe last time you referred to me as a sarcastic prison chaplain. If that's the case, then I don't think you'll be letting me guide you anytime soon."

"Who are you?"

"No one."

"I think that answer is actually copyrighted now, so you're going to have to do better than that."

The man looked at him now, deep-set brown eyes, burning bright with fire and wisdom. "What ideas do men have that they were not inspired to have? Do you think that you create? Truly create?"

Micaiah rubbed his eyes. "Fine. What are you doing here?"

"I'm making a candle." As he spoke, he went back to his work.

"Well, obviously, but why?"

"The same reason you are preparing to go to your death."

"I don't understand."

The man held up his candle, now eerily complete. "A candle gives of itself in order to produce light and heat. It gains nothing for its sacrifice." He set the first candle down and went to work on a second.

"Are you saying I'm about to burn out?"

"I am simply saying that your time is coming. But it is not here."

"That's...good. Isn't it?"

"You know that fire cannot be bound by Time or Bands."

"Please, I'm not in the mood for riddles."

"Maybe, but it's not like you have anywhere to be right this moment. Do you know it?"

Micaiah sighed. "Yes, I know fire can't be contained by Time or Bands."

"Everyone's candle burns out eventually. The candle burns and burns, only growing shorter and losing more of itself the longer it burns. Even the greatest fires, no matter how great they burn, only result in cold ash." He held up the two candles side-by-side. Micaiah saw that the first one had somehow become lit. "But, did you also know that while a candle gains nothing for burning, it also loses nothing—" He touched the wicks together. "—by lighting another candle?"

The man sighed, apparently pleased with himself, even if Micaiah had gotten off on the exit ramp a few miles back. After a moment, the man packed up his things. "Your time is coming, Micaiah Durvin. Even your candle will defy the Time you have wrapped yourself in, and it will go out." He stood and slung an old leather bag over one shoulder. Then he turned toward Micaiah and nodded solemnly. "But until then, you will light many, many candles. And the world will be a brighter, warmer place for it."

Micaiah blinked. "Sorry, was that supposed to be a compliment? Because if it was, I'll just take that *á la carte*, without all the doom and gloom that you packaged it in."

The man laughed. "You tickle my candle as well with your

ability to be in an impossible situation and still find it within yourself to bring laughter and joy into people's lives."

"That I think was a compliment. Or a thank you. In which case, you're welcome."

"Ah, fear not, Micaiah. All will be well."

Micaiah opened his mouth to say more when a noise down the corridor took his attention. A guard approached his cell and finagled with the lock for a second before the door swung open.

"Out," the guard commanded.

Micaiah looked back, but the man was gone.

A chill creeping down his spine, Micaiah followed the guard back through the corridors, past all the empty cell blocks which, just months ago, had been full to bursting. How many had died before even reaching the executioner's block? How many were now employed by the new kings of Time and hard at work out there? Another thought: if they knew that Micaiah was the one who isolated them, did they blame him for being unable to return to their families? How would things go over when they confronted Rifun and Cassius? His plan had been shaky to start with, and it wasn't getting any better.

Instead of returning to the courtroom, they took a different turn and ultimately ended up in what appeared to be an office of some form. Or rather, as the Victorians might have called in, a study. Where all the menfolk conducted their business whilst smoking pipes and cigars in regal smoking jackets in front of a roaring hearth above which hung an enormous painting of themselves, which of course included both arms and legs.

While Micaiah was offered no cigar, smoking jacket, or even fuzzy slippers, he was also not chained to the desk and beaten like he was last time. He wondered if he should feel hopeful about the situation.

A minute later, a huge side door opened and Rifun walked into the room, looking sorely out of place in his modern clothing. And, really, Micaiah would have expected him, of all people, to want to get into the spirit of things, costume and all. It wasn't like the other ten thousand aliens in the universe were going to know what was in fashion.

"Do you like it?" Rifun asked. "The room?"

"It's an improvement," Micaiah answered diplomatically.

"I designed and built it myself. Much better than doom and gloom from a medieval dungeon torture chamber, wouldn't you agree?"

"Guess that depends on who you ask. Regardless if I'm thrown in a black cell or put up in a luxury resort, I'm still going to a Time Trial." *I hope.*

"Yes, this is true. And while you may think me a cruel, heartless bastard, I do try to make my guests comfortable. As such, I am offering you this one opportunity for last meal rights. Anything you want, from an olive with the pit still in, to a six-course gourmet meal from ten different worlds."

Micaiah raised a brow. "You mean there are still cooks left?"

"Time does many wonderful things, but we are still only human, are we not? You think we've been stuck in here for six months with no food?" Rifun grinned. "As I said, I am trying to be nice and offer you some sort of dignity."

"Rather macabre to be compared to dignity, isn't it? The last meal you expect I'm going to eat while in this universe. 'Dignity' does not even begin to describe it."

"Call it what you will, but either the next words out of your mouth are your order, or you can go back to the black cells with no food at all."

Defiance was tempting, but his stomach won out. Not a lot of time had passed since breakfast, but between opening a portal, fighting a Tracker, and being thrown back in prison, he could use a good meal, especially if it would be his last one for quite a while.

So he told Rifun his meal order.

"Ah, and you'd like it just how your mother used to make it, right?" Rifun said pleasantly, nodding at a guard who ducked out of the room.

"No one could make it like she did," Micaiah informed him. "Not even me, not even Micah."

"Oh, I'm sure you can and do, but it's the psychology of it."

"So you brought me here to discuss the psychology of homecooked, childhood meals?"

"Of course not." Rifun took a seat behind the desk and motioned for Micaiah to sit also. "I am here because you interest me."

"I believe you said something similar when we first met. Problem is, I know who you are now."

"Yes, but you have not yet answered one question to my satisfaction. Why did you come back? You demand a Time Trial, knowing that the success rate overall is only about thirty percent, and the rate for humans is only two percent. More than that, you are so new to your disability that you can barely fend off a Tracker. What in the galaxy is going through your mind right now? It's not as if I killed your father or some similar, overtired story arc."

"No, but you are a cruel and evil dictator, you and Cassius both, guilty of crimes against the universe, who think they can somehow impose their own order into a universal system of chaos. If anyone has a Messiah complex, it's you two."

Rifun grinned, then. At one time, it might have been a pleasant thing, a sight to behold, something to woo fair maidens left and right. Now it was a bone-chilling expression, and Micaiah feared his answer.

"Do you think Cassius would have really gone for all the redecorating I've done around here? Do you think he ever cared for art and beauty the way I do? Do you honestly think he ever had a plan for after he became the Zero Hour with such absolute authority? He was a bottom-feeder who got lucky. He was lucky only because I made his luck for him, even if he didn't realize it. He was a bloodthirsty bastard, true, but he was also an unstoppable weapon."

Micaiah blinked, stunned. Rifun went on. "I always thought he was crazy, going on about the Akari. Until he demonstrated its power. Then, I knew I had to have it. It was impossible to work around him, so I decided to work through him. His little stunt through the Time

Portal the first time threw things off, but with Julianna also out of the way, it created the perfect mixture of chaos needed to create the Dispersal. That was when I really tested him, sending him to slaughter as many adversaries as he could."

"And keeping him in as the Zero Hour gave you access to every aspect of Time," Micaiah said.

"Oh yes. When he told me about the journal, I knew that was our key to power. So we returned to the cave, but it was nowhere to be found."

"When you came back out, it was modern day. Since it was almost election time, you had to keep Cassius in the system, but Lily figured out that there was one Hand where it shouldn't have been. And you tried to kill her."

"She's dead now, though, so what does it really matter?"

"Cassius is dead, too, isn't he?"

Rifun simply leaned back in his seat. "As I said, did he ever strike you as a Victorian kind of person?"

Micaiah shifted, trying to hide his disquiet. "But here's one thing I don't understand. I thought you weren't normally given to monologues."

"When it reveals my evil schemes for the future. I have done nothing more than simply recite the past."

"So what is to prevent me from killing you here and now?"

"For the simple fact that you couldn't if you tried."

Micaiah wasn't entirely sure what happened then, except that Rifun was proven right. He thought he might have launched himself over the desk at Rifun. He might have made contact. But his element of surprise was quickly negated by the fact that he had no weapons and he had no credible experience trying to fight with his leg the way it was. Rifun overpowered him easily, unleashing a fury that seemed rather unbecoming for the gentleman he purported himself to be.

In the end, Micaiah was left bruised and bloody and slightly disoriented, lying on the floor with no motivation to move. Rifun stood and brushed his long hair out of his face with no more regard than if he'd just done some heavy manual labor. He took a step back and made a motion. A guard hauled Micaiah to his feet with one arm and set down his meal on the desk with the other.

"For the sake of your brother and your friends," Rifun said, "I hope you do a lot better than that at your trial." He looked at the guard. "Take him to the black cells."

The guard grunted and started dragging Micaiah away. The last thing he saw in that posh office was Rifun sitting down and starting on the homecooked meal that was supposed to have been his. He sighed, foolishly thinking that if he was going to do something stupid, he should have at least waited until after the meal. His stomach growled angrily at him as he was taken out of the normal cell blocks to the wing of the prison that had remained a dungeon.

He was thrown into inky blackness that measured, if he remembered correctly, about ten by ten feet, just big enough for him to lay down. As he did, reluctantly, he looked up and saw that he could see his hand in front of his face. He had only to look to his right side to see two candles, flickering in the darkness.

# Chapter Twenty
## Ransom

After so many years of shag carpet and paisley, Walter was still stunned every time he walked in the house to find hardwood floors and tasteful decor. Even once the major renovation had been completed, he was still working on replacing the furniture. So far, only the flower power loveseat had been replaced as it had been arguably the worst offender when it came to furniture. There were still a couple tables, the TV, and one extra recliner that was almost never used, so he debated whether it needed to be replaced or tossed completely.

He rummaged around in the fridge a little for some food which he took out to his recliner. It had been a short day at the precinct. He'd been finally cleared and moved back to Homicide, but now there was some internal, higher up, administrative...political shakeup. He didn't know, but it happened every few years as the city government decided it needed to step in and do a better job of running the police force. So, schedules were changed around and people were moved around, and it ended up that today, Friday, he'd been able to get off at one o'clock.

Walter bit into his tuna sandwich and tried to think of anything that needed to be done before Tommen got home. Or, rather, Tommen and Becky got home. The two were almost inseparable—at least on Fridays, some Tuesdays, every other Wednesday, and one Sunday a month, when Becky wasn't plugging away at her sewing machine—and if they weren't both here at his house, they were over at her house, or they were out with friends. Walter sometimes wondered when Tommen even worked anymore, but the twins told him that he did work. He was still manager and still doing a good job at it.

It was probably just as well, Walter figured. Tommen needed a girl in his life, and Becky certainly gave him a run for his money. She was quite the little spitfire, able to whip up an edgy remark to just about any comment or conversation, and she knew how to take control and get what she wanted. That wasn't to say she was a brat, but she was determined to make sure that no one overlooked her or thought less of her because of her shortcomings.

Actually, Walter really liked Becky. In a different time, when high school romance had run its course, he might have said she was good for Tommen. Really good. But where the disadvantages of Tommen being a Timekeeper ended, there started the disadvantage that he was still an atheist. Some parts of Becky seemed to have worn off on him — he was far less prickly than he used to be and he seemed to be a little more open-minded — but Walter knew that no good could come of such a long-term relationship. The phrase "unequally yoked" came to mind. They ignored it now, for the most part, but they were both too stubborn for it to end well when that wall was finally breached and came down on top of them.

Still, Walter reflected as he took his dish to the sink, it was good for Tommen to have a girl, have a real, normal life. A life where he wasn't constantly looking over his shoulder or worried about his upcoming Timekeeper review or the things he would learn. He'd pestered Walter quite a bit at first to keep training him despite the upheaval in the Wheel. Now, after several months of being Suppressed, and especially after the incident during the school play, he no longer asked about it. He barely mentioned it at all.

The bus came right on time, its brakes almost as bad as the ones on Walter's car as they announced to the entire neighborhood that the bus was stopping. First came Becky, then Tommen after her, talking and laughing and carrying on. What in the world did they talk about for hours at a time? Didn't they ever run out of things to say? Walter tried to think back to his courtship of Paige, but it provided a poor reference. Things had changed since then.

They entered the house and kicked off their shoes, still chatting away. Only when Becky noticed Walter did they stop and do a double-take.

"Oh, hi, Mr. Forbes," Becky greeted.

"You're home early," Tommen observed. "Something happen at the precinct?"

"Yes, but it came form the top down," Walter answered. "I expect things might be a little different and unpredictable for a while."

"Oh. Cool."

And they kept right on going, down to Tommen's room, making sure the door was wide open.

Becky's parents had been leery of letting the two of them go anywhere alone, especially to one another's houses. Truthfully, Walter was pretty skeptical about it, too. Tommen was a professed atheist with no moral reason not to try and sleep with Becky, and while Becky was certainly forceful and stubborn, she was still a young woman who wanted to be loved and accepted, perhaps her more than most. Love and hormones did strange things sometimes.

It had taken some doing to convince Becky's dad that Tommen was as chivalrous as his claim to fame, and even then, the two were never allowed to be alone for more than an hour at a time. More than enough time for a couple horny teenagers to get it on and get it over with, Walter knew, but he figured some leniency was better than none. A show of faith as it were.

Walter only went along with it because he could randomly check in on them without them knowing. Without his Time abilities, Tommen couldn't Band and disguise their activities either. Still, it was a fine line and a dangerous tightrope to walk.

"So, how was school?" Walter asked, going and standing in the door to Tommen's bedroom. He hadn't played his video games in probably a year, but since Becky had come along and proven herself to be quite adept at console games in spite of her short fingers, he'd taken up the challenge. Right now, they were playing some racing game.

"Good," Tommen said, not looking at him.

"Finals are in a couple weeks," Becky said, also not looking at him.

"Are you ready for them?"

"Yeah, sure." Tommen shrugged. "Nothing too difficult."

"How about your AP Physics?"

"What about it?"

"Are you ready for that one? I seem to recall that you wanted to get into harder classes, and they'll only get harder from here."

"I know. I'm not worried; I got this."

Seeing he would get nothing more from him, Walter left the room. He figured he couldn't be too annoyed with Tommen and his apparent lack of respect for a decent conversation. He would have rathered to see this than the solemn, solitary moping that had overtaken him after Christmas. This, now, was normal and healthy for a sixteen year old boy.

Walter slowly let out a breath. What would happen if Tommen decided he didn't want to go back to Timekeeping? What if he decided that he just wanted a normal life, to live and love and not have to worry about all the side effects and consequences?

Walter plopped down in his recliner. And what would he do once Tommen moved out? What would he do once Tommen reached Master rank? Ever since he'd come out of the salt cave, his only mission in life had been to find his brother's son and keep him safe. He couldn't do that forever, and Tommen wouldn't want him to do that forever. He had to grow up sometime, but where did that leave Walter?

Life happened, and it was wearing him out. Maybe, just maybe, he should retire. Get Stoppressed, wait for the effects to wear off and he was normal again, and just live out the rest of his days. Maybe he should find a woman his age and do it right this time. Court her, marry her, love her properly.

It was a nice sentiment, one that apparently put him to sleep as the next thing he knew, his phone was ringing.

"Walter Forbes," he answered tiredly, not even glancing at the number.

"Walt, it's Micah."

"Tommen's not supposed to work today, is he?"

"No, no, he's fine. Actually, I'm calling for you."

"What's up?"

"Well, it's Cai. It'll be easier to explain in person."

Walter sat up. "I'll be right over."

Something about Micah's tone put him on edge. Micah was not given to mysterious, slightly cryptic calls that turned out to be either some kind of prank or nothing at all. If he called to say that something was wrong, especially if it involved Micaiah, then something was probably wrong. The fact that he wasn't panicking said that the shit hadn't hit the fan—yet.

"I'm heading over to the bakery," Walter told Tommen and Becky.

"Oh, okay," Tommen said, at least giving him a cursory glance. He couldn't Band, but his expression was curious to know if anything was wrong.

"Can I trust you two to be good?"

"Yeah, of course."

"Okay. Remember, honor system."

"We'll be fine," Becky assured him.

Walter wasn't worried about them being fine, but unless he wanted to hold them down and make them pinkie-swear not to have sex while he was gone, it was the best he was going to get out of them.

"All right. I won't be gone long." *I hope.*

He went out to the garage and got in the car, pausing a second before starting the engine. He needed to get the brakes looked at, he knew. Actually, he'd kind of been hoping to sell the car to Tommen before being forced to do anything else to the car. It was a little on the mean side, maybe, but what better way to really teach Tommen about car care and maintenance? It wasn't just about the gas and insurance, after all.

It would also give him a little extra play money when he went out to look for a new vehicle. Given the cost of the renovation and how much more it had cost than his initial expectations, he was going to be eating his own words when it came to buying a new vehicle. Normally, he didn't do a whole lot with his Time salary, but now that it was gone, he was starting to feel the pinch.

Well, Micah was waiting for him, and Walter didn't want to get another call halfway there that something bad had happened.

He tried to run through his mind a list of possibilities for what could be wrong. First, there were the physical possibilities that something was wrong with Micaiah's knee, or something else resulting from his amputation. Second, there could have been another Tracker attack and Micaiah was wounded. But with either of those options, Walter couldn't figure out why Micah would choose to be so mysterious about it. Yes, either one might be better explained in person, but at least mentioning the gist of what was wrong would have been helpful.

Of course, there was another possibility. Maybe Rifun or Cassius had returned and was holding one or both of them hostage and had forced Micah to make the call in order to lure him in.

Walter called Micah back.

"Are you coming?" Micah wondered.

"Am I on speakerphone?" Walter asked suspiciously.

"No."

"Where are you?"

"At the bakery."

"Are you alone?"

"Well, I mean there are customers in the dining room, and Jenna's working today, but...I'm confused. Why are you asking me these questions?"

"Just making sure of something. I'll be there in five."

He did sound confused, but also genuine. Micah wasn't exactly a stellar performer under duress. Something was wrong, but Rifun and Cassius weren't part of it. Or at the very least, they weren't present.

Traffic during the winter was easier to Band because there was less of it, and he could generally maneuver his way through with minimal difficulty. Traffic during the summer was futile to Band for the simple reason that it was so congested that there was nowhere to go. Sometimes, Walter was able to get lucky with a Slow Band, Banding the rest of traffic so it appeared that it was going faster, but there were still throngs of people to deal with.

In the end, it took a little longer than the five minutes that Walter had promised to reach the bakery. Still, upon arrival, he searched for anything that was amiss. Band wakes, remnants of a Tracker attack, a general disruption of daily life. He saw none of it. People still moved freely up and down the sidewalks, in and out of stores. There were no signs of distress that Walter could discern, and everything appeared to be completely normal.

Oddly enough, it put Walter on full alert. There was little worse than everything seeming normal, because that was when the worst problems arose. Trying to keep a neutral expression while remaining vigilant, he got out of the car and headed inside the bakery.

They were at the tail end of a decent mid-afternoon rush, catching those who had just gotten off work, those who had just picked up their kids from school, or just got a late lunch. Jenna worked the counter, and Walter could only assume that Micah was in the kitchen and Micaiah was in the office.

"Oh, hey, Walter," Jenna greeted. "Micah was looking for you, said to let him know when you came by."

"Well, here I am," he told her.

She retreated into the kitchen. A minute later, Micah appeared, wiping his hands on his apron. He looked stressed, Walter thought, even more than usual.

"Oh, good, you're here," Micah said.

"Got a little hung up in traffic."

"Yeah, why don't you come on back, and we'll talk?"

Micah was more than stressed, he was a nervous wreck. He was panicking internally and trying not to show it where his customers would see him. Worried, Walter followed him into the office where he all but ripped off his apron and collapsed into the chair. It didn't look like anyone had been in the office at all that day. The computer wasn't on, and all the pens, calculators, and other assorted office supplies were still tucked away in some semblance of trying to stay organized.

"Micah, what's going on?" Walter asked, now very concerned.

"Micaiah's gone," Micah blurted.

Walter blinked and shook his head. "Gone? What do you mean 'gone'?"

Micah took a breath and tried to collect his thoughts. "So, you've seen Cai recently, you know he's got his leg and, for the most part, his livelihood, right?"

"That's what it looked like. He's...he's not threatening suicide, is he?"

"Well, no, but his other idea is almost as bad." Micah sat up. "He's pissed, okay, about what happened."

"Well, we all knew that."

"And at some point in the last couple months, he's gotten vengeance on his mind." Walter could almost predict where this was going, and he didn't like it. Still, he remained silent as Micah went on. "So, in a nutshell, he's gone to kill Cassius and Rifun."

Walter leaned back in his seat. "Shit."

"It gets better. He's called for a Time Trial."

"Oh my God. Are you serious?"

"Believe me, I wish I wasn't. He's named me as the Stake."

Walter was incredulous. "And you accepted?"

Micah squirmed. "Well...yes. Actually, he asked me beforehand if I would."

Now suspicious, Walter folded his arms. "I get the feeling

you're not as innocent in this is as you think you are. Why don't you tell me the whole story?"

That caught Micah off-guard, more than Walter thought it would. There was a bigger story behind all of this, he was sure. His curiosity was piqued even more as, even though Micah started speaking and opening up, he still knew that he was lying about something.

"Okay, so a while back, Micaiah approached me with his idea for vengeance. He was just going to go back to the Wheel, kill the fuckers, and get out. Great, but not going to work. And I told him so. I thought that maybe, after a time, he'd come to his senses and drop it.

"Last night..." He squirmed some more. "Cai went out. He texted me later, said he wanted to meet somewhere. Well, I'm just going to skip over the boring details of what actually happened. There was a hooker involved, let's leave it at that." Walter couldn't help but smile. "Anyway, so after that's all over with, he tells me he's come up with a new plan."

"The Time Trial," Walter stated.

Micah nodded. "Yes. He says that they're so bloody that Cassius and Rifun wouldn't be able to refuse, and if the stakes were interesting enough, then he might have a chance."

"He's just starting to get around on his prosthetic. How does he expect to go from that to a Time Trial?"

"Hey, I said the same thing, but you know how he is."

Walter sighed and rubbed his eyes. "Okay. So what happened?"

"I told him he was crazy. He ignored me. I asked him what his 'irresistable' bargain was going to be. He said that if he won, Earth would be left alone. If he lost, we'd die. Pretty straightforward."

"Am I correct to assume that he has a real plan in mind?"

"Different? Yes. Better? Well, that's up for debate. He seems to think that I'll be able to hide a gun on me when I go in as the Stake, so that I can shoot the bastards on sight before they have a chance to even get started."

There were no words or gestures that could accurately depict how Walter felt at that moment. Micaiah was an idiot. There, that was one way to say it. He was going to risk, not only his life, but his brother's life, on some scheme of vengeance. Not to mention...

"Who did he call as Testimony?"

"Well...you, Tommen, and a friend named Doug."

"Fuck." And Walter was not given to such strong language. "Motherf—what business does he have volunteering my son like that?!"

Suddenly, before his very eyes, Micah disappeared. It was like a layer of dust was suddenly washed off of him and Tommen sat before him.

"The f—what?" Walter just about went backwards in his chair.

"Because it won't be Tommen going," Tommen-not-Tommen said, even in Tommen's voice. "Micaiah is more than you think he is, with abilities you can't even comprehend. Your son won't be going to the Wheel, but it will seem like he is."

Then Tommen disappeared, and Walter was left staring at himself. "Same goes for you, Walt. You won't have to do a thing, and you'll still be able to help save the universe. Now how does that sound?"

"I think it sounds all kinds of fucked up."

"It is. Which is why it'll work."

Kayla grinned as she shook off her Disguise of Walter, standing there in the door. Now it was Micah's turn to look shocked, dropping his Walter disguise there in his office chair and standing suddenly, only to fall right back in the chair.

"Wait, what?" he sputtered.

"I think that went well, don't you?" Kayla wondered. "I've always thought it was a lot like group therapy, but without the pressure of actually saying anything."

"Wait, so...what? You were Walter? But I called Walter. Or did I call you?"

"You called him, and he's on his way."

"What the hell am I going to tell him, then? I just..."

Kayla stood and stretched. "Don't worry about him." She cloaked herself in another Disguise. "I'll take care of it."

She headed out to the counter, dropping all of her Bands. Outside, Walter was just getting out of his car. Inwardly, she giggled. Disguise was always so much fun when used as a party trick. But there was the other side of it, too, when it could be used lethally. The only thing that could give away a Disguise were the mannerisms. She could look like anyone and speak in their voice, but she did not automatically assimilate a personality.

"Everything okay?" Jenna asked.

"Yeah," Kayla told her, hoping she could find the right mixture of fear and relief. "Everything's good. I'll man the front for a few minutes."

"Hey, suit yourself."

Jenna disappeared into the kitchen just as Walter walked into the bakery, looking somewhat concerned.

"Hey, Walt," Kayla-as-Micah greeted. "Here for a pastry?"

"You called?" Walter wondered.

"No, not recently. Why?"

Walter shook his head and put up a Band. "No, you just called me and said something was wrong with Micaiah."

"I did?" Kayla-as-Micah checked her phone. "My phone doesn't say it made a call. Here, let me see yours."

Walter handed over his phone. Kayla-as-Micah perused it casually and frowned. "Well, look at that. Apparently I did call you."

"But you say you didn't call me."

"You think it could be Rifun again?" Kayla-as-Micah wondered, handing him back his phone. "I mean, he did hack Tommen's phone, didn't he? Maybe he did the same to yours."

"That's what worries me. But why pull this kind of prank?"

"Maybe it's not Rifun. Maybe it's one of his cronies, trying to mess with you, get inside your head."

"See, that I might believe, except...it really did sound like your voice."

"There's a lot of editing software out there, Walt. If Rifun can remotely hack a phone to install an app to record phone calls, chances are, he has the expertise needed to take audio clips of our voices and string them together to sound however he wants them to. Or he might speak normally and use software to modify his own voice. I don't know, but the technology is out there."

Walter grunted. "I suppose. I don't doubt you, but it just seems strange to waste that kind of thing on a prank."

"Are you sure it's a prank? Where's Tommen?"

Honestly, Kayla hated playing it up this much, especially when she saw Walter's expression go from suspicious and trying to work out a puzzle, to absolute horror that he'd left his son alone, potentially unprotected. Walter dropped his Band and strode out of the store as calmly as possible to make a phone call. Kayla breathed a sigh of relief when she saw him do the same. A minute later, he walked back in.

"Everything okay?" Kayla-as-Micah asked worriedly.

Walter nodded wearily. "Yeah, he's fine. And, just for my own sanity, everything is all right with Micaiah, right?"

"Sure, as far as I know. I mean, he stepped out to get lunch and run a few errands. If you want, I can call him back here."

"No, no, that's okay. He can look after himself and call if he needs help."

Kayla-as-Micah grinned. "I think I know him a little better than that. After all, he's still trying to reclaim some of his pride. He got his bike out of storage the other day."

"Yeah, I've seen it."

"He's fine. I'm fine. Tommen's fine. You're fine. Everyone's fine. But even so, why don't you head home just in case? I'll keep an eye out here for anything amiss."

Walter hesitated. "I just could have sworn..." He shook his head. "Maybe it's time to retire. I'm getting too old for this shit."

"Aren't we all?"

After a minute, he nodded, thanked Kayla-as-Micah and left the bakery without buying anything. Kayla watched him cross the parking lot and get in his car, but he didn't take off right away. He waited a few seconds, still unsure. Finally he shook his head again, started the car, and left the parking lot.

Kayla-as-Micah ended up having to serve several more customers after he left, Banding several times to make sure she was grabbing the correct product and ringing it up correctly. It was strange, she thought, that for as well as she knew Micaiah, it was a whole different ballgame trying to impersonate Micah. True, they were twins and had similar general mannerisms, but the little nuances that made up their individual personalities, those were harder to master. It was even more difficult, she thought, in twins than in two strangers.

Still, she'd done well enough to fool Walter. That attested to either her superior acting abilities, or his state of mind. The jury was still out on how well Walter was coping with his time in prison, but after six months, Kayla figured he couldn't be doing too bad.

Once the last customer had been served, Kayla-as-Micah went back into the office, closing the door and shedding the Disguise. After another quick stretch, trying to shake off the "aftertaste" of a Disguise, she sat down in a chair, facing Micah.

"How do I know it's really you in front of me?" Micah wondered suspiciously.

"You don't, in all reality," she told him. "There is nothing you can physically look for that would give me away, were I currently Disguised. But, like Time, everything is shed when you sleep or go unconscious, and it's really hard to hold a Disguise under physical, mental, or emotional stress. And we're talking torture-level stress, not this, what you're experiencing."

"You think that the possibility of losing my brother isn't torture?"

"You think the possibility of losing my husband isn't torture?" Kayla raised a brow and put one leg over the other.

Micah sighed and rubbed his temples. "Okay. Fine. We're both stressed. What do we do about it? You're sure this plan is going to work?"

"No, I'm not. But I am as much as I can be."

"That makes no fucking sense." Micah leaned back in his seat. "This is fucking insane. I can't believe I agreed to this."

"But you did agree to it," Kayla reminded him. "And Micaiah is counting on you. He's counting on both of us. All of us."

"I know. I know, I know, I know. Okay. When is all this supposed to go down? You stalled Walter today, but he'll be back tomorrow morning, sure as shit, looking for his pastry. Eventually, he'll notice that Micaiah's missing."

"I can't imagine it will be too long before we get the summons. I've already arranged to intercept the summons for Walter and Tommen, assuming they'll be delivered through the normal route. Unfortunately, I don't know that they will be. We just have to be vigilant."

"Okay, so, assuming that everything does go normally, what happens? I've heard about Time Trials, I've been forced to watch one, but I've never actually had to take part. Thank God."

"It's actually as simple as jury duty. You get your summons that tell you where to be and when, and you better make sure you're there. And failing to appear for a Time Trial warrants a little harsher punishment than a fine and a slap on the wrist."

Micah folded his arms. "How do you know so much about Time Trials? I mean, I should probably know a little more than I do, but you're talking like you've been there, done that."

Kayla sighed. "Because I have." At Micah's expression, she continued. "A long time ago, before we were married, Cai and Rifun knew each other. When Cai first became a Timekeeper, Rifun approached him, much the same way he's approaching Tommen now. He tried to befriend, tried to scare, tried to threaten him into becoming his Akari Apprentice."

"But if I have the Akari, too," Micah interrupted, "why didn't he approach me also?"

"Because Micaiah convinced Rifun that you didn't have it in order to protect you. Rifun's crazier than a whole bag of cat ladies; Micaiah could see where it would lead, and he didn't want you to be part of it. Between that and his refusal to join Rifun—and, in retrospect, probably Cassius, too—Rifun got angry. Using Cassius' power as the Zero Hour, Rifun had Micaiah arrested. He might have executed him outright, but he wanted to give him one last chance to join him."

"So he sentenced Cai to a Time Trial."

"Exactly. He named me as his Stake. I told him—afterwards, of course—that he owed me big for putting my life on the line like that. And that was when he proposed."

"And you said yes?" Micah raised a brow and smirked. He looked just like his brother, Kayla thought. Hm. Imagine that.

"I slapped him first. Told him he could have just asked instead of going to such lengths to get me to say yes. But, yes, I said yes. Obviously."

"Well, that's my brother. Always a real Casanova."

"Shit. No kidding."

"So, you must have some insights into the whole Time Trial thing, right? How it works, what happens, all of that."

Kayla stood. "All you need to know is that it's a trap. The Bat and the Day are not natural. We don't know what they are, only that they seem to operate on their own Time frequency and are not affected by Time, though they may pretend to be. They're limited by the Akari, but even then, it's anyone's guess. When going up against them, it'll be a full physical brawl, count on that."

"That's not helpful."

She shrugged and headed for the door, but Micah called after her. "Hey, wait." She stopped and turned. "What if Rifun does intend to wait and make us sweat a little? Like I said, Walt and especially Tommen will notice that Cai's missing. What am I going to tell them?"

She hesitated. Then, "We'll deal with that when the time

comes. If it comes sooner than you can come up with a plausible story, well, the truth always works, too."

With that, she headed out, helping herself to a cinnamon roll and seeing herself out. When she got to her car, she dug out her phone and punched in a number.

"Hello?"

"Doug, it's Kayla," she said around a bite of cinnamon roll.

"You got the summons?"

"Not yet."

"Talked to Micah?"

"Just did. He's good on the Disguises, or as good as he's going to be given the circumstances. We just have to hope he won't lose it in the middle of the Trial. How are we doing elsewhere?"

"Hype can only go so far. Hopefully we get those summons before our loyal men-at-arms lose their enthusiasm."

"I think you underestimate them, Doug. It's only been six months, but that's a long time to just sit idly by. Far too long under Cassius' rule."

"I'll agree to that. Let me know when you get the summons."

"Will do. Thanks, Doug."

She hung up and drummed her fingers on the center console of the car. She still didn't like Doug, but he knew how to get things done, and that was what they needed right now. Sighing, Kayla finished off her cinnamon roll in silence, watching people come and go from the bakery.

She was just about to start the car and leave when she felt the pull of a temporal disturbance coming from the backseat. Slowly, she turned and only just stopped herself from screaming. A Tracker sat in the seat, some kind of rod in its mouth. It leaned forward, dropped the rod in the passenger seat, and was gone, only a slight temporal pull shaking the car. Then all the was normal.

Closing her eyes and trying to collect her frayed nerves, Kayla reached for the rod. It came apart easily and she arranged the projected screen so she could read it.

Well, these were the summons all right. Micaiah Durvin the Accused, Micah Durvin the Stake, Walter Forbes, Tommen Forbes, and Doug Templeton the Testimonies. She looked at the date. Saturday night.

# Chapter Twenty-One
## Summons

To say Tommen didn't want to fuck Becky would have been a lie, if he wanted to be honest, even as they sat there in his room playing video games. But he knew better than to try and go that route when: a) his dad still had Banding abilities and he didn't, and b) her dad would murder him regardless of any Banding abilities he had. So, yes, he did want to fuck her. If he wanted to be even more honest, a dozen different plans to get her to consent to it had already crossed his mind in just the last half hour. Unfortunately, none of them seemed plausible at this time. Becky attributed it to his gentlemanly, chivalrous nature; he attributed it to being powerless and having a healthy fear of death.

He heard his dad walk in the house a short time after saying he was going out. Must not have been too important, then. Maybe just a little cabin fever.

"Are you two still being good in here?" Walter asked, appearing in the doorway.

"What are you talking about?" Tommen said. "She's kicking my butt hard."

"Everything all right, then?"

"Sure, why wouldn't it be?" Becky wondered, glancing at him.

"Just making sure."

Tommen almost expected to get sucked into a Band so they could speak privately, but it never happened. His dad just stood there for a second, looking around the room, then left.

"He's weird sometimes," Tommen said.

"You're weird sometimes," Becky countered.

Well, there was that. Tommen was just glad it was only weirdness that plagued his dad. Tommen was no expert, but he was pretty sure his dad was doing all right after his ordeal, given what he could have been like.

But, in his distraction, the game got away from him, and Becky claimed another victory. Once she got done gloating, she set down the controller and lay back on the bed. Fuck, he wanted her. And there would be no Banding this time if he got a boner.

"I don't even play video games," she said, stretching and sitting back up. "Maybe it's all my sewing."

"Or you're lying and you secretly stay up late figuring out ways to beat me," Tommen told her.

"Well, there is that." She looked at the clock. "But I think it's about time I headed home."

Make no mistake, Tommen had great respect for Becky's parents and the way they cared about her and what happened to her; there were plenty of kids at school who could do whatever they wanted and their parents wouldn't care. It sounded great until you got the full story and realized that some of those parents were so indifferent as to not care whether their kid lived or died. So it was nice to see a good, solid family unit where parents cared for child. That did not make it any more convenient for Tommen, though, who wanted to spend more time with Becky. And he still wanted to fuck her. Where did one desire end and the other begin?

Still, they wrapped up their tournament—as if there was any way Tommen could win at this point—and Becky grabbed her things. They were supposed to have been studying together for Physics finals, but, clearly, nothing of the sort had gotten done.

"Heading home?" Walter asked as they crossed the living room, making for the kitchen to grab their shoes. Despite her usually strict rules on wearing her orthopedic shoes, Becky sometimes allowed herself a reprieve whenever she visited Tommen.

"Yeah," Tommen answered. "Don't worry, we're walking."

"Be safe out there."

"Yes, Dad."

He shut the door behind them, and they started out, Tommen carrying Becky's backpack. For him, it was nothing, but he could imagine it was quite a weight on her back.

"Sometimes I think your dad thinks we're still in middle school," Becky commented as they reached the sidewalk and turned left toward her house.

"I think he's just coming to terms with the fact that I'm growing up," Tommen said evasively.

Sure, that was one aspect of it, he was certain, but there was so much more to it. They'd both almost died last Christmas. They'd both almost died again just five, six months ago. They had stories and memories and knowledge and power that no one else could know about, and that was on a good day. But these weren't good days, and if they made any mention of such things, they could still die. Worse, they could die and no one would know. Chances were, they wouldn't even be able to defend themselves.

But still, it wasn't as if they were little kids where Walter had to remind them to look both ways before crossing the street. The whole being good and not having sex while he was out, well, there might be some substance behind that worry, but he didn't need to get weird about it. After all, Time was a gift, one which Tommen did not have access to presently, but that didn't mean that thousands of normal teenagers weren't fucking without their parents' knowledge.

To that end, however, Time was a gift, one that Tommen did not have access to presently, which meant he still couldn't hide himself if he let his thoughts run too wild. Better to rein them in and just be grateful that he was still dating Becky after, what was it, three, four months? His previous record was three weeks. The worst part was that he and Tanya had actually agreed that on their one month anniversary, they were going to lose their virginity together. Then she ended up going off to some church retreat or something and found herself new life and new purpose and whatever, and she broke the whole thing off.

He and Becky hadn't even had that conversation yet, and he wasn't sure if or how he wanted to approach it. He and Tanya had been dumb eighth graders still experimenting with the new words and concepts they learned in health class, and, up until her religious revelation, neither of them had any real moral restrictions. Becky, however, was a tougher nut to crack. He couldn't decide if her moral righteousness and purity was just a show since she still had to live with her parents, or if she actually held to those convictions. Asking her to sleep with him could either put him on her dad's hit list, in which case he would die within the month—by a liberal estimation—or it could send their relationship to a new level.

He figured he was going to have to keep going with her the way they were and just think on it some more.

As always, they said their goodbyes on the sidewalk before Dr. Polski met them at the door.

"How was studying?" he asked civilly.

"Good," Becky lied as she took her backpack from Tommen. "I kicked his butt." She ducked under her father's arm and went inside.

"Don't underestimate her," Dr. Polski told Tommen, his tone light but stare dead serious. *Translation: Don't underestimate* me. "She's a smart girl."

"I guess I have my work cut out for me," Tommen replied.

"And you're still being good?"

"Yes, sir. On my honor."

"You're only sixteen. You don't have a lot of honor, and that which you do have isn't worth much. Prove yourself and build your honor by being honorable."

"Yes, sir."

And the doctor shut the door in his face.

Walking with Becky meant shorter, slower steps, that way she wasn't running to keep up with his long stride. Walking home, therefore, only took about half the time. By the time he stepped in the door, his dad was just dishing out a plate of leftover chicken and potatoes for himself.

"Another successful journey to the lion's den, hm?" he said, amused.

Tommen shrugged. "I guess."

"So what are you going to do this summer when you won't have any studying to do?"

"It'll give me plenty of time to figure out how to beat her on those games. She's beating me at my own game, literally." Tommen got himself a plate and scooped out some leftovers for himself, waiting as his dad put his plate in the microwave.

"And what are you going to do the rest of the time? You're not going to spend the summer just playing video games. I know you're going to be working, but you need more than just work and video games."

"I know." He shrugged again. "I don't know, I'll think of something. My original plans kind of got overthrown in a bloody massacre."

His dad nodded, getting a distant look. "I know. And I'm sorry for that."

"Why? Wasn't like you could stop it."

But Walter was already gone. He was generally okay, but sometimes, the right thing said or done, and he was gone. He simply got his plate from the microwave when it was finished, got a fork, and went out to his recliner to eat in sullen, distant silence. Thankfully, his episodes didn't last long. And by long, that is, days at a time. At least by the next morning when he had to take Tommen to work—or supervise his driving anyway—he was alert enough to hold a normal, if awkward, conversation.

"You and Becky aren't sleeping together, are you?"

Tommen gave him a look. "What? No, Dad...why are you—?"

"Because you're a sixteen year old boy," Walter cut in. "Believe me, I know how you think. Answer the question."

Tommen sighed. "No, we're not. Okay, you know how I think, but do you know how she thinks? She's got like this armor of poisonous nails around her it seems like."

"That's good. But love is blind, and when you're young and dumb, you're apt to lower your defenses at all the wrong times for all the wrong people."

"You're saying I'm not right for her?"

"I'm saying you're too young to even know what that means. I just don't want to see you get hurt. Either of you."

"I get it. I mean, thanks, I think, but I get it. Pregnancy, STDs, the whole works. Believe me, we hear about it all the time at school." Tommen rolled his eyes.

"There's hearing, and then there's listening. Are you listening?"

"Yes!" Tommen huffed. "Yes, I get it. I do. We're not sleeping together. We don't even talk about it. Okay? Is that good enough?"

His dad was silent for a moment, and Tommen could feel the scrutiny. Finally, "Honor system, Tommen. I don't want to be your warden."

"Thank you." Tommen sighed. "What was up yesterday with you going out? It sounded sinister enough when you left, but then you were acting weird when you came back, too."

"You remember how Rifun or one of his minions hacked your phone?"

"Yeah."

"I don't know when or how, but they may have done the same to mine. I got a call yesterday which I could have sworn was from Micah, saying that something was wrong with Micaiah. But when I got to the bakery, he didn't have a clue what I was talking about. So I rushed home in case it was a ploy to get me out of the house and away from you."

"Oh." Tommen was suddenly sober. Yeah, that could have been a really bad thing, especially since Rifun had already demonstrated careless disregard for innocent bystanders. He'd already exposed Eric and Varad to Time, thus completely destroying their friendship. Why wouldn't he also use Becky against him, too, seeing how he had no Time abilities whatsoever to defend himself with? "So, did you find anything? Like, on your phone or his phone or something?"

"Nothing," his dad answered, sounding frustrated and tired. "As far as either of us could tell, both phones looked clean. Not that it means much, considering what technology can do these days."

Tommen pulled into the parking lot and was almost clipped from behind by a little silver car. Once the heart attack wore off, he found a parking spot and pulled in.

"That wouldn't have been your fault," Walter told him. "I would have given him the ticket. Anyway, have a good day at work. What time are you off?"

"Three, four-ish. Depends on how much they want to work me. I'll see you later."

When he got in the store, however, he noticed that something was off. There seemed to be, simultaneously, more and less chaos. Then he realized that the noise being made was only being made by one person. Peeking in the kitchen, he saw only Micah banging around. The office, with both blinds up, was dark.

"Hey, everything okay?" Tommen wondered as he punched in.

"Huh?" Micah looked up from his reckless rummaging in a cupboard. "Oh, yeah." Everything was not okay. "Hey, why don't you get started on the cinnamon rolls this morning?"

"Sure." Tommen tiptoed more than walked over to the appropriate area for the ingredients. "Where's Cai?"

"Oh, he, uh, he has a doctor's appointment this morning. I told him to go ahead and grab a few more hours of sleep."

"Is he okay? Like, his leg, I mean?"

"Well, he got his running leg, and I guess he had some question or problem that he wanted to go in to get figured out. But yeah, I mean, he's fine."

Something was not fine. Tommen wasn't sure if it was Micah, Micaiah, or something else entirely, but something was not fine, and Micah was having a hell of a time trying to keep composure and lie about it convincingly. At the same time, he was probably aware of his poor lying skills. So if he was still trying to lie despite knowing that it wasn't working, it was probably something he wanted to keep to himself, or keep between him and Micaiah. In the end, Tommen decided to let him have his lie for now and bring it up later if appropriate.

It didn't make morning production any easier, though, as they still had to crank out a ton of product. The good news was that Saturday mornings didn't get busy until later in the morning, so they had more time to be ready. Micah stayed in back, doing his frantic baking, made even worse by whatever was going on that he adamantly refused to talk about.

So Tommen stayed up front, serving customers and keeping the dining room clean. He'd overheard a few conversations between the twins about doing some redecorating, sprucing the place up a bit to make it seem a little more lively. A fresh coat of paint, some new decorations, small stuff to start. Then they might look at new tables, chairs, refinishing the floor. Micah wanted to redecorate, but Micaiah had pointed out that if they were going to do all that, why not just move to a bigger building? Maybe they should get out of the strip mall and into their own stand-alone building. Micah countered by proposing, not moving, but simply expanding. Keep this store, run by one of them, and open a second store across town, run by the other.

On the one hand, Tommen knew that opening a second store would be good for business. They were well-known and well-liked, so they wouldn't have trouble attracting customers. Plus, it would give the twins time away from each other. At the same time, the twins liked working together too much. It was their thing, their weird, brotherly bond of sorts. Because already being twins just wasn't good enough, apparently.

"Good morning, what can I get for you?" Tommen asked as a young woman walked up to the counter, brown hair pulled back enough that he could see the tan line on her forehead.

"Is it still morning?" she sighed, checking her watch. "I have so much to do today, you have no appreciation for it."

He immediately shut down internally. Just another adult, thinking teenagers are incapable of anything besides reciting useless information they learned in school, and sex. Ironically, even she couldn't have been much older than twenty-five, if that. Because graduation really changes people that much. *Yeah, you've moved on to a higher plane of existence in our rote reality. Let me show you something, babe. I'll show you more reality than you could possibly imagine.* He sighed. If only.

"Well, I think I'll have a cinnamon role and a small coffee, just cream."

Tommen got the cinnamon roll first, then went for the coffee. As he turned around, he caught her staring at him. Most customers did, of course, watching like hawks to make sure he got everything just right. But this stare, this was a stare more intent on him than the coffee in his hand. She was studying him, and he didn't like it. Still, he did not pause in his work and kept his composure as he rang up the order and took her cash. Then she headed to a booth and proceeded to get on her phone.

Maybe he'd imagined the whole thing. He'd been so relaxed lately that his paranoia was apparently feeling lonely. His dad's mysterious phone incident probably tipped it off, and now Tommen was seeing stalking and staring in the most ordinary things. She was just an adult who had been silently belittling him in her mind, staring at him to make sure he got her coffee just right, with only cream and no sugar.

He worked through the lunch rush, telling himself that all was well, except the woman just did not leave. By the time the lunch rush was over, she'd long since finished her cinnamon roll, and her coffee had to be either gone or cold. And yet, when he went to grab another coffee for another customer, he found the pot almost empty. The pot had been full when he'd served her, and there hadn't been enough coffee orders to drain the pot. When the line was finally gone, Tommen went back to the kitchen.

"Hey, Micah," he began casually, "if a person is Suppressed, he can still see visible Bands and stuff, can't he?"

Micah looked up, alarmed. "Yes, why?"

"Just wanted to make sure."

"Something wrong?"

*Only with you.* "I don't know. Got a customer out here who's had more coffee than she paid for. But I can't prove it."

Oddly enough, he seemed to relax. "Oh, okay. If that's all. Have you had lunch yet?"

"No. I was going to ask if I could go around the corner to the little Chinese place. I mean, if you can handle it alone. Honestly, you're not looking too good."

Micah waved him off. "No, no, I'm fine. I can handle it. Go ahead and go to lunch; just don't take forever."

Tommen nodded, removed his apron, punched out, and headed out the back door. He didn't normally like doing "off-campus" lunches, as it were. If he packed a lunch and stayed in, he got a paid lunch because then he could be called back into work to help. If he was going to be out and about and unavailable, he had to punch out. So he not only had to pay for his own lunch, but he also lost that extra half-hour of pay. But sometimes, he just wanted something different.

That's what he told himself, but if he was going to be honest, he more kind of wanted to get out of Micah's way. Honestly, the man was kind of freaking him out a little. If he just got out, got some fresh air, got away from the impending meltdown that was the younger Durvin twin, his sanity would be all the better for it.

"Hello, what can I get for you?" the cashier asked as he stepped up to the counter.

"I'll take some sesame chicken and teriyaki noodles with an egg roll," Tommen decided. "To go, with chopsticks."

His order was rung up and he was soon returning to the bakery, walking slowly so he could eat without spilling sauce all down his front. It wasn't bad, really, but he mostly got it just to break up his normal food routine, which usually alternated between good, homestyle 1800's Appalachian cooking, and quick junk like pizza, peanut butter toast, and TV dinners. One of these days, he figured he was going to have to break down and actually buy a hunting license. He'd been relying too much on his Time abilities to both catch game and evade the DNR. Maybe it was time he went back out and did things the right way.

His thoughts were cut short and his chicken almost ended up on the ground when he rounded the corner back into the alleyway, heading for the back door of the bakery.

A Tracker sat there, right in front of the door. This one seemed to resemble some sort of giant bulldog, but, you know, covered in slime, millions of tiny appendages, and had tentacles for ears, with a mouth that slobbered slime.

Tommen's breath caught in his throat as he weighed his options. With the distance, he might be able to run and get back to the front door, but that was a pretty hefty gamble. He might buy himself a second or two if he threw his food at it, either blind it or maybe give it something more tasty to chew on. As far as weapons, he was limited to a single pocket knife and two cheap chopsticks that were known to break just from trying to catch a wily piece of chicken.

In the time it took him to go through all of this, he also realized that it hadn't attacked him yet. Furthermore, there appeared to be something in its mouth, like a long rod or something. Was this thing about to come at him like a kung fu master?

It did not. Rather, it simply set the rod on the ground—still covered in slime—stood, and then it was gone. Tommen couldn't even say that there had been a portal or anything that it went through; it was simply...gone. After a moment of deliberation and standing on the sidewalk staring down an alley like a moron, he nervously fished for some noodles and cautiously took a step inside the alley. Then another, and another, always keeping an eye out for Rifun or Cassius or any of their minions.

He got to the bakery door and looked down at the rod. If the

Tracker had wanted, it could have attacked him and done whatever it wanted. The fact that it didn't did not mean that the rod might not be poisoned or lethal in some way, but he found it highly unlikely. As he reached for it, he paused. Hadn't he said it himself, though? The best way to beat a tough opponent was to establish a pattern and then break it? He would definitely run from a Tracker. Micah was armed, and he would definitely shoot a Tracker. But this rod seemed harmless enough. What if it wasn't?

He should tell Micah, see if he had any insight. At the same time, why was he so afraid of a rod? It wasn't more than eighteen inches long, looked like any ordinary steel pipe, just solid instead of hollow. Looking closer, he saw that there were two circular grooves at either end, but that was the only decoration on the entire thing that he could see.

Tommen positioned himself with his back to the door. Maybe he would have time to kick the door and alert Micah if something went wrong. At the same time, his absence would eventually alert him anyway. But still, he had to make up his mind. Was he afraid of the rod or not?

He touched the rod, and it sprang to life. It split in half long ways and separated. As Tommen watched, it became kind of like a tablet, but like out of some futuristic sci-fi movie, where everything was white and translucent and stuff. Then symbols began appearing which arranged themselves into normal Latin letters, then words, then sentences. Carefully, he picked up the rod and read the words.

"The traitor Micaiah Durvin, Lieutenant Timekeeper, Quadrant One, Parsec Eleven, Sector Five, System Four, Planet Thirty-Eight, Region Four, District Four, has been arrested and charged with treason against the Lord Zero Hour, the Hands of Time, and the Laws of Time, a crime punishable by death.

"The Accused has requested a Time Trial to determine his guilt or innocence. He requests as his Stake, Micah Durvin, Lieutenant Timekeeper, Quadrant One, Parsec Eleven, Sector Five, System Four, Planet Thirty-Eight, Region Four, District Four. For his Testimonies, he requests Walter Forbes, Captain Timekeeper...Tommen Forbes, Apprentice Timekeeper...and Doug Templeton, Gatekeeper Timekeeper and Runner...Region Four, District Two. Failure to comply will result in similar charges and punishment up to and including clock breaking.

"The Time Trial has been set at the following time, adjusted for local time: Saturday, May 31, 2014, at 2111 hours.

"Signed, the Grandfathers and the Hands of Time."

Tommen read through the notice three or four times, trying to wrap his head around it. Well, it certainly explained why Micah was acting so weird today. Had he known about this?

Tommen leaned against the door. Somehow, it just didn't even seem possible. Micaiah had been arrested and charged with treason, and he was sentenced to death. Just...what? How did that even happen? Tommen fully understood that, being an Apprentice, he was not privy to the goings-on of officers and the other higher ups. But he thought that they'd all been Suppressed and were trying to lay low. Yes, it was entirely possible that perhaps a Tracker had gotten to him and taken him back to Rifun's lair. But in what scenario did a Tracker get Micaiah and not Micah? Yes, both of them were tough motherfuckers, but if Tommen had to pick between the two of them, his money was always on Micaiah to be the one to survive.

Somehow or another, he got the rod-tablet closed and went back in the bakery. It wasn't busy, and Micah was rolling out some dough on the table.

"So, uh, is Micaiah coming in today?" Tommen asked casually. "After his doctor's appointment?"

Micah looked up. "Um...I don't know. He might have gotten tied up with other things."

"Other things, what do you mean?"

"Well, like running errands for the store, for himself. Between his 'vacation' in the hospital and getting his bike out of storage, he's rediscovered his freedom outside the bakery."

"Don't worry, I'm here."

Tommen turned as the back door opened and Micaiah himself walked in.

"I'm here," he repeated, sighed. "It's a beautiful day out, and you think I want to be cooped up in that office all day?"

"Exactly," Micah said, nodding at Tommen. A little too vigorously.

Tommen frowned as he looked at the elder twin. "You can't be Micaiah."

Micaiah raised a brow. "I can't? Who can I be, then?"

"I don't know, but this—" Tommen held up the rod. "—says that Micaiah is currently awaiting a death sentence."

Immediately, both twins froze and stared at the rod. So-called Micaiah broke first, nodding. "All right. You got me. Why don't we talk in the office? Micah."

The three of them headed into the office. As they skirted by the front, Tommen halted. Everything was stopped, frozen like they were in a Fast Band. People sat at tables, at the windows, a couple at the bar watched TV. Outside, people walked around. One person was just about to open the door to the shop. But through it all, there was no sheen of color like they were in a Fast Band.

"What is this?" Tommen wondered.

"Inside," Not-Micaiah said.

Panic alarms going off in his head, Tommen followed them into the office and shut the door. No Band was created, but still the breath was swept from his lungs as he watched Not-Micaiah appear to mutate in front of him, as though a layer of dust was being shaken off and all that stood before him was the same woman who had ordered the cinnamon roll and coffee.

"What the—?"

"You like it?" she asked. "Want to see me do it again?"

Tommen wanted to say no, but she did it anyway. It took a second for him to recall where he'd seen her before, then realized it was Micaiah's friend from the play. Dark skin, dark hair, great body. He took a step back. "What...the *fuck* is going on?"

"More than you can appreciate, Tommen."

"Who the fuck are you?"

"My given name is Aklaq, but most just call me Kayla."

Tommen shook his head. "Who the fuck are you, and what the fuck is going on? What did you just do? Are you, like, a fucking Harvester?"

"Not a Harvester. An Akari-bearer."

"Oh, fuck, we're back to this again? God..." Tommen trailed off, and Aklaq, Kayla, continued.

"I wish there was more time to explain, but we don't have the luxury of knowledge right now."

"I was already kidnapped by one religious whackjob. I don't need another." He turned to go.

"Do you think Micaiah is a religious whackjob?" Micah wondered. "Or me?"

Tommen paused and hesitated. "How do I want to say this? No, I can't. Not if I want to keep my job. I'm just going to leave now and pretend like I didn't see or hear anything."

"Pretending will get you nowhere."

He grinned, his hand already on the handle. "Then I won't pretend. I'll lie. After all, our lives are only stories. Doesn't matter if they're true or not; just make sure it's a good one."

But when he opened the door, Kayla was already in front of him. When he looked behind him, she was there, too. Looking ahead, she was gone. Looking back, she was gone. Looking ahead, she reappeared.

"That trick is called Imprint," she said. "The one before that was a Disguise." She moved forward, backing Tommen back into the office. "The Akari is Time unblemished. It is Time sentient. You ask to use it. Those like Cassius and Rifun and the numerous cults around the Akari think they use it, but really, it uses them."

Tommen rolled his eyes. "Fucking hell, you're all insane."

"Fine, I'll put it another way. The Akari is being able to see the full spectrum of color and waves across the universe. The cults are like seeing only through the narrow, human lens, red to purple and black to white. Time and the Time industry is like being color-blind."

"And you would know about that, would you?" He threw up his hands. "Fuck this, I'm out."

"You're too far into this already, Tommen. You've been summoned as a Testimony, and you made a deal with Rifun."

Now he stopped. "Is this his sign that he promised to send me?"

"Not likely, but he'll use it to his every advantage," Micah told him. "Time Trials are funny things. It's kind of like a regular trial, but if the defendant is found guilty, his lawyer and witnesses hang with him, too."

"What does that have to do with me?" Tommen wondered. "What's going on?"

"You may have guessed, but the universe has not been idle since Cassius and Rifun took over," Kayla explained. "It's been attempt after attempt to break in and kill them, but with no success."

"But Micaiah did find a way in, right?"

"Of sorts, but it's highly risky, as Micah just illustrated. The idea is that Micaiah would turn himself in and demand a Time Trial, naming his Stake and Testimonies as the four people Cassius and Rifun most wanted, in order to make the deal irresistible. But, before the Trial would officially begin, Micah, who would be smuggling weapons in with him, would shoot dead both Cassius and Rifun, since it is highly likely they would both be present, as well as any Grandfathers and guards also present. The problem is, if it fails, we all die anyway."

"What are you talking about you? You weren't named anywhere in the summons that I saw. It's my life on the line here. And Micah's."

"Micah, yes," Kayla acknowledged. "But not you. That's where the Disguise comes in."

Right before his eyes, Kayla seemed to don a layer of dust and Tommen was looking at himself just as clearly as if he looked in a mirror. When she spoke, it was with his voice. "I'll be going as you. Doug will be going as himself, and a third volunteer will be impersonating your dad."

Then she shed the layer, the Disguise, and was back to normal, or as normal as Tommen could expect her to be at this point. It left him reeling. So this was how Eric and Varad felt when they'd been exposed to Time. Fascinating.

"Okay, wait, so then, there's every chance that Micaiah isn't Micaiah. It's just a stunt double, but he has to lay low in order to avoid suspicion. Right?" Tommen said hopefully.

Kayla shook her head sadly. "How I wish that were possible, but the processing in the Judgment Wing is DNA-verified. Disguises are only a manipulation of appearance, what you might consider surface-DNA, and a trick of the eye. But if you were to test the DNA, no matter what Disguise I wear, it will still come back as me."

"And the rest of the people involved aren't held to the same standards? I mean, if you're going, knowing that you could die, and you had this ability — "

"But few do have this ability," Kayla interrupted. "Even fewer believe such a thing exists in any capacity. Harvesting is a severely washed-out holographic simulation of what the Disguises are, among other aspects of the Akari. Every part of the Time industry is a washed-out version. The DNA verification of the criminals is only for records; it has nothing to do with preventing impersonation. Therefore, there is no need to protect against something you believe to be a myth."

Tommen's mind went instantly to the warehouse. His dad had said that the Akari was a myth. Rifun was a cracknut cultist. He wasn't sure about this Kayla person, but the twins didn't come across as cracknut cultists.

He had no fucking clue what to make of all of this.

"The only time the DNA is taken from the Stake and the Testimonies is if they lose and they are sentenced to death. Then they might be discovered. With any luck, this will all be over before the

Trial even begins."

Tommen found a chair and slumped into it. "I am so fucking confused."

"I know," Kayla said sympathetically. "All of this was orchestrated in advance, and I'd even made arrangements to have your message intercepted, like I did your dad's, in order to keep both of you out of this." She hesitated. "You are an Akari-bearer, Tommen. One day, Micaiah and I had hoped to teach you, but not like this. Believe me, Cassius and Rifun messed up more than a few people's plans."

" 'Micaiah and I' you said," Tommen said, looking up.

She nodded. "You never asked my last name. It's Durvin. Micaiah is my husband."

"Fuck." He slipped farther down in his seat. He shook his head and laughed humorlessly. "Fuck. I just...damn." Beat. "So all those nights when he was leaving work early in order to go to bars and stuff...?"

"He was coming to meet me. We separated in order to keep Rifun off our trail."

Tommen glanced at Micah. "And you knew all this, right?"

Micah nodded. "I did. That's why I never said anything about it or protested too much."

"Fuck."

"It's a lot to take in," Kayla said solemnly. "Actually, you were never supposed to know at all, about the Time Trial."

"Well, now that I do know, what can I do? I mean, if you were going to replace me, there's no reason now — "

"No," Micah cut in. "That's exactly what Rifun is expecting. Your presence is his bait. You wouldn't be executed, but you would become Rifun's little servant, lackey, Apprentice — "

"His bitch?"

"Exactly. We're not going to risk losing you."

"You lose the trial, he finds out it's not really me, he comes for me anyway."

"It's a gamble," Kayla said. "All of this is a huge gamble."

Tommen shifted in his seat, trying to get back upright. "So what can I do to improve the odds?"

Kayla hesitated and glanced at Micah. This hadn't been part of their plans. They'd had everything outlined to a T, planned everything around Tommen and Walter being blissfully ignorant of the whole thing. But that wasn't possible now, so they had to reweigh their options, figure out what to do with the little bird who knew too much.

"First and foremost," Kayla began slowly, "your dad cannot know."

"Why not?"

"He's too fragile," Micah said. "There is no way he could mentally sustain such a blow, whether from just knowing what's happened to Micaiah, to knowing both of you had been called, to the Trial itself. It's too much for him to handle, I'm sorry to say."

The problem was, there was every possibility they were right. After last night, when an off-handed comment had sent him into one of his silent modes, the thought of going back to the Wheel, potentially back to the black cells, Tommen knew it would be too much for him to handle. He was cracked now; that terrifying possibility would shatter him.

"Okay," Tommen agreed reluctantly. "Okay. But I'll still have to call him and tell him that I have to work late or something."

Kayla nodded. "Fair enough. Why don't you go do that now and man the counter for a bit? We'll have to call Doug and see if there's anything we can do with you."

"Who's Doug?"

"Someone you'll meet later this evening. Go."

Tommen left the office, feeling dazed. Had all of that just happened? What the ever-loving fuck?

Oddly enough, the one thing he was fixated on the most wasn't the trial or any of that. It was the fact that Micaiah was married. Maybe they were fucking with him, but it seemed too out of place for the situation at hand. Micaiah was fucking married. Like, he had a wife. For better or worse, until death do us part, that kind of thing. His little escapades out to bars and clubs had all been a ploy to make him seem like a player, when he was really just going to meet his wife. Fuck. And they'd been doing that for, what, ten years now? Something like that?

"Excuse me. Young man."

Tommen almost startled as he realized that Time had resumed; whatever Band had been in place, he'd been released from it. Now a customer stood at the counter, waiting. Trying not to appear like anything was wrong or that his world had just been turned upside-down—or, at the very least, on its side—he went to meet her.

Micaiah was married. Holy fuck. And holy hell, his wife was hot. How in the world had they met in the first place, never mind get married? What was next, secret children running around who were going to be their backup force during this whole escapade? Was this Doug person one of their children? Was this going to go down in Time history as the Durvin Revolution? Or the Durvin Massacre?

It wasn't long before he got a few minutes to himself to call his dad.

"Hello?" Walter answered after a few rings.

"Dad, it's me," Tommen began.

"You off already? It's only one-thirty."

"No, Jenna called in, so Micah asked if I wanted to work a double. Are you okay to pick me up tonight?"

"Any idea when exactly you'll be out?"

"Um, well, Micah's kind of thinking we'll be busy, so, maybe around nine-thirty?"

His dad sighed over the phone. "Yeah, that's fine. I'll plan for nine-thirty; you let me know if anything changes."

"I will."

He hung up, unsure how he should feel about lying to his dad. Sure, he enjoyed a good secret spy, double-agent movie any day, and he was fairly certain that most people fantasized at least a little about being that spy or agent. Being part of a secret, underground organization, carrying out secret operations that the general public had no knowledge of, building a normal life as a pretense to throw everyone off, even their own family. It all sounded so heroic and awesome.

Interestingly enough, he already led that kind of life just being part of Time. He went to school, his dad was a cop, the twins were bakers, all of it a pretense to seem normal while they carried out secret operations as part of a bigger industry that most of Earth knew nothing about.

But what if, like Kayla and Micah seemed to be implying, there was another layer to all of this? What if there was some small, minuscule credence to be given to this whole Akari business? After all, was he going to trust in a failed system to tell him what was true, when that system had been overthrown by the very thing they proclaimed to be false? Or was he going to trust Micah and Micaiah, who he knew were generally calm, level-headed, and not given to wild religious fantasies? After all, the best way to destroy an ideology was to demonize it. Maybe the Akari really had been something decades or centuries ago, but the Hands had usurped it. Then you had the militant whackjobs like Cassius and Rifun who resorted to violence, while the calm adherents like the twins simply went underground, waiting for their chance to rise.

Fuck, what was this? An Illuminati conspiracy? Did these people have the end of the world date pinned down, too? It was way too ridiculous. Science and religion just didn't mix; they couldn't. It was like oil and water, and only one could slake your thirst.

It seemed to take forever, but Micah eventually called him back into the office. He did this, of course, by slipping the three of them into some sort of weird Fast Band that didn't suck the life out of him in the process.

"So, what's the verdict?" Tommen asked. "Can I go?"

"You're not going," Kayla repeated. "But you will be our last line of defense."

"I don't know how I should feel about that."

"Be glad you're being included at all," Micah told him severely. "Doug didn't want you anywhere near this, whether you knew or not; we came up with this as a way to at least make you useful and hopefully keep hurting Cassius and Rifun right down to the last possible second."

"Cool. So, what's the plan?"

"You are simply going to stay here in the office with a gun," Kayla explained. "If we come back out, let us pass. If it's not any of us, and especially if it's Rifun or Cassius, shoot the bastards. And don't stop until they're dead."

"That's it?"

"Think of it as the 300," Micah said.

"Like, Leonidas, Xerxes, that 300?"

"Yes. Portals are only so big; you can use it as a bottleneck. I think you understand how that works."

"I do."

"Rifun's gone to too much trouble to not want you alive," Kayla went on. "And he has no reserve for his own men. You can kill as many as you want and he's more likely to be impressed than offended. He'll take you alive, and that's the only comfort you have in this if we fail."

Somehow, Tommen still had his doubts. Rifun had had no qualms about shooting him in the boat; only Tommen's reflexes had saved him there. Plus, if Micah hadn't been there to pave the way for their escape during the coup, the Grandfathers would have killed him just as quickly as anyone else. Sure, Rifun had sinister plans for him, but he didn't seem overly concerned whether they came to fruition. He only added soldiers, and did not weep over the loss of his minions, especially not his potential minions.

"Because of the nature of the Wheel, how it's been sealed off, the portal will not stay open once we've crossed through," Micah informed him. "So when the portal opens again, you're going to have to make a judgment call whether it's us coming through or someone else."

That's what he was afraid of. Tommen could shoot on reflex, and he could shoot when he had time to ready himself, but he was less than confident in that bit that fell in between, taking that one second to decide whether that person coming at him was friend or foe. He was afraid he would lock up and be unable to decide.

"If you don't want to do it—"

"No, I'll do it," Tommen blurted. "I just...I don't know, it's just weird."

"We never wanted you to get involved in this," Kayla repeated. "One encounter with the Cult is bad enough, but two encounters in less than a year at your age, it's not fair. More to the point, it's not right."

"I can do it. I mean, between now and then, I think I can process it. You know, I'll think it over a little and I'll be good."

Neither of them seemed convinced, but he'd made his choice and they were all going to honor it. Kayla glanced uncertainly at Micah who shrugged and nodded.

"All right," she said. "If you think you can do it. But know that there's no shame in changing your mind."

"I won't."

Micah glanced at the clock on the wall. "We've still got seven hours before closing time. Go back out, do some work, and, as you said, think it over a little."

"Oh." That was it? They weren't going to bring him in on the rest of their plans? "Okay."

"I'll be out in the bit to help."

"Okay."

But the only thing Tommen could feel was disappointment, like he was finally being included in something awesome, and he was just given a rag and told to go dust the shelves. Well, he was only an Apprentice after all, in title only seeing how he had zero training in any new abilities. Speaking of abilities, he didn't even have those.

# Chapter Twenty-Two
## Waiting

Micaiah woke, and even then he wasn't sure. Somehow, he was fairly certain that there was more light generated from the inside of his eyelids than the murky blackness that lay beyond him. He sat up, head spinning, unsure if he was sitting on the floor or the ceiling, wondering how he could have such vertigo when he couldn't see anything.

It was all but impossible to tell how much time had passed since he'd been thrown in the cell. He'd once read an article about some cavers who had voluntarily gone under and spent up to six months in total cave darkness, in order to study its effects on the body. Neither of them had gone insane, but they'd had some contact with teams outside the cave who were responsible for their general well-being, food, water, and so on.

But those cavers had experienced strange side effects when it came to their circadian rhythm. One of them had slept for over thirty hours and woke thinking he'd just taken a brief nap. The other had slept for only about half an hour or so, but was convinced she'd slept for twelve to sixteen hours.

Micaiah tried to judge realistically how long he might have been down, but found that he couldn't. He knew it had been some time between being thrown in and when the candles went out, and then more time had passed until he'd fallen asleep. Actually, he wasn't even sure the candles had gone out on their own, now that he thought about it. Maybe he'd fallen asleep before they went out, woke up, and then fell back asleep. Or maybe his mysterious, sarcastic, prison chaplain friend had blown them out on purpose. Maybe he'd only been hallucinating that the candles were there and it didn't matter one way or the other.

He found a wall and leaned against it. Or maybe Rifun was playing with the perception controls in this cell. Who knew how much time had really passed? Micaiah could be in a Fast Band, and so years would pass inside his cell before he ever saw his trial, a way to try and break him. Maybe he was in a Slow Band, so years would pass outside his cell until he was all but forgotten and his friends and family considered him dead. That was the problem when you gambled with the devil; he didn't play by the rules you set down, and he knew every trick in the book. It was like trying to beat a bartender at his own drinking game.

Gingerly, he stood and stretched, feeling tight muscles protest and stiff joints crack and pop back into place. He sat back down in a heap. His knee was sore and his stump ached something awful. He'd never worn his prosthetic this long, and he certainly wasn't supposed to sleep it in, but he didn't dare take it off. The cell was small, true, but that didn't mean he trusted it to still be where he put it if he took it off for any length of time. Besides that, if he took it off, he was pretty sure the stump would swell and he'd never get it back on, at least not in time to go to the trial.

He let out a breath. So, Cassius was dead at Rifun's hand. He might have expected as much, really. Tyranny only breeds paranoia, especially among its leaders. He couldn't even say that he was surprised Rifun had been the victor. Cassius had been brutal and bloodthirsty, a menace to all, but Rifun's quiet power and aggression was more lethal by far. He'd been manipulating Cassius and orchestrating all of this from the very beginning, but where was that beginning? Some piece of the puzzle was missing to explain their involvement in the Cult, the Dispersal, and where did the salt cave fit in? How was it that this was all coming back around, Cassius and Walter, Rifun and Micaiah? How were they all coming back together again?

Micaiah sighed. *I think the Author is a sadist.* He looked

forlornly in the direction of where he thought his knee was. *At the very least, she enjoys cruel and unusual punishment.*

He looked around in the darkness, wondering which way the exit was. Not that it would matter since the door would be locked, and it would be flush with the wall so only those with the greatest tactile sensation would be able to find its seams. Some of the cells, like the one Walter had been locked in, had shackles. Even worse, the shackles had needles in them that stuck directly into the bloodstream. A nutrient stream would feed directly into the body, saving the time and hassle of having to prepare and deliver food to the prisoners, keeping them in the darkness that much longer.

So there was some hope, Micaiah figured. If he wasn't going to be put on prison life support, that meant Rifun was going to have to take him out pretty quickly to his trial. Unless he was given water, he couldn't be down here more than three or four days, really. Judging by the thirst already plaguing his throat, he hadn't been down much more than a day or two already. He nodded to himself. Yes, there was some hope yet that he would be out of here quickly.

Unfortunately, however, it did nothing for the present moment, and his hope was soon snuffed out by sheer boredom. Maybe there was something to be said for sleeping for thirty hours at a time. It would be like an old-school Slow Band, just passing the time away.

Micaiah shifted and shuffled until he got on his back, as comfortable as he could expect to be. It didn't take long for the darkness to do its work, and soon enough, he was out.

Micaiah knew he was dreaming only for the fact that there was light. The first few images or scenes were blurry, and he knew he wouldn't remember them, but gradually they sorted themselves out.

The sudden tide of emotion almost jolted him back to wakefulness, but he clawed his way back into the dream. He knew those streets and those alleys. He knew the roads and buildings and all the people who hurried along to some important thing or other while the children played freely, blissfully ignorant of the evils of the world.

Micaiah chased after his friends on two full legs, short though they still were, Micah always one step behind.

*"Fágfaimid, a MhacEoghan, beidh muid mar na cinn dheireanacha ann!"* Micaiah said, urging his brother forward. (Come on, we'll be the last ones there!)

A peddler had come to town. He attracted the children first with all manner of brightly-painted toys and shiny bits for the girls, and, of course, sugar candy for all. Then, once the adults had been roused from their stupor of routine work, the real wares were displayed for all to see.

*"A MhacEoghan, dean deifir suas!"* (Micah, hurry up!)

Micaiah dropped back and grabbed his brother's hand. Then he steeled himself and willed the two of them forward. It wasn't that they ran faster, necessarily, but it felt like it as they overtook the other children, being the first ones to arrive at the peddler's cart.

"Well, there's our first lucky lad," the peddler said. "What's this? Two of them? And they look exactly alike!"

*"Is mise Miach,"* Micaiah said breathlessly. *"Agus is MacEoghan sé. Is mo deartháir beag sé."* (I'm Micaiah. And he's Micah. He's my little brother.)

*"Is do charaid mé,"* Micah complained. (I'm your twin.)

*"Ach taim níos sine. Rugadh mé an chéad uair."* (But I'm older. I was born first.)

The peddler laughed. "All right, boys, settle down. Here you go, a couple of toy soldiers."

"Toy soldiers?" one woman asked, fuming. "Have you no shame, sir, after what we've been through? The Great War was bad enough without you peddling war to the next generation. Our children should not have to suffer such things, but I fear they will with the bad things happening on the mainland."

"My good madam, I mean no offense. I am simply a tinker, and I enjoy giving gifts to children and seeing them laugh."

"You have shiny bits and candy. Isn't that enough? Leave the war in the past where it belongs."

They continued arguing, but Micaiah was no longer paying attention. He and Micah were showing off their new toy soldiers to their friends, already coming up with a number of silly little games to play.

Later on, Micaiah and Micah were down at the beach, a good distance from the docks and the fishing boats. The peddler approached them.

*"An dtéann tú ar ár saighdiúirí bréagán as a cuid? Bean Mac Domhnaill?"* Micaiah mumbled. (Are you here to take away our toy soldiers because of her? Mrs. MacDonald?)

The peddler knelt in front of him. Micah wandered over. "No, young lads, I won't take away your toy soldiers, but I'm afraid I won't be returning to your town anytime soon. I came to say goodbye, and to say that I'm impressed by that little trick you did to get ahead of your friends back there."

"It's just something I do."

"Do you do other things like it?"

Micaiah shrugged. "Sometimes."

The man looked at Micah. "Can you do it, too?"

Micah shook his head. "I don't know how, and Cai won't teach me. He says it's for big brothers only."

The peddler chuckled. "Of course it is. Well, like I said, I won't be coming back anytime soon, but there will be other tinkers and peddlers. If you like, I know a man who might be interested in your little tricks. Maybe he'll pay you if you do them. And if you're both really good, he might teach both of you a few new tricks. How does that sound?"

Both boys perked up at the thought. "That sounds good."

"Right, then." The man stood. "I'll see if I can find him and maybe send him this way. I'll tell him to keep an eye out for the little twin lads. The older lad knows tricks, and the younger lad wants to learn a few of his own. All right?"

Micaiah and Micah agreed readily and watched as the peddler

turned and walked away, picking up his cart, and going on his way.

They never saw that particular peddler again, even later on in life once they'd been introduced to the Time industry. It was never clear, either, whether he'd actually reported the boys to Rifun, or if that had come much later from a different passerby.

Somewhere in the real world, Micaiah could feel himself returning to wakefulness. Painfully, he rolled over and managed to slip back under.

The little fishing village where they had lived later in life was gone. Not gone, as in, progress and industrialization had claimed it, but gone, as in, obliterated. Haphazard bombing had destroyed it, and the only thing that had spared Micaiah and Micah its wrath was their promotion. They'd been gone when it all happened, testing for their Journeyman status.

In a cruel twist of fate, having their home destroyed probably made it easier to leave, knowing there was nothing waiting for their return. A few of the villagers survived, but no one who really mattered. Their parents were gone for about a year by this time, and most of the older siblings had married and moved on, leaving the twins to basically take care of themselves and their father's fishing business. But with the bombing, business would crumble and there would be even less for them than there already was. Ireland was neutral, but secret underground war efforts were still made. After all, was there any reason to think they would be spared if Hitler conquered England?

It left the twins alone amid the devastation, their saving grace being their promotion. The world was a dangerous place, but, their mentors assured them, Canada would be their best bet. It was like America, but a little less of a target. So, the twins got on the first ship they could manage and sailed for Canada. They had to make their way west, to British Columbia, where their contact would be waiting for them.

It was not a difficult journey, but it was a painful one. In a world filled with chaos and uncertainty, the brothers had only each other to depend on. Still, they tried to make the best of it and tried to feel good about getting out and seeing the world, exploring this new place. The plan was to start in British Columbia—picking up bits and pieces from other Timekeepers along the way—head down the west coast of the United States, then continue south through Central America, concluding their journey around the future site of the Panama Canal.

They arrived in Vancouver no worse for wear, both of them hoping desperately that their contact would have a sign and flag them down. Otherwise, they had nowhere to go.

Of all the people they might have expected to meet them at the airport, none of them compared to what they actually got. She looked about their age, maybe a little older, five-foot-four or thereabouts. She had darker skin, like fine chocolate, and black hair that reached down to her waist even braided. But her gaze was as cold as the ice on the tarmac, this accentuated by the way she dug her nails into the paper sign reading "Durvin."

"Durvin twins, at your service, ma'am," Micaiah said as they walked up.

"Good, at least now I can put a face to a name." Her English was accented. She crumpled up the paper and tossed it away. "Patrick told me you were coming."

"Here we are." Micaiah tried to come off as friendly and non-threatening.

She merely raised a brow. "Aklaq, Master Timekeeper, Region Four, District One. I'll be showing you around the city a bit so you get acquainted with how things are done here. Then I'll take you to meet the District Captain."

"And what about the Lieutenants?" Micah dared inquire.

"They're posted in Alaska. I expect you might meet them, depending on how long you stay."

"Oh. Right."

She turned and started walking away, the twins trailing behind. "And if you really impress me, I might take you to meet another friend of mine." She glanced back. "But don't tell the Captain I told you that. He doesn't like my friends."

Micaiah wasn't sure he wanted to meet her friends if they were anything like her.

"One more thing." She stopped and turned. "If either of you check me out again, I'll rip your eyeballs out by their nerves. Got it?"

They got it.

Micaiah found himself laughing as he woke. God, looking back on it, it all seemed so hilarious now. Kayla had been so uptight and serious back then. Well, fuck, she could still inspire fear if she wanted to, but it all just seemed so...comical. Almost like it had all been just a dream.

As his eyes adjusted to the gloom, he was surprised and yet not surprised to find that there was light for his eyes to adjust to. Almost as expected, when he looked to one side, there sat his sarcastic prison chaplain, this time with three candles lit, pouring a fourth.

"Are you ever going to tell me who you are?" Micaiah asked.

"You know who I am," the man said simply, not looking at him.

"Do you at least have a name, or something I can call you, instead of 'hey, you' all the time?"

He shrugged. "If you wish. What would you call me?"

"I don't know. Steve?"

The man raised a brow and gave him a sideways glance. "That's the best you can come up with?"

Micaiah sat up and stretched, gasping in pain as his right knee seized in a charliehorse. He fell to his other side, rubbing and massaging the knee, gritting his teeth against the pain until it relaxed.

"You really shouldn't sleep with your leg on like that," the man said as Micaiah got back to a sitting position. "After all of this is over, I think you might need to see your physical therapist about that. There could be damage happening." He gave Micaiah a knowing look. "So, about that name."

"Well, if you're supposed to be my conscience, I guess I could call you Micaiah. But if I'm the only one who can see you, that might make me look and sound crazy. So I'll do the next best thing and name you after my genetic doppleganger. I'm going to call you Micah."

The man pursed his lips and nodded. "You could do that, certainly. But then, how would that look to those Outside?"

Micaiah paused. "Okay, fine, I can't call you Micah, or anyone else who's already been mentioned. And if I can't call you any of those, then what can I call you? I'm being serious."

"So am I. What do you want to call me?"

Micaiah sighed, frustrated. "Fine. You want to be mysterious, I'll play along. I'm going to call you Candlemaker."

"I think the word you're looking for is chandler."

"Fine. Chandler. There's your name."

"Very astute of you," Chandler observed mildly as he lit the fourth candle. "I wonder, what would happen if I stopped making candles."

He couldn't help it, Micaiah let out a loud groan of frustration. Chandler just smiled. "I am only joking. I will continue to make candles. After all, only light can ward off the darkness. No amount of your baking can do that, at least in a literal sense."

"Yeah, well—" Micaiah sighed. "—I don't know how much more of that I'm going to be doing."

"Why not? I have already told you that you're going to make it out of here alive. Do you not believe me?"

"I haven't decided on that one, but assuming I do survive, I just can't do it anymore."

"Do what?"

"I can't keep doing what I'm doing. Baking, day in and day out, running a business but going nowhere. I miss my wife; I hate having to sneak off to see her."

"You may wish to guard your words, lest they give you and her away."

"If I die, she will die as well. If I live, it will be because Rifun is dead. Nothing is gained by him knowing one way or the other."

"Fascinating logic. Please, continue."

"I want to have a real life, Chandler, outside of Time."

"Outside, even, of the Akari?"

Micaiah paused. "I don't know. Maybe. I just don't want to keep getting caught up in all this espionage and political intrigue and shit. It's exhausting, and it's already cost me a lot." He closed his eyes and tried to breathe evenly. "Just once, I want to experience real life. I want a wife and kids, I want a family and a regular job and all the things that people think I experience now that I don't. Because it's all an illusion, carefully crafted to hide my involvement in Time."

"When is the last time you went to a library?" Chandler inquired.

"If you don't count the Archives, fuck, it's been years."

"Hundreds of millions of people live their lives without Time, and even more without the Akari. They simply wake up, go and do, and at the end it's...the end. That's it. Nothing. Ka-put. No more. Happily ever after. Or not so happily, as is sometimes the case." He shifted position and poured another layer of wax into the mold. "But you...you are a different kind of story. Your story goes on, because it goes out."

"Where are you going with this?"

"Have you ever heard the story of the man in the cave with his shadow?"

"Um, yeah, I think so. He thinks the shadow is the truth until he turns around and sees the candle casting the shadow. Then he knows the candle is the truth."

"Exactly." And the fifth candle was lit. "You have seen the candle casting shadows. You will never be able to un-see it. You will try to tell others, to get them to look away from the shadows toward the light, and most will call you crazy. Even if you do end up sitting down, shutting up, and not speaking of the candle, you will still be sitting there, staring at it yourself, because it is beautiful and you know it is true."

Micaiah shifted position. "So, you're saying I should go dark and build a new life for myself and Kayla?"

Chandler gave him a curious look. "Seeing the light is the first step. And it is always good to try to bring others to it. But never discount the power of simply being, of sitting down and taking it in."

"Like the elevator experiment. Stare at something long enough and eventually others will get curious and look with you."

"Something like that."

Chandler licked his fingers and put out one of the candles.

Painfully, Micaiah made to stand and get closer, but the best he could do was a halting crawl. "Wait, Chandler, what are you doing?"

"There is another part to the candle in the cave that no one ever warns you about." Another lick, and another candle went out. "Sometimes, the flame is put out. For a time. The candle is still there, but if you cannot see it, how can you find it and know what you have found?" The third of the five candles went out. "What it needs is another spark, another flame to reignite the wick. But how do you explain what you need when no one either knows what you are talking about, or believes that it exists?" Micaiah's stomach twisted as the fourth candle was put out. "What happens when you are the only person in that cave who has seen the candle? Worse yet, what happens when you are not the only one who has seen it, but you are the only one who did not seek to destroy it and put it out?" Chandler licked his fingers a fifth time and looked at Micaiah. "Do you know what you must do?"

Micaiah's heart leapt. "Apparently I need to carry a few spare candles and keep a box of matches on me."

Chandler gave a sarcastic smile and shook his head. "Clever, but no. What you must do is—" And he snuffed out the last candle, throwing them both back into total darkness. "—you must become the light."

Being stuck in the cell might not have been bad, except Micaiah had grown used to the light. Now, accompanied by

Chandler's spooky speech, he found himself hyperventilating and afraid of the dark as it closed in around him. Was this how Walter felt each night as he lay down to sleep? Did he feel a nauseating sense of claustrophobia? Did he question whether the monster under the bed or the bogeyman in the closet might be true?

After a minute of uncontrollable fear, Micaiah started to come back to himself. He found a wall and slid down to sit against it. No, he had to think rationally. Nothing about his circumstances had really changed. He'd woken up in this black cell, and he was still in this black cell. In a few hours, he would probably be falling asleep in this black cell, too. Nothing was different.

He wasn't sure how long he sat there or if he'd managed to get more sleep, but the next thing Micaiah knew, the door was being flung wide open, light spilling in to illuminate every corner of the cell. Instinctively, he put his hand up to shield his eyes. Once he was able to look around without seeing spots everywhere, he put his hand down and tried to make out his guard.

"Room service," Rifun said sarcastically.

"You're feeding me?" Micaiah wondered, standing and limping painfully toward him, making sure to stand just out of arm's reach, suspiciously taking the tray which was held out to him.

"Time Trials are amusing, but only when the Accused actually tries to put up a fight and thinks he has a chance. There is more to be gained by an aspiring actor doing his best to win the stage, than a meager criminal sewn into the skin of a lamb and fed helplessly to the lions."

"I guess that's supposed to be an assurance that it isn't poisoned."

Not that it looked particularly appetizing, Micaiah thought as he took a few steps back to sit and eat. On a good day, it might have been mistaken for an attempt at split pea soup with ham and bacon. At best it tasted like old, soggy cardboard.

"If it had been up to Cassius, he would have killed you and sent out the summons to your friends to draw them here and kill them, too. No one would know, after all, what really happened. As far as anyone else would know, you'd simply failed the Time Trial and been subsequently executed. As for me, however, I am a man of my word."

"Here to strike a bargain with your dying and desperate prisoner, bringing food as a peace offering?" Micaiah sneered.

"I am not here to strike a bargain. I am the one holding all the cards. You brought the bargain to me, and what a bargain it is. I will admit, however, that I did have similar thoughts, especially when you named your Testimonies. You have already rejected me. Doug surely would, too. Tommen and your brother are the prizes to be won here, and your brother, I think it is safe to assume, slips from my grasp more and more with each passing day.

"But none of them would agree to anything if you were dead before the Time Trial even began. If they're going to agree to any bargain, best do it when they must honor a fair and square loss, hm? Besides, you may have guessed that life in the Wheel currently is very boring. I need the spectacle."

"How long have I been here?"

Rifun picked a bit of dirt from under his nails using a long knife. "A day, perhaps. Maybe more. You're lucky that the Executioner's Block with the Pit was already constructed when you arrived, or else you might have been sitting here quite a while. As it is, you will be the first to test it out in such a fashion."

"The Executioner's Block?"

"A far more efficient model of governing, I think. Rather than taking up valuable time and space in the Coliseum, or the Theater as it is now called, simply make it a separate sport for those who enjoy such things, and leave the politics to those who care. Things are getting back on track quite nicely, I think. As I said, you will be the first to test out the new model. I'm quite excited."

"Thrilled, I'm sure."

Micaiah did not want to seem overly grateful for the food and drink, but his stomach was sure thankful. He finished off the soggy cardboard mush and the water and set the tray aside. "So, the Day and the Bat are still around?"

"Oh yes, they are. You needn't worry yourself about that. Many things have changed around here, but your Time Trial will proceed just as all Time Trials have proceeded in the past."

Micaiah tried not to smirk. The goal here was to kill Rifun; getting rid of the Bat and the Day would just be a bonus. Slimy, shifty, two-timing sons of bitches anyway. There would be no great loss to see them gone.

"You have six hours until your trial," Rifun told him. "Regretfully, we have yet to fill the prison chaplain's position, so you'll have to make peace with God by yourself."

"I'm not worried," Micaiah said.

"Ah, banking on that 'Greater love has no man' and all that? Tell me how that works out for you."

"You first."

It was the only indication he gave that some plot was afoot, and he could tell Rifun was not amused by it. The tyrant got his familiar done-with-this expression and left the cell.

Before the door could shut completely, however, it was flung open again and two guards walked in. One was humanoid that was slightly smaller than him, the other a quadruped that appeared slightly bigger. Micaiah got to his feet to face them, not liking where this was going. As the guards approached, the door to the cell swung shut, throwing everything into blackness.

Micaiah stood there, waiting. He heard movement and he instinctively ducked, feeling a rush of wind over his head. As he turned, only shock caused him to stop long enough that a blow connected with his gut.

Then, suddenly, he could see. Not light of day kind of see, but he could see where the two guards were and what they were going to do. He could dodge blows and even get off counterattacks, allowing himself moments of Akari-Banding in order to get his leg under him where he needed it to be, learning to compensate and fight back.

Eventually the guards figured out that something was off, because they quickly switched from just pushing around a lowly prisoner to full-on seek and destroy. They did get in some good blows, but Micaiah was not as helpless as they thought.

Still, in a moment of smug satisfaction, the quadruped managed to trip him up as he took a step back, and the humanoid guard gave him what amounted to a full-body blow. Micaiah stumbled back, smacked against the wall of the cell, and fell, feeling the tray and all the dishes shatter on impact. He gasped in pain as some sharp edge pierced the back of his left arm, while another sliced across his hand. Another, more blunt object jabbed into his back and may have torn his shirt, but it did not break skin.

He might have expected more from the guards then, maybe for them to take advantage of his new wounds and poor position on the floor, but they did not. A few seconds after he landed, he heard shuffling across the floor and the cell door opened. Micaiah took a few seconds of that light to check himself over. The worst wound appeared to be the shard still sticking in the back of his arm.

The guards gave him a cat's regard, laughing at his wounds, and then shut the door.

Micaiah lay back, trying to catch his breath. Fucking hell, he didn't need to lose his arm, too. Chandler only said he was going to make it out alive, but he'd failed to mention in what condition that would be. He had no medical supplies, of the professional or improvised kind. If the shard had gone anywhere near his brachial artery, the last thing he wanted to do was pull it out without having some kind of tourniquet handy. He didn't even have a belt to use.

He closed his eyes, trying to figure a way out. After a second, it occurred to him that if the wound was really that bad, he should be going into shock. Or did that not happen until after the shard was pulled out and the blood flowed freely? Gingerly, he rolled his wrist and wiggled his fingers. Shockwaves of pain from both the cuts on his hand and the stab wound were sent racing up his arm, overwhelming the pain receptors in his brain. But he still did not pass out, and he had the presence of mind to note that this was like a paper cut compared to having his leg blown to shit.

Okay, so maybe it wasn't all that bad. Maybe he could just pull the shard out and keep pressure on the wound until it stopped bleeding. It was either that or else he was going to go to trial with a porcelain shard sticking out of his arm. Either way, he had to make his decision quick. Taking a breath, he reached for the shard.

"Are you sure you want to do that?"

Micaiah's hand immediately jumped away from the shard. Chandler had found him again, five lit candles all in a row.

"Is this going to be a regular thing with you?" Micaiah demanded.

"Only as often as you need it," Chandler replied.

"Fine, so what do I need now? More sagely advice? How about some bandages or something?"

"You keep asking who I am. I will tell you what I am not. I am not an errand boy to run and fetch and go and do at your will. I am here for you, to bring you what you need."

Micaiah rubbed his eyes with his good hand. "Proceed."

"Proceed to do what?"

"Enlighten me with your holy wisdom. You are from the Author, aren't you?"

"Aren't we all? I am simply here to provide inspiration."

"Yeah, well, candles might work for soccer moms who go to yoga five days a week, but for me—" He stopped himself.

Chandler raised a brow. "Yes?"

Micaiah paused, musing for just a moment. "Do I have to do everything myself, or can I ask you to help me?"

"That depends. What would you like me to do?"

"I'm going to pull this out. Do you know how to cauterize a wound?"

"There is that possibility."

Micaiah scooted over to Chandler and his candles, examining his wound in the light. It wasn't as bad as the darkness made him think it was, but with no bandages available, he was going to have to do something for it, regardless. He looked at Chandler who simply stared calmly back. Taking a breath, Micaiah grabbed the shard and ripped it out, crying out as it did not come out as smoothly as he would have preferred.

He gritted his teeth as Chandler took one of the candles and held it to the wound, burning the flesh and sealing the hole. Micaiah beat his fist on the floor as the seconds dragged on. Cauterizing was supposed to be done immediately, with intense and focused heat, not the pithy warmth of a candle.

Even after the wound was closed and Chandler took the candle away, the flesh still burned, and Micaiah had to hold it against the cool wall of the cell for several minutes for it to cool down. He was going to have to see a doctor about that when this was all over. He really didn't want to lose an arm, too.

"Okay, so, all that's left is the Time Trial," he sighed. "Fuck, but everything is different now."

"Yes, there is that," Chandler murmured, back to pouring wax into a mold. "If only there was some way you could get word to your friends."

"Even if I could, what would I tell them? The Wheel has entered its Renaissance era? Watch out for buckets of shit being tossed out windows? No matter if the Wheel looks like seventeenth century London or the mind-fuck is was before, it's still going to be a fight getting out."

"Very true. But Time Trials are as much about mental preparedness as physical."

"There's no way to truly mentally prepare for a Time Trial."

"There is if you've been through one already."

"Yeah, because that's making me feel better."

"And if it's not, why is it not? What's changed?"

"What do you mean, what's changed? Everything has changed. The locale, the judge. Even the rules have probably changed so that no matter what, Rifun always wins."

An idea came to him then, and Micaiah shifted position. "If you're real and not just a figment of my imagination, you could take a message to them, tell them I'm alive and what's happened."

"Physically, yes, I suppose I could."

"Will you?"

Chandler looked at him. "No."

"No? Why not?"

"As I said, I'm not your lackey. I am here only to provide inspiration."

"What the hell kind of inspiration are you providing me now?"

"I don't know. What kind am I?" He lit the sixth candle. For a moment, he watched them all burn, then, with a wave of his hand, snuffed them all out.

"No! Chandler!" Micaiah cried.

But there was no answer.

Micaiah sat back against the wall, confused and frustrated. He was going insane in here. He was talking to people who weren't there like some kind of crazy person. He'd even named his imaginary person. He wasn't even sure what that person was supposed to represent. His conscience, his guilt, some other aspect of him which he routinely denied and was now coming back with a roaring vengeance. It was supposed to be his inspiration, but he ended up doling out even more frustration.

He was insane. Even if he did make it out alive, he was going to go straight to the loony bin. He would never be seen or heard from again and no one would know if he was alive or dead.

Then another thought popped in his mind. Carefully, he put his hands on the floor and began to feel around, quickly locating the broken shards as well as the tray his food had come on, which Rifun had neglected to take with him when he left. Either it was a trap, or Rifun was entirely unconcerned. Micaiah decided it was the latter.

As his idea bloomed in his mind, he found that he could make out the shard and the tray in his hand. Slowly, he drew the shard across the surface of the tray. It wasn't like plastic cafeteria trays that might be found in schools and hospitals, but it etched just as easily.

The problem with the shard, though, was that it truly was a double-edged sword. The harder he pressed to etch into the tray, the harder it cut into his hand.

The tray was of an average size, but using a shard instead of a normal writing utensil meant the letters were larger, so he could not write as much as he wanted. Of course, in order to convey all the information he wanted would require far more than a few sheets of paper. Still, he diligently cut and etched, stopping occasionally to nurse the wounds on his hands.

That was the easy part. The hard part would be getting it out. First, there was the matter of the dampening field. It completely blocked Time portals, but the Akari could still get through, though with difficulty. Second, regardless of Time or Akari, places like the regular portal room, or Rifun's new portal room, were like black holes, funneling all the energy needed to create a portal into a centralized location. Micaiah was going to have to fight that pull in order to open up a portal anywhere else. Third, there was no way to know whether Rifun would know of his attempts. It certainly wouldn't be instantaneous, and who knew what would happen if he was caught?

But the worst he could do was try. He didn't know what time it was on Earth, but he knew the statistically most likely place that Micah would be at any given moment. Readying himself and using the Akari to feel out time and space, Micaiah took a breath and opened a portal.

It was less like opening a door, and more like the poor flickering of a screen that was trying to work but couldn't quite get everything up to snuff the way it was supposed to be. Were Micaiah himself trying to escape, stepping through would be a risky thing. As it was, though, he only needed it to be big enough for the tray to get through, and open long enough that he could quickly reach through and drop it on the counter.

His head was split with a migraine once he'd dropped the tray and slammed the portal closed. He closed his eyes and was momentarily grateful for the darkness of the cell. Well, it was the best he was going to be able to do. The only thing left now was the trial.

# Chapter Twenty-Three
## Time Trials

Tommen was just starting to wipe down the tables in the dining room when he heard a small crash in the kitchen. Micah and Kayla, still in conference in the office—or at least, he thought they were still in the office, doing something anyway—did not appear or otherwise shout to let him know everything was okay. So it was up to him to investigate. Normally, he would have been completely okay with such a task, but with everything that had gone on and was about to happen, he felt less like Fred, Daphne, and Velma, and more like Shaggy and Scooby.

When he got back to the kitchen, no one was there that he could see, and everything appeared to still be in its proper place. The only thing that appeared to be amiss was a few mixing spoons had clattered to the floor behind the prep table.

Breathing a sigh of relief, Tommen went around the table and starting picking up the spoons, tossing them haphazardly in the sink. He paused when he got to the last item. At first glance, it appeared to be like any average serving tray, found in schools and hospitals everywhere. When he picked it up, though, he found it was made of a slightly different material, though he could not say exactly what. But perhaps the most terrifying thing about it was the message that had been scratched into it.

For a second, he considered throwing the thing across the room like it was poisoned. Then he got a hold of himself, picked up the tray, and hurried to the office. Before he could knock on the door, however, the front door opened and he was forced to wait on a group of four who could not make up their minds for the life of them. He kept the tray on the counter next to the coffee pots, looking back every so often just to make sure it was still there, as if it was going to run away.

He got antsy as the foursome debated and deliberated and asked him for his recommendations and for various ingredients. Tommen obliged, even as he bounced on his toes, willing them to make up their minds and leave. Eventually they did make up their minds, but they still didn't leave, taking their chatty group to a booth at the far end of the dining room.

Released from his bondage, Tommen grabbed the tray and went to knock on the office door, opening it before he was invited in.

"Yes, Tommen, what is it?" Micah asked, sounding like he and Kayla had been arguing about the same thing for hours and he was both annoyed and relieved by the interruption.

"Micaiah's sent us a message," Tommen said, holding out the tray for Micah to snatch it away.

"*Athraítear an roth, Tá Cassius marbh, Táim beo. Cai,*" Micah read. "Wheel changed, Cassius is dead, I'm alive. Cai."

"Cassius is dead?" Tommen wondered. "By Micaiah or what happened?"

"If I had to hazard a guess, I'd say Rifun offed him," Kayla said thoughtfully. "Dictators don't share power and glory very well. And most likely, this has been Rifun's game the whole time; he was just using Cassius as a front."

Micah agreed. "It's the first part that's got me interested, though."

"What does that mean?" Tommen butted in. "Wheel changed? Wheel changed how? I mean, Sifura told me that the current—or previous—Wheel was the sixth iteration, but she also said that it takes a lot of time and talent to rebuild."

"It does. And being trapped in the Wheel with all of his portals exploded and out of commission, and with Cassius dead, I'll bet you that Rifun's had little else to do for the last six months."

"So what does that mean? Is it a good thing or a bad thing?"

"In our case, it's probably a bad thing," Kayla told him. "It means the layout has changed, the decor has changed, everything has changed. It's going to be a whole new maze in and out of there."

"But you can escape no matter what, right? I mean, Cai had to get this through somehow."

"Probably," Micah said.

"Probably?"

"It's the best we can do, Tommen. Nothing is guaranteed, especially now that things have changed. With Cassius dead, that means we have one less target to worry about. But that also means that Rifun is free to do as he sees fit with no one to answer to."

"But—"

"Tommen."

Tommen shut up.

Micah shifted in his seat. "You're not going either way. Neither is your dad. You will both be safe."

"Yeah, but that doesn't mean I'm not going to worry and try to help however I can."

"And we appreciate it. But your worry doesn't help our worry. We still haven't decided what we want you to do yet, but we're going to wait until Doug gets here to say for sure. What time is it?" He looked around. "Eight o'clock? He should be here pretty soon. Go back out to the counter or the kitchen or whatever you were doing."

Tommen sighed but nodded and ducked out of the room. He was very glad to not be in the direct line of fire this time, but still, was he wrong to worry about his friends and what might happen to them? He found his bleach water and went back out to wipe down tables. The annoying group of four had gone, but their crumbs remained, scattered about the table and on the floor. Grudgingly, he got a broom and got everything swept up.

What would happen to the store if the twins suddenly died? To the rest of the world it would seem they disappeared, but either way, the store would be ownerless and empty.

He tried not to think about it and instead started filling the mop bucket. It was almost full when he heard the front door open. Sighing and hoping it couldn't be heard up front, he went to the counter.

The man was not particularly tall, five-eight at the most, but he was built like a bull. He could have put Micaiah to shame. It wasn't that he appeared to be a bodybuilder, but everything about him said "fighter" like he'd once been an MMA fighter or something in his slightly younger days and still hadn't let that go. He kept his hair short, buzz cut, and his skin was tan from the sun, like he'd just spent the day yelling at wimpy new recruits as they did laps around a hot field.

"Tommen Forbes?" he wondered, looking at his nametag.

"Um, yeah. Are you — ?"

"Doug Templeton. Is Micah around?"

"Yeah, he's in the office."

"May I?" He went to the end of the counter.

Tommen shrugged. "Sure."

Say one thing, he was probably as good a salesman as a fighter. Five-foot-eight and he walked like he was ten feet tall and could sell ice to a polar bear after beating it at arm wrestling. He strode through the bakery like he owned the place, knocking on the door but not waiting for an answer before stepping inside. Tommen followed meekly.

"Evening, Micah, Kayla," he greeted.

"Doug," Micah acknowledged. Kayla just nodded once, looking pissed.

"I know I'm early, but I wanted to make sure we're all on the same page. Has anything new come about?"

"Well, Tommen's message was intercepted."

"By whom?"

"Tommen."

Doug turned, seeming to just realize that he'd been there the whole time. "Oh. So you know what's going on?"

"Vaguely," Tommen answered.

"He's not going," Micah clarified. "We were trying to keep him out of this entirely, but apparently we weren't thorough enough. Either way, neither he nor his dad are going to be part of this."

"I agree," Doug said solemnly.

Tommen blinked and folded his arms. "No."

"What do you mean, no?"

"I'm tired of being excluded."

"It's for your own safety, Tommen."

"If I don't know what's going on—"

Micah cut him off. "Tommen, the last time you tried to help, Rifun and Cassius lured you to a secluded area where they could have killed you if Cai and I hadn't conveniently showed up. You're not going. That's final."

"Is there nothing I can do?"

"We already gave you something to do."

"Yeah, stay here as your last line of defense. Sounds like you're just trying to get rid of me."

"In a sense we are. Because you're not going."

"Enough!" Doug barked. Everyone fell silent. "Tommen, I can see that you're a good kid and ready and willing to help in any capacity. But that's not going to happen, not here, not this time. You're going to stay here and wait for our return."

"But—"

"That's final. I am the one in charge here, so you listen and report to me, got it?"

Tommen sighed and rolled his eyes. "Fine."

"Let me hear you say it."

"Yes, sir, I understand."

"Good."

"Can you at least tell me how Time Trials work? Am I going to be sitting here for five minutes or three hours?"

Doug frowned, but nodded. "I suppose that would be all right. In any case, it's good to have basic knowledge of how the Time

Trials work."

"How they're supposed to work," Micah said lowly.

"Be that as it may, it's the only information we have to go on."

Doug found a seat and plopped into it like he was the king sitting on his throne. "So, from Micaiah's point of view, he is right now sitting in a cell in the Judgment Wing. If I had to guess, he's probably in a black cell." He shrugged. "Just the way Cassius is, I guess.

"When the time comes, Micaiah will be escorted out of the cell, out of the Judgment Wing. He'll be taken to the Coliseum where—"

"That's another thing, Doug," Kayla said, picking up the tray where it had gotten placed on the desk. She handed it to him. "Cai did manage to get a message out to us."

"It says 'Wheel changed, Cassius is dead, I'm alive,' " Micah told him.

Doug sighed. "Fantastic. This just keeps getting better and better." He shook his head. "As I said, we have only the information we have."

"So Micaiah gets taken to the Coliseum, or whatever it is now..." Tommen prompted.

"Right. In times now past, all of the Hands would be presiding, as well as an indeterminate number of Grandfathers, guards, and, of course, the Bat and the Day."

"Wait, the Bat and the Day? Both of them?"

"It's the only time you'll see them together, but yes. This is no small event. Anyway, the Coliseum—or its new equivalent—will be divided. Micaiah will be taken to one side, where the Hands and the Grandfathers et al would be. Each Hand would ask him a question regarding the nature of his crime—keep in mind, we're still talking about the past. Who knows what Rifun has done to it now?

"When Micaiah answers the question, one of the Testimonies must corroborate the answer in some fashion. If none can, or if it proves to be false, both the Testimony and the Accused, Micaiah, is beaten by the guards."

"What kind of questions do they—would they ask?" Tommen wondered.

"Where were you when such a thing took place? Do you know this person? Are you capable of such an ability? Standard questions in any trial, I should think."

"But, how would someone know if he knows a person or has such an ability or whatever?"

"Now you see why the survival rate is so low," Kayla told him sadly.

"More than that, after every five or ten 'wrong' answers as it were, the Accused must face off against either the Bat or the Day, where they are permitted to beat him within an inch of his life."

Tommen shook his head. "So this is basically just feeding him to the lions, and the questioning is for sport."

"Yes," Micah said. "And aside from the Hands and Grandfathers, the entire Coliseum is full of spectators, all drawn to the bloodbath."

"Shit."

"Once all the Hands have questioned the Accused, they may retire to deliberate the case, or they may rule on the spot," Doug continued. "And there are several verdicts that could come back. First, they may release him completely. No muss, no fuss, and as always, the Hands' word is law and he's free to go. Second, they could have him executed on the spot, in which case one of the Grandfathers would go down and kill him there. Third, they might leave it as a toss-up."

"What, they flip a coin?"

"The center barrier is removed, so Accused, Stake, and Testimonies can get to each other, and then the five of them are set against the Bat and the Day. If the Accused wins, he's free to go. If he loses, well, he's dead anyway."

"How is he supposed to win?"

"Very carefully. Honestly, we're not really sure."

Tommen shook his head. "Fucking hell."

"It's a terrible and brutal thing."

"But, I mean, if you guys are successful and kill Rifun and stuff, you do have the power to change things, right? Kind of the whole, power vacuum after a revolution and stuff? You can get rid of a lot of this, right?"

"Probably not as much as you might think."

"Why not?"

"For one, we have to take into account that there are more races involved than just humans. You think it's bad in America's government, trying to appease everyone? Try multiplying that by a thousand. There is no way to make everyone happy, true, but you have to include as many as possible. I think it's safe to say that a majority of the species in the universe wouldn't be happy to live by human rules."

"Well fuck them. They're not the ones risking their lives to overthrow a regime they're too cowardly to confront."

"Actually, they are," Kayla informed him. "When this is all over, maybe you'll get to meet a few of them. Believe us, we're not doing this alone, just the five of us. We're only brave, not suicidal. At least we're not trying to be."

"This is just way too fucked up. I mean, the Time Trial is one thing, but now it's like, you've got some kind of rebel alliance going and then there's that fucking...I don't know, Akari thing going, or whatever the fuck you're calling it..." He shook his head. "This is way over my head."

"And that's another reason we won't be able to change as much as you think," Doug went on. "Rifun and Cassius operated under the guise of being Akari-bearers. Whether or not they actually believe that they are is not important when it comes to forming a new government."

"Why not? I mean, you guys are the good guys, trying to overthrow the tyrant."

"Think of it this way," Micah said. "If Muslim terrorists suddenly took control of the American government tomorrow, and in, say, a year, another faction of Muslims were to overthrow them, even if those Muslims were the 'good guys' and the terrorists were the 'bad guys,' do you think too many people are going to see the difference? No. They don't care who saved them, but there is no way that they want more Muslim government. Make sense?"

Tommen reluctantly agreed, shrugging. "Yeah."

"If Rifun is the terrorist operating under the guise of being an Akari-bearer, few are going to appreciate a new government being set up and run by more Akari-bearers."

"What is the Akari anyway?"

"A discussion for a later date, I'm sorry to say," Doug told him dismissively.

"Whatever. What will you guys be doing since I'm obviously not going?"

"That's right you're not," Micah said.

"With any luck," Doug cut in, casting Micah an annoyed look, "we won't be shot on the spot. Normally, we'd just go to the Coliseum and announce our intentions, but this time around, I think it's safe to say there could be a full armed escort involved."

"How are you going to get guns in there, then?" Tommen wondered.

"Disguise has many uses," Kayla told him. "It's not limited only to people and living things."

"Shit. Is there a way to tell if it's being used?"

"Another time," Doug said severely. "I'm sorry, Tommen, but we don't have time to get into all the details. Once we get back, then we can sit around and chit chat about it."

"Okay. What else are you guys going to do?"

"We'll be taken to the Coliseum—or its new equivalent—and set up in our half of the arena. Micah will be taken to his own special spot where he will sit."

"What's the point of the Stake?"

"It's kind of a double-or-nothing bid," Micah answered, "and a risky one at that. In normal Time Trials, the Accused could stop answering questions at any time and hand it over to his Stake, essentially turning the questioning into a combat tournament, the Stake versus the Bat and the Day. If the Stake won, everyone goes free. If the Stake loses, everyone dies."

Tommen raised a brow. "These Time Trials are sounding more and more fucked up by the minute."

"They are. And they are rigged to be almost impossible to win, instead used more for providing entertainment and sport. There is no fairness here, only strategy."

"We can only assume that Micaiah's trial is rigged to be completely unwinnable," Doug said. "Or else, it's rigged in such a way that even if he does 'win' that he still won't really win, or walk away unharmed at least."

Kayla and Micah murmured their agreement.

"And how exactly were you planning to kill Rifun?" Tommen folded his arms and shifted his stance, trying not to let on how nervous this was making him.

"Element of surprise," Kayla replied. "We smuggle the gun in using a Disguise. Stake and Testimonies are brought in first, then the Hands, Grandfathers, and the Accused. We have to expect that Rifun will be expecting some sort of assassination, escape, what-have-you, but maybe not so soon. As soon as Rifun enters the arena, as soon as Micah has a shot, he takes it."

"Sounds...risky."

"We only get one shot," Micah said. "After that, the jig is up, and we either make a hasty exit or else we're all dead. There is no middle ground."

"And it will likely only make it harder to get off any more attempts in the future," Doug went on. "Fool me once, shame on you, and it'll be hell trying to get in a second chance."

Tommen nodded. "I could see that happening. You know, becoming difficult."

"No matter what, though," Kayla said, "we're not leaving without Micaiah, or else we're going to die trying." She seemed to say it more to herself than anyone present.

"So, that's it?"

"Were you expecting more?" Doug wondered.

"I don't know, it's just..."

"Too straightforward for you? Were you expecting some stealthy spying, political intrigue, secret assassinations, and a quiet change of power? And maybe a few women in there, too?" When Tommen blushed, he went on. "Life isn't like the movies, Tommen, at least not all the time. Some things really are as simple as they sound."

Somewhere deep down, Tommen got the feeling that there was more going on than any of them were letting on, but they weren't going to tell him. It was frustrating, really, to be excluded. Why couldn't they just give him their secret little details, that way he knew what to expect?

At the beginning of Tommen's freshman year, his class had been visited by several soldiers from various branches of the Armed Forces. They weren't recruiters, but speakers who went around to high schools, talking about the Army, the Navy, the Marines, and so on, and about other options besides the traditional college path. It was recruiting, but without the paperwork.

At the end of each person's spiel, the students had the opportunity to ask questions. One student, Mark, his dad had been in the Army. His unit had been out on some mission and the shit hit the fan. He lived, but he was severely wounded and subsequently discharged. According to him, if he had known more about what they were supposed to be doing, had gotten more information, shit could have been avoided and he wouldn't have been wounded. Mark wanted to know what the speakers thought about that.

The response was nearly unanimous. Shit hits the fan. It's a fact of life. It's a fact of war especially. There are no guarantees. The first line of defense is always the standing orders. Before they left, they should have been given some kind of "oh shit" plan to try and follow, and they should have all understood that plan. Leaving the safety of the base was the unwritten acceptance of "I understand and agree to the terms of use." If they came under fire, they had to get out from under it, whether by killing the fuckers who were shooting at them, or by escaping. They wouldn't have time to think and stand around and debate what to do. Barring that, they were to fall back on their training, use their wit and skill to escape and survive, get a message out and get rescued.

Walter operated under similar circumstances. A routine call to a noisy neighbor could turn into a domestic assault in record time, and he couldn't have time to stand there and think about what to do, who's doing what, and so on. He either had to neutralize the threat, or find a way to get to safety so he could call for backup and then decide what to do. He had standing orders to follow, and he would follow them. If he didn't, well, then, he risked litigation and a lynching from the rabid media who was all too eager to kill a cop's reputation these days.

If Tommen was right, that was about how this was going to play out. He was given information about the mission as a whole, what they generally hoped to accomplish, and he had his job; he was given information only as it related to his job. He didn't need to know what Micah or Kayla or Doug were doing because he wouldn't be able to help them anyway during the trial. He only needed to know what to do if he saw friend or foe. If he saw friend, great. If he saw foe, kill the fucker. And if all else failed, fall back on his training to try and escape.

"So, does all this mean that you're going to lift the Suppression?" Tommen wondered.

As if being reminded that he needed to pick up a dozen eggs at the grocery store, Doug nodded and did just that. It was like taking blinders off, or maybe dark sunglasses. Problem was, he'd been wearing those sunglasses for almost six months, and now the Time sunlight was blinding. He felt a headache start somewhere in the back of his brain, and he tried not to let it show.

"You're a quick study," Micah told him. "Don't forget that you're more apt to pick up things under pressure. If you do something you didn't know you could do, don't let yourself get stunned by it; it could cost you. Simply accept it and move on. Your life is at stake."

Tommen nodded. "I understand."

Outside, the service bell dinged, and Tommen jumped. Fuck, he almost forgot he was still at work. And they were open until nine yet. He glanced at the clock as he left the office. Eight-twenty.

"Hi, what can I get for you?" Tommen asked, trying to sound amiable and not nervous as fuck.

Seriously, how could anyone expect him to just be a part of this and still work at the bakery, selling loaves of bread and muffins and dealing with difficult customers, like nothing was wrong? In less than an hour, the bakery could be unofficially up for sale, its owners mysteriously dead, or at least missing. More than that, Tommen himself could be the subject of another feeding frenzy at the precinct. If Kayla was going to the Coliseum as him, and they were found out, it wouldn't end well. He was supposed to be Rifun's bait, but if the fish didn't get the bait he wanted, was there any reason to expect that Rifun wouldn't come for him? Worse, would he come for Walter, too?

Tommen ripped off the credit card receipt from the machine and handed it to the customer, along with a pen. Ten seconds later, she was walking out the door and the bakery was empty again. He let out a breath.

If he wanted to be honest, it might not have been so daunting except for his dad. Tommen might be taken, but only under such circumstances as Micah and Micaiah were probably dead, so worrying about them would be less traumatic. But what about his dad? Rifun might spare him—because if he didn't, then Tommen would have no incentive to listen to anything he said—but that only created a hostage situation in and of itself, didn't it? If Walter wasn't in the picture, Tommen really wouldn't have anything left to give a fuck about.

He shook his head, mentally beating himself that he would ever entertain such a thought. There was no way in hell he was ever going to listen to Rifun. He might be taken alive and he might be held for a long time to try and break him, but he was not going to listen to the man who'd tried to kill him and his dad, and now was probably going to at least try and kill two of his friends.

Tommen sighed and rubbed his eyes, trying to quell the headache. This was too fucked up. Life was so much simpler when he didn't have Time interfering with everything. He'd finally gotten the hang of it, having no control. He'd figured out when he needed to get to bed, when he had to get up, how to manage his days so he could go to school, go to work, get his homework done, and still have time to date Becky, even if he hadn't figured out how to sleep with her without his dad finding out. Or her dad, for that matter, which was the bigger point.

Now Time had to come roaring back to life, like a bull in a China shop, crashing around, breaking everything, make a mess of everything. It had gone past party tricks now, and he was dealing with some real life-and-death situations. What happened to the days when he was just supposed to become an Apprentice, train in the Arena, and learn how to capture, arrest, and turn in Runners? Had those days just passed him by, or had Rifun messed that up, too? Why did all of this have to coincide and make his life difficult?

"It's not fair, I know."

He turned to see Kayla behind him. "What?"

"It's not fair to put all of this on your shoulders, even what little we are giving you. It's why we tried to keep you out of this completely, so you wouldn't have to bear the burden of another Time catastrophe or encounter with Rifun."

"I'll do it, I mean—"

"Being willing and being able are not the same thing. You're sixteen years old, you think you can do it all. Problem is, you're more likely to break than bend."

"I can do it."

"Maybe after all of this is settled, if we win, then we can set up a more forgiving system."

"What do you mean?"

"One that will let you leave Time without fearing for your

sanity. Maybe, in the case of probationaries and new Apprentices, a system that will let you keep what you already know without further obligation."

Tommen shifted his stance. "You think I want to leave."

She raised a brow. "Don't you? You've gone from street magician and party tricks to heart-stopping life-and-death situations, with virtually no advancement in your abilities. You've held your dying father in your arms with only a hope and a basic Time ability to save him. You've risked civil war, clock-breaking. You've survived a military coup and you have faced down Rifun more times than should be considered lucky. And you're telling me that after six months of being terror-free—more or less—you're really that eager to rush headlong into yet another deadly encounter?"

Tommen sighed. He had no answer. No good answer, anyway.

"If you could give up Time right now, would you?" Kayla asked.

"I don't know," he answered honestly. "I have a life, I have a job, I have a girlfriend. And I think I've had my fill of heart-stopping life-and-death situations. But at the same time, I mean, I've always wanted to be a Scout. I want to go and see what's out there, explore new worlds, to boldly go, you know? If I don't have Time, I can't do that. And then what am I? I'm just some poor kid from West fucking Virginia."

"Maybe. But you've also done things no one else could dream of, gone places and seen things as yet undiscovered by most fiction authors and movie producers. And if you gave up Time, settled down, started a family, you would be able to tell them of these things."

"Then my family would put me in some godforsaken asylum."

"Or you could entertain and inspire them, just like the writings in your notebook. If you keep it all to yourself, it will only tear you apart."

"So...are you telling me I should give up Time or that I shouldn't?"

"I won't tell you either way. I would like for you to stick with it, enhance your Time abilities so one day you might advance into the Akari. But I know that too much too soon is just as likely to drive you away."

"What is the Akari anyway? I just want a straight answer on that. Give me the dictionary definition."

"Unfortunately, I can't give you that, because it is so much more. It's like asking me to define the universe and give two examples. It's less of an object and more of an experience, a lifestyle. There's a difference between observing it and being part of it. Regrettably, we only have time today for the former."

Tommen shook his head. "Why can't things go back to the way they were before?"

"When was that, when you were getting you ass kicked every day by Tyler Freeman?" When he looked at her, she grinned. "Micaiah tells me more than you think. He can be a prickly hard ass sometimes, but he watches out for you."

"I'd hate to think what he would do if he didn't like me."

"Fortunately for you, you don't have to worry about that."

Tommen sighed and looked around. "Guess I should start closing up and hope it's not the last time I do. This is the only place I've ever worked; I don't want to have to go out and find a new job."

"Ah. Well, Micah said to tell you not to forget the trash. Just because he'll be gone for a while doesn't mean you can slack off."

"Yeah, sure. I'll get right on that. But I do have one question."

"What's that?"

"If there's one Stake and three Testimonies, then who's supposed to be impersonating my dad?"

Kayla glanced at the clock. "He should be arriving shortly. Just keep an eye out and let us know when he arrives."

He shrugged. "Whatever. Guess I'll just start closing up shop."

"It'll be okay, Tommen. Don't worry."

She headed back to the office. Oddly enough, Tommen found that he believed her. Everything was going to be all right. They weren't exactly professionals, but they were highly-trained and skilled for what they needed to do. They had a plan, understood the risks, and they were willing to risk all for the hopes of freedom. It was kind of romantic, really, like watching movies about World War II—not movies from World War II with the actual bloody footage, but the Hollywood renditions of those movies, where there is the clearly-defined hero, the clearly-defined plot, the clearly-defined beginning and end. Okay, so the analogy sounded better in his head.

Tommen put off locking the doors under the last second, still hoping it wasn't the last time he would be doing so. But lock them he did. When he turned around, however, he found a man standing at the front counter. He was about five-foot-eleven, brown hair, neatly-trimmed mustache and goatee, average weight, average build. Looking at him, he was about as average and under-the-radar as any man could possibly be, really. Even his clothes were plain, standard business casual, wallet in the back pocket, phone holder on the plain fake leather belt.

"Are you the one they're waiting for?" Tommen asked.

"I expect so," the man said. "Micah, Doug, and Kayla?"

"In the office."

Tommen took the man to the office where the trio was waiting. If he was any judge of body language, Tommen might have said they were nervously praying. They looked up as the door opened and the man walked in.

"Junior, we were starting to get worried," Doug said.

"I wouldn't have been late," was all the man said to that.

"Tommen, this is Mike Junior," Kayla introduced. "He'll be impersonating your dad during the trial."

As if on cue, Junior donned a Disguise, and Tommen could have sworn up and down that his dad was standing right there in the office. It wasn't a costume or like a kid wearing a fake mustache and big shoes. It was, for all intents and purposes, his dad. But it wasn't his dad.

"Pleasure to meet you, Tommen," Junior-as-Walter said, in Walter's voice even.

"I'm not going to lie, that freaks me the fuck out. Is there any way to tell the difference?" Tommen asked.

"Mannerisms, mostly," Kayla answered. "There are a few other ways to tell, but we can't go over them at this moment."

"Should have been here earlier," Micah told Junior. "Could have gone over the plan one more time."

Junior dropped the Disguise. "Yeah? You're one to talk. Little Johnny-Come-Lately over here." He shook his head. "Still don't get why your brother didn't bring you in on this sooner."

Before Micah could come back with a sharp reply, Kayla stepped in. "It doesn't matter now. You volunteered to help us, Junior, so you can at least take this seriously—"

"I do," Junior protested.

"—and when we get Micaiah back, you can ask him why he chose to withhold information from Micah. Until then, we have a job to do."

The man sighed dramatically. "What time is the trial?"

"Nine-eleven," Doug answered. "I'd be willing to bet he chose that time for a reason."

"Well, be that as it may, is there a bathroom around here I can use beforehand? Nothing worse than running into pants-pissing terror and actually pissing your pants."

Micah gave him brief directions and saw Junior out the door with a glare to his back. "Maybe take the stick out of his ass, too, while he's at it."

"What's his problem?" Tommen wondered.

"He's always been a dick," Kayla replied. "But he's been even more of a dick since he was diagnosed with terminal cancer."

"Oh. Shit."

"Yeah."

"He can't, like, Band and—"

"Time is not medicine," Micah reminded him. "It won't cure him. Actually, it's more likely to speed his death."

"So, he's not going because he actually cares about Micaiah."

"He's going because he has nothing to lose," Doug told him. "Combine that with being a damn good fighter anyway, and he really is the ideal pick for this team."

"Sounds like you're going there just to sacrifice him."

"We try to follow your dad's example. Everyone goes home. Not everyone does, though. If anyone is going to volunteer for such a mission, it's going to be—"

"Death ground."

"Exactly."

It sounded cruel, but if Junior had nothing to lose but his life which was fast ending anyway, he would be exactly the guy they needed to be willing to run into a deadly situation. Didn't mean he had to be a dick about it, but Tommen figured he could understand where he was coming from.

Junior returned at nine-ten, receiving hostile and annoyed stares as he entered the office.

"I wouldn't have been late," was all he said.

The only reason Tommen knew that someone put up a Band just then was that he'd been watching the second hand on the clock and suddenly it stopped moving. This was not a Time Band, he knew, where its presence was obvious. This had to be an Akari Band, or whatever they claimed as the Akari. Tommen was still skeptical.

"Does anyone have any final questions?" Doug asked. "Once we don our Disguises and step through the portal into the Wheel, that's it. No more talk, no more questions."

He waited about thirty seconds, then nodded solemnly. "Then may the Author write us each a happy ending."

May the Author write us each a happy ending? Was that supposed to be some lame *Star Wars* ripoff or what? What kind of kooky Time religion cult thing was this? Tommen shook his head. This was all way beyond him. Maybe it was better that he wasn't going. Maybe he really should just sit this one out.

# Chapter Twenty-Four
## Escort

Donning a Disguise was kind of like getting into a full-body Halloween costume only to realize that the costume was actually a huge bear giving you a hug from behind. Then that bear turned into a parasitic alien that put tendrils all over into your body, so it turned into more like some sort of invisible, mechanical suit. Supposedly, the greater the change, and the more Disguises held at once, the worse it felt as the body tried to reconcile the body's normal DNA with all the "surface" changes as it were, changing the appearance and tricking the eye of outsiders, without actually changing the person. There were more technical and scientific terms to explain it, Micah was sure, but that was just a layman's observation.

He was thankful he wasn't required to wear a Disguise this time around, and he held no envy for those who did. Kayla having to masquerade as Tommen could not have been fun. He was taller, thinner, and had different parts which her body had to reconcile against her female frame. It was all an illusion, sure, but probably one of the more painful tricks in the book.

Junior had less trouble turning into Walter, though Micah was still questioning his acting skills. Would he be able to muster enough fear of the dark to pass Rifun's scrutiny? Even if Rifun himself didn't meet them until the Time Trial, Micah had little doubt that he would have spies everywhere, whether in some armed guard force, someone sneaking around in the shadows, or some form of mechanical fly camera. He would be keeping a careful eye on his prize.

Once all Disguises were donned and broken in a little—moving around, stretching, feeling—Doug stood. He handed

487

Micah a small pocketknife, no doubt the gun in Disguise.

"Here we go."

Micah was still inexperienced with opening Akari portals. Looking back, he realized that Micaiah had actually been teaching him quite a few things using the Akari, but without calling them such. They were simply "different techniques" or "something he learned from another Lieutenant who was training to be a Captain" or some such thing. As far as portals went, Micaiah had taught him enough that when it was needed, like escaping the Wheel during the coup, he was able, albeit just. But for the true concentrated effort, he was a bit of a drag on the rest of the team as they worked together to open a stable portal to the Wheel.

Really, it was him, Doug, and a little bit of Kayla-as-Tommen opening the portal. Time or Akari, it was still possible to identify who was doing what, and the last thing they needed was for Rifun to think that Walter was also an Akari-bearer. Or, worse, have him think that something was up and blow their plan before they even had a chance to fail at it themselves.

Micah wasn't really pessimistic about their plan—no more than he considered reasonable anyway—but he was nervous as all get out. For one, he was going to see his brother again. For two, it might be the last time they saw each other. Well, better than be separated forever and never knowing what happened to the other, though the way Cai had been talking lately, it sounded like he was ready for a new life, one that didn't involve seeing his brother for sixteen hours a day every day. Even so, that was better than being imprisoned by a madman, waiting to be fed to the lions just for sport.

It took some doing, but they got the portal open and stable enough to walk through. Micah was still nervous was they passed through, hoping it wouldn't destabilize, snap shut, and kill them all, and also hoping that Rifun wouldn't tear it apart and kill them all, or else send them to the Land In Between from which no one had ever returned. At this point, literally anything could happen.

But they made it to the Wheel unmolested and no worse for

wear, though Micah did trip over his own feet and went sprawling on the ground. Kayla-as-Tommen laughed even as Junior-as-Walter and Doug helped him to his feet.

"Are you all right?" Junior-as-Walter asked, and for a second, he sounded just like Walter. So maybe his acting skills weren't too bad.

"Fine," Micah answered. "I think." He winced as he put weight on his right knee. "A little tender."

Doug let out a breath. "We don't need this right now."

"I'm sorry. What do you want me to do about it?"

"At this point, there's nothing we can do about it. We just have to wait and see what happens."

"Well, other than the post-apocalyptic vibes I'm getting, this place doesn't seem like it's changed much," Kayla-as-Tommen observed. God, she was good.

And, really, she did have a point. They stood in the same portal room they'd transported to a thousand times in the past. Granted, parking seemed to be a little better nowadays, but the huge platform was still big enough for a thousand thousand portals and more to be opened at any given moment. The walls beyond, though now dim and almost invisible, were still struggling to operate, lights winking out, an occasional spark flashing here and there. The translator dispenser was still set in the wall, the symbols above telling all creatures in the universe what that hole in the wall did. Micah wondered if it would still operate, then decided it didn't matter.

The door-portal to the rest of the Wheel had been reconstructed, though not to the size it had once been. Before, it had been about like walking through an enormous garage door where a double-decker semi could get through; now it appeared to be just man-sized, maybe a little bigger. Maybe more like one lane of any given street.

"Well, we're still alive," Doug said, looking around cautiously. "I'd say that's a good sign so far."

They were alive, yes, and they were also alone. No guards had rushed into the room; no Trackers had descended upon them.

"If no one is here to meet us, I guess we better start walking," Micah decided. "Either way, we can't be late for the trial."

The group of four only got about six steps into the trek when they heard Rifun's voice, and a moment later he appeared, a dozen armed guards in tow.

"Sorry we're late," Rifun said, entirely unapologetic. "Got a little caught up in the construction and rebuilding and whatnot. Moving things around, it tends to get confusing. You understand, right? It's a bit like moving into a new house, or even just remodeling. Wouldn't you agree, Walter?"

"I suppose," Junior-as-Walter answered cautiously, but, more important, perfectly. He said what Micah might have expected Walter to say and just how he would say it.

"I have to admit, I'm a little surprised you showed up. After all, Akari-bearers aren't typically of the 'greater good' mindset. Micaiah came here to turn himself in and he offers me exactly what he knows I would want. But did he tell you that?"

"He's gambling the world," Doug said. Thankfully, he was playing himself because no one could quite match his Mr. All-That attitude.

"He's gambling your lives. To save the world. It sounds noble and yet, I am forced to wonder if there is some ulterior motive. What's really going on in that collective head of yours? One Akari-bearer in custody, one whom I have pursued for decades, one who has only recently discovered his potential, one who has yet to believe, and one who still thinks it's a myth. Quite an entourage. Of course, I might expect some sort of failed assassination attempt or coup, but this is hardly the force I expected to deliver the blow."

"Akari-bearers aren't exactly the violent type either," Doug told him. "You must have missed that day of class."

"Ah, such wit. I love it. And I'm sure I will also love whatever little plan you have for this trial later on. As you might expect, we don't get a lot of excitement around here these days. With that said, let's continue, shall we? Things to do, people to kill, planets to conquer."

As Rifun turned away, one of the guards said something. Rifun paused and looked back at the group, raising a brow. "Check them for weapons? What for? Even if they do have a small arsenal hidden under their shirts, they'll never get very far. Or are you saying that your entire force is unable to handle five meager humans? Of course, look what happened the last time. Shall I call in a few more hands so we can get them safely to the Time Trial?"

The guard grunted and said something more, which Micah took to be a "No, sir."

"That's what I thought," Rifun said coldly. "Bring them."

Somehow, Micah got the feeling that there would be discipline later for that guard. Actually, he found himself pitying the poor guard, too. He wasn't about to jump in and take a bullet for him—or it—or anything, but worse than living under Rifun was working for him. Did the guards around here ever question their choice as to which side they chose when they signed up for this gig?

His musings were interrupted as they stepped through the door-portal into the rest of the Wheel. The first couple rooms were of a similar appearance: dark, empty, kind of spooky. Once they got to the old marketplace hub, however—or what Micah thought was the old marketplace hub—things changed drastically.

"Holy shit," Kayla-as-Tommen said, echoing all their thoughts.

It was like they got transported back to ye olde England via kaleidoscope. Old shops and homes with Bavarian-inspired architecture lined cobblestone streets, portals open here and there in clustered neighborhoods, old English signs depicting the various marketplaces. Even the lighting had been changed to make it seem like a nice day, partly cloudy with a brisk breeze to awaken the senses. It was wonderful and yet unnerving. The biggest kick in the reality was the aliens meandering through these markets, secretaries and laborers working to make everything just so.

"If I would have known, I would have hired you to remodel

my house," Junior-as-Walter commented dryly.

"Ah, but redecoration is good for the soul," Rifun told him. "It provides a sense of peace and tranquility, once you're all finished that is. In the process, there is much anxiety and plenty of cursing to go around, regardless if you are remodeling a simple home or an entire dimension."

"Only Builders can look at the Core of the Wheel and live," Doug said. "How did you learn?"

"I was an architect once, you know. I loved seeing a project come together, seeing dreams realized. But my favorite part was taking bits and pieces of different architecture styles from all over the world, bringing them together into something unique and memorable."

"What does that have to do with—?"

"Why start from scratch? Find what you like, steal it, then file off the serial number, change the color from red to blue, and there you have it. Someone else did the dirty work and you profit from their labor."

So it wasn't really a Build, Micah figured. Building would mean that he had basically scrapped the entire dimension and had to start from scratch, building the new rooms, assigning and relaying spatial and temporal coordinates to both stabilize the rooms as well as connect them through portals. But then...

"If this isn't a Build," Micah began, trying to figure how to word it, "then how did you get all of this here? How did you turn all of that into all of this?"

Rifun chuckled darkly. "If only you had opened up Richard's journal when you had the chance."

"It was gibberish."

"I'm not talking about simply turning pages, I'm talking about Imprinting text and so much more, making the journal come alive to those who hold the key."

"And what did you unlock with this key?" Doug asked.

"A chest filled with treasure, but also more keys to more

chests. The key to unlocking the Akari itself."

*Isolation hasn't been good to him,* Micah thought. As he cast glances around the group, he could see the others thought it, too. Either he rubbed off on Cassius or Cassius rubbed off on him, but either way, now that Cassius was gone, there was no one left to keep Rifun sane. He no longer needed to plot and scheme, and he no longer had to compete with anyone for the absolute power he now possessed. With all the constraints and parameters and restrictions thrown off, he was free to do as he pleased and he'd gone insane. More insane, anyway.

"You do know how crazy you sound, right?" Kayla-as-Tommen wondered. "Like, seriously, you sound kind of like some kind of nutty, prophetic hermit or something."

Rifun glanced back. "Always quick with the tongue, aren't you? And always so blind to the consequences of your words and actions." Kayla-as-Tommen halted and got in a wary fighting stance, but Rifun simply laughed and kept going. "You thought I was crazy when I first told you about the Akari. But now you see that it is real and has real power. Why do you continue to doubt me?"

"It's not the Akari we doubt," Doug said smartly.

"My sanity, then? 'Oh, goodness, Rifun, locked up for so long in the Wheel, his mind has finally gone.' Is that what you think? But tell me this, then. Which do you fear more? An insane man with unlimited power, or a sane man with that same unlimited power?"

*Worse,* Micah mused silently. *I fear an insane man who thinks he's sane and has that unlimited power.*

The lower marketplaces were similar to the marketplace hub, cobblestone streets and ye olde English architecture, but there had been fewer buildings and more market booths, all of them reminisce of a Shakespearean play, waiting in eager anticipation for the Merchants to return. They left those behind and entered into the intermediate marketplaces, another drastic change.

"Did you never consider becoming an architect or a landscaper?" Micah wondered aloud.

"Your brother asked me the same thing," Rifun replied. "I was an architect once. I designed buildings that were more reminisce of temples to the gods; men looked upon them and wept."

*So what happened?*

The intermediate marketplaces were certainly comparable to such things, Micah thought as they passed through gardens of such grace and beauty, he wouldn't have been surprised if they just happened upon Buckingham Palace or some such place. Hedges both square and sculpted, flowers of all varieties from a hundred hundred worlds, water features running from ceiling to floor and around every wall, huge boulders of natural shape or carved with reliefs or into statues, all of it accompanied by the same feeling of a sunny day, like all was right with the world. Here, the Merchants' booths were a little more sophisticated, built of wood and stone, polished and primed, ready to display modest wares from lands far, far away.

"If this is the intermediate marketplace, what's the auctionhouse look like?" Junior-as-Walter murmured.

"Would you like to see it?" Rifun asked, sounding like a child, eager to show off his painting from art class that day.

In all reality, it was difficult trying to pin down Rifun's true motivations. Not that Micah would have pitied him at this point, considering the crimes he'd committed against the universe, but there should have been some reasoning behind it, even a bad one. Hitler blamed the Jews. It wasn't a good reason, or even a substantiated one, but it was a reason. Micah certainly believed that some people were truly, genuinely evil for evil's own sake, but he wanted to exhaust every other explanation before jumping to something that serious.

They did not have to go far to leave the intermediate marketplaces for the auction hub, and it was exactly as Micah thought it would be: like they'd just waltzed right into Buckingham Palace. It wasn't actually Buckingham Palace, but someplace that made Buckingham Palace look like some peasant's house. It almost seemed like reverse alchemy, as if gold would turn into lead were it brought into such a place.

It took a moment for Micah's eyes to adjust and be able to comprehend that they were indeed standing on water. On closer inspection, they were standing on some sort of glass or other plane so clear, it was as if it disappeared. The walls were of a dark, well-oiled wood, with a grain pattern that made it look like water was continuously falling down its face. Or, maybe water really was falling down its face. An enormous set of stairs opening up in front of them, made of polished stone that looked as though it had been cut from a single block. The same dark wood plated the steps and formed the banister. A woven runner tumbled down the center of the stairs, red with a golden border, brown trim, and some wildly complex pattern down its center. Around the room, various portals were open to the many auctions yet to be had.

"Holy shit," Kayla-as-Tommen said again. "Someone's got too much time on their hands."

"Building is only part of my to-do list," Rifun explained. "It helps me relax after a long day of looking after the rest of my affairs."

"Yeah? And what are those? Butchering children and destroying entire planets?" Junior-are-Walter growled.

"When you are cleaning your house, do you mourn for every ant, spider, cockroach, and fly you kill? Isn't their eradication necessary to actually cleaning your house?"

"Is that all we are to you? Ants?"

"Everyone in the universe would like to believe themselves special, that somehow they will be the ones to make a difference. Somehow they will be the ones remembered. Battle is naturally bloody, coups no different. And there are plenty of pawns to go around. Those who survive may be useful, and use them I have. Others have been executed. It is the nature of war. And history is written by the victors."

"You are not the victor, not unless the Author says so. And what fate awaits you if you are not the victor the Author intended?"

Micah could see instantly that Rifun was not happy with Doug's answer. His stance changed and his gaze turned murderous.

For a moment, Micah was afraid he would order his guards to murder him right then and there, Time Trial be damned. Kayla-as-Tommen looked back and forth between the two, looking like he wanted to run but not daring to move. Junior-as-Walter kept one eye on the two of them and one eye on the guards surrounding them. The guards had sensed something was up, and they were moving into battle-ready position. This could get real ugly, real fast. And they hadn't even made it to the trial yet. *Good going, Doug. Lecture us about blowing cover and you might have done just that yourself.*

After a minute or two of crackling tension, Rifun relaxed. He backed down from his threatening pose, but kept his gaze firmly locked on Doug. "If your body and your abilities are as strong as your convictions and as quick as your tongue, you may have a shot at surviving the trial to come."

That was that, and they made for the door, moving purposefully. The tour was apparently over, now they were going to get down to business. Micah let out the breath he hadn't realized he'd been holding and hurried to keep up, minding his knee.

"You all right?" Junior-as-Walter inquired.

"Fine," Micah said shortly. He looked at Doug. "What was that? You could have gotten us killed before we even got started."

Before Doug could answer, Rifun beat him to it. "Fear not, young Durvin. You were never in any danger. Yes, I considered ordering him beaten or some such thing, but then I decided that watching you struggle in vain in the Time Trial would be far more rewarding. And who knows, maybe I will be pleasantly surprised if you do manage to win and pull this off today. Things get boring quickly when they always go your way."

Micah couldn't decide if his words were forlorn personal observations, or a threat. Maybe Rifun was expecting something to happen and he was warning them not to get too comfortable in their plans. Micah felt the hair on the back of his neck prickle with fear and anticipation.

It didn't take long for them to get out of the marketplaces and into what seemed to be a town square. They'd regressed from the palace back to regular ye olde English town, thrown in a kaleidoscope blender and spit out to match the mind-fuckery of the Wheel. Micah saw portals scattered here and there, all with signs. One marked the Archives, another the Judgment Wing, and so on. But there was one sign he didn't recognize, and that was the one that was open, morbidly, in the gallows. The symbols were actually etched into the wooden frame, and if Micah read right, they were the ones for Judgment, Grandfathers, War or Battle, and Death.

"The Hands really were greedy sons of bitches," Rifun said. "They always had to have all the fun. And by fun, I mean they micromanaged the shit out of everything, and left the Grandfathers to, what, break a few clocks? In my new system of organization, it is the Grandfathers who govern and oversee the Time Trials, and they have their own special arena in which to conduct them. I call it simply the Executioner's Block, or the Pit."

Micah took an even breath. This could get real ugly, real fast. He did not have time to hesitate or reconsider before they moved through the portal into the Pit.

It was, true to form, a pit. Where everything else in the Wheel's Rebuild had thus far been one of old architecture and extravagant beauty, this was where all the emptiness, anger, and hate ended up. It was like a coal mine had been hit with a nuclear bomb, then roughly carved out to look like some ancient gladiator pit, or maybe a dog fighting arena. There was seating all the way around with a significant drop into the arena itself, much like the old Coliseum, but this time coming in from above rather than coming up from below. It was meant to be a bowl, a descent into Hell itself.

The path they took ran around the top outer edge, so seats were accessible from anywhere, but there was a secondary path that took a sudden drop down, and they followed a winding, poorly-carved spiral staircase down, down, into the suffocating blackness of an old coal mine.

"You okay?" Kayla-as-Tommen asked when he tripped over

something in the darkness and pitched forward.

"Yeah, yeah, I'm fine," Micah said, glad the darkness hid his embarrassment.

They reached the bottom of the stairs and found themselves in a larger cavern with a long tunnel stretching out from one wall, likely leading into the pit. A single torch lit the cavern as the light from the arena was dim at best. Almost as expected and yet still surprising, the Bat was there to meet them.

"The Bat?" Junior-as-Walter wondered anxiously.

"Of course," Rifun said, matter-of-fact. "Who else would I trust with such a job?"

"I didn't think you trusted anyone," Doug said.

Rifun's expression said that Doug was walking a fine line with his patience. Still, he spoke, saying, "And I never thought you capable of loving anyone but yourself. But I digress."

That got Doug a little flustered, and Rifun moved on.

"So, this is how things are going to work from now until the trial actually begins. You will be taken to your own special holding cells to wait. Someone will be by to properly process you. I'm still working out the finer details of all the paperwork involved, so you will have to be patient. It is highly advisable that you answer all questions thoroughly and honestly.

"When everything is in place, you will be escorted from your holding cells to the appropriate place in the Pit. There will be the introductions, formalities, all that fun stuff that we all love to hate. I've thought about keeping it for nostalgia purposes, but I might scrap it after today. We'll see how things go. Then, after the formalities, we'll discuss how the trial is to proceed." Rifun gave Micah a look. "I don't know how much your brother told you about how Time Trials work, but just know that it will do you no good now."

That was not a comforting thought. That was not a comforting thought at all. Micah felt sweat snake down his back and under his arms where the gun-as-pocketknife pressed against him in his belly band holster. It had been the only place where he could get to it quickly without it looking obvious to the casual observer. Hey, he was a guy, got an itch and he's going to scratch it. And also pull out a .45 ready to shoot the tyrant responsible for them being there in the first place.

What was even less helpful, however, was the fact that the Pit seemed to use the same technology as the Judgment Wing, where the force fields required special stamped access, either a one-way or a two-way stamp to get through. No surprise, they were all given the one-way stamp. Micah glanced nervously at Doug. He could see the gears turning the Doug's mind as he struggled to reformulate a plan where they wouldn't get all the way to the end and die because of a fucking force field.

They hadn't anticipated this. This was all way too different. A few minor changes, some decorative repairs, that was one thing. This was a whole new ballgame. What if they were forced to go along with the straight Time Trial, no evil schemes or anything? Did they have the power and resources to be able to defeat the Bat and whatever other obstacles Rifun decided to throw their way? Micah could feel his blood pressure rising. This was not good. This was very not good. They had to come up with something and fast.

Hands stamped, the Bat opened the first gate, the same way he had for the last however many centuries he'd been working as the veritable Gatekeeper for the Hands. Rifun left the group then, and the guards escorted the four of them down the tunnel and into the Pit.

It looked very much like the Coliseum and the Seat of the Hands—or the old Seat; who knew what it looked like now?—but with a doomsday, mysterious ancient civilization, post-apocalyptic feel to it. Pompeii came to mind, actually. Everything looked like it might have been active and lively at one point, but now it was just...dead. Covered in ash and dead to the universe, Time wreaking havoc on it.

The biggest difference between the old Seat and the Pit was that the Pit had cells with wrought-iron gates barring each one. It wasn't difficult to imagine that, on Earth, there might have been lions or bears kept in them, just waiting for the gate to open so they could go charging out to kill and eat whatever man-prey had been sent into their domain.

Micah was separated from the others, then, taken to his own cell. He figured he was about at the halfway point, fitting for the Stake who might have to go either to one side or the other, in a normal Time Trial that is. The others were taken to a cell on the other side of the Pit, about two cells down.

He was left there. There wasn't even a stone bench to sit on, not even a rock. Gradually, he made his way to the floor, stretching out his leg and inspecting his knee. It didn't really hurt when he pushed and poked, only when he put weight on it, and even then it wasn't bad. Walking around the Wheel had aggravated it, but if he had to guess, it wasn't anything an ice pack and a couple days of light work wouldn't help to remedy. That was assuming he even made it home in order to procure an ice pack.

Fuck, this was actually happening. There was no way out of this except to win. He was going to have to—

He jumped as the gate opened. It took him a second to realize that it was a secretary who'd entered. Not a guard, not a Grandfather, but a secretary. Micah had always been a little suspicious of them, but there had been no more welcome sight since coming here. This one was almost humanoid, except for the four legs with more flippers than feet, amphibious skin, spindly arms with three webbed fingers, and a face that reminded Micah of an elephant seal he'd seen at a zoo one time.

It handed him a translator which he put on and set up.

"I am here to process you," the secretary said. "Stand, please."

The secretaries had never been the most lively bunch. They generally worked with about as much enthusiasm as the work crews from jail that went out to dig ditches and do other menial labor. It was usually best to not engage in conversation and just let them do their mundane jobs. This secretary, however, was past even that level of boredom. Micah was no expert of whatever alien species it was, but he was willing to put money that the emotion being conveyed here was misery. This secretary wasn't doing its job because it was a job and it had to do its job, but because it was living under threat that if it didn't do its job, punishment would ensue. Death, clock breaking, familial hostage situation, who knew? It was modern, intergalactic slavery; something was keeping this secretary here, and it wasn't the perks and benefits. Was there a way to exploit that misery? Micah briefly debated the ethics of such exploitation.

"What is your name?" the secretary asked, opening its little information-gathering device.

"Micah Durvin."

"Origin?"

So Micah gave the secretary the coordinates for Earth, his species, his Time rank, a brief history of his Time training, his Akari rank, a brief history of that training, and a small book full of other information he wasn't sure was relevant in any way to the situation at hand, or any situation which might arise in the Wheel or Time. Maybe it was just busywork. Maybe Rifun was seeing what kind of fun he could have, what kind of information he could get from them.

Then the secretary did something he didn't expect, or at least didn't expect until the trial was supposed to be over.

"I require a flesh sample in order to obtain your DNA for review."

Alarm bells went off in Micah's head. *Red alert! Red alert! Abort! Abort! Abort! This is not good! This cannot end well! Run! Go! Hide! Flee!*

But there was nowhere to run. He couldn't leave the Pit if he wanted to. If the guards or the Bat didn't kill him, the force field surely would. Ultimately, he had no choice but to offer out his hand so the secretary could take a small flesh sample, like a diabetic pricking his finger for the meter.

He might have hoped for a little mercy, in that the secretary would have to take the sample elsewhere to have it verified, but the little information-taking doodad seemed to have a built in separator and analyzer. Through the screen, Micah could see the flesh and blood being stripped down to the cellular level, then even more as it dug for pure DNA. When it found a strand it liked, he watched as it streamed quickly over the screen, all the bonds and other scientific terms he couldn't remember.

In a way, it was fascinating, to see all the little itty bits that made him who he was, what he looked like, and then to think that he shared that with one other person in the universe, his twin brother.

Unfortunately, the machine seemed to realize this as some sort of error message came up.

"It says your DNA is already in the system," the secretary said. "Under a different name."

"I'm a twin," Micah explained. "My twin brother is the one on trial today."

The secretary made a motion. "I understand. I will make the necessary corrections. There is one more question I must ask."

Micah sighed. "What's that?"

"In the event of your death, are there any special instructions you would like me to convey?"

Translation: Do you have any last will and testament? Do you have any last words? Would you like to be buried, cremated, or possibly eaten?

"No," Micah decided finally. "I don't have any special instructions. If I die, then my brother is dead, too. And the dead don't care."

"Of course. Thank you for your patience."

The words were spoken more of formality than gratitude, and in the same melancholy tone that, were the secretary human, might have told Micah that he — or she — was going to go home, crawl into bed, and commit suicide. It was not a friendly thing, not something he wanted to dwell on. Was the situation here really that awful?

Micah considered everything he'd seen thus far. Rifun had killed Cassius which meant he had total control. He treated the guards like shit, and he was probably going to have words with the one guard who'd questioned him. There was no reason to think he held any special regard for the secretaries. What hell did he put them through just to make sure the Wheel kept turning?

What was worse, how many of the guards and secretaries in his employ had been eager volunteers to start with? How many of them had been duped into thinking that everything was going to get better? Furthermore, how many of them had been pressed into this slavery, told they would live but only if they served? Shit, they would have been trapped here with the rest of them for the last six months. Did any of them have homes?

Micah shook his head. He couldn't get sentimental about it now. He had a home, and there was every chance that he might not go back to it tonight. He had to stay focused. He had to take this time and figure out a way to work around all the setbacks so far. There was the force field, the Bat, the guards, the new layout of the Wheel... Really, the only difficult obstacle was the force field. If he could get past that, the rest was fluff. If he was more practiced in opening up an Akari portal, even that would be less of a problem, but he didn't have the skill for that yet, not on his own.

He went to the gate and looked across the Pit to the cell where the others were being kept. They were in so much trouble with the DNA being taken before the trial. Kayla and Junior would be found out right off the bat. What would Rifun do to them? Kill them? Break their clocks? Would he hold them hostage until Tommen and Walter could be summoned? Would he simply substitute them in the trial? Micah found the last one a little hard to believe. Bringing Tommen had been their best bait; Rifun wasn't one to settle for second-best. Not now.

Micah made laps of his cell, telling himself that it was thoughtful, constructive, active planning and not worried pacing that was only making his knee hurt more. Problem was, he was only lying to himself. After a few more laps of empty-headed thoughtlessness, he forced himself to sit and stretch his leg.

This was all going downhill, and that hill was like an avalanche over ice. He went back to the gate, just waiting for the guards to go rushing in and drag Kayla and Junior out of the cell, if not kill them outright. Micah could hear the blood pounding through his ears. His shirt stuck to his back and sides from the sweat. If not for the Disguise, the belly band and gun-as-pocketknife would be completely visible.

What would they do to him when they found out Tommen and Walter were not Tommen and Walter? Likely, they would assume that it had all been a collaborative effort, which it had been. Could they plead out, say they had no idea? Would that work? Or would it only make the punishment hurt more?

To his utter amazement, nothing appeared to happen. The secretaries went in, did their interviews, took their DNA samples, and left. No alarm was raised. No one screamed in pain as they died. It all went exactly according to plan. Micah took a few steps back, hoping the shadows would hide his nervousness and confusion.

Disguises only tricked the eye. It wasn't so much an absolute manipulation of DNA, like what creepy scientists did in a lab to goats and cows and most of the world's food supply, but more of a..."tickling" of the DNA, as one Akari-bearer had once put it. It was certainly possible to get down into the nitty-gritty of such things and truly manipulate one's DNA, but that involved time and effort and patience, as well as a general education in advanced genetics. A Disguise was a quick and dirty, temporary way of doing basically the exact same thing, but only based on set parameters, that is, impersonating someone versus just manipulating certain aspects. There was more to it than that, a far more detailed explanation, but the point was, the DNA that showed up on the secretaries' little devices would not have been Tommen and Walter, but Kayla and Junior.

So why not raise the alarm? Micah batted around several possible explanations. First, the secretaries simply hadn't gotten a DNA sample. Maybe the Testimonies just weren't as important as the Accused and the Stake, or maybe they didn't have time. Somehow, he found the likelihood of that a bit on the low side. Second, the secretaries did get the DNA sample, but it really had shown up as Tommen and Walter. Maybe Doug had been able to manipulate the devices themselves, change the readings. Micah still wasn't clear on the visibility of using the Akari, but as far as he knew, Rifun would be able to, but the secretaries wouldn't. Doug could have done anything and they wouldn't have known. The plausibility of that was only as high as Micah was correct in his assumptions, but he still wasn't well-versed in the Akari, even after five months.

Of course, he might have entertained a third thought if he thought it likely. Maybe the secretaries had taken the sample and gotten the mismatched results, but they also knew that Kayla and Junior were powerful foes against Rifun. The secretaries weren't exactly living it up under Rifun, wanted him gone, so they chose not to say anything. Maybe the secretaries were their invisible ally, a link to the outside universe if they needed one. Not that it would do them much good now, except maybe to get rid of these one-way hand stamps?

*Damn you, Cai, why couldn't you have told me about all this sooner?* Micah thought, finding a modestly comfortable position in which to sit, massaging his knee and hoping it would feel better in time for the trial. As Lieutenants in Time, they could combine their abilities, double their strength with half the effort, a nearly unstoppable force — for Lieutenants, that is. But now, when it came to the Akari and when it mattered most, Micaiah was all but incapacitated and Micah was left dangling over the edge, about as useless as Tommen had been to the original murder case.

He couldn't have been sitting for more than five minutes before he stood again and went to the gate, looking out across the Pit toward the cell where the others milled about. As far as he could tell, the three of them were still in there, Doug, Kayla-as-Tommen, and Junior-as-Walter. None of them appeared to be limping or coddling wounded areas. Doug spotted him looking, but if he made any kind of significant motion, gesture, or said anything, it was lost to Micah. Did he dare yell out to him, see if they could commune? Or would that only invite a beating of some form?

Micah returned to where he'd been sitting and resolved to stay sitting until the trial actually started. Better to just stay put and not cause trouble, at least not yet. Of course, the longer he sat there, the more he thought that Junior had had the right of it, going to the bathroom before they left.

# Chapter Twenty-Five
## Release from Darkness the Prisoner

There were days when Micaiah wished he would have taken up an instrument. To take all the hours of dedicated practice, trial and error, attempted improvising, and turning that into something as beautiful as music, it seemed a venture worth investing in.

The harmonica, for instance. Now there was something he could get into right about now. It wasn't loud, wasn't particularly disruptive, and it would keep him entertained while he sat in the darkness, waiting to be taken to trial. He might have asked for his mp3 player, but figured Rifun would deny him that request. For one, it would provide some light when the black cells were meant to be, well, black. And then there was that whole clause in the user agreement about not using it to make a nuclear weapon. Micaiah was still trying to figure out how that could be done, and whether it would be possible to do here in the black cells, to free himself without simultaneously blowing himself up.

Of course, that only applied to situations from which he could not feasibly escape. If he really, really wanted to, he could chicken out and escape. It would be difficult, the portal almost as risky as the trial, but he could do it. He might even be able to come back and rescue the others, too, if they were already here. At the same time, if the others were already here, escape ought to be the last thing on his mind because then it would only turn into a hostage situation, or maybe even an outright slaughter. At this point, he wasn't willing to put any action as being beyond Rifun's capabilities.

He sat with his back to the wall, left leg bent, right leg stretched out. God, his leg hurt, but the last thing he needed was to lose any little pieces and parts in this cell, and have his prosthetic come off right in the middle of the escape, or at all. But one thing was for sure, as soon as he got back, he was going to take the stupid thing off and rest his leg for a few days. He'd hobble along on crutches around the bakery and probably spend most of his time in the office, but he couldn't leave it on much longer.

At the same time, he doubted he would be at the bakery much longer either. Too much had happened, and he was too restless. It was time to get away from it all, go off the Time-grid, and live. Take Kayla with him, and settle down properly. Buy a house, have kids, raise a family, all the things they should have done from the very beginning, before Time and the Akari had taken over their lives.

Micaiah rubbed his face, fairly certain he was smearing dirt but uncaring of appearances at this point. The guards had been back half a dozen times to beat up on him a little here and there. It wasn't anything huge, like the fights Tommen got in at school, but more like a punch here, and kick there, a little pushing around, just enough to make him afraid and question himself. So, while he was sure he was covered in bruises, he was otherwise unharmed.

Chandler had not returned, and Micaiah wondered whether he had ever really been there. He knew that people would eventually hallucinate when left in the dark, except Chandler had come in right off the bat. What's more, he'd even appeared in the light, when Micaiah had been kept in the regular holding cells. So far, Rifun hadn't said anything, hinted at anything, or made any veiled threats about it. Either Rifun couldn't see Chandler—therefore, Micaiah was crazy—didn't know about him—which seemed improbable but not impossible—or else he refused to acknowledge him. But who was Chandler that Rifun would not acknowledge his very existence? For a man on a quest to conquer the universe, and making sure that everyone everywhere knew he was in charge, that did not seem very likely.

Therefore, Micaiah was insane. Maybe he'd been on this path for a while and only now was it beginning to manifest itself outside his body as hallucinations. Maybe losing his leg had fucked him up more than he knew. Maybe he should get help when this was all over with. But if he was crazy, and he was afraid that he was crazy, and he was wondering if he needed to see help for being crazy, was he still crazy? Fuck, but psychiatry confused him.

He tried to find some way to anchor himself in reality, something to hold onto. He obviously had no good way to tell how long he'd been in the cell, or how long it was until he would be taken out to trial. If he couldn't find a root in the past, maybe he could find a root in the future.

Where would he and Kayla go to live? Obviously, they couldn't stick around West Virginia. The general consensus was to at least get out of the District, if not the whole Region. Maybe they ought to go to District One, Alaska and Western Canada, at least so Kayla could visit her home and see her people again, even if she could not feasibly be part of them anymore. The Inuit were not especially technologically advanced, but they had their family ties. Although, despite being one hundred percent pure Inuit blood, Kayla would be seen as an outsider with no clan ties. Okay, so maybe that was a bad idea. No need to make her feel that bad about herself. He would have to ask her what her thoughts were about it.

Instead, maybe they could go back to his homeland. The little fishing village where he grew up had been rebuilt and was more commercialized than ever, but it was still home. They could take a tour of Ireland, see the sights, maybe extend that vacation to Europe. Maybe they really would leave the Region, become European Timekeepers for a while. Wouldn't that be something? Kayla had always wanted to visit Spain and Greece, and Micaiah thought that the Netherlands and Denmark might be pretty interesting.

So there. Once this was all over and their blood pressure was back within a normal range, he would take his wife on a right proper honeymoon vacation. Six months minimum, anywhere they wanted to go. Theoretically, they wouldn't even have to worry about flights and airfare; if they could get the right coordinates, they could just travel by portal. Fewer lines at the airport, less hassle with security, and they wouldn't have to get up at shit o'clock in the morning to try and catch the flight. Plus they could spend more time vacationing and less time worrying about any possible delays that might crop up. After all, traveling to Europe, one day was spent just getting there, and another day was spent just getting back. Two extra days, right there, thanks to portal travel.

Micaiah let out a breath, unsure how well he liked this anchoring business. It was good to pass the time, but it did nothing for his mood. No matter what, first he was going to have to make it through this trial. All of his brilliant, romantic plans were all moot if Rifun wasn't taken out of power. Today, right here, in this trial.

"Your time is coming," Chandler had said, "but it is not now."

How much stock did he want to put in the words of a hallucination? Was it meant to be a declaration of fact, and all would go according to plan? Or was it meant to be a comfort, something to take his mind off the worrying? If it was meant to be the latter, it wasn't working very well.

He rubbed his face, dared to rub his eyes, glad he didn't rub dirt into them. He had to get out of here. He had to get out of the darkness, out of this cell. He was tired of waiting. He had to get to his trial, get through the formalities and bullshit and kill Rifun.

Fuck, was this how Walter felt on nights when a storm knocked out the power and killed his night light? Was this how he felt when even the thought of total darkness crossed his mind? Have to run, got to get out, got to escape. Run, run, run, flee, flee, flee, get out, get out, get out. What a miserable existence, to be afraid of one of the few things in the universe that was, well, universal. It was one thing to fear it as a child, but to have such a deep-set fear as an adult...that did things to a man. Micaiah could only hope it wasn't happening to him now.

He closed his eyes and took a breath, let it out slowly. He had to stay calm, had to think rationally.

He nearly jumped out of his skin as the door opened.

*No, Cai, don't let it get to you. Don't let them break you like they broke Walter. Stay strong, and endure. Your trial has to start eventually.*

Except Walter had been kept in his cell for a perceived year in the space of only a day or two.

Micaiah braced himself for another fight, but this time, the door did not swing shut and enclose him in darkness. This time, his guards hauled him to his feet and bade him walk, or limp as the occasion demanded. They took him out of the cell, winding back through the asylum and the regular cell blocks. He might have expected to be taken out to the trial, but they made a detour. Ten steps in, he knew where they were going.

His suspicions were proven correct as they opened a couple lavish doors and he was again deposited in Rifun's posh study. It looked the same as before, absolutely exquisite, except this time there was a tray of food set out on the desk. Daring to take a step closer, Micaiah saw it was the food he'd ordered the last time he'd been here, but never got to eat because he foolishly decided to attack Rifun before lunchtime. It looked untouched. His stomach growled.

As he took another step toward the food, a familiar voice spoke. "Do sit and eat. I did promise you a last meal, didn't I?"

Micaiah looked around, his gaze settling on Rifun, sitting in a large wingback chair facing the roaring hearth. He still did not wear a smoking jacket or any kind of Shakespearean costume like Micaiah might have assumed. Still a sweatshirt, jeans, long hair pulled back in a simple ponytail. There wasn't even a cup of tea or a cigar on the little coffee table.

"Cassius was the smoker, not I," Rifun said, as if reading his thoughts. He stood. "Though he preferred a pipe."

"Having second thoughts about killing him, are we?" Micaiah wondered as Rifun approached.

Rifun nonchalantly walked right by him, sitting in the large chair at the desk, gesturing toward the seat across from him, where the food sat. "Please. Eat. I insist."

"Is it going to kill me?"

"Only one way to find out."

Considering all the ways Rifun could have killed him so far, Micaiah highly doubted he would stoop to poison. Still wary, though, he sat slowly and cautiously started eating. Three bites in, his stomach got the better of him.

"That's more like it," Rifun said. "Now I don't feel so bad about discussing business."

Micaiah swallowed. "What kind of business?"

"The business of your — how shall I say? — rescue? Conspiracy? I'm really not sure what to call it other than clever. In a normal Time Trial, it might have even worked."

Micaiah felt his stomach sink, but he wouldn't let the realization reach his face. "This is a Time Trial, isn't it? Isn't the whole point of it to fight for my freedom?"

"Of course. According to some specific parameters. Your Testimonies, for example."

"What about them?"

"You named Tommen and Walter as your Testimonies, two of them anyway."

"Yes?"

"Except, they're not the ones who showed up. But they looked like them. It took me a little time to go back to the journal and do some research, but I think I found what they were doing. It's called a Disguise, isn't it?"

Micaiah met his stare, trying to look disinterested. "I've heard of it."

"The one Disguised as Walter is Michael Junior, another rather prominent Akari-bearer, though a bit difficult to work with, am I right?"

"That's the nice way of putting it."

"Yes, it's too bad about his diagnosis. I'll bet that's why you chose him. He's dying anyway, so what difference does it make if it's today or a year from today?"

"And then there was the other one. I found it a little hard to believe, but apparently it's a woman impersonating Tommen, did you know that?" Micaiah elected to remain silent. "Aklaq White Bear. A decent Akari-bearer, true, and quite a looker, I must say. Though I have to ask, why bring her along?"

"Too few sixteen year old boys in the ranks; she was the only volunteer who could get Tommen's Disguise to fit her frame properly."

"Ah, so there are limits to it. A good thing to know. I shall have to write such an addendum when I am finished translating Richard's journal."

"What are you going to do to them?" Micaiah asked, too afraid to know but too afraid to not know.

Rifun shifted in his seat. "So far, I haven't done anything. The secretaries did their job processing them for the trial and brought the discrepancies to me for review. Needless to say, there has been something of a rain delay in the trial proceedings, but you brought that on yourself." He folded his hands together, tapping his fingers, or the fingers he still possessed. "I thought of a number of things I could do. I could kill them, maim them, inflict other bodily harm upon them. I could throw them in the black cells, inflict some psychological harm on them. I could take you out to them, kill you in front of them, inflict some psychological harm on them and send them home, having made my point. Really, there are a number of things I could do, so I'll just leave most of it up to your imagination. But, do you know what I am going to do?"

"Clearly not."

"Yes, that's right, you've been locked up, haven't you?" He smirked. "I have decided that, in light of this rather irritating turn of events, I am going to do...nothing."

Micaiah raised a brow. "Nothing?"

"Let me rephrase, I am not going to expose them or harm them in any way thus far. Such a clever plan, one that might have slipped me by if I hadn't changed the rules of the trial just that little bit. I want to see how it's going to play out. Can they really pull off their

Disguises and make me truly believe that they are who they pretend to be?"

"It's worked so far."

"Indeed. However, I cannot let this go completely unpunished. So we're going to change the stakes a little."

This could get real ugly, real fast. Micaiah braced himself for some outrageous terms, trying to come up with some kind of counteroffer.

Rifun grinned. "Look at the wheels turning already. What am I going to ask, and how can he counter? How can he negotiate so that there is as little loss of life as possible? I like that. All right, here are the new terms. If you win, Earth remains insignificant and cut off from Time for good. Time, Akari, all of it, sealed off forever. You and your brother — and Doug, since he surprisingly appears to be the only honest Testimony this time around — return home. Mike and Kayla, however, stay here with me."

"No. They go home, too," Micaiah said firmly. "If Earth is to be sealed off, they will be of little threat to you."

"I have to punish them somehow. Besides, Mike is going to die anyway. Or is it that dear Kayla means something to you, but because you don't want to be thought of as playing favorites, you include Mike only as a courtesy?" He chuckled. "Oh, now this does add a new layer to the game. All right, I won't make them stay here. But I'll tell you what will happen. Mike gets his clock broken up to the point where he's a drooling idiot. He won't even know he's dead until he's dead."

"And Kayla?"

Rifun leaned forward in his chair, resting his arms on the desk. "I get to fuck her in front of everyone. What's more, Isthim is going to be there. As a *vodrak,* she is capable of pushing all Borelian poisons, including the one for sexual arousal and stimulation. I'm going to fuck your girlfriend, and she's going to like it."

For the second time in as many visits, Micaiah launched himself at Rifun. For the second time is as many visits, Rifun won. At least Micaiah had gotten to eat his food this time, though it was small comfort.

Micaiah lay on the floor, the wind knocked out of him. As he tried to get up, Rifun simply knelt and put a boot on his chest and he obediently stayed down.

"Those are the terms for if you win," Rifun stated. "Wait until you hear what happens when I win."

Micaiah spit at him, missed. Rifun blinked and dramatically wiped his face, his expression unreadable. Then his fist flashed out and caught Micaiah in the jaw. And he was speaking again.

"When I win, you—and Walter still—are going to be my servant lackeys. I'm not going to break your clocks beyond your inability to perceive time because I want you to experience and remember everything you've done and failed at. Doug I haven't decided if I'm going to kill or make him a clock-broken lackey. Tommen and Micah are going to be my Akari Apprentices. Mike, I might just put him out of his misery. Throw him in the ring with the Bat, perhaps. And as for your girlfriend, well, fuck her enough times and eventually, maybe I won't need Isthim's influence."

Rifun did not let him up right away, instead waiting for a guard to come and restrain him. He knew that Micaiah was hell-bent on tearing his throat out now, and he was taking no chances.

"Take him to the Pit," Rifun ordered. "Lock him in the holding cell and retrieve the Day. When the First Grandfather arrives, begin the trial, whether I'm there or not."

"What are you going to be doing?" Micaiah hissed. "Hiding?"

"Being the master of the universe is a lot of work. You might have an idea of what it's like, running your own business. Managing personnel, overseeing supplies, advertising and reaching out to all your customers, it's hard work. I have a few deadlines to meet, so I'm going to go and get a little work done, then come and watch the end of the trial."

Rifun made a small motion, and the guard turned, jerking Micaiah along with him.

Rifun wasn't even going to be at the trial. He'd turned the proceedings over solely to the Grandfathers and made himself just a spectator, free to come and go as he pleased. If he didn't show up at all, then this whole plan would have been for nothing. Had he planned it this way from the beginning, or did the revelation of the Disguises change things? Had he suspected an assassination attempt and was thus removing himself from the situation?

Was there any way they could force him to come? Could they refuse to move or do anything until he showed up? Would it work, or would they simply be beaten or killed? Would Rifun suspect something? He was already on high alert, so why not? Maybe he wouldn't show up until the very end, where they were all too beaten and bloody to be any sort of threat, that way he could safely gloat over his victory.

Micaiah couldn't shake the horrifying image of that bastard fucking his wife. Worse, he would be using Isthim's sick Borelian poison to manipulate and influence her so she had no choice but to enjoy it as she'd never enjoyed sex before, all to torture Micaiah. If he had to stop anything, he had to stop that. God help him, even if he had to kill his own wife so she wouldn't have to endure a lifetime of being Rifun's drug-raped whore, he would do it. He would have no choice. Oddly enough, it seemed the only merciful thing to do. Despite Rifun's affinity for theater and drama, Micaiah had little doubt that he wasn't a gentle lover.

Fuck, he had to think of something and quick. But what? He was being taken to trial right now. The guards were all but dragging him down the corridor to the Judgment Wing lobby while his thoughts raced and plans came poorly into focus.

Well, maybe things were better with Rifun knowing. Now they didn't have to pretend and tiptoe around the facts. The next question became, then, would that knowledge be made public? Rifun had said something about wanting to be convinced that Kayla was Tommen and Junior was Walter, which implied that no one else was going to know of their little deception. What would happen if Micaiah gave it away arbitrarily? Rifun had already set the gambling stakes, so he wasn't likely to just go back on them and have everyone killed. Maybe he gave the man too much credit.

They exited the Judgment Wing, landing back in the town square of some unknown English town from 1600. It was uncanny and a little disconcerting. Still, Micaiah tried to keep his thoughts focused. He had to think of a way out, but the only way out was in. In order to save his friends who were, presumably, waiting in the new Time Trial arena, he had to go into the new Time Trial arena. And yet, there was no hope or comfort in walking up to a gallows, regardless if there was a noose or a portal in the frame. He could feel the eyes of the secretaries on him, the first sacrifice in the Pit.

Once through, he paused for just a moment as he looked around the Time Trial arena, but his sightseeing was short-lived before a guard roughly shoved him forward, almost sending him sprawling over the edge into the stadium seating, possibly to his death in the arena below. Even from the top, it looked like a pretty wicked drop.

Somehow, the whole place put Micaiah in mind of Fight Club, even though it looked more like some archaeological dig from Pompeii. Dark, dismal, a cruddy makeshift arena for a sport with no rules. How fitting, he supposed. With Rifun in charge now, it was just as likely that the Time Trials no longer had any real rules either.

Strangely, though, Micaiah found himself comforted, like stepping into a familiar pair of shoes. In a way, this took him back to his prize-fighting days. It had been kind of like Fight Club, in that it had been more of an underground loosely-organized sport that no one really talked about, but it had been widely attended. Most of the attendees were poor folks who had only a few pennies to bet on this man or that man, but every so often, a rich man would drop by. Most often in disguise, the rich man was most often looking for a strong man who could carry out some dastardly deed—vandalizing a competitor's store or bank, robbery, even murder. Their bets were the ones worth fighting for.

Most often, Micaiah was just in it because he thought it would prove he was tough and make him even tougher. And he did win quite a few of his fights. He had no choice or else he and Micah would have starved, or so he believed. Once or twice, he had compromised his morals and taken a rich man's bet, won a fight and so had to go out and do a little vandalism or petty theft or some such thing.

Framing the Time Trial in that manner seemed to make it more bearable, at least in his mind. But, one small trip and a stumble only reminded him of how different life was now. He'd always been light on his feet, but only when he had two feet. These days, he had a foot and a stump. He could walk, but that was about it. He couldn't have beaten Rifun in a fair fight if he tried. How in the world was he going to hope to take on the Bat and the Day?

Well, he figured, it was time to start pulling out a few party tricks. If Rifun hadn't known about Disguises, maybe there were other things he hadn't figured out yet about the Akari. Pull enough animals out of the magic hat, eventually you'll find one that no one has seen before. Micaiah ran his tongue over his teeth. Okay, so the analogy sounded better in his head.

Perhaps the only good thing about this was that Cassius was already dead. Rifun had done half their job for them, now they just needed to accomplish the other half. There just seemed to be some sort of gap between the now and the done.

They seemed to circle the outer edge of the pit arena several times before finally finding the path they were looking for, or maybe it just seemed like a long walk, the way Micaiah's knee was hurting. Maybe if his holding cell had some light, he could take his leg off and relax his knee a little. Not likely seeing how as soon as he took it off, his knee was likely to swell and then he'd never get the stupid thing back on.

The path took a sharp turn down and Micaiah found himself tripping and stumbling down what may have been a poorly-constructed spiral staircase. It was dark and hard to tell, but the guards kept him upright, if roughly so. And they continued down,

down, until Micaiah was sure they were much deeper than the floor of the arena. Just when he was beginning to question their destination, the staircase ended and the dark tunnel opened up into a cavern lit only by a single torch. A tunnel branched off through one wall and was gated on both ends. And who should man the wheel but the Bat himself?

As the guard and the Bat conversed, Micaiah was acutely aware that he lacked a translator. Not that it was imperative that he know what they were saying. They could have been chatting about the weather or planning to take him out back and kill him; either way he was stuck with no good way to fight back. When had he decided this was a good idea again? Oh, right, when he was sitting in a hotel room, feeling pretty good after some good sex and still hell-bent on vengeance against the man who'd cost him his leg.

So...when did this plan start turning into the good idea he'd been envisioning?

As if things weren't already difficult enough with Rifun not even attending the trial and the new arena looking more and more like a bowl to drown them in, Micaiah's plans were thrown off even more when the Bat brought out an all-too-familiar stamp. Of course there would be a force field in place. If the rules were to fight to the death, cut off all routes to escape and make it a fight to the death.

Once again, he had no choice. If he wanted to get in, he needed the stamp. If he wanted to get out, he either needed to bring down the force field or else get the two-way stamp. Neither one seemed terribly likely as the Bat started cranking the wheel and the gates lifted. The guards escorted Micaiah down the tunnel, through the force fields which now sealed him in.

The tunnel ended, but it did not open into the main arena itself. Instead, he found himself in a small round alcove with a gated cell on either side, the arena opening out in front of him through another arch. Judging by the angle, he guessed this was one of the arena "corners." As one of the guards worked to unlock one of the cells, Micaiah looked out across the open arena. There, about halfway down on the opposite side, he thought he might have spotted Micah. He couldn't see the others, but judging by the way Micah was fixed on a point elsewhere in the arena, he guessed the others were in their own separate cell.

Then he was shoved into the cell with no one to catch him when he fell. Damn it, but he was clumsy today. Or maybe it was just the uneven ground. He was going to have to get better at this fast or else he wasn't even going to make it to the opening part of the trial before he killed himself. The guard said something, which could have been anything from a sarcastic comment to an outright threat, and the entire troupe left.

Again, Micaiah was alone, but at least this time he had light. This time, he had purpose. Now all they had to do was retrieve the Day and the Grandfathers and the trial would begin. No more of this kept in the dark waiting for news. This was actually happening. It was terrifying and yet a relief. Suspense probably killed more people than the trials ever could, and the anxiety associated with this...

He couldn't have been in the cell more than five minutes before the gate opened again and a secretary entered, walking on four flippered legs, holding some sort of information-gathering device in hands with webbed fingers, looking at him around an enormous appendage which might have been a nose, but from an elephant seal or something. The first thing it did was hand him a translator, which he took gratefully and quickly set to his liking.

"Thank you," he told the secretary, figuring there was no need to be rude to someone who was likely just one of Rifun's many slaves.

"I am here to gather information," the secretary said blandly.

Didn't Rifun already have his life story in the palm of his hand? Wouldn't he have already read his biography by now, taken notes, read the companion study guide, taken the intellectual college study course, written his dissertation, and become an expert? Why was he sending this secretary to gather information that was already known? Well, maybe it was for the official Time Trial records. After all, this would be the first one in this arena, so he had to set some kind of precedent.

"All right," Micaiah sighed. "Fire away."

The secretary gave him a funny look—but then, every look was a funny one with a face like that, in Micaiah's opinion—but began its report.

"Full name."

"Micaiah Durvin."

"Origin."

"Quadrant One, Parsec Eleven, Sector Five, System Four, Planet Thirty-Eight, Region Four, District Four."

"Species."

"Human."

"Time rank?"

"Lieutenant Timekeeper."

"Give a brief history and description of your Time abilities."

"What?"

Since when did Rifun need that? Since when did anyone need that sort of information? Didn't "Lieutenant Timekeeper" say enough about the abilities he possessed, or could possess? Ask an Apprentice that sort of question, maybe a Journeyman, but a Lieutenant? The whole prospect was almost infuriating, and he even considered refusing to answer. Well, if he was going to die or be made a servant, it wouldn't matter since he would be stripped of his abilities anyway. If he won and Rifun died, there would be no need for this information. So he did answer the question, but he did not answer it fully. He left out things here and there. If Rifun was going to take this as gospel, best to have a few tricks in reserve.

"And your Akari rank?" the secretary asked, with about as much enthusiasm as it had asking for his name.

"Excuse me?" Micaiah wondered.

"Your Akari rank. It is per the Faharoa's request."

The Akari-bearers didn't really have "ranks" among the general population. There were the beginners, who might be likened to Apprentices. Micah was one such Apprentice. Then there were the leaders like Doug, officers of sorts who had a four-tiered hierarchy. Micaiah was neither of those. He was simply...an Akari-bearer. Each of them had different gifts and different specialties, though they all wielded the same core abilities.

He fumbled for an answer. "Um, Akari-bearer. I don't really have a rank."

Again, the secretary gave him a look which he could not interpret seriously. He scolded himself for such shallow humor, but it was the only thing he had right now.

"Give a brief history and description of your Akari abilities," it said, again with zero enthusiasm.

Micaiah let out a breath and ran his tongue over his teeth, considering. Finally he shook his head. "No. I am refusing to answer that question."

"You must answer it."

"No." He smirked. "And if Rifun wants an answer to that question so badly, he can come down to the trial and get it from me himself."

The secretary seemed uncertain how to proceed. Finally, it entered something in its information device and moved on to a series of questions which seemed, to Micaiah, to be only fluff, information for information's sake. Those he answered, sometimes giving sarcastic answers which only served to confuse the poor secretary. After what seemed like half an eternity, the secretary put away its device and called out for a guard to open the cell gate.

"The Time Trial will begin soon," the secretary informed him. "The Grandfathers will come, as will the Day and the Bat. I will also pass along your message that you wish to meet with Rifun in order to discuss your answers."

Then it was gone, leaving Micaiah to wonder if there had been some sarcasm in that last little bit. Was the secretary serious and it was actually going to retrieve Rifun, or had it caught on to some of the sarcasm and tension between the two? Well, fuck. *There you go again, Micaiah, your big mouth getting you in trouble again. And this time, it's a little more important than some shitty child labor laws. How are you going to get out of this one?*

But there was no use worrying about it now. That done and past, now he had to worry about the present, take everything as it came. The time for planning was coming to a swift end and he had to be prepared to think on his feet.

Then another thought occurred to him. What if Rifun learned how to use Disguise? What if he figured it out before the trial and sent someone in his place, a decoy that would take a bullet while he would remain completely unharmed? Was Micaiah crazy for thinking so? Only as crazy as Rifun was paranoid, and that camp was growing every day.

Shit, but what if it did happen? They could launch their plan, spring their trap, and lead their revolution, all against the wrong guy.

Micaiah found himself pacing painfully around his cell, trying to separate paranoid what-if fantasies from real plans and contingency plans for the contingency plans. When he stopped to think about it, though, he realized there wasn't much of a difference between the two. Rifun had the upper hand here; he had every advantage. Unlike the warehouse, he also had the home field advantage. And where he'd had five guys and Walter had had two whole teams, now Micaiah had five guys and Rifun had a fucking army. Was there any way for this to not go horribly, horribly wrong?

The more he thought about it, the more likely it seemed that this would be the suicide mission his wife had predicted from the beginning. Was he really that foolish? What kind of man was he that he let revenge blind him that much? His options were sorely limited already, and they were dwindling fast.

By the time he came back to reality from his pity party, he realized that life had come into the arena. The whole place seemed to shake, like a burned out building with too much weight still in it, ready to collapse. Micaiah kept his head down as dust and dirt fell from the ceiling in small puffs. He grunted as a small rock fell and hit his shoulder.

Outside, he could hear shuffling and the general din of activity. Were these the Grandfathers coming in, or did the Wheel actually have a large enough population to warrant a full audience for this spectacle? Maybe attendance was mandatory.

Micaiah recalled his last Time Trial, decades ago. The Coliseum had been absolutely packed, shoulder-to-shoulder, no bathroom breaks, death from heatstroke, can hardly even breathe, packed. The noise of it had been terrible, too, almost deafening. When everyone had been moving and talking and carrying on, it had been like a football stadium, the Superbowl to end all Superbowls. It had taken a good twenty minutes to get everyone to quiet down and stop talking, but even then the din of general noise—a shuffle here, various bodily functions there, one person rubbing against another—had made it so the Hands could hardly be heard.

The noise as he heard it now in his cell did not seem to match that kind of noise. Really, it did not even appear to approach that level as he could still hear himself think. If he had to compare it, he would put it somewhere between Little League championships, and minor league open practice, or maybe an early game. After all, there were some pretty dedicated Little League fans out there; better to aim high.

He looked up as the gate creaked and opened, and the same secretary walked in.

"I was only joking about telling Rifun to come," he said, still unsure if he believed his own words.

"Indeed," the secretary said. "He informed me that he would be joining the trial later. I am here for a preliminary assessment."

"Keeping a record of all my injuries now, that way they can tally up the new ones later?"

Nevertheless, Micaiah stood and went to it. He expected some kind of physical workup—vitals, pat down, something of that nature. He was unprepared for the secretary to wipe away the one-way stamp on his hand. He was about to question it when the secretary took out a stamp from its cloak; if he guessed right, this was the two-way stamp which would see him out of the arena, regardless of the force field.

"We know why you are here," the secretary told him. "We know what you are doing. If you wish to succeed, you will need this." It hid the stamp back in its cloak. "Know that you have friends here, Micaiah Durvin."

He studied the secretary, looking for any evidence of humor or treachery, but alien expressions were notoriously difficult to read. Finally, he nodded. "Thank you. If we succeed, we will not forget this. What about the others?"

"They have been remarked. Your friends would not have been given away to Rifun, except that I was not the one to examine them. Not all secretaries are friends here. Some are loyal to Rifun, for reasons I do not understand."

"Are any of you armed?"

"No. Rifun disarmed everyone but his army; he is in total control."

"Well, he can't get rid of everything, and everything can be used as a weapon. Get creative if you have to. Gather your friends and be ready. Hopefully this won't take long."

The secretary dipped its head. "I will do as you have said. If Rifun is captured, would you like the honor of killing him?"

Micaiah hesitated. "Normally I would say yes, but every moment that Rifun is alive and allowed to think and plan is another chance he'll escape. As I've told everyone else, if you get the shot, you take it. Do you understand that?"

"I understand. Now I must go, or they will suspect that something has happened to me, or that we collaborate."

Micaiah nodded and took a step back. The secretary said some formal farewell or another and left, just as bland and unenthusiastic as when it first walked in.

He wasn't even sure what to make of the exchange, really, except that the secretaries were as miserable as he might have expected them to be. Therefore, they had allies if and when push came to shove. If the secretaries could undo the dampening field, then some of them and any other enslaved Time Agents would be free to help. With Time at their beck and call, guns or other variations thereof were pretty much useless in a fight. Not to say there weren't any, but experience had taught him that small, short-range weapons were more effective: knives, wires, brute force and fisticuffs, that sort of thing. The only reason they were even using a gun to assassinate Rifun was because there was no way in hell they would get close enough to try anything else.

He sat and pondered the situation as the noise from the field grew louder and the shaking persisted. They had allies in the secretaries, but not all of them. So it would be largely a matter of paying attention only to the person in front of them, whether they were assisting or attacking. In the chaos, it was entirely possible that there would be friendly fire deaths.

Before he could sit and think on it too long, he heard the noise outside die down, though it would never completely go away. There was a little more movement, some more shuffling, this feeling more rhythmic, more militaristic, as if a troupe of new recruits from bootcamp marched overhead. Then it was quiet. A moment later, he could hear speaking, but could not make out the specific words.

The gate to his cell opened again, and who should walk in but the Day, in all its fucked-up giraffe...vine...peacock...incestuous glory? There was no nice way to describe the Day, but it didn't seem to be making a social call, looking for girl chat and fluffy compliments.

"The First Grandfather has arrived," the Day informed him. "The Time Trial is beginning."

"Really? I thought for sure I bought my tickets to the Super Bowl. Guess I'll have to contact the seller and get a refund. He did seem a bit shady, but the deal was great. Now I know why."

The Day was unmoved. Was it really too much to have a scary Time-immune creature from the bowels of the universe with a reasonable sense of humor? Micaiah thought it had been a great joke, but his audience was a bit stale. Still, he reluctantly stood, ignoring the throbbing in his knee. The time for planning was gone. Once he stepped out of his cell, it was do or die. Problem was, he wasn't willing to bet on either.

# Chapter Twenty-Six
## The Day

Micah couldn't say how long he sat in his cell, but he knew he began to wonder whether these cells were outfitted like the black cells, to change the prisoner's perception of Base Time, make it seem like forever when it had only been a day. Maybe it was to make him even more nervous, but there was an art to creating suspense. If there was no suspense at all, then there was only glory, bravado, and suddenly it was all over. For as anxious as Micah was, he knew that there had to be a healthy dose of fear and anxiety in order to truly savor a victory.

On the other hand, if there was too much suspense carried out over too long of a period, the suspense died. Micah was beginning to feel his anxiety just start to wane when the gate started creaking open and he almost jumped out of his skin. Jump scares in movies were overrated, but in real life they were probably one of the worst.

It was only the elephant seal secretary. "I am here for a preliminary."

Preliminary what? Micah wanted to ask. But he stood and approached. If he had to guess, it seemed female. Not that he was any expert, but he definitely got those vibes off it. "What do you need to know?"

"I require your hands."

Curious now, Micah held out his hands. His breath caught when she wiped away the one-way stamp and brought out a small box from a hidden pocket in her cloak. She flipped it open to reveal a two-way stamp. She hurried stamped his hand and stashed the stamp and box back in her cloak.

"You have friends among the secretaries," she told him, "but not all secretaries are friends. Rifun knows of your deception, but he is going to play along anyway. You must do the same."

Micah nodded. "Duly noted. Have you seen the others?"

"I am visiting them next, then I will see your brother. He is in the holding cell for the Accused. It is located in that corner." She gave a brief, almost imperceptible gesture toward one corner of the Pit where another tunnel seemed to dig under the walls.

"What's our best bet to get out of here?"

"If you assassinate Rifun, there will be chaos. You must take any way you can."

"I was afraid you'd say that. Thank you for your help."

"I hope it is enough." And she left.

Well, she really couldn't have made it any worse, Micah thought. Other than maybe giving them false hope so they thought they could go through the force fields when they really couldn't, so they would only electrocute themselves trying to escape. Or was he just being paranoid? He examined the stamp. Everything about it seemed genuine, as far as he could tell. Maybe this was the break they needed, a boost in friends and firepower. They just had to hope no one noticed the little change.

He snapped his hands behind him as the gate opened again, but it was no secretary this time. Now it was the Day, the grotesque giraffe-peacock bastard. There was a time when Micah had been fascinated by the Day and maybe even thought it pretty, or homely at least. Now, given the circumstances, it was just an ugly fuck-up of nature, and the lighting certainly didn't help its image.

"The First Grandfather is here. The Time Trial is beginning. Come."

Micah had thought that there was quite a bit of noise coming from outside his cell, but he'd forced himself to stay seated and try to relax as much as he could. Now, being led out into the Pit, he saw that there had indeed been noise and movement.

The Pit was packed. It was like all the tickets for the FIFA

World Cup had been given away this year, with complimentary lodging and airfare and still more people were let in to fill the seats. Supposedly, in a normal Time Trial, the crowd would be a mix of Time Agents from around the universe, as well as a few secretaries, maybe a few guards, and the Grandfathers were there automatically. This crowd, however, was nothing like that. The majority of those in attendance were Grandfathers, beating out guard attendance only just. There were secretaries in the mix as well, though decidedly fewer of them. For every ten Grandfathers, there appeared to be nine guards and one secretary. Not that it made him feel any better.

*We're here to assassinate Rifun, but we're sitting in a pit of vipers.* Even if they did somehow pull off the initial shot, the Grandfathers would be on them in a second. There was no way they would be able to run or escape. And what happened to the Wheel then? Did the whole thing collapse? Did this "First Grandfather" figure become the new leader? Fucking hell, but a Grandfather in charge of the Time industry? Now that was a scary thought. Not that he'd be around to witness it.

The Pit had been modified since they were initially brought in. Not ten steps from his cell, a platform had been erected. It was perhaps ten feet high, six feet by six feet, about as plain a box as could be imagined, like a CGI element in its earliest stages of conception. Stairs just as plain and square and boxy as the platform itself wound around the four sides, and Micah was made to walk up them. His knee had just started to feel better as he was sitting in his cell, but now the pain came roaring back to life as he limped forlornly up the stairs to the top of the platform.

Thankfully, a chair awaited him at the top, but what was less comforting was the chain and manacle. The Day made him sit, then clapped the manacle on his right ankle. He would be going nowhere today. Fuck, did Rifun have to think of everything? Paranoia really was frightening to behold, especially when it made sense.

He looked around the Pit, tried to read it, analyze it, find some hidden weakness, an Achilles heel. Was there some secret passage they could utilize, something other than the obvious tunnels and escape routes? Was there a servant or secretary door that would send them out the back?

Three smaller platforms were set up in line with his, about fifteen feet apart, the same six by six, but only about four feet high, each with a chair and a chain. In relation to the Pit, they were about a third of the way down from where the secretary had said Micaiah was being held. That space was a good thirty by twenty yards, maybe a little smaller, completely open, likely to allow room for Micaiah to face off against the Bat and the Day.

*I hope you know what you're doing, Cai,* Micah thought, sighing. *Because you are going to get your ass kicked after the first question.*

A moment later, Doug, Junior-as-Walter, and Kayla-as-Tommen were led out of their cell to their respective platforms. Doug and Kayla-as-Tommen resisted the chains a little, but they were shackled in just as securely as Micah. Junior-as-Walter put up little resistance, a perfect reaction from a man who'd spent far too much time in prison and in the dark. Except now, they were only pretending for the benefit of the audience. Rifun wouldn't be fooled. Maybe it was all a game to him and he wanted to see how things played out if he didn't say anything.

*Thank God for spies and double-crossing secretaries.*

Micah and the others exchanged uncertain glances, all thinking the same thing: this was not how this was supposed to go. This was supposed to be easy, well, easier. Rifun wasn't supposed to be so smart or so cunning or so well-prepared. He was supposed to get overconfident and give them free reign, enough to see them run around, supposedly, in vain. He wasn't supposed to get paranoid, remain crafty and clever, and come up with everything that could potentially stop an escape. Nothing about this plan was really going right so far, and they hadn't planned for it all to go wrong even before it got underway.

So then the question became: what the fuck did they do now? Did they try to play by the rules, hope they won and hope Rifun upheld his end of the bargain? Or did they try to improvise, still try to carry out their plan, and, ultimately, die trying? Neither option seemed particularly viable right now.

Micah did not have long to dwell on it before he saw the Bat emerge from his tunnel and wait in the gateway. A second later, one of the Grandfathers from the Grandfather choir they were facing stood. Was this the First Grandfather that was spoken of? As Micah studied the seating, he saw it probably was, as two seats were elevated just a little more above the rest. It was not easily seen because of the sheer density of bodies in the seats.

Any remaining doubt was erased when the Grandfather raised its hands and threw back its hood. It was Isthim. Because who else?

"This is the Time Trial of the Grandfathers and Faharoa Rifun versus Micaiah Durvin," she announced, her voice carrying across the entire Pit. And still, the only thing Micah could think was, *Faharoa Rifun?* "Bring forth the Accused."

Micah looked toward the tunnel the secretary had mentioned. For a long moment, as he strained to see in the darkness, he could not make out anything at all. Then he saw the hulking form of the Day, a split second before he could make out Micaiah walking just in front of him.

Put nicely, Micaiah looked a wreck. The first and most obvious thing was that he was limping. Bad. Micah didn't think he'd limped that bad since he first got his leg after the hospital stay. As he got closer, Micah could see his knee was swollen pretty good, too. This on top of how dirty and sweat-stained he looked, to say nothing of the bruises. He looked as though he'd already gone ten rounds, and now he was going to go ten more at least. There was no way he was going to make it. He couldn't. They had to intervene. But where was Rifun? In the entire crowd, Micah couldn't spot him. Unless he was wearing a Grandfather cloak. Oh, this just kept getting better and better.

Micaiah stopped and stood before the Grandfathers.

"Your name," Isthim commanded.

"Micaiah Durvin." Say one thing for Cai, his spirit appeared to still be in tact. They hadn't broken him, despite their apparent attempts.

Micah batted around an idea, whether he wanted to Akari-Band and try to talk to him. Unlike Time Bands, Akari-Bands were invisible except for those who knew what to look for. The problem then became whether Rifun or Isthim knew what to look for. If they did, and they caught Micah Banding, what would they do? Would they just rip his Band to shreds, or would they punish Micaiah for some form of disobedience? Thinking about it, Micah couldn't recall any rules saying he couldn't Band.

So he did, gathering Micaiah in with him before he could answer whatever question Isthim had asked of him.

"Cai," he said to get his attention.

Micaiah turned. The right side of his face seemed to be the only part of him that wasn't scratched, bruised, or beaten.

"The hell have they done to you?" Micah asked, standing at the edge of the platform, as far as his chain would allow.

"Nothing good," Micaiah admitted.

"Are you okay? I mean, well—"

"No worse for wear, but my knee is killing me."

"Yeah, mine, too. But mine doesn't seem nearly as bad as yours."

"Ha ha, funny." Micaiah rolled his eyes and shook his head, then he got serious. "Listen, Rifun knows about the Disguises and our little deception."

Micah nodded. "That's what the secretary said."

"Did it re-stamp your hand with the two-way stamp?"

"Yeah. And the others. We're good to get out of here. Assuming we can." He indicated the chain.

"Blow the fucker off if you have to. You do have the gun, right? Or did they take that, too?"

"No, they didn't find it. Or if they did, they only found a little pocketknife. Probably they let me keep it to see if I might actually try something with it."

"Well, it'll come as a surprise, all right."

"Where is Rifun?"

Micaiah sighed. "He won't be coming, not until later. Best guess, after the questioning, but before the verdict."

"Cai...you think you can last that long? If those bruises are any indication, I can't imagine the Day and the Bat are going to be much easier, or much nicer."

"Agreed, but at this point, I don't have much of a choice."

Micah racked his brain. "The Day and the Bat are immune to Time. Are they immune to the Akari?"

"I don't know. Believe me, I'm going to be trying every trick I know. My biggest concern is Rifun."

"Yeah." Micah nodded sadly. "Stay safe, brother. I'll help in any way I can."

"I know."

Reluctantly, he released the Band. Several things happened then. First, Micaiah began to answer whatever question Isthim had asked of him. Second, he was cut off but an unearthly growl, like a leopard snarling right before an attack. Looking around, Micah saw that it had come from the Bat, and the nightmarish creature took a few steps forward. On the other side of the Pit, the Day also advanced menacingly.

"Enough!" Isthim snapped. "What is the meaning of this?"

"The Akari has been used," the Day growled, and the Bat hissed in agreement.

"Has it?" Isthim did not seem impressed. "Well then, I imagine you are going to have your work cut out for you, a little challenge during combat. I would hate to see him lose too badly."

And that was that. The Day and the Bat were dismissed back to their original posts, neither one looking pleased. Actually, Micah thought they looked ready to defy her orders and tear Micaiah apart anyway. And yet, they'd just given up a wealth of information.

First, the Day and the Bat could see the Akari at work. Second, they were so repulsed by it that their first instinct was to attack. That could be either good or bad for Micaiah. Before, the combat had been simply part of the Time Trial, an expected segment during the play. Now they were fueled by some boiling rage, one that drove them from incapacitating Micaiah to make a point, to outright murder regardless of what the rules said.

Micah glanced at Doug who was on the platform closest to him. Doug did not look at him, and his expression was unreadable. Was he having the same thoughts? Was his tactically-trained mind already running through a hundred scenarios, cataloging the information and working out how to exploit it? How Micah wished he could Band again, just them two—or even all five of them—and ask, but he didn't dare risk another outburst from the Day and the Bat. The first time had angered them, but Isthim had still kept them under control. What would it take for them to defy her and go straight for the kill?

Micaiah was being asked the same questions that Micah and the others had been asked, his Time rank and training, and so on. Micah noticed that when he talked about his Akari rank and training, that the Day and the Bat started shuffling and growling again, like a couple of mad dogs, straining against a chain to run at him and tear him to pieces.

"This is the first of the new Time Trials, under the direction of Faharoa Rifun," Isthim went on, having finished preliminaries with Micaiah.

"And where is Faharoa Rifun?" Micaiah interrupted.

Isthim gave him a look that Micah wasn't sure how to interpret. Irritation, hostility, murder, apathy? "He has other matters to attend to presently and will join us later. However, that is why he has turned control of the Time Trials over to the Grandfathers. As the First Grandfather, I will be presiding over this affair."

There was no way this was going to end well, Micah thought, trying to relax in his chair and not pace a worried circle at the end of his chain. The four of them were chained up and useless, and Micaiah himself was too weak. The Day and the Bat would kill him before Rifun ever arrived.

"As such," Isthim went on, "there will be a new way of doing things here. They are as follows:

"First, the Accused will be introduced, which we have done.

"Second, the Stake and the Testimonies will be introduced, and I will explain their general roles. Their roles may change depending on the trial proceedings." *Translation: I'll say what they are supposed to do, but I'm making it up as I go along.*

"Third, the terms of the agreement will be named, so all may know what to expect if you win or when you lose."

Her word choice was not lost on anyone present.

"Fourth, the questioning of the Accused will commence."

"How do you expect to do that when you murdered all the Hands?" Micaiah sneered.

"This panel of Grandfathers will do well as a substitute," Isthim answered easily. "And unlike the former Time Trials where each Hand asked one question for a maximum of fifty-one questions, we will continue asking questions until we are satisfied with our judgment."

Micah swallowed. So they had the power to make this as short or as long as they wanted, get it over with after ten questions, or drag it out and see just how long Micaiah would last before effectively putting him out of his misery. This wasn't a trial, it was a game. A sick, twisted game. Micah was forced to wonder who had really developed the new rules: Rifun, or Cassius before he died.

"Once the questioning has ended, judgment will be carried out immediately."

If Rifun wasn't going to join this party until after questioning but before judgment, that meant they only had a tiny window of opportunity to kill the bastard, assuming he showed up at all.

"And now introducing the Stake and the Testimonies," Isthim continued after a sufficient pause. "For the Stake, we have Micah

Durvin, twin brother of the Accused. He is a Lieutenant Timekeeper from Earth." She went on to give the coordinates again, his training, his Akari rank and training, all the information that he'd given to the secretary earlier. "The Stake is free to stand in for the Accused at any time, if asked."

It was then that Micah wished he would have been a little less clumsy upon entering the Wheel. If his knee wasn't throbbing like it was now, he would have switched places with his brother right then and there. Forget what Micaiah said about being brave and strong and fighting his own battles; he was too weak. Not that Micah expected there to be a dramatic difference regardless of who fought. The Bat would tear him apart just as soon as he would tear Micaiah apart.

"Introducing the Testimonies. Doug Templeton, Gatekeeper and Runner."

Again with the coordinates, rank, abilities, and other introductory nonsense. When she finished with Doug, Micah's stomach twisted at the thought of what could happen when she looked at Junior-as-Walter.

"Walter Forbes." There was a sneer in her voice, but she was going along with the Disguise. "Captain Timekeeper from Earth."

Junior-as-Walter looked around appropriately, but mostly kept his head down in apparent resigned defeat. But Micah could see the strain on his face. If Rifun and Isthim knew the game, then the game ought to be over. Let them testify as themselves. Junior and Kayla knew Micaiah better than Walter and Tommen. But then, that, too, was part of the game. How much did they know, and how much were they supposed to know when they were Disguised? Even now, Rifun was going to turn the tables on them. Oh, this had been a bad idea from the start.

"Tommen Forbes," Isthim said. "Apprentice Timekeeper from Earth."

When it came to the Akari, Walter was simply listed as having no affiliation and no abilities. Tommen was listed as a prospective recruit with questionable abilities.

"The Testimonies serve as credible witnesses and alibis," Isthim explained. "They also serve as motivation for the Accused to answer his questions honestly and thoroughly."

Yes, this could get real ugly, real fast. Kayla-as-Tommen nervously glanced at Walter who looked at Doug who simply stared at Isthim, as if sizing her up and searching for a weakness.

"The terms of agreement of this Time Trial are as follows." Micah turned all his attention toward the Borelian at the front of the room. "If the Accused is successful in defending himself over the course of questioning to the satisfaction of the Grandfathers, he is free to return home, along with Micah Durvin, Doug Templeton, Walter Forbes, and Tommen Forbes. Their world, Earth, will be sealed off from the Time industry forever. They will have no further contact with any aspect of the Wheel or the Time industry, or any races involved therein."

It wasn't a bad deal, actually, Micah thought. The problem was getting there.

"However, due to unforeseen circumstances regarding the summoning of the Testimonies, an addendum has been made to these terms." *Translation: That's what we were going to offer you, but because you fooled us, we have to punish you for it somehow. Nothing personal, we just have to send a message to everyone else in the universe.* "Should the Accused be successful, he will retain all rights to the aforementioned terms, however, Michael Junior and Aklaq White Bear, being Runners in Time and Master Akari-bearers, also of Earth, will be summoned here for punishment before being released with the Accused. Michael Junior will suffer clock breaking of the most severe form. Aklaq White Bear will be brought before Faharoa Rifun where he will have his sexual pleasure with her before releasing her back home."

Isthim looked right at Kayla-as-Tommen as she said it, and for a full three seconds, Micah was certain she was going to drop the Disguise and launch herself at the pink bitch. Even Junior-as-Walter and Doug looked rather displeased by the whole thing.

"If the Accused is unsuccessful," Isthim went on, clearly very self-satisfied, "he and Walter Forbes will have their clocks broken unto an inability to wield Time, and they will remain as Lord Rifun's personal servants until the end of their days. Micah Durvin and Tommen Forbes will become Faharoa's willing Akari Apprentices, to be personally trained by him. Doug Templeton's punishment will be at the discretion of Lord Rifun, based on the proceedings of this trial."

*Translation: Rifun hasn't made up his mind what he wants to do with you, so play nice and he might be merciful.*

"Also, pursuant to the aforementioned unforeseen circumstances, Michael Junior and Aklaq White Bear will be summoned for their punishment. Michael Junior will face off against the Bat in the Pit in single combat. Aklaq White Bear will be brought before Rifun to remain as his mistress of sexual pleasure. Do all agree to the terms?"

"No!" Kayla-as-Tommen blurted, taking a step forward. For a second, she seemed to realize what she'd done, but she pressed on. "You can't treat women like that! She's done nothing wrong! She's innocent in this. You can't—"

"Hush!" Isthim barked. Kayla-as-Tommen shut up. "The question was not one for you to answer, though I and the Faharoa admire your persistence and outspokenness."

*Translation: It was a rhetorical question for formality, not because we're here to negotiate.* But at the same time, Micah was impressed; the outburst could have come from Tommen as much as Kayla. Still, before things got ugly and Kayla-as-Tommen had to be forced to sit, she retreated to the chair.

Before them, Isthim shifted her stance. Back in control and all was well. "Now then, if all parties are satisfied, then we may begin with the questioning.

"Here is how the questioning will work. A Grandfather will ask the Accused a question. If the Accused decides to answer, one or all of the Testimonies or the Stake must corroborate the answer to the satisfaction of the Grandfathers. If the corroboration is unsatisfactory, or the Testimonies are unable to corroborate, the Accused must face either the Bat or the Day in single, non-lethal combat. The outcome of said combat will determine the sway of the answer." *Translation: We'll only believe you if you win.*

"At any time, the Accused may forgo a question and elect to fight. Or the Accused may ask the Stake to stand in his place. Single combat by the Stake is more heavily weighted, counting for two answers." *Translation: Hope your champion is stronger than he looks.* "The Stake may not stand in more than twice in a row.

"The questioning will continue for no less than one question per Grandfather, until such time as the Grandfathers are satisfied with a judgment." *Translation: We've already made up our minds; we're just here for a show. As long as it's interesting, we'll let it keep going.*

"If there are no further questions or interruptions as to the proceedings of this trial, then questioning may commence."

Micah swallowed nervously. They'd originally planned for Rifun to be dead already. He was supposed to have walked in with the Grandfathers and be seated there next to Isthim. Micah was supposed to have already shot the fucker. He wasn't supposed to have "other things" that needed tending to. He wasn't supposed to have appointed someone to stand in his place. He was supposed to be here, now. Why wasn't he here now?

Because this was part of his game. This whole thing was a chess match. Rifun had wiped out most of the board and they were still losing pieces left and right. Now he was moving in for the kill.

"Micaiah Durvin," the first Grandfather began, "less than one year ago, you were caught snooping around the Archives looking for information related to the Dispersal, specifically high-ranking Timekeepers and Harvesters. Is this true?"

Micaiah glared at him. "It is."

"Who can corroborate?" The Grandfather glanced over the four of them.

"I can," Micah said. "I was with him."

For a moment, the Grandfather was silent. Then, "This answer is unsatisfactory."

So that's how this was going to be, Micah thought woefully as the Bat advanced toward Micaiah. This was a game of save your own ass. By corroborating, Micah was condemning himself in the process. Plus, the confirmation, while true, just gave them an excuse to declare it unsatisfactory and so punish Micaiah by making him fight the Bat anyway. Whereas not answering would have resulted in the same thing. This was a no-win situation.

He watched helplessly as the Bat took a swing at Micaiah using one of its wings for cover and distraction, coming out of a whirlwind maneuver and clocking him straight to the face. Micaiah stumbled backwards and fell hard, gasping for air. The Bat screeched shrilly, but backed off. Apparently it wasn't as fun as anticipated, but maybe that would work in Cai's favor.

Before he'd even picked himself up off the floor and gotten back to an upright position, the next Grandfather was ready and asking his question.

"In that same time frame, it was reported that you sought information about Faharoa Rifun and the former Zero Hour Cassius, seeking to overthrow them. Is this true?"

Micaiah groaned as he stood, wobbly on his right leg. "No."

"Explain."

"Seeking to overthrow them would imply that they were already in power. I was trying to stop them from gaining power in the first place. Rifun was no longer a Hand, and Cassius was a Zero Hour by cheating."

Micah didn't even get a chance to speak in Micaiah's defense before the Grandfather declared, "The answer is unsatisfactory."

This time it was the Day who advanced. Micah went to the end of his chain, but that was all he could do. Fuck, but he wished Rifun was here now so he could shoot the motherfucker and end all this.

But then the question became, would it really end? Or had Rifun set everything up so that even if he died, his empire would carry on? At this point, it seemed the logically paranoid thing to do.

The Day was not seen as often as the Bat, but there was no

reason to think that it was any less powerful just because it was slightly less frightening. In fact, it used every bit of its peacock-like charm to distract and confuse, keeping its head high until the last second when it used it as a battering ram, first knocking Micaiah to the side, then plowing into his chest, sending him flying a good ten feet, again landing hard on his back in front of Doug's platform.

"Cai!" Micah cried. "Cai, come on, get up!"

Spirit was a wonderful thing to have, but it meant little if the body was weak. Micaiah let out a breath, coughed a few times, and managed to get back to his feet. Two questions in and he was already whipped. This did not bode well. Even if Rifun walked in now, Micah shot him, and the whole revolution and overthrow of the regime went exactly as planned, was Micaiah even strong enough to make the escape?

The next Grandfather was already waiting to ask its question. Judging by body language under the shroud, it was waiting quite impatiently. Micah could already see that no matter the answer, it would be unsatisfactory.

"During one of your trips to the Archives, you and your brother were apprehended and held in the Judgment Wing under suspicion of Running and treason. How did you manage to escape your holding cell?"

Micaiah took a breath, winced. "We didn't escape. Walter came and bailed us out. It was just a misunderstanding."

"Walter Forbes?"

"It's true," Junior-as-Walter said, just loud enough to be heard. "I was summoned and questioned, and it was ruled a misunderstanding. We were trying to—"

"The answer is satisfactory."

Micah was stunned, but he could see the relief on his brother's face. He could breathe, even if was only for ten seconds. The next Grandfather stood.

"You were also found to be in possession of pages from a journal deemed heretical by the Hands of Time. You were reportedly looking for someone to interpret them and so put you in contact with Faharoa Rifun and former Zero Hour Cassius. Is this true?"

Wait, so were they charging him with treason from both sides of the empire? Whatever crimes he'd committed against the old Hands—even if Rifun had done them himself at the time—he was being held responsible for them. And whatever crimes he'd supposedly committed against Rifun's new regime, he was still responsible for them? What kind of double-standard was that? Nevertheless, Micaiah nodded and answered, "We had the pages, yes. We wanted to know what was in them, why they meant so much to Rifun."

"The answer is unsatisfactory."

So was he being punished for being in possession of the pages and wanting to know what they were, or because he hadn't joined Rifun because he had those pages? Micaiah spoke before the Bat could get more than two steps toward him.

"I call my Stake."

Micah's heart skipped a beat. He was going to have to face the Bat. Of course, that was his role as the Stake. And he would gladly help his brother out, especially seeing how he was already beaten. But still. He was going to face the Bat, this thing of nightmares who saw—well, heard all, knew all, was immune to Time and hated the Akari with white-hot passion. He became light-headed at the thought as a secretary moved swiftly up the steps to his platform to unlock the chain on his ankle.

He hadn't even gotten off the last step before the Bat was on him, and before Micah could even process what was happening, he was on his back in the dust. The pain didn't come for a few more seconds. His breath caught in his throat as he was made aware of some very unnatural openings in his skin, especially around his chest and shoulder area. Once his head came back to him and he was able to take a small inventory, he found that the Bat had sliced him open with its three-toed talons, one set of marks ripping open his left shoulder, the other his right breast, his shirt torn to shreds.

He couldn't even remember what happened. Had he even tried to defend himself? He gave an incredulous look toward the others, but they seemed just as shocked. What the...?

Gradually, Micah got to his feet and looked around. He wasn't even five feet from the platform steps. Feeling confused, conspicuous, and not a little pissed, he slunk his way back up the steps toward the chair. A secretary followed him and dutifully replaced the shackle.

The Grandfathers continued their questioning, but Micah found himself preoccupied by his new wounds. They still hurt, sure, but it was reduced to a dull ache. The wounds themselves weren't that bad, so he must have hit his head, or else it really had happened just that fast.

Micaiah got lucky, as he managed to go three questions in a row where his answers were deemed satisfactory. Apparently he was feeling good enough that by his next unsatisfactory answer, he elected to take on the Day himself. To no one's surprise, he was dispatched with time to spare and not a mark on the Day.

"Micaiah Durvin," the next Grandfather began, "it is reported that you once attempted to rally a force of Hands and anyone who would listen, in order to march against Faharoa Rifun and former Zero Hour Cassius. What happened to this force?"

"At the time?" Micaiah said. "Rifun fled into a quasi-dimension of his own making, such that we were unable to penetrate it and get inside without severe risk of loss on our part. So we abandoned the mission."

*There was also that time where I had the rallying force ready to come to aid,* Micah thought. *But I called it off because Rifun had taken you hostage as well.* He sighed, wondering if he'd done the right thing. They were supposed to be Timekeeper officers, fearless, ready to give their lives. But at the same time, they were not soldiers. And as Micaiah had said on many occasions, he wasn't going to risk his life for a corrupt system. Looking back, Micah also couldn't remember if there had been any good way to have kept the force and saved Micaiah's life. It felt so long ago now. Back when things were much simpler.

But whether it was the force they were supposed to have had at the airport or at the warehouse, it was still a crime against Rifun. Regardless of how honest Micaiah was being, crimes against Rifun had to be punished. His answer was deemed unsatisfactory, and the Bat came out to play.

Micaiah almost seemed resigned to getting his ass kicked by the Bat, but he still got in a weak defensive posture. It seemed to have moved past the game phase of the trial, and now they had entered the routine phase. They just had to keep going long enough to make sure all the Grandfathers got to ask him a question. Though if Micah had to hazard a guess, if there were more than fifty Grandfathers on the panel—which it certainly looked like there were—they weren't going to make it all the way.

It was painful to watch his brother get his ass kicked. Had Micah not been chained, he would have jumped down into the arena and tried to help. Instead, he could only watch as Micaiah managed to dodge the first swipe, but was too slow for the quick one-two punch follow-up. He was easily knocked off-balance, but before he went down, the Bat got in a couple more blows, taking Micaiah's head and smashing it against Junior-as-Walter's platform.

Micaiah went down. The four of them peered over their respective platforms, all straining to see. Micaiah was not moving. From his poor vantage point, Micah couldn't even say if he was breathing. After a minute of silence, a secretary approached and lightly examined him.

"He is alive," the secretary reported. "He is only unconscious."

On the platform, Isthim huffed angrily and folded her arms. It looked unnatural, and Micah wondered how much she had picked up from Rifun as far as gestures, body language, and slang went. Still, there was nothing unnatural or even unusual about the dark stare on her face as she studied Micaiah's unmoving form. Micah waited silently, as if making any sound might send her off on a rampage. Would she declare the trial over? Had they just lost everything?

"Return him to his cell," she decided finally, sounding none too pleased. "And the others. We will recess the trial for now; I must have a word with Faharoa Rifun."

*Translation: This trial isn't as fun as we'd hoped. Now I have to go and ask Rifun what he wants to do to make it more fun.*

It was the best news Micah had heard so far. He didn't even wait sullenly. Once the secretary unlocked the ankle shackle, he bolted. He ran down the steps just as fast as his body would let him, breaking out in a dead sprint once he hit the ground, sliding to a stop beside Micaiah as a couple more secretaries got him on a stretcher. A guard advanced toward him, but Isthim recalled him.

"He will do no harm," she said. "Let them have their petty moment. It may be the last one they get together."

Her words held more truth than Micah wanted to admit as he followed the secretaries back to Micaiah's cell where they laid him on the ground and left, the gate grinding shut behind them.

"Cai? Cai, can you hear me?" Micah asked, shaking him a bit.

But Micaiah was out cold. Micah sat back on his heels, mind racing, trying to figure out what to do, what could be done. He looked him over briefly, taking note of the most obvious injuries, but being unable to do anything about them except Band them lightly. The best he could do was maneuver Micaiah's shirt off him and try to manage some of the bleeding, even if most of it was past its worst stage. He would have used his own shirt, but he still had to hide the band and the gun-as-knife.

"Come on, Cai, you got 'em right where you want 'em. You can beat these slobs. I know you can. For fuck's sake, you call yourself a prize fighter? What are are you doing out there? Come on, show 'em what you're made of."

Micaiah's lips moved and a breathy sigh escaped his lips, along with a few words Micah couldn't catch. He leaned down. "What?"

"I said, fuck you," Micaiah whispered.

He still didn't open his eyes, but he started to come around a little. Either that or he was still unconscious but speaking nonsense. Was that possible? Micah decided it didn't matter, but a few seconds later, his brother's eyes peeped open.

"Is he gone?"

"The Bat? Yeah. He knocked you out, so Isthim called a recess. You're back in your cell."

"He didn't knock me out."

"Then what...you Banded? But the Bat nearly killed you just for — "

"Internal Band, not external. Just enough to make it seem like I was out cold."

"So it was a trick."

"I had to take a break, get out of there." He sighed. "I can't keep going much longer."

"I'm surprised you made it as far as you did. But there's got to be forty more Grandfathers, all waiting to ask you questions."

"I know. There has to be something we can do."

"Why don't we just escape? Open a portal, grab Doug and the others, and just get out of here? Cai, at this rate, you're not going to survive, regardless of whether Rifun attends the trial or not."

"He'll only pursue us. And it won't be him, but he'll send someone or something. This is our only chance."

"No, it's not. There will be other chances. Even this chance isn't working out quite like we'd hoped. And if we escape, then we should be able to hide out for at least long enough for you to rest and heal."

Micaiah shook his head. "No. It's only delaying the inevitable. We end this here and now, or we'll be running forever."

Micah took a breath and let it out slowly. "Okay. I can't change your mind, but there has to be some way to get you a fighting chance. The Bat and the Day hate the Akari. Is there any way to use that against them?"

"Maybe. If I can just get ten seconds to think about it." He shifted and gritted his teeth against the pain. "Ah, but you're right. This is not going how we planned it."

Micah helped him to a sitting position, keeping him upright until the dizziness subsided. "How's your knee? It looks...swollen."

"If the Bat or the Day or anyone else here doesn't kill me, I think my doctors just might," Micaiah said, forcing a weak laugh. "But I think I can take them on a little easier than the people here. Call it a hunch, but I don't think they like me very much."

Well, at least his sense of humor was still there somewhere. Before either could say more, however, the gate opened and Isthim walked in.

"So, you survived," she observed, looking down her nose at them.

"Surprised?" Micaiah wondered wryly.

"The Faharoa has decided to be merciful and offer you a chance to peacefully surrender."

"Surrender?" Taking a breath, Micaiah stood. As he did so, he Banded and Double-Banded and Pinpoint Banded until his open wounds had healed shut and his bruises reduced to fresh pink skin. Micah noticed he was gentler with his knee, maybe still getting used to the new physiology in his residual limb, for while he took down the worst of the swelling, some still remained. "Honey, I'm just getting started."

Isthim sighed, seemingly unimpressed by his party tricks or sudden display of bravado. "Very well. You have made your choice. Faharoa Rifun has decided to come down to the trial now, to oversee your humiliating defeat. The Grandfathers are returning. When they are seated, you will be fetched."

"Best news I've heard all day."

She left them then. As soon as she was out of sight, Micaiah Akari-Banded the two of them, pulling it tight around them.

"It was always a trick," Micah said. "You knew that if you were going to lose too quickly, Rifun would have to come down to witness your demise."

"Precisely," Micaiah told him.

"First shot I get, I take?"

"No. Not since you have those shackles. I'm going to humor him for a question or two, get my ass kicked some more, then I'll call you to stand for me the next time. What do you think of your vantage point on the platform?"

"It's the best one I'm going to get. Anything lower and I'm just firing into a sea of black shrouds."

"Once you're free, if you have the shot, take it."

"What about Doug and the others?"

"If the key secretary is friendly, enlist their help. If not, get on those platforms and blow the fucking chains off the platform. Whatever you have to do. But you'll have to make it quick, because all hell is going to break loose as soon as the first shot is fired. I have a feeling the Bat and the Day are each going to come for one of us."

"I was afraid you were going to say that."

"Just like we planned."

Micah nodded uncertainly. "Just like we planned."

The Band was dropped and the gate began opening. The twins bro-hugged, hoping it wasn't the last time they would see each other. The Day walked in, as hostile as ever, murderous gaze looking back and forth between the two. "Faharoa Rifun has arrived, and the trial is set to begin again. Come with me."

# Chapter Twenty-Seven
## Metamorphosis

The twins were led back into the Pit, each one gripped roughly so they couldn't try anything smart. Micaiah was deposited in the same place he'd fallen while Micah was taken back to his platform. His knee still throbbed and a headache was starting to blossom in his mind. Shit, he'd been through way too much today. He would have given anything to be back at the bakery with a long line out the door, all them angry customers, each with a different complaint, some serious, some total bullshit. That was entirely preferable to being in this situation now.

He grunted as he felt the pinch of the manacle around his ankle. Dutifully, he sat down in the chair and looked around. The last of the stragglers in the crowd were making their way back to their seats, and Doug and the others were already in their chains and chairs. Up front, the Grandfathers had reassembled, but this time, Rifun sat in their midst, on the raised platform next to Isthim. He scrutinized the whole thing, like an Olympic judge looking for any reason to knock off a few points of a performance. Except too few points in this performance would end in death. He and Isthim exchanged a few quiet words. After a minute or two, whatever cue they'd been waiting for, Isthim stood and the Pit grew deathly silent.

"The Accused, Micaiah Durvin, is awake and has recovered," she announced. "Faharoa Rifun offered him a chance to surrender, but he has refused. He has elected to continue with this Time Trial and see it through to its end. Therefore, we will pick up exactly where we left off. Noble Grandfathers, you may continue your questioning."

A thousand things were going through Micah's mind at that

moment. What if Rifun somehow discerned their plan? What if he decided to change the rules on the fly? What if he wouldn't wait four or five more questions before declaring the whole thing unsatisfactory and Micaiah had lost? What if, what if, what if? There were too many what ifs, too many variables, too much unknown. Micah hated it, and he still had to act on it and make that split-second decision to reveal himself and shoot Rifun, hopefully killing him this time.

"It was reported that you, Micaiah Durvin, assisted Tommen Forbes in his petition to the Hands of Time, including giving him ideas to convey that would result in the Hands overtaking the Grandfathers and potentially causing a Time civil war. Is this true?"

"It is," Micaiah answered, glaring at Rifun.

Problem was, that had actually been a very serious crime with very serious repercussions, regardless of who was sitting in judgment over them now. It was like planning to assassinate the president, or maybe some tyrannical dictator—North Korea or, say, for instance, the new Dictator of Time. The guy might be a tyrannical dick, but the crime was still serious, and every aspect of it had to be thought out. Why were they doing it, how they were going to pull it off, what was going to happen afterwards, who was going to take over, how could they ensure sympathizers wouldn't retaliate, how were they going to make the new system better than the old one?

Maybe they had erred when they neglected to consider all those aspects when preparing Tommen for his petition. It had helped them in the short-term, true, but this long-term stuff was a bitch, and she was biting them in the ass in a way Micah didn't really appreciate.

As expected, Micaiah's answer was deemed unsatisfactory. The Day moved toward him. This time, though Micaiah appeared much more with it, prepared, even. He managed to dodge the first and second blows, even took the third hit and turned it around on the Day, striking it. With the Day stunned, more from the fact that it had been hit than the hit itself, Micaiah was able to get in several more blows. Unfortunately, though, the Day was just too big and too heavy for him to effectively knock down, where one simple move by the Day saw him flat on his ass. Another small hit sent him skidding painfully along the ground on his back.

Micah looked at Rifun, trying to read his expression. No doubt Isthim had told him that Micaiah was a miserable failure and could barely stand on his own, never mind try to fend off a small attack. Rifun watched everything with a gaze as stony as his silence. He was watching, analyzing, calculating, plotting, scheming. Micah looked down at Doug who was looking at Rifun, no doubt doing the same thing.

Doug glanced up at Micah once, a brief glance, but the question was as big as the nose on his face. *Why haven't you taken the shot?* it wondered. Micah simply gave a tiny shake of his head. Doug watched him a moment longer before turning his attention back to Rifun.

Micaiah managed to squeeze out one more satisfactory answer. Micah had to wonder if there was a pattern to the satisfactory and unsatisfactory answers. Was it just random, the Grandfathers flipping the metaphorical coin just to keep Micaiah guessing? Was there some sort of pattern to it? Were there Grandfathers in the ranks who could care less for Rifun's personal vendetta and truly wanted to see some form of justice done, as barbaric as this seemed? Were they just sadistic, adding in satisfactory answers just to keep things going as long as they could?

"Is it true that you sought the cure for the Borelian poison, that you could undermine the Borelians and the Grandfathers and establish your own industry to compete with Time?" the next Grandfather inquired.

"No," Micaiah answered. "I wanted to find a cure in order to save my Captain and my friend."

"The answer is unsatisfactory."

Of course it was. Because there always had to be some ulterior motive that somehow involved dominating the universe or the Time industry. Because love was clearly something only humans experienced. Micah sighed internally and watched as the Bat advanced.

Which one would Micaiah make him fight? The Bat who had already demonstrated scary speed, or the Day who was simply a huge rolling roadblock with exceptional distraction skills? Not that he intended to fight either, seeing how he was hoping to get off his shot and kill Rifun before ever leaving the platform. As Micaiah did his ten-second dalliance with the Bat, Micah tried to gauge his shot. From his vantage point, his only options were head and neck; everything else was too dodgy amid a sea of black shrouds. If he went for the neck, there were a number of vitals he could hit there: the jugular vein, the windpipe, the spinal cord, all of them instant or near-instant kills. But it was a smaller target. If he aimed for the head, even if he didn't kill Rifun instantly, it should incapacitate him long enough for Micah to get up there and finish him off in a few minutes. He mulled this over in his mind, acutely aware that his time was coming up fast.

The battle — or "scuffle" may have been a more appropriate term, if one didn't want to go straight to "ass-kicking" — ended quickly enough, with another loss for Micaiah. Supposedly, the overall success rate for Time Trials, the former ones anyway, was about thirty percent. For humans, it was only one or two percent, if that, and Micah found himself wondering just what in the hell those humans had to do in order to train to fight the Bat. Seriously, were they super bodybuilders or something? Micaiah worked out, and he was having a hell of a time.

Still, Micaiah picked himself up off the floor, casting a quick glance at Micah, one that told him to be ready. Micah gave an almost imperceptible nod in return and fixed his gaze on Rifun. The next one was his.

Actually, the next one turned out to be a satisfactory answer, and the Grandfathers moved on. Micah absently scratched at his ankle, then his thigh, hoping that his "scratch" under his arm wouldn't be anything of note to anyone.

His plan was suddenly foiled as the next Grandfather to stand completely blocked his shot of Rifun. Thankfully, Micaiah seemed to realize this, so when his answer was deemed unsatisfactory, he elected to face the Day himself. The false start had made Micah's heart jump, and he hated himself for it. He had to be prepared, be ready to fire the shot that would be heard 'round the universe, the one that would surely cause the entire Pit to erupt into chaos.

Micah absently scratched at a scab on his arm, peeled it off, made it bleed. Well, damn. But he noted that every time he moved, fewer and fewer people were interested. They no longer cared to be notified of his every cough, sneeze and itch. Micaiah got up off the ground.

The next Grandfather stood. Micah couldn't say what the question was, he was just waiting for it to be declared unsatisfactory. He glanced nervously toward the Bat, poised and ready to strike. The creature could smell the weakness as Micaiah was beginning to wear out again.

"The answer is unsatisfactory," the Grandfather declared.

"I call my Stake," Micaiah said, breathing hard and looking at his brother.

Time seemed to slow then, and not because of any Band. Micah looked around the Pit, trying to judge his exits as well as the crowd. There were a lot of Grandfathers here, even if they weren't part of the questioning panel. They were dangerous enough of their own, but there were also armed guards in the ranks, too. Micah itched his shoulder, pulled at his shirt collar as if checking for some sort of rash or allergic reaction. The elephant seal secretary walked up and bent to unlock the manacle.

"Get ready," he hissed.

She looked up at him. "I'm sorry?"

He hoped his expression was enough to convey his meaning, but body language was not always a universal thing. He stepped out of the manacle, but he did not get down off the platform.

"Micah Durvin, you have been called to stand in for the Accused," Isthim told him, sounding very annoyed.

He nodded. "I know. I heard you. There's just one little

problem, though."

"And what's that?"

He scratched under his arm, reaching for the gun. "I'm not Micah Durvin."

Several things happened at once, then. First, Micaiah shed his Disguise, glad to finally be free of his little brother. Below, Micah also shed his Disguise, and Junior and Kayla revealed themselves on their respective platforms. Second, Micaiah touched the knife, dissolving its Disguise. In one fluid motion, he drew the gun, aimed, drawing on the Akari to Band and give himself just a few more seconds to make sure his aim was true, and fired at Rifun. He saw Rifun's head snap back at the same time the Pit erupted into chaos.

Everything began moving at once. Isthim screamed and knelt beside her fallen master. The Bat and the Day advanced on Micah who scrambled onto Doug's platform to get out of the way as much as possible. All around them in the Pit, Grandfathers, guards, secretaries, all stood up and started shouting, confused and outraged. What had just happened? Who did it? What was going on? What happened now? Who was going to stop this?

Micaiah took the opening to make a calculated leap from his platform onto Doug's. It was less than perfect and he had all the grace of a bull. He made it, but he was too unaccustomed to his running leg yet and he fell, almost sliding right off the platform. As he pulled himself upright, he did a quick inspection of the prosthetic. Oh, his doctors were going to kill him, assuming he survived this ordeal long enough to care about his doctors.

Originally, he'd thought that the elephant seal secretary had run off, just as confused and afraid as the rest of the secretaries seemed to be. A moment later, before Micaiah could blow the chain off Doug's platform, she appeared, keys in hand. Once Doug was free, she looked at him. "I will free them. You must flee."

"Don't worry," Doug told her, choosing now to flaunt his ego. "We've got reinforcements coming."

"Well, they can show up at any time," Micah said, looking

around nervously.

The confused crowd seemed to have gotten their heads together and now they began pouring down from the stadium. As they did, however, Micaiah observed a strange phenomenon: they weren't all on the same side. As expected, he saw secretaries fighting secretaries, but what he hadn't expected was divided loyalty among the guards. Maybe Doug had planted a few of their forces in the ranks, just to confuse things.

But perhaps the thing that stunned him the most, so that he almost forgot what he was doing, was the sight of even the Grandfathers fighting amongst themselves. Micaiah could believe that Doug was able to plant operatives in the secretaries and the guards, but if the Grandfathers were fighting each other, it was because they were truly fighting each other. Due to the shrouds, it was impossible to say what separated them or who was on which side, but if it kept them occupied and away from them for a while, long enough for them to escape, Micaiah was okay with it.

He stuck with the elephant seal secretary, moving from platform to platform, giving her cover while she hastily unlocked the shackles. When they made it to Kayla and got her free, Micaiah pulled her into his arms and kissed her.

"See, I told you everything would go according to plan," he told her nervously.

"So far, but we still have to escape," she reminded him. "We have to get up there and make sure Rifun is dead, or else all of this was for nothing."

"Agreed. How are we going to get up there, though?"

They were surrounded by fighting of one form or another. As meager humans, they might have been able to slip through, except they always ran the risk of friendly fire, plus the Day and the Bat were still in there somewhere.

Micaiah didn't get a chance to think about it too long before he found himself swept off his feet, his chin hitting the platform hard before he was dragged off. He twisted in the grip of a very pissed off guard who raised its weapon for a death blow. Out of nowhere, Kayla launched herself at the guard, clinging to him like an octopus. She took the guard to the ground, disarmed him, and killed him with his own weapon, something resembling a battle ax. As she stood, she took out two more guards who advanced on her. When she finally got five seconds to breathe, she held out a hand to Micaiah and helped him to his feet.

"Damn it, woman, you're making me look bad," Micaiah said.

"You do that just fine on your own, dear," she teased. "Now then, which way?"

"I think we just have to get to the top, then we can step down into the seats."

Problem was, that was a suicide mission. Just as they had set Tommen to be a watchdog at the portal and bottleneck the enemy, so the passageways leading up out of the Pit could also be used to bottleneck anyone trying to escape, to say nothing of the gates on either end of the tunnels.

"We can't go through the tunnels," Kayla said, reading his thoughts.

"Then we'll have to use the Akari, use Gravity," Micaiah decided.

"Cai, that's unstable and unpredictable."

"We're in the Wheel. Physics don't apply here. And in case you haven't noticed, this is not a very stable environment anyway. We have no other options."

The Akari was many things that Time was not, and the power of the Akari was not limited to Time; it encompassed all realms of physics. Problem was, some aspects were more unstable than others and more difficult to control. Time was easy, or maybe it just seemed that way because of how commercialized and widespread its use had become. Gravity was a more fickle beast. Manipulating those forces was kind of like trying to balance two eggs on top of each other.

Micaiah chose a spot on the wall where the fighting seemed the thinnest, but it was about halfway down from the platform where

Rifun was killed. He used his gun for quick clearing, while Kayla used her newly acquired battle ax to mow down a wider path. He paused once, briefly, just to admire his wife as she went full commando and went to town on anyone who dared approach her with a weapon raised. She was a sight to behold, and Micaiah found himself glad that they were on the same side.

His admiration lasted only half a moment before he dove back into the fray and followed her. The crowd had thinned enough so he could breathe, and he picked his spot on the wall that seemed the safest to attempt to scale.

Time was easy. In its most basic and easiest use, one could Band oneself. It only affected the Time he himself was standing in. Later, it could be honed and strengthened and used to include others in Bands, as well as a vast array of other abilities.

Gravity was not so easy. Even in its most basic form, it had to be manipulated along a path. Micaiah could jump and affect the gravity around a small area, but for such a feat as scaling this wall, he had to affect all the gravity along the path he was set to take. If he didn't, and he hit a patch of unaffected gravity, he would go plummeting back to the ground. Needless to say, manipulation of Gravity was not an easy or effective way to fly. Plus, he still had to get Kayla up with him, which was a whole different aspect of it.

"Think you can do it?" Kayla wondered.

"Don't have a choice," Micaiah said, backing up.

In another, less stressful instance of having to use Gravity, Micaiah had found that, while a running start was not necessary, using it and activating Predict was particularly helpful when trying to determine the path he need to take and manipulate. Kayla followed his lead.

"Ready?"

He didn't wait for a reply, but he started off. Immediately, he knew it was probably a bad idea. He'd had his running leg for all of two days, and he wasn't ready for the strain and impact. The Pit was not a treadmill, and a full sprint was not an easy jog, to say nothing of the jump he was going to have to do. He tried to push those thoughts away and focus only on what needed to be done, but doubt still niggled at his mind.

He set the Gravity effects in motion as soon as he was able to see Predict and get the two in sync. If it worked, they would land safely in the bottom row of seats. If it failed, they would go plummeting thirty to forty feet, likely to their deaths. It was not a comforting thought.

"You got this," Kayla told him, as if sensing his anxiety.

Micaiah was not prepared for jumps of any form, but he had no choice. He set Gravity, found the point of ignition, and they jumped together. It was like bouncing around on the moon, and the unpredictable change in gravity did go over well with Micaiah's stomach. His throat locked and he could feel his heart pounding wildly in his chest. He tried to stay in line with Gravity and Predict, but the fear of being out of control in a physical environment he didn't understand was terrifying. Beside him, he could tell Kayla was having similar reservations, but she also had a more determined resolve.

Then they landed. Safely. In the bottom row of seats. Well, Kayla landed safely, hitting the breaking point of the gravitational field and being dropped to the ground like a sack of potatoes right at the very end. Micaiah also hit the threshold and dropped, and his inexperience with his leg saw him ungracefully to the ground, his knee in a most uncomfortable and painful position.

"Are you okay?" Kayla asked, moving toward him and standing to keep him covered. It was a miracle she hadn't landed on her ax and split herself in half.

"Fine," Micaiah told her, repositioning his leg and getting unsteadily to his feet.

He looked around, trying to determine the easiest and safest route to the front of the Pit. In the end, he figured one way was as good as any other, and they set off along the row.

Fighting in the rows was different than fighting on the ground. In a way, it was easier since they had only to push their foes over the wall. On the other hand, there was the point that if they themselves were pushed over the wall, neither of them were skilled enough with Gravity to make that a non-issue. Micaiah silently resolved that he was going to have to study up a little more on it, just in case some shit like this ever happened again. But that was for a later time, and they pressed forward.

The fighting in the Pit seemed to be thinning, and their path to the front became clearer and clearer. Micaiah tripped over more than one body, but thankfully none of them reached up to grab him and drag him down. Truth be told, that was always a fear of his, when walking among the dead, that one or more wasn't really dead. Maybe he watched too many zombie movies. He needed to cut back on that shit; it was messing with his thinking.

"Do you think it's over?" Kayla wondered, looking around and seeing the battle appeared nearly at a close. Judging from the way they hadn't been immediately apprehended, Micaiah wondered if they'd actually won. Was it possible that everything had gone according to plan?

"I don't know," he answered cautiously. "We're about to find out, though."

They approached the front of the Pit where the panel of Grandfathers had sat in judgment of the Accused. The elevated platform had seemed very minor when the Grandfathers of all shapes and sizes had occupied it. Seeing it now, empty, it was a pretty significant difference, a platform for the viewing ease and pleasure of Caesar and his chosen favorites.

Grandfather bodies were scattered about the platform, each one having his shroud pulled back to show the face of the dead. Many were Borelians, but there were other races mixed in as well. Had they all been real Grandfathers, or had some of them been planted within the ranks? Micaiah decided it didn't matter now.

They approached the platform and looked behind the lip, on the ground.

"Shit," Micaiah hissed as they knelt beside the body.

It wasn't Rifun, despite the very obvious hole in the middle of his forehead. A human man of approximate size and build, yes, but not Rifun.

"It was a Disguise," Kayla growled. "He wanted to see what was happening, but he didn't want to get involved. He was testing us."

Micaiah shook his head in disbelief. "How do you beat someone who knows all your tricks and has learned how to use them against you? He could be anywhere."

"You think he knows what's happened?"

"I would be more surprised if he didn't."

"You think he's going to flee again?"

After a moment of consideration, Micaiah shook his head again. "No. Not this time. He's finally gotten what he always wanted; he's not going to give it up so easily."

"If that's the case, then we're sitting ducks in here. We have to get out."

"Agreed. We have to find Micah and the others. We've done all we can; it's time to let this revolution sort itself out."

Getting back down into the Pit was considerably easier than trying to scale its walls, but that didn't make the trip any less harrowing, trying to manipulate Gravity into gently easing them to the ground instead of just dropping them. But they made it down, no worse for wear.

"They could be anywhere," Kayla said.

"You want to split up?"

"No way. Fool me once, shame on me. Switch places with your brother without telling anyone, and I'm not letting you out of my sight."

Okay, so maybe she had a point. Micaiah grinned stupidly even as they made their way through the battlefield, the need for cutting and hacking dwindling sharply.

They found Doug along one wall, cornered by a couple of Grandfathers and not having a very easy time of defending himself.

Just knowing about Borelian proximity poisons and being prepared was enough to negate ninety-nine percent of the effects, but without knowing exactly what color the Borelian was made it so the effects could still drip in, bit by bit.

Kayla dealt with them swiftly, splitting their heads open, covering herself and Doug in blood. She was already pretty well-soaked, but Doug still cringed at the thought. The man was a boxer: ring, referee, rules of the match. He wasn't a freelancing battle warrior like Kayla, accustomed to survival at the top of the world, battling bears and walruses and a whole host of other creatures also trying to survive.

Maybe that was a little exaggerated, but the point was there. Doug was shaken, and she was not. Micaiah approached, hoping he appeared friendly and could calm him down a little.

"Is Rifun dead?" Doug asked, seeming to remember himself.

Micaiah shook his head. "No."

"He survived?"

"It wasn't even him. Rifun Disguised someone else to look like him. He was never here to begin with."

"Shit. So we still have to find him and kill him."

"Yes," Kayla confirmed. "But it looks like we may have tipped off something of a civil war in here."

"It's hard to love a dictator," Doug said. "I knew we had friends, but this surprises me. Still, Rifun has more of an army than this at his disposal. Battle's not over yet."

"That's what worries me," Micaiah agreed. "We have to find the others and get out of here."

"Junior is dead."

"What?" Kayla wondered.

Doug nodded. "He was determined to go down in a blaze of glory. So he did. He went down under four Grandfathers; I saw it myself."

Micaiah shook his head. "I don't know whether he's a sorry bastard or a stupid one."

“Doesn't matter. He's a dead one now.”

“What about Micah?”

“I haven't seen him.”

*That could be good or bad,* Micaiah thought. “I have to find him.” He looked at Kayla. “Stay here and guard Doug.”

“Last I saw, he was over there.” Doug pointed toward the tunnel that led to the cell of the Accused.

Micaiah took a breath and started that way. He'd long since run out of extra clips and resorted to grabbing whatever was at hand, usually the weapon off of a nearby body. But he knew that it was a dangerous thing to get trapped anywhere, especially in a tunnel or, worse, one of the cells.

But that was exactly where he found Micah, trying a bottleneck technique in the cell of the Accused, with unexpected success. He'd managed to stack a dozen or so bodies and effectively barricade himself inside. With half a dozen guards all focusing on him, Micaiah was able to cut down four of them before the other two realized what was happening. When they became distracted, Micah finished them off.

“I figured you would come for me eventually,” Micah said. He was slick with sweat and exhausted, taking a minute to drop his sword-like weapon and sit against the cool cell wall. “You could have come a little sooner, though.”

“Yeah, I'll make a point of that next time,” Micaiah told him.

“Is Rifun dead?”

“No. It wasn't even him. He used a Disguise.”

“Shit.”

“That's what I said. Come on. We found Doug; we have to get out of here.”

“No argument from me, boss. What about Junior?”

“Dead. Four Grandfathers.”

“Good for him, I guess, that it took that many. Still, I guess if you're going, better to go out on your own terms.” Micah held out a hand and Micaiah helped him up. “Okay, I guess I'm ready. Let's get the fuck out of here."

They stepped around the bodies of the guards and headed back out to the Pit where the fighting was largely subsided. Doug and Kayla were waiting in the same spot he'd left them.

"Good to see you're all right," Doug said diplomatically as they approached.

"Is it over?" Micah asked, looked around. "Did we win?"

"We won this battle," Kayla said suspiciously. "But if we didn't kill Rifun, there are a lot more to come in the near future."

The activity in the Pit seemed to be dying down. Those who had been planted by Doug now removed their disguises, some as simple as secretary or Grandfather cloaks, or various guard rank insignia, others literal Disguises. Some of their allies, however, hadn't been plants by Doug, but actual secretaries, guards, or Grandfathers, turned against their master for whatever reason. On any other day, they might have gone after those planted, but for now, they were under a kind of truce. The enemy of my enemy and all that. Right now, Rifun was still the common enemy.

Before Micaiah could suggest they leave, however, something caught his attention. He looked up to see a new wave of guards and Grandfathers flooding into the Pit, and they didn't look like they were worried about fighting their own, nor did they appear to be very friendly. They did not swarm down into the Pit, but they did fill every inch of the seating and upper walkway.

"Oh...fuck," Micaiah said.

After a moment of tense scrutiny, the Grandfathers began to part, a not so straight path for the man who'd arranged the whole ordeal. Rifun walked out to the platform, regarded the dead man who was not him, and looked out across the open Pit. He had the look of a man who'd just gotten done watching a particularly intense and very good sporting event, where both sides were comprised of excellent athletes of comparable skill, and the game had gone on for a few extra exciting innings.

"My, my, my, what have we here?" he said casually, almost

able to make Micaiah believe that he had just stumbled haphazardly into the scene. "I knew Time Trials were exciting, but I never imagined they could get this exciting. We really should do this more often, I think." Then his expression changed into something that was too familiar. "But then, that isn't what you hoped to accomplish here, is it, Micaiah?" He looked at him. "Micah? You and all your little friends came here for the sole purpose of assassinating me and bringing my empire to a glorious end."

"That was the idea, yes," Kayla said matter-of-factly.

"Had we the time, I would be interested to know what you take me for. An overconfident fool, perhaps? Do you think I haven't anticipated that such attempts might come to pass? Do you think that some haven't already tried to kill me with no obvious success?"

"You ever think that you talk too much?" Micah told him.

Rifun grinned and Micaiah cuffed Micah in the back of the head. "Keep your mouth shut, idiot."

"Ah, yes, I have always been given to monologues. But if a monologue conveys no information—such as a dastardly scheme or vile threats—is it still a monologue, or just a man talking to himself? If so, does that make me the fool regardless? But I digress. Your little revolution was fun and interesting to watch, and it told me who my dissenters are, so if they will kindly remove all shrouds and other disguises?"

Grudgingly, false and turncoat Grandfathers, guards, and secretaries removed all remaining evidence of their disguises and get-ups.

"That's better," Rifun said. "Makes it much easier when you know who you're trying to kill and can see them. So then, this is how this is going to play out. I already gave you one chance to surrender. Clearly, you have no such interest. Similarly, I have no reason to think you won't try this ever again, or that friends and family will not attempt something similar if I send you home alive, even with your clocks broken. Therefore, these guards and Grandfathers here, they will be coming down to kill you all. And I am going to end this madness once and for all."

"There will always be more," Doug cut in.

"Perhaps. But not today." And then, in a manner that was all too familiar, Rifun took a step back and let the Grandfathers advance. "At your leisure."

Kayla hefted her battle ax, but Micaiah could see the weight was starting to wear on her. Doug got in a boxing stance, but there was no ring, no referee, and no rules. Micah rolled his neck and shoulders, but he was already exhausted. Even Micaiah felt like he'd gone a few more rounds than normal from his prize-fighting days.

"Don't worry, guys," Doug said as the Grandfathers advanced. "Help is coming. We've been here long enough that I think I understand the spatial-temporal coordinates of this room."

"Then stop psycho-babbling and open a portal," Micah told him impatiently.

"Cover us," Kayla told him.

They moved to the center of the Pit, Micah taking up his sword while Micaiah, Kayla, and Doug worked on opening a portal. Doug led, feeling out the spatial-temporal coordinates of the Pit and trying to connect them to some other place in the universe. Once he had the coordinates located, Micaiah and Kayla met him and worked to strengthen the connection, looking for anyone on the other side who could meet them. Micaiah tried not to get distracted by the advancing Grandfathers. The traitors from Rifun's forces kept them at bay, but only as long as there were a few of them. As more and more filtered in, that wall would crumble like New Orleans under a hurricane.

"Any time now guys," Micah said nervously.

They found one person on the other side of the potential portal, and a tiny portal about the size of a fist opened up. Then there were two, then three, then five on the other side. When the coordinates solidified, the portal opened wide.

Micaiah, Kayla, and Doug jumped out of the way as a small army came barreling through the portal. There was no chance to warn them about friends this side of the portal, and a few of the helpful guards and Grandfathers were cut down in accidental friendly fire. Micaiah pushed his way into the foray and dragged Micah out before he could be cut down or trampled in the chaos.

"Where were these guys before?" Micah asked.

"On reserve," Doug replied. "If we could win with the force we had, great. If not, better to not show all our cards too soon."

"But you, sir—" Kayla said, poking Micaiah. "—are still in trouble for throwing in that wild card."

Micaiah sighed. "Can we talk about this later, honey? We're kind of in the middle of a battlefield."

"That is very true," Doug said, jumping out of the way as one entanglement got a little too close to him. They moved out of the way, trying to get toward a small open area where they might be able to speak.  Gradually Kayla was shuffled away in the chaos, but Doug seemed not to notice. "And we should seek shelter as soon as possible. Now that we have the coordinates—"

"No." Micaiah shook his head. "No, we're not running. We rallied this force, so we ought to be here fighting with them."

"We did our job—"

"No, we didn't," Micah interrupted. "Our job was to kill Rifun. In case you haven't noticed, he's still alive. We have to complete our mission."

Doug glanced around at the two of them. Micaiah wasn't sure what to make of him in that moment. The man was a brilliant tactician and a good thinker when it came to war and strategy. So why was he suggesting running away now, except...?

"Fine," Cassius said, shedding his Disguise of Doug and drawing an ancient French rapier in one hand and a twelve-gauge shotgun in the other. "Guess I'll just kill you here."

The man had no grace, no flourish, no stance or balance like one might find in a studio.  He was all brute force and heavy muscle, his battle cry coming from deep in his chest and causing Micah's throat to tighten with a strangled sort of sound.

Cassius made as if to go after Micaiah first, then turned on Micah, aiming the shotgun in order to get him to jump out of the way and directly in line with the rapier. Micah skidded and twisted at the last second to avoid being skewered, but the blade still found skin and blood blossomed from the wound.

Without even hesitating, Cassius continued to move the rapier, catching Micaiah's pilfered sword and parrying so that the shot from his pilfered gun was equally useless. The bloodthirsty man jumped back so that the twins were suddenly facing each other.

Cassius shifted his stance as if he would charge both of them, then paused for half a second, his attention caught elsewhere. Kayla was a short distance away, still fighting, but with a clear line of sight. He raised the shotgun.

Clumsily, Micaiah leapt at him. He didn't have to do much, just get him off-balance, which he managed to do. The first shot went wild. The two of them stumbled to the side together. In a moment of clarity and rage, he took his sword and stuck it in flesh. Cassius snarled in pain, but it turned to a howl as they landed on the ground and the blade went deeper.

Standing, Micaiah saw the blade had gone into Cassius' chest, under the ribcage, likely puncturing a lung. Blood bubbled up from the man's mouth and he wheezed sickeningly.

"All you Akari-bearers are cowards," Cassius burbled.

"How long were you Disguised?" Micaiah demanded.

"Long enough." Cassius' words were becoming faint and the light was going out of his eyes.

"Where is Rifun?"

"Long gone by now."

"Where is Doug?"

"Long gone. As you will be."

Then he died. Micaiah let him fall to the ground, then took another knife and cut his throat just to be sure. No other Disguises came off; this had been the real Cassius.

"He was in on it from the beginning," Kayla said, forcing her way back. "That's how Rifun knew what we were planning and how to prepare for it. That's how he was able to gain the upper hand."

"If we had gone with him to hide, he would have killed us," Micaiah said. "As it is, if Cassius has been impersonating Doug this whole time, then we have to expect that Rifun knows the location and firepower of every Akari-bearer, including the Akarin fortress. We have to find him and stop him."

"Cassius said Rifun is long gone," Micah pointed out. "Where do we even begin?"

"Somewhere that isn't here."

The Pit, even for its size, was too small to contain the magnitude of the battle, and it had spilled out into the rest of the Wheel. Maybe from it above, it would have been apparent who was winning or losing, but in the thick of things, it was still too close to call.

"How are we going to get out?"

There was no good place to safely use Gravity to try and get out, and the tunnels were akin to suicide. They were distracted for several minutes by a couple guards attacking them, but, when those were dispatched, they were left in the same predicament. Then Micah spoke.

"What about the portal room?" he suggested. "It still has enough power to channel the energy so we're not shouldering all of it, and the portals to the rest of the Wheel have been restored. We can start there and make our way back in, give the place a good canvassing."

Micaiah glanced at Kayla who shrugged and nodded. "It's the best idea we've got."

He looked around again, trying to find any other way. If Rifun was hiding, he would be holed up in his little study in the castle known as the Judgment Wing; they'd be leaving the fighting only to jump right back in again. Problem was, there was only one way in and out of the Pit, where the rest of the Wheel at least had two or three or ten portals going here and there.

"All right," he conceded. "Let's do it."

They fought their way back across the Pit toward the cell of the Accused. The bodies were still piled up in front of the cell and the area appeared to be undisturbed. As expected, it took far less time and energy to generate a portal back to the portal room, though it still took more than normal as the stress and strain of battle had not been good to any of them. They stepped through, then had to force it closed so no one could follow them. Moving from one place to another within the Wheel meant that the physical toll was less strenuous as well, though the stress and strain of battle had not been good to any of them. Micah sat on the floor, Micaiah massaged his knee, and Kayla dropped her battle ax with a sigh of relief. After a quick five-second breather, they stood and started moving through the Wheel, hunting for Rifun.

# Chapter Twenty-Eight
## The Bat

Micaiah figured that he was a pretty forgiving guy on a regular day, even if he was still an asshole, someone who would extend mercy simply because it was easier and less work than going to the hassle of arresting, processing, and delivering a Runner to the Grandfathers for judgment.

Today was not a normal day, and Micaiah extended no mercy, except maybe to his fellows. To any guards or Grandfathers he caught fleeing, he cut them down with hardly a second thought. For his fellows, if he saw them struggling, he would cut their throat if he thought it best. If there was still hope, he took a moment to render ten-second aid, then moved on. The closer they got to the thick of battle, the less kindness he dispensed.

He fought more out of irritation than anything. This had gone far past its usefulness, and the reason why only served to infuriate him more. They'd been duped, had at their own game. Doug was dead, and they'd been dealing with Cassius the whole time. They had told him any number of Akarin secrets, given him the blueprints to every building, the password to every computer account, the keys to every vehicle...Why not just hand everyone over on a silver platter?

His own grudging logic told him that they had done just that, without even realizing it. Cassius had infiltrated the Akarin who knew how long ago, impersonated a man no one liked but would still trust with their lives. They followed him into battle, believing it was for a worthwhile cause, while at the same time, Cassius and Rifun took Micaiah's plan and worked their own magic. They would lure the Akarin forces into a hopeless battle, wipe out the majority of their

571

army, and still have the coordinates to go back and do the clean-up. It was disgusting, and Micaiah was just as guilty as the rest of them for not bothering to do any sort of double-checking. Sure, they could Disguise themselves, but why had they behaved as if the enemy couldn't do the same?

The fighting had made its way into the auction hub and some of the intermediate marketplaces, and Micaiah had a fleeting thought that it was a shame that all the beautiful architecture was going to go to waste in a spray of blood and guts. Rifun really should have stayed an architect; he would have lived longer.

The closer they got to the Judgment Wing hub, the less they were able to just skirt around the battle and keep going. Sometimes, they were able to simply push their adversaries away; other times it was more of an actual battle. Micaiah had once read that a skilled knight in the Middle Ages could defeat an opponent in four blows or less of his sword. Comparatively speaking, he figured he was doing pretty good, down to an average of ten or so, though it did nothing for his stamina.

"I don't see Rifun anywhere," Kayla shouted over the noise. At some point, she'd traded her heavy battle ax for something that kind of looked like a bowstaff, but with a sword at each end. It was lighter, anyway, and a more effective ranged weapon.

"Rifun is the coward, not Cassius," Micaiah said. "He won't be in the thick of things. He'll be holed up in the Judgment Wing."

"If he's here at all," Micah pointed out.

"He'll be here. He won't surrender until he knows things aren't going his way."

*And we haven't had our duel,* Micaiah thought. This was like Walter and the warehouse all over again, but on a much bigger scale. Rifun has his plans, makes his demands, shows his hand. But once again, things weren't going as he had planned, or so it seemed. He would run and hide, reappearing only if things wound up in his favor, or when his chosen favorite chased after him. First, it had been Walter, and he'd been made to fight Isthim. Now it was Micaiah's turn, and he was determined to butcher the pink bitch and take Rifun out once and for all.

They reached the Judgment Wing hub and were immediately separated as an enormous club came down and split the ground just in front of the portal. Whether or not it was intended for them didn't matter, as the guard who wielded it dispatched his initial foe in the next blow, then turned his sights on the three little humans who had just shown up to the party.

Micaiah couldn't say what alien species he was, only that it severely put him in mind of *Jack and the Beanstalk* and what lay in the castle in the clouds, club and all. He was glad to have his running leg on him, but what he wouldn't have given to have two functional real legs. As it was, his role in the fight seemed to be limited to keeping the beast distracted so Micah and Kayla could hack away at it. In the end, it was like a large animal being attacked by a swarm of wasps, and the lumbering giant fell.

"Was he with us or against us?" Micah asked, going up to the dead alien and kicking it just to be sure.

"At this point, I don't know that it matters anymore," Micaiah answered honestly.

Looking around, it was hard to tell. The only thing that was certain was that the Grandfathers were the bad guys. The guards were divided, and the few secretaries who dared enter the fray were also divided. The Akarin army was fairly familiar with one another, but with no definite uniforms or any regalia to look for, it was anyone's guess in the heat of battle. Rifun was human, so any aliens not familiar with humans or the fact that they three were against Rifun might consider all humans the same, regardless if they were technically on the same side.

"Micah, you were taken to the Judgment Wing," Micaiah said, looking at his brother. "Is that where Rifun is most likely to hide?"

Micah shrugged. "I would imagine so. It's where he kept his evil lair."

"It would make sense for him to be hiding there," Kayla said, fending off another foe. "All he needs is a two-way stamp to get in, then he can destroy the stamps to keep everyone else out. These guys—" She swung the bowstaff-sword out and dispatched another attacker. "—we can fight. But there's no way we can get past those force fields."

Still they fought to get closer to the Judgment Wing, moving along a wall until they reached a staircase that took them to another wall, and around they went until they got on the same plane as the portal. Then it was another war and a half to get closer to the portal; each step was a small battle, and Micaiah could feel his strength waning.

"What about a portal?" Micaiah wondered. He looked at Micah. "We've both been inside the Judgment Wing, in the holding cell area where we deliver Runners. We could try to open a portal there."

"The dampening field is too strong," Kayla told him. "The Judgment Wing field was always the strongest because of the force fields. Even with the Akari breaking through the first layer of the dampening field, there's no way we could get inside without someone on the inside meeting us halfway." She looked at Micah. "The most we'd be able to do is your little portal to get a message through."

Micaiah grunted. There had to be a way in. That was too easy of an escape, and yet it was the most perfect one he could think of. With all the cells cleaned out of prisoners, there would be no one on the inside who could—

"I might know who we can reach," Micah said suddenly. "I met him in the black cells."

"Are you sure you met him, or is he a hallucination?" Micaiah asked warily.

Micah faltered. "Honestly, I don't know. But what's the worst that could happen? We get through the first layer and we bump off the second layer, just like we would normally. We have to give it a shot."

Kayla nodded. "Okay. Come on. It'll probably be easier to try when we're not fighting for our lives every three seconds."

There was some truth to that, but that didn't mean it was easy getting to the Judgment Wing portal. When they stepped through, only Micaiah's quick reflexes—and the Akari—saved them all from being decapitated, or worse, touched by a Grandfather. They jumped and rolled away, Micaiah unable to stick the landing and crashing most ungracefully, but still getting away.

When they stood and turned, they saw that Isthim was their attacker, and she was on a murderous rampage. She was a *vodrak* Borelian, capable of pushing the entire poisonous spectrum of her species, and she was utilizing it to its fullest potential. She no longer wore her Grandfather shroud. She no longer wore her gloves or her jacket. In fact, she wore nothing at all, baring everything in its pink, poisonous glory. Completely untouchable.

Her first advance was on Micaiah. Then, in the space of half a second, her color changed and suddenly she was moving like a snake, bending, turning, twisting around until she was all but facing completely backwards from the hips up. She grabbed Kayla's bowstaff-sword, yanked it from her hands, and tried to use it against her. Kayla leapt out of the way. Micaiah tried to go after her, and the only thing that saved him when she turned the blade on him was his awkward gait, giving out at the last second and sending him stumbling into the floor. He almost went headlong into her shins, but managed to control his fall enough that he was able to fall away and keep rolling until he was out of range.

"You guys keep going and find Rifun," Kayla said. "I'll deal with the pink bitch." With a growl, she slid a knife out of her boot. "Bring it, honey."

Truthfully, Micaiah would have much rathered watch the catfight, but there were more pressing matters to attend to. In a moment of distraction as Isthim tried to decide who to go after, Kayla got a good swipe in, but hitting nothing lethal. Isthim hissed and turned her full attention on Kayla.

"Come on," Micah said quietly. "It'll take both of us."

It would take both of them and all their energy, Micaiah knew. They would expend so much energy trying to get to Rifun that they wouldn't have any left to spare to fight him.

Micaiah let his brother take the lead on opening the portal. Breaking through the first dampening field was the easy part. After that they had to find someone on the inside to get them through the force fields. Micaiah wasn't sure about trusting this mission to something that could easily be a hallucination, but it was the only thing they had to go on. Sweat streamed down Micah's neck and forehead as he searched and searched but only found walls. Just as Micaiah was ready to suggest they give up, something caught.

"Wait, wait, wait," Micaiah said before Micah could strengthen the bond and open a portal. "How do we know that's your friend and not Rifun planning to suck us in and chop our heads off?"

"Because I know him," Micah answered. "It's him. He'll help us."

Still skeptical, Micaiah lent more of his strength to the portal and it opened in front of them, struggling at first, then finally stable enough that they dared to enter.

They didn't die walking through, and no one was waiting to kill them. Looking around, Micaiah surmised that they were in the first room of the cell blocks, beyond the two force fields of the main tunnel, beyond the force field that separated the cells from the rest of the Judgment Wing. He turned around and saw someone standing there in the corridor. A man with dark skin and black hair, his clothes looking like something out of the seventeenth or eighteen century, what a common man might be expected to wear. He had a pack slung over one shoulder.

"Are you Micah's friend?" Micaiah asked.

"I don't know," the man said. "Am I?"

And he vanished. Right before their eyes, he was gone, faded away like some bad movie effects. Micaiah looked incredulously at Micah who shrugged. "He does that."

"And you trust him?"

"He got us in and didn't try to kill us, didn't he?"

Well, there was that.

"Okay, fine, you have a point. Do you remember the way to Rifun?"

"I remember," Micah said lowly.

There was also the point that they didn't know for sure that Rifun was here. Maybe he'd holed up in his new iteration of the Coliseum; there was every chance that he'd turned that into a well-fortified castle, armed, stocked, and provisioned so he could survive for years. And what if he was there? They'd had to go to great lengths to get into the Judgment Wing. How were they going to get out? Kayla, most likely, but what if...what if she didn't prevail against Isthim? Guilt knotted Micaiah's stomach and he chastised himself, telling himself that he should have stuck by her side and fought with her.

One cell block looked the same as any other, Micaiah thought, but Micah seemed to know where he was going. They went down one corridor, turned, went down another, up and down a few flights of stairs, this way and that. Perhaps the thing that most set Micaiah on edge was the fact that they hadn't run into any guards. None whatsoever. Not even a night guard asleep at his desk. The whole place was more deserted than a ghost town.

"And here I thought this place was scary when it was full of angry prisoners," Micah said softly, as if any noise might negate their good luck.

Micaiah just grunted his agreement as they turned another corner and found themselves heading toward the black cells. "Are you sure you know where we're going?"

"Yeah. It's right around this corner."

Before they actually entered the asylum, he stopped and turned, and they were presented with the most opulent set of doors Micaiah had ever seen. Forget being real wood, these things were like whole trees, tall and majestic, polished until they were almost mirrors, every corner and all the carved designs. He was willing to bet that the fixtures were solid gold and not just brass. He whistled.

"He really doesn't spare any expense, does he?"

They didn't stop to admire the architecture long, however, though it took both of them to open just one of the doors. Once inside, Micaiah felt wholly inadequate. It was like walking into a lord's castle, the opulence displayed. And here he was, walking in sweaty and dirty and not a little bloody from all the foes he'd been cutting down. The place reeked of luxurious living, and he found that it made him sleepy. He'd been doing a lot more work than he intended to do today, and one of those plush chairs was calling his name.

"Okay, we're here," he said, trying to break his mind away from sleep and back to the mission at hand. "Now where is Rifun?"

"Oh, don't worry about me. Though if you'd done any sort of preliminary search of the room, you might have noticed me."

There was movement from one of the chairs and Rifun leaned forward to set a drink on the coffee table; it looked like a proper glass of brandy, too. Or maybe scotch. Something for the elegant man who was above the beer and ale of the commoners. After a moment, he stood and walked around the chair to stand before them.

"I'd wondered how long it would take you to beat your way in here. Do you want to know what I came up with?"

Micaiah took a step forward. "Rifun Ndolo, for the charges for treason against the Hands of Time—"

"Three hours, forty-one minutes, and twenty-two seconds," Rifun continued, not moving. "I must say, it is a bit disappointing. Personally, I was betting more on an hour, maybe two if the fighting got really bad.  But really, I expected more from you, especially since Banding is fully within your capabilities."

"—and crimes against the universe, including coup, holocaust, unlawful imprisonment and enslavement, unauthorized used of Time, and misrepresentation of the Akari—"

" 'Misrepresentation of the Akari'? I beg to differ, and I had no idea that was a crime recognizable by the Laws of Time."

"—I, Micaiah Durvin, Lieutenant Timekeeper from Quadrant

One, Parsec Eleven, Sector Five, System Four, Planet Thirty-Eight, Region Four, District Four, and Core Akari-bearer, hereby arrest you. Seeing how there seems to be a lack of proper justice system and due process—"

"And the fact that the Grandfathers work for me anyway."

"—and because I'm sure no one will put up too much of an objection, I will also act as judge, jury...and executioner. Rifun Ndolo, I sentence you to die."

Suddenly he was flying across the room as if hit by a car. He wasn't even able to comprehend what had happened until he was picking himself up off the floor. Micah was by his side in an instant, coming under him and helping him up until he was able to get his bearings.

"I'm sorry," Rifun said, "but did I say that I was ready to surrender? You and Walter have worked together for far too long, I think; you're starting to act like him. It's not bad until you start to look like him, but this is pretty darn close." Now he started moving, meandering toward them like a cat. "You know, this is all starting to look very familiar. Where have I seen this before? Ah, yes, the warehouse. Except it was Walter beneath my shoe instead of you."

"I was thinking the same thing," Micaiah said.

"Oh, good, so we both know what's going to happen."

"You're going to send one of your minions to distract us while you get away, or that's what you're going to try to do."

"Tell me, have you ever heard the definition of insanity? It's where you keep doing something the same way over and over again, expecting a different result each time. My problem last time came only when I did not stick around to make sure that Walter died. Between you and me, though, I'm glad he didn't. He's too much fun. You, however, I have no problem with killing."

Rifun got within six feet of them and stopped. "So, here's how this is going to work. I'm going to go into the next room—"

Micaiah made a sudden move then, trying to Band and be fast enough and strong enough to throw Rifun off and plunge a knife into his chest. He got a small slice in, but Rifun was faster still. In one deft movement, he managed to break Micaiah's wrist, take the knife, then turn it on him and stab him. Micaiah was able to wiggle and twist enough that the knife did not hit his spine, but a kidney shot was nothing to sneeze at. He made a small noise and sank to his knees when Rifun released him.

Micah knelt beside him. He was shaking.

" 'Tis but a scratch," Micaiah said hoarsely, sitting back on his seat.

Micah went after Rifun, then, raising his arm to strike, but Rifun caught him easily and soon had him pinioned, cheek pressed against the wall.

"That was very rude," Rifun said. "From both of you. You interrupted me. Now then, as I was saying, I'm going to go into the next room. Things are going to get very violent and very messy, and I would just be in the way. You understand. You're going to be facing off against an old friend of yours. Too bad your brother got injured beforehand, because you could have really used him, I'm sure. So, I guess it'll just be you alone against the Bat."

"The Bat?" Micah huffed, trying to breathe as Rifun leaned heavy against him.

Today just kept getting better and better, didn't it? Rifun got off him and released his arm. He turned and walked away toward another door. Micah took several long steps toward him, ready to go up and just snap his neck, when suddenly something crashed into him from the side in a flurry of talons and wings. He didn't even know what ability he was reaching for as he invoked the Akari, but whatever it was, it was enough to blind the Bat and cause it to get off him and stumble back, screeching and clawing at its eyes.

Micah stole a glance in Micaiah's direction. His older brother appeared to still be conscious, slowly dragging himself toward the wall, hand on the knife still lodged in his abdomen. So, he was okay. For the moment. Micah just had to keep the Bat focused on him so he wouldn't have to worry about Micaiah.

The Bat came at him again with the same scary speed demonstrated in the Pit. Micah remembered a time decades ago when he'd been testing for his Apprenticeship and had to face off against the Bat. That had been scary enough, but to see now how much it had been holding back? That gave a whole new meaning to pants-pissing fear.

Micah dodged the Bat's next blow and only just managed to slip to the side, though not without receiving the blade's end of a third strike, a red line appearing on his cheek. He danced back a step or two, trying to figure out if he had any kind of advantage. The Akari was great for distractions and party tricks, but he had no clue on how to really use it as a weapon. The best he could do was use the Bands to give himself enough time to get away from the Bat when it struck.

He did his best to keep the fight to one side of the room, but the Bat's full wingspan was a good twenty feet or so, so his radius of destruction was significant. Half the time, Micah was just trying to watch out for them, never mind try to do anything else, and the battle drifted closer and closer toward Micaiah. Once, Micah managed to grab a metal floor lamp and crack it against the Bat's head, but it never seemed to faze the creature. If nothing else, it enraged it further, sending it on a small rampage that destroyed most all the furniture in the room.

Micah tripped over one of the broken pieces and went sprawling on the floor, rolling away as the Bat brought a huge wing down to crush him. Micah had fought geese before—more to the point, they'd attacked him and he tried to fend them off—and those bastards could do a number on a person. The Bat's wings, he had little doubt they could kill.

As he stood and whirled around, trying to keep one eye on the Bat and one eye on Micaiah, he saw the huge double doors open and Kayla walked in. In his distraction, the Bat made a grab for him, but Micah jumped out of the way, heading for Micaiah, whom Kayla just noticed.

"What happened?" she demanded. "Are you okay? Babe, how

are you feeling?"

"I'm fine," Micaiah said strongly. "In fact—" He pulled the knife out. "I'm more than fine."

Micah saw that the knife wasn't as bloody as might be expected. Micaiah shed another layer of Disguise, but the only thing that seemed to change were his clothes. He lifted his shirt to reveal protective plates, like Kevlar, but for knives instead of bullets.

"Fuck you, asshole," Micah said, cuffing him in the back of the head. "You mean I've been facing the Bat all by myself because you—"

He didn't get to finish before the Bat came crashing between them. Micah grunted as one of the wings hit him in the face; his only saving grace was that it had been a glancing blow and not head-on. Still, it sent him reeling. He heard a screech of pain then, and the Bat took a step back, Micaiah's knife buried in the joint at the base of its left wing, blooding dribbling down its side.

The Bat backed up until it was about in the center of the room, the twins and Kayla surrounding it. Only Kayla had a weapon, her bowstaff-sword.

"Isthim?" Micaiah wondered briefly.

"The bitch?" Kayla raised a brow. "It took me longer to break into this place."

Her words were oddly comforting, Micah thought as he picked up a piece of broken furniture—a splintered table leg with as sharp an end as he could find. Kayla handed a knife off to Micaiah. The bat swung its massive head around, looking from person to person. Then it pulled an oddly human trick. First it looked at Kayla, but it sprung backwards, turning and twisting and catching Micah off-guard. He was driven to the floor, but the Bat was thrown off-balance by the loss of function in its left wing. It landed awkwardly, allowing Micah to wriggle his arms free to grab at his weapon of choice and try to stab it, trying to find an artery or other lethal strike.

The splintered piece of wood wasn't sharp enough or strong enough to penetrate the Bat's leathery hide, but Kayla's bowstaff-sword and Micaiah's knife were. Micaiah went for the joint of the other wing. Kayla might have been going for a head or neck shot, but the Bat was too quick, moving away to a safer spot. Fortunately, she pulled out of the blow before she accidentally skewered Micah instead.

Micaiah helped Micah to his feet and they faced the Bat, standing near the hearth in a defensive position. It seemed to be torn between having second thoughts about facing them, and going full kamikaze, killing them all even if it meant its own death.

"The thing that I don't get," Micah said, addressing the Bat, "is how you got mixed up in all this. I mean, the Dispersal and any number of little civil wars throughout all of Time history, and you have never given an inch, never taken a side. What makes this one so different? What is your role here?"

"My role is the same it has always been," the Bat hissed. "My job is to keep the Akari out of Time. Time will war with itself, and I care nothing for it. My sole purpose is to destroy the Akari."

"What about Rifun?" Micaiah wondered. "He claims to wield the Akari; why not kill him?"

The Bat hissed again, differently this time, until Micah realized it was laughing. "Rifun is a fool. He does not wield the Akari. The power he holds wields him. One day it will consume him. But as long as he was working against the true Akari-bearers, I was willing and obligated to support him."

"The Day, too?" Kayla asked.

"And the Day."

"What about the Grandfathers or the guards? Or even the secretaries?" Micaiah inquired.

The Bat sneered. "Let them have their petty wars. I care not. My only job is to destroy the Akari and those who wield it. And that I shall do, even if it means giving up my life to do it."

With that, he was on them again, a wild animal forced into a corner and fighting for its life. Except this was not so simple; this was a murderous demon out to kill and destroy. It went for Micaiah in the middle, but lashed out with wounded wings, driving Micah and Kayla back. Kayla tore open its wing with her bowstaff-sword while Micah rolled away, looking for a weapon that might actually work against this beast.

The Bat tossed Micaiah to the side, throwing him into Kayla and sending them both stumbling back, tripping over broken furniture and landing on their asses, the bowstaff-sword tumbling from Kayla's hand. As the Bat advanced, Micah took a breath and made a break for them, scooping up Kayla's weapon and swinging it around to stop the Bat. The end made contact, but not enough to do much more than scratch the Bat's face. In that moment of distraction by a small wound, Micah gathered his strength and thrust.

The bowstaff-sword hit the bat just below its right eye, crunching bone and piercing brain. Still the thing did not die. It stumbled back, screech, reeling, clawing at its face and trying to pull the weapon out. In that moment, Micaiah darted forward, yanking one of the knives out of the Bat's wings and stabbing it in the chest. Kayla was the one who made a grab for the other knife and, when the Bat was less active and writhing, stepped forward and delivered the killing blow. She did more than just cut its throat, she took the little knife and went to town, not stopping until the blade had broken but the head was off. When she was done, she let the head drop and so did she, taking a seat against the wall, sweat mixing with the fresh blood.

"And that's how you do that," she breathed.

Micaiah nodded wearily. "I'd kiss you, but there's an audience."

"Compared to the shit we did in that hotel room?" Micah said sarcastically, folding his arms and rolling his eyes. "Shit. Rifun."

"I'll wait here," Kayla said as the twins picked their way to the door to the second room.

Micaiah opened it. The room was empty. It looked similar to the other room, except there were no other doors here, no way that Rifun could have escaped except via portal. Cautiously, they entered the room and looked around. Micah was the one who spotted the note on the table.

" 'My dear Durvin twins,' " he read. " 'If you are reading this, you have once again proven your battle prowess in defeating the Bat. Congratulations. I never liked it anyway and always figured it was plotting against me in secret, so you have merely done me a favor. I suppose that means I owe you one, but then, you also killed Isthim. We're just going to call that even.

" 'Clearly, you have also noticed my escape. Does it really surprise you that much? You call it cowardice, I call it strategy. Without Cassius to puppet around, I must figure out new ways to master the Akari and bend others to my will. I cannot do that if I am dead, which I surely would be if I had stayed and allowed myself to be captured by you. The only redeeming part of this is that I still have the journal.

" 'This has been a fascinating tale to tell, and I look forward to reading about it later. Maybe then I will figure out what I did wrong. Until then, I must bid you adieu, as I hear the fighting coming to a close. Congratulations, Micaiah, on becoming so proficient with your prosthetic leg. Clearly, the Author favors you more than I realized. I expect we will meet again in the future.

" 'Most affectionately yours, Rifun Ndolo, former King of Time.' "

They stood in silence for a minute after that.

"He's an asshole," Micaiah said. "I wonder if he realizes that."

"I think he flaunts it," Micah agreed.

"I don't know about you, but I'd take that as a surrender."

"What, because the head of the Bat wouldn't be good enough?" Kayla said from the doorway. "And the fact that we do still have Cassius' body lying dead in the Pit?"

"True," Micaiah acknowledged. "But even if we did get them, how would we show them off in such a way that everyone would know the battle is over?"

"And we don't have Rifun's head, which might pose a

problem," Micah pointed out.

"Maybe. But objects can be Disguised just as well as people."

"Rifun is alive, though."

"He's on the run," Kayla said. "He's powerless. And we need to bring the Wheel back under control, like, yesterday. I agree. We take the Bat's head, and Cassius, and find someone else's head to Disguise as Rifun's just long enough to show that he's at least out of power. Then we can worry about pursuit later."

The twins were reluctant, but ultimately agreed. They couldn't take much more fighting, and if the battle went on much longer, there wouldn't be anyone left to run the Wheel, let alone populate it. First and foremost, they had to bring back law and order. They turned and headed out of the room, grabbing the Bat's head as they did.

"How did you get in past the force fields?" Micaiah asked as they walked back through the cell blocks.

"I got in the computer and shut them down," Kayla answered. "Believe me, with all the records wiped, it's a lot easier to navigate the system."

"But you said it was harder to get in than it was to defeat Isthim," Micah said, confused.

"She acts all big and bad, but she relied too much on her reputation to instill fear in her opponents and throw them off. I just said fuck it and killed the bitch."

Micaiah grinned and put his sweaty, bloody arm around her sweaty, bloody shoulders. Micah looked away.

With the force fields down, it was considerably easier to get out of the Judgment Wing than in, and when they emerged into the hub, fully expecting a raging battle, they were met with the cold desertion of an empty battlefield. Well, not quite deserted, but close enough as the dying were put out of their misery and the bodies were looted for weapons, money, anything that could be taken. A few opportunistic Harvesters made rounds, Harvesting those that could be Harvested, stuffing the Time Capsules in pockets, sleeves, anywhere they could be hidden.

"The war is over and the capitalists emerge," Micah observed dryly.

"Indeed," Micaiah agreed. "Come on."

The scene that greeted them in the Pit, however, was something entirely different. At first, Micaiah thought something terrible had happened, some explosion and now people were running, screaming, trying to escape. After a moment of observation, he realized that it was actually a celebration, the bottom of the Pit turned into an enormous bonfire.

"Shit. Cassius' body was down there."

"We know," someone nearby, another human, said. "That was the one we used to start the fire."

"So...we won."

"If by 'we' you mean the Akarin, yes. We won. Does it surprise you?"

*A little.* "Are all the bodies being burned?"

"There are too many to bury, and they would rot long before they could be sorted to return to their home worlds."

*Similar to what happened to Lily,* Micaiah thought ruefully. Not all the bodies had been returned, and he was sure hers had been returned only so Rifun could snub Walter and show off that he'd finally accomplished one of the things he'd set out to do.

"Hey, that's the Bat, isn't it?" the man said, gesturing toward the head in Kayla's hand. "You...killed the Bat? Seriously? Like, you killed that nightmarish motherfucker and decapitated it? Sweet! Hey, where's the rest of it? We should throw that thing on the fire and see how it would burn."

"It's in the Judgment Wing," Micaiah told him. "Force fields are down."

"Hey, cool. I'll just—"

Micaiah caught him before he could push past them. He looked at the man, hoping he could convey the severity of the situation. "This was not a game. This *is* not a game. This was a battle. People fought and died here. Most of them, I didn't know, and neither did you. That's what makes it easy to dismiss. And believe me when I say that it's real easy to make the other side out to be faceless bad guys, but they weren't. They had lives and families and homes. Some of those homes are Unengaged, and those families will never have any idea what happened or why. They did what they had to do, what they believed what right. They didn't all make the right choice. Some, like the Bat and Cassius and Isthim and some of the Grandfathers, those you can celebrate, because they are the ones who birthed this evil. But don't assume that all who fight, do so freely. They're not like us. They are deceived."

The man said nothing, simply met his gaze with a sudden sober determination. He nodded finally. "Yes sir. You said the Bat's body is in the Judgment Wing? I'll just go and bring that here."

Micaiah released the man. "Get a few to help; he's a heavy fucker."

The man left.

The three of them glanced at each other.

"What do we do now?" Kayla wondered.

Micah sighed, feeling fatigue spread through his limbs. "Might as well throw that thing in the fire. The war was over before we ever got out here."

Micaiah shook his head. "The battle was over, but the war continues. As long as Rifun and those like him exist. As long as the Bat and those like it exist."

"What was the Bat anyway?" Kayla asked. "I was never able to find anything on it, what it was, where it was from, nothing. The Day either."

"We may never know. But at least we know they can be killed just as readily as the rest of them."

Kayla grunted and went off to toss the head in the fire, trying to avoid getting pushed around by those celebrating around the fire, as well as those in a much more somber mood.

"Dude," Micah said. "Your wife is hot. Like, holy shit, she is amazing."

"Yeah, but she's also all mine. I let you borrow her for a little while when we were still masquerading as each other, but if you want her, you're going to have to go find your own."

"Where the fuck am I supposed to find a woman who is that smart, that talented, and that bad ass? Not to mention that hot. Holy fuck, dude."

"No, I'm the one doing the fucking. Besides, I thought you were the one objecting to that little stint in the hotel room? What was it, only yesterday you were complaining about it?"

"A guy can change his mind, can't he? I don't know, something about watching a sexy lady wield a battle ax and mow through bad guys...it kind of turns me on."

"Any woman even looking at you turns you on. And she wasn't looking at you, she was looking at me, or she thought she was."

"Yes, but in the moment, she was looking at me."

Micaiah stepped forward and took Micah under his arm, mussing his hair until he begged for mercy. Micah took a step back, shaking his head and laughing. "Okay, I guess I may have deserved that. I am your little brother, after all."

Micaiah shook his head. "No, you're not my little brother. You're my twin."

They bro-hugged, but Micaiah wouldn't let him go immediately, instead pausing a moment to whisper, "You just happen to have been born three minutes after me."

Micah pulled back and playfully punched him in the ribs a few times.

"Hey now, battle's over," Kayla said, walking up. "Holy blazes, that fire is hot. Is there anything else we really need to do here?"

"I don't know," Micah admitted. "I mean, I feel like there should be some kind of meeting or something to figure out what to do next, but even if there was going to be a meeting, it's unlikely we'd be called to be part of it."

"Agreed," Micaiah murmured. "We may have killed Cassius

and the Bat, but now it's back to business, and Earth is still a very small player in the Time industry. There are worlds out there that have been completely devastated by this madness. Our opinion is neither asked for nor relevant. We might as well just pack up and go home."

"What, and leave the deliberating to a panel of bureaucrats?" Kayla asked, not moving from her spot even as the twins started to walk away. "That's what got this whole mess started was leaving the power in the hands of those who couldn't be seen, touched, or talked to in any way but worship."

"Okay, so what do you want to do?"

She let out a breath. "I don't know, but we should do something. We can't let it get this bad again."

Micaiah sighed and went to her, put his hands on her shoulders. "I know you really want to save the universe, but I'm going to save you the trouble and tell you that it will always get this bad again. The universe is imperfect. It is selfish and greedy and full of a lot of bad things and bad people. We can't save it. We can try to make it a little better, but we can't save it. No matter what we do, there will always be conflict."

"I know..."

"Why don't we head home, get a shower—God knows we need one—get something to eat, get some sleep, and then we can figure out what to do next. Okay?"

"Okay. Can I at least keep the bowstaff-sword?"

Micah snickered and Micaiah rolled his eyes but grinned. "Yes, you can keep the bowstaff-sword. As long as you promise not to use it on me."

"Done."

"You seem very confident in that," Micah observed as they turned and headed out of the Pit.

Kayla shook her head. "After fifty years of marriage, if I was going to kill him, I would have done it by now."

"Gee, thanks, dear," Micaiah said. "I think I'll take that as a compliment."

As they walked through the Wheel, it was hard to believe that all of that had really just happened. Micaiah had woken up in prison, gone to trial expected and expecting to die, started a revolution, won said revolution, and now they were going home for a shower and a bite to eat. It was relieving and yet terrifying. Shouldn't he be afraid, shaking, plagued by living nightmares? Or did that come later? Or had his soul grown so calloused to such things that he no longer saw them as significant? Just another day, just another battle to fight. Be ready to die, or else live and move on to the next one.

The thought was disconcerting, but even as he pondered this, he found himself overwhelmed momentarily in his senses. He glanced at Kayla and Micah and saw they seemed to experience the same thing. After a minute, he managed to pinpoint the feeling as the dampening field over the Wheel being taken down and his sense of Time returning.

"The rebuilding has already begun," Micaiah observed. "I don't think it will take long for talks of government and reopening to begin."

Kayla grunted in frustration but said nothing.

As they made their way through the Wheel, clean-up had begun. Bodies were being gathered, stripped of all possessions, and carted away to be burned. It seemed a cruel thing to do, but with Rifun's total wipe of the system and the chaos that the industry was in, there just wasn't time or manpower to identify and return them all for proper ceremonies. Micaiah picked out a couple humans, but he had no knowledge of them and wouldn't know what to do with them if they were suddenly thrust upon him, his responsibility to make sure they got back to their Districts and their families. So he passed them by, and the bodies were carted away.

By the time they reached the portal room, it was already back in business. Micaiah estimated probably a hundred or more portals were open for business, creatures and aliens of all races moving in and out, to and fro, working hard on the clean-up and restoration. It put him in mind of the time the bakery caught on fire and they'd brought in contractors to do the heavy work they couldn't do themselves. He'd Banded the store, forcing the poor guys to pull extra long days so they could reopen sooner. It all seemed to long ago, and so unimportant.

"Now we just have to hope Tommen doesn't cut us down the moment we walk through," he said dryly.

Opening a portal now was considerably easier, and the three of them might have even put too much effort into it, as if expecting to kick down a solid oak door and finding only a bedsheet, the momentum carrying them clumsily through into the bakery office. Micaiah's first instinct was to go for a chair and rest, then figured he didn't need all the blood and dirt rubbing into his office chair that he sat in every day. He forced himself to stand.

"Everyone okay?" he asked as they forced the portal closed. He looked around. "Where's Tommen?"

"This might explain it," Kayla said, picking a note up off the floor. " 'You said my dad couldn't know about this, so in the interest of not telling him, I had to go home with him when he came to pick me up. If Rifun is going to come for me, he's going to come for me regardless of where I am. And if you guys are running scared, there's nothing I'm going to be able to do to help. Sorry. Tommen.' "

"Well, he's right," Micah stated.

"We never planned to have him here anyway," Micaiah said, stretching. "We only gave him the job to get him out of the way."

"It's better that he went home," Kayla agreed. "And I would be more surprised if he was still here. It's three in the morning."

"Fuck, and we have to be up in an hour and a half."

"Oh, please, have you never heard of Time?"

"I need a shower," Micah said, moving stiffly for the door. "And a solid eight or ten. So you can either Band me or I'm saying fuck you to work tomorrow."

"Agreed," Micaiah sighed. "I'll see you at home."

Micah said nothing, just headed out the door. A minute later, Micaiah heard the back door open and close. He turned to Kayla.

"So."

She raised a brow. "So...what?"

"My place or yours?"

"Cai...I'm tired. I stink like blood and shit. I just want to go home and get a shower and get to bed. I'm not even hungry right now."

"I know. So I'll ask again. My place or yours? We've just survived a Time Trial, a revolution, and a hell of a lot of heart-pounding, pants-pissing action where any move could have been our last, to say nothing of how we dispatched the Bat. Okay, the *Bat*." He took her hands in his and kissed her. It was probably the foulest kiss he'd ever tasted, but just the fact that he was still able to kiss his wife at the end of the day helped to override his revulsion. "I want you with me tonight, even if we don't have sex."

She let out a breath and relaxed, almost to the point where he was afraid he would have to carry her outside. "Well, when you put it like that, why don't we go to your place? You're always bragging about how nice it is and what a great deal you guys got on it. I want to see it."

"All right. Come on."

They left the store, initially surprised to see Micah still there, until they realized that neither of them had their vehicle. Micaiah's bike was still at home, and Kayla had elected to take the bus.

"Guess I really will be going home with you," Kayla observed.

Per Micah's orders, they went back inside to grab some large garbage bags to put over the seats in order to avoid contamination. As they pulled out into the street, Micaiah started laughing.

"What's so funny?" Kayla wondered.

"If we get pulled over tonight, we're going to be arrested under suspicion of being fucking ax murderers," Micaiah said.

All three of them were laughing then. It was amusing, but not that much. Mostly they just needed the comic relief, something to laugh at for its own sake, a way to drive away the horror they'd just witnessed and been a part of. Was there any such thing as a normal life after this? Could things ever go back to the way they were before?

No, it couldn't, Micaiah decided. Life was about making irreversible decisions. The decision to pursue Time. The decision to pursue the Akari. The decision to marry Aklaq. Now, the decision to start a revolution and depose a tyrannical dictator. All of these things defined him, and there would be no going back.

Kayla was less than impressed with their house on the outside, but stunned when she walked in the door and Micaiah flipped on the lights.

"I'll give you the grand tour after we get cleaned up," Micaiah told her.

"Yeah," she agreed, then stomped her foot impatiently. "Well, fuck. I don't have a change of clothes."

"You can wear something of mine for tonight."

"Hey, no mushy romantic stuff while I'm standing right here," Micah said, pushing past them to get down the hall to his bedroom.

"But we can do it later when you're trying to sleep on the other side of the wall, right?" Micaiah teased.

"Fuck you, Cai!"

"That's my job!" Kayla informed him, laughing. She shook her head. "I am so fucking exhausted."

She followed Micaiah down to his bedroom at the end of the hall. She remained in the doorway while he went to the dresser to grab a fresh change of clothes.

"God, your room is so...boring," she said, looking around with a disgusted expression. "Have you ever heard of interior design?"

"Yeah, I think my wife does something like that, but I work too much, so I don't see her enough to ask for decorating tips." He straightened and tossed her a few items of clothing.

"You have a skinny ass, too," she said, unfolding the pair of boxers he'd tossed her way. She tossed one pair back. "Just give me a pair of sweatpants or something with a drawstring."

He sighed dramatically and went back to rummaging, trying not to get everything in the drawer dirty. "Just can't please you for anything."

"I'm sure that's something we can work on later."

He handed her a pair of old sweatpants, grabbed a spare plastic bag from his little trash can, laid it out on the bed, then sat on it and started taking his prosthetic off. He gasped with relief when it finally came off and his knee could breathe again.

"Does it hurt?" Kayla asked.

"It did," he confirmed, massaging the stump that was red and raw in some places. "I think I'll have to go a few days without the prosthetics."

"Was that one damaged at all?"

"Oh, I'm sure of it, but I'll look at it once I'm out of the shower." He might even just be a terrible person and put it off until morning. Fuck, he was sore and exhausted. Judging by the black and red plume that went down the drain, he was dirty, too. Still, he forced himself to relax as Kayla scrubbed his back.

"I like your house," she said. "I really do."

"Should have come here more often," Micaiah said.

"Hey now, you were always the one saying how we couldn't be seen together like that, because of Rifun and Cassius and this and that."

"Doesn't mean that I was right necessarily."

"Then what does it mean?"

"Just means that I have to work a little harder to make up for the time lost."

He grabbed her playfully and she squealed. Outside, Micah beat on the bathroom door. "Whenever you two are done being weird, I need to get in, too."

Micaiah raised a brow and turned back to his wife. "Don't listen to him." And he bent to kiss her.

# Chapter Twenty-Nine
## Breaking News

Ow was work?" Walter asked as Tommen got in the car. He looked exhausted from working a double.

Tommen shrugged. "Okay. I mean, it got a little interesting toward the end, but...whatever."

"Yeah? Interesting how?"

"Just...stuff."

"Stuff like...bad stuff between you and Becky?"

"No. No, nothing like that. No, we're cool. We're good."

"Okay. Stuff like...something happened to Micaiah, some piece of bad news?"

"Um. Y-you might say that. Something like that. Yeah, that might be a decent way to put it."

When Tommen got evasive, Walter got suspicious. It was even worse when the twins were involved, and they hadn't informed him of anything lately. He racked his brain, trying to come up with reasons why the twins and his son would be conspiring together without him. He didn't think he'd forgotten any birthdays—Tommen's wasn't until August, and Walter's birthday had already passed. Well, Father's Day was coming up, so maybe there was some kind of conspiracy there, though Tommen had never been big on "Hallmark holidays" as he'd called them. He barely tolerated his own birthday. A sudden Father's Day conspiracy would be way out of character.

"So are you going to tell me what's going on, or am I going to have to guess?" Walter asked after a minute of silence, Tommen squirming a little in the passenger seat.

"I, uh, I would be surprised if you were able to guess correctly."

"That sounds more like a challenge than a deterrent to me. Micaiah isn't going to lose his knee or the rest of his leg, is he?"

"No, nothing like that. I mean, not in like the official, go to the hospital sense sort of thing. Maybe. It depends."

"He..." Walter paused, wondering if he wanted to voice his fears aloud. Well, Tommen was almost a man grown and certainly no stranger to sex or Micaiah's lifestyle. "He isn't going to die of a deadly STD, is he?"

Tommen gave him a weird look. "No, not that I know of. I can't imagine he'd tell me that sort of thing anyway."

He nodded. "Okay, just wanted to be sure. He and Micah aren't fighting, are they? I know they fight as brothers as such, but it's not anything bad, is it?"

"Well, there was a disagreement, but it wasn't anything huge. I mean, they really didn't have time to be mad at each other with everything else going on."

"Everything else? Tommen, you're not making sense. What happened?"

Tommen squirmed in his seat. "Uh, they said I couldn't tell you..."

"Why?"

"Because...reasons..."

Even as he fidgeted, Walter could appreciate the dilemma. Tommen was battling two aspects of his personal code of chivalry, loyalty to one's friends and keeping their secrets, and loyalty to one's family and being open and honest. Finally he sighed and said, "They only said you couldn't tell. Would you tell me if I was able to guess correctly?"

"Yeah." Tommen nodded vigorously as he pulled into the garage. "Yeah, that I would do. But like I said, I would be shocked if you could guess."

"Well, I guess as long as they haven't done anything stupid

like go after Cassius and Rifun alone..." He looked at Tommen who suddenly looked guilty. "They...didn't go after Cassius and Rifun alone, did they?"

"Um...yes?"

He paused in the door into the house. "What happened?" When Tommen did not answer right away, he added, "Tommen, I'm not holding you responsible for their actions. And if they told you not to tell me, I'm taking it as you following orders from a ranking officer. Except I outrank them. Now I'm telling you, since you said you would tell me if I guess correctly, to tell me."

Tommen relaxed a little then, and answered, "I don't know how it started or the whole story. I guess that last night or this morning, Micaiah went to the Wheel and turned himself in to Rifun. He demanded something called a Time Trial."

"Oh my God," Walter said, turning away.

A Time Trial? Really? On a good day it was only self-righteous suicide. For Micaiah to do it in his condition, with the way things stood in Time and in the Wheel, he could have saved himself the effort and cut his own throat. Tommen was silent as Walter paced the living room a few times, trying to blow off steam and collect himself. Finally he collapsed in his recliner and motioned his son forward. "Okay. What else?"

"The plan was supposed to be that Micah would stand as his...Stake? And me, you, and someone named Doug would be his Testimonies or something. But the summons to me and you were supposed to be intercepted. Yours was, but I got mine, which is how I know any of this. I wasn't supposed to know either."

"When you talk about Doug, do you know his last name?"

"Um, Temple-Something."

Templeton. He was a Gatekeeper-trained Master, but his political views were usually a little too extreme for the Hands' taste, and he often elected just to fly under the radar of the Time industry. He was classified as a Runner, but as long as he didn't cause trouble, he could live peacefully. What in God's green earth was Micaiah doing with him?

Walter sighed and rubbed his eyes. "Not showing up for a Time Trial is punishable by death or clock breaking. They may have intercepted the summons, but how did they expect to pass off me and you not being there?"

Tommen shifted uncomfortably. "Because we did go. And we didn't. They used something called a Disguise."

"What, like hair and makeup?"

His son gave him an incredulous glance. "No. I mean, we're talking like a total Disguise. Some guy named Mike was Disguised as you, and he looked and sounded just like you. Like, clone-level stuff here."

"So he was a Harvester?"

"No! Not like that. They said..." He hesitated and shrugged as if trying to just pass it off as insignificant. "They said it was an Akari ability." When Walter hesitated, he went on. "I don't know about that, but that was some serious shit. I saw it with my own eyes. Mike was you, and someway, somehow, Kayla turned into me. It freaked me the fuck out!"

"What have I told you about your language? Now then, who's Kayla?"

Tommen blinked. "She's...Micaiah's wife."

"Micaiah isn't married."

"Hey, that's just what she told me."

"Do you believe it?"

"Well, yes. I mean, if you're going into a life-and-death situation where you're not likely to survive, love and sentiment is only going to cloud your judgment and make it harder to win, especially if the Time Trial is as big of an issue as everyone says it is. In that case, it's better to have a clear head. There is nothing gained by her claiming to be his wife when she's not."

Walter sighed and leaned back in his recliner. Apparently, total isolation from Time and being Suppressed hadn't been good to the twins if they'd gone this far off the deep end. It wasn't even that they were talking about doing dumb shit like this; it was that they'd actually done it. Come morning, Bakery na hÉireann would have no owners. Walter would have to file a Missing Persons report, knowing full well that it would never get solved. Tommen would not only be unemployed, but he would be forever scarred. His bosses, his Lieutenants, his friends, who had always been so good to him, had lost it and went off on a suicide mission, trying to be martyrs for a cause for which he, Walter, had nearly died to keep from killing his boy.

"Are you mad?" Tommen wondered cautiously.

"Not at you," Walter told him. He shook his head. "Why did they tell you not to tell me?"

"They..." Tommen looked guiltily at his feet. "They said you were too fragile after your ordeal in the black cells. They said you would never be able to handle it." He got defensive again. "Like I said, I mean, I got my summons on accident; neither of us was supposed to know about this."

"I get it, Tommen. I do. It's not your fault."

"Are you...what are you going to do to them, if and when they get back?"

Walter rubbed his eyes again. "They're not coming back, Tommen. Time Trials are suicide for a human. If Cassius and Rifun are overseeing them, they will most assuredly die. There is no way around it." He let out a breath. "Go to bed. Might as well cancel your alarm, too. There will be no work for you in the morning."

He didn't like telling Tommen that, didn't like the way his expression twisted into understanding. The twins weren't coming back. They were going to commit suicide, all for a lie and a hope. After a minute, Tommen just nodded and went off to bed. Walter watched him go.

Maybe what was worse, what really got him about the whole thing, was the reason they gave for not telling him. Walter didn't deny that he had problems, and being locked up in the black cells certainly hadn't helped him out any, but he wasn't fragile. He still went to work, still did his job, still went into battle beside his brothers in blue, come what may. He didn't stand back from the scene just because the house was dark and deserted; he toughed it out, did his job, and had his nervous breakdown later, when he was alone and could deal with it in his own time and his own way. The shrink was still watching him, but even Tequila acknowledged that he was improving.

Walter headed to bed feeling rather dejected. His two best friends had just jumped off a bridge, and Tommen had been the one to see them go. He was going to have to appoint two new Lieutenants for the District. How did he even go about doing that now, Time the way it was? What if he just didn't appoint new Lieutenants? Everyone was Suppressed anyway, so it wouldn't matter.

He woke up feeling like he hadn't slept at all, punching off his alarm clock and dragging himself through his morning routine. When he checked on Tommen, he found his son still fast asleep, blankets kicked to the floor, every inch of the bed covered by his tall, skinny frame. First he'd been kidnapped by religious terrorists, then he found out that his bosses apparently bought into that fiction, too. Keep it up and he was never going to be anything but a cold, bitter atheist for the rest of his life. A shame, really, considering Becky seemed to have been working some real good in his life.

Walter went to work, mentally preparing for another day of speeding tickets, graffiti, and noisy neighbors. Fourth of July was coming up, which meant fireworks and alcohol, most often at the same time.

It was around eight o'clock when Jim Standish met him at his cubicle, swirling his coffee just so. "We've been here for three hours and you still look like someone killed your dog. What's up?"

"Oh, just...nothing. Personal stuff."

"Everything all right? Tommen okay? I mean, I know he's going to be a senior —"

"Junior."

"Junior? Well, either way, he's not beating up on your too bad, is he?"

"No, it's not him. Other stuff."

Standish took a drink of coffee and studied him for a moment. "You're okay, right? I mean, I didn't want to say anything because I didn't want to pry, but I know you've been talking to the shrink regularly since that incident last winter—"

"I'm fine," Walter told him shortly, looking at him. "I'm fine, Tommen's fine, that's all fine. It's other stuff."

"Uh-huh. Have you been to the bakery to get your pastry yet this morning?"

He sighed. "They're closed."

"No, they're not. I just drove by there on my way back in from a run; they're open and bustling with business."

"You're kidding. And...both twins are in there?"

"Well, I mean I only drove by; I didn't actually stop in to check. But it looked like one of them was on the counter, and the other was probably in the kitchen."

Before Walter could say anything more, his cell phone rang. It was Tommen.

"Hello?" he wondered.

"Dad, it's me." Tommen sounded like he'd just gotten out of bed. "Hey, so, um, Cai just called and was wondering where I am. I was kinda supposed to open today. Do...you mind if I go in to work?"

Walter sat back in his chair. "Are you able to get a ride?"

"I should be able to. Or I can just Band and walk. Um, Micaiah lifted the Suppression."

Damn that man. Arrogant bastard. He rubbed his eyes. "Yes. Go ahead and go."

"Okay. Do you want me to say anything about last night or what do you want me to do?"

"No, don't tell them. I'll have a talk with them later."

"Oh. Okay. I guess I'll see you later then."

"You sure everything's all right?" Standish asked when Walter hung up.

"I'm fine," Walter repeated irritably. He stood. "I'm going to head out for a bit."

Standish got out of his way, and Walter went out to his cruiser. Maybe a little fresh air and a quick road patrol would do him some good. Deal with something easy, something besides this fiasco that was exploding out of control only in his mind. As he pulled out of the parking lot, his phone rang again.

"Detective Forbes," he answered levelly.

"Regina DeWitt, Manager Timekeeper, Region Four, District Six," the woman on the other end introduced. "Did I catch you at a bad time?" Her tone was sarcastic, suggesting she didn't give half a damn if he was in the middle of an active shooter standoff.

"Not at the moment. I wasn't aware that Region Four had a Standing Manager."

"Well, we do. As of about forty-five minutes ago. I'm working on getting Captains reinstated in all the Districts. At least you're alive and well."

"This time, yes. But I get the feeling you think I know more about the situation than I actually do."

"At least you're aware that there is a situation."

"Do I get a debriefing, or are we going to play vague, passive-aggressive word games all morning?"

He could hear Regina breathing on the other end; she sounded as frazzled as he did, except he didn't even know why he was frazzled. Finally, "Cassius is dead, and Rifun has been removed from power. The Wheel is free from their terror; rebuilding efforts are already underway."

"I expect you're going to tell me that my Lieutenants had something to do with it."

"They were the instigators of this whole event. Supposedly, if rumors are to be believed, they even managed to kill the Bat. However, your name was attached to this incident. Micaiah Durvin was taken to a Time Trial—at his own request after turning himself over to Rifun—and listed you as one of his Testimonies."

"That is one rumor I had heard, but I did not understand what it was in reference to," Walter said, only half-lying. "But in that, is there some sort of accusation or charge being brought against me or my Lieutenants?"

"Not yet," Regina replied. "And I'm less inclined to take any action against you for the sheer fact of who they were running with in their little revolution."

"I heard Doug Templeton's name being tossed around."

"Yes, him and his band of less-fanatical-than-Rifun Akari-bearer group. I'd call them a cult, but Cassius and Rifun redefined that for us."

"Agreed. Although, I have to wonder, when you're going up against an adversary like Cassius and Rifun, why wouldn't you take all the help you can get? Fanatics they may be, but if they can fight, they can fight."

"It's the fact of it, though, Walter. I shouldn't have to tell you that. When you ask for the public's help in solving a case, are you asking for their vigilance and their tips, or do you literally want them to come into the office and work beside you?"

"Mm, point taken. But the fact remains that Cassius and Rifun are out of power at the least."

"Yes, I suppose."

"You don't sound too enthusiastic about it."

"One tyrant is dead, another gone. But they were the absolute authority, the only ones in power. Right now, teams are working to restore the Wheel and make it accessible like it once was, restaff it and so forth. Once the nostalgia and the fuzzy feelings are gone, what's going to fill the power vacuum? *Who* is going to fill it?"

"I don't know. That's above my paygrade. Yours, too, by the sounds of it. But at this point, I don't think it could be worse than what we've just endured."

"You're walking a fine line right now, Walter. Don't forget that you are still responsible for the actions of your Lieutenants. Oh, and before I forget, they're fired. Since we're in a power transition right now, I'm removing them from their post. I'll leave replacements up to you, but they are terminated as of this moment."

"Understood. I'll be sure to let them know."

"You do that." Click.

Walter tossed his phone in the passenger seat. Just over the course of the conversation, his attitude had changed. Originally, he'd been planning on going to the bakery and ripping them both a new one. Now that Regina had sufficiently attacked them, questioned their character and their actions, and fired them, he felt the need to defend them and find out exactly what the hell happened.

As Standish had said, the bakery was open for business and full of people. He guessed Tommen had Banded and walked to work, because there was no other way he could have beaten Walter there. He was on the counter, and Walter watched Micah deliver a tray of something to the front display case.

After a moment of consideration, Walter got out of the cruiser and headed inside. He waited for probably ten minutes behind half a dozen people. Tommen had spotted him almost immediately. Micah came and went a couple times, but if he saw Walter, he gave no indication of it.

"*S'mae,*" Tommen greeted when he finally got up to the counter. "*Does?*" (Hi. Pastry?)

"The twins in?" Walter asked.

Tommen's expression changed then, conveying an understanding that now the grown-ups were going to be having a discussion, and things were probably going to change. He nodded and went back to call for Micah. Walter noted that he only asked Micah to come up front, not necessarily that Walter was looking for him.

"Morning, Walter," Micah said, drying his hands as he approached the counter. "Pastry for you?"

"Where's Micaiah?"

"He might be coming in later if he's feeling better; otherwise, I think he's taking a sick day."

"He wasn't hurt too bad from last night's excursion, I hope?"

Now Micah's expression changed. He nodded slowly. "So you

heard?"

"I did." Maybe it was better not to mention that Tommen had told him. Instead, he opted for, "The new Regional Manager called me this morning. Said there might be something we need to discuss."

"Right. Well, like I said, Cai's at home. And as you can see, we're a little busy right now. Can we do this later?"

Walter considered his options. Then, "I'll swing by your place after you guys close. If you can give Tommen a ride, I'll pick him up there."

"Works for us. We'll see you later, then."

"Hey now, I'm not leaving without my pastry."

He tried to sound friendly, put Micah's mind at ease, try to convey that he wasn't going to whip them, however much he felt like it. Still, Micah seemed unsure about the whole thing, retrieving the pastry and ringing him up, as nervous as a teenager on his first day of work. Walter still thanked him before going on his way, walking out to the cruiser and sitting there for a minute, chewing thoughtfully.

Judging by Micah's demeanor, whatever endeavor they'd gone on, it wasn't about trying to usurp him or go over his head, inasmuch as they begrudged him as Captain. Leaving him out had been a matter of principle, thinking him too psychologically unstable to handle a bloody Time Trial and ensuing revolution. He was still debating the legitimacy of that one. Running into an active shooter situation or other deadly scenario was one thing; getting caught up in a war was quite another. He tried to tell himself that he could have handled it just fine. Maybe in the heat of the moment, he could have. It was afterward that he had a hard time convincing himself of.

Walter spent the day batting around different ideas and theories, in between calls from other Districts. Some wanted to know what happened, others just called to inform him of some power change or other office appointment. By lunchtime, all the Districts had at least a Captain, with three of them needing Lieutenants, his included.

The twins had been his Lieutenants for a decade or more.

They had a good relationship, a system they could work by whenever something came up. During the murder case, he only had to hand them some piece of information, and he knew he could trust them to run with it and get what he needed. Not only would he have to re-learn that with two new Lieutenants, but there were no other Lieutenant-trained Timekeepers in Charleston. Everything would have to be done remotely. Call him old-fashioned, but Walter preferred working with people in person, especially his immediate subordinate officers.

But the Manager had spoken. He had to find new Lieutenants.

He got off shift a little before the bakery closed, so he took the time to go home and change out of his blues. Maybe if he wore something a little less formal and imposing, their conversation would be less like an interrogation. To that end, he also made himself something to eat. There was little worse than trying to get information on an empty stomach. It made him cranky, or so Standish had said on multiple occasions.

When he finally got out to the twins' house north of town, he saw that both cars and Micaiah's motorcycle were parked in the garage—or the metal tent that passed for a garage anyway. The light in the living room and the TV appeared to be on, and there was some indistinguishable movement inside. Outside, Tommen was fighting with the pull string on the lawnmower.

Taking a breath, Walter got out of the old Cadillac and went to the front door that led to the kitchen. He intended to knock and let himself in, but he had only to knock once and the door was opened for him, Micah standing back to let him in.

"For a few minutes, we were wondering if you were going to show up," Micah said. "Then we realized that we still had your kid, so we knew you would come eventually."

It was poor humor, delivered nervously. Elsewhere in the house, Walter heard Micaiah's voice. *"A Mhicah, tá leathcheann ort. Lig an fear taoibh isteach."* (Micah, you're an idiot. Let the man inside.)

Walter took off his shoes and went into the living room. He

was less than prepared for what he found there.

Micaiah lay on his stomach on the couch, covered only by a blanket at the waist, ending at his knees. From shoulder to waist, he was covered in dark purple bruises and cuts of varying severity. His leg stump looked red and slightly swollen, and his lower left leg seemed to be in about as good a shape as his torso.

"Quite a sight, isn't it?" he mumbled into the pillow.

"Why don't you Band and heal yourself?" Walter wondered.

"Because I'm taking a fucking sick day. And if I'm going to take a fucking sick day, I might as well be fucking sick. It's as much for the internal damage as anything." Stiffly, he rolled back just enough to show off a place on his left side where it looked like he'd been stabbed. "Micah's not in much better shape, really, but he did choose to Band his wounds."

"So you really did it. You went and killed Rifun and Cassius."

"The Bat and Cassius," a new voice said.

Walter turned and had to do a double-take. She was about five-four, five-five, around one-twenty or so at a liberal estimate. Her skin was chocolate, hair and eyes black. She had a small towel in hand and went to the kitchen, grabbing a cold pack from the freezer and wrapping it in the towel before taking it and placing it on Micaiah's back.

"You must be Kayla," Walter guessed.

"Aklaq White Bear Durvin," she introduced. "But yes, most call me Kayla."

He looked at Micaiah on the couch and Micah in one of the recliners. "I have a feeling there's something you guys aren't telling me."

"You wouldn't believe us if we told you," Micah said, trying to relax.

Kayla got a couple hot packs and warmed them up in the microwave. Then she wrapped them in towels, handing one to Micah and taking on for herself while she collapsed in the other recliner.

"Considering that you three look like death, I imagine there has to be some sort of explanation," Walter replied, grabbing a chair from the dining room. "How about we start with something easy, like why you didn't tell me—after how many years have we known each other?—that you're married, Micaiah?"

Micaiah laughed hoarsely, face still buried in the pillow. Painfully, he got himself flipped around on his back, moving the cold pack to the area around his stitches. "That's the least easy thing about this."

"You have to start somewhere. Might as well start there. When did you get married and why wasn't I invited?"

"I've been married longer than I've known you, Walt," Micaiah said, grinning stupidly. "But Rifun has been stalking us for years. During and after the Dispersal, we weren't sure what was going to happen, what he might do, so we made it a point to not be together-together, as a married couple."

"So you're implied playboy lifestyle was always an excuse just to see your wife? What the hell was Rifun stalking you for?"

"The same reason he's stalking Tommen now; he's looking for Akari-bearers."

"Why not stalk Micah, then, too?"

"I managed to convince Rifun that Micah wasn't an Akari-bearer; he wasn't the one he was looking for."

Walter folded his arms. The twins had never been less than honest with him up until now, and yet he found it difficult to swallow that there was more to them than met the eye. "What happened in the Wheel? More importantly, why were you hanging around Doug Templeton? Or why was he hanging around you?"

"It wasn't Doug," Micah said after a moment of solemn hesitation. "Cassius Disguised himself as Doug in order to get close to us. We're still trying to work out a timeline of exactly when he made the switch."

"Cassius may have been a Harvester, but he was also black. Doug was white. You might be looking at years to—"

"We're not talking about Harvesting, Walt," Micaiah

interrupted. "We're talking about a Disguise. It was the original Harvesting, before Time came in and corrupted it. With a Disguise, you can pretty much pull off anyone you want, regardless of genetics. It's not foolproof, but close enough. Mike Junior Disguised himself as you, and Kayla Disguised herself as Tommen in order to get into the Time Trial."

"You're talking about something Doug—or someone else—taught you as a Manager or a Gatekeeper?"

The twins glanced uneasily at each other, but it was Kayla who answered. "We're talking about the Akari. Not the one you're thinking of, that fabled legend of some Time Holy Grail, or the one Rifun thinks he's following and using."

"Is there any other?"

"There is the real one," Micaiah said simply. "The one we used to get into the Wheel in the first place, Disguise Junior and Kayla as you and Tommen, open a portal to bring in an army to find the Grandfathers and the guards, kill Cassius, break into the Judgment Wing without stamps, kill Isthim and the Bat. Normal Time could not have done what we did. If it could have, it would have already."

Walter leaned back in his seat as best he could, trying to absorb and digest everything. Cassius and Rifun were nuts; that much had already been proven over and over again. Micah and Micaiah weren't nuts, well, no more than anyone else, he supposed. They were humble bakers, hard workers, excellent Lieutenants, and critical thinkers. They didn't just say something because they liked to hear themselves talk, or buy into something because some smooth-talking salesman told them to.

At the same time, though...this was ludicrous. It was like trying to add a third camp of Holy Grail hunters. In the one camp, there were the legend-lovers, those who liked the thought and the story, but knew it was just a legend. In another camp, there were those who actively sought the Holy Grail, driven by obsession until they exhausted their entire life savings and destroyed any and all credibility they had, whether archaeologically, historically, or financially. Now the twins were claiming a third camp, those who actually had the Holy Grail and used it on a regular basis. It was just impossible. Something like that would have to make the news; someone would blow the whistle and call attention to them.

But then, what if the revolution was that whistle blowing? If everything they said was true, what did that mean for the future of the Wheel and of Time? The legends always spoke of the Akari's great power. They also said that the Akari didn't play nice with others.

Walter mulled it over, trying to reconcile everything in his mind. He knew he'd Suppressed the twins. They should not have been able to even Band their way to work, much less break into the Wheel which had been sealed off, or lift the Suppression which had been instilled on them from the Manager. At the same time, however, Micaiah shouldn't have been able to collapse those portals like he did. Such abilities were reserved for Wardens and Dominion Timekeepers.

"So what actually happened in the Wheel?" he asked finally.

So the three of them gave him a fairly detailed version of events, starting with Micah Disguising himself as Micaiah, getting into the Wheel and turning himself in, demanding a Time Trial. They described the new Wheel layout and the Pit. They detailed Rifun's Time Trial format. They talked about the shot that did not kill Rifun, but a decoy he'd sent, and the first wave of battle that ensued. Then there was Rifun's reveal as he brought in the rest of his army. The trio explained how they discovered that Doug wasn't Doug, and that they'd killed Cassius. They described hunting Rifun through the Wheel. Kayla talked about her short-lived duel with Isthim while the twins broke into the Judgment Wing and made for Rifun's study. They finished with their battle with the Bat and returning to the Wheel to find that the Pit had been lit up to burn the bodies of all the fallen, no room for funerals.

"When we got back, it was three o'clock in the morning," Micah finished. "We all took showers, then Micaiah Banded me so I could get some sleep. Then he started noticing his wounds weren't as superficial as he originally thought, and he decided he was just going to take a sick day." He Banded. "Personally, I think he just wanted to fuck his wife."

"Do you blame him?" Walter asked, stealing a glance at Kayla.

"Stop gossiping about me," Kayla hissed, breaking into the Band and tearing it apart. "I know what you're talking about in there."

Micah blushed and Walter grinned, but Micaiah was laughing. "Should have called you Aklaq Porcupine Durvin." Kayla pointed a threatening finger at him, but he only laughed harder, stopping only when his stitches made themselves known. He sucked in a breath. "This gives whole new meaning to 'bursting at the seams.' "

Walter went to Band him and stop the sick day nonsense, but when he tried to feel for Micaiah's place in time, he found that there was something like an invisible force field keeping him out. Micaiah apparently sensed his attempts, because he shook his head. "Time can't touch me when I'm in the Akari. Or at least, it would take a lot more force than what you're trying to use."

Walter retreated, unsure of how to respond. Instead he changed the subject. "So Rifun got away."

"He did," Micah confirmed reluctantly.

"Did he make any threats? 'I'll be back' or anything?"

"He's too smart for that," Kayla said. "He knows enough not to give away his plans. If we don't know his plans, we can't make plans of our own."

"I was afraid you'd say that. Did he ever mention Tommen at all?"

Micaiah explained the bogus bargain he'd made over the Time Trial, about Tommen becoming Rifun's Akari Apprentice. "That was the last time Tommen was mentioned by name, but he did say something about, even though he was defeated, he would still be looking for ways to master the Akari and bend others to his will. I don't think we have any reason to think he won't come after Tommen again. It just might not be right away."

So, once again, the one they wanted to kill the most got away.

At least Cassius was dead, but that thought brought little comfort seeing how he'd only ever been the puppet in the first place.

"The Wheel is going to be doing some heavy remodeling over the next few months," Micah was saying. "It's going to be at least until the end of the summer before things are any semblance of normal again. But we'll be here to help you, as your Lieutenants."

"You're not my Lieutenants anymore," Walter said quickly. He noted their stunned and hurt expressions. He hurriedly added, "Regina DeWitt from District Six is the new Regional Manager. She got word of your escapades and greatly disapproves of them. As of this morning, you've been removed from your posts. She said she'd leave the new nominations up to me, but you two are not allowed to be Lieutenants anymore, not while she's Manager."

"What a bitch," Kayla said incredulously. "We risked our asses so she can be appointed to that fucking post—and have it actually mean something—and she fires them."

"I didn't say I agreed with her, but that's what's been done."

"Do I get to keep my vacation time, at least?" Micaiah asked.

"Fuck you, Cai," Micah told him.

"You've been saying that a lot since we got back, but have yet to actually do it."

Out of the corner of his eye, Walter saw Kayla roll her eyes and shake her head. He looked at her. "So will you be sticking around a while?"

"I expect so," she answered. "Someone has to keep them in line."

"Where are you from?"

"Well, that depends. Officially, I'm listed as District One, Alaska and Western Canada. Problem is, as a Native American, or First Nations as we're called in Canada, I'm part of the unofficial, still-unrecognized District Nine that encompasses the tribes. So, take that how you will."

Walter nodded uncertainly and turned his attention back to the twins. He expected they might have been doing a little physical bro-fighting, but neither seemed physically up to the challenge. So they settled for sharp tongues and sharper words. They quieted when they caught him staring.

"We're sorry we didn't tell you about the plan," Micah said. "But you're not an Akari-bearer, and Time would have been useless."

"And...?" Walter prodded.

"And...we weren't sure how you would handle it. Psychologically," Micaiah confessed. "Especially if you thought Tommen was going. Even if you knew it was Kayla, we weren't sure how the visual of Tommen there would affect you. Not to mention what could happen if you didn't come back. In the end, we just decided it would be better for you to sit this one out. We made a judgment call." He paused. "You can't fire us from our post at this point, but we understand if there is some punishment we have to endure."

Walter hesitated. "Part of me does want to punish you in some way, for going behind my back and lying—or intending to lie—and because of your lack of faith in me, even if it is plausibly justifiable. The other part of me wants to reward you for taking a chance, killing the Bat and Cassius, and restoring the Wheel, or helping to get that started. And because you did try to consider both Tommen and myself when considering how to protect him from Rifun in this whole deal. Speaking of which, where is Tommen?"

Micah grudgingly pulled himself to his feet and went to the window. The days were long, but the sun was starting to sink behind the mountain peaks, casting long shadows over the valley. He opened the window. "Tommen! Hey, Tommen!" He waved a hand. "You can come in now. Yeah, it looks great. Thank you."

He got back to his seat just as Tommen walked in the door, his shoes caked in dirt, grass, and other debris. Once he kicked off his shoes, he fished around in his pockets for his hearing aids and slipped them back in place.

"Oh. Wow," he said, stopping in his tracks when he saw Micaiah. "Are you...okay? Can you not Band and stuff?"

Micaiah sighed. "Just leave it alone, Tommen."

Tommen glanced at Walter who nodded once and indicated a chair for him to sit in. "Is everything okay? Like, you guys aren't in trouble or anything, are you?"

"The new Regional Manager fired them," Walter said. "They're no longer Lieutenants."

"Apparently, we're lucky to not be classified as Runners at this point," Micah threw in.

"What does that mean? Do you have to leave or something?"

"No, it just means that we won't be part of any Time-side investigations in the future, not like we have been in the past."

"And officer communication will be more on the phone and online, less in person," Walter finished.

"So you won't be coming to the bakery as much."

"Oh, I still expect to get my pastry every morning, but no, I won't be stopping by with cases and asking for investigation and information."

"Oh. What happens now, then? Am I still an Apprentice and stuff?"

"You are," Walter confirmed. He didn't miss the look Micaiah gave him, though. It was one of questioning and curiosity, but also a little fear. Micaiah had just revealed himself—or proclaimed himself—to be an Akari-bearer, one whom Rifun had been stalking for years to try and recruit. Now Rifun was stalking Tommen for the same reason. How did they handle the situation? "You are still a Time Apprentice."

"Yeah, but..."

"But what?" Kayla prompted gently.

Tommen kind of hunched his shoulders and rolled his eyes. "I still don't really know if there's a God or anything, and Rifun is still nuts, but...what about this whole Akari business?" He looked at the twins. "You guys are weird, but you're not crazy. And I know some of the shit that I saw just in the store before you left. I mean, there's got to be something there. And if I had to choose between you teaching me about something and Rifun, I'll take you two any day."

Micah looked back at his brother. *"Is dóigh liom gur mhaith linn."* (I think he likes us.)

Micaiah nodded. *"Mise freisin."* (Me, too.)

Tommen turned his gaze back to Walter. "But I don't know how you feel about it. I mean, you always said that it was a myth and should be treated as such."

"I know," Walter said, nodding. "But I would be remiss if I said that, given certain evidence, I'm not sure quite where I stand on the subject. But I think it's safe to say that if my prickly atheist son is swayed by something, then there might be some credit due somewhere."

"So how do you want us to proceed?" Micaiah asked.

"For right now, I think we should just sit tight and wait to see how this all plays out in the Wheel. I imagine there will be some sort of meeting or election or something come up quick to establish a working government. Once the worst is past, then we'll figure it out from there. Sound good to everyone?"

No one had any objections. Walter stood and stretched. "Are you guys sure you're okay for tonight? You look like you're about ready to drop dead."

"We'll be fine," Micah told him.

After a moment of hesitation, Walter bid them good night, and he and Tommen headed out to the car. Tommen was close to getting his road test and his license. God, how time flew.

"So, what did you think about all that?" Walter asked.

"I don't know," Tommen admitted after a minute of silence. "I mean, Micah and Micaiah aren't crazy. They're just not. You know, a month ago, six months ago, I would have dismissed them as being a little weird and maybe not doing so well in Time isolation, but then…I saw things, Dad. I saw Kayla turn into me and speak with my voice. I saw Junior turn into you, and he moved just like you. They were able to break into the Wheel, which no one was supposed to be able to do. Fuck, Micaiah even broke out of the Wheel, exploding portals, trying to save you and the others, and he lost his leg and shit." He shook his head. "I don't know what to think."

Oddly, Walter's first thought was that maybe Becky was having a positive effect on him. He'd gone from "There is no God," to "I don't know if there's a God." Becky was a squirrelly little spitfire, but she was sharp as a tack and just as ready with questions of her own as answers to Tommen's questions. That apparently made him more open to the possibility of there being more out there than just the physical universe. Of course, Walter still wasn't one hundred percent certain on this whole Akari business. But like he'd said, if his prickly atheist son was curious, there might be something to it.

They rode the rest of the way in silence, each lost in his own thoughts. The last twenty-four hours had been more tumultuous than the last almost six months of nothing. Even the Tracker attacks seemed pretty tame by comparison.

When they got home, Tommen headed to his room to start his homework, and Walter went to relax in his recliner for a few minutes. Hopefully he didn't fall asleep. But with the way his thoughts were going round and round, that didn't seem likely at the moment.

Ultimately, what all of this meant was that things were going back to normal. The Wheel would build its government, eventually, Time would resume, and things went back to the way they were before. Walter would be the District Captain, and he would answer to Regina DeWitt, as terrible as it was. They would go back to chasing Runners, feuding with the Harvesters, arguing with the Hands, and training Apprentices.

Down the hall, Walter could just hear the faintest music coming from his son's room. He was growing up, and he would be moving on here pretty soon, leaving dear old dad behind. Then what did Walter aspire to? Decades of waiting for his nephew to appear, ten long years of raising him, trying to keep him on the straight and narrow, raise him as his pa would have wanted. He was going to be an empty-nester within three years. Then what?

He spent the first part of his life as a criminal. Now the second chapter was coming to a close, him entertaining Time as long as it suited him. Did that make him selfish, using Time only as long as it benefited him? Did that mean that he hadn't really changed at all since his younger days?

But Time had slowly ceased to be of use to him, especially in light of the events of the last year. The revolution in the Wheel had come, but things would not truly be the same. They'd reached a turning point as well, with Rifun bringing the Akari—whether real or not—and its zealous cult followers to the forefront of the imagination. Micah and Micaiah, always so docile and, for lack of better term, uninvolved, now coming out as part of a separate Akari movement, determined to be rid of Rifun and his gross violence in the name of the Akari.

Maybe there would be a Time Renaissance, a revival of sorts, and thousands would flock to the Akari and its followers. Maybe there would be a secondary revolt, as fearful and angry Time Agents sought to destroy anyone who even uttered the name. But things would not be the same. Time was losing its place in the universe.

Walter sighed and hauled himself out of his recliner, making for his bedroom. Maybe it was time for him to retire from this Time business. He could see Tommen off to college before going dark one last time, and rebuild himself one last life. Physically, he only appeared to be in his late forties, early fifties. He could get in a couple more decades of honest work while waiting for the effects of Time to wear off, and he could enjoy his retirement like any good American. He might find a nice little cabin in the woods, or buy an RV and just tour the country. Either would do.

He looked in on Tommen briefly, watched him turn off his stereo, put away his homework, and set his hearing aids on their charger. He'd been doing so well over the last six months. He had school, he had a girlfriend, he had a job. He had a life. Did he really want to throw it all away just in the hopes of learning about something that had done nothing but try to kill him so far? Did he still hold out hope that he could be a Scout and explore the universe, going to places untouched by Time?

After a moment, he headed to the bathroom to get ready for bed. It was ironic, he thought. So many people wished for more time. More time to study, more time with family, more time for hobbies. He himself had the ability to bend Time, to effectively "make" more time in a day.

*Time has had its way with me,* he mused bitterly, spitting toothpaste into the sink. It had tossed him around, chewed him up, and spit him out. Now he was ready to be done with it all. *Just a couple more years. Tommen's got two more years of school, and then he's off on his own. Take a little time to go dark and rebuild your life, just one last time. It doesn't even have to be a continuation of this one. It doesn't even have to be true. It's all about the stories we tell, after all.*

"Are you done?"

Walter was jerked from his thoughts as Tommen leaned against the door frame. "Huh? Oh, yeah." He wiped his mouth and paused. "You're sure you're okay?"

"Yeah, why wouldn't I be?"

"Just making sure." Walter pulled Tommen close to him in an awkward embrace. "I just want to make sure you're okay and keep you safe."

"Um...Dad...you're kind of freaking me out. Are you okay?"

Walter let him go. "I expect so. I'm just tired. I'll see you tomorrow when you get off work."

"I don't work tomorrow; I work Tuesday."

"Then I'll see you when I get off work."

Because Tommen was an adult now, and they discussed work schedules instead of school schedules or Little League schedules. God, this was all too much to handle. Walter closed his bedroom door and collapsed onto his bed. He was fine. Everything was great.

# Chapter Thirty
## Tiers and Fears

Morning came too early, as it always did. Walter grudgingly punched off his alarm clock and lay in bed for a minute longer. Three seconds into the day and he already had a headache. That's what stress did to him apparently. He'd been under way too much stress in the last twenty-four hours or so. Strange thing was, he not only had nothing to do with it, but it didn't concern him at all, and everything that had happened was, fundamentally, good stuff. So why did his body seem to think it was under the same stress it had been when Tommen was kidnapped? A curse of old bones, perhaps. Old bones and a wizened mind.

Grudgingly, he made his way out of bed and started in on the morning routine. Shower, shave, coffee, breakfast with the morning paper. His hours had been cut, so why did he still have to get up so damn early? Why not let him sleep in until eight or nine o'clock?

As always, he checked on Tommen before he left. He'd finally stopped growing at about six-foot-one, and while he was a prolific eater, he was still skinny as a beanpole. And still he managed to sprawl out over his blankets and take up every square inch of his bed, not even flinching when the sliver of light passed over his face. Walter searched his memory but couldn't recall that he himself had ever been so skinny or slept so soundly. Of course, when he was Tommen's age, he usually spent his nights either in jail, in a cardboard box, or in bed at a brothel; he'd had to sleep lightly.

He headed out to the car, looking around at half a dozen projects he'd started while on vacation. He'd been determined to build his own cabinets instead of buy them, woefully unprepared for all the specialized tools he needed. Trim had seemed an easier endeavor, except the sheer amount of trim he needed for the whole house. Now, as before the time Tommen cleaned out the garage, the projects were left to die in their own sawdust. Maybe he should just give up on it for now. Maybe in his next life he'd be a carpenter.

So far, everything appeared to be progressing smoothly, no vicious clashes between various factions warring for power. But then, the liberation had only happened yesterday. It was probably going to take a while for anything to get sorted out. As it was, he still had to consider his options for Lieutenants. Maybe he could do that in between calls and paperwork at the precinct.

"Morning, Walt," Standish greeted, meeting him at the coffee pot. He raised a brow. "You sleep last night?"

"Just," Walter replied. "If they're cutting our hours, why do we still have to get up at shit o'clock in the morning?"

His attempt at sarcasm worked, or it appeared to, as Standish scoffed. "I hear ya, man. Believe me, I wish I could sleep in until ten or eleven. The only reason I don't move to second shift is because of my wife."

"Yup. Tommen is my reason; I like to see him at the end of the day."

"What are you going to do with him over the summer? He's driving here pretty soon, isn't he?"

"Already got his road test scheduled for the end of August, right after his birthday. It's his gift to himself."

"Assuming he passes."

"I think he will. He's a good kid, good driver. For a sixteen year old."

"There's the rub, isn't it? Well, I'll see you out there at some point I expect."

He left, and Walter headed to his cubicle. After a brief perusal of his emails and a few follow-ups, he started in on choosing his Lieutenants. By that, he brought up a list of all the Lieutenant-trained Masters in District Four. It was all cataloged in the Time Agent website, password protected and secured by superior technology and nerdy Time Agents from all disciplines.

Well, they weren't savages. With the technology available to them in the Wheel, why wouldn't they have their own localized database for such things?

There were six in the District, not including the twins. It should have made the decision easier, but it only really made it harder. He knew all of them, of course, and knew they were all sufficiently trained. But he liked having his Lieutenants close by. It wasn't that he was always trying to intrude and micro-manage, but when he needed something done or need to bounce ideas off them, he wanted to do it in person, not just over the phone or through email.

Wayne Jade was from South Carolina, currently stationed there because of his service in the Coast Guard. He would certainly be an asset to have, up until he got moved to another Coast Guard base. Walter didn't think that happened often, but the last thing he needed was to wake up one morning, go looking for him for some urgent thing, and find that he'd been moved to Michigan, or California. Or Alaska.

Esther Thomas hailed from Maine, a regular 9-5 girl in the corporate office setting. Having a female Lieutenant wouldn't be a bad idea; she would be able to go places Walter and the twins hadn't been able to in cases past. But still...Maine was so far away. The only reason is wasn't part of District Three was because, quite simply, Quebec. Quebec demanded their own District, and they just tolerated having to share one with Newfoundland and the other eastern Canadian provinces. At the same time, proximity might make it easier to communicate between the Districts if necessary.

Luke Gros lived in Florida, worked as a lifeguard and surfing instructor. He seemed like a nice enough guy, but it reminded Walter too much of Kyle. Kyle was a nice guy, too, but there was always that aspect of Running that would stick with him wherever he went. It wasn't a fair association, or assumption that all surfer dudes were lazy, useless Runners, but Walter was smart enough to recognize his prejudice and elect to steer clear of future conflict until said prejudice had been otherwise resolved.

Alex Randal was the closest of the six, living in Virginia. His file was sparse, stating only that he was from Quantico, Virginia. There was only one reason to list his residence as Quantico, and that was working for the FBI. Now that would be the guy to have. Problem was, his file also stated that he was currently training for Captain status. That didn't necessarily mean he was coming after Walter's position, but the thought was unnerving.

Gabriel Emmanuel Martinez also lived in Florida, a Cuban defector. His file stated that he intended to move north to New Jersey, but there was little issue there since New Jersey was also in District Four. Having someone who spoke Spanish and could communicate with Regions Two and Three might be valuable, plus his defection from Cuba certainly showed he had the guts to do what was necessary. At the same time, though...New Jersey...

Zeke Waters was the last one on the list. The newest and youngest Lieutenant-trained Master, he made his home in Georgia. He listed his occupation only as "self-employed" which could mean any number of things. On the one hand, he could be like the twins, owning his own business and being very responsible and successful. On the other hand, it could be a catch-all for a dozen different attempts at trying to achieve the "Work from your own home and earn a hundred grand a week with no effort!" dream found in numerous scams on the Internet.

Walter leaned back in his chair and reviewed the list two or three times. He had a pretty good idea of who he wanted, but he would have to stalk them online a little more, and he would definitely have to call and interview them.

After a minute or two of staring at the computer screen, he got up, stretched, and headed for the break room to refill his coffee. He really should stop drinking the stuff; it was terrible for him. Nevertheless, he stirred in his cream and sugar, taking a few minutes just to himself before returning.

He'd no sooner sat down than a call came in for some noise complaint. He conversed with the lady on the other end amiably enough, but groaned when he hung up, Banding and taking a few minutes to himself before actually dragging himself out to his cruiser. Oh, today was going to be a long day.

He'd no sooner returned from the noise complaint than his cell phone rang. It wasn't Tommen or the twins, but the number was still familiar. Half a second after he answered, he realized who it was, and he wished he'd just let it go to voicemail.

"Walt, it's Gina," the Manager said, her voice sharp for already moving on to familiar forms of address.

"I'm going over the candidates now," he told her. "I know I'm a little old-fashioned, but please, humor me. I'm going to call each of them to interview them. Then I'll get back with you."

"Excellent. Will that be before or after Voting Day?"

"Voting Day?"

"Mm-hm. The powers that have been rebuilding the Wheel the last couple days have apparently worked out some new governmental system they want to try. But in the spirit of democracy, they're going to open up the initial vote to everyone."

"Everyone, as in...?"

"From probationaries to officers, every single Time Agent who is still alive is allowed to vote in this special election. Which means your boy gets a voice in this, too."

"So I deduced. What kind of 'new system' are we talking about?"

"A tiered system, somewhere between U.S. government and Hidalian government; have you ever heard of them?"

"No, not that I recall."

"Well, I'm still trying to wrap my head around this flow chart, but it looks like the power is no longer concentrated into two major groups—the Hands and the Grandfathers. Now it looks like they want to break it up, move things around. Truth be told, I think it's actually more efficient than it looks."

"That depends. How over-reaching is it going to be?"

"Only time will tell, Walter. I'll email you the flow chart if you want."

"Please. When is the actual Voting Day?"

"Wednesday, all day."

"Okay. Guess I can't complain if I don't vote, especially with an election this important."

"I was thinking the same thing. Until then, Captain." Click.

Walter found his cubicle and slumped in his seat. This was all happening way too fast. He needed time to process it. Well, technically, he could just make the time to think it over, but still. This was all happening way too fast.

After a minute or two, he got back into the Time Agent database and looked up the contact information for each of the Lieutenant-trained Masters. He did not call Alex. Wayne and Luke did not pick up. Gabriel asked to reschedule for a better time, which he did. As for Esther and Zeke, well, he'd only been impressed with one of them.

By the time he got done with all that—and that done between his normal police officer duties—it was just about time to go home. Damn, but the day just felt like it had flown by, which was a good thing considering how it had started out.

What most people didn't know was that, even without exposure to Time, the average person could still manipulate Time in minuscule ways. For example, "a watched pot never boils" and "time flies when you're having fun" weren't just pithy little sayings. There was a little truth to each of them. Walter just happened to be able to take both of them to extreme levels.

Before he left the precinct, he called the twins. It was Micaiah who answered the phone at the bakery; no surprise there.

"So, are we un-fired?" he asked, sounding almost cheerful and amused. Maybe having his wife around did him some good.

"Sadly, no, but I do have other news." He briefly explained the new Voting Day process, as well as the concept of a new governing system.

Micaiah whistled. "Big changes coming down the pipe, then. We should have done this years ago. But what do you mean that it's going to be a 'tiered' system?"

"I'm not entirely sure, but it looks like the Hands will no longer be able to congregate all of them in one place, with exception of the Inauguration. From what I can see, each Hand or a group of Hands will be permitted to oversee their charge and no others. For example, during reviews, such as Tommen's, he would only be overseen by the Hand of Training and Reviews and the Hand of the Timekeepers, not all fifty-one of them. An officer's review would also see the attendance of the Hand of the Officers. At least, that's how I understand it. And each Hand would have secretaries under them dedicated to assorted tasks in that area, giving the secretaries a little more power as well."

"Well, it's certainly different. Sounds more like the president and his Cabinet, and I'm not sure how I feel about that."

"It can't be worse than what you just freed us from."

"True, but that's a pretty lousy standard to use, isn't it? I can't say I don't like it, but I also can't say I do like it. Guess we'll just have to wait and see. Let me know how it goes."

"Well, here's the other thing. Voting is wide open this time. Every Time Agent from probationary to officer is allowed to vote. Which means you and Tommen are allowed to be there."

"Damn. Is that out of some gesture of good will, or was the Time population really reduced that much?"

"The numbers are still coming in, but from what estimates I've heard, we're at about one-tenth the size we were, speaking across the universe, but it's hard to get an exact number."

"Shit. Guess it makes sense that the first order of business would be to establish order. What do we know about the candidates?"

"Nothing. I haven't even gotten that far. I just called to update you on what's going on."

"Much appreciated." He let out a breath. "Things are

definitely going to change, that's for sure."

"We can only hope for the better. Well, I'm just about to head home to my kid. I'll see you Wednesday."

"You're not coming in for your pastry tomorrow?" Micaiah sounded hurt.

"I have interviews to conduct tomorrow. And I really need to knock off the ten pounds those things put in my pockets."

"Oh, sure, blame the pastries. All right, we'll see you, Walter."

Walter hung up, logged out of his computer, punched out, and headed home. Monday evening traffic wasn't bad compared to Friday traffic, but it was still worse than winter traffic. When the roads got gridlocked, he either had to get creative and feather his Bands, or else give up on Banding entirely and just go with the ice flow.

Tommen was already home when he walked in the door, just finishing up washing his dishes.

"Hey," he greeted.

"What's cookin'?" Walter wondered.

"Um...some meat. Pulled pork. There's some leftover in the fridge."

"Please, Tommen, I know you're a poacher. What is it?"

Tommen blushed but shrugged. "Coon." He added quickly, "Forest coon, not city coon."

So he was back to his antics again, Banding in order to go illegally hunt some meat out in the wild. If the fur wasn't out in the garage — which it wouldn't be, because it would be too warm — then the only other place it could be was...

Walter's eyes started watering when he opened the fridge. Yup, that's where it was.

"Sorry," Tommen murmured. "It'll be out of there in a day or two."

"Yes, it will." He hurriedly removed the container of leftover "pulled pork" and the loaf of bread and shut the refrigerator door. "How was school?"

"Okay. I mean, it's finals week, so...yeah."

"And when are your finals?"

"AP finals are Wednesday. Regular classes are Thursday and Friday. Why?"

So, while he ate his sandwich, Walter again explained the new changes in the Wheel, about the tiered system as he understood it, and especially about the once-in-a-lifetime offer for Tommen to vote as an Apprentice.

"Whoa, so this is like, serious stuff," Tommen said when he was finished.

Walter nodded, standing and taking his plate to the sink. "It is."

"How do you feel about it? Like, do you think it's okay, or it might be a trap, or what?"

"I really can't say. Believe me, I'm not exactly thrilled at the idea of going back to the Wheel."

"So you're not going."

"I didn't say that. I just said I didn't like the thought of it. As for the new system they're proposing, I can't say either way. It'll either turn out really well, or it's going to devolve back into the system we all know and hate. Either way, I'm asking if you want to go."

"Heck yeah, dude. Well, unless you don't think I should?"

"If I thought that, I wouldn't have asked."

"Yeah, dude, I'll go. I want to go. If I have this one chance to make my voice heard, I'll take it. Who are the candidates?"

"Well, that's another thing. I don't know."

"Oh." Tommen frowned and was silent for a minute. Then, "Well, I'm still going."

"Do you want to go before or after school? How do you feel about your AP final?"

"Oh, I'm totally good on that. I mean, I can't be totally, completely prepared for it, but I'm not worried. Actually, I mean, if I wait until after school, I'm just going to be thinking about it all through the final."

"And if we go before school, you're still going to be thinking about it all through your final."

Tommen shrugged. "I guess. Point is, you're the one who let the genie out of the bottle."

Yes, there was that. After a moment, he spoke again. "If we can go before school, I think that would be better. I mean, I've got to see how this works."

"All right," Walter said calmly. "We'll go before school. We've got until Wednesday, though, so don't get too excited and mess up your studying for your finals."

Tommen headed to his room. Without turning, he said, "I'm not worried."

In hindsight, Walter wondered if it had been a good idea to tell Tommen about the whole thing, or at least the part about every Time Agent being allowed to vote regardless of rank. Maybe he'd been hoping that he would refuse, say he wasn't interested. Maybe he was hoping he'd been scared enough at the last inauguration that he wouldn't want to go back during such events. But Walter knew his son better than that. Despite being proven wrong time and time again, Tommen was still an invincible sixteen year old boy, or he thought he was. He could take on anything, and his word was gold. His voice was going to be heard, dammit. He was going to change the universe.

Walter's enthusiasm was at about the same level as any of his visits to Lily's condo before her death. Walking into a pit of starving wolves had been preferable to going to visit her, and that was about how he felt now about going back to the Wheel. If Tommen hadn't agreed to go, he probably wouldn't have either.

At the same time, though, did that make him a coward, and unfit to serve as District Captain? It was one thing to not want to return to the Judgment Wing, but to not want to return to the larger Wheel, the hub of the Time industry for the entire universe, that was absurd, especially for his position. So, Tommen or no Tommen, he was going to have to suck it up and do it, come what may.

He pondered this and tried to mentally prepare himself for the trip, even as he interviewed the rest of his Lieutenant candidates the following day. With exception of Alex, who was training to become a Captain anyway, and Zeke, who was less than impressive as a regular human being, all of them were decent candidates. Each had his strengths and weaknesses, advantages and disadvantages, assets and deficiencies. It was a matter of judging which deficiencies could be overlooked, and which advantages outweighed the disadvantages. Regina hadn't told him he had to pick by Wednesday, but her tone had suggested he do so.

Perhaps his biggest advantage that he could foresee going forward was the need and ability to communicate. In his opinion, they had to stop acting like tiny sovereign Districts and bring everyone together as Districts within the Region. Then the Regions had to come together under the Gatekeeper as a planet. Let each govern himself, but not as an island. They needed to stay in constant contact and build a network of offense and defense against whatever insanity came their way. If shit happened in the Wheel again, they needed to be able to pull together and not be sent scrambling like they were last time. Proactive, not reactive.

He called the bakery.

"Bakery na hÉireann, Micaiah speaking," Micaiah answered.

"Cai, it's Walt."

"Everything all right for tomorrow yet? There hasn't been another coup already, has there?"

"Not that I know of. I was calling to let you know that Tommen and I are going to the Wheel tomorrow morning before he heads off to school. If you and Micah want to meet us there, I'll introduce you to our new Lieutenants."

"You want us to meet the bastards taking our jobs?"

"It's not their fault. Your better bet would be to take it up with Regina."

"Aye, well, let's just say she's stopped returning my calls. Personally, I'm expecting a Cease and Desist letter in the mail any day now."

Walter couldn't help but chuckle at that. "Of course. Anyway, what do you say?"

"Aye, sure, I'll come meet them. Might as well know who's going to be signing my paychecks. Was that all you needed?"

"I reckon so. How's your...wife? I still can't get over that."

"Oh, she's great."

"You sound better, too."

"Well, let's just avoid the details, shall we?"

"Yes, let's." Regardless of actual age, Micaiah was still a young man, Kayla a young woman. He didn't need to know the details. "We'll be going to the Wheel at about six-thirty."

"We'll see you there."

Walter did his best to concentrate on his work, but it was hard. To his coworkers, he simply said that he was ready for his day off. That wasn't entirely a lie, but going to vote in a high stakes election wasn't exactly what he had in mind. Doing it twice in one year, given what had happened the first time, he was liable to have an aneurysm if anything went wrong the second time.

"When are we going to the Wheel?" Tommen asked as he got in the car after Walter picked him up from work.

"Six-thirty," Walter replied. "Micah and Micaiah are going to meet us there."

"They said that they'd been replaced, that they're no longer the Lieutenants of the District. Is that true? What happened?"

"It is. The new Manager doesn't appreciate what they did, and she thinks it makes them volatile and untrustworthy. I don't like it, but her word is law now."

"Oh. That's dumb. They did more for us than she did."

"I didn't say I agreed with her, only that that's what she said."

Tommen shook his head and scoffed. "Whatever. I don't think I'll be able to sleep tonight, anyway. I'm too hyped up."

"Believe me, it's nothing to get excited about. And you still have school tomorrow. You need to try to sleep."

Apparently, adrenaline didn't go as far as it used to; Tommen was in bed, sound asleep by eight o'clock. Walter shook his head as he turned away from his bedroom door and returned to the kitchen for a last bite to eat before getting ready for bed himself. He still wasn't keen on going back to the Wheel, but he figured he'd pretty well mentally steeled himself for the occasion. Who knew, maybe going back and finding everything the way it was would calm him down some. Maybe it would make his imprisonment seem more like a bad dream instead of a hellish reality.

Too soon, however, his alarm clock was going off. Even on his days off, he just couldn't catch a break. He'd barely slapped it off before his door opened and Tommen poked his head in. "Are you awake?"

"Just barely," Walter growled. "How long have you been up?"

"Since, like, four. I'm ready whenever you are."

Walter should have been the one saying that to him. Still, he shooed Tommen out of his room, then began the slow trudge of the morning routine. He Banded through most of it, taking extra time to wake up and get motivated. He was not looking forward to this. At all. His blankets were calling his name; he should heed them.

"Hey, Dad, come on," Tommen said, peeking around the corner into his bedroom. "Breakfast is ready."

"You go ahead and eat," Walter told him. "You're the one taking exams today, not me."

"Yeah, but who knows how long we'll be in the Wheel? And what if the Food Court isn't back up and working yet? We could starve!"

"I find that highly unlikely. Go out and eat. I'll be out in a minute."

By the time he did get out to the kitchen, Tommen had scarfed his way through probably half a dozen eggs, a quarter pound of bacon, half a dozen slices of toast, and a dozen or more sausage links.

"Didn't realize you were testing for Harvard," Walter observed, getting his own plate and snatching up some meager pieces before they were inhaled by the black hole that was his teenage son.

"Come on, let's go," Tommen goaded, Banding to get

everything cleared, then hurrying to get all the dishes done, finishing just as Walter took his last sausage link in hand.

"Wash this, then we'll go," Walter told him.

Tommen did so, anxiously. Then the portal was open and they entered the Wheel.

Opening the portal was more difficult than Walter remembered it being, but whether that was from some part of the portal room still malfunctioning or because he was out of practice, was difficult to say. As he got his bearings, Walter felt his heart rate and blood pressure go sky high. This might not end well.

The portal room itself didn't appear different, but something about it had changed. It wasn't until they got up to the translator dispenser that Walter realized what it was. It was smaller. There weren't hundreds of thousands of portals open, and it hadn't taken them twenty minutes just to get to the front of the room. Looking around, if he had to hazard a guess, there were maybe ten thousand portals total, two hundred rows of fifty maybe.

Walter turned and startled as Micah and Micaiah stood behind him. A moment later, Kayla joined them.

"Sorry, boss, didn't mean to scare you," Micaiah said. "You doing okay?"

"Yeah, fine," Walter told him, hoping he sounded convincing. "You? I see you got your prosthetic back on."

"Yeah, I think a couple days off did some good. And how are you, Tommen? Ready for your first election?"

"Absolutely!" Tommen answered, grinning hugely. "I can't wait."

"Don't get too excited yet," Kayla cautioned. "We don't know how this is going to all turn out. I won't believe it until I see it, and that sort of thing."

Tommen nodded vigorously, but Walter could see the excitement hadn't been dampened in the least.

"So when do we get to meet our replacements?" Micah asked.

"I haven't seen them yet," Walter answered. "But we just got here. What's changed?"

"Multiple portal rooms," Kayla answered. "Openly Engaged civilizations now have their own portal room where they can keep portals open indefinitely without taking up room elsewhere. There are others, but that's the overall gist, not having to walk half a marathon just to cross the room."

"Well, that's one good change so far. What else?"

"Come and see."

It was like walking into Shakespeare meets *Relativity*. Whelp, wasn't hard to guess who did the interior decorating around here.

"Wow," was all Walter could manage. "I had a few ideas of what this place could look like, but this was not one of them. I don't know if I like this or the stale theme better."

"Say a lot of things about Rifun, but he had a taste for the classics," Micaiah said sourly. "The Time Agents are pretty well divided on whether it should be kept or changed. Some like the change, others think it has to go because Rifun did it."

If he wanted to be honest, Walter wasn't sure which side of the fence he fell on. On the one hand, it would always remind him of Rifun and the atrocities that took place here. On the other hand, it really was a very beautiful setup, in spite of the weird physics of the Wheel.

They made their way through the marketplaces, each level a different landscape from some Shakespearean play, Walter was sure. He also noticed that there were more marketplaces, each one divided more precisely.

It wasn't until they reached the "village square" that the extent of the population depletion made itself known. In January, the Judgment Wing hub and every room for five portals had been crowded, if not suffocatingly packed. Today, it just felt...empty. It was nauseatingly crowded to be sure, but nowhere near the level it used to be.

So it was still a small miracle that Walter spotted Gabriel and Esther in the throngs of people. He flagged them down, and the seven of them retreated to a quieter room.

"We were afraid we had missed you," Gabriel said.

"The feeling is mutual," Walter agreed. "Micaiah and Micah Durvin, this is Gabriel Martinez and Esther Thomas."

"Glad they're not computers," Micaiah said, shaking their hands in turn. "I'd hate to think our jobs got automated."

"So, you are the ones who killed Cassius and chased away Rifun?" Gabriel mused, looking at Micaiah's leg and nodding solemnly. "Thank you. You are brave. I'm just sorry our new Manager couldn't see it."

"I'm not bitter. It'll give me time to catch up on other things."

They exchanged pleasantries and small talk for a minute or two. Walter had a hard time deciding whether Micaiah was totally bullshitting Gabriel and Esther, or if he really was fine with the whole thing. How had his mood gone from thunderclouds with patches of sunshine, to not a cloud in the sky? Walter couldn't believe that it was all thanks to Kayla. If it was, it wouldn't last long. If it wasn't, then he was still holding out on Walter. But why?

"We should probably get moving," Walter suggested after a moment. "A lot has changed. I don't want to get home to find out that the non-passage of time no longer exists."

"Agreed," Esther said. "Let's go."

They moved back into the market square that now housed portals to the Judgment Wing, the Coliseum—or its new rendition—the Food Court, the Archives, and the Pit, if Walter remembered the story right about the portal in the gallows. Once there, it was anyone's game, and they soon found themselves separated. Tommen kept close to Walter and they eventually found some semblance of a line which they pushed their way into.

"So, how does this work?" Tommen wondered.

"I only know how it used to work," Walter answered uncertainly. "It could have changed."

"Even if it has, how did it used to work?"

So Walter explained how the election and voting process used to go, from checking in, to getting stamped, to the long walk down the vault tunnel, to the room with three doors. He explained walking into the voting room and how that worked.

As he spoke, Walter noted that Tommen was not the only one who seemed excited. The whole atmosphere of the Wheel was thrilling anticipation. Every Time Agent was present, every single one of them invited to vote, regardless of rank. Not only that, but they were all going to be part of this new governing system; they were all going to have a say in what happened in this new Wheel, all have a part in how this all started out. Hopefully they didn't trip at the starting line.

Even though the population had been reportedly reduced so dramatically, it seemed to take a long time to get in to vote. Walter remembered thinking that maybe he should have eaten more for breakfast. Looking at Tommen, he didn't seem fazed one bit.

Eventually they got in, and again Walter felt his blood pressure spike. Everything looked exactly as it did before, but this time there were no enormous voting "scoreboards" as it were. There was just the line and the secretary at the head. Walter did notice, however, that the secretary's cloak was a different color, a cream color trimmed with dark gray, the secretary symbol embroidered huge on the back and smaller on the front.

"Name and coordinates." Even the secretary sounded eager for the results.

Walter gave him the information, unsure how he was going to make it down the tunnel with the way he was feeling. Already he was dizzy and a little light-headed. Holding his hand out to be stamped certainly wasn't helping things either. When he was cleared, he turned and walked stiffly toward the vault door. He couldn't walk away, stop, or look back. But he did manage to get away with waiting for Tommen to catch up. *Just keep talking to him, and just keep walking,* he reminded himself. *It will all be over soon.*

"So, we just walk in the third door and vote?" Tommen wondered.

"Basically, yes," Walter answered, hoping he sounded somewhat normal. "We have to enter one at a time, though. Everything is completely private. The screen will open up, and you can adjust it however you want. Then you just follow the directions. It's really not complicated."

"Cool. Are you okay?"

Was it that obvious? "Yeah, fine."

"Oh. You just seemed a little..."

"Yes...?"

"A little on edge is all. But, I mean, if you're fine, then you're fine."

It was an easy out, and Walter knew it. He might have pursued the argument further and actually try to convince Tommen he was fine, but not only was that a lie, but he was spared the discomfort as they reached the room with three doors. Like everything else lately, it had a Victorian vibe to it, but the three doors remained the same. They stepped aside as a couple voters exited their booths. Walter made sure Tommen got in all right—not that it was a terribly difficult thing to walk through a portal—then stepped in the next available booth.

The familiarity of it helped ease Walter's racing heart, and he took several deep breaths before approaching the screen. It turned on, and that was about where the familiarity ended.

Before, it had simply been a seemingly endless list of positions, with another endless list of candidates for each. This time around, however, it came up like a computer directory, with folders and files. Difference was, the folders were the various "departments" in the Wheel now, and the files were the positions being voted for. Thankfully, along the bottom was a "Take the New Tutorial" option.

Even the voting cycle was different now, it seemed. Rather than having all the Hands on the chopping block every eleven-slash-seventeen years, it would be one-third of them up for a vote every four-slash-six years for twelve-slash-eighteen and a half year terms. Walter was both disturbed by the longer terms, but amused by the concept. He wondered if Micaiah had truly backed away from this as he had claimed, or if he'd implanted a very Earthling idea in the minds of the creators. As for this first election, all the offices were starting out at the same time. In four years, there would be a lottery to determine the first one-third on the chopping block. In another four years, there would be a second lottery. Then it would be all set.

Also new was the concept of voting for head secretaries in the various departments. Under the Hand or Hands, three secretaries were to be voted on and given power. Similarly, the First Grandfather was now a candidate, and three under him were also up for a vote. Furthermore, the First Guard and ten under him were candidates as well. However, where the Hands would be replaced by one-third every four years for twelve year terms, the Grandfather and secretary candidates would only be voted on every eight years period. The guards would be voted on every ten years. No rotation or mix-and-match there.

On top of all of that, it was no longer a straight yes or no vote for the candidates, but a ranked vote, one through five. He would rank his top five choices for a candidate, and as each one got eliminated, his vote went to the next one in line. If none of his candidates made it to the "finals" as it were, it went to a lottery. That could be good or bad, he thought, but it was certainly different. And anyway, it didn't look like there were too many candidates for any one position. Yet. Give it a few decades, and the pool might grow larger.

And then, even with all of the changes so far, as he began voting, Walter discovered that the votes were weighted based on his personal engagement in Time. The Hand of Primitive and Unengaged Civilizations did not represent his world, so his vote was only worth half of what the vote would be by someone from a Primitive and Unengaged Civilization. On the flipside, his vote for the Hand of Timekeepers was worth twice what Tommen's was because he was an officer, and a secretary's vote for the same position would only be worth half a vote.

It was enough to make Walter's head spin. No wonder the voting seemed to take so long despite the smaller crowd. They'd all come in expecting something familiar and easy to use, and they'd gotten a system that had been flipped around and turned upside-down. It was halfway to ridiculous.

At the same time, though, it helped to calm Walter's anxiety. He was uncertain about the new program, but his earlier fears about being back in the Judgment Wing were momentarily quelled.

After a few problems, oopses, and missteps, he got the hang of the new system and how it worked. Actually, he rather liked it. He wasn't really a computer or technology person, but this he could figure out and use without too much trouble.

He finished and left the voting booth, unsure of how he should feel. Bewildered, yes, from all the changes. Amused, at how those changes so closely resembled Earth-side government. Lost, feeling like he was going to be left behind as a relic of an old way of doing things. Terrified, because he was still in the Judgment Wing. Confused, wondering if he should wait for Tommen or if he'd already voted and headed out.

Walter waited for a minute or two, then started back down the tunnel. He noted that the closer he got to the vault door, the faster he walked, until he was almost running. Then he was through the force field, but he didn't stop until he was out of the Judgment Wing completely. He needed some fresh air.

Maybe he should resign. With all the power at hand still up in the air, he could slip away quietly. He wouldn't even ask to be Suppressed at this point, just relieved of his officer duties. Just long enough for him to collect his head and figure out what he was going to do. Bad enough he felt as bad as he did just standing in the Wheel; he didn't need that to start bleeding back into his normal life, too. He didn't want to go back to the shrink again.

The crowd was thinning, but Tommen was still nowhere to be found. Walter started looking around the Wheel, figuring he might have gone exploring to see what all had changed. He was a little surprised to find him waiting at the portal, ready to go home.

"I would have thought you'd be out exploring," Walter said.

"I did, a little," Tommen replied, nodding. "I don't know how I feel about it, though. I mean, it looks great. Seriously, it puts my lame stage set to ultimate shame. But at the same time..."

"Rifun is the one who built it."

"Right. I just...how does someone that talented go that wrong?"

"I wish I knew. I deal with it on a much smaller scale at work, and I still don't have a good answer for that."

"I just don't understand." Tommen shrugged. "But either way, I guess I have to go to school at some point today, right?"

"That you do. You have your finals, and I don't want to see you tripping at the finish line."

"Oh, please, it's only tenth grade."

"And if you want to go into the eleventh grade next year, you're going to take those tenth grade finals. Let's go."

They stepped through the portal, landing back in the living room at home. It was a rougher ride than Walter remembered it being, and he stumbled into his recliner until the world stopped spinning.

"Need me to drive?" Tommen wondered.

Walter let out a breath and sat up. "You're driving anyway. Just give me a second." Grudgingly, he got to his feet.

"When will we know the results?" Tommen asked as they got in the car and he backed out of the garage.

"Normally, it's within twenty-four hours of the voting booths closing. This time around, who knows? But, Regina will call me, then I'll called the tw—the Lieutenants, and they'll spread the word."

Tommen glanced at him briefly from the driver's seat. "Still thinking of the twins as the Lieutenants, huh?"

"It's going to take some getting used to, that's for sure. But that's not to say that I might not still go to them in a pinch." When Tommen grinned, Walter added quickly, "You didn't hear me say that."

"Okay, okay."

"I'm serious."

"I get it. My lips are sealed. I know nothing."

It was the best he was going to get from him, but Walter trusted his son. He'd been through too much to not understand when something was important.

"Are you riding the bus home or to work?" Walter wondered.

"Um, I don't work today, because of the finals. Micah and Micaiah think I should take a break and focus on the tests."

"Well, they're right—"

"But, me and Becky were going to go out for ice cream at the little shop just down from the school. You know, as a celebration for passing the AP Physics exam."

Walter had his suspicions that it was more of a celebration for their four-month anniversary. Walter couldn't speak for Becky, but it was Tommen's record, and they appeared to still be going strong. How would this play out over the summer? Popcorn, anyone?

"Is that okay with you?" Tommen was saying.

"Huh?"

"Me and Becky going out for ice cream. Is that cool with you?"

"How are you getting home?"

"Her mom is going to meet us there. She can take us back to her place, and I can walk home."

"What time?"

"Probably early. Becky wants to do some studying for her classes, but we don't share any other classes, so she wants to do it alone."

"You two are being good, right?"

Tommen rolled his eyes. "Yes, Dad. And she says that I should probably study for my exams, which, so what? I'm not worried; they're not hard."

"Uh-huh." Walter didn't miss the way Tommen evaded the question. Either they weren't being good, or else Tommen was just shy about the subject. The jury was still out. "What do you think of your exams? Your English grades haven't exactly been stellar."

"It'll be fine. Besides, all I have to do is get a D- for the entire class and I still pass."

"Maybe so, but you remember that discussion we had about grades and scholarships? Remember the part where you wanted to go to a really nice, really expensive college? You might be a science whiz, but scholarships and grants look at your grades as a whole."

"I know, I know. I get it. I'm still not worried about it."

Walter wasn't convinced, but they were pulling into the school parking lot. Tommen parked—a little lopsided, but still within the lines—and got out of the driver's seat. As he grabbed his backpack, Walter got out and went around to the other side.

"Got everything?" he asked.

Tommen sighed. "Yes, Dad. It's only the AP Physics exam. Pencils and calculator. I got this."

Walter nodded slowly. "I know you do."

"Why are you giving me that look?"

"What look?"

"That look like you're sending me off and we'll never see each other again?" Tommen tried to force a smile, but it didn't seem to want to come. "It'll be fine. It's just exams. I'll be okay. You'll be okay."

"Right. Well then, Mr. Smartypants, I expect to see 100% written in gold on top of your exam when you get it back."

Now his son grinned as he shook his head, said some sort of farewell, and went inside.

Walter got in the car and chastised himself, both mentally and verbally. He shook his head. "He's too young for this shit. He shouldn't have to be the man. He shouldn't have to comfort me and tell me everything's going to be okay. I should be doing that to him. With his girlfriend, with his college prospects, with his Timekeeping. I should be the one doing all of this, not him."

Even as he left the school parking lot, the inner voices

wouldn't stop tormenting him. He was a loser, a fraud, a trembling child, a hopeless murderer. One little flick on his Achilles heel and he was reduced to a sniveling fool who had to be comforted by his sixteen year old son who had already done more than most men on their deathbeds. It wasn't fair. It wasn't right. He needed to get his act together and do something about this. He needed to take control.

To any casual observer, the drive home was rather quiet and peaceful. In his mind, though, the war raged on, his demons versus his resolve. He parked in the garage, gave a casual glance toward his projects that he either needed to finish or dispose of, and went inside.

*See, you leave those, too. Because you can't fulfill any promises you make.*

*I found my nephew and raised him as my son.*

*And you almost died to protect that stupid secret. How much pain could you have spared Tommen if you had just confessed? Who knows, maybe he would have forgiven you. But, yeah, it was definitely worth it to die instead.*

Walter went to the living room and collapsed in his recliner, knowing full well that he was probably going to fall asleep. In a way, he was hoping to. He couldn't deal with these voices and fits of mental rage, the way it tore him apart. Anxiety, depression, they weren't just for teenagers, and adults didn't always handle it well either.

He tried to sleep, but his mind wouldn't let him. After a while, the demons ceased their assault on his character, instead beginning a single chant. It only got louder the more he ignored it. In the end, he gave in. Hauling himself to his feet, he went into his bedroom and got in the nightstand. He grabbed the pill bottle that sat next to the gun, popped two in his mouth, then settled in to bed.

# Chapter Thirty-One
## New Hands, Old Enemies

Tommen headed into school, buzzing with excitement. He'd gone to the Wheel and had actually been part of the elections. He'd gotten to see the rebuilding, cool in its own right, but still unnerving that it was Rifun's handiwork. He'd gotten to see what the new governing system was going to look like. He wasn't too well-versed on all the Earth-side systems of government, and he certainly didn't know much about any other governing systems in the universe, but from what he had been able to discern, the power in the Wheel was much less centralized and much more localized. Every Hand would no longer oversee every aspect of the Wheel. Rather, only the Hands pertinent to various operations within the Wheel would be in charge of those operations. He no longer had to worry about the opinion of the Hand of Harvesters, because only the Hand of Timekeepers governed him now.

"You look happy," Becky observed as she met him at his locker. "Are you actually excited for exams today?"

"Heck no, are you kidding?" He grinned. "I'm looking forward to what comes after."

"I see." She raised a brow, but couldn't hold the expression long before she dropped it and grinned. "Well, I'm excited for that, too. Come on, they're serving breakfast to all the AP students."

Tommen was about to say that he'd already had a huge breakfast, until he realized that he was hungry again. Had they really been in the Wheel that long? It didn't seem like it. Damn Physics, anyway. Still, he dutifully followed her to the cafeteria where he got a muffin, a bagel with cream cheese, sausage, eggs, hashbrowns, a buttery biscuit, plus one carton of orange juice and one carton of milk.

"You must be hungry," Becky observed as they sat. She had only a muffin, some eggs, some sausage, a biscuit, and a carton of milk. She checked her insulin pump as she always did before eating, then proceeded to pray over her food — and Tommen's, she'd once told him. There was no reason his food shouldn't be blessed. She also prayed for the exam, though Tommen was forced to wonder about that one. Why would God bless a science exam? Wasn't that like a Christian going out on the street corner and handing out *The Origin of Species*, or an atheist handing out Bibles?

The first time he'd tried eating before she finished praying, she'd kicked him in the shins. It might not have been so bad, but her orthopedic shoes were a force to be reckoned with; he'd had bruises there for four days. So he put up with it instead.

"You ready for the exam?" she asked, picking up her fork.

"I don't know." Tommen shrugged. "I mean, I'm not super worried or anything, but I'm not overly confident either."

"Does it have something to do with what happened last semester?"

"It could." Last semester, he'd thought he had been totally prepared for the exam, and he'd blown off most of the studying. Problem was, even though the material was only over things learned in that semester, some of the knowledge and equations were built off of things from the first semester which he'd missed. On top of that, he'd been without his Banding abilities. So not only had he been unprepared for the material, but he'd been unable to do anything about it, that is, cheat. He counted himself fortunate to have gotten a B+ on it.

"Well, I think we've been studying well," Becky went on, "and I'm pretty confident that I can do it. I'm not the fastest, and I won't be the first one done, but I'll get there."

They only had all day, after all. All the normal exams were just under two hours long from start to finish. The AP exams were done in four parts. The first two parts were the longest and would take them to lunch, while the second two parts were shorter and would see them to the end of the day. They wouldn't even be able to join the rest of the school for lunch, but they would have their own separate lunch. Aside from bringing snacks and their own lunches—ham on rye with a good dose of mustard for Tommen—they would also have a catered option, similar to the breakfast they ate now.

As breakfast was wrapping up, Mr. Layman the principal got up in front of the students gathered and gave some short speech about how proud he was of each of them and how they were a credit to the school, their families, and themselves. It was meant to be a feel-good speech, but Layman didn't do feel-good. He didn't hand out flowers; he handed out detentions, suspensions, expulsions, and a good dose of Marine Drill Sargent for each of them.

Then they were dismissed to their respective tests. The classes were shuffled around a little so the AP tests could be moved to a wing of the school that could be shut off from the rest in order to cut down on noise and mischief. The AP Physics exam, therefore, was actually held in one of the math rooms.

AP exams were run like prisons, Tommen thought, as each student was made to empty all pockets and show any and all scrap paper to the proctor. All papers had to be blank, all pencils had to be plain, all snacks had to be kept out of arm's reach, all water placed where it could not potentially spill on the test, and they were especially not allowed to smuggle in drugs up their ass.

That wasn't to say some of them didn't get creative. Calculators were high-tech things these days, and anyone who'd spent even a few class periods just fiddling with them could figure out a way to store information in them like a small computer. Formulas, laws, concepts, even images, all of them hidden under unassuming file names such as "Math Symbols," "Biology Tools," or "Graphing Help." Tommen had never needed to know these tricks before, when he could just Band to create more time or even get a glance at someone else's test, sometimes the answer key. But when he'd been Suppressed, he'd had to learn a few things, and fast. Now he had both to fall back on.

There were only eleven students in the class, which meant that they were able to sit at least one desk away from all the other students. Tommen picked a back corner, but watched as Becky chose a desk across the room. She was all business now.

The proctor was not Mrs. White, but an official Advanced Placement Course Exam Proctor—seriously, how did someone get a job like that?—who was unbiased and, in Tommen's opinion, uncaring. His only job was to hand out the tests, read the boring ass intro text about the testing rules, and make sure they didn't cheat.

Truth be told, Tommen didn't remember a whole lot about the test, other than he felt more prepared for this one than the last one. He still found himself perusing those little hidden files stored in his calculator, and occasionally Banding so he could peruse the tests of a couple people he felt might know a particular answer. But otherwise, he found the test to be easy enough, or as easy as one could expect from an AP Physics exam.

"So, how are you feeling about this whole thing?" Tommen asked Becky when they were dismissed for lunch. He grabbed his ham on rye, scarfing it down so he could get to the catered portion of the lunch.

"Okay," Becky replied. "I mean, I studied like crazy, but I still never really feel ready."

They got their lunches and only just finished them before lunch ended and everyone was called back in for round two.

The first couple parts were the longest ones, but the parts that came after lunch seemed much more difficult, Tommen thought. There came a point for every AP student during the exam where, no matter how dedicated and brilliant he was, he just wanted to say "fuck it" and walk out the door. It had very little to do with the difficulty of the material, but the slogging monotony of reading four story problems that were all the same except for one little piece of information squished somewhere between lines thirteen and fourteen. Missing that one little piece of information meant certain death. By the time the end of part three of the exam rolled around and they took a break for snacks, water, and bathroom, Tommen had reached his "fuck it" point. Or, as Becky had once said, his give-a-dam broke.

Still, he slogged through the last part of the exam. He did his best, to be sure, but his brain was fried. When they were finally dismissed from the exam and the school, he wasn't even sure he could make it to the ice cream shop. And he hadn't even been doing any real physical activity.

"One thing's for sure," Becky said as they got their ice cream dishes and sat down at a picnic table to eat them, "I feel a lot more confident about my other exams."

"No kidding." Tommen shook his head. "That was almost ridiculous. Cruel and unusual punishment."

He said it to make her laugh, but his own words sounded hollow to his ears. Taking a test wasn't cruel and unusual; it was just a pain in the ass. Being locked in a prison in the dark for a year, that was cruel and unusual.

It wasn't long before a familiar blue van pulled into the parking lot and Becky's mom got out.

"*Szia, gyerekek,*" she greeted. "*Hogy ment?*" (Hi, kids. How did it go?)

"*Jó, Anya,*" Becky answered. (Good, Mom.)

"*Az jó.*" She nodded. "*Hogy vagy, Tommen?*" (That's good. How are you, Tommen?)

"*Fáradt,*" Tommen told her. (Tired.) He'd picked up a smidgen of Hungarian and Hebrew from his time at Becky's house, but he was sorely limited in anything but the basic greetings and pleasantries.

"I understand. But it's good for you. Well, if you're not done with your ice cream, I might just grab something for myself real quick."

She bought herself a small cone and joined them at the table. They talked about the test for a bit, then headed back to Becky's house.

"Normally, I would invite you in, but I still have to study for my other exams," Becky explained as he walked her to the door.

"If you're not ready by now, you never will be," Tommen told her.

"Maybe, but why take chances? I'll see you tomorrow."

He nodded. "Okay."

Four months in and she still wouldn't let him kiss her except on the hand or on the head, and it was still a little strange to have to get down on one knee to hug her. Then he was walking back down the mosaic walkway to the sidewalk.

Surprisingly, he found his dad in the garage, apparently working on one of the many projects he'd abandoned over the years. If he had to hazard a guess, this was the trim project that he was currently working on. He looked up as Tommen walked up the driveway around the car. He straightened, stretched, and turned off the power tools.

"What are you doing?" Tommen wondered, as if he couldn't guess.

"Figured I'd try and finish a few projects before I tossed them completely," his dad answered. "Good news is, the trim is almost all cut. Now I just need to get up the motivation to go to the store and get some stain and a few tools to attach it. Plus the whole moving the furniture bit."

"I see. Hey, good luck."

"How'd your exam go?"

"Long, boring, difficult as hell."

His dad raised a brow. "What does that even mean?"

Tommen shrugged. "I don't know. It was tough is all."

"Ah. And how was ice cream with Becky?"

"Good. Tasty. In more than one way."

"Uh-huh. I'd tell you to be careful of how you talk about her, but I think you'll figure it out if she ever heard you saying something like that."

*Yeah, because she'd kick my ass, and any further punishment from her dad would be a kindness.* "I know. I was just saying." He shook his head. "Any news on the elections?"

"Nope, not until the voting is done, and it's supposed to be all day. Tomorrow is the soonest we'll find out."

Of course, it was too much to hope that Walter would shake Tommen awake at twelve-oh-one to tell him the results and let him know what happened next. Even when Tommen texted him from the bus asking, his dad simply replied that there was still no news. Something about the results needing to be recorded officially. Then they would be coded fluidly, like the tablets in the Archives, so they were available in all languages and could be distributed all at once. Or something.

So Tommen went to school like normal. Today was a full day for the first through third period exams. Seeing how he'd already taken his AP Physics exam, he would be spending that time in the library with Becky.

His third semester classes included Law and the Courts first period, Geometry C second period, History 10B fourth period, and Mechanical Drafting fifth period.

Of course, his dad being a cop, Tommen was expected to be able to practically teach the Law class. Even more embarrassing, his dad had actually come in one day to give a short lecture on crime, how it was investigated, and what happened once a criminal was apprehended. He was less than thrilled about the exam, but he certainly knew his stuff. Well, he knew his stuff on the criminal and police procedure part of it. When it came to the actual court side of things, pre-trials, trials, sentencing, appeals, and so on, he was a little more sketchy.

He was equally as enthusiastic about Geometry. He wasn't really a spatial reasoning kind of person. His inherent sense of direction, his internal compass seemed to be about as dodgy as his moral compass, at least according to his dad. He preferred real mathematics, equations, formulas, variables, things he could manipulate. Yeah, Pythagorean theorem was great and all, but throw in a picture of a triangle and he got all sorts of confused. So he just did what he could and hoped it would be good enough.

Lunch came after that, longer than normal to give students a chance to recover and prepare for their third exam of the day. Tommen took his lunch directly to the library, seeing how he was going to end up there anyway. After a minute, Becky joined him.

"You don't have any of your books," he observed. "You're not going to study for fourth and fifth exams?"

She shook her head. "No, not while my brain is still recovering from first and second. And like you said, if I don't know it now, I never will."

"Well, I didn't say never."

"Doesn't matter. I'm sick of studying anyway."

Tommen was about to say more when his phone chirped for a text. It was from his dad.

"Results are in," was all it said.

"Good or bad?" he replied.

"Don't know. This election cycle was so short, I wasn't able to really feel it out and form an opinion. Either way, our new leaders have been elected."

"When is the inauguration? Or are they not doing that anymore?"

"No, they're doing an inauguration. It's at eleven o'clock tonight, though. Do you still want to go? You have your exams tomorrow."

"Yeah I want to go! I'll just take a nap or something."

This proved easier said than done, and Tommen found himself lying in bed at nine o'clock — having gotten in bed at six o'clock — and he still hadn't slept for any length of time. He didn't even feel tired. His mind just kept going around and around in an endless cycle of thoughts. The results had come in, and now they were going to inaugurate a new government and a new style of leadership, one that was more fair across the board with less corruption. The results had come in, and now they were going to inaugurate a new government with leaders they knew nothing about, and their blind hope that it would be better than Rifun and would obscure any evil and corruption still lurking in their midst.

It was 2014 Earth-side, and already the political gears were grinding, gearing up for the 2016 elections. And what elections they were, or would be, holy shit. Tommen hadn't paid much attention to the 2012 elections, was barely aware of the 2008 elections, and anything before that was completely lost on him. So it was fair to say he didn't know jack shit about the American elections, how they worked, how they compared, or anything at all that the candidates were campaigning on. But damn it if he knew what misery, corruption, and revolution smelled like.

He wasn't sure if he just lost track of time, or if he'd actually managed to sleep, but the next thing he knew, his dad was knocking on his door.

"You awake?" he asked.

"Yeah," Tommen sighed.

"Did you sleep?"

"I don't think so."

"Still want to go?"

"I didn't just waste four hours or more of my life to not go."

"Come on, then, let's go."

Tommen pulled himself out of bed and followed his dad out to the living room. "Are Micah and Micaiah going?"

"They are."

Walter stopped suddenly, and Tommen nearly ran into him. "But know one thing," Walter said, turning. "Have no illusions that this is going to be all sunshine and roses just because it's new and we're coming out of a very bad time. There is every chance that this could go horribly, horribly wrong, just like the first time. Be vigilant. If anything seems out of place, tell me, and we'll leave. I'm not going through all this again. You understand?"

Tommen nodded. "I understand."

"Good."

Then the portal was open. Tommen thought it was a little

rougher ride than in the past, but at least they made it through. Not that he particularly enjoyed having the air sucked from his lungs and feeling almost as dead and exhausted as he had leaving the AP exam, but they made it through.

It was still difficult to imagine that there were multiple portal rooms now. How did the portal rooms know where to put the portal as it was being opened? How did they know that a portal from Earth went to this particular room, but a portal from, say...okay, so Tommen didn't know of any Fully Engaged worlds, but how did the portals transmit those portals to a different room? Was it really as simple as programming the coordinates? He let out a breath. He should have paid more attention in Physics.

Whatever the reason or the cause, it was kind of nice to be in a smaller portal room so they didn't have to walk a whole marathon just to make it to the translator dispenser. Of course, being such an important day, they still had to wait in line behind a thousand other aliens all thinking the same thing.

"Have you seen the new Coliseum, or whatever they're calling it now?" Tommen asked.

His dad shook his head. "No, I haven't."

The unsaid part of that statement, however, was something along the lines of "and I'm afraid to find out." And why shouldn't he be a little on edge? The last time any of them had been in the Coliseum, the government had been overthrown by a madman, and it had been subsequently used to detain, separate, enslave, and-or slaughter hundreds of millions.

They got their translators and started following the crowd through the Wheel. All around, Tommen could see that people were getting ready for life to get back to normal. Merchants were setting up their stalls, Harvesters negotiated with Auctioneers. Even Timekeepers and Scouts seemed deep in amiable conversation, or as amiable as could be found between a Timekeeper and a Scout.

After a moment, Tommen was able to put a name to the energy that had encapsulated the Wheel: hope. People had hope. They no longer milled about in the dull drudgery of everyday life, or in fear of the Hands or the Grandfathers. They had hope that things would change for the better. With any luck, that hope was not unfounded.

Tommen was pretty excited, too, honestly. He just wasn't sure how excited he wanted to be. He counted himself lucky that he'd gotten away the last time, and then only because Micah happened to find him and drag him along. Even once they'd gotten out of the Coliseum, it had been a fight to escape the Wheel. So, yes, Tommen was excited for the new inauguration and all the possibilities that went with it. But he was cautious and always made sure he knew where to go to hide and how to get back to the portal room. Even if he had ended up in the Engaged portal room where the portals would all be open, he could still go through and use his translator to generate a small atmospheric shell to keep him safe for a time, if necessary.

He hoped he was just being paranoid; he was good at that, too. Looking around at the shuffle and bustle of aliens of all shapes and sizes, it was impossible to tell intent just by body language. What was acceptable to one was a grave offense to another. Like an American giving someone a thumbs up in Greece. The smallest thing misinterpreted could set this whole thing askew.

"If we get separated," his dad began as the crowds got thicker the closer they got to the new Coliseum, "use your instincts, and remember everything I've taught you. When you return to the portal, don't wait for me, but hang your translator on the rod so I know you've gone through."

"Got it," Tommen answered, but his words were carried away by the din of the crowd.

Pushing, pulling, shoving and elbowing, the herd plodded along. Strange to see aliens traipsing about in the gardens of *Romeo and Juliet,* moving among hedges and statues. Did any of them appreciate the history and the culture associated with the new decor, or did they see only the work of a mad tyrant? Could any of them even say where the inspiration came from, what planet even?

Moving along, he was also forced to wonder what the general

opinion of humans would be going forward. He suddenly had a moment of clarity as he realized this was probably how Varad's parents had felt when they decided to move back to India. They'd done nothing wrong. They were loved by all who knew them, and they did their part to be inclusive. But Tommen remembered something Varad had said about the news focusing only on Cassius' and Rifun's nationalities. "They know I didn't do anything, but eventually the details will fade and only the association remains. Pretty soon, they don't know why they don't like me, only that they think that I'm hostile and violent."

Tommen thought he'd been overreacting, but now he thought he might begin to understand. For right now, Cassius and Rifun were still known well enough that the hatred for them was focused. But eventually, someone would figure out where they had come from and how to identify others of the species. After a while, it didn't matter if only two out of seven billion humans had committed some crime in the Wheel, it had been humans who took over the Wheel. Watch out, boys, humans are dangerous sons of bitches.

From what he could gather from surrounding conversation, no one had been inside the new Coliseum. Well, some had, but they were currently in there now and mum's the word. If that was the case, Tommen guessed the interior couldn't be too bad. Either they'd been impressed enough to keep it the way Rifun had it, or they'd torn it down and replaced it with their own new creation. Whatever the case, it was going to be a surprise for everyone on the outside.

"Stay close to me," Walter said as they got within sight of the portal.

Tommen nodded, but studied his dad for a moment longer. His tone was reminisce of the time they'd gone to the airport to meet with Rifun and exchange the old miner's journal for Eric and Varad. He was expecting danger. Worse than that, maybe, was that he'd learned from both that experience and the shootout at the warehouse, so his paranoia was even greater than Tommen's right now. Seeing how red he was, his blood pressure was probably through the roof.

Then they were through. And holy shit, was the new Coliseum a sight to behold.

The rest of the Wheel was obviously Shakespearean, or Victorian at the very least. Everything was very posh, very regal, very wealthy, everything designed to let the meager peasants know that they trod among royalty.

The Coliseum was nothing like that. It couldn't even be called a Coliseum anymore. Tommen wasn't sure what he wanted to call it.

When he'd been taken captive and held in the cave, Rifun had mentioned that he was from Madagascar, the product of a native woman and a "more civilized" European. This new Coliseum was certainly a reflection of his early childhood.

Tommen had never been to Madagascar, or anywhere in Africa for that matter. His information was limited to biased news stories about political goings-on, the incredible cinematography of *National Geographic* and *Discovery*, and half a dozen fake reality shows. There was always an element of truth in each, but they never really captured the whole picture.

Rifun had captured the whole picture. He'd had to modify it a little in order to accommodate some of the larger alien species, but otherwise it looked like a true-to-form Malagasy village from a time before the "more civilized" world invaded. This particular locale featured a wide open space of hard red clay surrounded by thick jungle vegetation. Mountains rose in the distance even as the rest of the landscape sloped downward. The sun was a non-entity, but light came from somewhere. There was the noise of wind and wild animals, but no wind to be felt or animals to be found. The crowd moved across the hard-packed clay along a trail that initially rose, then dipped suddenly, a valley spreading out before them.

The closer they got, the more Tommen saw that there appeared to be multiple distinct village sections, all positioned in such a way as to make up one larger villager. It put him in mind of his excursion to Sifura's world, except this was planned all in one go versus over generations of trial and error.

The first village section they approached was comprised of mere shade shelters, grassy roofs but no walls. Carved into a head beam were symbols for "secretary," "enter," and more that he was not entirely familiar with. So this was the spot where someone would meet with a secretary and be directed to the appropriate section.

There were other sections that they did not explore, where the huts were made of reeds and vegetable fibers, and larger buildings were constructed of deep red clay bricks with thatch roofs. Tommen saw symbols marking the lower courts in one section they passed. Given how the Wheel used to work and what the new system of governing looked like, he guessed that there would be more of a flow chart to things and less of a linear model. This was a government complex with multiple offices, not the king's throne room where one man spoke gold. What had Rifun's plan been exactly?

"Holy shit," he said. "I was not expecting this."

"I'll agree with you there," his dad said, nodding. "Rifun definitely put some hard work into this. Say a lot about him, but he had an eye for design. It's just too bad he engineered his own downfall."

Tommen grunted in agreement. At the same time, a small thought in the back of his mind wondered if Rifun hadn't been right, at least part way. Yeah, the genocide was terrible and unforgivable, but what about the rest? What could a man do when he was lost in a crowd so big that no one heard his ideas? What happened when that crowd told him to shut up and play by the rules? What happened when that crowd, despite its own grumblings, ended up defending the very system they purported to hate just as much as he did? No one was willing to do anything about it, whatever they claimed. So Rifun did something about it. He silenced the crowd by, well, silencing them. He made a fundamental, radical change to the order of things. Once again, a little sketchy on the mass murder, but what if this second revolution would bring about the peace he was trying to achieve? On top of that, again, sketchy genocide aside, what if his ideas had come through to fruition? What if they really worked?

Tommen shook his head as if to clear it. No, he couldn't afford to have sympathy for anything Rifun did, may have done, was doing, or would do. He was a killer, a brutal psychopath who murdered many individuals and slaved countless more. His love for Shakespeare and his homeland only proved it, using it as a way to insulate himself in his own insanity.

They ended up on the other side of the large village, over a ridge, in the shadow of the mountains. Did Madagascar have mountains? Tommen wasn't sure. Highlands, maybe, but he couldn't recall ever hearing about mountains on the African island. Well, what did he know?

The amphitheater they descended into was decidedly less than authentic to the scenery, though it had been disguised to look like it, carved out of the hard clay. For the stage, instead of old Greek stone, this appeared to be made of a combination of fibers and clay bricks, even though, in reality, it would never hold the volume and weight of those in attendance.

"Good news is, it looks like we'll have more options for escape this time," Walter mused, looking around at the wide open area. "On the other hand, it won't matter much because there is still only one way in and out."

"True, but you'll notice that there's no dampening field here," Tommen pointed out.

Indeed there wasn't. Tommen could still acutely feel the passage of time, could still Band. If he looked around and was able to focus well enough, he could even call up Predict in order to see the projected path of a moving object. This time around, everyone was armed, but no one was defenseless.

Across the amphitheater, just off to the left, there were more fibrous huts, four to be exact. They weren't large, and Tommen could just see the outline of a portal shimmering in each of the door frames.

"All the old Hands are dead, and if the Bat is dead, it's reasonable to think the Day is gone, too," Tommen said. "Who do you think will be hosting this?"

"I don't know," his dad answered. His disposition was difficult to gauge. He looked like he was trying to have a good time, but some internal war was making it difficult for him.

They did not have to wait long to find out. At first, no one noticed the secretary emerge from the hut farthest from the amphitheater. From his vantage point, Tommen could just make out six legs, though it walked like a dog. After a minute or two, he recognized it as one of the secretaries who had taken him to his review, the Labrador-looking one. It reached center stage and stood upright on its two hind legs with perfect balance. It took a second or ten, but those gathered quickly quieted down.

"Welcome," the secretary began. "We are gathered here today to present to you the new Council of Hands, those who will govern the Wheel and the Laws of Time. A terrible tragedy has occurred here recently. And everyone is to blame. We allowed our greed to blind us to the corruption that flowed through the Wheel like blood. Those who spoke up, we struck down. In the midst of our petty pursuits, a single man was able to destroy everything we thought we knew."

The secretary looked around. "It does not matter whether you were a Dominion Timekeeper, a Triage Harvester, an Investor Merchant, anyone who worked closely with the Hands, or whether you were a Runner who actively opposed the Hands at every turn. We allowed the system to become corrupt and stay corrupt, creating a system where seats were bought and sold to the highest bidder, where those we commissioned to keep us safe were punished for doing just that. It is no secret that that system was on a constant cycle of war, but a wheel that spins while going downhill, still goes downhill.

"To that end, a new system has been put in place. It is no longer one man with one word that governs all. Rather, you will be governed by those who are one of you. Harvesters have no business with Timekeepers, and Scientifically Superior and Fully Engaged Civilizations have no business with Scientifically Primitive and Unengaged Civilizations. You will conduct your own affairs. There will, however, still be a Zero Hour. As before, the word of the Zero

Hour is absolute, but it is not final.

"There are many changes that have yet to be disclosed, and to do so today would take more time than we would wish. Instead, we will name our new Hands. They will be the ones to pass down the information."

"So far, it doesn't sound too bad," Tommen commented.

"Very true, but always be skeptical," his dad cautioned. "I'm not going to be too celebratory until we make it back home, and I'm back in bed."

Even as he said it, Tommen felt fatigue creeping over him. Well, he was going to get less sleep, but he was going to sleep well, anyway.

"We will begin with the new elected positions," the secretary was saying. "First, the guards."

The reception was half-hearted to say the least. According to Micaiah, there had been division among the guards during the battle; not all had supported Rifun. That didn't mean that they were well-liked by the masses. Walter had once said that corrections officers were ten times more likely than police officers to be killed by a freed inmate. The police made the arrest, but the inmate saw only the corrections officer day in and day out. Here, the guards had been the ones to trap people in the Coliseum. The guards had been the ones to shuffle the prisoners to the Judgment Wing for processing, then back to the Coliseum to be enslaved or murdered.

The secretaries were next, and they seemed utterly thrilled to be where they were, finally gaining power and having a say in things. Even the Labrador seemed impressed and proud of them. At the same time, did that make the Labrador the new Bat? He or she wasn't named as the First Secretary, or any of the other elected secretary positions, so either it had been a lottery for the spokesperson position, or else their new Hand lackey was the Labrador.

When the Grandfathers were ushered out to be introduced, they were met with hisses and screeches and boos and all manner of disapproving noises and gestures. And why not? It was like making a bunch of atheists or Satanists part of the board of elders at a church. One thing of note, however, was that none of the elected Grandfathers were Borelians. Furthermore, even once they were officially named and charged with their duties and position, they remained unshrouded. Only when they were gone did the Labrador stop to explain.

"Secrecy was but one fuel that fanned the flames of corruption and deceit in the old system. From now on, neither the Grandfathers, nor the Hands, nor any other position will be shrouded. All will see the faces of our leaders. Our leaders will be held accountable to us by sheer visibility, among other things. No longer will we be kept in the dark like ignorant pups."

The reaction to that was mixed, but mostly positive. Tommen rather liked the idea of being able to see those who governed him. Especially when the time came around for his Journeyman review. Or if he had to file any future petitions.

Then it was time for the Hands themselves to be named and introduced. As with the others, they were all brought out at once, made to stand stage right. Tommen wasn't sure if their arrangement was intentional or simply haphazard depending on where they ended up. As the Labrador named each one, the Hand would step out and swear the oath of office. When done, the Labrador would thank them, and they would move to stage right.

But there was one face which Tommen did not expect to see. He wasn't even sure he was seeing right, until the Labrador called her up.

"The Hand of Scientifically Primitive and Unengaged Civilizations. Sifura. Quadrant Two, Parsec Nine, Sector Five, System Twelve, Planet Nineteen."

Tommen leapt to his feet, momentarily startling his dad. Yes, it was her! She'd made it; she'd escaped! She walked forward on her two enormous hind paws, making some gesture or another as she took her oath of office. Then she was done and moving off to the opposite side. Tommen tried to call to her, but his voice was but one among thousands.

"Maybe you'll get a chance to talk to her afterwards," his dad suggested.

"I want to know how she survived," Tommen said, sitting back down. "I mean, by all accounts, when she and the other Hands left the last inauguration, they were slaughtered as soon as they walked back through the tunnel."

"As I said, maybe later."

"Later" quickly turned into "a hell of a long time" as the Hands were finished up and the Labrador gave some small confirmation that she had indeed been voted on by the secretaries to be the replacement for the Bat and the Day. In actuality, there were four such Hand lackeys now, and the others would be seen in due time as their shifts came around. Each one would follow a particular cycle of Hand election so that none would have the power or influence that the Bat and the Day had.

To say the inauguration ended as quickly as it had began would be an outright lie. It did not end quickly in any sense of the word. The Labrador kept talking for a minute or two, reiterating some statements, and generally seeming about as comfortable speaking publicly as Tommen was; she just didn't know how to end a ceremony. Even after she did finish, there was still the problem of getting out. Leaving the Amphitheater was considerably easier than leaving the Coliseum, but the crowd just would not disperse.

Some wanted to stay and mill around either in the seats or just around the edges, making it impossible for anyone wanting to leave to actually leave. Others went down to speak to the new Hands, or try to. Tommen got about three rows down before he lost sight of Sifura. When the crowd only got thicker and thicker, he decided that trying to force his way in or wait in line just wasn't worth it.

"Not going to try and see your girlfriend, huh?" his dad teased when he rejoined him.

"She's not my girlfriend. She just helped me out in a big way, and I was curious to know how she survived."

For the first time that night, his dad managed a smile. "I know. I'm picking on you."

Gradually, the crowds thinned. Some left the area completely while others wandered around the village, exploring the new way of doing things. Tommen and his dad were just heading that direction when he saw something out of the corner of his eye. He turned and was almost bowled over by Micah who slipped on the clay which, by sheer volume of people and being worked by the crowd, had turned into mud. A moment later, Micaiah appeared as well. Apparently he'd been chasing Micah and the collision was entirely coincidental. Tommen had his doubts.

"Hey, you guys made it," Micah said, still grinning as he picked himself up and held a hand out to Tommen. He was covered in thick red clay where he'd fallen.

"Yeah, we did," Walter confirmed. "We would have joined up with you guys if we'd found you."

"We've been here for a while," Kayla said, approaching.

"We came in on the tail end."

"So, what do you think of the new digs?" Micaiah asked, folding his arms. "I kind of like it, actually. Don't like the guy who built it, but the concept is neat."

"It's less claustrophobic anyway."

Tommen sighed and stepped away until the crowd swallowed him up and he was able to get away. They were supposed to be leaving, not standing around chit chatting like all the other obstructive aliens in the place. He was tired. The inauguration had taken way too long. He still had two exams to take.

The Hands were still swamped, so he moved farther off until he was standing at the edge of the trees, now fully engulfed in mountain shadow. Still he heard the wind and the animal noises, but he felt and saw none of it, as if it were merely an audio track.

Still, it was a beautiful landscape. Almost made Tommen want to climb up there, see if there were any caves to explore, see if he could actually go climbing or caving, see just how much detail Rifun had put into this place.  And it couldn't go on forever, could it? There had to be a wall or some kind of limit somewhere out there.  If not that, well, Madagascar was an island after all.

"Beautiful, isn't it?"

He looked to his right to see another human standing at the tree line. He was about six foot, maybe a little shorter, a bit soft but not explicitly fat, black hair, brown eyes, long sleeve shirt and jeans.

"It is," Tommen confirmed. He nodded at the man's clothes. "Kinda cold where you're from?"

"A bit chilly, yes." Tommen had his translator set to Welsh, but with the proximity, he could tell the man was speaking French. Quebec, then, perhaps. "Is your home warm?"

"Getting there. I mean, it's nice, but it's not overly hot."

The man nodded. He still hadn't even glanced at Tommen. "You know, I miss this view. They say that young people are incapable of appreciating beauty and art. I'm quite a bit older now as you might imagine, but even as a young man, I could stare at this view for hours."

Red flags went off in Tommen's mind. "And what view is that?"

Now the man looked at him and grinned an all too familiar grin. "The view from my village on the north side. Where the more civilized Frenchmen came to spread their civilization and the seeds thereof."

Tommen turned and opened his mouth to speak or shout or raise an alarm, but suddenly he felt like his throat was closing, and the most he could manage was a squeak. As he glanced at the man, who was Rifun, he shed one Disguise or donned another, Tommen didn't know. He just knew that this was Rifun speaking to him, but he was wearing the faces of a hundred different men in order to avoid detection. The face and body he wore now put Tommen in mind of Mr. Morris if he'd been taller and a little thinner.

"Did you really think that I would just go off and hide in some hole, waiting for the manhunts to find me? When you have the power to Disguise yourself as anyone and go anywhere, why wouldn't you? Cassius walked right into the Akarin base and stole their leadership. I am the most wanted man in the entire universe right now, and yet I can walk right into the inauguration of the new Hands. I can be anyone, go anywhere."

"Then go to Hell," Tommen rasped.

"And that's another thing. Did you think that because I am out of power that somehow our deal is null and void, and you owe me nothing? We have an agreement. I saved your dear daddy and saw you through your review. You owe me."

"Fuck off."

"The more you resist, the more painful it will be. I did warn you of 'dropping like flies,' didn't I?" Tommen took a breath but stopped struggling and trying to speak. Gradually, Rifun released whatever Force choke he had on him. "The timeline may have changed. The locale and overall manner of your new training may have changed. But our deal and your training have not changed. I will still send you a sign, when I am ready for you. If you don't respond, well, I don't think I have to try and prove my record to you. And in the future, dear daddy will be lucky to be any more than a vegetable, and Micaiah will be losing a lot more than just a leg. Do you understand?"

Tommen glared at him. "When are you going to give up?"

"I never give up. I always win."

"You lost your power."

"Temporarily, but I am still alive. The only thing that will stop me now is death."

"And what's to stop me from telling everyone that you're here and need to fucking die?"

"Because as soon as you open your mouth to do so, you'll be dead. And even if I decide to let you raise an alarm, by the time anyone notices and comes to investigate, I'll be long gone. So consider your actions carefully."

Tommen was silent for a moment as he tried to come up with

something, anything. "I'm going to tell them. You know I will."

Rifun grinned, donning another Disguise. "I would be heartbroken if you didn't. It makes the game that much more interesting, especially if you got the twins involved. I almost want to make it an order and tell you to tell them. What's that going to do to your little plan, hm?"

Tommen glanced up the hill where he could just make out his dad and the others still talking.

"Don't forget," Rifun went on. He donned yet another Disguise. "I can be anyone. And I can go anywhere. I'm like Santa Claus. I see you when you're sleeping; I know when you're awake. And I know if you've been bad or good, so you better do as I say or else more people are going to die."

"I don't think that's how the song goes."

"Perhaps, but do you doubt me?"

No, he didn't, and that was the worst part.

"Watch for my sign. And heed my warning. I think I'm being overly generous even giving you one."

Again Tommen looked at his dad on the top of the hill. When he looked back, Rifun was gone.

"You look pale," Micah observed when he rejoined them. "Hills a little bigger than you thought they were?"

"Um...no." He felt light-headed and dizzy. "Just..."

"Is everything all right?" his dad demanded, studying him.

"Yeah, just...Rifun was here." That made them all take a step back. "He was Disguised."

"What did he say? Did he threaten you?"

"Kind of. Nothing really new. He just said that even though he's not in power anymore, that our deal still stands. He said he would be sending me some sort of sign and I would do well to pay attention to it. His exact phrase was 'dropping like flies.' "

Tommen didn't remember much after that, only that Walter and the twins and Kayla had some sort of serious discussion. Then they were going back through the Wheel. No conspiracy, no murders, and certainly no genocide. Everything had gone exactly as it should have this time. Except for the part where Rifun showed up and no one knew about it.

They returned to the portal room and dropped off their translators. Before they could go through their portal, however, Walter paused.

"He didn't hurt you or try anything, did he?" he asked severely.

Tommen shook his head. "No," he lied. "Just verbal threats. Which I certainly believe he'll carry out. But for the moment, I think he realized that he was on the defense in there, regardless of his attitude."

"He didn't say anything specific about going home or about anyone in particular?"

At first Tommen thought he was speaking about himself or the twins. Then it occurred to him that Becky might be on the hit list now, too. Fuck. How was he going to keep her safe? Still, he shook his head. He was exhausted. "No. He just said to wait and watch for the sign, whatever it is and whenever it comes."

Walter let out a breath and nodded. "Okay. Well, I'll send the word out, and we'll keep a lookout. We'll be ready for him, wherever he resurfaces next. All right?"

Tommen just shrugged and stepped through the portal. It was a hard recovery, but it seemed to work with him as he stumbled to his bedroom, crawled in bed, and was out like a light.

# Epilogue

So, how was that for an inauguration?" Micah sighed, pulling himself into a recliner while Micaiah and Kayla opted for the couch.

Micaiah rubbed his eyes and tried to stay awake. He was sick of these baker's hours, even if he worked fewer of them these days. "The inauguration was fine. It was that bit afterwards that has me worried."

"Not like we can do a whole lot now that we've been officially demoted."

Micaiah shook his head. "No. We're not going to accept that. We're going to do what we've always done. Find a way to find an answer."

"Hoping the new Hands and the new Grandfathers might be a little more willing to work with us Timekeepers now?"

"I'm not talking about the Timekeepers."

Micah studied him for a second, his mind mulling over his words, even as he didn't want to believe them. "What are you talking about then?"

"I'm talking about doing some research off the books, in Time's peripheral vision. I'm talking about the Akarin."

"You mean...?"

"We're going in, Micah," Kayla said gently. "Now that all this mess has come and gone, we need to go and help with the cleanup. We need to do it now more than ever, especially since Cassius' treachery was uncovered. We need to find out if anyone else was impersonated and root them out. Then we have to work to rebuild the trust that the Akarin—and the Akari—once had."

"Why can't you do that in your off-time?"

Micaiah hesitated. "It's going to be our primary concern, at least for a short time. Once the bulk of the mess is cleaned up, then we're planning on dropping off the grid for a while. No Time, no Akarin, just us."

He could see Micah was struggling to comprehend his words. It would be the first real time that they'd really been apart. But at the same time, it would be the first time that Micaiah and Kayla would really be together. No more running in fear, no more hiding, no more Disguises and playing games, no more pretending to be perfect strangers meeting in a bar. They would have a life together. God help them, but they were hoping for kids, too. And all that would be without Micah.

"You've been planning this for a while." It was a simple statement of fact.

Kayla nodded. "We have. We were planning this even before Rifun took power."

"And there's nothing I can do to try to talk you out of it? Listen, man, if you wanted to stop being a baker, I wasn't going to tell you no. It's wearing on me, too."

Micaiah grinned. "No, it's not that. It's just...it's time for me—for us to move on. This time, it just means that you're not coming with. Doesn't mean you can't visit. I'm not going to deny that I have a twin brother."

Micah sighed. Micaiah hated to see the hurt and defeat, but it was the way things had to be. Finally Micah nodded. "Do you know when exactly?"

"We'll be tying up loose ends this summer, but we're aiming for New Year's. We'll spend our last Christmas here, then move on."

He let out a breath. "Okay. I get it. Maybe it's time I moved on away from my brother, too. Doesn't mean I won't still try to talk you out of it, though."

"I wouldn't have it any other way."

So you may have noticed that there is no preview for the next book. This is primarily because adding an extra chapter is becoming rather cumbersome. The main book itself is getting to be incredibly long. We're topping two hundred thousand words in this book alone, and it's still not the longest one in the series. If I continued to include the next chapter, eventually we'd be looking at over eight hundred pages. If there isn't enough in the main book itself to capture your attention, having one more chapter isn't going to cut it. Plus, I think there is getting to be enough extra material to keep you excited for the upcoming installments. Walter's book, *Of Saints and Sinners*; some short stories, deleted scenes, reading guides, and more available on the website; plus a host of goodies.

All this to say that the series isn't over just because I didn't include the first chapter of the next book. In fact, it's all just getting started. With this revelation of Micaiah, not only being married, but part of this secret society, it adds a whole new dynamic to Rifun's takeover. What is the Akari? What does it mean to be an Akari-bearer? What fctions are there and how do they relate to one another and the Time industry? What does the Time industry do now that this long-perpetuated "myth" is suddenly a reality? Where has Rifun gone and what does he have planned for Tommen?

Book five, *Free Time*, is going to expand on all of these ideas and introduce a swath of new characters to love and hate, including one of my favorites (but I'm going to be mean and not tell you his name yet). A lot of questions are going to be answered and events are going to be set in motion. Where books one through four have been a lot of action and a lot of immediate needs addressed, book five sets a new tone for the series, where a lot of the nebulous motivations and character development come into focus and, I think, where things really start to ramp up.

I could go on, but I don't want to give too much away, and I think it would only frustrate you, Reader, and get you mad at me. Just know that things are going to change and expand wildly.